THE GREEN HILLS
of Snowdonia

From Across the Ancient Waters © 2012 by Michael Phillips
The Treasure of the Celtic Triangle © 2012 by Michael Phillips

Print ISBN 978-1-62029-787-2

eBook Editions:
Adobe Digital Edition (.epub) 978-1-62416-102-5
Kindle and MobiPocket Edition (.prc) 978-1-62416-101-8

Cover Photo: www.shutterstock.com, gfdunt

Published by Barbour Publishing, Inc., P.O. Box 719, Uhrichsville, OH 44683, www.barbourbooks.com

Our mission is to publish and distribute inspirational products offering exceptional value and biblical encouragement to the masses.

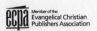

Member of the
Evangelical Christian
Publishers Association

Printed in the United States of America.

THE GREEN HILLS
of Snowdonia

MICHAEL
PHILLIPS

BARBOUR
PUBLISHING

—A Note Regarding Locale—

Whenever one is blending fact and fiction, certain disclaimers and clarifications are necessary. Everything that follows is fiction, the characters, the setting, the story. Authors are often asked about the locations in which their stories take place. Some settings are truer to the reality of place than others. I have searched high and low to find the settings of some of George MacDonald's Scottish novels, only to arrive at the conclusion that those settings existed only in the author's mind. In the case of his novel *Malcolm*, however, the details of locale in the story match precisely the reality in and around the northern Scottish village of Cullen. Readers do the same with my books, with similar results. Some are based on factual places, others are not. In the case of *From Across the Ancient Waters*, the location of the story is set along the north coast of Wales. But the specifics of the villages and coastline and roads have been changed and adapted for the sake of the story. If you visit North Wales, you will *not* find a village called Llanfryniog or the promontory of Mochras Head or Westbrooke Manor or the cave on the beach. The setting, as well as the story and characters, is entirely fictionalized.

The Region of Gwynedd, North Wales
at the Northern Expanse of the Cambrian Mountains

Caernarfon Bay

Mt. Snowdon

S
N
O
W
D
O
N
I
A

Yr Aran

Moel Hebog

Moelwyn Mawr

Blaenau
Ffestiniog

Moelwyn Bach

Lleyn Peninsula

Penrhyndeudraeth

Porthmadog

Traeth
Bach

Harlech
Castle

Moel
Ysgfarnogod

Tremadog Bay

Burrenchobay Hall

Llanfryniog

Barrie Cottage

Rhinog Fawr

Mochras

Head

Westbrooke
Manor

Yllethr

Moelfre

Diffwys

Dolgellau

Barmouth

Barmouth
Bay

Cader Idris

Wales

Liverpool Bay

Anglesey

Flint

Wrexham

Barmouth

Welshpool

Cambrian Mts.

Cardigan

Brecon Beacons

Swansea

Newport

Cardiff

From Across
the
Ancient Waters

DEDICATION

To Robert James Nigel Halliday,
A man of integrity, truth, and depth of character,
whom it is an honor to call my friend.

PROLOGUE

The Fate of the Rhodri Mawr
1791

*T*he blue-green sea of the Irish Ocean between the treacherous coastlines of eastern Ireland, northern Wales, and southern Scotland could be as placid as any of the thousand inland lochs for which the three Celtic lands were known.

Saint Columba had been borne safely over it to Mull more than a millennium before. He had carried a new spiritual destiny to Scotland's western isles, which would spread throughout all Britannia. But when the seas of the north Atlantic rose in unexpected fury, beware to all who challenged them, whether conquering Roman or Viking, whether Irish saint or Welsh pirate. At such times, the waters of this Celtic triangle, no respecter of persons, sought victims to add to its ancient tomb of the watery deep.

Such a fate had come suddenly upon the vessel of dubious reputation known as the *Rhodri Mawr*.

A fierce blast from the north bent the struggling ship's aftermast dangerously toward the slate-gray waters of an angry sea. The imposing craft, stalwart and fearsome when sailing out of Penzance two days before, now bobbed like a plaything as it bottomed into a trough between two giant swells of St. George's Channel. The leading edge of the second wave rose ominously then sent its white-tipped crest

9

smashing into the prow with such violence that it seemed the ship's massive stem must burst into matchsticks from the blow.

The front third of the ship disappeared as if swallowed whole. Two seconds later it reappeared out of the tumult. Somehow it was still in one piece. Water pouring over the sides, the pointed bowsprit shot toward the sky. The swell that had swallowed it now spewed the boat as a mere toy upward in a dangerous arc.

Thus repeated the downward crash and heavenward flight of the two-masted English brigantine as it had for hours. Each disappearance between titanic billows seemed to all appearance its last. Only by a miracle had it managed to remain afloat so long. Helpless against the elements, its crew was too exhausted to think what terror must be their inevitable portion. The gods were in control now. Such men as these, however, had not spent their lives befriending whatever deities made the fate of men their business. Nor was it likely that a heavenward flight would be the final journey of their souls. It was doubtful any would live through the descending night or that the *Rhodri Mawr* would enter safe harbor again.

The secret of Dolau Cothi seemed destined for a deep, black, unknown grave somewhere near the home of the giant serpent *Gwbert-ryd*, whom superstition credited with such violent storms and the shipwrecks that resulted from them.

Water was not just threatening from below but also from above. Rain slammed onto the deck with a ferocity that made visibility impossible. The crow's nest had been abandoned hours before. Nothing could be seen from it. No man could survive atop it.

The *Rhodri Mawr*'s crew had ventured into these waters on a mission now forgotten in the battle for survival. As the storm rose quickly, the captain thought to find some sheltered inlet in Cardigan Bay. But the anger of Gwbert-ryd swept upon them rapidly, turning every inch of this Celtic sea into a frothy boil. No shelter was to be found. Had they only known that the drift of the current had taken them northward into Tremadog Bay and that they were now floundering within three hundred yards of the rocky coastline, it might have been different. But through the falling mist, none knew how close safety lay.

The bow slammed into another wall of water yet more violent than the rest.

"She's taking water!" cried one of the mates, clinging desperately to a ragged end of hemp to keep from being sucked overboard.

With the wind roaring and the tattered remains of sails flapping, his warning was lost to the prince of the power of the air. The nearest of his fellows had been thrown onto the deck thirty feet astern.

A sharp crack sounded.

The tall front mast swayed dangerously. . .rocked the opposite direction. . .then another splintering crack. Suddenly the thick round timber lay across the deck in the sea. Even if she survived the storm, no ship could navigate without its rigging.

It mattered little. The next instant a tremendous wave slanted high over the bow, battering the side with mortal force. Another shattering blow followed to starboard. A deep groan creaked below deck.

Those aboard seemed destined to live out the poet's words of the ancient rime:

> With sloping masts and dipping prow,
> As who pursued with yell and blow
> Still treads the shadow of his foe,
> And forward bends his head,
> The ship drove fast, loud roared the blast,
> And southward aye we fled.

The *Rhodri Mawr* pitched dangerously to port. It took but one more split. Now the aftermast snapped from its base and tumbled overboard. The stem could no longer absorb the blows from the raging sea. Side-timbers began to splinter. Within seconds the forehull of the *Rhodri Mawr* was breaking up. Now indeed did the sea set about in earnest its business of making matchsticks of this once sturdy vessel.

"Over the side!" sounded cries from all parts of the ship. "Save yourselves. . .she's tearing apart. . .we're going down!"

In panic, most of the crew leaped overboard to keep from being knocked unconscious on the lurching deck. Within minutes the brigantine's three lifeboats were in the water. Whether they would fare better than the mother ship was doubtful.

There was one on board, however, who did not so hastily leap to his doom. He would outwit the legendary serpent of the deep with more than a brief prolonging of his own life. He had seen the signs an hour before as the winds whipped up the frothing cauldron. He knew what must be the result. He knew these waters better than his fellows. From the shape and flow of the waves, he had deduced what even the captain had not realized, that land could not be far off.

As his mates struggled above deck, he descended into the depths, to the captain's quarters, empty now except for its most precious cargo. With the floor pitching and yawing under his feet, he lugged a great black chest from the closet. The thing was nearly too heavy to lift. He could not hope to swim a foot bearing it. The contents would sink faster than a great iron anchor. But there might yet be a way to save the treasure within it.

With all his might, he lifted the reliquary and struggled toward the stairs. Inch by inch he made his way up then onto the next flight. A great crash sent the box from him as he toppled onto his back. Luckily its lock held. He scrambled to his feet, retrieved his booty, and continued toward the sea-deck. Hearing both masts crack, followed by shouts everywhere, he knew the ship's fate. If he could just get himself and the box overboard.

He reached the air to see lifeboats being tossed from above. All about, his fellows were scrambling overboard. No one paid him heed. None saw what he lugged behind him.

Another lurch of the deck sent the chest from him again. Picking himself up, he dragged his bounty toward a mass of corked netting. Hastily he wrapped it amid several folds, securing the strands to its precious load.

The *Rhodri Mawr* swayed one final time then lurched sideward. The motion flung him off his feet, over the bulwark, and into the sea, tangled in a mass of cord and chest and hemp and cork. Bobbing up into the dim light of dusk, he gasped for air. A length of cord remained connected to the bulwark. In seconds the sinking ship would pull the chest and netting and himself down with it.

A wave dashed him below the surface. He sent his fingers groping toward the sheath at his side. As his head surfaced again, his hand bore aloft a shiny blade. He plunged through the netting toward the ship.

A minute more and the *Rhodri Mawr* capsized to its side. Half its deck was now underwater, its keel exposed, the lower hold filling rapidly.

As the ambitious pirate felt himself pulled down in the sinking vortex, three quick slashes from his knife released him safely from the doomed ship, adrift with a lifecraft of cork and netting.

Thirty seconds later, the mighty vessel above him tipped farther and slowly sank out of sight.

The rocky shoals of this coast were unforgiving. It took not many minutes for the squall to reduce the three lifeboats to floating debris. Futilely gasping for breath between twenty-foot waves, those of the crew who had trusted them found themselves clinging to mere scraps of wood. Most would not be heard from again. As they had given their lives to the sea, the depths now became their final resting place. If the serpent Gwbert-ryd was near, he must certainly be satisfied with this day's work.

The great hull slowly settled to the bottom and came to rest almost in one piece. There the waters, though frigid, were calm. After its gallant struggle, the *Rhodri Mawr* could finally rest in peace.

Under the water it rumbled on,
Still louder and more dread:
It reached the ship, it split the bay;
The ship went down like lead.
Stunned by that loud and dreadful sound,

Which sky and ocean smote,
Like one that hath been seven days drowned
My body lay afloat:
But swift as dreams, myself I found
Within the Pilot's boat.

And now, all in my own countree,
I stood on the firm land!
The Hermit stepped forth from the boat,
And scarcely he could stand.

No one ever saw the tangled mass of ship's netting, held afloat by great balls of cork no storm could sink, bobbing up and down as it bore two parcels—one human, the other filled with that which men would kill for—away from the wreckage toward the coast of Mochras Head, overlooked through the mists of the storm, by the green hills of Snowdonia.

PART ONE

Stranger in North Wales

1867

ONE

Strange Benefactress

$\mathscr{A}$ girl of indeterminate age stole with stealthy step into a narrow lane leading perpendicular to the central dirt road of a coastal village in North Wales.

Whether she had just pinched a sweetie from the post or a half-penny roll from the baker, the quick furtive glance behind as she disappeared from view of the three or four humble shops of the place would surely prompt an observer to think, whatever her business, that she was up to no good.

The tiny flaxen scamp was soon swallowed by shadows of high stone rising on both sides of her. Immediately she broke into a run.

Noiseless as they were swift, her steps took her quickly through the buildings of the village. Moments later she was racing across a wide green pasture. Several black-and-white cattle grazing in its midst paid the flight of the girl no heed.

In truth, the small Celtic lass was no thief at all. That her two hands and the single pocket of her threadbare dress were empty gave all the proof necessary that nothing untoward had taken place during the three or four minutes in which she had darted into the village and out again unseen. In actual fact, her exit had been made with one less encumbrance on her person than she had entered with. Her errand on

17

this day had been one of giving not taking. She had been discharging a debt of kindness from her young heart.

The only evidence left behind that she had been in Llanfryniog at all was a small bouquet of wildflowers—dandelions and daisies mostly, with a few yellow buttercups sprinkled among them—plucked on her way into the village from the field next to the one through which she now ran. She would have left something of greater value on the latch to Mistress Chattan's side door if she had had it. But the blooms were free and abundant, available to all for the having, and the only gift she could afford to bequeath. Flowers were thus the normal commodity of the unusual commerce in which she engaged.

At this hour of late afternoon, the front door of the inn swung back and forth on its hinges every few minutes. This was the time of day when the region's miners came to relax with their afternoon pint before trudging home to their suppers. Already the place was bustling with animated talk and laughter as ale and an occasional whiskey flowed from Mistress Chattan's hand. The tiny bouquet on the door of the lane that opened into her private quarters remained unseen for some time.

What manner of woman it was who thus served the men of the mine their daily ration of liquibrious good cheer was an inquiry that would have provoked heated discussion among the respectable wives and mothers of Llanfryniog. Though they were no more genteel than she, they were far from pleased that their husbands made such regular visits to her establishment. That the thirsty miners and fishermen of the region contributed so much to the health of Mistress Chattan's cash box was as much a grief to their wives as it was a boon to the innkeeper. No one knew Mistress Chattan's antecedents. Neither were they inclined to ask about them. But the women were suspicious. They would cross the road if they saw her ahead, like the priest and Levite of old, in order to pass by on the other side, little knowing what curses and imprecations she muttered under her breath against them.

Having left the small floral token of goodwill, not fragrant but nonetheless precious in the eyes of Him who made girls and flowers and surly old women together, one would assume the recipient and the girl on intimate terms and that the discovery would bring a smile to the good Mistress Chattan's lips.

In fact, only the day before the proprietress of Llanfryniog's single inn—which boasted only three little-used rooms but whose pub contained six frequently used tables—had given the girl a rude whack along the side of the head. This had been followed by a string of harsh words that ought not to be heard from a lady's lips.

But Mistress Chattan was no lady. And when she discovered the small nosegay on her door later that evening, a silent oath passed those same lips, more vile than anything spoken against her customers' wives. She knew whence came the gift and was anything but grateful.

On one thing were the wives of Llanfryniog and Mistress Chattan agreed—the young imp and daughter of Codnor Barrie was a menace.

Half the women of the village, like Mistress Chattan on this day, had at one time or another been the recipient of some such insignificant remembrance, usually wildflowers, from the strange benefactress of Llanfryniog. To chastise her or tell her to mind her own business, in the words of Solomon, only succeeded in heaping burning coals upon their own heads. Where one nosegay had been the previous day, a larger one would be found the next.

Most had learned that the best way to keep little Gwyneth a safe distance from their homes was to bite their tongues. Their policy was either to ignore her or treat her with distant civility. Rebuke or anger acted as too ready an incentive to the girl to repay evil with kindness—a sentiment they would all have endorsed in church every Sunday but which, when they found themselves on the receiving end of it, they found disconcerting in the extreme. Where she had come by such an absurd notion, they could only guess.

"There goes the Barrie girl," said one of the village wives to her neighbor over the low stone wall between the gardens at the back of their two cottages.

Both women paused a moment and watched as the unruly head of white sped through the field of green.

"Aye," sighed the other. She added a significant click of her tongue for emphasis. "But where does she come by her strange ways?"

"From her mother, some say."

"Mere gossip. No one on this side ever saw the mother."

"She must have been an ill one, to have given the world such a girl."

" 'Tis the auld grannie, if ye be asking me."

"She's no grannie to the lass."

"Who's kin is she, then?"

"The father's, I'm thinking. Though what relation I can't rightly say."

"What of the girl's mother, then?"

"They say she was cursed with the evil seed."

"Where did you hear such a thing, Niamh?"

"From them that know."

"Nobody knows who she was, except that she came from over the water, where the man should never have gone looking for a woman. I hear she had the blood of Irish kings in her veins."

"Now 'tis you who's spinning tales, Eilidh. How would an honest man like Barrie have got such a wife? Whether her blood ran blue or no, I can't say, but 'tis more likely that of knaves."

"Aye, ye may be right. There's rascals and kings alike above us."

"Whatever the color of her blood, the mother passed *something* to the girl that was not altogether of this world."

"Unless it came from her daddy."

"Codnor Barrie? No, I'm thinking it must have come from the mother or the grannie's side."

"No matter. 'Tis with us now. And none can escape whatever it be till she's gone back to wherever she came from."

TWO

The Gray Cliffs of Mochras Head

*T*he course taken by the girl as she disappeared from the two observant busybodies led south of the village. Beyond the grazing cattle behind her, she ascended a gradual slope of uncultivated moorland and soon arrived onto the precipitous promontory known as Mochras Head.

Having completed her errand of grace, she skipped merrily over the terrain of gentle green as if possessing no care in the world. That the plateau across which her steps carried her overlooked a peaceful sea from a height of at least two hundred feet above the craggy coastline caused this Celtic nymph no alarm. She had roamed every inch of these regions since she could walk. The mystery of the sea lay in the depths of her being. Her soul felt its majesty, though she knew not why. These high perches above it were her favorite places in all the world.

Her father taught her that the cliff distinguishing this seawardmost point on the eastern curve of Tremadog Bay was not to be feared, and she trusted her father. Only she must keep three paces from it, he said. From there she might feast upon the blues and greens and grays of the sea to her heart's content and dream of what lay beyond.

Though they knew nothing about her, everyone in the village knew that the girl's mother had come from across these waters. Codnor Barrie loved the sea for his mysterious wife's sake. His daughter shared the mother's blood and was likewise a child of the sea. The father saw in young Gwyneth's countenance daily reminders of the only woman he had ever loved. He knew that the sights, sounds, and smells of the water drew the girl and made her happy. Whatever evil the women of Llanfryniog attributed to the radiance shining out of them, the far-off expression in Gwyneth's pale young eyes kept the melancholy memory of his wife quietly alive in the humble man's heart.

The girl paused and stooped to her knees. She then stretched flat onto her stomach and propped her chin between two small fists. There she lay and gazed out to sea.

It was a warm afternoon in early June. The fragrance of the new spring growth of grass on which she lay wafted gently on the warm sea breezes. What rose in her heart as she lay on the grassy carpet were feelings and sensations no words could explain, no images contain. The world's splendor exhilarated her spirit. For Gwyneth Barrie, that was enough.

How long she lay, she could not have said. When the sun shone and school was over and her papa was at the mine, time did not exist. The sea stretching out like an infinite blanket of green, the moor above it, the hilly woodland rising away eastward toward the peaks of Snowdonia—these all comprised the imaginative playground of her childhood. She was at home on every inch of the landward expanse of them.

The sea beyond, however, remained an intoxicating mystery. She could stare at it for hours. Yet still it withheld its secrets.

She knew that her mother had lived somewhere on the other side of it, and that she had been born in her mother's country. That connection with her unknown origins, and with a mother she had never seen, made the sea a living thing in her soul.

Inland from the girl at a distance of some five or six hundred yards, two riders on horseback trotted slowly down the road toward the village. The gray and the red they rode were well groomed and exquisitely outfitted. The two young people were themselves dressed in riding habits that none of the local peasantry or miners could have afforded for their sons or daughters. Their two hats alone might have cost a month's wages for half the working men in the village.

"Hey look, Florilyn," said the older of the two, a youth who had just turned eighteen. He had seen the girl walking along the promontory as they came onto the plateau. "There's the witch-girl! How about some fun!"

"Like what?" answered his sister, younger by two and a half years.

"To see the little scamp try to outrun a horse!"

"Go chase her yourself, Courtenay," said the girl called Florilyn. "She gives me the shivers. Besides, she's afraid of no animal. She would just stand there and let you charge straight at her."

"Then I'll run her down!" Her brother laughed.

"And have Rhawn's father to answer for it!"

"He wouldn't do anything to me. Father wouldn't let him."

"You might be right. But I have no intention of making the girl angry. She'd probably put a curse on us or something. Suit yourself, but I'm going to see Rhawn." She urged her mount forward down the incline.

A few seconds later her brother followed. Bullying is not a sport enjoyed in solitude. He wasn't quite brave enough to upset the strange child by himself.

THREE

Unknown Ancestry

Having no idea she was an object of conversation between Lord Snowdon's son and daughter, the girl they had been watching rose and continued on her way. After some distance, she turned toward the great blue expanse below her and suddenly disappeared over the side of Mochras Head.

At this point along the promontory, she *was* allowed within three paces of the edge. For between the northern and southern extremities of the rocky face, the cliff had worn inland through the eons, creating a slope seaward from the plateau noticeably more gradual in its descent. Down it a well-worn path crisscrossed back and forth until it reached a sandy beach. The inviting narrow strand was approximately forty yards in width at high tide between water's edge and the bluff and stretched away in both directions under the shadow of the lofty headland.

Down this sloping trail the girl now made her way. She bent occasionally to pluck a wildflower from amongst the rocks beside her or kick at a pebble beneath her feet. Three minutes later she ran down the final winding slope and emerged onto the white sandy shore, bright almost to brilliance as it lay between the blue-green of the sea and the gray-black of the rocky promontory. Her descent was not unlike that of the wide-winged sea birds—whose antics she glanced up at now and then with hand to forehead. She never tired of watching as they played on the currents and breezes between the cliff and water, occasionally dropping from great heights to the sea, almost paralleling the very trajectory she had herself just taken.

The joys of exploration and discovery of late afternoon were no doubt heightened by the fact that her days were not entirely filled with happiness. School was a painful ordeal for Gwyneth Barrie. She was slow of speech and insecure among the other children who were quick to make her the object of their derision. That she never defended herself and silently accepted the teasing of other children in the village as the natural order of things, invited their jeers all the more.

Her stature, too, tempted cruelty. As it has in all times, the smallest and least aggressive in the animal kingdom are singled out by others of their kind for intensified scorn. Poor Gwyneth had the misfortune to stand a head shorter than any other boy or girl her age in Llanfryniog.

No one but her father knew exactly how old she was. Everyone considered her several years younger than she was. The women who had suckled her, as they grew to fear her, had done their best to forget. The years, however, passed more quickly than they realized. Most assumed her eight or nine. She had actually just turned thirteen.

Pure white hair—lighter than was altogether natural, the old women said with significant expressions—added yet one more visual distinction to make her, in the eyes of young and old alike, more than merely different but *peculiar* from other children.

Codnor Barrie, stocky, muscular, and a harder working man at the slate mine than most, stood but a few inches over five feet. It was therefore no surprise that his daughter should also be a bantam among her peers. He had suffered similar indignities in his own childhood and youth. It had been assumed that by some quirk of nature his two average-sized parents had produced a dwarf for offspring. But Codnor grew into manhood manifesting no dwarflike attributes other than a simple lack of height.

None in Llanfryniog had ever laid eyes on his wife. Assuming from the daughter that she must have been as tiny as he, they would have been shocked to see her on her wedding day in Ireland, neither short nor blond, towering four inches above beaming young Codnor Barrie.

Notwithstanding his diminutive stature, in all other respects the Welshman, widowed less than two years later, had lived a normal life. This did not stop two or three of the low-minded men of the village from thinking that he, like his daughter, came from an inferior class of humanity. After several pints of stout in Mistress Chattan's pub, such boors often made him the object of their base jokes, exactly as their sons did his daughter.

Courage, however, is measured by other standards. Young Gwyneth possessed more valor than any of her schoolmates among the things of *her* home—whose roof was the sky and whose furnishings and friendships were provided by nature itself. It required no fortitude to ridicule the defenseless. But let the heavens open and unleash their torrents, let thunder roar and lightning flash, and young Gwyneth Barrie was out the door of the school into the midst of it, rapture in her eyes. All the while her classmates cowered near the black cast-iron stove waiting for the tumult to pass.

Likewise not a youngster among them would tempt fate by walking toward the hills at dusk for fear of the water-kelpie of the mountain lakes. *Gwberr-niog* was known to come out only at night. They were as terrified of waking his hunger for human flesh as the fishermen who braved the waters of the Celtic triangle were of arousing his cousin-beast Gwbert-ryd. Gwyneth, however, romped and played among the trees and hills near her home as happily with a moon overhead as the sun.

Nor would any of the boys and girls of Llanfryniog on the cheeriest of days have crept among these rocks and caves where Gwyneth now frolicked beneath the promontory. Legends of dead pirates and live beasts abounded. Her own fearlessness only confirmed in the eyes of fellows, schoolmaster, and old wives of the village alike that Gwyneth Barrie exercised a closer acquaintance with the dark forces of the universe than was healthy in normal people.

Fear being a healthy ingredient in the human constitution, Codnor Barrie's daughter possessed her appointed share. But she was well on her way at an early age to recognizing what *should* be feared and what should *not*, a vital distinction to a life of contentment.

Thus was young Gwyneth Barrie suspected of being preternaturally abnormal from other children—a view given credence by the impediment of her speech—freakish, queer, perhaps not quite "all there" according to Llanfryniog's gossips. Even the calm sagacity of her countenance, it was assumed, hid something sinister. Had she been a prankster, mean-spirited, or a giggly simpleton, she would scarcely have been given a second thought. That she spoke little, and was *better* than other children, made her an object of mistrustful and dark speculation.

Her light hair, shooting out from her head in the disarray occasioned by being raised by a man not a woman, surrounded features pale but full of health. Out of their midst gazed wide, knowing, trusting eyes of deepest blue green. Their shades were as changeable as the sea itself. At one glance, they seemed to reflect the blue of heaven, at another the emerald green of several inland lochs at the height of spring's snowmelt.

Young Gwyneth's ageless face was one any thoughtful grown-up would pause over with mingled admiration and question. In truth, who could not admire the graceful loveliness of childhood, a beauty still dormant but waiting to blossom? In the midst of their awe, however, rose the riddle of those empyreal eyes. They surely possessed some secret that might be worth knowing but which would not be easily discovered. The face bore a complexity of expression only a true Celt could recognize. And then only one who knew the old mystery of the ancient race.

That her dead mother was no native to Gwynedd and, said some without a wisp of evidence to back up the claim, was more than a little disreputable herself strengthened the conviction that the odd child, if she was not one already, was well on her way to becoming a witch. The child's tongue was cursed. That alone was a sign that must be heeded. No good would result when she came of age.

Hopefully before then she would disappear from among them.

Codnor Barrie himself came from a decent Welsh family. He was mostly respected among his fellow workers. He had no complaint against him other than falling in love with an Irish lass who had borne him a witch-child and then promptly died for her trouble. The poor widower was left alone with his baby. The good little man may have named his daughter for the Snowdonian region of Gwynedd. But that could not prevent her being what she was.

Once her peculiarities became evident, Barrie was offered no more help by the women in the village such as they would have given any other poor father with a daughter to look after. Those who had nursed and bathed her in infancy now feared for the day the curse of the growing girl would come upon them. They wanted nothing to do with her. The Christianity so deeply embedded in their Celtic blood was heavily laced with superstitious remnants of the paganism out of which it had grown. They trembled at the sight of her floral bouquets as maledictive charms against the doors of the village from the nether regions.

The mother's untimely death, though rarely spoken of, was never forgotten. What could it be but a verdict from on high? It was only a matter of time before similar judgment was rendered upon the daughter. Doubtless some ill-fated misfortune would eventually fall upon Barrie himself for allowing the evil to invade Snowdonia from across the Irish Sea.

FOUR

Secrets of the Sea

G wyneth ran to the water's edge and skipped merrily along it for some distance, then slowed. She realized that the tide on this afternoon lay uncommonly low. The flat, wet expanse of sand was much wider than usual. She gazed all about then returned in the direction from which she had come. She passed the end of the path from above then continued northward where a rocky shoreline gradually encroached on the expanse of sand until replacing it altogether. A stormy few weeks had prevented her coming here for some time. With the tide so low, she could again explore the crags and boulders and caves at the water's edge.

Two or three minutes later she was scrambling about the base of the rocky headland, scanning the small pools left by the tide for tiny sea creatures and plants. Living things of all kinds and species gladdened Gwyneth's heart. Hers was a continual search to discover new forms of life she had never seen before, whether insect or flower, weed or bird, tree or unusually colored rabbit. On this day what drew her attention where sea met land happened to be the limpets, sea snails, mussels, tiny crabs, whelks, cockles, and water bugs made newly accessible in the swirling eddies of the extraordinarily low tide.

The tide on this day lay lower than it had in years. The waves of previous weeks against the rocks and inlets of the promontory had rearranged the sandy floor of the caves and beach. The largest of the boulders remained unchanged. Yet the surface beneath Gwyneth's feet was different as she scampered over it. Some rocks of great size previously exposed were nearly covered with sand. Others whose mere tops were partially visible before had been to all appearance thrust upward into the light of day. With every rise and fall of the tide, new changes came to the coastline.

She walked into the largest of the caves, which sat at the foot of the sloping bluff where the beach sand mostly gave way to rocks and boulders. Its height was sufficient that she could explore to a distance of thirty or forty feet inside it without bumping her head. It was one of her regular haunts, though only when the sea was calm and never when the tide was in its flow. Smooth slate walls beside her as she entered glistened black from constant salty spray.

The tide was still in retreat, and on this day there was no cause for concern. Gwyneth knew the signs of the sea, knew when danger was present and when it was not. She never allowed curiosity to compromise safety. She was, in truth, more "there" of intellect and savvy than most of the villagers had any idea.

If she was different than other children, the distinction came more likely as the result of genius than fatuity. Like most genius, however, it was invisible to the commonplace mind and would be slow to reveal itself. Whatever rare gift she possessed yet lay at rest, growing, deepening in the invisible recesses of her character, awaiting the kiss of a prince to bring it awake in power.

By now the shadows of afternoon were lengthening. The westerly sun cast its slanting rays against the cliffs of Mochras Head. It had not yet descended far enough on its daily journey to hover at the horizon and throw its light directly into the yawning mouth the girl had just entered. But dim visibility shone inside the cave as the tide approached low water.

Gwyneth walked gingerly into the blackness, hands spread in front of her. As well as she knew the place, subtle changes in the sea floor made her cautious lest some stone or wall of rock loom before her unseen.

All at once her toe caught something half buried at her foot. She stumbled and fell onto her stomach and elbows at once. She cried out softly, more from surprise than pain, as she hit the wet-packed floor. Quickly recovering herself, she rolled to one side on the sand and lifted one knee.

Suddenly a terrified shriek echoed through the darkened chamber.

A foot away, two dark eyes were staring straight at her!

Black and vacant, however, they were eyes that saw nothing. The human skull, whose empty sockets leered silently in the blackness, lay two-thirds buried in the sandy cave floor. Thin light from the cave's mouth played eerily on the polished bony cranium. That its season for seeing was long past only heightened the dread of the hideous spectacle.

Gwyneth sprang to her feet and sprinted for the safety of sunlight. She did not once glance back in the direction of the macabre object uncovered by the storm. Not easily frightened, Gwyneth's young heart now clutched at her chest with the horror of the unknown.

Lightning and rain and legends of lake creatures were one thing.

Dead human heads with black holes for eyes were another!

She dashed across the open sand, turned for the promontory, and scrambled frantically along the narrow trail. All the way up the rocky bluff the way she had come earlier she ran as if her life depended on it.

Reaching the plateau above the sea, she scarcely slowed. With what remaining speed her feet possessed, she set out across several fields and then over the wide moor toward the stone cottage at the edge of the hills where she and her father made their home.

FIVE

Lord and Laborer

F rom a high vantage point overlooking plateau, town, harbor, and the coastline of the sea for miles, two watchful eyes beheld the curiously speedy retreat of the girl away from Mochras Head inland across the flat moorland below.

It was not his custom to walk alone on the rolling hills and solitary high meadows of his estate. He was not a great walker. He preferred the back of a horse for transport to his own feet. But afternoon tea had precipitated a disagreeable dispute with his wife. Roderick Westbrooke, the Viscount Snowdon, had therefore sought the out-of-doors, not for whatever solace it offered but merely to get away from the house. His annoyance required movement to quiet itself.

Though his stables were well stocked with suitable mounts for any occasion, he was in no mood for a ride. It was too late in the day for that. He had wandered out with no particular destination in mind. He ambled aimlessly up from the house, kept on longer than planned, and now a mile from the manor still had none.

Lord Snowdon paused at the sight below him. He stood observing the flight, now across the road that connected the village of Llanfryniog to the main north-south thoroughfare. At length the blond-headed figure disappeared from his view.

Gradually he now made his way down the slope he had climbed. Descending a dense thicket of pine and fir toward a stream where it passed through a corner of his estate, he eventually completed a wide arc back toward the front of the house.

If only it *was* his estate, he mused sardonically. . .in *all* ways. That his name appeared on the title was such a mockery when he possessed no means by which to rule and enjoy life as a lord and viscount ought to be capable of.

The ridiculous inheritance laws could be so confounded unjust. They gave a man property and title but no means to use them if those means had been squandered before his time!

He had known all that, of course, when he married the earl's daughter. *Her* wealth and *his* property seemed made for each other.

He had not paused long enough at the time to consider the consequences if she ever proved stubborn. Now he found himself on the horns of that very dilemma.

Technically, of course, it *was* his estate. The ground itself, the land, the house were entirely his possession. But what good did property by itself do a man? He couldn't *spend* dirt or trees or grass or the stone blocks of which the manor was made.

He had to find a way to win her over to his point of view. . .or else find some other means to raise the cash he needed. The opportunity before him was one he mustn't let slip by. True, it was only a yacht. But he had his heart set on the purchase. Yet without his wife's funds, the thing would be dashed difficult, if not downright impossible.

❧

Meanwhile, the child Roderick Westbrooke had seen reached the stone cottage of her home and burst inside. Her father had only moments before returned from the slate mine north of the village. He spun around at the sound of the door nearly crashing off its hinge.

"P–P–P–Papa, Papa," stuttered his daughter. "Th–th–th—"

"What is it, Gwyneth, my child?" asked Barrie as he calmly

approached with open arms. He had long ago learned that to soothe his daughter's agitation was the quickest remedy for the difficulty of her tongue.

"It's a. . .a h–h–h–h—"

Her father sat down and took her lovingly into his lap as if she were as young as the villagers thought her. He smiled with reassuring patience.

"Th–th–th–there's a head, P–P–Papa," she finally blurted out. "It's b–b–b–buried in the s–s–s–sand."

"Where, Gwyneth?" asked Barrie calmly.

"In th–th–th— In the c–c–c–cave, P–P–Papa."

"Where, Gwyneth?"

"B–by the w–w–water. I stumbled over it and fell d–d–down."

Her father stroked her wild hair and gently rocked her in his arms. Gradually she calmed.

"Are you hurt, little one?" the miner asked.

"No, Papa," Gwyneth replied, leaning her head against his chest. Already the cave apparition was beginning to fade. Since she was not one ruled by fear, neither did she cling to it on the rare occasions it visited her. She was happy to let it go. She would soon laugh at the memory.

Assuming his daughter had seen some oddly shaped stone, or perhaps come upon a fragment of sheep bone fallen from the plateau above, Barrie thought it best to avoid further mention of it.

The two chatted casually a few minutes.

"Shall we have some tea, Gwyneth?" asked the father at length.

"Yes, Papa," she replied, jumping down from his lap. "I will boil water." She ran across the floor, picked up a small iron kettle, and dashed outside.

Her father rose and followed her toward the small kitchen that occupied half of the larger of the cottage's two rooms. Upon arriving home, he had restoked the stove with coal and already begun water boiling for potatoes. He now bent to check the fire again then tossed in a second small shovel of fuel from the scuttle.

A moment later, Gwyneth lugged in the kettle of fresh water. She placed it on the stove.

He tossed a handful of potatoes into the iron pot, now beginning to steam, beside it. "Did you get bread from Grannie, Gwyneth?" he asked.

Her face fell. "I forgot, Papa," she answered. "I meant to after I went down to the sea. But I forgot and ran straight home instead."

"No harm done. We shall go see Grannie together while the potatoes boil."

Adjusting the flue of the stove, Barrie turned and took his daughter's hand. They left the cottage together and made their way down the sloping hillside toward the sea and to the village of Llanfryniog.

SIX

Trouble in Glasgow

A sneaking figure of a lanky youth of sixteen sprinted along a wide Glasgow street. The echo of tinkling glass from a breaking shop window faded behind him. In his hand he clutched the booty he had retrieved through it.

He had no need of the antique sterling silver mug. Neither did he have the slightest interest in whatever money it might fetch. The shiny object struck a momentary fancy as he passed, nothing more. Mere seconds after spotting it, a brick from a nearby alley crashed through the window. The next instant he was sprinting along Gallowgate, mug in hand and a smile of youthfully devilish triumph on his face.

The mere thrill of theft drove him. It had been brought on by neither necessity nor upbringing. The lad's training had in fact instilled an altogether different set of values than those of the lifestyle in which he had been engaged for the past year or two.

Unlike the most common of thieves, this youth came of wealth. His was a home highly respected in the city. He had been given all the privileges of his station yet was now doing his best to mock them. Like many adolescents—ruled by a lust for autonomy, seduced by premature self-reliance, possessed of self-gratification, and eschewing common sense in the choosing of associations—he had reached fourteen and suddenly found the constraint of goodness intolerable. Within another year, he had burst its bonds altogether. The adventure upon which he had now embarked contained just enough danger to act as a stimulant to his rebellion.

His only creed at present was to make mischief and to do that which was certain to be "disapproved of." That such self-indulgent behavior could make anyone truly happy was doubtful. Nevertheless, such was the lad's modus operandi. And he had given himself wholeheartedly to it. Whether the training he had received in his early years would in time reemerge to reverse the present decline of character, he alone would be capable of determining.

Clinging to the stone building at his left, he shot into a narrow close leading away from the wide thoroughfare. He could not help smiling to himself at how absurdly easy crime really was.

Suddenly his eyes shot open, and the smile disappeared from his lips. Thirty yards in front of him stood a policeman!

His running feet clattered to an echoing halt on the cobblestones. The evening fell momentarily silent. The boy stood as one paralyzed. His eyes drifted down to the large mug glistening in his hand.

With cocky nonchalance, he turned and began to saunter in the opposite direction. He had only taken a few steps, however, when he heard the policeman's booted feet behind him. They were coming with steadily increasing tempo in his direction.

He wasn't about to wait to see how this turned out!

In one quick motion, he tossed the mug clanking onto the stones of the alley, then turned and sprinted back for Gallowgate. He could outrun any policeman in Glasgow. He had no intention of being caught with the evidence.

"Stop. . . Hey, you!" shouted a voice behind him. "Stop, I say!"

Calling out again and with whistle blaring, the policeman broke into a run. But though he took up the chase with vigor, the lanky legs of youth quickly widened the distance between themselves and the middle-aged bluecoat.

A quick glance by the young rogue over his shoulder confirmed that he was out of danger. He continued at full speed, however, as the whistles and shouts gradually faded behind him. Around a corner he flew, along a long block, across the deserted street, left again, and—

Suddenly a great crash was followed by exclamations of astonishment and cries of pain. The teen went sprawling over the rough stones of the street and landed in a heap against a brick wall. Angry curses burst from his lips as he began to pick himself up.

Before he could completely recover, a great hand seized the scruff of his neck and hauled him back to his feet. "Ay, 'tis you, is it, young Drummond?" said an unmistakable voice attached to the bulky frame he had collided with. "I thought as much. Ye'd be advised tae watch oot a mite better whaur ye'd bound."

"Yeah, yeah," the youth replied testily. "I might say the same for you, coming round the blind corner without letting a bloke know you're there. Just let me go, will you!"

"I want tae ken what ye're aboot runnin' through the streets this time o' the evenin'."

"I'm about nothing that's any of your business!" shot back the boy. He struggled in earnest to free himself, but to little avail. His captor was three times his size. The lad threw a nervous glance over his shoulder.

As he feared, soon another set of feet came running heavily toward them. "Stop him, Forbes!" shouted the exhausted pursuer. He lumbered to the scene, breathing heavily. "Keep a tight grip on him or he'll bolt."

"He's aye gaein' nowhere, officer," replied the policeman called Forbes. "I've a good grip o' him. Noo, young Drummond," he said, turning again to the boy, "why dinna ye tell me what ye've been aboot like I asked ye?"

SEVEN

The Village

The village of Llanfryniog of North Wales spread out in random disorder away from the main street running through its center.

Several shops—the post, a baker, a dry goods store, a butcher, and a green grocer—were supplemented by a dozen or more homes that boasted an assorted miscellany of goods in their windows. Most of their offerings—from sweeties to tobacco to eggs, milk, potatoes, turnips, apples, candles, jams, and an infinite variety of homegrown and homemade products—could be purchased for a penny or two, but rarely more than a handful of shillings. Even this latter, however, would have been a considerable sum for most who passed by and gazed at the simply offered wares. There were also a variety of services available from a blacksmith, a cobbler, and a doctor from their homes on the outskirts of town.

The school and the chapel, the same white-harled steepled stone edifice serving for both, stood at one end of the town. Beyond it the single wide street turned toward the harbor, gradually narrowed to a single lane not quite wide enough even for two farm wagons to pass, and skirted the coast northward for another mile before veering inland to connect again with the main road north where it led a course around the waters of Traeth Bach.

At the opposite end of town, walkers through Llanfryniog passed two other churches, symbolically facing each other from opposing sides. The wide thoroughfare then continued straight south, rising through farmland above the sea toward the plateau of Mochras Head. There, like its northern counterpart, it wound back inland to reconnect to the north-south road connecting Blaenau Ffestiniog in the mountains near Snowdon with Barmouth where the River Afton emptied into Barmouth Bay.

Near the top of the Mochras slope, a private avenue led off the main road east and inland into the foothills. An imposing iron gate across it with gatehouse beside stood some fifty yards off the main road. From this impressive entryway, the approach led along a winding tree-lined course of some half a mile up a continuing incline to Westbrooke Manor. The largest mansion for fifty miles sat at the base of the Cambrian range, which, as the hills surrounding it increased in height, led some miles inland to the southern peaks of Snowdonia.

Though it was a mere village housing a thousand people or less, its proximity to Westbrooke Manor, as well as the small natural harbor in the protected waters of Tremadog Bay, gave Llanfryniog the distinction of being of ancient date and of a certain historic importance. Centuries earlier it had been a sort of sister village to Harlech, the administrative seat for the surrounding coastal area. That Harlech Castle—built in the late thirteenth century by Edward I, dominating the region for centuries, and considered by some the most perfect castle design in all Britain—was now reduced to a stupendous but impotent stone shell took nothing away from the historic tradition of both towns.

Notwithstanding that serious judicial functions had long since passed to the larger cities of northern Wales, Llanfryniog continued as home to a lay magistrate, whose duties were largely at the behest of the viscount and involved minor civil matters. It was his daughter, in fact, whom the viscount's son and daughter had come to town on this day to visit. Neither viscount nor magistrate, however, benefited from the services of a local policeman. For that they must depend on

Porthmadog to the north or Dolgellau south and inland, both about fifteen miles distant.

It was not a serious deficiency. The need for either serious law enforcement or legal proceedings in such a rural oasis, where farming, fishing, and slate mining occupied most of the waking hours of its working men, was rarely felt. That they enjoyed their stout, and occasionally partook of more than their wives might have wished, belied the fact that these were good men, devoted to family, church, and the friendships that bound their community together. Nearly to a man, in spite of conflicting religious affiliation, most would have given their lives for any other. They would indisputably have bound together in common cause against any foe, no matter what the odds, whether real or imaginary.

If the Celtic blood of their ancestors had inbred a troublesome flaw into their collective nature beyond an occasional hot temper, it was an affinity for the bizarre, the paranormal, and the occult. Their religion, whether Catholic, Anglican, or Protestant, was so laced with superstition as in some respects to be scarcely distinguishable from the paganism of its ancient origins. The staid memberships of both Catholic and Church of England houses of worship, along with those of the more enthusiastically minded Methodist chapel, could all have quoted chapter and verse from the lexicons of doctrine that had been drilled into them from their infancies why the other two were false expressions of Christianity and theirs the true.

In actual fact, however, all three tended to see God as an almighty magician and shaman, rather than as the loving Creator-Father of humankind. Ritual, doctrinal legalism, and the idea of vicarious sacrifice passed down from humankind's prehistoric ancestors remained the pivotal elements of their creed, not obedience to the commands of the Creator-Son nor the sacrifice of self-will He exampled.

This grotesque intermingling of the Christian Gospel with medieval druidism presented a particularly frustrating challenge to the truth-loving ministers and priests who came among them through the years. Sadly, it also provided a singular opportunity toward manipulation and mind control for those pulpiteers of less honorable repute.

As if in visible manifestation of this occult religiosity that existed in the very air of the place, a small house constructed mostly of wood, whitewashed on its exterior, stood near the heart of the village. It had been built at the intersection of two narrow lanes—out of the way of most foot traffic and carefully avoided by those whose routes took them in proximity to it. The very architecture of the dwelling bespoke mischief if not outright devilry behind its weirdly appointed and colored exterior. A steep-slanted roof was accented by curious ornamentation at the four corners and with a spooky weather vane atop it. The purple paint on doors and window frames and an assortment of statues about the garden, including trolls, fairies, goblins, and a miscellany of bizarre figures and gargoyles, all indicated dubious if not outright evil intent.

The scrupulously avoided dwelling might easily have been a dwarf's cottage from some fairy tale transplanted out of the depths of Germany's Black Forest. How it came to be *here*, in this Welsh village where gray stone predominated, no one knew. That it predated by half a century or more its present occupant was certain. Yet almost by seeming preternatural contrivance of the gods, or of powers from more subterranean regions, the place had apparently been perfectly designed for its present mistress, even though she had been in Llanfryniog only a dozen or so years.

A small wood sign above the door, ornate with Celtic symbolism, snakes, contorted animal shapes, and leering faces, read: MADAME FLEMING, PSYCHIC—FORTUNES AND FUTURES FORETOLD.

None in the village knew why the enigmatic "Madame Fleming" had chosen this coastal village to set up her shop of doubtful wares or where she had come from. No one for a moment thought the name on the sign her *real* name. She was rarely seen. When she did chance to be about—with long flowing dresses of bright colors, sashes and scarves and kerchiefs of reds and pinks and oranges and purples about the head, and gaudy jewelry dangling from ears and neck and wrists—there was no mistaking her. Rumors abounded about the woman's age. These ranged from fifty to one hundred and five.

How she supported herself was an equal mystery. About this, even more rumors were part and parcel of the undercurrent of talk that circulated among the women of the place. Ideas were as far reaching as that she possessed independent wealth, to the existence of a dead husband of means, to her being "kept" by the viscount with whom she shared a secret he could not afford to come out.

If Madame Fleming, so called, had not come of gypsy origins in Bohemia or Bulgaria, she certainly looked the part. Except that gypsies, as associated as they were with sorcery and clairvoyancy, did not generally stay so long in one place, pay their bills, and establish themselves in communities it was their intent to fleece. That the woman had been here for so long and that no charge of misconduct or failure to meet her obligations could be laid at her doorstep argued for other antecedents, perhaps halfway reputable, than of gypsy tradition.

Neither man nor woman, neither miner nor fisherman, neither lord nor lady nor commoner was ever seen coming or going from her establishment. Yet she remained a distinct presence in the midst of the town and always paid baker and butcher in cash. The whole thing was an enduring mystery.

A private door opening into a dark and narrow lane leading away from the central district of Llanfryniog afforded ample means for further gossip. That it was never locked, and its hinges kept well-oiled for reasons of silence and secrecy, added credence to the rumors, despite all appearances, that she actually had paying customers. Some of them were said to be regular, including those who sought consultation from as far away as Chester. But there were also said to be some among the local populace who walked to and from her back door unseen from their own homes less than five minutes away.

At this time of night, with summer nightfall descending, though an occasional clandestine caller might extend his or her hand in the light of a flickering candle to have its lines read by the shadowy Madame

Fleming, it was Mistress Chattan's establishment on the main street that was doing the brisker trade.

By this time, the two young riders had returned to the mansion up the hill that was their home and were concluding an uneventful dinner in the dining room of Westbrooke Manor with father and mother, Lord and Lady Snowdon, the viscount Roderick and his wife, Katherine.

EIGHT

Ale and Information

*T*he evening wore on. Dusk deepened.

One by one the miners, having had what drink they could afford, left the inn for their wives, potatoes, tea, and, if they were fortunate, children who loved them and appreciated their hard work to put what meager provision they could on their tables each night.

A scruffy man probably in his fifties, although with features hard and difficult to assess, cast a look about the deserted street of Llanfryniog then walked into Mistress Chattan's inn. He was not a man who even had a place to go. He had left home at fifteen and never returned. He had not seen his father nor mother again. If he regretted his prodigality, he had never admitted that fact.

It takes humility to face the regrets of life honestly, and this was a man who had not yet become acquainted with the eternal imperative of humility. When he had had enough of the seafaring life, he had betaken himself to a career in subterfuge and charlatanry—turning whatever information came his way, or that he could coerce out of others whether willing or unwilling, into profit to himself. His methods had become more ruthless through the years, as befit the atrophy of whatever conscience he once may have possessed. He was a man better avoided.

He walked inside and quietly took in the two or three men seated at one of the tables. He walked slowly across the floor and found a chair at the far end of the room. His business would keep until they were gone.

An aproned woman approached, large though her step was soft. Hair graying slightly, her face showed weariness from the long day. She was, however, always eager to oblige a new customer.

The man glanced toward her.

"It's not a room you'll be wanting, I'm thinking?" said the woman.

"Just your darkest ale," replied her visitor.

She turned away. A minute later she returned with a tankard.

The man began to sip slowly and in silence.

One by one the other men rose. With a few final words to the proprietress, they gradually wandered out.

At last the stranger and Mistress Chattan were left alone.

"Another ale, if you please, my good woman," he said.

She brought it.

He tossed a half-crown coin on the table. It jingled in a circular motion until it fell silent.

Mistress Chattan scooped it into her fleshy palm. "I will bring you back what's due you," she said.

"Keep it," said the man. "There'll be another to add to it if you can provide me with a small piece of information."

Mistress Chattan's eyes narrowed imperceptibly. In her business, where talk was cheap and where the liquid inventory of her stock-in-trade tended to loosen tongues, she had come by more than her share of secrets. Some were harmless; some not so. That it was in the nature of her position to occupy the occasional *rôle* of confidante was in truth one of the perquisites of her profession. Over the years she had, by subtle art, by attentive ear, and by skillfully placed sympathetic comment, gained much information that might be useful to possess.

Indeed, Mistress Chattan knew far more about Llanfryniog's people than they had any idea. She possessed two or three juicy secrets concerning which she was biding her time until some profitable opportunity presented itself. At such time, she would either divulge what she knew or, if the price was right in the opposite direction, vow on a Bible, which meant nothing to her, to keep silent forever.

Giving away information, however, was another matter. She was a woman who knew how to guard her tongue. But as the man had rightly surmised, what she might or might not know could be had. . . for a price.

"Make it a gold sovereign," she replied after a moment. "If it lays in my power, I will tell you what I know."

"You are a shrewd one, if not a shrew."

"If you think to hurl insults at an honest woman, you best keep a civil tongue in your mouth," she spat. "One more such word and you'll get nothing from me."

"Tut, tut, lady, I was paying you a compliment. I shall give you your pound and one, then. It's easy money for you. All I want to know is where to find an old man by the name of Drindod."

"There's Drindods and there's Drindods," she replied cryptically.

"Toy with me and you'll lose your sovereign."

"There's at least six Drindods within a mile of my door. Another ten within five."

"This one's called Sean Drindod."

Mistress Chattan took in the information without divulging her chagrin. She did not like the look in this fellow's eye. Nor did she know where the old man could be found. She had heard the name. But she knew nothing more. And she had no doubt that this man would come back and slit her throat if she played him false.

"You can keep your sovereign," she said reluctantly. "If you want to know where old Sean Drindod is, you'll not hear it from my lips. But for what remains of the half crown, I will tell you of one in town who knows things. For a sovereign she will tell you what she knows."

"How do I find her?"

The stranger to Llanfryniog left Mistress Chattan's inn a few minutes later and sought the dark lane. Through quiet hinges no one heard, he was led into a secluded parlor. There a candle and incense burned in the gathering darkness.

The low conversation that followed between the stranger and the clairvoyant proved satisfactory to both parties of the exchange.

NINE

Drastic Measures

A Glaswegian man and his wife sat silently at a well-appointed supper table. A third place setting had been prepared. The chair before it was empty. They had waited until dark but had finally gone ahead with the meal. Every swallow, however, was made difficult by the concern visible in their eyes and by the ache eating at both their hearts.

It was not the first time the two had eaten late and alone. Yet upon every successive occasion of their son's absence, deeper anxieties arose concerning what might be the cause.

The house in whose dining room they sat was of obvious culture and refinement. The man's study upstairs, though lined with bookshelves, was sufficient to contain but half the volumes in his possession. Books spilled into most of the other rooms of the house, including this. On an ornate sideboard sat a handsome silver tea service. Furnishings everywhere bespoke wealth.

All such comforts, however, this man and woman of God would have traded in a heartbeat in exchange for the opening of the eyes of him for whom both now silently prayed.

Their affluence had been sought by neither. It was the mere result of the circumstances in which they found themselves.

The man's father was an earl. Though the title would not pass down at his death, he had already split most of what remained of his fortune, after what he had given away, between his son and daughter, keeping only enough for him and his wife to continue the missionary endeavors to which they had devoted their latter years.

In truth, the earl's son and his wife possessed a healthy fear of the balance of their account in the Clydesdale Bank. Unlike most couples of means, they took no pride in it nor based a moment's security upon it. The unusual man and woman regarded their wealth as a holy possession, not theirs at all but rather a stewardship that had been placed in their hands. It was not theirs to spend but rather to *administer* by prudence, prayer, and wisdom. They were of that exceptional breed in the spiritual realm, rare but thankfully not extinct any more in their own time than such were in the Lord's, though as infrequently found in society at large as in its churches—a humble and unpretentious man and woman of wealth.

"Where *can* he be, Edward?" said the woman finally. The question came from her mouth in scarcely more than a whisper. Either words or tears *must* at last burst from her mother's heart. For the moment she preferred the former.

Her husband shook his head. The only possible response was a pregnant sigh born of anguish too deep to find expression.

Nothing more was said. They continued to eat sparingly.

Their silence was interrupted fifteen minutes later by a knock on the parsonage door.

At the sound, the woman's hand unconsciously clutched at her heart.

The man rose quickly and strode from the dining room to the front door. He opened it and saw a policeman standing on the porch.

"I'm sorry tae be disturbin' ye, reverend, sir," said the transplanted native of Inverness who had come south years before and now wore the blue of a Glasgow bobby. "I'm afraid I found yer laddie up tae nae good again."

Beside him, with the large highlander's grasp firmly around the boy's bicep like a vise, stood the young thief. The expression of profound vexation on his face could not have been less indicative of repentance.

The vicar glanced at his son. His expression betrayed nothing. But his heart ached within him.

Behind him his wife approached. It was all she could do to avoid tears. She knew they would only make her son despise her the more.

"Thank you, Constable Forbes," said the vicar. "We are greatly indebted to you."

"Beggin' yer pardon, Mr. Drummond," added the policeman in an apologetic tone, "this will be the last time I'll be able tae bring the lad home tae ye this way. The next time, sir, it will be the tollbooth for him, even if he is but a lad."

"I understand."

"And there will be a bill comin' for tonight's damage."

"I understand, constable. Thank you very much. We will take him now." The vicar stepped forward, took his son by the arm, led him inside, and closed the door.

"Percy, *why* do you do these things?" said the vicar's wife once they were inside. Her voice was soft, though urgent. At last she could hold in her emotion no longer. She looked away and began to weep.

The boy struggled to free himself from his father's grip, but the man's quiet wrath was smoldering. He had finally had enough of his son's foolish antics. All fathers, no matter how long-suffering, how loving, how patient, have their limits. Vicar Edward Drummond's had finally been crossed. "Answer your mother!" he said angrily. He shoved the boy down in a chair and stood towering above him.

His son shrugged his shoulders. "I like to," he said insolently. "I enjoy outwitting the stupid policemen. I would have gotten away tonight if I hadn't stumbled, and if there hadn't been two of them."

"It's a game to you, is that it?"

"Of course it's a game. What else would it be?"

"How can you ask that after all we've taught you. . .all we've given you?" said Mrs. Drummond, bursting into sobs as she collapsed in a couch across the room.

"It is pointless to argue," said the vicar. "I don't know what evil spirit has overtaken you, or why. I do know this," he added in a tone of greater finality and resolution than his son had ever heard, "we *will* have no more incidents like this evening's."

The youth glanced up briefly then away. His father's words jolted him out of his testy nonchalance. They sounded eerily like a threat.

"I will *not* rescue you from your own folly again," the vicar went on. "If you persist, you *shall* find yourself in jail like Constable Forbes said. If it comes to that, I will not bail you out. Is that understood?"

The sixteen-year-old son sat sulking. He realized he had pushed his father too far. He had never heard such a voice of command. His father rarely became angry. It was obvious he had aroused something more dangerous than mere anger. That was righteous indignation.

One of his father's favorite sayings from the Bible was, "Let your yea be yea; and your nay, nay." His father was not merely a man of his word. He made no idle promises—or threats. What he said he would do, he would do.

The minister's son realized he had best lie low for a while.

"Go upstairs to your room," said the vicar after a moment. His voice had calmed but rang with no less authority.

Percy rose and went. To say that he *obeyed* would hardly be accurate. Mother and Father wondered if he had ever truly laid down his own will for the chosen purpose of doing what another commanded him. In the present case, however, the boy recognized the expediency to himself of departing his parents' presence at the earliest possible opportunity. This he therefore did.

To be banished to his room at sixteen, like a child, was a profound humiliation. But young Percival Drummond, though he may have been a rebel, was no fool. He was enough of a realist to know that his room at home was better than any of Glasgow's jail cells.

The parlor fell silent. Supper was by now long forgotten. Mrs. Drummond's breathing occasionally caught on a lingering sob.

At length her husband turned from where he had been standing still as a statue. He walked slowly to the couch. He sat down beside his wife and placed an arm gently around her shoulders.

"What did we do wrong, Edward?" she said in a broken voice.

The vicar sighed deeply. How many times had they asked that question of themselves during the past year? "I don't know, Mary," he replied softly. "If it continues, I don't see that I shall have any other option but to resign my vicarage."

"Surely that cannot be God's will."

"Nor can it be His intent that the son of the parish minister is running through the streets of Glasgow as a common burglar. Sadly that seems exactly our situation."

They remained silent a few minutes more.

"What would you think of our sending him to my sister?" said Drummond at length.

"In Wales—you mean. . .to stay?"

"I don't know—perhaps for an extended visit. The country might do him good. School will be out in a few weeks. At the very least, we could try it for the summer. When fall comes, we can see what the situation is then. School is doing him no good anyway."

"Do we really want to send him away from home, Edward? What if he doesn't return? I don't think my heart could take losing him at sixteen."

"We have as good as lost him as it is," rejoined her husband. "The city is trying its best to corrupt him. I fear for his soul if *something* is not done. The country has been known in some cases to exercise a therapeutic influence. Whether it can exorcise his spirit of foolishness and rebellion," he added with another long sigh, "I do not know."

His wife nodded. Her heart was breaking for her son. She was willing to consent to anything that might help. "He would never agree to it," she said.

"I shall give him no alternative," rejoined the father. "He is young enough that he is still dependent upon us for everything. I often wonder if he would have been better off had we been paupers. If his salvation requires it, I will cut him off without a farthing."

"Knowing that he stands to inherit all we possess, he would bitterly resent it."

"He is possessed with a spirit of resentment anyway. I doubt we can make it much worse. Character is the only inheritance worth giving. At present our son is in fearfully short supply. I would sooner give away my entire half of my father's fortune than allow Percy to squander it to his own demise. Hopefully time will not make such extreme measures necessary."

"I am in favor of anything that might help," his wife replied. "What do you think your sister's husband will say?"

The vicar smiled. "My brother-in-law is a man I can never predict," he said. "Roderick might refuse our request. On the other hand, it would not surprise me if he took a liking to Percy. That Roderick makes no claim to being a man of religion and has always looked down on me for my profession, would give him and our son something in common. They might find themselves forming a friendship on the basis of their mutual antipathy toward me!" he added, chuckling at the thought. "In fact," Drummond said, rising from the couch, "I like the idea so much, I think I will go up to my study and write Katherine straightaway."

TEN

Evil Night

*T*he night in Llanfryniog grew late.

Wispy elongated fingers eerily bisected a near-full moon only recently risen above the silhouette of the mountains to the east. The ethereal thin horizontal clouds did not substantially reduce the light from its pale glow but did portend this night's omens of sinister intent.

A powerful man, whose appearance might have indicated him one of the region's slate miners but whose hands and mannerisms indicated other means of gaining his daily bread, had let the evening pass until an hour when respectable persons had taken to their beds. Leaving Madame Fleming's, he now slunk through the deserted streets of the coastal Welsh village. The occasional lone bark of a dog was the only sound that divulged life.

He was careful that his steps were not heard. None saw him sneaking among the shadows of their abodes on his nefarious errand. It may have been unwise to talk so freely to the woman he had just left. But unless he was a poorer judge of character than he thought, she would not talk. If that changed, she could easily be bought off—or eliminated.

His own connection to the man he had come to Llanfryniog to find had come about years ago by one of those chance encounters destined to alter the course of life forever after. While most of the others in the

Dolgellau pub that night dismissed the drunken man's stories of pirate treasure with the laughter of their own whiskey-soaked brains, he had been sober enough for his ears to perk up.

For the next hour, he had listened attentively across the dingy tavern. An hour after that, he followed the man out and struck up what conversation was possible in his wobbly state.

It was enough to convince him that there existed more than a grain of truth to the man's story.

He had carefully arranged to meet Drindod again. . .and again, professing friendship and standing him drinks—the surest way to an alcoholic's heart. Gradually he learned more. He had not learned enough, however, to lay his hands on what the man claimed was the key to the location of the booty, a certain gold coin of exceedingly ancient date.

He had patiently waited all these years without success. He had tried every means of persuasion possible to loosen the old fool's tongue. He had craftily spoken with every septuagenarian and what few octogenarians remained within fifty miles, carefully and without betraying his intent.

But years continued to pass.

One by one they went the way of all flesh. Whatever knowledge they possessed passed with them. Fewer and fewer remained from that fateful century when fortunes were made—and hidden.

He had finally discovered where the man was from. After Drindod's retirement from the seafaring life, he had followed the old salt back to the home of his childhood.

Then came a day when he realized the time could be delayed no longer. If he did not act soon, it would be too late. He would be left with nothing. He did not intend to let this night pass without discovering more about the mysterious coin.

Pausing momentarily beside a wall of stone, the figure now hurried across a wide dirt street then along it another hundred yards. Though a conglomeration of cottages were scattered about inland, the buildings thinned northward along the shoreline beyond the harbor. With stealth he approached the seaward side of the street. Light from the moon was shielded by the low building in front of him.

The Fleming woman's description matched the place exactly. He crept toward its corner, paused briefly, then moved around it and temporarily into the thin glow. He did not hesitate. He set hand to the door and quickly entered. No homes in this region possessed locks.

A sound of startled wakefulness from the occupant was brief. "What are. . . Who are you?" he said in the darkness.

"Shut up, old man," growled a low voice at the bedside. It made no attempt to disguise itself.

"What are *you* doing here, Rup—"

A large hand clamped over the aged lips. "Quiet, I told you!" rasped a whisper which could not hide its menace. "Get up. You're coming with me."

The sleeping old man could hardly argue. Already his unwelcome visitor had rousted him from bed and was dragging him from the cottage in his bedclothes. The old man of eighty struggled feebly as he was pulled from his home. But the hand across his face prevented so much as a peep from escaping his lips.

Twenty minutes later, away from the village on a lonely expanse of shoreline and beyond the hearing of all save the waves, which never slept, at last assailant and hostage stopped.

The younger of the two released his prisoner and threw him rudely to the sand. "I've been patient all these years," he said. "Now I want to know where it is."

"I don't know what you mean," said the old man. He attempted to climb to his knees.

A rude kick sent him toppling over on his back. "You told me there was a coin."

"A small thing, of no value."

"You said it would lead to the rest."

"I was drunk. I didn't know what I was saying."

"Maybe the whiskey loosened your tongue to tell the truth."

Silence was his only answer.

"Where is it, Drindod! I want it. . . . I want it all!" He bent to the sand and raised his hand to strike.

"I told you before. The old man was dead by the time I saw him."

"Then how did you get the coin?"

"I never had it."

"You said you saw it."

"Only once. And just for a moment. I could never get my hands on it."

"But you know who has it. Tell me and I may let you live!"

"She has it!" the old man burst out, at last divulging his secret of many decades. "She's had it all along."

"Who? Tell me!" cried the younger man. He grabbed Drindod with a huge fist and viciously yanked him to his feet and within six inches of his own leering face.

"Little. . .little Bryn," whimpered the old man in terror. For the first time in three-quarters of a century he spoke the nickname of his childhood acquaintance of that fateful day.

"I've never heard that name! Who are you talking about?"

"I tell you, the girl has it. She would never give it to me. It was she who found the body. She was just a little girl."

Enraged at what he took for another lie, the hysterical prodigal seaman clutched his prey by the throat. A loud whack sounded across the wrinkled cheeks. The blow sent the weak old man sprawling again to the ground.

A few more wrathful attempts to coerce the information from him gave way at length to the full force of the younger man's fury. The struggle was brief. Soon all that could be heard was the rhythmic inflow of Tremadog's waters.

Five minutes later a shadowy figure, alone now and unseen of human eye, scrambled across a few rocks and up onto the moor. It then hastened northward away from the village.

Behind him, on the very shore whose secret had possessed him in vain for seventy-six years, lay the form of him who now followed the salty old pirate to a place it might be hoped was better than this.

ELEVEN

Condemned to the Country

*T*he first sensation to reach sixteen-year-old Percival Drummond's ears the morning following his arrival in the Gwynedd foothills of North Wales was the sound of a bird chirping somewhere in a tree outside his window.

He and his father had reached his uncle's home by coach after dark the night before. A round of tedious reintroductions to relatives he had not seen for five years had been punctuated by looks from his two cousins, Courtenay and Florilyn, that did not invite optimism about his prospects. Boring conversation followed on stiff chairs with tea altogether too strong for the occasion. Mercifully he had finally been allowed to retire for the night to his new quarters.

A prison cell would be a more apt description! Maybe he had been wrong—a Glasgow jail *might* have been better!

How would he possibly live through the summer in this country wasteland?

Perhaps after his father left, Percy thought, he could steal some money and make an escape. There might be some fun to be had out of this after all!

He turned over sleepily, stuffed his pillow over his head, and did his best to go back to sleep. But it was no use. The blasted bird was too close, too loud, too persistent. If he had a gun, he would shoot the infernal thing. If it insisted on waking him every morning, he would see about getting one! His uncle surely had a well-supplied gun cabinet somewhere about the place.

Reluctantly he climbed out of bed, dressed with the enthusiasm of one preparing for his own execution, and left the room. He descended to the main floor of the house. He heard voices coming from the breakfast room. The last thing he wanted was to see anyone.

The gnawing in his stomach, however, reminded him that such a thing as food existed and that sixteen-year-old boys consumed great quantities of it. He therefore walked along the wide corridor toward the sounds and entered. He found his aunt and uncle and father seated about the table.

"Ah Percival—good morning!" exclaimed his uncle.

"Hello, Uncle Roderick," he replied with an imperceptible nod. He did not offer much of a smile to accompany it.

"Come, Percival," said his aunt Katherine, beckoning him to one of the empty chairs. "The tea is just come."

Percy approached and sat down. Somberly he took the plate offered by his aunt and helped himself to generous portions from the contents of several platters on the table.

"I see nothing to be gained by glossing over the affair," said Edward Drummond as his sister poured tea into Percy's cup. "I have been explaining to your uncle Roderick and your aunt Katherine exactly the nature of, shall we say, our *problem* with the authorities in Glasgow. Should you think to dupe them, Percy, rest assured that I have urged watchfulness. There are no false pretenses about your presence here. They know what you have done and exactly why I have requested that they take you in for the summer."

Percy busied himself with breakfast. He saw no advantage in making a reply. His father's words rankled, but an argument now would not help his cause.

"Don't worry about a thing, Edward," put in Westbrooke with

blustery confidence. "We shall have an amiable time of it. Although I dare say the country life may be more dangerous than you bargained for," he added, laughing.

"How do you mean?" asked the vicar.

"Tilman Heygate, my factor, came to the house early this morning to tell me that the body of an old man was found on the shore a mile south of the harbor just after daylight by one of the village fishermen."

"Who, Roderick?" asked Mrs. Westbrooke in alarm.

"Old Sean Drindod."

"The poor man!" she exclaimed as her hand came to her mouth.

"Drowned?" asked the vicar.

"No, actually. That's the curious part," answered Westbrooke seriously. "Seems his neck was broken."

"What happened?" asked his brother-in-law.

"No one knows. There appears no sign he'd fallen among the rocks. I'll ride into town later this morning and speak with the magistrate. At the moment it appears he was murdered."

His wife gasped as her face went white. Silence fell around the table.

Lord Snowdon quickly resumed his zestful spirits. "I assure you such occurrences are most out of the ordinary." He laughed, though his wife's face remained pale. "As I said, Percival will be most welcome. We shall make a man of the young Scotsman! Once he has a taste of the country life, you may never get him back to Glasgow."

"Thank you, Roderick," replied the vicar. "You cannot know how much this means to Mary and me."

"It is the least we can do for your brother, is it not, Katherine?" replied the viscount. He glanced briefly across the table to his wife. "If the lad proves troublesome," he said, throwing Percy a quick wink and grin, "I shall hire him out to one of my tenants to help with the sheep shearing or send him to sea on one of the fishermen's boats. Eh, Percival, my boy? Hard work and country air—that's what's wanted. We shall provide both in good measure."

Lord Snowdon's words rang a little hollow in his wife's ears, seeing as how he had never taken the slightest interest in making a man, as he put it, of his own son, who would sooner have jumped over the moon than soiled *his* hands in the matted wool of a dirty sheep. But the moment her brother's letter had arrived from Glasgow with its request, the viscount had perceived his opportunity to reestablish himself in his wife's good graces. Well knowing her family's notions of spirituality and Katherine's fondness for her older brother, Westbrooke determined to assist her side of the family in the matter of their wayward son. Secretly he hoped for the result of his wife's loosening up her purse strings. Toward that end he would make himself everything an aristocratic country uncle should be to a Glasgow-bred youth. Thus he would win favor with the brother-in-law *and* his wife.

Whether eighteen-year-old Courtenay would greet the presence of his city cousin with equal jubilation was doubtful. He had behaved himself last night. Yet from the moment Percy's eyes met those of Courtenay Westbrooke, his elder by a year and a half, it was clear that a contest for supremacy was inevitable. Courtenay's fifteen-year-old sister, Florilyn, was every bit the equal of either boy in feisty self-centeredness. But she would gain her ends by wile rather than bluff. She possessed the face and physique of an eighteen-year-old, with cunning and coquetry in equal measure. She was already turning more heads among local old youths than either of her parents had any idea and had bewitched several to attempt foolhardy exploits to gain her notice.

That both young Westbrookes were as spoiled as money could make them was as much a grief to their mother as it was object of humorous jocularity to their father. The viscount was not a man for whom character was life's highest ambition, either for himself or his offspring. Even now, with the evidence before his eyes every day, he yet remained oblivious to the danger he continued to perpetuate by pampering his son and daughter in their self-indulgence. Westbrooke was of the school that taught a man to get what he could and watch out for number one. His foresight, therefore, was not altogether perceptive in the matter of what he might be passing down unto the third and fourth generations of his progeny.

The axiom "Lead by example" works in many directions. The result generally reinforces tendencies already well established within the garden of personhood. A good example is not usually sufficient to counteract a bad one willingly emulated. In this case, as their father was the stronger personality of the marital union, the children had taken his model as their standard. Neither Courtenay nor Florilyn had any desire to become a saint. Both appeared likely to be granted their wish.

Breakfast concluded, Percy wandered back to his quarters. Alone again, he stood for a moment gazing absently out the window, then turned again into the room and threw himself on the bed. It was less than twelve hours since their arrival. Already he was bored silly.

His father found him unmoved forty minutes later.

Their good-byes were stiff and awkward. Hoping for a word or glance or gesture that might indicate a softening in his son's soul, the vicar remained a moment more beside the bed.

But none came.

Drummond turned at length and left the room. Tears gathered in his eyes as he made his way down the hall.

An hour later he sat in the coach on his way to the train that would take him back to Glasgow. *God,* he prayed silently, *his mother and I have done the best we knew. It certainly did not turn out as we had hoped.* He sighed disconsolately then added in an inaudible whisper, "Do what You can for him, Lord. Fulfill the words of the proverb that he will one day return to the training we gave him."

Shortly after lunch—a strained affair with aunt and uncle now that he was alone with them—Percy wandered out behind the great house. He had seen neither of his cousins since the previous night and was glad. As much bluster as he tried to wear, he was, after all, still a boy in many ways. One would think that city life might have made him more worldly wise than his country-bred cousins. Just the opposite was in fact the case. Without any noticeable spiritual component to their existence, in spite of their mother's efforts, and a sense shared by both of their own superiority as wealthy son and daughter of a lord, Courtenay and Florilyn had matured rapidly in that ugliest of character flaws—hauteur. They were in love with themselves.

Percy Drummond, on the other hand, had grown up as the only child of a manse. That fact alone had shielded him from many of the very influences bearing such foul fruit in the personality gardens of his cousins. He at least had *heard* values espoused that, though he now eschewed them, had been part and parcel of the soil in which his being had sent down its first roots.

Percy's rebellion was a phase of youth. The conceit of his cousins was more deeply endemic to their natures. It would thus be more difficult to purge.

TWELVE

The Stables

For the rest of the day, which seemed fifty hours long, Percy wandered about, did his best to avoid human contact, returned to his room, stared out the window, lay on his bed, wandered out again, and nearly went mad with boredom.

The family did not gather for dinner as the viscount and Courtenay were gone to the neighboring estate. A buffet had been spread out in the dining room. Percy ate with his aunt, though the conversation was mostly one-sided on her part.

Slowly the evening wore on. Dusk descended on North Wales. A gorgeous sunset rose over the sea to the west but was lost on Percy. Alone in his room, he stared out the window into the dusky gloom. All below him the house was quiet. It had been since the striking of ten. Everyone had long since retired.

It had been a warm day. The evening remained warm as well. Percy's window stood open. Straight out from him, midway up into the sky, a few reminders remained of the brilliant reds, yellows, oranges, and purples of the sunset that had come and now were gone. No noticeable disturbance of the air came to his face. Yet he felt the faintest tingling of the sea somewhere about his nostrils, borne inland on breezes too light to be felt by the skin. He continued to gaze in the general direction of the ancient Green Isle of Ireland, which was supposed to be out there somewhere. Closer at hand he could just barely make out the fading dividing line between the blackening green of sea and the faint dimming goldening blue of sky.

What was on his mind, even sixteen-year-old Percival Drummond himself could not have said. He was young for introspection and unaccustomed to the exercise though its season was approaching. How far away and long ago Glasgow seemed—another world from this.

He reflected on the incident that had sent him here in the first place—the theft of the sterling mug. It was not the first such incident.

What had possessed him to do such things? So remote it now seemed in his memory.

What caused the reckless streak within him? Was his rebellion directed against his father? If so, again came the question—why? Did he resent his father's profession? Had he been trying to discredit him, make him look foolish in the eyes of his parishioners?

For now, such questions remained unanswered.

The only sounds coming from outside were crickets, turning the darkness into their own chirping symphony. From the stables behind the house, whenever the crickets paused to rest their leggy instruments, the occasional stamp of horse's hoof or snort of nose and lips broke the silence.

He knew his father had sent him here to change. But now the question rose, and with it an inexplicable annoyance: Did he *want* to change?

A last vestige of insurrection rose within him.

I am who I am, Percy said to himself with mounting indignation. *I am not my father. I am no one but me. I shall do as I please! Nothing will change me!*

He turned from the window and took several restless paces into the room. Realizing there was no place to go, he turned toward the window again.

He swore under his breath, hardly pausing to reflect that his father, peaceful man though he was, would whip him if he heard such from his lips.

He closed the window with a bang, angry at the crickets, angry at the tomfool of a horse who was keeping the stables awake, angry at the peaceful and fragrant air, angry at the sea, angry at the mountains, angry at his father for sentencing him to this ridiculous place.

He spun around and walked toward his bed and threw himself on his back. Mercifully sleep eventually brought an end to the tedious day.

Percy awoke the following morning, fleetingly thought himself back in his bed in Glasgow, then realized with a sinking feeling that his waking had brought a return of the bad dream.

His second morning in Wales passed much like the first. By noon he was going so mad with cabin fever that he had to get out and find *something* to do.

After lunch he left the house again, determined to find some way to pass the afternoon.

In truth, Percy was more insecure than he let on. He was not quite sure of himself here. He was out of his element and could not help feeling a little ill at ease. He fancied himself more a man of the city than he actually was. Whether he would allow that insecurity to be transformed into humility, or would encourage it to fester into smoldering bitterness against his father—the most natural, though illogical, target of youth's imagined grievance—only he would be able to determine.

Once outside, Percy walked around one wall of the huge stone manor house. He soon found himself among hedges and roses and flowers. As yet they held little fascination for him. He was not alive to the mysteries of growing things. Realizing he had entered an enormous garden, he turned and retraced his steps.

Give him the streets of Glasgow and he would be at home anywhere. But here in the country—with limitless space in every direction, with green all about, with the blue vault overhead, without people and with only solitude and emptiness, and with such blasted quiet everywhere—he didn't know what to do with himself.

He kicked petulantly at the gravel beneath his feet. He had to do *something*.

He made his way aimlessly toward the opposite side of the house. Soon he found himself wandering in the direction of the largest of several outbuildings surrounding the manor. From the sounds and smells and general look of them, he realized that he was approaching the barn and stables. Though he knew how to ride as well as a half dozen city lessons had made him capable, it could not be said that he was a great horseman. But if he was going to spend the holiday here, he thought to himself, he would probably have to acquaint himself with this place. He continued toward the buildings.

The wide wood-planked door of the largest barn stood open. He walked inside.

Dim light and the mingled aromas of hay and horseflesh were the first sensations to reach his eyes and nose, followed almost immediately by a more pungent bouquet, at once enchanting and repulsive depending on one's love or antipathy toward all things equine. It was the strong smell of manure.

A snort or two sounded from deep in the darkness. Percy glanced about, sniffing with some discomfort. Gradually his eyes accustomed themselves to the shafts of dusty sunshine slanting through the doors at each end and several openings high along the walls.

Suddenly a voice he could barely understand broke the silence.

"You'll be Master Percival Drummond, I'm thinking," said a crusty, thick Welsh tongue.

Startled, Percy spun about. Ten feet away stood a lanky man of fifty-five or sixty, clad in blue work trousers, boots, and worn green shirt. His sleeves were rolled up to the elbow, and his hands clutched a pitchfork.

"Uh, yes. . .that's right," said Percy, recovering himself.

"Pleased to make your acquaintance," said the man. "It's Hollin Radnor you're talking to, my lord's groom. Were you wanting a ride, Master Drummond?"

"Well. . .sure, I suppose so—if you don't mind."

The groom turned and ambled deeper into the huge barn.

Percy followed, continuing to look about as his eyes adjusted to the surroundings.

"Your second day at the manor, is it?" asked the man.

"Yes, it is."

"No better way to acquaint yourself with the country than on horseback. Here's just the one for you, Master Drummond." He paused beside a waist-high stall. Inside stood a light grayish-brown mare, with a white forehead star and two white stockings on her forelegs.

"What's its name?" asked Percy.

"Grey Tide," replied Radnor. He pulled down a saddle from the rack nearby and lugged it to the stall. "Like the water of the sea after a storm."

"Not wild like a storm, I hope," said Percy. He could not prevent his tone betraying a hint of nervousness.

The groom laughed lightly. "Don't you worry about a thing, Master Drummond. She's the gentlest creature in the place. Though's she's fast enough with Lady Florilyn in the saddle. For today, you just enjoy a quiet ride to get your bearings of the estate and hills."

Satisfied, though still a little fearful, Percy watched as the groom opened the stall, spoke a few words in Gaelic, then proceeded to saddle the mare.

He had never ridden other than on the flat grass of Glasgow's city parks. He had never been more than a mile from the stables where he took his few riding lessons. Nor had he ever ridden alone. He was still trying to decide if this was such a good idea when, a few minutes later, the groom led him through the back door of the barn to stand near the mounting block.

"All right, then, up you go," said Radnor, offering Percy a hand.

Still wondering if this was wise, Percy slowly mounted.

"Follow the road there up the hill," added the groom, pointing ahead of him. "In half a mile you'll come to the high gate. After that you'll have the whole of Snowdonia in front of you!"

THIRTEEN

On the Slopes of Gwynedd

*F*ollowing the groom's instructions, Percy rode tentatively away from the stables.

He had hardly gone a hundred yards, and was still within the precincts of house and garden, when suddenly the form of his cousin appeared from behind the trunk of a great beech tree. If her unexpected movement startled the mare called Grey Tide, the animal showed no sign of it other than a brief upward jerk of the head.

"Where are you going?" asked Florilyn Westbrooke. She stepped into their path, reached for the rein at the mare's nose, and stopped her.

"Just for a ride," answered Percy.

"Where?"

"I don't know. . .nowhere. Just there—up in the hills, I suppose."

"You must be a skilled horseman."

"Not really. Why?" asked Percy.

"To go out alone. . .on our wildest horse."

"The man back there in the barn—I've already forgotten his name—he said she was perfect for me."

Florilyn saw the quick look of anxiety that passed through Percy's eyes as he spoke. She met it with a mischievous smile of her own.

"Oh. . .Hollin?" she said with pretended innocence. "One thing you

70

will learn is that he is the biggest liar around here."

"Why would he—"

He did not have a chance to finish his question.

As quickly as she had appeared, his cousin now leaped aside, ran to the back of the horse, and gave its rump a great swat, followed by a piercing shriek.

The mare lurched forward, nearly throwing Percy backward onto the ground. Desperately trying to keep his seat, he grabbed frantically for any piece of mane or saddle his hand could find. The next moment he found himself hanging on for dear life as Grey Tide galloped out of the grounds. Florilyn's laughter echoed in his ears.

In less than ten seconds, which nevertheless seemed a lifetime, his mount slowed. Gradually she resumed a gentle walk away from the house. Knowing full well that his cousin was still watching behind him, Percy did his best to regain his composure after the brief scare and do so without looking back.

Vowing to get even with the little vixen the first chance he got, he tried to relax. Slowly the manor receded in the distance behind him.

After passing through the eastern gate of the estate ten minutes later, Percy found himself on open hillside. He continued at a slow walk. Now that it was behind him—and now that he had survived it!—the memory of his brief skirmish with death atop a galloping horse filled him with a sense of exhilaration. As a result, he quickly gained confidence as he went. This was nothing like the lessons he had had at twelve on the Clydebank. He had to admit it was an agreeable sort of activity once he was comfortable enough to trust the beast underneath him.

For one accustomed to the rolling hills and dales of Ayrshire, the countryside over which Percy Drummond now made his way might not have appeared scenic or beautiful. To the young Glaswegian, however, though he would persist yet for a while in trying to convince himself he hated the rugged and mountainous aspect of the place, it could not help but strike into him a vague sense of awe.

Beautiful, perhaps, it would not be called by some, but wild certainly...

big, high, even magnificent. If rugged starkness possessed an allure not found either in city street or tidy countryside, that appeal might explain why the ancient race of Brythonic Celts, now known as the Welsh, had made their home here. He supposed the area through which he now rode was like the highlands of his native Scotland. But in his two or three sojourns up Scotland's western coast with his parents, he had never paid much attention to the scenery.

At present grass grew under his mount's four iron shoes. Upward ahead in the distance, however, stone seemed the chief characteristic of the landscape, here black, there containing reddish hues, but mostly gray. He continued to make his way through low-growing shrubbery and a few small woods. The highest ridges ahead, however, were so rocky as to appear mostly bare.

Several peaks loomed rather than towered in the distance. They were not of particularly great height, though remnants of snow could yet be seen on one or two. The topography rose steadily eastward from the sea into the northern reaches of the Cambrian Mountains, of which Percy could now see the summits of Rhinog Fawr, Yllethr, and Diffwys stretched out as in a line some four or five miles inland. The lower slope of Moelfre was nearer at hand and partially obscured the latter. Blue billows of clouds drifted lazily in the blue expanse overhead.

It was altogether a lovely summer's day for a ride. Had Percy Drummond been more a friend of nature, he would have derived immense pleasure from it. If the truth were known, he was actually enjoying himself more than he was likely to admit. He was more than a little proud of himself for holding his seat for so long as well as he had. The spectacular grandeur about him could not help but prick certain hidden regions of soul to which it was designed to speak.

Northward out of sight from here, the range of inland peaks rose amid craggy precipices and high-notched passes through the range to its highest point, Wyddfa, "nesting place of the eagles," known in English as Mount Snowdon. The treeless granite gray peak from which the region took its name overlooked the whole of North Wales. It was the highest summit in Britain south of the Scottish highlands, second only to Ben Nevis, with which it shared an uncanny likeness.

Percy found himself riding for some time along a trail that gradually and circuitously ascended upward and northeastward. Whether it was actually a trail or not, the horse followed it on her own. Cresting a small rise, he heard the tinkling of bells.

A moment later, a rambunctious flock of sheep suddenly appeared nearly upon him, scrambling and bleating their way along the ridge. Seconds later Percy found himself in the middle of a tumultuous sea of white. Neither horse nor sheep paid the other heed, though the mare paused while the little white balls of wool passed, scurrying and baaing around her feet.

A stocky lad followed behind the flock, a black and white sheepdog at his side. "*Prynhawn da,*" he said as he came near. "*Sut mae?*"

"I'm sorry," replied Percy with a confused expression. "I'm afraid I don't understand you."

"Then 'tis I who should be apologizing," said the boy with a smile. "I said good afternoon to you. Fine day for a ride, it is."

"Yes—thank you. I had no idea anyone else was nearby," said Percy. "I must admit you startled me. I'm not too good on a horse."

"Looks to me you are doing right fine. I shall get my sheep out of your path as quickly as I can."

He cried out in the strangest voice Percy had ever heard, uttering some unintelligible mixture of command and singing chant. Whatever its meaning, the animals all understood the ancient Welsh tongue. The sheep burst into a frenzy of motion, scooting along at suddenly doubled speed. The dog leaped eagerly into action and scampered about at their heels with sudden frenetic urgency.

Percy took the young shepherd for several years older than himself, though he was in truth seventeen. His stout frame was not as tall as Percy's, yet broad and muscular. The brown, leathery skin of face and arms, from constant exposure to the harsh coastal elements, gave an appearance of age beyond his years.

"The name's Stevie Muir," the boy said. "I live over the hill there." He pointed behind him.

"I am Percy Drummond," said Percy.

"New to Llanfryniog?"

"Visiting," answered Percy.

"Da. Then let me say *'Croeso i Cymru'* to you!"

Confusion on Percy's face was his only answer.

" 'Welcome to Wales,' in your tongue."

"Thank you," nodded Percy.

"I best be on my way." The boy called Stevie laughed. "My little flock is already leaving me behind!" He broke into a jog to catch them, whistled once, then turned. "You'd be welcome for a visit anytime," he called back. "We're over the rise there, in the little crook of the next valley. . .a little stone cottage."

"Thank you," said Percy.

Stevie waved then turned and hurried after his sheep.

Percy resumed his ride in the same direction. A short distance farther up the gently rising slope, he paused and turned around in the saddle to take stock of where he had come. Whatever might be the horse's condition, his own hindquarters were sore. He would gladly have dismounted and walked awhile. He was not at all confident, however, that he would be able to get back up on the mare by himself.

Spread out below him, at a distance now of perhaps two miles, stretched the coastline. Between the ocean and himself sat his uncle's imposing stone mansion of Westbrooke Manor from which he had come. The eight-foot-tall stone-block wall of the boundary of the estate meandered across moor and through field, into woodland, and a good way up this same slope and out of sight, in a great circumference of four or five miles surrounding the great house. From this distance the estate did not appear so huge. In truth, however, the viscount's property measured in the thousands of acres. Only a portion of it lay enclosed by the high stone wall in the immediate vicinity of the manor.

Lord Snowdon owned most of the village of Llanfryniog as well, and nearly all its cottages and the poor homes Percy saw scattered about the moorland and into the hills. His tenants paid him, through his factor, semiannual rents. Though they could at times prove difficult to bear, they were not so crippling as they might have been. His people considered the viscount a reasonable man, though generally stern and aloof. Most harbored no reason either to love or hate him. That they did not tremble when they saw his factor approach on horseback was a good sign. Though neither did they smile.

The sea today offered the beholder intriguing shades of blue and green. From the high vantage point of his ride, the white stretch of sandy beach below the bluff straight ahead of him was obscured from Percy's view by the cliff edge. Farther to the right, however, the sand surrounding Llanfryniog inlet, at the southern extremity of which the body had been found, and the slate roofs of the village beside it, glistened in the westerly afternoon sun. Sails of a few fishing boats from the harbor dotted the surface of Tremadog Bay, as the waters were known between Point Mochras and the peninsula of Lleyn, faintly visible at a distance of some fourteen to sixteen miles to the west. Northward from Percy's outlook, the spires from another great country house, constructed of more reddish-looking stones and appearing like a castle from this height, rose above the coastal moorland.

As he gazed about him, Percy realized that he had come a good distance. He had better return down the slopes. If he wanted to know more about these hills, he would find out another time. He had already ridden farther than he intended.

He urged his mount on. Perhaps the mare now sensed the direction he wished to go, for she veered to the left and they began a descent, where they would circle around and return to the estate by the front gate. He decided that Grey Tide was the horse of choice for him. She seemed to know that he trusted in her.

FOURTEEN

Nosegay from a Tiny Friend

*A*nother hour passed as the lone rider from Glasgow made his way out of the hills on a course roughly southwest. His route brought him below the estate on the wide moorland plateau overlooking Mochras Point as it sloped down to the inlet and village. Feeling relatively at ease in the saddle by now, though tired, he even urged Grey Tide into an occasional light trot for a few moments.

Mostly occupied with the ground in front of him, he glanced up to see a small girl a hundred yards ahead walking casually toward him. With seemingly aimless step, she was apparently on her way to nowhere. She stooped to the ground every now and then. As he drew close, she glanced up, stopped, beheld him steadily as he came toward her, then shielded her eyes from the sun and smiled.

"H–h–hello," she said sweetly, stuttering as she spoke. She did not seem embarrassed by the fact.

Percy reined in and looked down from his high perch. "Good afternoon to you," he said, returning her smile. He did not realize it, but it was the first intentional smile he had sent in the direction of another human being in a long while. That of the girl, along with the wide trusting gaze of her deep azure eyes, was so infectious there was nothing to do but return it.

"W–w–what are you doing riding G–G–Grey Tide?" the girl asked, patting the horse's wide stomach without hint of fear.

"You know this horse, do you?"

"I know all the horses at the m–manor."

"Do you indeed! Why is that?"

"Because I love horses. I love all animals."

"Do you live at the manor?"

"No," replied the girl. "I live over there." She pointed behind her, but Percy could see nothing. "That is where I have *my* animals," she added, turning back toward him.

"Do you have horses?"

She shook her head. "I wish I did. M–m–most of my friends are smaller. But why are you riding one of Lady Florilyn's favorite horses?" she asked.

"I am her cousin."

"Oh!"

"I am here to visit for the summer."

"From where?"

"From Glasgow."

"That is a b–b–big city, isn't it? I think I have heard of it."

"A *very* big city," laughed Percy.

The girl's eyes widened. "Have you been to London?" she said. "I want to see London someday."

"I am sure you shall," rejoined Percy. "And Glasgow, too. Perhaps you shall visit me there one day."

Her face brightened yet more. "Visit *you*?" she said.

"And why not? I am *here*. Why should you not go *there* when you are older?"

"My father is poor. How would I get there?"

It was a turn in the conversation Percy had not anticipated. He had merely been making conversation. "Those things have a way of working out," he said breezily, glancing about.

The girl's silence brought his gaze once more down to her face. Her wide round blue eyes still stared straight up into his. "Grannie says always greet a stranger with flowers," she said simply.

"So—" Percy smiled, in the absence of suitable reply, a streak of wit seizing him—"you consider me a stranger, do you?"

"I've never seen your face before."

"Then what do you intend to do about it?"

"Give you the flowers I picked for you, of course," replied the girl with an innocent smile. She brought her hand from her side. "Here," she said, reaching up and handing him a small handful of tiny wildflowers.

Percy hesitated as he took them. The heart of the sixteen-year-old rebel was suddenly touched by the kindness of the child-stranger. He hardly knew what to say. He hadn't expected such a response to his attempted humor. The droll smile faded from his mouth as he spoke again.

"Surely you meant these for someone else?"

"I picked them for you," she replied simply, still gazing into his face with wide, innocent eyes. "Now that I have given you flowers, I must know who you are. What is your name, so I shall know whom to ask for when I go to Glasgow?"

Percy could not help laughing with delight. He hardly even noticed that as she had grown more comfortable talking with him her stuttering had lessened. This girl was absolutely too charming! The fact that he was out in the middle of the countryside, so far from the city where he was accustomed to behaving like a surly youth, brought out of him responses very different even than he would have expected.

That the girl herself—at one moment so young, at the next seemingly ageless in her innocence—had evoked his laughter and the unexpected feelings that had gone with it was not a fact he paused to consider. As they spoke, their respective ages of thirteen and sixteen—the girl such a child in the eyes of the boy, the boy such a man in the eyes of the girl—did not enter the matrix of either's consideration. Both could have been fifty; both could have been five.

"My name is Percival. . .Percival Drummond, at your service," replied Percy at length. "My friends call me Percy."

"What would you like *me* to call you, Mr. Drummond?"

"You must call me Percy. What is *your* name?"

"Gwyneth Barrie."

"Then, Gwyneth Barrie, I am happy to make your acquaintance." Clutching the floral gift in his left hand, he bent down from the mare's back and extended his right as far toward her as he could.

She reached up and placed her tiny palm inside his and shook it.

Percy pulled away his hand, sat back upright, and looked for a moment at the humble bouquet. Again the thoughtful mood swept over him. "But. . .why did you pick these for me?" he said.

"I saw you coming," replied the girl.

"You didn't know me when you picked them. Surely you don't give flowers to *every* stranger you pass."

"Only those who are going to become my friends."

"You knew that about me?"

"Of course."

"How did you know?"

"I saw on your face the look of a friend. So I picked them for you as you rode toward me."

Percy gently lifted the tiny nosegay to his nostrils. He breathed in of the earthy fragrance in which was hidden the faint perfume of something sweet. When he looked up, already the girl had left him and was making her way up the hillside.

Percy stared after her then turned around in the saddle with a mysterious smile of question on his lips and slowly continued on his way.

FIFTEEN

Cardiff

I tell you I've seen it with me own two eyes!" said a raspy voice.

The candle in the center of the table between the two men danced on the hard-bitten, deep-chiseled miner's face. The light revealed eyes nervously in motion lest unwanted ears venture too close.

"Maybe you have, and maybe you haven't," said the other. His tone was calm and measured. "But I pay nothing without seeing it with *my* own two eyes."

The corner of the darkened pub fell silent. The man who had just spoken, his accent betraying that he was no native to this region, sat doing his best to swallow his annoyance. The other, whose accent was barely intelligible to his ears, took a long swallow from the tall mug in front of him. The Englishman had come here to make what he understood was a simple arrangement with a longtime Welsh coal miner of greater cunning than most of his fellows gave him credit for. The man was said to possess information his employer had been seeking. He had not been told the fellow was an opportunist and shyster as well.

Most of the business conducted within the buildings, offices, and storefronts of Bute Street in the burgeoning Welsh city across the channel from Bristol at the mouth of the River Severn had to do with one of two things—coal or shipping. This port, which at the beginning of the nineteenth century had been little more than a township, had grown rapidly with the industrial nation's hunger for coal. Cardiff was well on its way to becoming a great metropolis and seaport. It sent around the world that valuable black commodity from the nearby mines which lay in abundance beneath the mountains north of the city. English, Irish, and Scots flooded daily into South Wales, brought here by industry. They were now as numerous in Cardiff as its native Welshmen.

Neither coal nor shipping, however, was on the minds of the crusty miner or Englishman across from him. The two had been engaged in low conversation in a darkened corner of a cellar pub half a block off the busy Cardiff thoroughfare long enough that the Welshman had downed a pint of dark strong beer and was well begun on a second. With the other paying, he would consume as much as quickly as he was able. It was not the sort of establishment in which the Englishman felt altogether comfortable. He had heard stories about Cardiff that did not put him at ease. But he had been told he would find the man here. He hoped the information he possessed would make it worth his employer's while.

"And see it you shall," the miner said, "but it's far to the north, in that part of Wales called Snowdonia. I won't take you there without five crown up front. Then it'll be fifty quid more when your own eyes flash at the sight."

"They told me you were a thief, Bagge," said the Englishman. "Now I believe them. But you'll not get a brass farthing from me without *some* kind of proof."

The miner smiled, if such it could be called. Though he had scarcely enough teeth left to make much use of, his lips parted in devious delight. A low chuckle rumbled in his throat. A Cardi was known for having short arms and deep pockets, and this old-timer took the Englishman's comment as the highest form of praise. To outwit an Englishman in any financial transaction represented the ultimate triumph.

The man called Foulis Bagge brought a dirty hand to his chest and patted the outside of a ragged grimy coat once or twice with significant expression.

"Are you telling me you. . .*have* proof?" asked the other.

"Right here," replied Bagge, patting his coat again.

"Let me see it."

"Let me see the five crown."

The Englishman hesitated a moment then reached into his own vest pocket and retrieved a small handful of coins. He placed ten on the table between them.

In less than a second they were gone, swallowed up in the miner's blackened hand with the marvelous speed of a frog's tongue snatching a fly from midair.

With the coins secure in an unknown receptacle somewhere among his garments, he now slowly drew back the flap of his coat with one hand. The other crept slowly and mysteriously inside it. His fist emerged a moment later, clutching a small leather pouch. Untying its neck with deliberation, occasionally sending his cunning gaze across the table, he held it out to allow the other man a brief peep inside. The Englishman's eyes widened at the sight. Even in this dim light there could be no mistaking the contents.

The five crowns, however, only purchased him two or three seconds. Suddenly the bag withdrew, was yanked shut, and disappeared after the coins.

"This came from the place you told me about?"

"It did."

"You could lead me to it?"

"For fifty quid, Sutcliffe, I'll carry you there on me own back."

After a few minutes more conversation, the Englishman rose and departed the pub, leaving the toothless Welshman to his third pint. He squinted briefly as he climbed the dirty stone stairs back into the sunshine then turned again into Bute Street.

After a block's walk, he stopped and stepped quickly into a large, handsomely appointed black brougham whose owner had been waiting.

The moment the door closed behind him, the driver above called out to his team of two. The windowless carriage jostled into motion.

"Well?" said the man seated inside.

"He is exactly what I expected, crafty as a Cardi and twice as greedy."

"Will he do it?" asked the other, whose voice left no doubt of his aristocratic upbringing.

"I think for the right price our slimy friend Foulis Bagge would do anything, including sell his own grandmother. But he would tell me nothing without ten half-crown coins in his greedy fist."

"A small price. You paid him?"

The man nodded.

"Did he provide you a map?"

"No. He said he had to lead us there himself. He did show me what he purports to have taken from the place with his own two hands."

"He will take us there, then?"

"That was the agreement. But I warn you, he will double-cross us in a minute if he sees his opportunity. He may have to be killed once we know the exact location."

"Again," said the other, "a small price to pay. You made arrangements to meet again?" he added.

"He will wait to hear from me."

"Good. It seems the time has come for us to make closer approach to the owner of the land in question."

Sixteen

The Festive Board

*T*he atmosphere around the lavish dinner table that evening at Westbrooke Manor was noticeably cheerier than could be claimed as the normal custom.

Young people are notoriously skillful at moodily subduing meal conversation into irritable and sullen silence, invariably preferring anyone else's company to that of their parents and anyone else's conversation as well. On this occasion, however, the addition of Percival Drummond to the Westbrooke family ensemble promised amusement to his cousins and provided at least a slim potential of conversational interest for their parents.

All except the youngest were seated promptly at seven thirty as a staff of two began to ladle out a colorless cabbage soup. Florilyn entered a minute later and took the last remaining seat, which happened to be opposite their guest. She did not look at him, though Percy was staring daggers at her.

Percy waited, not quite sure what protocol would inaugurate the proceedings. When his uncle at the head of the table picked up his soupspoon, he assumed that no formal prayer would be forthcoming. A glance in the other direction, however, revealed his aunt momentarily bowing her head.

The same instant Florilyn looked up. Her eyes came to rest on his face. Percy observed the movement and turned toward it. The expression that met his was not what he expected. It was a sly smirk, not particularly subtle. Florilyn's glance flitted toward her mother then back again, as if making silent sport of old-fashioned religious predilections. The expression carried with it the assumption that Percy was of one mind with her in finding the private moment of prayer humorous—as if they mutually shared a slightly naughty joke.

Now whereas Percy would have been the first to ridicule the faith of his own father and mother, and that not merely in private for he had in fact been doing his utmost to *publicly* ruin his father's reputation along with his own, the slight against his aunt annoyed him. Whether he found himself taking his aunt's part against his cousin because of the incident earlier in the day or whether some unexpected remnant of the spiritual training of his formative years suddenly rose to the surface unbidden, Percy Drummond himself would have been the least able to say.

It is a well-known fact that, removed from the parental objects of their rebellion, many temporary prodigals find themselves not nearly so antagonistic to the faith of their upbringing as they thought. They surprise both themselves and their parents by growing closer to the parental tree than seemed possible at the height of their youthful independence. In the end, their roots extend deeper into the soil of their early years than anyone would have expected.

Though perhaps invisible forces might even now have begun probing his soul, however, Percy was aware of no sudden spiritual epiphany. He simply did not like his cousin making fun of his aunt. He understood the look perfectly, and it rankled him. He gave it no answering reception by sympathetic expression of his own. He would not, even by the subtlest passing glance, play his aunt false.

Detecting by his blank stare that she had been rebuffed, Florilyn was clearly not pleased. The expression that followed added yet more to the spirit of worldliness that was all too apparent, even at fifteen, dripping from her countenance.

All this passed in less than two ticks of the second hand on the giant clock on the wall behind Roderick Westbrooke.

Percy waited in respectful silence. As soon as he saw movement from his aunt out of the corner of his eye, he took up his spoon with the others.

"So, Percy, my boy," boomed the viscount from the opposite end of the table, entirely oblivious, as he was to most of the internal dynamics at work in his family, to the brief drama that had taken place between the cousins, "how did you find your first day in Wales?"

"Fine, sir," replied Percy, looking toward him with an effort at a smile.

"What did you find to occupy yourself?"

"Percy went for a horse ride, Daddy," chimed in Florilyn in a mischievous tone.

"Did he now? Good for you, Percy, my boy. Did you accompany him, Flory?"

"No, Daddy," answered Florilyn in a tone of affected injury. "He seemed to want to be alone. He galloped off before I had the chance to ask if he wanted some company. It hurt my feelings, actually. . . . After all the rain, I had been wanting someone to go for a ride with."

"Don't forget, dear, this is Percy's first day here. We must be patient and allow him time to get used to his new surroundings. What do you say, Percy. . .perhaps you can take your cousin along next time? I dare say she won't slow you down much."

"Yes, sir," replied Percy, smoke coming out his ears.

"I don't know, Daddy," said Florilyn. "I'm a little unsteady on the back of a horse. I might not be able to keep up with him."

A flinch of the eyes shot her way from her brother, accompanied by the hint of a sportive grin.

"Nonsense," blustered her father. "You'll find we're not so bad," Westbrooke went on to Percy in a jovial manner. "Perhaps not so sophisticated as your city friends, but you must give us a chance. How about you, Courtenay," he said, turning toward his son. "Good to be home from the university, I'll warrant. How did you spend your day?"

"Colville and I went shooting in the forest," replied Percy's older cousin.

"Any success?"

"Not much. A couple of pheasants and a rabbit."

"Ah, well—the big game have probably retreated into the mountains for the summer. You'll have to take Percy out with you next time."

Courtenay vouchsafed no reply. Instead he busied himself with his soup. What he thought of his father's suggestion, he kept to himself. As the meal progressed, however, he thought that perhaps his father had indeed hit upon something.

Though but a year and a half separated them, he had grown up considering his cousin a mere child along with his sister. The teen years had done nothing to convince him that he ought to modify that assessment.

Yet in one of the inane displays of the animal kingdom, the male ego is compelled—in ways often foolish and rarely revealing manhood's true strength—to demonstrate superiority over its fellows. Ironically this impulse is stimulated all the more by insecurity. The greater the self-doubts, the more overpowering the drive to prove prowess. On the other hand, a young man with sufficient self-confidence that his budding manhood is not threatened by his peers, with nothing to prove, has little desire to strut the peacock's tail of his ego. Paradoxically, the more cocksure a youth shows himself, in all likelihood the less of a true man he is on his way to becoming.

The moment Courtenay Westbrooke learned that his cousin was coming for the summer, and why, an undefined resentment began festering within him. That Percy looked and acted like such a stripling— he was fully six inches shorter and two stone lighter than himself—yet had been in trouble with the police, had actually, if he had heard the thing right, once spent a night in jail, made him resent him all the more.

He had never run afoul of the law, thought Courtenay. He had never been in trouble, never been arrested, never been sent away for the summer. Part of him envied Percy the roguish reputation that preceded his arrival. Yet in a perverted way, he also despised him for it. Hardly having subjected his motivations to the scrutiny of logic, Courtenay was anxious to prove, to himself and to Percy, that whatever his exploits in Glasgow, his fair-skinned little cousin wasn't as tough as he might think.

"How are you with a gun, Percy, my boy?" asked Westbrooke, turning from his son to their guest. "I take it you know how to use one?"

"Yes. . .of course," replied Percy hesitantly. The fact was he had never held a gun in his life, much less pulled the trigger of one. Guns had not been allowed in the vicarage. To his knowledge, his father had never owned one.

"What did you learn in town about poor Mr. Drindod?" asked Percy's aunt as the soup was cleared away and steaming platters of beef, vegetables, and potatoes were carried in from the kitchen and set before them.

"Nothing," replied her husband. "No one knows a thing. The man was simply found facedown on the beach half covered by the tide."

"Did you talk to Mr. Lorimer?" asked Katherine.

"I did." Westbrooke nodded. "He knows no more than I do."

"What's it about, Father?" asked Courtenay.

"One of the old fishermen from the village—he was apparently killed on the beach last night."

"Oh!" squealed Florilyn. "A murder—how exciting!"

"Florilyn, goodness! What a thing to say!" exclaimed her mother.

"What's wrong with it, Mother? Nothing fun ever happens around here. I think it *is* exciting."

"It is dreadful. . .the poor man."

"We don't know for certain it was murder," the viscount went on. "There are no obvious signs of it, no clues, as it were. He was too far from the bluff to have fallen. If there was a struggle of some kind, the evidence was washed away long before the body was found."

"The *body*. . . I like that!" said Florilyn exuberantly. "It sounds like a mystery novel! Is it allowed to call it a *corpse*, Daddy?"

"Florilyn, good heavens!" expostulated her mother a second time. "We have a guest. He's going to think we are a family of heathens."

"I don't care, Mother. Besides, I *am* a heathen, so why shouldn't I talk like one?"

The viscount roared with laughter at the humorous repartee. He hardly paused to consider what his reaction to his daughter's uncouth tongue indicated of his sensitivity toward his wife.

Percy was also enjoying it. He could not help an inward smile. It was not that his momentary loyalty to his aunt had faded. But neither could it be denied that he found his cousin's irreverent and sassy manner more or less in harmony with his own. But he was still furious at her. He would not give her the satisfaction of seeing him smile at her antics.

"What are you going to do, Daddy?" asked Florilyn enthusiastically.

"There isn't much we can do," replied her father. "I wrote today and reported the matter to the authorities in Dolgellau. Whether they will send someone to investigate, I don't know. Otherwise, he'll be given a decent burial. God bless him and take care of his soul is about all there is to it."

"Oh pooh, Daddy," Florilyn said with a laugh, "you don't believe any of that."

"What are you talking about, Flory?"

"That business of God taking care of his soul. You just pretend for the sake of what people will think. You go to church and sit there and make a pretense of paying attention. But I know you're looking at your watch waiting for the boring sermon to end. The man on the beach is dead, and that's all there is to it, don't you mean? You don't *really* think he's still alive somewhere. Nobody believes that anymore."

She had finally gone too far even for her father. The viscount's superstitions toward matters of religion were deeply enough embedded that he dared not cross them. Whether there was anything to it all, he hadn't a clue. But like many an unbelieving man of so-called religion, he saw no reason to take any chances.

A brief shudder coursed through him at the words that had just echoed about his table, as if his daughter's audacity was tantamount to a curse against the gods and would bring retribution down upon them all. "Of course I do, Flory," he replied, unaccountably ruffled by her perceptive assessment of his usual outlook of a Sunday morning.

"Then where is he, in heaven or hell?"

"How in blazes should I know? I'm no priest. I didn't even know the man."

"What do you think, Percy?" said Florilyn, turning and staring across the table with large, inquiring, devilish eyes. "You're the son of a minister. You probably know all about such things."

Taken by surprise, Percy had no leisure to prepare himself for suddenly finding himself on the spot.

Glad to be off it himself, this time his uncle did not rescue him.

"What do I think about what?" he said.

"Whether the dead man will go to heaven or hell."

"I would say the same thing as Uncle Roderick—how should I know? I suppose it would depend on what he believed."

"Do *you* think there's a heaven and hell, Percy?" she asked, blinking her large eyes playfully several times with feigned sincerity.

"I don't know. I suppose I don't really know what I believe."

"Doesn't Uncle Edward preach about heaven and hell all the time?"

The question took Percy off guard. He found himself thinking a moment. "Actually," he said slowly, "now that you mention it. . .no, he really doesn't. I don't think I've ever heard him preach a sermon about heaven and hell."

"What does he preach about then?"

"I don't know. . .doing good, being nice. . . He's always talking about doing what Jesus said. That's one of his favorite phrases."

"What does that mean? How can anyone do what Jesus said?" laughed Florilyn. "Why would anyone even want to?"

"I don't know," replied Percy a little testily. "I'm not claiming to know what it means. I'm just telling you what he says, that's all."

He suddenly found himself in the uncomfortably weird position of beginning to defend his father against his cousin's nettlesome barbs. He didn't like it. He had no interest in pursuing this line of conversation or being on the receiving end of his cousin's irksome interrogation.

Without planning it, he turned to Florilyn's brother at his right. "Who's the chap you went hunting with?" he asked.

"Colville?" said Courtnenay. "He's our neighbor."

"Colville Burrenchobay," added the viscount, relieved to have the opportunity to wrest the conversation away from his daughter. "His father owns the land adjacent to mine, northward."

"I saw what looked like a castle when I was riding," said Percy, "about two miles away, I would say."

"That's it." His uncle laughed. "Burrenchobay Hall. Hardly a castle, but an imposing edifice indeed. Colville's a year older than Courtenay. His father represents Gwynedd in parliament. But we try to forgive Trevelyan his odd politics. The boys grew up together. I doubt there's a square inch between Blaenau Ffestiniog and Barmouth you two lads haven't explored together, wouldn't you say, Courtenay?"

Courtnenay nodded.

"Well, if you're the horseman Florilyn seems to think, Percy my boy," the viscount went on, "I'm sure you will learn your way around the hills in no time. No better place in all the world to ride."

"I ran into a fellow today with a flock of sheep," said Percy. "But the horse didn't seem to mind them."

"You'll find sheep everywhere in the fields and hills," rejoined his uncle. "The horses ignore them. Who was he—did he tell you his name?"

"Yes. . .uh, let me see—Stevie. . .something like that, I think."

"That's Stevie Muir," said Florilyn. "A big, ugly oaf if you ask me."

"He seemed nice enough," said Percy. "He invited me to visit him."

"Oh, ick!" exclaimed Florilyn. "I wouldn't set foot in that filthy cottage where he lives! All those poor people are so uncivilized. Their floors are nothing but dirt! Can you imagine how dirty everything must be? Ugh!"

At the end of the table, Katherine Westbrooke hardly tasted the food on her plate as the meal progressed. Listening to what came out of her daughter's mouth was mortifying and humiliating to her sensitive mother's ears. She excused herself with the pretext of a headache when the meal was over, declining coffee and dessert, and apologized to her brother's son for her departure.

Seventeen

Westbrooke Manor

*P*ercival, only son of Edward and Mary Drummond of Glasgow, had visited Westbrooke Manor but once prior to this in his life. That was so many years ago he scarcely remembered other than hazy recollections of the place. The last time he had seen his Welsh relatives was five years before in Scotland.

Lord Snowdon's estate spread across the sloping incline up from the moorland plateau above the sea toward the inland hills. From the house, therefore, one could command a view of most of the region seaward, as well as north and south for some distance. Approaching the estate from the village, as one entered the front gate the great house could not actually be seen. A thick wood lay between the gate and the manor, comprised mostly of pine and fir, as well as magnificent specimens of ancient beech, oak, and chestnut.

The drive wound through these trees until it emerged suddenly into a vast clearing. This expanse spread out on both sides, still sloping gently upward. At the far end of it, the manor rose majestically, presiding over lawns and trees and hedges and gardens. A lovelier setting could hardly be imagined. As the drive approached the enormous house, it was lined with flowering ornamentals of plum and cherry and crab apple, at the bases of whose trunks grew all manner of bulbed and perennial flowers, low-spreading lithodora, and several varieties of heather.

Reaching Westbrooke Manor, the gravel drive widened into an expansive stoned elongated circle, around whose circumference exploded at this time of year a profusion of color, from roses and azaleas to multicolored pansies, alyssum, lobelia, violets, violas, daisies, and an abundance of other blooming things, scattered and planted among one another seemingly heedless of pattern. Their diverse colors and foliage mixed and flowed together in chaotic beauty. In the middle of winter, the sight would not have been nearly so inviting. But in early June, it was a sumptuous feast for the eyes.

The house itself—of gray stone and slate, intermingled with red brick from England, here and there with iron and copper work accenting the colorful mosaic of its design—stood as an impressively beautiful estate, whose draftsman must surely have enjoyed himself. Originally constructed in the late sixteenth century after union with England had reduced the defensive requirements of the castles and great houses of Wales, Westbrooke Manor represented one of the oldest and largest such structures where aesthetics and functionality replaced solemnity and starkness as the paramount architectural concerns.

The front face—opening southward and with columned entryway inset from the remaining plane of the building—and west wing boasted perhaps more windows, larger and of unusual design, than any mansion in Wales. These afforded magnificent views, when weather permitted, of the entire coastline. The architect must surely have cherished a particular fondness for the ornamental potential of the openings he set among the stone walls of the massive building. Its windows were the eyes into the soul, if not of Westbrooke Manor's present occupants, then surely into the man who conceived it. They were clearly the singular visual highlight of the place.

The manor's windows represented enormous variety of size, shape, and framing material. No more than three were alike. Even these possessed tiny crafted individualities that revealed themselves only to the most diligent scrutiny. While the primary object had been to give the manor's inhabitants a view outward, this unique architectural feature also granted the visitor a striking sight as he beheld the house upon approach.

Great double doors of solid oak planking three inches thick, each measuring four feet in width and eight in height, ornately framed and studded in black wrought iron, were overspread with a great stone plate upon which the Westbrooke coat of arms was carved. This was surrounded by miscellaneous heraldic symbols, swords, and roaring and leaping beasts from both the world of men and fairy.

Away from this entryway around to the left along the west wing and extending northward behind it, a rambling, curved mossy stone pathway led toward an area near the house, which from the position of the house relative to the sun, remained shady during most daylight hours. Among the trunks of spaciously placed sycamores, beeches, and chestnuts, grew a distinctive variety of ferns and other plants, mostly now showing off their thick foliage of green. This was the winter garden. Those of its contents that flowered—only perhaps a fourth of the whole—had been placed here for their wintry blossoms, which came into prominence when the deciduous giants above them dropped their leaves to let in the cold, thin light of the winter months.

The oak doors of the manor opened into a large hall of high ceiling. Around its tall wood-paneled walls hung guns, swords, stags' heads, a few faded tartans, and other similar ornamentation. The effect gave a visitor at first glance more the appearance of a hunting lodge in the Scottish highlands than a family home. Full-length suits of armor stood opposite one another as silent sentinels guarding the two far corners. Two corridors extended from this entryway, one to the right and one to the left. Directly ahead a wide stairway swooped down, slightly curved though not circular, from above.

Most of the family's more comfortable living quarters were located up this grand staircase and to the left, on the first floor of the west wing, whose windows overlooked the sea. There was no limit to parlors and drawing rooms in the west wing of the ground floor either. The kitchens and servants' quarters occupied most of the area to the right of the entry hall, comprising the remainder of the main south wing and the small east wing.

Two dining rooms, a great formal banquet hall outfitted in paneling and wainscoting to resemble the hunting motif, and a smaller room, warmer of atmosphere and of floral tones, sat directly to the rear of the entry hall. It was in this latter where the family's meals were taken. Both dining rooms looked out on the courtyard enclosed by the three wings of the manor, kept tidily manicured by the viscount's gardener, Stuart Wykeham. A breakfast room of immaculate white walls and ceiling and black floor tile also faced the courtyard.

The second floor of the manor sat mostly unused now except for a multitude of bedrooms and storage rooms, the viscount's private study, and an ancient armory in which he took special pleasure.

Roderick Westbrooke had not always prided himself in being master of the family estate. His father, the seventh viscount Lord Snowdon, was already old when Roderick was born and was dead before his only son reached his teen years. Whatever family fortune might once have existed, it had been unwisely invested, spent, squandered, and gradually used up in the generations prior to the present viscount's life.

Nor did young Roderick help matters with regard to his own financial future by leaving Wales in 1830 at sixteen as a pampered aristocratic heir intent upon seeing the world, ostensibly, he said, to seek what he called his fortune. In reality all he succeeded in accomplishing was to dry up what remained of the stipend guaranteed him by his father's will until he should come of age at twenty-five and inherit the title and property that went with it.

He was gone for five years—traveled extensively on the continent, remained a consequential year in Ireland, and returned under somewhat mysterious circumstances to Wales at twenty-one, virtually penniless and peculiarly dispassionate according to those who had known him before. At the same time, however, he was no more at peace with himself. Something ate at him. But he confided in no one.

One thing was clear upon his return—Roderick Westbrooke was a boy no longer, though still four years from becoming master of the estate. Whether he was older and wiser from his voyages, adventures, and amorous escapades or merely older would require the rest of his life to determine. His mother remained trustee of the estate until he inherited at twenty-five.

He met the wealthy daughter of the Glasgow earl in 1845 when in the northern seaport on a minor matter of business. On the surface, they made an odd match—he the thirty-one-year-old man of the world, she eight years younger, well-educated but untraveled, and the daughter of an earl whose chief reputation lay in his unconventional religious views. That the religious family possessed money added in no small measure to the attractive young Katherine Drummond's charm in Roderick Westbrooke's eyes. Yet in fairness to his motives, she did cause his heart to beat with something resembling affection again, and he persuaded himself that he loved her. Katherine, on her part, found the nobleman from western Wales more dashing than he really was. Like many young women, she did not inquire too deeply into his character beyond what appeared on the surface. She convinced herself that she was in love with him, which she probably was, however unwise that love may have been. They were married two years later.

Their two offspring—Courtenay, cut from the same cloth as his father, now eighteen, and Florilyn, fifteen—rather than infusing the bloodline with the spiritual tradition brought into it by their mother, appeared to be going to seed along with the former Welsh lineage of their descent.

Gradually the faith of Katherine Westbrooke waned under the constant pressure of her husband's unbelieving churchgoing religiosity. She held out hope during their early years of providing their two children *some* spiritual grounding. She discovered, however, that weekly church services were a singularly ineffective means of doing so, especially under the shadow of worldliness with which the viscount's outlook on life infused the home.

Katherine continued to love her husband and made of it a good enough marriage for both. Yearly, however, her grief deepened at the realization that though they continued to attend the Church of England socially as a family every Sunday, her son and daughter were growing into pagans of the first order. What heartache must surely follow, either from the grave or more eternal regions, for those scions of spiritual families who spurn the good soil implanted into them and choose the world's way instead.

Whatever evils might be laid at the charge of their paternal pedigree, Courtenay and Florilyn Westbrooke at least had the benefit of a maternal rootstalk of godliness to stand them in good stead as they developed. This bloodline, however, both were learning to despise. Their father's influence had certainly been formative. But scorn of spiritual things is entirely individual. Thus, the downward spiral of character was given most of its energy by the power of their own self-willed choices. None of the three—father, son, daughter—had the slightest notion that the demon called "playing with religion" had nearly entirely taken them over.

Katherine wept in her room for an hour after Florilyn's ridiculous exchange at the dinner table. How could they do Percy any good, she thought through her tears, with her own children adding to the problems of her brother's son with such dreadful ideas of unbelief?

What would Edward think of her if word reached him of what faithlessness reigned in Snowdonia!

Eighteen

The Generations

$\mathcal{A}$ cold front blew in off the sea, keeping most of the inhabitants of Westbrooke Manor indoors for the next several days.

As Percy walked up the main staircase, returning to his room at the distant end of the west wing's second floor, he glanced about him at the paintings on the walls. He realized for the first time that many of these people were in a way related to him, even if distantly and by marriage.

Who were they? he wondered.

He paused at the landing between the ground and first floors, his attention suddenly arrested by a penetrating look in the eyes of the portrait of one particular woman. She stood as if eternally gazing over the entry hall below with a mysterious expression.

"Having a stroll about the old place, eh, my boy?" came a voice behind him. Percy turned to see the viscount striding toward the base of the staircase.

"Yes, Uncle Roderick," he replied. "It has been raining so steadily all day I had no choice but to get my exercise indoors."

"Shrewd thinking," said his uncle, climbing the stairs toward him. "The rain here can be insufferable. But it always clears, have no fear. What do you think of the old woman, there?" he added, pointing up to the painting in front of his nephew.

"She has an unusual countenance," answered Percy. "Her stare stopped me cold as I passed. I felt like she was actually looking at me."

His uncle laughed. "It's my grandmother," he said. "Well her eyes *might* stop you in your tracks!"

"Why is that?"

Westbrooke lowered his voice mysteriously and leaned close to his nephew. "They say she possessed the second sight," he said into Percy's ear.

An involuntarily shudder swept through Percy's chest at the words. "What's that?" he asked.

"A Scotsman like you. . .never heard of the second sight, my boy? But I forgot, your family's religion probably disavows the existence of such fancies. It's the Celtic blood of the ancients that still lives in these hills. Surely you know of our great old Welsh ruler, Rhodri Mawr, and our warrior king who fought the English in the early fifteenth century, Owain Glyndwr."

"I've heard of them, that's all," replied Percy.

"Great men if you believe your history," rejoined Westbrooke. "Legends abound of their mystical powers. It's a power that lives on, especially here in the north in Gwynedd and Snowdonia. They roamed these very hills, you know—Mawr and Wyddfa. They say it occasionally gets into folks even today, the second sight, I mean. They say it enables them to see things other people can't see. Some say they can even predict the future. Runs in family lines, they say."

"Do *you* have it, Uncle Roderick?"

"Me—good heavens, no!" The viscount laughed with a shudder at the thought. "No one around here lays claim to such clairvoyance. Well," he added with a chuckle, "other than the old hag in the village. But then she's a different story altogether." He glanced away briefly, as if something had distracted his train of thought. "It's mostly all superstition," he resumed quickly. "Nothing to put stock in. But come," he added, "let me show you the armory."

He led the way up the main staircase to the second floor, then to the right and into a part of the house Percy had not yet seen. "Neither Courtenay nor Florilyn have any interest in the family's history," he said as they entered the room. "Perhaps I shall be more successful in arousing your fascination."

Percy glanced about. Every wall was covered with weapons and implements of battle of many diverse kinds—swords, guns, axes, knives, daggers, lances, coats of mail, leather jerkins, two more full suits of armor, ornately carved and painted shields, and a crossbow.

"It was something of a hobby of my grandfather's," said the viscount as they strolled leisurely about the room. "He was the husband of the lady downstairs with the probing eyes. Perhaps I have inherited his interest. What do you think?"

"It's fabulous, Uncle Roderick," replied Percy, gazing about at the walls.

"It's one of the largest collections in Wales. Look out here," he added, walking to the east window of the room. "If you are partial to mountains rather than the sea, this window affords the best view in the house."

Percy followed his uncle to the window. The two stood side by side, gazing out for a time.

"If I'm going to make a Welshman out of you, you will have to learn to love those hills," said the viscount at length. "Sometimes, on the clearest of days, I stand here and gaze on Mount Snowdon away up there to the north."

"Can you really see it from here?" asked Percy.

The viscount nodded. "It's eighteen miles and requires ideal conditions," he said. "On most days all you can make out is mist and clouds. It's then," he added, laughing, "when you definitely need the second sight!"

He and his uncle chatted easily for another ten or fifteen minutes as they moved about the room.

"Come and have a look about any time, Percy, my boy," said Lord

Snowdon at length. "Feel free to explore the whole place. My house is your house, as they say," he added, laughing.

"Thank you, Uncle Roderick. You have been very kind to me. I appreciate your generosity. Thank you."

"However, I am afraid I need to leave you for now. I was on my way to my study when I ran into you on the landing. There is an important letter I need to answer. I hope you don't mind."

"No, of course not."

Left alone, Percy wandered about a few minutes more. He then left the armory and drifted along the corridor toward the library. He had only been inside it once since his arrival and was not a great reader. But on a rainy day like this, what else was there to do but find a book to occupy the time?

He had no idea where his cousins were or how they occupied themselves when housebound. He didn't really care. Neither had shown much interest in him. He had the feeling Florilyn was avoiding him until his anger over the incident with Grey Tide simmered down.

He entered the library. It was deathly quiet. He assumed himself alone. Slowly he wandered through the shelves lined from floor to ceiling with books.

Suddenly a movement startled him. There was his aunt seated in an alcove reading. She laid aside her book and glanced up at his approach.

"Hello, Aunt Katherine," he said walking toward her.

"Hello, Percy."

"I didn't know anyone else was in here."

"A gloomy day, is it not?"

"I suppose I should be used to it. It rains in Glasgow all the time, too. Still, you're right, it is rather a depressing sight outside."

"A perfect book day, that's what I call days like this."

"What are you reading?" asked Percy.

"Actually, a book your father just brought me—a novel by one of your fellow Scotsmen whom he has been taken with in recent years."

"Not that MacDonald fellow?"

"Why, yes it is!"

Percy chuckled. "My father and mother are always talking about him. Now that you mention it, I recall hearing them say they were planning to send you something of his that had just been published."

"What kind of books do you like?" Katherine asked.

"I don't know. I don't really read much."

"Have you read any of MacDonald's?" she asked?

"No," laughed Percy. "I figure if my parents like them, I probably wouldn't! We haven't exactly been seeing eye to eye lately."

"You might surprise yourself and actually like them," suggested his aunt.

"They're huge, long novels, aren't they?" said Percy. "I have seen several about the house. They look boring. I doubt I would be able to wade through something like that."

"Your father and mother are terribly fond of him. They are constantly waiting for every new title. If you don't care for the novels, maybe you would enjoy his fairy tales."

"Children's stories!" laughed Percy. "You're right—that would probably be just the right thing for me."

"I said fairy tales, not children's stories," rejoined his aunt with a smile.

"What's the difference?"

"All the difference in the world when the author is George MacDonald."

"Well, maybe I should," chuckled Percy. "Got to have something to occupy my time on a day like this, I suppose. Perhaps you could recommend something for me."

"I will be happy to," smiled his aunt. She rose and walked across the room and disappeared between two tall bookcases.

Percy followed.

Ten minutes later, his aunt had resumed her seat in the alcove with her book. On the other side of the library, Percy was slouched in a small couch that sat adjacent to a window looking out north from the manor, one leg slung up over the side rest, reading a book of much different fare than he had ever dipped into before, that his aunt had selected for him to try.

Nineteen

Altercation

Lord Snowdon sat in his office perusing the letter that had arrived two days before. He had read it over at least ten times but still could not satisfy himself that he had gotten to the bottom of it. The thing seemed straightforward enough. His naturally suspicious nature, however, could not prevent him from wondering if it was as simple as it appeared on the surface.

The Right Honorable, the Viscount Roderick Westbrooke, Lord Snowdon, he read yet again.

My Lord,

I have the honor to request your indulgence on a matter of some importance to me, though perhaps to no one else. I can only hope that you will treat the fancy of an aging sentimentalist with confidentiality and will consider my request with the same seriousness with which I make it.

Having spent some of the happiest years of my life as a boy romping the hills of Snowdonia with my father, it is my desire at this late stage of my life to build a small cottage on a meadow that I particularly cherished which sits on the slopes of one of Gwynedd's lesser peaks. Investigating the matter, I find that the property in question lies within and almost at the boundary of your own estate. I am hoping that its remote location and relative insignificance among your vast holdings will encourage you to consider selling it to me.

I can assure you that my plans would in no way encroach on your privacy. I would seek to gain access by obtaining a right of way eastward through public lands from the main road between Blaenau Ffestiniog and Dolgellau. To put the matter in its simplest terms, you would not even know I was there.

I would purchase whatever amount of land you would graciously consent to part with up to a thousand or more acres. However, if a transaction of such size is impossible, I could carry out the plans for my small cottage with as little as twenty.

I am a wealthy man and believe I can make the transaction well worth your consideration. I am willing to pay anything within reason.

I am,
Sincerely and gratefully yours,
Palmer Sutcliffe

Westbrooke set aside the letter, leaned back in his chair, and exhaled a long thoughtful sigh. *Who is this man?* he wondered.

He reached for the copy of *Debrit's Peerage* on his desk and flipped through it but found nothing. He would have Tilman Heygate institute further inquiries.

Was it possible that this letter had come to him as manna from heaven, to meet his ongoing financial need? His wife's refusal in the matter of the yacht he had hoped to purchase remained a burr under his collar. This fellow Sutcliffe's proposal could make him independent of his wife's miserliness once and for all.

The wheels of the viscount's brain began to spin with increased momentum. How much could he reasonably ask for twenty acres? Such land was probably only worth ten or twenty pounds an acre. Surely Sutcliffe was no fool. Perhaps he would pay double, even triple that. But a few hundred pounds would hardly relieve his dependency on his wife.

Five hundred pounds. . .a thousand pounds? Even that would but temporarily ease his financial straits.

But a thousand acres! The thought of parting with such a sizable chunk of his holdings brought almost a physical pain to his chest. And yet. . .if he could raise, say, ten thousand pounds, he would be sitting pretty. For such a sum, however, he would have to give up a good deal of land.

How much would he be willing to let go of? Everything depended on how determined this Sutcliffe was on obtaining the specific land he mentioned. . .*his* land. . .and how wealthy he really was. If he asked too much, the man could simply build his cottage elsewhere. Land was cheap in Snowdonia.

The viscount drew in another deep breath. He would have to handle the matter with delicacy so as not to push too hard. As onerous as was the thought of parting with any of the estate's ground, this was the opportunity of a lifetime to gain financial independence.

He rose and left his office in search of his factor.

As Westbrooke contemplated the potential change in his fortunes, outside the sun was winning a brief battle against several swirling gray clouds, aided in the contest by a stiff wind off the sea. It now emerged bright and, for the present, victorious.

Seeing the change, the viscount's son left the house for the stables, thinking of a ride. The rain had put him in a surly mood. It would doubtless be a miserable afternoon for whichever horse he chose to bear him to help ameliorate his inward vexation at the world.

The sun's rays sent their life-probing radiance through the windows and into the house and into souls that were more malleable than that of young Courtenay Westbrooke. Little bubbles of God-shaped joy burst from hearts of servants and gentility alike. Gladness returned, and with it an occasional song came to the lips of housekeeper, maids, and cook.

Percy Drummond felt it, too. On the couch in the library, he had begun to doze. The sudden warmth as the sun shone on his face through the window brought him back to himself. An afternoon nap is a much different thing to a fifty-year-old than to a sixteen-year-old, for whom the very thought of sleep when the sun is shining is an abhorrence. Percy laid down the book of fairy tales, which had nearly fallen from his hand, got up, and left the library. He had no definite purpose in mind. He only knew that the sun and fresh air drew him and he must be out in it.

He left the house a minute or two later and drew in a satisfying breath of the chilly, damp air. Almost the same moment, he heard the fearsome shriek of a horse. A dreadful mad frenzy had just erupted. Thinking that either man or beast must be in some terrible trouble, he broke into a run and sprinted toward the stable yard as the earsplitting whinnying rose in fury.

Percy flew through the door of the barn. After the brightness of the sun, it took several seconds for his eyes to adjust. He was aware of frenetic kicking and stomping and flying dust. Men's voices were raised in argument. Drowning them out, however, continued the horrifying screaming of a beast either in terror or tremendous pain.

Courtenay had come in some time earlier and, not finding the groom, had set about saddling his horse carelessly and in haste. The moment he mounted the nervous and highly strung Gelderlander, the horse began to back and rear. Courtenay gave him a vicious cut with his whip. The poor beast went wild, plunging and kicking.

Hearing the racket, Hollin Radnor hurried in from outside as the viscount's son was bringing his whip down a second time. "Don't punish him, my lord!" implored Radnor, hurrying forward. "You'll drive him madder than he is already!"

"Get back, Radnor," yelled Courtenay, "or you'll come in for your share with him!"

The viscount's son was a good horseman in the sense of being able to hold himself in the saddle in almost any circumstances. Yet he knew little about horses. He had not learned to love them as among the noblest creatures of the animal creation. To him, they were mere beasts of burden to be compelled into obedience. If it took cruelty to achieve that end, he would not withhold it.

One of his father's horses had been put down years before because Courtenay, at twelve, had ridden it to such exhaustion, whipping it beyond all hope of endurance, that the poor creature had simply collapsed and shattered both its front legs. Even then, angered at having been thrown, he withdrew his whip and attacked the animal as it lay dying. Alas, the intervening six years had taught him nothing about curbing his temper.

But Hollin Radnor did love horses, if not more than his own life, perhaps close to it. Ignoring the young lord's command, he ran to the horse's head and set about desperately trying to calm him.

Courtenay's rage as he looked down on the insolent servant overpowered good sense and common decency together. A series of blows from the whip descended on head of groom and horse together.

Almost the same moment, Percy rushed in.

"My lord, my lord," Radnor cried as the blows fell relentlessly on him, "the curb chain is too tight! The animal is suffering great pain. Please, my lord. . .hold off him and allow me to loosen it!"

Percy now ran toward them hoping to protect Radnor from further blows.

Seeing his cousin take the groom's side added contempt to Courtenay's dudgeon. The next blows from his whip were directed at Percy.

"Stop. . .stop, Courtenay!" howled Percy. "If you don't stop hitting Mr. Radnor, I'll—"

"You'll what?" cried Courtenay scornfully. "Get back. This is between me and him." Another whack fell from the whip against Percy's cheek and forehead.

A stinging pain on his face brought his blood to a boil as hot as his cousin's. "It's between you and me now!" Percy yelled. "Stop, I tell you, or I'll throw you from that horse!"

A peal of derisive laughter filled the barn. But it is unwise to laugh at an angry man. Percy rushed toward Courtenay, took hold of the nearest booted foot, and with a great shove pitched him backward over the thoroughbred's side. Taken by surprise at Percy's daring and strength, Courtenay did not keep hold of the reins. He tumbled to the ground with a great thud and groan.

Radnor led the crazed and terrified horse a little way off and struggled to slacken the twisted chain that had been biting into his jaw. The poor animal was dripping with sweat, his flesh quivering and trembling, still prancing and jerking his head about. Radnor gradually soothed him with whispered words and the gentle touch of his hand.

Percy stood above Courtnenay waiting.

Recovering his shock, his cousin leaped to his feet. "You will pay for that, you little rotter!" he cried, squaring off against Percy with fists in the air. "Do you really think you are any match for me?"

"Probably not," replied Percy, his gaze warily fixed on Courtenay's eyes and fists. "You may beat me to a pulp, but you will not touch that horse or Mr. Radnor again."

"You think you can stop me?"

"I *will* stop you."

Courtenay leaped forward with marvelous speed. The fist of his right hand smashed into Percy's forehead with such lightning force that Percy scarcely had a chance to blink. A second pounded into his cheek at the edge of his nose and drew blood.

Percy staggered back, dazed, and toppled to the dirt floor.

Seeing blood coming from his nose, and with Radnor leading the frothing horse outside, Courtenay thought better of pursuing the battle on either front. "Let that be a lesson to you," he said down to Percy where he lay. "You stay away from my horse. You stay away from everything of mine, or it will go worse for you next time!" He turned and stormed from the barn.

By the time the incident had passed, the sky had darkened again. The weather remained fitful for the remainder of the day.

TWENTY

Devious Invitation

*T*he conversation around the dinner table that evening at Westbrooke Manor was noticeably subdued.

No word had reached either husband or wife about the day's altercation in the barn. There had been talk among the servants, however, for Hollin Radnor had sought one of the maids to bandage his face and arms. Though he divulged nothing about the cause of his wounds, the girl who tended him came of a family that considered horses almost equal in the family to the children. Her father was universally regarded the most knowledgeable man concerning horseflesh in the region. She knew the mark of a whip when she saw one. Everyone at the manor knew the young master's proclivity with the leather. Speculation had run rampant ever since.

Some of this talk came within the hearing of Florilyn Westbrooke. She was a girl for whom secrets existed but for one purpose—that she might find them out, discover their source, and use the information gained to work mischief in the lives of those involved. This she would do by any and all means that lay open to her cunning and wiles. She was a pixie, a knave, an inciter of annoyance, what the French would call a *provocateur*. To disrupt, confuse, frustrate, sabotage, and irritate was the spice of her life.

The moment her cousin entered the dining room, she divined the truth. Percy's forehead and cheek were badly swollen and bruised. A thin cut extended along the opposite cheek up to and across half his forehead. She knew as well as Padrig Gwlwlwyd's daughter what the cut of a whip looked like. Her suspicions were all but confirmed when Courtenay came in a minute later, favoring one leg but without a mark on his face. Both boys wore serious expressions. Neither looked at the other throughout the meal.

"You must have had an interesting day, Courtenay," said Florilyn with a twinkle in her eye.

Her brother did not reply.

"I thought you were going for a ride earlier," she went on. "I was watching, but I never saw you leave the stables. Did you have some kind of trouble?"

"I decided not to go," said Courtenay moodily.

Florilyn turned to her cousin. "What happened to *you*, Percy?" she said. "You look a mess."

Percy shrugged and went on with his dinner.

"Did something happen, Percy, my boy?" now asked the viscount. For the first time, he seemed to take note of Percy's face.

"Just a little accident," answered Percy. "I fell in the barn."

His uncle did not press the matter, though Katherine appeared concerned.

Florilyn, however, was not about to let it go. She continued to bait both boys throughout dinner. But to no avail.

Later that evening in her room, Florilyn's lust to know what had happened between her cousin and brother gradually gave way to a yet deeper puzzle. Why hadn't Percy said a word about the incident? What could account for such behavior? If Courtenay had so much as spoken an ill word to her, she would have been ranting with accusations to their parents at the first opportunity, trying to get even with him.

She knew good and well that Courtenay had given Percy those cuts and bruises. Why his silence? Was he afraid of getting more of the same from Courtenay if he squealed?

Somehow she thought not. Percy was smaller than Courtenay, that was true. But she doubted he was afraid of him. Percy carried himself as one who knew how to handle himself in a tussle. There had to be more to it.

Did some twisted form of gallantry prevent him from blabbing? Twice now he had refused to blame either Courtenay or her. What was the reason for his silence? Did he possess some peculiar code of conduct that barred accusation. . .even when it was deserved?

Not knowing nearly drove her mad. She was determined to loosen Percy's tongue one way or another.

By morning Florilyn had made up her mind what to do. She needed to get Percy angry. Angry enough to retaliate. What was the fun of being mean to him if he wouldn't fight back? Even if it meant getting in trouble herself, making Percy lose his temper would be such a sweet victory it would be worth it.

The rain passed through Wales and the sun came out, gloriously and warm the next morning. By noon, most of the meadows and fields were dry enough to consider riding again.

Percy was surprised to hear a knock on his door shortly after he had returned upstairs from lunch. There stood Florilyn in her riding habit. "I know you probably hate me for what I did the other day," she said, dropping her eyes.

"I don't hate you," said Percy. "I would just like to know why you did it. What do you have against me, anyway?"

"I don't know. Sometimes I just get that way and can't help myself. But would you like to go for a ride today? I promise, I won't swat your horse."

Percy thought for a moment. It wasn't much of an apology. But he was dying to get out of the house, and he was leery of doing so alone lest again he encounter Courtenay, which he was not anxious to do.

"Don't worry," she added with a winning smile. "I'll give you the gentlest mount in the stables."

"All right," he said, forcing a smile. "Just let me change my clothes."

"I'll meet you at the barn," said Florilyn, turning to go.

The two met in the stable yard twenty minutes later. Florilyn led the way inside. Percy followed.

"Prynhawn da, Miss Florilyn. . .Master Drummond," said the groom. He turned to greet the two young people in the midst of the empty stall he was cleaning.

"We're going for a ride, Hollin," Florilyn said.

"Will you be wanting me to saddle two horses, Miss Westbrooke?"

"I will do it, Hollin," she replied. "You go do something else. Leave us until we're gone."

The groom did as instructed, though he ambled from the barn slowly. He glanced back every so often as if delaying until he could see which horses they planned to take.

But Florilyn, who had experienced the old man's interference before, waited until he was out of sight. She then proceeded to saddle two mounts while Percy looked on.

She led the horses out to the mounting block. After handing Percy the reins of a reddish bay mare that she introduced as Red Rhud, she herself mounted the mare called Grey Tide. Percy managed to get up into the saddle alone, a feat he pretended to take in stride without displaying his profound satisfaction at the accomplishment.

They left the stable yard. Quickly Florilyn led the way down a sloping path through the gardens and trees, continuing in the direction of the sea. A few minutes later, they emerged onto the uncultivated fields and open moorland east of Mochras Head. Already Florilyn was a considerable distance ahead.

Percy gave the mare a touch of his heels. She darted skittishly forward, her four hooves prancing over the grass as if the ground was red hot. Percy jostled about but did his best not to show his concern.

Soon, however, Florilyn slowed, waited for them to catch up. She then veered southward. In a huge gradual arc, she led the way across moor and field until they had come around 180 degrees and were bound on a course almost due east in the direction of Moelfre and Yllethr.

They rode for an hour or more into the hilly forested regions, skirting north of the two peaks, making many turns and changes of direction, uphill and down, along streambeds, following a good-sized river for a while, then through meadows, here and there entering forests so thick there was scarcely room for the horses to pass single file through the branches.

Percy had not an idea where they were or in what direction they had been going. For all he knew, they could have been anywhere in Snowdonia. Had he been asked to point in what direction lay the sea, he might have turned around in a complete circle and scanned his surroundings without being able to settle on any of the 360 degrees of the compass.

He was thoroughly and completely lost.

No words were spoken between them. Though Florilyn led at a relaxed pace, she never allowed Percy to draw alongside. This was fine with Percy. Despite the apparent change in her attitude, he had no particular desire to exchange small talk with his cousin.

In time they reached what appeared to be a small green valley that sat between two ridges of hills that angled together and met a mile or two farther on in front of them. Whether it was truly a valley or a high plateau somewhere in the depths of the Cambrian Mountains would have been hard to determine. It was so protected and out of the way, it was impossible to tell anything about the surrounding terrain beyond the two ridges and the thick forest through which they had come at one end of the expanse. Wherever the place was, it was so remote that not a living creature was to be seen.

Percy had seen no sheep or cattle for an hour, though plentiful deer and rabbits were hiding among the trees.

They began to cross the flat grassland.

Suddenly with a shout, Florilyn leaned forward in the saddle and burst into a gallop. Hair streaming behind her, within seconds she was fifty yards away.

Red Rhud required no encouragement. With a tremendous burst, she shot after Grey Tide.

A cry of terror escaped Percy's lips as he lurched back in the saddle. Frantically grabbing at the saddle edge, he held on for dear life. Tearing up clods of the soft turf with her hooves and throwing them up behind, his mount flew across the ground.

Florilyn persisted in the reckless sprint toward the far end of the grassy flat then reined in, laughing gaily as she threw her head around.

Percy rode up out of breath, white-faced and angry. His mare slowed, though still pranced with spirit. The brief gallop, far from expending the great creature's energy, had only excited it the more. "I nearly fell!" he exclaimed.

Florilyn did not reply, only smiled. Her coy expression gave away nothing. She turned in her saddle and rode on at a slow walk.

Percy pulled alongside about to speak again then judged it best for now to say nothing. Maybe she *hadn't* done it intentionally. It certainly wouldn't do to anger her when he was at her mercy and so far from the manor.

Percy's respite from the precarious gallop, however, was short-lived.

Even more rashly than before, again Florilyn shouted to her horse and burst with astonishing acceleration into another madcap gallop. "Race you to the ridge!" she shouted over her shoulder.

"I don't think—" began Percy.

It was no use. His words gave way to a piercing wail of terrified surprise. His own steed had again bolted, exactly as Florilyn knew she would. The two mares, so different in temperament, were actually twins. A great rivalry existed between them, a fact the viscount's daughter had decided to exploit on this day.

Looking behind her, Florilyn saw the response she had expected. She dug her heels into Grey Tide's sides and urged the mare to the full measure of her speed. For the gentle horse Radnor said she was, with her mistress on her back, few horses in all the region of Llanfryniog could equal her for raw speed.

Clutching reins and saddle as he was wildly tossed about on Red Rhud's back, Percy made a gallant effort to keep his seat. He might have succeeded, too, had their way continued on level ground.

But Florilyn had other designs. Unlike Percy, she was not a bit lost. She knew exactly where she was, knew the precipitous terrain that lay up the steep slope ahead. She knew, too, what must be the inevitable result with Red Rhud straining every muscle of her great flanks to overtake her twin.

Florilyn kept on, therefore, as fast as she dared, flew into the trees at the far end of the flat and up the incline that began almost immediately. Over fallen logs Grey Tide leaped without breaking stride, across a stream eight feet wide, and through another level of about fifty yards. There she swung the mare sharply left. If Percy behind her managed to keep in the saddle over the trees and stream, the steep path she followed for the next two hundred yards would surely prove too much for his novitiate equestrian skill.

She dared not look back. She would have to be able to profess innocence to her father that she did not know when she might have lost him. Therefore, she leaned forward, hugging her chest to Grey Tide's long neck to keep in the saddle herself and scurried the rest of the way up the near vertical ascent. Reaching the crest, she straightened again in the saddle and galloped along the top of the ridge for some distance.

Soon she heard Red Rhud behind her and gaining. She suspected the cause well enough—that the burden on the red mare's back had been reduced at some point along the way by exactly the weight of a sixteen-year-old Glaswegian.

Finally Florilyn glanced back over her shoulder. It was as she thought. Red Rhud was flying toward her riderless.

She laughed, thoroughly delighted with herself, and eased back on Grey Tide's reins. Red Rhud came alongside. Keeping up a swift canter, Florilyn now led the two horses on a slant down the opposite side of the ridge, thinking herself well out of sight of any human eyes, and then in a westerly direction that would take them back to the manor.

TWENTY-ONE

Heaven-Sent Guide

*T*he final steep ascent had not been necessary to achieve Florilyn's end.

Percy had barely managed to cling to his seat as Red Rhud leaped the first fallen tree across her path. But repeating the feat when the mare went airborne a few seconds later, landing on the opposite side of the wide stream with a great jolting earthquake of a bounce, proved impossible.

Luckily the water flowed through a grassy section of wood or he might have been seriously hurt. As it was, when Percy looked up from the soft grass where he found himself after his inglorious tumble to see Red Rhud disappearing through the trees in the distance, though his back would feel it tomorrow, the chief injury he had suffered was to his pride—actually not a bad injury to sustain. As humility is its opposite, for a humble spirit to emerge within the human character usually requires that pride be dealt a series of painful blows by the hammer of circumstance, and Percy had just had one to his.

He took stock of himself, realized nothing was broken, then drew in a deep breath and climbed to his feet. He knew the general direction his mount had gone. He could still hear her hooves thudding in the distance as she made for the ridge. He had no doubt Florilyn would be waiting for him at the top with an insufferably obnoxious grin.

He set off trudging up the hill. It took Percy some fifteen or twenty minutes, after a much steeper climb than he had expected, to emerge into the clearing along one of the two ridges he had seen from the field below.

He stopped, breathing heavily, and gazed about. There was no sign of Florilyn. The entire world was still and quiet.

He turned around, looking back and forth and in every direction a second time. His initial bewilderment slowly turned to anger. The vixen had deserted him in the middle of nowhere!

Nor did he have the slightest notion in which direction lay the sea, the village, or the manor. Beyond the two ridges, which seemed more or less to join a quarter or half mile away, lay an endless series of forested hills, broken here and there in the distance by a few higher peaks. Had he known the the region better, he would have been able to identify these hills as sitting in a near straight line between Mount Snowdon in the north and Calder Idris farther south. From their relation to one another, it would have been an easy matter to tell whether he was looking north, south, east, or west. But as he was not familiar with the northern Cambrians, he had no idea. Nor, for the present as it beamed down from overhead, did the sun accurately suggest to Percy his bearings.

In every direction he looked, the outlook was identical. He was not high enough to see the sea beyond any of the ridges or ranges. He might walk for hours and only succeed in getting farther from home and more deeply into what could be dangerous mountains. He did not relish the thought of spending a night out here alone. Snow was not unheard of in June. And no doubt more wild animals came out after dark than he cared to meet.

An evil oath began to rise to his lips. But it never reached them.

A sound interrupted it, as if sent from heaven to answer the cry for help it did not occur to him to lift to the One who knew where everyone was.

"She's g–g–gone, M–M–Mr. Drummond," a voice said simply.

Percy spun around in terror, as if the preternatural silence had been broken by the roar of a lion rather than the gentle timbre of one of God's angels. But the stupendous relief of finding himself not alone rushed in to banish his fear.

There stood his stuttering young friend who gave bouquets of wildflowers to strangers!

"Gwyneth!" he exclaimed. "What in God's name are you doing here?"

Percy spoke more truth than he realized.

"I have been w–w–watching you and Lady F–Florilyn as you rode," she said, coming toward him with a smile.

"Where is she now?" asked Percy.

"She is gone, M–M–Mr. Drummond. She kept riding b–back down there." Gwyneth pointed down the hill.

Percy followed her arm but could see nothing.

"I knew you had b–been thrown, so I w–w–waited for you. Are you hurt, M–M–Mr. Drummond?"

He answered her with a smile. "I don't think so," he said. "Did Florilyn see you?"

"I would not have let her see me."

"Why not?"

"She would have said cruel things."

"Well," said Percy, his self-deprecating humor rising to the surface as he began to feel better about his predicament, "it would appear I am not much of a horseman."

"Y–y–you were riding my lord's w–w–wildest m–mare."

"You don't say," said Percy with significant tone. "His *wildest* mare?"

"R–R–Red Rhud throws everyone except L–Lady Florilyn."

Percy chuckled at the revealing information. Though calming under the mesmerizing girl's peculiar power, he was still irritated enough to find little humor in Florilyn's deception.

"How do you come to be so far from home?" he asked.

"It is not so very far. B–b–besides, I know every inch of these hills."

"Are you not afraid to wander them alone?"

"No, Mr. Drummond."

"Can you lead me back to the manor?"

"Of course. Come, Mr. Drummond," she said, walking to his side and taking his hand. "I will show you." She led the way down the hill, Percy followed as if he were a compliant child, laughing at the incongruity of it. She treated him as if he were a full-grown adult, yet she carried herself with the maturity and self-confidence of a fifty-year-old.

Who could not be charmed by such a one!

Before they had gone far, Gwyneth let go of Percy's hand, paused, shielded her eyes from the sun with one hand, and looked down in the opposite direction. An expression of question crossed her usually placid countenance.

"What is it?" asked Percy.

"Nothing," she replied thoughtfully. "I saw some men off there a few weeks ago. They weren't from around here. I did not like them."

"Were they so close you could see their faces so well as to know whether you liked them or not?"

"I was not close. But I could tell they were not good men."

"How?"

"I don't know. I could tell."

Intrigued, Percy did not press the matter. In another minute Gwyneth was scampering down the hillside with Percy beside her.

They descended the ridge and within minutes were surrounded by overspreading boughs of pine and fir. Percy saw no hint of a trail anywhere. "How do you know where to go?" he asked.

"Because I know where we are. I know the sea is this way," she answered, pointing in front of her. "I walk everywhere here. I cannot get lost."

"You have been in this exact place before?"

"Of course. This is near one of my special places."

"Your. . .'special places'?"

"Yes. I have many special places where I go to visit animals and visit God and visit my mother."

"I don't know what you mean," said Percy.

"My mother is dead, Mr. Drummond."

"I am sorry, Gwyneth. I didn't know that."

"She is with God. So at my special places, I go to be alone and visit them and talk to them."

"And one of them is near here?"

"Yes, would you like to see it?"

"I would, yes. . .very much. But isn't it a private special place?"

"It is *my* special place. So I can bring anyone to it. Remember, Mr. Drummond, you are my friend now, not a stranger. The flowers made us friends. So I can show it to you."

She continued to lead Percy through the thick wood. They came a few minutes later to a little brook. It was no more than a foot or two wide and could have been easily stepped across. Instead, Gwyneth turned and led Percy along the edge of it. They were still descending from the same ridge where they had begun.

The brook was swift and noisy, splashing over rocks and pebbles, creating tiny little waterfalls as it went. Its water was brown and foamy from the mountains and hills of peat through which it came.

They continued another ten or fifteen minutes. The downward slope grew less steep as they reached the bottom between this ridge and the next one westward. Through a dense growth of pines they went in single file, until it suddenly opened into a clearing.

In front of him, Percy beheld a secluded meadow in the midst of the wood. It was perhaps twenty yards wide and fifty long, flat and grassy. The brook they had been following flowed through the center of it, where it tumbled into a pond that was deep enough, because the water was brown, that the bottom was not visible.

Gwyneth stopped and gazed about. The smile of pleasure on her face said clearly enough that her heart was full of delight to share her discovery with a friend.

"It's beautiful, Gwyneth!" exclaimed Percy. The sound of his own voice almost startled him. Except for the gentle babbling of the stream, the place was so secluded that utter stillness reigned. "This must be your special place."

Gwyneth nodded.

"How did you find it?"

"I came upon it when I was exploring in the woods. So I kept coming here and made friends with the animals."

"Animals come when you are here?"

"Only deer and rabbits. I don't think they will come today because they don't know you. They will be afraid. It took them a long time before they realized they didn't need to be afraid of me. Come and sit by the pond. That's where I sit when I come."

Percy followed her across the grass, and they sat down.

After a minute or two of silence, Gwyneth spoke. "God, this is Mr. Drummond," she said simply.

Surprised, Percy looked over at her.

Gwyneth was staring into the pond. "I'm sure You know him already," she went on, "but he has not been here before. He is a good man. He is kind to everyone. He is visiting at the manor, but they are not kind to him. Mummy, I want you to know Mr. Drummond, too."

Percy listened spellbound. He did not want to intrude upon one of the most unusual one-sided conversations he had ever heard in his life. For one who had always associated prayer with his father's prayers from the pulpit or at the table, the simplicity of Gwyneth's conversation with God was almost too much to take in. Especially hearing her speaking to God about him!

This was, as Percy had said, Gwyneth's own private place. No one else in the whole world, or so Gwyneth thought, except now for Percy, knew of it. Sitting here, not necessarily thinking or praying about anything in particular, but *feeling* it, silently moved her with the invisible music of creation. She did not always talk aloud when she came to the pond in the wood. She spoke as she did on this day so that Percy could share in her thoughts.

When Gwyneth felt the silent mysteries of the world and felt the tunes of God's music inside her, all creation made her happy. At such times her whole being was at prayer, for she was swallowed up in the expansive presence of God Himself.

There are those who only associate what they call prayer with formality and words and churches and mealtimes and public worship. But from a young age, Gwyneth had intuitively known, though no one had taught her, that all motions of heart and brain sent heavenward were prayers, for they went into the heart of Him who treasured the uplifted thoughts of His children.

After some long minutes of silence, Gwyneth stood. "We should leave now, Mr. Drummond," she said. "We have a long way to go. I want to be home before my papa gets home from the mine."

They left the meadow on the opposite side from where they had entered it and started up the next in a series of several ridges that still lay between them and the sea.

"Your father works in the mine, does he?" asked Percy as they went. "A coal mine?"

"No, Mr. Drummond. The slate mine. There is no coal here, only slate. There is a gold mine, too, somewhere not very far away, but my papa works in the slate mine."

"There is gold in Snowdonia?" said Percy in surprise.

"Yes, but not as much as slate."

"Gold is more valuable."

"My papa says that, too. He says that much of the gold of Snowdonia lies under the hills where no one has yet found it."

"Does he know where? Why doesn't he look for it?"

"Papa says that dreams of gold cannot buy potatoes. But slate can because it is no dream. Grannie has seen real gold, though I have never seen it."

Before Percy could question her further about the remarkable turn the conversation had taken, they entered a dense grove of trees. They were occupied for some time getting through it with a minimum of scratches.

By the time they came near the crest of the final ridge an hour later, Percy was feeling the effects of the afternoon's ride and walk. He would definitely sleep well that night!

They had been climbing steadily through a rocky hillside of pine. Ahead they appeared nearly to have reached the top of the incline.

Gwyneth stopped. "We have come to another of my special places," she said.

Percy glanced about but saw nothing to distinguish the hill they had been climbing. "Where?" he said.

"Right there," answered Gwyneth pointing in front of them. "Just ahead, at the top of the hill, there between those trees. We will walk through them, and then it will be downhill the rest of the way."

"What makes this a special place?"

"You will see when we get to the top. Come."

Gwyneth had brought Percy along this particular route for the very purpose of the overlook that was suddenly about to present itself when their vision rose over the crest in front of them. She had discovered it years ago and never tired of the stunning revelation as her head came up slowly over the top of the hill.

With Percy beside her, having no idea what was coming, Gwyneth continued slowly. They emerged through the trees at the crest. Two or three more steps brought their eyes above it. . .and lo! There was the whole of the coastline spread out below them in the glorious splendor of late afternoon.

The great ocean seemingly stretched out before them to infinity from the Lleyn Peninsula ahead and to their right, into the distance where their vision finally failed somewhere in the direction of Barmouth Bay to their left. Below them the plateau of Mochras Head extended out into the deep blue of Tremadog Bay. From this vantage point of a mile or more from the shoreline, and so high above it, the sea and all the countryside inland was eerily silent. A gentle breeze off the ocean met their faces as they came over the rise. Faint reminders of salt spray were borne upon it. The wide panorama, so alive yet so silent, appeared as a painting rather than the resplendent reality it was.

The silence surrounding them was deeper than silence, a *full* silence because the whole of North Wales lay in front of them. It pulsed with the energy of being, of life, yet no sound, not even of the gulls soaring along the cliffs at the shoreline, reached them.

Percy had never beheld such a sight. As the view overflowed his senses, a sensation stabbed his soul with an almost physical longing for something he desired but felt he could never attain.

The reaction that followed was not what Gwyneth had expected.

He stood gaping for a few moments at the majestic overlook, slowly shaking his head in wonder and disbelief. Then suddenly he broke into laughter. "Gwyneth!" he exclaimed. "You did it. You brought me out of the wilderness, from wherever we were to. . .just look. . .to here! There's the manor! There is the sea—glorious, blue, radiant! I'm back. . .you brought me home!"

Without warning, he turned, grabbed her two hands, and began dancing and skipping about with joyful abandon.

Gywneth giggled with childlike happiness.

Round and round they danced in the clearing between the trees. Finally Percy let go, spun around one more time for good measure, then threw himself on what sparse dry grass grew at the crest of the ridge and stared out toward the sea.

Slowly Gwyneth lay down beside him.

It quieted again. Neither spoke. They lay side by side perhaps ten minutes. The dome of the sky overhead appeared to meet the edge of the sea at the horizon in an unbroken continuity of blue.

But the line between them was not as unbroken as it seemed.

"Can you see Ireland?" said Gwyneth after some time.

"No," said Percy. "Is it really out there?"

"Yes—straight across the ocean."

"Can you see it?"

"I think so," said Gwyneth a little hesitantly. "Sometimes I imagine I can when I really can't. But from here on the clearest of days I *know*

I see it. There is a tiny bit of haze today so I cannot be completely sure."

"Maybe you have the second sight," said Percy, more lightheartedly than serious.

But Gwyneth took in his words earnestly. "Papa says I do," she said. "I don't even know what it means. But look—surely you can see the tiny bumps of land out there. . .at the edge of the ocean."

Percy squinted and sent his eyes back and forth. "Yes. . .there it is," he exclaimed. "I do see it—you're right!"

"You must have second sight, too, Mr. Drummond."

Percy laughed. "I doubt that. So, that is Ireland across there?"

"Yes. My mother was from Ireland."

"Was she indeed?"

"Yes. My father married her in Ireland. He says she was really Welsh, though I don't understand about all that. I was born there. Then we came back here to Wales, though I was just a baby and cannot remember. There was a terrible storm at sea, and my mother died. So when we arrived here, my father and I were alone."

"I am sorry, Gwyneth," said Percy. "It must be hard not to have a mother."

"I don't know what having a mother is like. But I have the best father in the world. Perhaps God knew that I could do without a mother for a while. But I will see her again."

They lay a few more minutes in silence. The scents of the sea breezes continued to drift up the sloping moor to meet them. The peace of the world enveloped them in its embrace.

TWENTY-TWO

Gwyneth's Offer

$\mathcal{A}$s Percy and Gwyneth romped down the ridge toward the plateau of Mochras Head, laughing and talking gaily, they were being watched.

Exulting in her supposed triumph over her cousin for the two hours since she had returned to the manor, Florilyn had been eagerly awaiting Percy's arrival. If he somehow managed to find his way home before dark, she could not wait to greet him face-to-face and watch him lose his temper with her.

She knew he would not hurt her. But if she could make him yell at her—or even swear aloud!—she would count the day a wonderful success. If she could somehow badger him into doing so in front of her father or mother, whose movements she was carefully watching for exactly that purpose, so much the better. A victory over a rival, in her opinion, was infinitely sweeter if he could be humiliated in front of witnesses. She never took out her revenge on her brother in private. She hoped to do the same with her cousin.

Seeing him now coming toward the manor with the tiny white-haired brat, Gwyneth Barrie, however, filled her with sudden uneasiness. Something didn't look right.

They were laughing! Percy didn't appear the least bit upset!

128

"Well, Gwyneth," Percy was saying, "I thank you for a most enjoyable afternoon. . .and for rescuing me! If you hadn't been watching out for me like a guardian angel, I would still be out there wandering around in circles. I shall be more careful in the future when Florilyn baits me into a race."

"Do you think you will race her again, Mr. Drummond?"

"I don't know. I hope not!" Percy laughed. "It's humiliating being trounced by a girl—no offense to you."

"Would you like to beat her in a race?"

"Would I ever!" Percy laughed again. "But that's easier said than done. As irritating as she is, she happens to be very good on the back of a horse."

"You *could* beat her."

"How?"

"I could teach you," said Gwyneth simply.

Percy stared back, wondering if he had heard correctly.

"You. . .could teach me to ride faster than Florilyn?"

"Yes, Mr. Drummond."

"You know horses that well?"

She nodded.

"I should say, you know how to *ride* that well?"

"Yes, Mr. Drummond. I could help you learn to ride like the wind."

Percy could not help himself. He broke out laughing at the delicious humor of the suggestion. The girl was such an innocent! But she had not yet said a word to him that was untrue. He had already come to feel a supreme confidence in whatever she told him.

What did he have to lose?

"You're on, Gwyneth Barrie," he said, still chuckling at the thought. "I accept your offer."

Gwyneth glanced toward the manor and realized they had come closer than she had intended. She thought she had seen Florilyn by the house watching them. She paused, suddenly nervous, then began to leave him.

"G–g–good-bye, Mr. Drummond," she said as she started walking away. "You can find your way from here."

"Where are you going all of a sudden?" said Percy.

"Home. L–L–Lady Florilyn will be angry with you if she sees you t–t–talking to me."

"Don't worry, Gwyneth." Percy laughed. "We won't worry about her. You may talk to me anytime."

"But she d–d–doesn't like me. I don't want her to g–g–get angry with you. G–g–good-bye."

"Thank you again, Gwyneth," said Percy after her. "Where will I find you so that you can give me those riding lessons?"

"Ask for G–G–Grannie in the village," replied Gwyneth. "She will t–t–tell you where to find me."

"What horse should I bring when I come to you?"

"Any of them, M–M–Mr. Drummond. I know all the horses. I can t–t–teach you to ride any of them f–f–fast. Mr. Radnor will help you. He is my friend. He will keep our s–s–secret."

As suddenly as she had appeared on the ridge in the wilderness, she ran from him and within seconds had disappeared from sight.

Percy did not see his cousin again until that evening. Her gloating turned to pique; she had walked back into the house in the huff of defeat. She was still filled with ire when dinnertime came.

Percy's spirits, on the other hand, remained high as he took his chair at the table, a fact that enraged Florilyn all the more. She had deserted him miles from home for the express purpose of making him angry. But he seemed happier than ever!

She made several juvenile attempts to bait Percy into tattling on her. But they only succeeded in making her look foolish. None of the other three had an idea what she was talking about. In truth, he had spent such a delightful afternoon with Gwyneth Barrie that he was actually thankful for the fall off Red Rhud's back. Florilyn's antics were beginning to strike him as more humorous than spiteful.

"You seem cheerful tonight, Percy," said his aunt as the meal progressed. "You must be enjoying the turn of warm weather."

"Very much, Aunt Katherine. I had begun to wonder if summer would ever arrive."

"Well, it seems it has. I am enjoying it as well."

"How did you occupy yourself, Percy, my boy?" said the viscount.

"Florilyn and I went out for a ride, didn't we, Florilyn—a *very* long ride."

"Splendid! There, you see—I knew you two would hit it off if you just gave her the chance. Florilyn is a dashed good horsewoman, you know."

"Yes, I have discovered that," said Percy with a wry grin. "Certainly out of my league! I'm not near the horseman she is, that's for sure."

"Where did you go?"

"Actually, I'm not altogether sure, Uncle Roderick," laughed Percy. "We headed off into the hills. I became so turned around I had no idea which way home was. I was completely lost! We were gone hours and hours. But luckily I wasn't left out there *alone*. That would have been frightening. Can you imagine, being out in the hills and not knowing your way back. . .and with night coming on?" He cast Florilyn a glance and a wily wink.

The expression on her face indicated clearly enough that she was not appreciating his humor. She did *not* like the tables being turned. Now it was *her* turn to feel the smoke coming out her ears.

"But 'all's well that end's well,' isn't that what old Bill Shakespeare says?" Percy added. "Here we all are, safe and sound. It was an extraordinary day. In fact, I can't think when I've enjoyed myself more."

"Excellent," said the viscount, obviously delighted that the cousins were all hitting it off so well. "Your father and mother will be pleased that the country air is agreeing with you. You shall have to write them, Katherine," he added to his wife at the end of the table, "and tell them that Percy is enjoying himself here with us."

TWENTY-THREE

The Draper's Shop

*T*he fair weather continued. At last, it seemed, perhaps summer had decided to grace North Wales with its presence for an extended stay.

The next days would have been spectacular for riding in the hills. But Percy had had enough of horses' backs for a while. He was eager to take Gwyneth up on her offer but needed to let his body recover from its bumps and bruises. By the morning following his adventure in the hills, his back was screaming from the fall. When he was ready to get on a horse again, he would sneak away from the manor alone.

He spent a couple of days recuperating, mostly indoors. During that time, he finished the book his aunt had suggested he read. One of the stories in particular had moved him in a way he could not explain. He finished it and felt tears rising in his eyes. He had to put the book down until he recovered himself, wondering what on earth had come over him. Unaccountably, for he had never done such a thing in his life, when he was done he immediately began to read the story over a second time.

On the third day, feeling better, he decided to walk to the village and acquaint himself a little more with his summer's surroundings. It was surely no Glasgow, but he was curious to feel the pulse of life in the place.

As he made his way down the entry from the house and thence along the road through the sloping plateau toward Llanfryniog, he stooped now and then to pluck a few wildflowers from the roadside. He smiled at the reminder of Gwyneth Barrie's endearing habit of greeting strangers. If he saw her today, he would return her kindness from three days ago with a bouquet of his own making!

He reached the village, by now clutching a good handful of wild daisies, bluebells, and assorted bits of color and walking with a jaunty step. He passed several villagers who nodded and smiled as they passed, though with the unspoken question in their minds—who was he? Percy returned their smiles. After so long in the city, the simplicity of their guileless country faces touched him with honest sincerity.

In the normal course of human relationships, it is to those older, wiser, more knowledgeable, more experienced to whom one looks with respect and honor as befit their years. Percy had never had what in any sense could be called a *mentor* in the things of life, mainly because thus far he had eschewed the mentor God had intended for him. Yet something very strange had slowly begun to infect him—that was the subtle influence of one *younger* than himself, and one in his view a mere child at that! The thing was absurd on the face of it, impractical, laughable, unheard of.

And yet. . .he could not deny that the forceful pressure of Gwyneth Barrie's outlook on life and the world had come to exercise a hold on him. She was like no one he had ever met—a mountain-nymph, a fairy-child, a tiny cherub of mystery who roamed fields and hills and ubiquitously turned up in the most unexpected places and said the most unusual things. Yet a fairy-angel with such a sensible streak to her whimsical nature that she asserted with perfect calm and confidence that she could teach him to ride a horse like the wind!

Percy broke out in a peal of laughter at the reminder of Gwyneth's offer. Two or three women glanced toward him from across the street. Young men who walked along laughing to themselves were best avoided. They hurried by, casting him skeptical glances.

Since his walk out of the hills with little Gwyneth, then with the haunting, tear-luring story he had read coming on the heels of it, everything began to *look* different—nature and the faces of humanity most of all. In some inexplicable way, Percy found himself seeing all about him through Gwyneth's fearless, trusting, unassuming pale blue eyes. He found himself wondering what *Gwyneth* would say to this, what *Gwyneth* would think of that, whether she would laugh at something he said or make one of her otherworldly comments that jolted new regions of awareness awake in him.

Percy had walked down to Llanfryniog on this day with neither specific purpose nor destination in mind, thinking simply to explore the town, perhaps walk to the harbor and along the shore. He was not yet a great friend of the sea as are most who live on the borders where water meets land in the daily dance of its tides. But he was *beginning* to love it because he knew from how she gazed across it that Gwyneth loved the sea. Seeing it through her eyes, what could he do but love it? And thus, almost without his realizing it, the sea subtly began to woo him with its hypnotic allure.

He passed several shops as he made his way casually along, looking absently into their windows. As he came to the draper's, he paused. A handsome buggy and single horse stood in the street tied to the rail next to it. In the window a display of brightly colored spools of ribbon caught Percy's eye. He looked down at the clump of flowers in his hand. He was seized with an idea, broke into a smile at the thought, and went into the shop.

The bell above the door rang as he entered. The shopkeeper was engaged across the room with a woman whose back was to him. Beside her, a girl about his own age turned at the tinkling bell. The smile, not yet faded from Percy's lips, met her glance. She thought it meant for her and returned it.

Percy came into the shop, saw a girl smiling at him—and a very pretty one at that—and walked toward her. "Hello," he said pleasantly, mistaking her look. "Are you one of the shopkeepers?"

"Oh, no," she said, laughing lightly. "I'm here with my mother."

"Oh, sorry."

He saw her eyes flit toward the bouquet in his hand.

"For a friend," he said. "I came in to get a piece of ribbon to tie it with."

"A friend. . .a *girl*?"

"How did you guess?" Percy said, laughing.

Now Percy Drummond, when he was not being surly to his father or mother, and though the lines of his countenance were still in the process of developing, was an extraordinarily good-looking young man. His features yet remained a little delicate, even, it might be said, bordering on the feminine. His face did not yet require the razor. A thick clump of light brown hair fell over a low forehead, on this day mostly obscuring the remaining evidence of Courtenay Westbrooke's whip and fist, though the bruise on his cheek was still prominent. His nose and lips and jaw were unremarkable but well-formed, not yet showing the pronounced angles that manhood would bring. In spite of the visible bruise, and in a way perhaps almost enhanced by it, the overall effect, accentuated by a winsome smile, was more than moderately attractive to a young woman of fifteen.

Rhawn Lorimer was exactly such a girl, herself prettier than she had a right to be. The fact that she knew every boy or girl for ten miles around but did not recognize Percy made him all the more interesting in her eyes. And that he was carrying a bouquet for some *other* girl immediately set the wheels of her inquisitive brain spinning about who the lucky recipient might be.

Before she had the chance to coax more information out of him, a tactic at which she was singularly skilled, her mother moved down the counter, occupied in the examination of something she had just been handed, and the shopkeeper behind it addressed an interrogative expression to Percy.

"Hello," said Percy buoyantly. "I saw some ribbon in your window. I would like to get some. How do you sell it?"

"By the foot," replied the woman. "It is over here," she said, leading Percy across the shop. "There are a number of colors. It is a penny a foot."

"Oh, I see. All right, then. . .I think I will take, let me see—" Percy dug in his pocket to see what coins he had. His father hadn't left him much money, but he certainly had enough for a few lengths of ribbon. "I think I would like three feet each of the red, the yellow, and the blue. And would you please cut off six inches from the red. I'll use it right away."

The woman went to find her scissors.

The magistrate's daughter approached Percy again. "That will be a lot of ribbon for such a little bouquet," she said.

"Oh. . .that," said Percy. "I decided to get some extra. The girl I am buying it for will love it."

"She must be a lucky girl."

"Actually, I think I am the lucky one!" Percy laughed.

Unknown to either Percy Drummond or Rhawn Lorimer, Courtenay Westbrooke was riding—calmly and on a different horse than the flighty thoroughbred—through Llanfryniog just about the moment the shopkeeper had spoken to Percy. He was on his way back from Burrenchobay Hall and had taken the long way through the village to check at the post office for his father. For several days the viscount had been impatiently expecting a telegraph from his factor, whom he had sent to London. Courtenay saw the carriage, recognized it, reigned in, tied his horse beside it, and went into the shop.

He came through the door just in time to hear the fading echo of Percy's laugh and to see the answering smile, which he took for one of fascination, on Rhawn Lorimer's face.

Courtenay strode forward but did not look toward the latter in greeting. A thundercloud gathered on his brow.

Percy saw him and turned away. But it was too late. Courtenay grabbed his shoulder from behind and spun him around.

"Hi, Courtenay," said Percy, trying to sound friendly. He had no idea what had caused the angry expression on his cousin's face.

"I thought I told you to stay away from what's mine!" said Courtenay heatedly.

"Uh. . .yes," said Percy in a confused tone. "You made that quite clear. I haven't touched your horse. I haven't so much as looked at it."

"I don't mean that. You stay away from my girl."

"Your. . .girl?"

"That's what I said. I don't want you looking at her any more than I do my horse."

Out of the corner of his eye, Percy saw the horrified look of mingled chagrin and indignation on the girl's face where she stood staring at Courtenay. Immediately he divined the truth. Irritated afresh at Courtenay's bluster and presumption, his calm demeanor left him. "You're not actually telling me that you are comparing *this* beautiful young lady to your horse?" he said, feigning innocence but with obvious sarcasm in his words. "She deserves better than that, Courtenay. I think you owe her an apology."

"What she deserves for talking to the likes of you," Courtenay shot back, "is between her and me, and it is certainly *not* an apology. I am telling you to stay away from her!"

Incensed to hear herself spoken of as if she were chattel, Rhawn Lorimer at last found her voice. "How dare you, Courtenay Westbrooke!" she said. "You have no right to call me your girl."

"What are you then?" rejoined Courtenay brusquely.

"Maybe I don't want to be called your girl any more than I want to be compared to your horse. You have no right to talk to him that way either," she added, glancing toward Percy. "We don't even know each other. He just came into the shop a minute before you. You can't go around yelling at everyone I meet. You owe *him* an apology!"

Momentarily ruffled by the stares of the two women and Miss Lorimer's rebuke, Courtenay realized he might have overreacted. But he was not sufficiently chastened to have learned his lesson. "Look, Drummond," he said, "if you know what's good for you, you will remember what I said. And you," he added, to the girl, "you stay away from him." He turned and stormed out.

Whatever dignity Courtenay Westbrooke may have entered the store with was certainly in tatters as he left. And he had accomplished the shredding entirely on his own. Jealousy is indeed one of the stupidest of demons. The louder it cries, the more it defeats its own ends. By threatening Percy in her presence, Courtenay only succeeded in elevating Rhawn Lorimer's interest in the handsome young stranger a hundredfold. Without his childish rant, she might well have forgotten the incident.

She was not about to forget it now!

Added to Percy's good looks was now the increased fascination of both underdog and forbidden fruit. Thus, as he left the shop a few minutes later with his bouquet and ribbon, her eyes followed him with keen attentiveness and feverish curiosity.

Who could he possibly be?

TWENTY-FOUR

The Magic of the Sea

Percy had planned to ask the shopkeeper who Grannie was that he might deliver his bouquet while it was still fresh. In the flurry of events with Courtenay, however, it slipped his mind. When he remembered, he turned momentarily again toward the shop. But as Courtenay was still in town and just walking into the post up the street, he thought better of it.

He set out instead in the opposite direction and continued on his course from earlier. He passed the chapel and school at the end of the village, followed the bend of the street seaward, and soon found himself approaching the small but serviceable sixteenth-century harbor that was now home to several dozen small fishing vessels.

A week ago, Courtenay's blustering threats would have filled him with anger. But now he could laugh them off. What did he care for his cousin's petty jealousy when there was a world to enjoy!

A few fishermen were about with their boats and nets. Small groups were clustered here and there talking among themselves. It was a small harbor, not in any sense a center for commercial fishing like the more sizable ports of the Wales west coast. But the local fishermen kept families, friends, and nearby villages supplied with fresh mackerel, salmon, and haddock. It therefore served its purpose bravely and kept

139

the worst of the sea's storms from eroding the shoreline—as important a function as providing a home for the many-colored boats that rested in its protected waters when not being employed in the fish-laden waters.

Percy spoke to a few men as he passed. Their greetings were more reserved than those in the upper town, in keeping with the two women who had seen him laughing to himself. These fishermen were a rugged lot who remained wary of strangers considerably longer than did Codnor Barrie's daughter. They eyed him skeptically as he wandered on, all the more so that he was carrying a handful of posies bundled with a short red ribbon. It was not the sort of thing, in their opinion, that *men*, or even boys on the way to becoming men, did. Whoever he was, with that fair face and with flowers in his hand, the lad had sissy written all over him.

Leaving the harbor, men, and boats, Percy made his way along the sandy shoreline, walking southwest at the water's edge in the direction where Mochras Head protruded into Tremadog Bay. As he went, the shoreline rose inward gradually where he came again even with the village. As he continued, it rose to become a hilly bluff then gradually by degrees a sheer cliff that separated sea from the plateau above.

The sea was calm. Its wavelets splashed gently landward, foam-topped, and ran up the gentle incline of sand until, their momentum spent, they slowed and receded back toward their home to meet the next coming toward it in the endless ebb and flow that made the sea, wherever it met land, a *living* thing. The sensations of sound and movement and smell wove their subtly intoxicating spell over the minister's son from Glasgow.

The tide was probably halfway in. Percy walked along perpendicular to it, his shoes imprinting themselves in the wet sand in an uneven line behind him that might have been made by a wobbly drunk as he wandered in and out at the edge of the shallow foamy flow. The rhythmic resonance of the water to his right, the cries of the gulls flying overhead, punctuated by an occasional louder crash of waves on the distant rocks, made a music in his soul different than anything he had heard from the pipe organ in his father's church. It was the music of nature, the symphony of the universe, the sounds of whose instruments he had only lately begun to recognize. He was not merely seeing through Gwyneth's eyes, he was hearing the call of creation through her ears. The sights and sounds of the world were coming *alive* and stirred his heart.

Gradually the sand underfoot gave way to pebbles, then larger rocks, until the beach was no more. Ahead he saw clusters of larger rocks and boulders and seaweed-filled pools and submerged muscle-encrusted stones, with eddies of the tide swirling in and among them with unceasing motion and undulation, where lived a whole oceany universe of tiny creatures. Assuming his way blocked to further exploration, Percy was about to turn back when a sight arrested his attention in the distance.

In the middle of the cliff face that had risen on his left, perhaps half a mile ahead, a speck of white was moving down from the plateau above against the gray of the rocky cliff. At first glance, he took it for a gull. But the back-and-forth movement could surely be no graceful bird in flight. *It must be a sheep,* he thought. As he stared further, however, he realized it was too small for a sheep.

Suddenly he knew that speck of white!

He continued on, stepping carefully across the uneven rocks and stones and climbing around the increasingly difficult obstacles in his path. He slipped a few times as he worked his way through the boulders that filled the space between the water and promontory, doused his boots more than once in slippery tide pools, but finally succeeded in arriving onto the surface of another expanse of flat sandy beach.

By now the promontory on his left had risen to considerable height. Four hundred yards ahead the white head of his mysterious but delightful friend reached the shore.

"Gwyneth!" he yelled and broke into a run toward her.

In truth, Gwyneth's eyes, whether from the second sight or careful observation, had seen Percy on the beach almost the same moment she had begun her descent down the bluff. She was not certain it was Percy. From that distance the features of his face would have been more difficult to descry with certainty than the Irish coastline from the overlook where she and Percy had gazed toward it over the sea.

Her heart beat a little more rapidly at the sight, for she *hoped* it might be him. But she was not sure until he called her name.

Her young heart leaped again. But she did not run across the sand. Rather she continued walking slowly toward him. Her heart had begun to be stirred, too, but for different reasons than Percy's.

Percy reached her a few minutes later. He ran toward her out of breath and stopped. "I can't believe I found you!" he exclaimed. "I had hoped to. I was going to ask in town how to find Grannie, but I forgot. I brought you these." He handed her the bouquet.

Gwyneth blinked back something that sought to rise in her eyes. Flowers always moved her. To her they were tiny windows into the soul of God's creation and made her happy. But flowers exchanged between friends meant even more. She gave flowers all the time. But no one had ever given *her* flowers—no one except Grannie.

Her heart was touched to be on the receiving end of such kindness. "Thank you, Mr. D–D–Drummond," she said softly as she took them. "You are more k–k–kind to me than anyone has ever b–b–been. It is a pretty ribbon."

"Oh yes, I almost forgot!" Percy dug into his pocket. "Look, I bought you some more—three pieces in different colors. I thought you might like to use them when you make your bouquets." He held them out to her.

Gwyneth stared at the lovely gift in disbelief. Was she being given a bouquet and a gift besides?

"Here, take them, Gwyneth," said Percy. "I bought them for you."

"Thank you, M–Mr. Drummond."

"And about this *Mister* Drummond business," laughed Percy. "I thought we settled all that the first time I saw you in the hills. I told you that my friends call me Percy. Surely you qualify as my friend by now! I'm only sixteen—I'm hardly a mister yet. Don't you think you might call me Percy?"

"I can try, Mr. Drummond," said Gwyneth simply. "But it might be hard. You *seem* so much like a man."

Percy laughed again. "I suppose I shall be one someday. But not yet. Just promise me you will try."

"I promise," said Gwyneth. "Would you like to see the cave where I found the pirate's skull?"

The words slammed into Percy's brain as if he had been hit by a train. She could stop a conversation so abruptly with the most unexpected statements!

He stared back with a look of incredulity. "A. . . *pirate's* skull!" he exclaimed.

"That's what Grannie said it was when I told her. Papa didn't believe it. He thought I had seen a dead animal's head. But I knew it was from a man. I could tell. Come, I'll show you where I saw it."

She led him along the beach back toward Llanfryniog. Percy had run right past the cave's mouth only a few minutes before but had not seen it. Moments later they crept into the darkened opening.

"The water is almost too high," said Gwyneth. "I never go inside unless it is low because I don't want to get trapped inside."

"You found a skull in here?" said Percy, his voice echoing into the darkened chamber.

"It was buried in the sand."

"What became of it?"

"I don't know. I've never seen it again. I think the water washed it away. But I have been a *little* afraid to come here since. I have only peeped inside, just in case the pirate is still there. Grannie says there is pirate gold somewhere, if only we could find it."

Was there no end to this girl's surprises?

"Pirates. . .*and gold*!" said Percy.

"That's what Grannie says."

"How does she know?"

"I don't know. Grannie knows many things. But sometimes it is hard to understand what she means."

"Let's go inside and look!" said Percy excitedly.

"I am nervous about the water," said Gwyneth. "It will rise into the cave soon."

"The tide comes in so slow, it won't bother us."

"Sometimes a big wave comes in all at once. It is high enough now that that could happen. I am very small, and I have to be more careful about the water than bigger people. It is too dark to see inside anyway. And there is no gold in the cave. I have been all the way to the back of it."

"How do you see well enough to be certain?" asked Percy.

"When the sun shines exactly right at the end of the summer, it shines all the way to the very back wall. Then you can see everything. That only happens for a few days, when the sun is coming straight into the cave's mouth from the water. That's why I know there is no gold in the cave."

On this day the sun was too high in the sky for its rays to probe inside the cave more than a few feet. Having come out of bright sunlight, all Percy and Gwyneth could see was blackness.

"I think I want to go now," said Gwyneth, walking back outside.

Percy followed, turning the remarkable series of revelations over in his mind. "Where were you coming from," he asked, "when I saw you from back there? It looked like you were climbing down the cliff."

"A trail comes from the top," replied Gwyneth.

"Can you show me? I'll go home that way instead of walking back through the village."

Again they turned along the beach, continuing past the place where two lines of footprints coming from opposite directions still showed the place of their meeting in the sand. They walked past them toward the base of the trail.

"So, Gwyneth Barrie," said Percy as they went, "when will you begin teaching me to ride like the wind?"

"Whenever you like, Mr. Drummond."

Percy looked at her with a stern smile.

"Whenever you like...*Percy*," said Gwyneth shyly, her face reddening.

"That's more like it! How about tomorrow, then?"

"All right."

"Where shall I meet you?"

"On the beach there where you came from," said Gwyneth, pointing back toward the harbor, now probably a mile distant. "Between the harbor and the rocks. Lady Florilyn never walks along the sea. She will not see us there. I don't think she likes the ocean. I love the ocean."

"I know you do. I think you love it because of your mother."

Percy's statement made Gwyneth thoughtful. "I don't know," she said slowly. "I have always loved the water. Perhaps you are right and that is why."

"Then the beach below the village it is," said Percy. "I will be there as soon after breakfast as I can get away. I will ask Mr. Radnor to saddle a horse for me."

They made their way up the steep trail from the beach to the plateau above, then struck out across the open moorland in a direction that led toward Westbrooke Manor and finally parted.

TWENTY-FIVE

Secrets of Nature

$\mathcal{A}$s soon as he had finished breakfast on the following morning, Percy slipped out of the house for the stables. He had never yet seen Florilyn in the breakfast room. She was not an early riser. To his relief this day was no exception.

Hollin Radnor was out with Stuart Wyckham pruning some of the hedges around one of the gardens after their vigorous spring growth.

Percy walked toward the two men. "Good morning, Mr. Radnor," he said cheerfully. "I think I am ready for another ride. Would you mind helping me saddle a horse?"

"Certainly, Mr. Percy," replied the groom. He set aside the shears. "I will be back in a few minutes, Stuart," he said.

Then he and Percy walked together toward the stables.

"Fine day indeed for a ride, Mr. Percy," said Radnor as they went. "Going out alone, are you?"

"For now," replied Percy. "Though I suppose you never know who might turn up, eh?"

"Which horse do you fancy, sir?"

"The gentle one you recommended before. Grey Tide, I believe she was called. I got on well enough that first day. I'm not keen on going out on Red Rhud again!"

146

"Yes, sir—I heard what happened. I would have prevented that unpleasantness if I had been able, Mr. Percy."

"Well, no harm done. I survived it. Still, I think a gentler mount will suit me until I am a little steadier in the saddle."

"Grey Tide is a wise choice, Mr. Percy. You will do fine on her back."

Fifteen minutes later, after a detailed lesson in horse saddling, Percy rode off in the direction of town. The morning was still chilly. But Percy was full of the jubilation of life, added to by the exhilaration of sneaking away from the manor without Florilyn knowing it. Exuberantly he even encouraged Grey Tide into a trot two or three times on the way down to Llanfryniog. He was still timid about allowing the mare to cantor or gallop. Hopefully before long, with Gwyneth's coaching, that would change.

He found Gwyneth walking along the shore south of the harbor waiting for him. He rode up beside her, reined in, and dismounted. "Good morning, Gwyneth," he said. "It looks to be another fine day."

"And the tide is low," she said, turning toward him with a smile. "It is good for riding."

"Do you ride here often?"

"We do not have a horse. I do not have many chances to ride."

"But you know how to?"

"Horses are my friends. I have always known how to ride."

"Well then, teacher," said Percy with humor in his tone, though he meant the word with an endearing respect, "how do we begin?"

"You must show me how you ride first," said Gwyneth. "I have seen you from far away. Now I want to see you close."

"I shouldn't have dismounted," Percy said, laughing. "I still have a hard enough time getting in the saddle." With some difficulty he climbed back up. "What do you want me to do?" he said.

"Can you gallop?" asked Gwyneth.

"I've never galloped on purpose," answered Percy. "The only time I've ridden fast was on Red Rhud, and she threw me off!"

"Can you try?"

"I will try."

Gwyneth stepped back.

Percy gave a few kicks into Grey Tide's flanks and flipped at the reins. Grey Tide eased forward into a gentle cantor then gradually, as Percy kicked harder, into a halfhearted gallop, with Percy bouncing clumsily about in the saddle. He reined back after a short distance, turned the mare around, and returned to where Gwyneth stood. He stopped and looked down at her.

"To ride fast," she said, "you need to lean forward. You sit up too straight. That's why you bounce around. If you are bouncing up and down, the horse knows you aren't secure. If it knows that, either it won't do what you want or you will fall off."

"I'm *not* secure!" Percy laughed.

"But you will be. When you are secure, the horse will know it. Then it will do what you tell it. So first you must lean forward. And sit higher in the saddle, with your knees bent. You must feel the horse with your knees, not your bottom."

Percy tried to adjust himself.

Gwyneth continued to suggest this or that until she was satisfied with his seat for the present. "When you want her to go," she went on, "press into her sides with your heels. Don't kick—just press in with your heels and knees and lean forward. Then talk to her, tell her to run, and stroke her neck."

"Why don't you show me?" said Percy. He jumped down.

"You'll have to help me get up," said Gwyneth.

Percy took her foot in his hand. She reached up for the saddle with her hands as he lifted her. She was so unexpectedly light that he nearly flung her up and over the top. But Gwyneth recovered and landed gently in the saddle with the grace of a cat. Her feet did not reach Percy's stirrups, but she hardly noticed.

She took told of the reins, then leaned forward, stroked the big mare's neck, and spoke a few whispered words into her ear. "Now watch, Percy," she said. "I will press in with my knees to keep me balanced.

I am hardly touching the saddle, you see. . .and give her a little nudge in the sides with my heels, and lean forward. . ." She spoke again into the mare's ear, "Dash on, Grey Tide. . .dash on!"

Though her command was soft, Grey Tide bounded with several steps into gentle motion. Quickly the pace increased. Within seconds she was at top speed and flying away from Percy down the wide sand glistening wet from the retreating tide. Huge clumps flew up behind her hooves as their echoes pounded through the morning air.

Percy gazed after her in astonishment that one so small could command such a powerful beast with so few words and movements. Until that moment, he had taken the proposed riding lessons more as a lark than that he really thought he could ever beat Florilyn in a race. Suddenly he realized, all things being equal, Florilyn would have no chance against Gwyneth. So why couldn't he learn to ride as fast as she?

Had it not been for the rocks and boulders enclosing the harbor portion of the beach to the south, Grey Tide and her tiny white-haired rider would have quickly disappeared from sight. As it was, while he stared in wonder, Percy saw them make a wide semicircular arc on the sand that, because of the tide, was fifty or seventy-five yards wide. Gradually they came flying straight back toward him again.

Horse and rider were truly one. The motion of Gwyneth's tiny frame flowed in a harmony of exquisite precision with Grey Tide's movement. Elbows out, knees flexed, her frame parallel with the horse's great neck, her body floated with fluid ease as if riding on a cushion of air. As they flew toward him, Gwyneth slowed the mare so gradually that Percy never once saw her use the reins.

A few seconds later, the huge horse stood panting beside him, great puffs of white pulsing from her nostrils in the chilly morning air. Gwyneth's face was flushed with animation, her eyes wide with joy, a smile of ecstasy on her lips.

"Gwyneth," exclaimed Percy, "that was marvelous! I had no idea you could ride so fast."

"I told you I could ride fast."

"Yes, but. . .*that* fast! I've never seen anything like it. How do you do it?"

"When you move up and down, holding by your knees instead of bouncing in the saddle, in exact rhythm with Grey Tide's back, she will scarcely feel you. Then you will be able to ride as fast as me."

"I can't imagine that." Percy laughed.

"Your motion must be smooth with hers," said Gwyneth. "She will not feel you. She will be free. When Grey Tide is free, there is no horse at the manor faster. Now you try it again," she added, swinging one leg up and around the mare's back and slipping to the ground.

Again Percy mounted.

"Remember, feel Grey Tide's motion," said Gwyneth. "Move gently up and down. Do not let her feel you bounce in the saddle."

For the next hour, Percy rode up and down the beach, sometimes fast, sometimes slow, trying to follow Gwyneth's instructions. She watched and told him this or that to try next. By the end of his first lesson, he did not feel much improvement. Although he had begun to know what she meant when she spoke of moving in concert with the rhythm of the horse, to achieve his goal would take much practice.

They parted, and Percy rode back through town. By now the morning was well advanced. The sun was high and warming the earth, luring from the grass and trees and shrubs and dirt and water the fragrances of the wonderful time of late spring that was the month of June. For the first time in his life, Percy felt relaxed and confident enough on the back of a horse to enjoy himself. It was still early. He was not anxious to return to the manor. Instead he struck out inland over moor and field toward the hills east. He was curious whether he could find Gwyneth's special high place with the spectacular view.

He rode slowly up the plateau. After a good deal of exploration along the ridge, he found the spot he had been looking for. He dismounted, tied the horse, and sat down looking out over the sloping plateau and coastline.

His mood grew thoughtful. His father came to his mind. With

it floated into his consciousness an unexpected sense of fondness. Poignantly Percy realized that things were changing within him. Thoughts of his father were no longer irksome in his memory. Instead they drew him with emotions he had not felt in years. It reminded him of how much he had once loved his father and enjoyed nothing more than being with him.

Where had these new feelings come from? What could be the cause of these strange sensations? Were they really *new*. . .or was he just feeling again sensations he had lost from long before?

A hunger after something beyond him, something he could not have described, had come awake in his heart. When it had begun, he could not have said. Once he was aware of it, he realized it had been there from his first week here. It was, in fact, the beginning of the greatest transformation in all the universe, though Percy did not yet know it as such. He had heard his father preach about such things. He had never dreamed that the very movements of soul his father described would one day come upon him.

Was Wales the cause of it—the walk through the hills with Gwyneth. . . lying on the top of the ridge, at this very place, overlooking the moor and sea and sky. . .walking along the sand at the water's edge. . .seeing the faces of humanity through newly loving eyes—or had it begun even before?

He came to feel a strange mystery in the world. It seemed full of meaning, yet a meaning he could not lay hold of. He perceived a whispering of unknown secrets in the wind that now came up the moor from the sea to greet him. He was stung with a consciousness of inexplicable rapture at the cry of a gull or the song of robin and sparrow. He took joy in every sunrise, felt a poignant sadness in the oranges and purples and reds of the sunset. He felt there must be something wonderful beyond and inside and above him. What could he do but ask, "What can it all mean?"

Wherever he turned, the bewitching loveliness in the face of the world met him. The scents the wind carried from field and forest and sea were sweeter than ever wind-borne scents from Glasgow's streets and lanes and the deserted alleys he had roamed during the darkest days of his prodigality.

He sat on the high ridge for perhaps an hour. When he remounted Grey Tide and started back down the hill, he was still not ready to return to the manor. He was too *full*. The last thing he wanted now was to run into Florilyn or Courtenay or his uncle.

He descended the ridge and made his way across the plateau, then struck out along the promontory of Mochras Head. By now the tide was well on its way in, the beach below where he had walked with Gwyneth yesterday almost covered. The splashing and crashing of the waves against the rocks below echoed up and met him and filled his consciousness with the undefined pleasure of being.

As he went, the breeze coming off the water braced his face with a welcome chill, as if it had something to say. The sea glistened below as if it knew something it would be good for him to know. Its waves broke on the shore with words in a strange tongue he could not understand. Their watery echoes plunged into his heart and made him both happy and sad.

Creation reveals itself in secrets, but as secrets that are outer cloaks of truths waiting to be discovered. All around, in leaf and grass and cloud and rain and flower, the world whispered into his heart. It said that life could be a good thing, and that somehow God was in it all.

The world suddenly seemed so full of joy. But in truth the joy he felt was within *him*. Something was coming awake in the soul of Percival Drummond, something that had lain as an embryo of God's creation, waiting to flex the seed-life of its being and break the sleepy shell of its chrysalis, that a new and higher form of being might emerge. What was it but *life* itself struggling to come awake within him.

He had begun to uncover the truths that lay beneath creation's secrets.

TWENTY-SIX

Secrets of Man

While Percy was riding along the headland, Lord Snowdon sat in his study perusing the telegram that had finally arrived from London the previous afternoon. He had been stewing over it ever since.

Not only had Heygate learned that Palmer Sutcliffe was business manager for mining magnate Lord Coleraine Litchfield, but he was a forty-two-year-old business manager at that. He was a young man in the prime of his career. The fellow was a Londoner, born and bred, had probably never been to North Wales in his life...and was certainly not on the verge of retiring so that he could spend his leisure time in some cozy little cottage nestled in the Snowdonian mountains!

The letter from Sutcliffe had been a ruse, a fabrication of lies from beginning to end!

Litchfield's interests, for such the fellow Sutcliffe was certainly representing, were in mining. Neither was Sutcliffe's boss anticipating retirement anytime soon. Whatever he was up to had profit at the bottom of it, not nostalgia for the bygone happiness of childhood.

What did they take him for—a fool whom they could scam into selling off a piece of property for a few shillings? Whatever it was they thought lay beneath his property—and the logical assumption was coal—he wasn't about to let some greedy Englishman waltz in and help himself!

It was time for a response. The viscount wrote:

Dear Mr. Sutcliffe,

It has come to my attention that you represent Lord Coleraine Litchfield in his business dealings and mining interests. I have only to assume, therefore, as you do not appear near retirement age yourself, that your recent letter expressing the desire to purchase a small portion of my land was sent on behalf of Lord Litchfield.

Is his motive personal, or do business pursuits make my land of interest to him?

I am,
Sincerely yours,
Viscount Roderick Westbrooke

A week later he received the following reply:

The Right Honorable, the Viscount Roderick Westbrooke,
Lord Snowdon.
My Lord,

Please forgive the subterfuge of our previous correspondence. I asked my manager and assistant Mr. Sutcliffe to draft the letter you received, expressing sentiments that are dear to my heart. Knowing the speculation my name invariably raises because of my extensive business interests throughout Britain, I told him to make the request in his own name. It was foolish of me. I see now that I was wrong not to be entirely candid with a man of your experience and good reputation. I apologize. Rest assured, however, that my motives are as stated, and my interest genuine.

Despite the fact that we have gotten off, as it were, on the wrong foot with one another, I hope you will consider this a new

beginning and will consider my request to purchase a piece of your
land as outlined in the previous letter with sincerity.

> *I am,*
> *Humbly yours,*
> *Lord Coleraine Litchfield*

By now, however, having stewed on the matter for another week
and having carried out further research, Westbrooke's suspicions had
nowise been alleviated. Indeed, they were greater than ever.

As a result, Litchfield received a second and more pointed communication from Lord Snowdon:

Lord Coleraine Litchfield,
My Lord,
   I am deeply appreciative of the straightforward manner in
which you have explained the letter from Mr. Sutcliffe. While I
can assure you that I am not on principle opposed to selling a small
portion of acreage from my estate and would happily entertain an
offer, I would have to know more details regarding your purpose in
such a proposed transaction. The image of a cozy retirement cottage
nestled in the mountains is appealing. My instincts, however, tell
me that there must be more to it than that and that the candor you
spoke of has probably not yet been entirely forthcoming.

> *I remain,*
> *Sincerely yours,*
> *Viscount Roderick Westbrooke*

Litchfield swore lightly as he read; then his fist slammed down
on his desk. This was not going to be as easy as he had hoped. He
would have to consider his next move with care. To tell this provincial
Westbrooke *everything* could spell doom to his whole scheme.

TWENTY-SEVEN

Shoes, Horses, and Friends

*C*odnor Barrie's daughter usually kept to the side streets when walking through Llanfryniog. Thankfully Grannie's cottage lay where she could easily reach it and keep mostly out of sight.

This girl of far-seeing eye but faltering tongue could welcome harshness from the elements of God's world with glee. But meanness from those of her own kind was a harshness far different that she could not understand. She was child enough to be hurt by the lashes of unkind tongues. She thus kept to herself within the shadows of the village, although this habit contributed all the more to her reputation among the more low-minded of its inhabitants.

She climbed, on this summer's day, from the grass and rocks down to the southern sandy tip of the Mochras Head beach, removing her shoes the moment she hit bare sand, and now wandered along it northward in the direction of the village. She climbed through the rocks halfway along more easily with bare feet than Percy had with his shoes. Before reaching the harbor in which the few boats were tied at the northeast end of the protected bay, she turned and scampered up the beach onto one of Llanfryniog's outlying dirt streets, still carrying her shoes. From there she ran in the direction of Grannie's cottage.

A few jeers and taunts came flying as she passed, mostly from school classmates, whose idleness led them to no good. But a friendly voice soon brought her swift barefoot steps to a stop.

"Hey there, young lady," it said. "Where'll you be bound in such a hurry?"

Gwyneth turned toward the wide doors of the blacksmith's shop, which stood open to the day's sunshine. "H–h–hello, Mr. Radnor," she said as she caught her breath. "I'm on my way to Grannie's."

"She's a fine woman, your Grannie."

"N–not everyone thinks so," replied Gwyneth, walking toward the Westbrooke groom, one of her few friends in the place.

"Not everyone has eyes to see people as they are," he rejoined with a smile. "But I know what she's made of. Are you taking your shoes to the cobbler?" he added, nodding toward her hands. "He won't be working today, I'm thinking."

"No. I took them off s–s–so I could feel the sand in my t–t–toes."

"The sand is one thing, hard streets are another."

"The shoes are more uncomfortable than the stones. I'd n–n–never wear shoes if I didn't have to!"

"The mare's done," said a voice behind them. The next moment appeared from the shadows the hulking form of the smithy. With a blackened leather apron tied around his thick waist, rippling muscular chest and arms bare and perspiring from his work over the fiery forge, leather reins held in his gloved hands, the huge man led the horse out into the street with a slow *clop, clop, clop* behind him. His great black eyebrows creased and his eyes darkened as he saw with whom his customer had taken up conversation. He handed the reins to the groom and turned inside without another word.

"You see you're not the only one concerned about shoes," said Radnor as he began walking along the street with Gwyneth at his side. "But I came to the horse cobbler to get a *new* set of shoes for Red Rhud, not get them taken *off* like you did yours. Would you like to lead her?"

"Oh, yes!" exclaimed Gwyneth. "M–m–may I really?"

With a smile, the groom handed her the reins.

Gwyneth dropped her two shoes on the hard-packed dirt then took the reins with one hand and with the other gently stroked the long face and nose and whispered a few unintelligible words to the mare.

Radnor picked up her shoes and resumed on his way.

Gwyneth followed, speaking quietly to the great beast at her side. Despite her occasionally wild behavior with a rider on her back, the huge mare gave every appearance of being perfectly content to be led by such a tiny girl. "W–why does Red Rhud need new shoes?" asked Gwyneth at length.

"To keep from picking up pebbles and getting bruises in her hooves."

"Don't the nails hurt?" said Gwyneth, who had watched the shoeing process many times at her father's side.

"Nay, lassie. The smithy-cobbler knows what's good for horses. He would never hurt them. It's like our own Master does—sometimes things that *look* like they hurt keep us from worse trouble in the end."

"That's like something Grannie would say."

"A fine and a wise woman," rejoined the groom. "She's one who knows the ways of the Master. And, young lady," he added, "it seems we're nearly to her door." He took several steps toward the cottage in front of them then called into its open door, "I brought you a visitor, Mrs. Barrie!"

An elderly woman appeared a moment later. She shielded her eyes from the sun as she emerged from inside. "Who's your great friend there, Gwyneth dear?" she said.

"Red Rhud, Grannie."

A smile spread across the old woman's face. She and the groom shook hands and exchanged a few words. "Won't you join Gwyn and me for tea, Mr. Radnor?" she asked.

"You sorely tempt me, Mrs. Barrie," he replied. "I fear my charge here would lose her patience. She'll already be wanting her oats, I'm thinking."

"Then you must come back another time."

"I promise." He nodded as he took the reins from the girl's hand.

"And here will be *your* shoes, young lady," he said.

"Thank you for letting me hold the reins, M–Mr. Radnor."

The groom chuckled, gave Grannie a wink, then continued out of town.

Gwyneth and the old woman went inside.

TWENTY-EIGHT

Sabbath

*T*he day happened to be a Sunday, the Calvinist "Sabbath" for those attending the worship service at the Methodist chapel at the north end of town, and in the two houses of worship to the south, "Holy Day" for the Anglicans and "High Mass" for the Catholics.

Percy Drummond had been in North Wales three weeks. After declining two previous invitations, he had at last decided to accompany his aunt and uncle and cousins to church. Being of the aristocracy, they were staid and respectable members of the Church of England.

All the shops of the village were of course closed. But Kyvwlch Gwarthegydd, blacksmith and village atheist, made certain that he was vigorously and noisily at work in his blacksmith's shop every Sunday between the hours of ten o'clock and noon. Any home or farm for probably three miles north, south, or east, might set their clocks weekly to the 10:00 a.m. hour. At the very moment Big Ben began to strike in Westminster, the rhythmic *clank, clank, clank* of hammer on anvil likewise began to toll loudly from Gwarthegydd's shop. His choice of this hour was chosen because it was at ten o'clock that the first of the three church bells pealed out from the Methodist chapel, and he did his best every Sunday to drown them out. He was mostly successful, too, as he was at 11:00 a.m., when the two dissonant knells from

160

opposing sides of the street at the opposite end of town announced the commencement of their services.

The clanking continued, on and off, for the duration of all three services, to the supreme annoyance of the more spiritually minded of the clergy and laity of Llanfryniog. They considered the sound to be the very drumbeat of the devil from hell itself standing in brazen opposition to the truth of almighty God, whose existence the heathen blacksmith so flagrantly denied. Not a few sermons through the years had used the background discord as a fitting object lesson to rail against those who openly mocked God and the fiery retribution of judgment that awaited them.

Neither did Hollin Radnor often spend his Sundays in church. He did not as a rule find God's presence much in evidence in any of Llanfryniog's three houses of worship. He visited them all from time to time, not so much looking for God, for the groom knew where *He* was to be found, but looking for kindred hearts that might know Him after the same manner in which he had himself grown to know Him. It was not an enterprise that had been crowned with much success through the years, but he remained hopeful of occasionally discovering such a one. No doubt that he was doctrinally fluid and nonsectarian in his acceptance of the men and women from all three congregations contributed in large measure to the fact that none of them accepted him as one of them. In such assemblies, it was always who was "one of us," not who was "one of God's."

In fact, there was no man to be found in all Snowdonia who *knew* God on the intimate footing of daily obedience more than did Lord Snowdon's humble groom. As is often the case in such instances of godliness, however, few recognized that fact. As he left Grannie's cottage and made his way back up the street and out of town on the back of the newly shod bay mare, he was surprised to see the manor's three cousins walking along toward him.

"Good day to you, Master Courtenay, Miss Florilyn, and Master Percy," he said, tipping his hat as he passed.

Percy greeted him warmly. A patronizing nod was all that came his way from the other two.

The appearance of the three youths a few minutes after noon on the main street of Llanfryniog was not difficult to explain. It being a warm day, as they were approaching the buggy at the conclusion of the morning's service, Percy announced that he was going to walk home. Having nothing better to do, and vaguely thinking that perhaps it might present her an opportunity to get back at Percy somehow for the grudge she was still nursing against him, Florilyn said she would join him. Inwardly chagrined at the thought, Percy could hardly object.

Instead of following the direct route home, it was Percy's intent to take the long way round along the beach and, if the tide was low enough to permit passage through the rocks near the cave, to continue on and up the bluff path. It only took a moment's reflection to cause him to relish the thought of Florilyn trying to keep pace with him over the rocks and through the tide pools in her Sunday shoes. He and Florilyn, therefore, set off toward town.

They were surprised a few seconds later to hear Courtenay's steps running to catch them. Upon reflection, he thought the day might present an admirable opportunity to visit the Lorimer home, *without* Percy in tow, and soothe whatever ruffled feathers might remain between himself and the magistrate's daughter.

Roderick and Katherine Westbrooke found themselves in consequence riding home in the buggy alone.

Twenty-Nine

Homegoing

On this same day in Glasgow, a faithful minister who had given his life in service to the Church of Scotland was struggling mightily to reach the end of the morning's service.

The day's reading had been taken from the fifteenth chapter of the Gospel of Luke. He had managed, with more than one throaty hesitation, to get through the poignant passage of scripture. But the sermon had progressed with increasing difficulty.

He had, of course, anticipated for some time that this Sunday was coming and known what would be the morning's text. He had agonized over it all week. More than once he had all but decided on the coward's way out of his intensely personal difficulty. He would have one of the church elders give the New Testament reading. That would keep him from having to utter the words in public that stabbed his heart with pain: *"I will arise and go to my father, and will say unto him, Father, I have sinned. . . ."*

Avoiding the text itself, he would then dust off one of the stale sermons from his seminary days, written with the intent of impressing professors rather than moving hearts. Or perhaps he would follow the script in one of a half dozen volumes on his shelf of sermon outlines and notes. He would gloss over the powerful passage with a few dusty truisms. His words would thus be guaranteed to keep his own tears at bay and, at the same time, to put his listeners to sleep. One thing they would certainly never do was rouse so much as a flutter of homegoing, right-making conscience-movement in the heart of whatever unrepentant prodigals might be listening in his congregation.

He knew as well as any man who had asked God for insight into the human condition that prodigals of all ages were alive and well in his parish. He knew that thirty-, forty-, and fifty-year-old prodigals needed to repent no less than their younger counterparts, before the matter of their prodigality became of internal import. Some, it was true, delayed their homecoming until it was too late to say the healing words. How deep must be their grief and how bitter their tears before God to realize their fathers were no longer alive to receive them into a loving embrace.

Still...such must repent and arise...they *must* repent and go to their fathers.

Homegoing is imperative, whether in this life or the next. Homegoing is the eternal imperative, the overarching *must* of the universe.

How fortunate for those thirty-, forty-, fifty-, and even sixty-year-old prodigals, perhaps who have grown comfortable in their prodigality, who awake, alas, late in life, but not *too* late, thank God, with their fathers still alive. For they could go to their aging parents, hearts of young and old breaking together, and whisper the eternal words, "I have sinned." However late it comes, they have the opportunity to hear the father's long-awaited, "I love you, my child. You have always been forgiven. Welcome home."

Yet for most of his listening prodigals, those who bury the rebellion of youth in the deep recesses of consciousness as a blurry dream from long ago, it was easy to allow life simply to "go on" and not look back. These never face the heart-probing reality of what their words and actions inflicted into the hearts of those who sacrificed themselves on the altar of parenthood. Many indeed drift back into relationship with their elders on such a superficial foundation. In the presumed maturity of their own adulthood, the hostility of early years fading, they assume it enough to be on "speaking terms." But as long as the underlying schism remains unhealed, it is *not* enough. Relational drift cannot eradicate the roots of rebellion. Only repentance can accomplish that. Outwardly respectable, these never take account before God for the hubris of their early years with the words, "Father, Mother. . .I sinned against you. I am sorry. I want to be a true son, a true daughter to you for the years I have left."

The vicar knew there were such comfortable prodigals in his church, because they existed everywhere. As the consequences of this unseen prodigality swirled through his mind, the question rose in the heart of Edward Drummond: Could he, in good conscience, deny them the opportunity of being challenged to "arise and go" because of the frail tenderness of his own suffering father's heart? In the end, he had realized that the answer was no. He had to issue the challenge of Luke 15, whatever it might cost him personally.

And surely it *would* cost him. The image of father and repentant son was too personal, too close to his own breaking heart. Yes, it would *cost* him! But he could not shirk his duty. He could not shirk the truth. Thus he would not shirk the challenge.

With that decision came an even greater realization. He had to confront the reality of Luke 15 for *himself*. With his own son adrift in prodigality, did he, Edward Drummond. . .did *he* still believe in God's goodness, in God's infinite fatherhood, in the welcoming embrace of the Eternal Heart of Forgiveness?

He could only answer that question by confronting the Fatherhood of Luke 15 in all the anguish it might cause his own heart and in all the glory of its eternal resolution.

Truly no man nor woman can apprehend the full pathos of the prodigal story who has not stood as the waiting, praying, seeking, hurting, eager, long-suffering, grief-stricken, shattered yet patient parent of Luke 15—who has not stood on the road day after day, wept night after night, and gone out again morning after morning to stand on the road. . .waiting for the return of son or daughter.

THIRTY

Grannie

*A*fter leaving church and passing Hollin Radnor on his way out of town, the three cousins from Westbrooke Manor made their way casually through Llanfryniog's streets. A few others were out, mostly young boys with nothing on their minds other than that favorite pursuit of the weak-minded—seeing what amusement might chance their way now that they had been released from the prison of Sunday morning.

Still not having seen much of the town, Percy struck off the main street with Florilyn trailing after him. Courtenay followed as well since they were moving in a general direction that would take him where he was bound. Soon they were lost in a maze of twisting and turning lanes and streets.

Percy paused to stare down a side street where an oddly shaped purplish building caught his eye. Brother and sister continued sauntering along. They came to an open door through which they heard the *whirrrrrr* of a spinning wheel.

"Look, Florilyn," said Courtenay. "The old witch is spinning."

A girl walked out the door. When she saw who was standing in front of her, she turned and hurried back inside. But it was too late.

"Hey, th–th–there, funny-looking little Gw–Gw–*Gwy–neth*!" taunted

Courtenay. "Visiting the old w–w–w–witch today?"

Florilyn laughed at what she supposed her brother's wit.

Gwyneth turned and planted her feet firmly. "G–G–Grannie's not a w–w–witch!" she said. "Y–y–you should be ashamed of yourself, M–M–Master C–C–Courtenay!"

"Did you hear th–th–that, Florilyn?" laughed Courtenay. "This little brat thinks I ought to be ashamed of myself! You know what I think?" he added, turning back toward Gwyneth and glaring down at her. "I think it's *you* who's the w–w–w–witch! Ha! Ha! Ha!"

By now Percy was approaching and saw who they were talking to. "Cut it out, Courtenay," he said. "She meant no harm. Hello, Gwyneth," he said, smiling down at her.

"She's just the little village idiot—that's what she is."

"Leave her alone," repeated Percy.

"What—is she a friend of yours now?"

"That's right—she's a friend of mine."

"So that's how it is! That explains everything," laughed Courtenay. "I'm hardly surprised. And she *is* a witch. Didn't you hear her stutter?"

"That doesn't make anyone a witch."

"Listen to the city boy!" Courtenay spat back. "Even if she's not a witch, she's a half-wit." He touched his index finger to the side of his head and winked at his sister.

"I tell you there's nothing wrong with her," said Percy angrily. "That's the trouble with cowards like you, Courtenay. You don't know how to pick on someone your own size."

"You're calling me a coward?"

"For making fun of a girl half your size—that's exactly what you are."

The words were unwisely spoken. Seconds later Percy found himself on the ground groaning. A little more on his guard after the incident in the barn, this time he managed to sidestep the quick jab from his cousin's hand. But Courtenay was not merely bigger than Percy, he was twice as cunning. Missing with his fist, he gave a lethal swipe with his foot. Percy's legs went out from under him, and the next instant

Courtenay's booted foot landed two well-placed kicks into the side of his ribs.

Brother and sister continued on their way laughing at the two fools behind them.

Percy rolled over and tried to sit up in the dirt of the street, while Gwyneth ran inside the cottage. A moment later she stooped beside him, this time with no fistful of flowers but holding a moist cloth. She handed it to him. He took it with a smile of gratitude and wiped at his dust-covered face.

His two cousins were not yet out of sight. Glancing back and witnessing the tender scene, they could not keep themselves from the temptation to add insult to injury. They walked back toward the cottage.

"Percy, Percy, baby Percy!" chanted Courtenay. "Witch girl taking care of baby boy from the city!"

Florilyn was laughing so hard by now that she could scarcely contain herself. This was sweeter revenge than she had hoped for!

Suddenly a great shooing and scurrying interrupted the laughter and taunts. A woman by appearances ancient beyond years ran from the cottage with a torrent of shouts. In truth she was but eighty-one, old enough to be wise yet still robust enough to hold her own against the viscount's troublesome brood. She held a great broom in her hand and came flying into the street like an old Celtic warrior from whose stock she had come. Heedless of their father's status in the region, she whacked and swatted at the two young Westbrookes, whose character she knew well enough. "Get away from here, you two troublemakers!" she cried, landing a powerful blow with the blunt handle of her weapon on Courtenay's head.

"Ouch. . .hey, you old witch!" he shouted, jumping back. "Stop it! I'll send my father down here after you."

"I'll give him the same," shot back the woman, "if he tries to harm a hair on another body's head!"

Wham! came another strike from the broom.

"Get on home! You two are no better than a couple of street urchins!

Whatever happened to gentlemen and ladies?"

"Come on, Florilyn," said Courtenay. Now that he had recovered himself, he found himself a little cowed by the rumors he had heard of the old woman. "Let's leave Percy to the two witches."

They ran off down the street, laughing again, though not quite so gaily. They were superstitious enough to be nervous about having a run-in on God's day with one of the devil's presumed workers of iniquity.

Gwyneth took Percy by the hand and tried to pull him to his feet.

"Goodness, goodness!" said the old woman, out of breath from the battle. "Come inside, the two of you. What you need, young man, is some strong hot tea."

"Grannie, this is my friend, Mr. Drummond," said Gwyneth as they entered the darkened cottage. "He's from Glasgow."

"Is he now! Well then, welcome to Grannie's house, Mr. Drummond," she said as Percy followed them inside. "You must have these violets I picked just this morning," she added. She set down the weapon-broom and took a tiny clump of purple from a water dish on the table. "No stranger comes to my house without flowers to make a friend of him."

Percy and Gwyneth glanced toward each other and smiled.

"Thank you," said Percy. He took the tiny bouquet and lifted them to his nose as he sat down on the straight wood chair the woman pulled toward him. "Are you Gwyneth's grandmother?"

"No, young man, I am Gwyneth's great-great-aunt. Her father is the grandson of my husband's brother. They're all gone now to their home with the Lord, all except the lad, Gwyneth's daddy."

The old woman set about the tea making. At her side, Gwyneth assisted with the familiar routine.

"I hear rumors," said Grannie as she worked, never embarrassed to speak her mind before either lord or peasant and especially before friend, "that in Glasgow you're not much better than your two cousins." As she spoke she glanced over her shoulder to where her guest sat holding the wet cloth to his face.

Percy was so shocked by the unexpected words that he did not answer at first. His only reply came in the form of the reddening of his cheeks.

"Sometimes the Lord must turn the tables on us," she went on, "so that we see ourselves as we really are." She glanced toward Percy again. This time she gazed deeply into his eyes. "No," she added with a knowing nod, "you are not one of them. The difference is not hard to see. You've just been a mite confused about some things. But there's the look in your eye of one who knows right from wrong. You are of the truth, I'm thinking."

Grannie sat down and said nothing more. Gradually she seemed to drift away to some distant time in the past.

Gwyneth quietly finished the tea preparations. She handed a cup to Percy then laid the tray on a small table beside Grannie's chair.

Percy remained thoughtful over Grannie's words. He *did* know right from wrong. The woman was right. He had been no better than his cousins. He deserved more than just a kick in the ribs. He deserved to be in the gaol right now. He would be, too, if his father wasn't a respected vicar.

Gwyneth had inherited Grannie's straightforward tongue as well as the Celtic clarity of her vision. "What's bothering you, Grannie?" she asked after a few more minutes. "Why are you so quiet?"

"Did you not hear about poor old Sean Drindod, dear?"

Gwyneth nodded. "Papa told me."

"He and I were two of the few left from the old century, you know," said Grannie. "When someone you've known all your life goes on to their next home, it makes a body thoughtful."

Percy detected from her tone and the faraway expression that had come over her countenance that there was more behind the old woman's mood than her brief explanation revealed.

THIRTY-ONE

A God to Call Father

*B*y the time Sunday came to Glasgow, the vicar doubted he would survive the morning without tears.

"My friends," his message had begun, "I would like to speak to you this morning about reconciliation. It is what the Bible calls *unity*."

He paused to allow the word to sink in. He was also trying to settle his own thoughts.

"I believe," Drummond went on, "that unity is what God cares about more than anything in the world. Jews the world over remind themselves daily that God is one.

"It is a mighty truth—God is *one*. God's nature is singleness, oneness...unity. For things to be one as God intends...for relationships within God's creation to reflect their Creator, all discord, all separation, all disharmony...these must be brought together, made *one*. Everything in life, everything in the world, must be made one, because God is one.

"Reconciliation is the goal and purpose of God's heart. He would have His created beings reconciled with His Father-heart. That is the ultimate oneness, the ultimate unity. Until this reconciliation is perfected between God and His created universe, all within that creation is at strife."

Drummond paused and drew in a deep breath. His eyes closed briefly then opened, and he continued. "But this unity is not a reconciliation that can take place in some grand and sweeping way between *mankind* and God. It is a reconciliation that takes place individually—one man, one woman at a time. It takes place in *my* heart, not mankind's heart. And it takes place in *your* heart, not the whole world's heart.

"If God is anything," he went on, "He is our Father. We have in this parable before us no mere story of a broken family. Our Lord here offers us a picture of the entire scope of the human drama. In a mere twenty verses, we are given a microcosm of the grand epic of the biblical saga. A loving father gives his children all they could ask for. Instead of being content with this provision, one decides to seek his fortune outside the loving abundance of this home. He squanders the inheritance that is his, at length returns to his father, repents of his foolishness, and is happily restored.

"This morning, however, it is not the son's sin that I want us to focus on, but rather the father of this wonderful parable. For if we can truly see into the heart of this man whom Jesus described, we discover a picture of God found nowhere else in the Bible.

"Look, my friends—see the parable with new eyes. How does *God* respond when we return to Him?

"The Lord's words tell us God's response upon the return of a single wayward prodigal to his father's home. They are more beautiful even than the son's humble repentance. They are among the most important words in the Bible, for they tell us what God is like. 'But when he was yet a great way off, his father saw him, and had compassion, and ran, and fell on his neck, and kissed him.'

"See the father of the parable! He is waiting with a great smile on his face, a smile of welcome, arms outstretched. He is not waiting to judge or punish his wayward son; he is waiting to embrace him and kiss him and love him and be all the home a father can be to him.

"The image makes my heart swell. God is waiting for us! He sees us coming even while we are yet far off! He runs *to* us. Can you grasp it—God running to us to throw His arms around us and kiss us in welcome!

"How different is this from the austere image of God presented by the old theologians. Does this sound to you like the God of the hellfire evangelists who rant about sinners in the hands of an angry God, about sinners being dangled over the flames of hell?

"Of course not. The Father of Jesus Christ does not demand that we repent in sackcloth and ashes before He will deign to look down upon us from His almighty throne, wielding thunderbolts of retribution if we do not. He is a *loving* Father, a *patient* Father, a *good* Father, a *forgiving* Father.

"Of course there are consequences if we refuse this reconciliation. But they are consequences we bring upon ourselves, consequences He observes with tears in His eyes. They are not the consequences of vengeance, retribution, and wrath. They are consequences of our own reluctance and stubbornness.

"In Luke 15 we are presented the Gospel in its fullness: Our Father is a good and loving and forgiving Father. He is the perfection of that broken and incomplete fatherhood that we all experience in our earthly families. Our earthly fathers are incomplete and broken. They have hurt us. We who are fathers have done a poor job of it and have been broken and incomplete examples of what God intended. We, too, have hurt our sons and daughters.

"But earthly fatherhood, in its imperfection, is intended as a reflection of what lies beyond. It is meant to lead us to our true Father. It is thus the human doorway to God Himself. In spite of its flawed nature, it is the most important relationship in the world for us to get *right*. We must make *our* hearts right with our fathers and mothers that we can be right with God.

"God is the *perfection* of the broken earthly image. He is everything we hoped our fathers would be, all we wanted them to be. He is the perfection of all that lies in your father's heart and mine to be to our children that which we were incapable of being. He is a God whom to call *Father*. Not Monarch, not Terror, not Judge—though He can surely be those to those who continue to refuse Him—no, nor Tyrant nor Despot. . .not even Holy, though He is that, not even Omnipotent, though He is that. . .but He whom Jesus taught us to call 'Abba, Father!'

"*He is our Father.* And He waits for our return. In the embrace of His love is our home. There only is it possible for us to find the home in which we were created to live.

"That is where unity originates—in my heart and yours. The words of the prodigal are the universal words of the reconciliation of the universe. They are the words by which we acknowledge our disconnection from our Life-Source. They are the words by which we return to oneness with God, who is nothing more nor less. . .than our *Father.*"

Drummond paused again and drew in a deep breath and closed his eyes briefly.

"It takes humility, great humility to seek reconciliation," he went on after a moment. "Yet *humility* is the doorway into reconciliation. The prodigal son, whose story Jesus told, looked around and realized he was eating with pigs. He had had such dreams! He had been so eager to claim his inheritance and to live life, as we of this modern age say, *on his own.* But where had it brought him in the end? What did he have?

"Only loneliness. He was eating with pigs!

"When he realized it and admitted it. . .then was born in him the *humility* that leads to reconciliation. That humility, that swallowing of pride, that recognition of what he had sunk to, led him home to his father. It is humility that leads us home.

"It is that same humility that leads us to reconciliation in our lives. Humility, my friends. The humility to say to one we have wronged, to one who has wronged us, to one with whom misunderstandings have separated us for whatever reason. . .to say, 'I no longer want to be disconnected. I do not want to be apart from this one whom I once loved.' In humility I am ready to say, 'I will arise and go to my brother. . .my sister. . .my mother. . .my daughter. . .my father. . .my son.' I will say, 'With all my heart I desire again to be in relationship with you. I am sorry to have failed in loving you, but I will try to love you again.'

"The humility to acknowledge, 'I do not want to be separated one day more. I will arise and go.'

"Humility, my friends. Humility to recognize that life is not what we had hoped. Humility to recognize that life is full of mistakes, that we have made our own share of them. Humility to apologize. Humility to arise and go to the one we have hurt. Humility to go to one who has hurt us.

"Humility is the doorway, my friends. It is the door to all healings, the door that leads to our brethren, the door that leads to our sons and daughters and mothers and fathers and our friends. . .the door that leads to the heart of God."

Drummond stopped. He glanced around for a moment and exhaled deeply. It was obvious he was spent. The church was silent.

THIRTY-TWO

Cryptic Words

*I*n the humble cottage of Llanfryniog, Codnor Barrie's great-aunt continued to stare into the fire. She had not yet poured out a drop of tea from the pot.

At length the old woman began to talk. Her speech was soft and faraway. "He wanted to take it from me," she said in scarcely more than a whisper, "thought he had a right to it...but I wouldn't give it to him... wouldn't tell him where I'd kept it this many a year."

The words were cryptic and strange. Percy asked no questions. Even after three weeks, he was still a stranger to this place. Nor could he keep from his brain reminders of his cousin's claim that the old woman was a witch.

As Grannie rocked gently back and forth, she continued to say odd things in an otherworldly voice. Percy could not prevent a certain sensation upon neck and arms commonly known as feeling one's flesh crawl.

Gwyneth busied herself around the cottage. She seemed to pay her aging aunt no heed. She had heard such oddities too many times to consider the words strange.

"Old man said it was *all* mine if only I could find it...out there, he said, though Sean always thought I knew more than I was telling... resented me having it...never know what fate your steps will lead you to, the old pirate said. . .now look where Sean's have led him. . .dead on the same shores. . .just like the old sea dog we found."

The cottage fell silent. By and by Grannie came to herself. She glanced about, saw the tea, reached out her hand and touched the lukewarm pot, then gave a little chuckle. "Have I fallen asleep in my chair?" she said.

"You were talking about the old man again, Grannie."

"Ah." She nodded. "It's no wonder, after what happened to poor Sean. My mind's been turned toward that day ever since I heard the evil news. Shall I put on a new pot?" she added, rising again to her feet.

"I have to go home, Grannie," said Gwyneth. "I have to make tea for Papa."

"Don't forget the bread then, child," said Grannie. She rose and picked up a fine brown loaf from where it stood on the table.

Percy rose also. "Thank you for the tea," he said.

"The door of my cottage is always open to you." Grannie smiled. "I hope you will visit me again. Gwyneth, dear," she added, "here's the loaf for your papa."

By now Gwyneth's shoes were back on her feet, and she had both hands available for it.

Grannie's two visitors walked outside. Wondering if his cousins were still about, Percy glanced up and down the street. When he turned back, Gwyneth was already making her way homeward out of the village, carrying the large round loaf under her arm. Percy hurried after her.

"Where are you going, Percy?" she asked as he jogged up to her side.

"Home with you first."

"W–w–with me!" exclaimed the girl in delighted surprise.

"I'm going to make sure Courtenay and Florilyn aren't sneaking about somewhere waiting to hurt you. Once you are home, then I'll return to the manor."

"Thank you, Percy. N–n–no one's ever looked after me like that before."

"You've taken care of me twice now," laughed Percy. "Isn't it time I returned the favor?"

They continued out of Llanfryniog and up the rising plateau. Gwyneth felt safer with her grand knight beside her than she thought she had ever felt in all her life. She talked the whole way, explaining to Percy about every inch of the terrain about them.

THIRTY-THREE

Arrows of Prayer

*D*rummond concluded the remainder of his sermon quickly, endured the handshakes and smiles and well-wishes at the door, then escaped with his wife to the solace of the parsonage.

She felt the ache of his heart. She said nothing, merely slipped her hand through his arm as they walked home. The mother, too, shared the universal parental heartache of unrequited love.

"What do you think, Mary?" He sighed at length, still reflecting on his own message. "What were the father and mother doing the whole time their son was reducing himself to such foolish straits?"

Both pondered the question as they walked.

"Even as I was speaking," Drummond went on, "I found myself considering the parable from that light, wishing our Lord had spent more time on the *parental* side of the tale rather than following only the son. Now that we find ourselves in such circumstances, I am hungry for a specific example."

"What could the father and mother do but pray?" suggested his wife. "It seems all other means of parental influence were taken from them."

"Except keeping arms ready to open themselves," added the vicar with a sad smile.

His wife nodded.

They reached home and went inside. Mary put on water for tea. In ten or fifteen minutes, husband and wife sat down together with steaming cups in the parlor of the parsonage. Oddly, for this man and woman of God whom so many in the city looked to as pillars of spirituality, Edward and Mary Drummond were in truth lonely at such times. Their family was broken, and they knew it.

"Did we do the right thing, Mary," said Drummond at length, "by sending Percy to the country?"

"I truly believe so," she answered. "Here he was only becoming wilder by the day. A city's ways are not healthy for a rebellious spirit."

"The country can sometimes allow God's voice to get through more directly." Edward nodded. "I only hope our son will open himself to its influences."

"God has people everywhere," rejoined Mary. "Percy will come into contact with those the Lord will use to help his eyes open."

His wife's words caused the vicar to burst into spontaneous prayer. "Oh Lord, our Father," he said, "we ask You to bring our dear Percy into contact with Your people. May they touch his heart in ways even he perhaps does not see."

They fell silent for several moments.

"Your prayer reminds me of that wonderful sermon you preach from time to time about arrows of prayer," said Mary. "It is truly one of the profound truths God has revealed to you—how we can launch prayer arrows up into God's heart and then must trust Him to resend them down to earth where He will in His time, turn them into arrows of light and clarity in human souls."

"Even miraculously sending the answer arrows occasionally *before* the prayer arrows are launched." Edward nodded. "*Our* notions of time are nothing to God." Edward became thoughtful. "Your mentioning that. . . ," he mused. "You know, I honestly don't know if I have prayed that prayer for our own Percy."

"Lord," Mary began almost immediately, "wherever our dear Percy is at this moment, whoever he is with, whatever he is thinking, we ask that You would be there beside him, inside him—speaking, wooing, luring him to Your heart. Send arrows of clarity into his thoughts, pleasant reminders and fond memories."

"Give us fortitude and courage to trust *You* to be Percy's Father in our place," added Edward. "Send piercing arrows of light into his heart. Accomplish Your perfect will and desire in his life."

"And in ours," added Mary softly. "As painful as this separation is, dear Lord, we ask You to perfect Your will in us through it. Bring Percy awake. Send bursts of revelation into his consciousness. Illuminate truth within him. Wake him to You, God—to the Father You want to be to him."

"Give us courage," prayed Edward, "to trust You and to believe that You love our Percy far more than we do. Remind us that *Your* arms ache more for him than ours."

"May we *keep* trusting You for him no matter how long it takes," added the mother.

"Help us believe more deeply than our frail flesh seems capable of that You are infinitely more Percy's Father than *we* are his father and mother. Help us, God our Father, to believe that You will not rest until he acknowledges himself the son he was created to be."

Mary kept her head bowed in silent prayer. When she heard a trembling sob escape her husband's lips, she laid down her cup and went to him.

The two wept together. Their tears accompanied the cleansing painful knowledge that they had truly given their son into the hands of the Father of them all.

What comfort it would have given them to know that their prayers were indeed already being answered. But God's comfort, like His arrows of clarity into the human soul, He sends in His perfect time, that heartache, too, may accomplish its appointed purpose in the hearts of His faithful ones.

THIRTY-FOUR

Gwyneth's Friends

*C*odnor Barrie stood in the door of his cottage waiting for his child.

The moment she arrived with Percy, Gwyneth told him excitedly of the events of the day.

"I'm very thankful to you, young man," said her father when Gwyneth paused for breath. "Surely you'll join us for tea."

"I only just had tea at Grannie's," laughed Percy. "I probably should be getting back to the manor. They may wonder about me—Sunday dinner and all. I mustn't offend my hosts."

"It sounds as if it is already too late for that, young man. That is if you consider the young brood your hosts as well."

Percy laughed. "I do not. I will offend the two of them anytime I can! But my aunt and uncle are very kind to me."

"The viscount is a decent man. I have no quarrel with him. But you'll not leave without a thick slice of Grannie's good bread to keep you company across the moor," added Gwyneth's father, taking the large loaf from his daughter.

"It smells peculiar," said Percy hesitantly. "I noticed it on the way. What kind of bread is it?"

"Laverbread—seaweed, oatmeal, and bacon fat."

"Hmm. . .maybe I should try it next time," said Percy.

"Percy, please don't go yet," implored Gwyneth.

"Why not?"

"I want to show you my animals."

"Your pets?" he said, glancing about for a dog or cat.

"My daughter has more than a few pets." Barrie laughed. "She keeps what can only be called a small zoo. Animals flock to her like to no human being I've ever seen. It's uncanny. I truly believe they see her as their master."

Already Gwyneth had taken hold of Percy's hand and was tugging him around toward the back of the stone cottage. Percy was surprised to see a large fenced enclosure extending far behind the cottage. In it scampered the most diverse array of creatures he had ever seen.

At sight of the girl at his side, they all scurried and scuffled and bounded and pattered toward them from inside, bursting into a cacophony of screeching, squealing, barking, chirping, meowing, and happy caterwauling. From somewhere a whirring of bird wings whisked toward them overhead.

Percy laughed at the wild and joyous greeting.

"Is it feeding time?" he exclaimed.

"They always greet me like this," said Gwyneth simply. "They think I'm their mother."

Percy later learned that the fence had been built merely to keep wild animals from the mountains *out* rather than to keep Gwyneth's friends *in*. Most would have remained near the dwelling of their mistress without any enclosure whatever.

To one side, a small cluster of pens and kennels served as hospital to those animals presently being tended for injury. If such a thing as communication between species occurred in the animal kingdom, surely Gwyneth's animal hospital gave credibility to the theory. Weekly it seemed some creature appeared with a gash on its side or with a wounded leg or broken wing or sliver in its paw, somehow knowing that this was the place where help would be given. Nor did the creatures flinch when Gwyneth approached to examine paw or wing and administer the nursing care so instinctive to her nature.

Around the outside of the pen, a half dozen deer grazed contentedly on the lush grass of the moor. Some would return to the mountains when night fell, others would leap over the fence into the compound, there to spend the night with racoons and rabbits and dogs and chickens and other of their diverse fellows of the animal kingdom.

In Gwyneth's zoo all creatures were at peace. No harm came to any. A spell of goodness lay upon the place. For they behaved in Gwyneth's presence as perhaps did the creature friends of that first man and woman in the garden so long ago.

"Don't you love all the creatures God made?" said Gwyneth as they walked back to the Barrie cottage.

"I don't know that I thought about it much before. When you live in the city, nature isn't something you think about."

"You're not in the city now. Maybe God sent you to the country to learn to see what He has made."

"God didn't send me to the country."

"Who did?"

"My father."

"That's the same thing," said Gwyneth.

"How do you mean?" laughed Percy. "God's not my father."

"Oh, isn't He?" rejoined Gwyneth, astonished that Percy would say such a thing. "What else is He then if He isn't your father?"

"I didn't mean it like that. I mean, of course I suppose God created everyone. I meant He isn't my *own* father, you know, like my *real* father."

"Grannie says I have two fathers. She says that Papa is my father so that I will learn to look up to know my real Father."

That night as he lay on his bed reliving the day's incidents, Percy's thoughts came to rest on young Gwyneth Barrie.

Meanwhile, across the moor in her own cottage, Gwyneth Barrie also lay awake, eyes wide, thinking about Percy. She would not have believed it had she been told that he was thinking of her.

New sensations filled her tender heart. That another person besides Grannie, Hollin Radnor, and her papa had befriended her, stood up for her—even been attacked for her! The very notion rose so mightily in her consciousness as to render sleep impossible.

And a young person besides! Someone not her own age, yet not so *very* much older, she thought. Percy was the same age as many of the boys and girls in the village who made fun of her.

In Gwyneth's eyes, the boy was not a boy at all, but fully a man, a giant eight feet tall, a prince, a warrior, a defender of the helpless. In the short time she had known him, young Percy Drummond had become Gwyneth's hero, her knight in shining armor.

She would never fear to walk Llanfryniog's streets again. She had as good a papa as ever lived. She had as kind and wise a grannie as ever it pleased God to give a girl. And now she had a new friend who had come from Glasgow and was afraid of nothing.

What Percy would have thought had he known himself viewed as the answer to a young girl's prayers would have been interesting to inquire. He had for some years been in the habit of scorning his father's spirituality. Now his new friend saw him as God's special gift just for her.

God, thank You for Percy! prayed Gwyneth simply, then turned over and, with a smile on her face, was soon asleep.

THIRTY-FIVE

Conflicting Affections

*C*ourtenay had been so successful, he thought, in patching it up with Rhawn Lorimer on the previous Sunday that he pressed his advantage with an invitation to luncheon with his family at the manor later that week.

It was a spontaneous gesture. Only upon later reflection did the potential awkwardness, even danger, of the situation present itself to Courtenay's suspicions. But he could hardly retract it, nor could he tell Percy to get lost for the day without in all likelihood incurring the viscount's anger. His father had, to both son's and daughter's profound annoyance, developed a soft spot for his nephew. He and his sister had to be a little careful what they said in their father's hearing.

Courtenay's reservations would have increased tenfold had he divined Miss Lorimer's true reason for accepting the invitation so eagerly. Having successfully ascertained the identity of the mystery boy she had encountered in the draper's shop and learning where he was living for the summer, she was far more anxious to see him again than she was Courtenay Westbrooke, with whom the association, on her part, was more the result of proximity to her best friend than genuine affection.

Had Courtenay been a gentleman, he would have taken one of his father's buggies to pick up his guest prior to the luncheon. But he was of the school that said let the girl come to him. And as Percy showed no sign of disappearing, he was secretly hoping that maybe Rhawn might not make an appearance anyway. She was, however, like Florilyn, an expert rider. She arrived on horseback almost exactly as the hour of twelve began to strike on the clock above the stable yard.

Hollin Radnor heard her approach and went to meet her. He helped her dismount and saw to the horse while Rhawn walked to the front door of the manor. There, next to the doorpost, hung a bouquet of wildflowers, tied with red. She recognized the ribbon immediately.

So, she thought, *the young man's affections were closer to home than she had realized!* Was he really falling for his own cousin?

But what an odd place to leave a bouquet. Their rooms were so near each other, why not put them on her own bedroom door rather than out in the open where everyone would see them?

Courtenay had been watching the front of the house from an upstairs window. The moment he saw Rhawn riding up, he dashed downstairs to the front door. He wasn't about to risk her running into his cousin again without him around.

Even as the echo of the bell faded, he opened the door to greet her. The smile meant for Rhawn Lorimer died on his lips as his eyes fell on the bouquet hanging almost directly in front of him.

"What in blazes is that?" he exclaimed, hardly aware of his rudeness.

"It would appear that *someone* in this house has a secret admirer," replied Rhawn, more than a little surprised by the intensity of his reaction. "Hello, Courtenay—my goodness, you look like you've seen a ghost. Not exactly the greeting I expected."

"Oh. . .right, sorry—yes, hello, Miss Lorimer," said Courtenay, trying to recover himself, though continuing to stare at the bouquet out of the corner of his eye. "The impish little tramp!" he muttered under his breath. He grabbed the flowers and flung them across the stones of the entryway. "People like that need to mind their own business!" Again he struggled to regain his composure, laughed nervously, and led his guest inside.

"Not a very nice way to treat a gift to your sister," said Rhawn in a humorous though confused tone. She was both bewildered and amused by Courtenay's bizarre behavior.

"She needs no gift from the likes of *that*!" rejoined Courtenay. "And neither do I!"

Having no clue what he meant, Rhawn Lorimer followed Courtenay to the dining room. Florilyn and her mother were already present.

"Good afternoon, Rhawn," said Katherine. "I am so glad you can be with us today."

"Thank you, Mrs. Westbrooke," said Rhawn with a pleasant smile. "Hi, Florilyn," she added to Courtenay's sister.

Though Rhawn was dying to get Florilyn off to one side of the room to ask about Percy out of Courtenay's hearing, the far door opened almost immediately. Hope of further conversation was cut short by the entrance of the viscount and the object of her curiosity himself. Uncle and nephew were laughing and chatting like the best of friends.

"That's a good one, Percy, my boy!" roared the viscount. "I'll have to tell that to my friends in London. Nothing like Glasgow humor! Oh," he added, glancing about, "it would appear we are the last to arrive. All here, what? Ah, Miss Lorimer," he said, taking note of their guest, "welcome, welcome! How is your father?"

"Very well, sir. He sends his regards."

"Good, good—thank you. Give him my best, of course. You have, I take it, met our guest for the summer, my nephew. . . ," he added, gesturing toward Percy.

"I. . .uh," Rhawn began. With Percy's eyes staring straight through her, she suddenly found herself at a loss for words.

Percy quickly rescued her from the difficulty. "Miss, uh. . .Miss *Lorimer*, is it?" he said, "and I ran into one another in town. Courtenay," he added, turning toward his cousin with the hint of a smile, "you remember the day, I'm sure. Unfortunately, we were not actually introduced."

He turned now to face the young woman directly. "Hello," he said, extending his hand, "I am Percival Drummond."

"Hello, Mr. Drummond," said Rhawn, taking his hand and clinging to it an imperceptible moment longer than propriety demanded. "I am Rhawn Lorimer. I am extremely pleased to make your acquaintance. . . at last."

"The pleasure is all mine, Miss Lorimer," rejoined Percy, withdrawing his hand lest Courtenay get any ideas.

Indeed, Courtenay had been watching, though absently. He was still a little shaken from having been the recipient of one of the witch-girl's voodoo bouquets. He had actually been turning over in his mind whether tossing it on the ground had been a good idea. Weren't such things supposed to be burned or otherwise destroyed to mitigate their occultish power? Thus, the looks being sent toward Percy by Rhawn Lorimer uncharacteristically escaped his notice.

By the time they were all seated around the table, Rhawn's fluttering eyelids had calmed themselves. But her eyes remained busily glancing back and forth between Percy and Florilyn to see what kind of expressions passed between the two lovebirds. Observing nothing to titillate her interest, however, as opportunity presented itself, she tried to urge the conversation into the proper channels. "Do you come to Wales often, Mr. Drummond?" she asked, ignoring Courtenay's displeasure at her question.

"I haven't been here in years," replied Percy. "I can hardly even remember the last time—when was it, Aunt Katherine? I was just a wee lad, as we say in Scotland."

"I think you were about five," replied his aunt.

"What brings you here this summer?"

"That is. . .uh, a little awkward to explain. My father thought perhaps a change from city life would be good for me."

"Percy got in trouble with the police," chimed in Florilyn merrily.

"Goodness, Florilyn!" exclaimed Katherine. "Must you be quite so frank? Think of Percival's feelings."

"That's all right, Aunt Katherine," said Percy. "No harm done. Besides, Florilyn is right."

"There is no reason for her to air the family's dirty laundry," persisted Percy's aunt.

Rhawn Lorimer was enjoying the exchange immensely. She had apparently stumbled into the middle of a juicy family secret!

"I don't mind so much," said Percy. "No sense in trying to hide it. Yes," he added, turning to Rhawn, "I was behaving foolishly in the city. To keep me from getting into deeper trouble, my father asked my aunt and uncle if they would take me in for the summer. They agreed and have been very gracious to their wayward nephew."

He glanced toward the two with a genuine smile. His pleasant expression did much to ease Katherine's annoyance.

"Miss Lorimer's father is our local magistrate, Percy, my boy," boomed the viscount. "Better watch your step around her!"

"I will be very careful," Percy said, laughing.

As the meal progressed, Courtenay was anything but pleased with the direction the conversation around the table seemed determined to go, with Percy at the center of it. But he found himself unable to do much about it other than ask Rhawn if she wanted a ride after lunch. Even that, however, after her halfhearted consent, she foiled by asking Percy if he and Florilyn rode together. She was far too interested in the blighter to suit him.

When the two girls were alone in Florilyn's room later, the moment the door was closed behind them, Rhawn turned to Florilyn. "He's an absolute dream!" she said excitedly. "How did you get so lucky?"

"What are you *talking* about?" said Florilyn with a confused expression. "*Who* are you talking about?"

"Your cousin. . .Percival, of course."

"You must be joking!" Florilyn laughed. "Why would I be lucky?"

"To have someone like that fancy you, of course."

"Percy. . .fancy *me*? Ugh, what a sickening thought!"

"You don't like him?"

"I can't stand him!"

"Now it's you who must be joking."

"I'm not," insisted Florilyn.

"What about the flowers he left you downstairs?"

"Percy?" Florilyn's tone was more disbelieving than ever.

"Yes. A little bouquet tied with the very ribbon I saw him buying at the draper's shop. He had flowers with him that day, too. He said they were for a girl. I never dreamed it was *you*."

"When was that?" asked Florilyn a little more seriously.

"A week ago maybe."

"He never gave me any flowers."

Rhawn stared back at her in surprise. "Then who are the flowers downstairs for if he didn't mean them for you?"

"What flowers downstairs?"

"I told you—a bouquet hanging on the door outside. Courtenay saw them."

"What did he do?" asked Florilyn.

"He got really angry and threw them on the ground. He was acting very strange."

Florilyn did not reply. A brief shudder went through her as she recalled the incident in town after church.

But Rhawn took little notice of her change in mood. "Don't you think your cousin is good looking?" she asked.

"I don't know," Florilyn replied distractedly. "I suppose. I never noticed."

"How could you *not* notice?"

"Well, now that you know he's got no interest in me, if you're so sweet on him, you can have him. But what about Courtenay?"

"What about him?"

"What about, you know. . .you and him?"

"Oh, Courtenay's okay, I guess. But that was before I saw Percival. What kind of trouble was he in with the police? I think it's exciting! Was it something really awful?"

"I don't know. I doubt it was so bad. He's not very brawny. I can hardly imagine him being in serious trouble. But I did overhear my parents say that if they didn't take him in for the summer he would probably wind up in jail."

"*Jail*. . .that is exciting. He doesn't *look* like a criminal."

"He's still a boy if you ask me. Courtenay's already beat him up twice."

"Why?"

"They just don't like each other. Courtenay hates Percy even more than I do. If you even look at him, it will make him furious."

"So I found out at the draper's shop. I will just have to be careful."

"You'd better start now," rejoined Florilyn. "He's probably already waiting for you down by the stables to ride you home. If I know my brother, you are going to have a lot of explaining to do for the way you were fawning all over Percy at lunch."

Rhawn smiled. "I can handle your brother."

THIRTY-SIX

Market Day

Summer weekly market day began in Llanfryniog in July and would continue every Saturday until the harvests were in and the leaves of autumn began to fall.

It was still early for most produce, though strawberries were at the height of their season. Besides the strawberries, new potatoes, carrots, turnips, and homemade cheeses and jams, most of the featured items were handcrafts the village women had been making through the winter and spring months, as well as small trinkets and sweeties to tempt the children. Not that there was much money to be made. Barter was more common than cash. Nearly everyone grew their own potatoes and carrots.

But it was a tradition of long standing, more social than economic in the life of the community. No one for miles would miss the first market day of each new summer, when all manner of local wares were available on the grass in front of the chapel and school building. It was not unheard of for animal flesh to trade hands as well.

Nor would it be Wales without music! Though the school term had finished several weeks earlier, the children all came together on this day to sing from the school steps several songs they had practiced the previous spring. They would alternate throughout the day with choirs from the three churches and a dozen or more fiddlers and accordionists.

By noon of the first Saturday of July, the town was full with movement, bustle, and activity. Singing could be heard in the distance. A variety of aromas from fires and kettles tempted hungry stomachs to part with a few pennies in exchange for their lunch. Booths and tables and games and amusements and handcrafts and all manner of hand-knitted wool caps and socks and sweaters and scarves for sale were spread out everywhere.

At one end of the field were tied a few pigs, sheep, and horses to see what offers might be made. Already Kyvwlch Gwarthegydd and Padrig Gwlwlwyd and a handful of men were clustered about a pure white five-year-old stallion, examining teeth and legs, hooves and flanks.

As he felt more and more at peace with himself in the country and at home on his uncle's estate, Percy had taken to roaming the region with increasing freedom. His comfort upon the back of one or another of the viscount's horses, though he had not ventured out again on Red Rhud, had greatly increased. In Llanfryniog, he made acquaintance with a growing number of the villagers. Despite the fact that he was well known by the youths of the place as little Gwyneth Barrie's defender, that he was Lord Snowdon's nephew caused most of the older townspeople to give him the benefit of any doubts they may have had in regard of his peculiar relationship with the strange girl. A few, in fact, secretly admired his championing of Barrie's daughter. This general prejudice in his favor was aided by his cheerful disposition, as well as by the fact that he was so likable and unlike the viscount's two children, neither of whom had made themselves particular favorites with anyone.

Hearing about market day, Percy was not about to miss it.

As much as they gave every indication of despising him, for reasons difficult to explain, both Courtenay and Florilyn were reluctant to leave their cousin on his own. In actual fact, the lives of the two scions of the Westbrooke name had grown a little tedious of late. When Courtenay was not shooting or riding with Colville Burrenchobay or pressing his attentions on Rhawn Lorimer, he had very little to occupy himself during the long days of summer. He did not read, did not ride merely for enjoyment. The sea, the mountains, the village, the forests held no fascination for him. Much the same could be said of Florilyn. Both were too wrapped up in themselves to find delight in the world about them.

The three young people were therefore often found together more often than could be accounted for by cousinly friendship. Courtenay and Florilyn kept track of Percy's movements and, motivated as much from boredom as interest, almost followed him about. If he chanced on some amusement, they did not want to miss it. He found them a nuisance. But he could hardly tell the son and daughter of his hosts to leave him alone. So he went about his affairs, and not wanting to be left behind, they tagged along, sniping at him with derisive comments.

Percy, newly alive to the delights of the country, was eager to be out exploring and walking and riding, talking to the servants, meandering through the town, encountering new people, making friends, engaging the old fishermen in conversation as one by one they overcame their reticence toward him. To her great disgust, Florilyn had once even seen him helping Hollin Radnor cleaning out the horses' stalls, talking away to the groom as if they were old friends!

In spite of such revolting tendencies, Percy brought an energy and enthusiasm to life at the manor that slowly rubbed off on everyone, staff and family alike.

Both his cousins accompanied him into town on this day also because they knew that Colville, Davina, and Ainsworth Burrenchobay were planning to be in Llanfryniog after lunch. The five aristocratic youths of the two neighboring estates were capable of far more mischief en masse than singly. Davina Burrenchobay, at thirteen, was too young to interest Courtenay. But she idolized Florilyn, and the viscount's daughter found her attentions gratifying. They offered Florilyn, too, the occasional opportunity to try out her seductive wiles on Davina's nineteen-year-old brother, Colville.

They had not been in town long before Percy disappeared. By then neither Courtenay nor Florilyn cared. Half suspecting where he might have gone, they would not have followed him anyway. That Courtenay had managed to run into Rhawn Lorimer allayed his anxiety about Percy in that regard. From somewhere, Davina Burrenchobay came running excitedly toward them. Before she knew it, Florilyn had been deserted by both brother and cousin and found herself walking along with thirteen-year-old Davina chatting away and ten-year-old Ainsworth traipsing along behind.

"Where's your brother?" asked Florilyn.

"I'm right here!" piped up Ainsworth eagerly.

"I mean your older brother, you goose," rejoined Florilyn.

"I don't know," replied Davina. "I think he's over there somewhere looking at a horse. He's always looking at horses."

Meanwhile, Percy was enjoying a cup of tea with Grannie in her cottage. With every visit, he learned more about the village, about Gwyneth and her father and why Codnor Barrie had been in Ireland when Gwyneth was born. He also continued to pick up tidbits of interest about the family of his aunt and uncle with whom he was spending the summer.

"Will Gwyneth be here for market day?" he asked.

"She doesn't take to crowds," replied Grannie. "You know how people are to her, poor lass."

Florilyn and the two younger Burrenchobays continued to wander about aimlessly. In the distance, Florilyn saw Courtenay and Rhawn. She increased her pace in their direction. The two younger ones followed.

By the time Percy arrived at the festivities an hour later, the sheep-shearing contest was in full swing. A hundred or more spectators were cheering on their favorites. Percy moved toward the noisy commotion and was soon swallowed by the crowd.

"Hoy there, Mr. Drummond, isn't it?" said a voice at Percy's side.

Percy turned to see his sheep-herding acquaintance from his first ride into the hills. "Hello, Stevie," he said, shaking the other's hand. "Are you one of the contestants?"

"Aye, I am. How is your summer?"

"Good…very good."

"I am still waiting for that visit to my house."

"I haven't forgotten." Percy laughed. "Seeing you again…I will make a point of riding out your way next week."

He saw Stevie glance behind him. A serious expression came over the shepherd's face. Percy turned to see Florilyn walking past them at the side of a large youth. She pretended not to notice as they moved beyond the crowd. She was smiling and laughing and carrying herself with a flirtatious air.

"I don't like to see your cousin with the likes of him," said Stevie.

"Why, who is he?" asked Percy.

"That's Colville Burrenchobay," replied Stevie.

"Ah, yes. I've heard of him. He's a friend of my cousin Courtenay's."

"Not the sort of fellow I would want my sister or daughter keeping company with. I'm concerned only for Miss Florilyn, you understand. I don't know what my lord Snowdon is thinking to allow it."

"I don't think he pays much attention to what his son and daughter do."

"All the more reason he should."

"Is the bloke really so bad?" said Percy, watching the two walk off together.

"There are stories that find their way back from the university," replied Stevie. "That's all I will say. Oh, I just heard them call my name!"

"Best of luck to you!"

"Don't forget that visit." Stevie ran off.

Percy inched his way to the front of the throng for a better view. As he did, out of the corner of his eye he noticed Florilyn and Colville Burrenchobay moving out of sight behind the chapel. He was soon caught up in Stevie's performance with the sheep. By the time Stevie flung the coat of wool in a single piece away from the skinny little white body that emerged from beneath it, Percy was cheering and yelling with the rest.

"Well done, Stevie!" he exclaimed when Stevie approached at the conclusion of his effort. "Will you win, do you think?"

"Who can say? I was third last year. Some of the men have been at it decades more than me. It will take me years to catch them. If I manage to get in the top five, I will have had a good day of it."

"Is your father here? Does he participate?"

A sad smile came over the young shepherd's face. "No, I'm sorry to say," he replied. "He used to be the shearing champion of all Gwynedd. But he's not well just now, you see. He doesn't get out anymore."

As they were talking, Percy was surprised to see Rhawn Lorimer walking toward them. She was alone. "Hello, Percival," she purred. She glanced toward Stevie. Her nose crinkled squeamishly.

"Miss Lorimer," said Percy. "Quite a day, eh? Do you know Stevie Muir?"

"Everybody does," she answered, not attempting to disguise her repugnance. "Would you like to walk with me, Percival?" she added.

If she had thought to win Percy's affection by being brusque with Stevie Muir, the magistrate's daughter had misjudged her prey. Nevertheless, by that subtle art at which young women are so skilled and of which young men are so oblivious, in less than a minute Percy found himself cleverly drawn away from his shepherd friend and the sheep-shearing crowd together. He glanced back, but Stevie was already swallowed up by the activity.

"What are you looking at?" asked Rhawn.

"I was just wondering where Stevie disappeared to," replied Percy.

"Who cares about *him*?"

"I care about him."

"Florilyn says you're friends with the little witch-child, too. Are you friends with all the local riffraff?"

"Riffraff?" exclaimed Percy. "What are you talking about? They are people. God made them no less than He made you and me. Yes, I am friends with Gwyneth and Stevie. They are two of the first people I met here. I like them."

Percy hardly realized that the words out of his mouth might well have come from his father. Had he been paying closer attention, he would probably have wondered what was becoming of him. They continued to move farther from the crowd.

"What about me?" said Rhawn in a coquettish tone, moving close and brushing Percy's side.

"You're a nice enough girl, Miss Lorimer, I suppose," replied Percy. "But I hardly know you."

"Do you think I'm pretty?"

"What kind of question is that?" laughed Percy. "You don't go around asking people if they think you're pretty."

"All the other boys think I'm pretty."

"I am sure they do. All I am saying is that I want no trouble with Courtenay. He told us to stay away from each other. So I'm not exactly sure what you are doing. What if he sees us?"

"Do you take your orders from Courtenay?" baited Rhawn.

"No. But he's bigger and stronger than me, and with a temper I don't particularly want to upset. He's already put me on the ground twice. I'm no idiot. I'm not eager to experience it again."

"Wouldn't it be worth it. . .for me?"

"Honestly, no. Sorry. I don't want to hurt your feelings, but if you are Courtenay's girl, I have no desire to interfere. I certainly have no intention of getting beat up for you."

"I'm not his girl," rejoined Rhawn with the hint of a pout.

"If Courtenay thinks you are, then—"

What Percy had been about to say was interrupted by the scream of a girl's voice. It came from behind the chapel. Percy bolted toward it.

He rounded the corner of the stone church to see Florilyn struggling in the arms of the same youth he had seen her with earlier.

"Just a simple kiss, Florilyn," he was saying in a voice that revealed aggression. "I know you're in love with me!"

"No, I'm not! Colville. . .let me go!" cried Florilyn.

Obviously provoked, the young man pressed his advantage. He grabbed her tight and pulled her face to his.

Another scream sounded. Somehow Florilyn struggled to loosen herself sufficiently to free her arm. A great whack struck Colville Burrenchobay's cheek.

Florilyn was stronger than it might have seemed, especially when aroused to fury. Burrenchobay's eyes filled from the sting of the blow. "You little vixen!" he cried. "You will pay for that!"

However he thought to retaliate was preempted as Percy flew into their midst.

"Hey, what the—!" exclaimed Burrenchobay. In the torrent that followed, he forgot that he was in the presence of a young woman, if not quite yet a lady.

"Stand back, Florilyn!" said Percy in a commanding voice as he separated them. "Get away!"

Whether Florilyn had really been shocked by Colville Burrenchobay's advances, only she could say. The strength of his grip had, in truth, frightened her just a little. She, too, had heard the stories to which Stevie had alluded. But like many foolish maidens, she found playing with fire tantalizing, thrilling, and dangerous. She greatly overestimated her ability to keep from burning her fingers. She had been as much to blame in the clandestine affair as Burrenchobay, perhaps more so. Yet with a squire suddenly rushing in to protect her honor, as it were, notwithstanding that it was one whose interference she would have scorned had she taken the leisure to stop and think about it, what could she do but back away and see how the thing turned out?

"You will regret your insolence, whoever you are, you little cur!" shouted Burrenchobay in a rage.

He was not one who stood on ceremony, nor who cherished qualms of etiquette about taking on someone half his size. Charging like a wild bull, within seconds Percy yet again found himself on the short end of a brief but violent scuffle.

Florilyn saw nothing of it. She raced from behind the chapel, only stopping when she met Rhawn Lorimer coming around the side of the stone wall.

"What—" began Rhawn, seeing the look of fright on Florilyn's face.

Behind her she heard the yells and saw the fight well enough. It did not last long. A minute later, Colville Burrenchobay had disappeared.

The two girls walked slowly to where Percy was sprawled out on the grass.

"What happened?" said Rhawn.

"Colville tried to kiss me," replied Florilyn. "I screamed. Percy, like the nincompoop he is, ran in and tried to rescue me."

"That hardly sounds like the work of a nincompoop," said Rhawn. "No one's ever rescued *me*."

They approached. Percy still lay motionless.

"Is he. . .dead?" said Rhawn, her voice trembling at the word.

Slowly Percy opened his eyes. He saw the faces of the two girls staring down at him. "Ohhh!" he groaned in pain. "I definitely do not think I am cut out for country life." He groaned again and tried to move. "These blokes here are lunatics," he said. "They'll knock your block off at the drop of a hat. I'll never survive the summer."

Florilyn could not prevent an inward smile. He was always saying something funny.

So relieved that nothing appeared broken, both girls stooped down and tried to help him sit up.

"I'm all right," said Percy, drawing in a deep breath. He breathed in and out a few more times where he sat on the grass. "Whew," he sighed. "That was one big, strong guy. Remind me to keep out of his way."

Rhawn broke into laughter to hear Percy feeling good enough to make light of it. Florilyn joined her, but her laugh was mingled with anxiety for herself and what would be the upshot of the incident.

"You two can go," said Percy, struggling to his feet. "I don't want you to get in trouble on my account. That's all I need, to incur Courtenay's wrath now as well. Why don't you go and have fun and pretend this never happened. I'll find my own way home. . .like the proverbial dog slinking away with his tail between his legs."

THIRTY-SEVEN

Mixed Fortunes

O nce again at dinner that evening, Percy's facial condition was the object of comment and question. He did his best to brush off the questions, but the viscount was noticeably concerned.

When his uncle began hinting at talking to Styles Lorimer about investigating the incident, Percy knew he had to come clean before it went any further. "It's really nothing, Uncle Roderick," he said. "I got into a row with Colville Burrenchobay, that's all."

"Oh. . .I see. Hmm. . .not a lad to tangle with, Percy, my boy," said the viscount seriously. "He's twice your size, I dare say."

"I will be more careful in the future, sir, believe me."

"What were you fighting about?"

Florilyn's face sought the table. She felt her cheeks redden and was afraid to look up without betraying herself.

"Nothing much," said Percy. "Just a difference of opinion. It was my fault."

"I can hardly believe that," rejoined the viscount.

"It's true, sir. I am sorry if I disappoint you."

"No, no, Percy, my boy—think nothing of it. Boys will be boys. Young Burrenchobay is well known to have a hot head."

The meal progressed. The mood remained subdued. Florilyn said

202

almost nothing. For once Courtenay seemed to be enjoying himself more than the rest of the family.

Most of those attending the market day gala had gotten wind of the fight behind the church. Young boys smell a fight a mile away. Any scuffle to lads under twelve is like catnip to a cat. A few had managed to catch glimpses of the tail end of it, and the exciting news spread like a brush fire.

Not having discovered Rhawn Lorimer's treachery toward himself in the way of her advances toward Percy, Courtenay was delighted with the turn of events with regard to his friend and cousin. And he could not help but enjoy watching his sister squirm in hopes that her part in the incident, which he learned later from Colville, would not come out.

Later in the evening as he was walking slowly down the corridor to his room, one arm noticeably drooping at his side and very much looking forward to his bed at last, Percy was surprised to see Florilyn standing waiting for him. The expression on her face was one whose acquaintance Percy had not made before. In a strange way, he hardly recognized her. He approached and nodded in silent greeting.

Florilyn glanced down at the floor. She was clearly embarrassed.

He waited.

Finally she looked up at him. "Why didn't you tell my father it was my fault?" she said.

"I didn't know it was."

Again Florilyn glanced down at the floor.

"*Was* it your fault?" asked Percy. "It didn't look that way to me. He was behaving badly to you—certainly not like a gentleman."

"No one has ever accused Colville Burrenchobay of being a gentleman," rejoined Florilyn. She looked up. The gaze that met Percy's was earnest and sincere. "But I was flirting with him," she said.

Percy took in the information without comment. He was not surprised. "What would it have accomplished to blame you?" he said after a moment. "Your father doesn't need to know. . .that is, if you learned your lesson."

"I hope I have," said Florilyn, obviously uneasy. "Daddy would have whipped me if he knew. Well, thank you, I guess." She forced a smile, though the effort seemed to strain the muscles of her face to their limit.

She turned and left Percy at his door pondering the unexpected exchange with his cousin.

Percy remained out of sight for a few days, nursing his wounds for a third time and vowing to keep clear, whatever the circumstances, of his older cousin and his wild friend from Burrenchobay Hall. If he didn't find a way to keep out of the way of these two crazed young Welshmen, his father would have to come fetch him from the hospital!

Several days later he ran into Florilyn outside the house. He and she had not spoken since the previous Saturday night.

"Would you like to go for a ride?" she asked.

Percy smiled skeptically. "So you can get me thrown and ditch me again?" he said, half playfully, though not *entirely* playfully.

"No, I promise. You can lead the way."

She *sounded* sincere. Percy thought for a moment then nodded.

"I may regret this," he said. "But. . .all right. I'll take you up on your offer."

Twenty minutes later, the cousins rode out of the stable yard. True to her word, Florilyn allowed Percy to lead. They took the same two horses as before, but this time Percy was on Grey Tide, and not once did Florilyn increase her speed. They led the two mounts slowly down the entry drive side by side, and then Percy turned onto the main road and down the slope of the plateau toward Llanfryniog.

"You seem steadier in the saddle," said Florilyn.

"I've been riding quite a bit," said Percy. "I'm getting comfortable with it."

"That's good."

"We should have another race before I return to Glasgow. You did rather take advantage of me last time."

"That wasn't really a proper *race*."

"Maybe the next one can be."

Florilyn smiled. Her expression was difficult to read. "Do you really think you could keep up with me?" she said with a hint of playful banter.

"Maybe not. . .not now. But perhaps by the end of the summer."

"Is that a challenge?"

Percy did not reply. He met her coy smile with one of his own.

They reached the village and clomped leisurely along the hard-packed dirt street between the stone buildings lining it on both sides. Most of the people they passed, to Florilyn's surprise, greeted Percy by name. He led the way through town, past the chapel, all evidence of the previous Saturday's festivities gone, and down to the harbor. They continued onto the sand and a short distance along it then turned back up again into town. Returning through the village, Percy led randomly through several side streets and lanes where the two horses occasionally had to walk in single file.

"What is that strange building there," asked Percy, pointing to his right down a narrow lane, "with the funny roof and purple doors and windows and all the statues about?"

"That's Madame Fleming's house—the fortune-teller."

"A fortune-teller? You must be joking!"

"No, really," replied Florilyn.

Suddenly her face lit. "Percy!" she exclaimed. "Let's go get our fortunes told!"

"I don't—"

"Oh, let's. Can we, please? I've always wanted to. I would be afraid to go alone. But with you, I wouldn't be. Oh, let's do!"

Though he had never once spoken with them about such things, somehow Percy knew that his parents would strongly disapprove of his setting foot inside such a place as Madame Fleming's. His father would also remind him, as the man and the older of the two, that if it lay within his power, he had a responsibility to protect his cousin from harm.

Yet the youthful spirit of adventure proved an irresistible lure. For once Florilyn was being nice. He didn't want to snub her only request on the first day she had made an effort to have fun with him. He thus found it impossible to deny her.

They turned and made their way down the narrow lane. Suddenly the village grew quiet around them. To their ears, the *clop, clop, clop* of the horses' hooves echoed louder than Kyvwlch Gwarthegydd's anvil on Sunday morning. It seemed to announce to everyone within earshot what they were about to do.

Florilyn glanced around nervously. Her father would probably whip her for this, too, if he found out. But she was determined not to back out now.

Slowly they approached the house. Percy shuddered as he looked at the steeply slanted roof with its weird ornaments at the corners and the occult weathervane at the apex. All around the house, the assortment of statues of goblins and dwarfs and trolls silently seemed to shout, "Stay away; there is evil here. Come if you will, but leave the past behind. Here lies your future. . .and it may fill you with dread."

They came to a halt and slowly dismounted. Even the two horses seemed ill at ease and moved about with jittery feet. They tied them to a nearby rail.

Percy glanced along the adjacent street. He could just see one wall of Grannie's cottage a hundred feet away. He thought to himself that he would rather visit her. But it would take a more than moderate-sized miracle to get Florilyn into that house of light. Yet she was eager to visit this house of darkness in front of them and was already halfway from the street to the door. Reluctantly he turned and followed her.

They walked onto the porch. Percy glanced at the sign above the door, ornate with snakes and horrid-looking animals and faces. MADAME FLEMING, PSYCHIC—FORTUNES AND FUTURES FORETOLD, he read.

Florilyn rang the bell. "I hope no one sees us!" she whispered. "My parents would kill me if they knew I was visiting the old hag."

The door opened. A face appeared, shrouded in darkness from behind. Percy shivered at the ghostly sight. The woman's countenance was pale and wrinkled. Out of deep, dark sockets, eyes of black shone above lips painted bright red. A purple-orange scarf of silk covered the hair above the face. From the woman's ears hung gaudy ringlets of gold and silver.

A tingle of terror swept through Florilyn's body. "We have come to get our fortunes told," she said, her voice shaky. "May we come in? I don't want anyone to see us."

"Come in. . .come in, my sweets," said the woman. "Your fortunes told is it you're wanting? You've come to the right place." She opened the door just wide enough for them to squeeze through then shut it noiselessly behind them.

Peculiar aromas assaulted them, and sights too strange to be told. Candles flickered throughout the room. Burning incense was so thick as to hover over them like a visible cloud. It was not sufficient in itself, however, to completely overwhelm the smell of the old woman herself. The interior of the place was furnished with peculiar ornaments and statues and furniture such as surrounded the exterior. Silks and tapestries covered the windows and hung throughout in the dim light, along with beads and draperies and a few paintings. The only item of immediately recognizable design was a bookshelf that stood against one wall, filled with books of dubious origin and purpose.

"Come, my sweets," said the woman. "Come through and sit with Madame Fleming." Her voice was old and scratchy, thick with Bulgarian or Russian accent. That it was fake was a fact lost entirely on the wide-eyed cousins. The good Madame Fleming was as Irish as any self-respecting leprechaun, but she carried off the gypsy charade to convincing effect.

She led them into a small anteroom and waddled around a table that sat in the middle of the floor. A single candle burned in its center. She eased her plump frame into an upright chair on the far side of the table. "Sit. . .sit down, my sweets," she said.

As if they had been expected, two empty chairs awaited them. They sat down opposite her.

"So it's your futures and fortunes told, is it?" she said again.

Florilyn nodded.

"It will be a shilling each, then. . .in advance."

Even at the best of times, the good Madame Fleming's sign would never have read, FORTUNES TOLD AND FORTUNES MADE, for there was not great money to be had in her chosen line of endeavor. But she would do well for herself on this day. The quoted price was three times her going rate. Like a spider in her lair, she had seen the two innocents coming through a slit in the curtain hanging over one of her windows and knew well enough who they were. If the inmates from the manor up the hill intended to purchase her wares, she would make them pay as befitted their means.

Percy and Florilyn looked at one another. Neither had considered the practical aspects of the case. Florilyn had not so much as a ha'penny on her. Percy always carried a few coins, but two shillings was unexpectedly steep. Regretting his acquiescence to this questionable enterprise all the more, he dug into his pocket and took out everything he had. "I'm sorry," he said, looking over his meager resources. "It looks like I've only got one shilling sixpence." He began to rise. "Here, take the shilling. You can tell hers. I don't need my fortune told."

"Sit. . .sit, my sweet," said the woman. "I am feeling generous today. A shilling sixpence it is. You shall both leave knowing what your futures will bring."

Percy laid down the coins. Quickly they disappeared across the table away from him in the midst of a large fleshy palm.

Slowly Percy sat back down.

"Give me your hand, young lady," said Madame Fleming.

Tentatively Florilyn held out her hand. A tingle of electric current surged through her at the touch from the woman's leathery fingers. The psychic closed her eyes. Her lips began to move but remained silent. Florilyn stared with eyes as wide as saucers. The candle flickered and shadows danced on the walls and ceiling. There was no other movement, no sound.

After what seemed an eternity, the woman's lips stilled. Her eyelids quivered and slowly opened. She leaned forward and peered intently into Florilyn's hand. She began mumbling again to herself, running one finger up and down and across the lines of Florilyn's palm.

"I don't know who you are, young lady," she said at length. Her voice was thick from the East and full of exotic mystery. "But I see a great change coming to you. An inheritance that is yours will be taken away. Another will be given you in its place that is greater yet. Evildoers will try to take advantage of you and steal what is yours. But you will find love, and one will be faithful to you, though he is the least in your eyes. He will be your protector, and thus you will gain your inheritance in the end."

"What does it *mean?*" said Florilyn, trembling with the terrible thrill of mystic unknown.

"I cannot say," replied Madame Fleming in a voice of hidden wisdom. "The eyes of the oracle only pass on what they see and what secrets the hand divulges." Keeping Florilyn's palm clasped in the fingers of her own right hand, she reached toward Percy with her left. "And now you, young man."

Percy hesitated.

The woman's open hand stretched toward him.

"No," said Percy after a moment. "I don't want you looking at my hand."

"There is nothing to fear."

"I am not afraid. But I—"

His father's face rose before Percy's mind's eye. The expression was calm and purposeful. It steadied him. His father was staring into Percy's soul. Suddenly Percy realized that he *loved* his father and knew that his father was a *good* man and full of truth.

"No," he repeated. "I do not think my father would be pleased."

"Your *father?*" chided Madame Fleming. "Are you not your own man?"

"I am my father's son," said Percy. He rose. "Let's go, Florilyn."

"Wait," said Madame Fleming. "Even without your hand, I can see that though you are poor, you shall be rich, for you will find love and wealth together where you least expect them. Yet great pain will accompany the journey where you will discover—"

"That's enough," said Percy. "I will listen to no more. Florilyn, I am going." He left the anteroom and walked back through the large dark room toward the door.

Terrified to be left alone, Florilyn pulled her hand away, jumped up, and hurried after him.

Back in the sunshine of the street, Percy drew in a deep breath and exhaled. He felt as if he needed to rid himself of the spell of the place.

"Why did you rush out like that?" said Florilyn. "It was just getting interesting."

"She gives me the creeps. I didn't like being there."

"What about everything she said?"

"It means nothing. They just make that stuff up," said Percy. "Let's get out of here," he added as he took Grey Tide's reins and hastily mounted.

Inside the strange abode, Madame Fleming chuckled to herself as again she peeped through her window at her jumpy young customers. They would be back. She had given them enough to whet their appetite with all that nonsense about inheritances and evil people and wealth and love. She knew her words would worm their way into their minds, especially the girl's. The day would come when she would want to know more. Today's purpose had only been to bait the hook.

Her most lucrative profits were derived from repeat visits.

THIRTY-EIGHT

Below Stairs

A gentle knock came to the open stable door behind Westbrooke Manor. "I say, Hollin, my auld frien'," sounded a voice thick with accent from the north, "be ye ben?"

"Ay, is that you, Richard?" replied Radnor. "I'm inside—come in, come in!"

" 'Deed, 'tis me," said the visitor, Richard Hawarden, entering the darkened barn. "Ye maun hae kenned my tongue, I'm thinkin'."

"There's no mistaking the tongue of a Scot any more than there is that of an old Welshman," rejoined the viscount's groom. He walked out of the dark with a smile and a hand extended to his longtime friend from Burrenchobay Hall. "What brings you all this way from the Hall?"

"Jist yer ain stables. 'Tisna anither finer in all Gwynedd, as a'body kens."

"Lord Snowdon takes pride in his stock, that's the truth," remarked Radnor. "What is it you need?"

"A four-horse harness. Sir Armond has taen it intil's heid tae hae a jaunt aboot the coontryside the morn's morn wi' ane o' his Lonnen frien's frae parliament an' a' the rest o' 'em. He wants t' tak oot twa coaches wi' four, an' we haena but the ane harness."

"I think I have just what you'll be needing. But it's nigh eleven.

211

Come inside and join us for tea."

The groom led his counterpart from the neighboring estate out the door and toward the kitchen. Already the cook was pouring out eleven o'clock refreshment for the rest of the servants.

"You brought a guest, I see, Hollin," she said. "Welcome to you, Richard."

"Thank ye—and hoo are ye, Mrs. Drenwydd?"

"Well as can be expected," replied the woman in her customary fashion.

The two grooms sat down. Presently Broakes, the butler; Stuart Wyckham, the gardener; Mrs. Llewellyn, the housekeeper; and Deaken Trenchard, the viscount's footman, all entered. Greetings with the Burrenchobay groom were exchanged all around. They had just started on a loaf of sliced bread when Percy came through on his way outside.

"Tea, Master Percival?" asked the cook.

"Oh, that is very nice of you. But no, thank you, Mrs. Drenwydd," he replied, "I'm off for a ride." He shook hands with each of those present in turn.

She introduced him to their guest.

Hollin Radnor slowly uncoiled his lanky frame and rose from his chair, thinking to accompany Percy out to the stables.

"Stay where you are, Mr. Radnor," protested Percy. "I'll saddle her. I think Grey Tide is used to me now."

"I'm happy to—"

"Don't worry. I've watched you do it a dozen times. I'd like to try it myself."

The groom sat back down with a smile.

Percy left the kitchen and headed toward the stables.

"A muckle daecent chap, it seems tae me," remarked Sir Armond's groom.

Nods went around the room.

"A pleasant smile on the lad's face as weel. An' he gie me a fine grip o' his han'."

"I only wish the lad of the house were as interested in horses as his cousin," remarked Radnor.

"Or anything else for that matter," added Stuart Wyckham.

" 'Tis jist hoo things stan' at oor place," rejoined Hawarden. "Seems the yoong ones are the wairst o' it fer manners. I dinna like tae be aroun' when Master Colville comes wantin' a mount, though he comes searchin' fer me if I'm nae there. He'd ne'er dirty *his* fair hands saddlin' a horse! Luckily he's tae be off soon."

"To the continent, I hear," said Mrs. Drenwydd.

"Ay."

"The viscount and Sir Armond have spoken of a match between the two, I hear," now put in Lady Katherine's housekeeper.

"Master Colville and Lady Florilyn, you're meaning?" asked Trenchard.

"I'm not saying I approve," answered Mrs. Llewellyn. "But who else would I mean?"

"Never!" rejoined the cook.

"Dinna be so sure, Mrs. Drenwydd," rejoined their guest. "Talk aroun' the Hall is that they've aye ta'en a fancy tae ane anither. Mightna e'en need the father's tae show themselves in the matter."

"Meaning no disrespect to the Hall, Richard," persisted the cook, "but Sir Armand's eldest isn't fit to be husband to *any* woman, least of all our Lady Florilyn. We all know what happened on market day, though none of it's come within the ears of the viscount or Lady Katherine, poor woman."

Hawarden did not reply. In truth, he had more reason for agreeing with Mrs. Drenwydd's assessment of Colville Burrenchobay than any of the viscount's people knew.

"What about the two younger ones, Richard?" asked Broakes.

"Master Ainsworth and Mistress Davina—a mite better than their brither, I'm thinkin'," replied Hawarden. "But they're still carryin' the blue blood o' their kind. And ye ken what that means. An' they're yoong yet. Takes the teen years tae reveal character, ye ken. Canna say much afore the testin' o' pride an' independence rear their heads."

The butler nodded, joined by Mrs. Llewellyn. She knew the three Burrenchobay children well enough. She had served there some years before coming to the Westbrooke household. She had heard rumors of the proposed match for years, and she feared for Miss Florilyn.

"'Tis the same here," remarked the cook. "Our young lady's already getting a long nose toward her inferiors, as she judges us. Though I can't think where she got it. Her mother's the kindest soul a body could meet."

"She got it from watching her brother, make no mistake," gruffed Broakes. "He's had the long nose of superiority since he could walk. He didn't need the teen years for *his* character to show itself. It was there long before."

"If she's not out riding," said Mrs. Llewellyn, adding her own critique of the young mistress, "it's every day she's wanting this dress pressed or her room cleaned or her bedclothes freshened."

"I daresay, what's to become of these young ones when their parents are gone?" sighed Wyckham.

"What do we care?" rejoined Llewellyn. "By then we'll be gone as well."

"They may be what they are," remarked Radnor, returning the conversation to their houseguest, "but the young man from Glasgow is a gentleman. It is nice to see in one so young."

"It is indeed," assented the butler. "The other afternoon he called me by name. 'Mister Broakes,' he said. And he's always got a kind, 'Thank you,' for me."

Nods and comments went round the room.

"Ay, he does the same with me," said the housekeeper. "He *thanks* me for doing up his room! Who's ever heard of such a thing?"

"Did you not hear him speaking to me just now in that respectful tone?" added the cook.

"I never saddle his horse without a kindly word of gratitude," nodded Radnor.

"His father's a preacher, you know," said Mrs. Llewellyn. "Lady Katherine's brother. That must be where he comes by such respect."

"I begin to wonder if the stories we heard of him be exaggerated," added Broakes. "I can't imagine the likes of *him* in trouble with the law."

"And why shouldn't they be exaggerated?" Mrs. Drynwydd nodded. "It's Courtenay and Florilyn we hear speaking about him. They're jealous of their father, if you ask me. It's clear the viscount's taken a fancy to the lad."

"Hollin says he knows how to talk to the horses," interposed the gardener. "That says a good lot about a man, young or old—isn't that right, Hollin?"

"Indeed so, Stuart," nodded Radnor.

"He was afraid of them at first, as I hear it," chuckled Trenchard.

"At first, maybe," said Radnor. "But a young man who can learn from his fear is on his way toward manhood. You saw yourself, he's not afraid of them now."

Tea completed, the little company gradually broke up.

Hollin Radnor and Richard Hawarden rose and ambled back out to the barn to finish the business that had brought the latter to the manor in the first place. They found Percy just completing his initial effort to saddle a horse by himself. Both grooms checked the straps, pronounced the job well done, and sent him off on his way with praise for his effort.

THIRTY-NINE

The Tea Cake

*T*he day dawned especially warm. Gwyneth had walked with her father to the slate mine early in the morning. She treasured every moment with him, even so simple an activity as walking him to work. Clouds over the mountains indicated rain, perhaps not that afternoon but surely by the next day.

Their conversation had been happy. Barrie kissed his daughter good-bye and turned to enter the quarry. Gwyneth's spirits were high as she stopped in at Grannie's for breakfast tea, her normal custom when accompanying her father to the mine.

No visit to town on Percy's part, whether to look in at any one of the half dozen shops or to pass through to the shore, there to chat with one of the friendlier fishermen or watch them coming and going from their trade, was complete without a visit to Grannie's cottage. There a warm pot always sat near the flame—awaiting the arrival of visitor, whether friend or stranger—with fresh tea leaves ready in the canister on a nearby shelf. Many days found Percy gone from the manor by midmorning and not returning until evening tea, chatting with Grannie, often with Gwyneth waiting on them hand and foot, exploring the town, or visiting with his widening circle of village friends.

Such associations, though ridiculed by his cousins, increased all the more his uncle's affection for his nephew. In truth, the viscount found it difficult to sympathize in heart with the humble folk of the region. Seeing how well the son of his wife's brother was received gave him a certain vicarious sense of satisfaction. It was as if, through the boy, he was a little more doing his duty by his people.

Gwyneth skipped and danced her way through the narrow lanes toward the east side of the village. Suddenly something pelted her from behind.

"Look, Eardley, it's the idiot-girl!" said the boy whose hand had just released the stick that had hit her back.

Percy's ride into town on this day was a little later than usual. Gwyneth was already on her way home from Grannie's as he rode between the two solemn church buildings at the south end of town. He heard a few shouts in the distance but thought nothing of it at first.

"Been to visit the witch, idiot-girl!" yelled a second taunter. "Ha, ha, ha! Let's get her, Chandos!"

The two boys, thirteen and twelve respectively and well known in the village for their pranks, sprinted after Gwyneth.

She might have returned to Grannie's, but that would only bring the trouble down on them both. And besides far-seeing eyes, Codnor Barrie's daughter had been blessed with two of the fleetest feet in all Llanfryniog. She could easily outrun the boys across the moor. She was confident they would not pursue her beyond the edge of the town.

Gwyneth turned and flew.

News of the incident outside Grannie's cottage between the cousins from the manor had spread among the youth of the town as rapidly as had reports of the fight behind the chapel on market day. Everyone for miles knew about the Westbrooke cousin, and the younger ones were wary of him. That he had been ready to take on the likes of Courtenay Westbrooke and Colville Burrenchobay convinced them that they would do well to keep clear of him.

Notwithstanding the account that both older boys had soundly thrashed the Scotsman, today's two young hoodlums had cast a few quick glances about to make sure Percy was nowhere near before commencing their attack against Gwyneth. Unfortunately, they hadn't looked closely enough.

Suddenly the sound of a galloping horse swooped toward the two boys. When he realized what was happening, Percy hardly stopped to consider whether he was capable of a fast ride through Llanfryniog's narrow streets. As it turned out, his practice had paid off.

He caught up to the boys, reined in, wheeled around, and leaped to the ground before they could flee. The two stood momentarily paralyzed as Percy walked toward them. Both thought of making a dash for it. But they knew that one of them would be run down by the big sixteen-year-old and that he would find the other soon enough.

"You blokes have a problem?" said Percy as he approached.

"No, sir," replied the younger of the two.

"What are your names?"

"Eardley White," replied the one who had spoken.

"And you?" he said, glancing toward the other.

"Chandos Gwarthegydd."

"Are you the blacksmith's son?"

"Yes, sir."

"Do you think your father would want me to tell him that you were trying to hurt a girl half your size?"

"No, sir."

Percy looked the two over a few seconds. "All right, then," he said, "I am going to tell you this once. If I hear that either of you have been bothering little Gwyneth again, I will come find you. Do I make myself clear?"

"Yes, sir," they said in unison.

"I will expect you to spread the word that anyone who even thinks of hurting her will have me to deal with. Do you understand?"

"Yes, sir."

"Then get out of here."

They ran off.

Percy returned to his horse and looked about. Though Gwyneth had glanced over her shoulder long enough to see Percy flying to intercept her pursuers, by this time she was nowhere to be seen. Percy's first instinct was to ride after her. But he knew the speed of her feet, as well as the rest, and that she was now safe. He was more concerned for her aunt. He did not trust the two scamps. Watching him leave town, they might retaliate against Grannie. He rode, therefore, to her cottage and spent the next hour there.

Rather than going inside when she arrived home, Gwyneth made her way behind the cottage to greet her friends for the day. She would never understand the meanness of her schoolmates. She did not fear them, at least too much. But she could not understand why people were not kind to one another.

In the large enclosure, her menagerie came bounding and romping toward her, each awaiting its turn as she sent a small hand probing through the fence to pet nose and head and speak to each by name. Two dogs came barking up from behind, eyes aglow, tails whisking back and forth, wet pink tongues seeking any part of her person to lick, jumping and whining impatiently for their share of the attention.

When she was able to free herself, Gwyneth walked to the smaller pens. Two orphans here were her special concern of the moment, a gull from the sea and a small gray rabbit. The gull had immediately allowed Gwyneth to hold and feed it. She had found it trapped in a bit of some strange kind of netting down on the shore. She managed to free it, though its wing was broken. Speaking gently, she had carried it up the steep path and back home.

The rabbit she had discovered one day at her doorstep, limping and with signs of blood on its coat. Unlike the gull, it had been skittish and afraid of her touch. Wearing his leather gloves, her father managed to capture the little creature and place it in a pen. Gwyneth had been feeding it daily ever since. After two days she was able to hold the timid little thing in her arms and feed it grasses and flowers from the meadow.

She opened the pen and gently removed the furry little rabbit who had by now been given a name. "You understand what it is to be afraid, don't you, Bunny White Tail," she said softly, walking about stroking behind its soft, furry ears. "I know you were afraid when you came here, weren't you? You know now that there is nothing to be afraid of, because I am here to take care of you. I am not afraid, either, for God has sent someone to take care of me, just like He sent me to take care of you."

Most of the larger beasts left for hours and days at a time, some by day, others by night, to feed and forage as best they could in the wild. Gwyneth's father could not afford to buy grain to feed all the small animals in her care. But he managed to keep a supply of corn or oats or meal on hand at least to prevent the starvation of the chickens and injured creatures. The former repaid them with a steady supply of eggs. As for the latter, he only hoped his generosity would somehow be credited to him in the eternal scales by which the world is sustained. He certainly could ill afford extra expenditures.

Barrie was on good enough terms with many of the local farmers that a decent supply of usable hay and grain came his way. He and Gwyneth visited the harvest fields every autumn to glean what they could when the harvesters had completed their work. On most such days they pulled a large cartload of broken stalks home at the end of each afternoon's effort. After threshing out what grain could be salvaged, they stored their own little harvest in the loft of the shed beside their cottage for use throughout the winter.

On this day, Gwyneth's thoughts were not on her animals. She was thinking instead of Percy. How could she repay him for his kindness? After she had come home from the village an idea struck her—she would bake him a fine sweet tea cake!

She set about almost immediately mixing the ingredients—just as she had learned from Grannie—and placed the tiny loaf in the coal oven to bake. An hour later it was nearly ready. She opened the oven door to check her creation. By then its aromas filled the cottage. Gwyneth patiently waited another ten minutes. Again she opened the iron door.

The top was a perfect golden brown.

With careful hand slipped inside a great padded mitten, Gwyneth removed it and set it on top of the stove to cool. Now she just had to find a way to get it into Percy's hands. She had sneaked onto the manor grounds without being seen to leave the forgiveness flowers for Master Courtenay and Miss Florilyn. But she could hardly leave a cake hanging from the doorpost!

She went to the front door, opened it, and gazed out across the moor in the direction of the manor. Rain clouds clung to the mountains. She would have to watch for him. If she didn't see him today on his way back from the village, perhaps he would visit Grannie's tomorrow.

Midway through the following morning, Gwyneth Barrie's keen eye was rewarded. She darted inside. The next instant she was dashing across the moor as fast as her legs could carry her.

Percy had emerged from the manor gate, on foot this time, when Gwyneth saw him. As he turned onto the Llanfryniog road, he heard a high voice calling his name. He looked around to see Gwyneth running toward him through the field of grazing cattle between himself and town, white hair streaming behind her appearing almost golden in the sunlight. He stopped and waited.

"Good morning, Percy!" she said sweetly then paused to catch her breath. "I baked you a tea cake!"

"Why, Gwyneth, thank you," said Percy. "What's the occasion? It's not my birthday."

"It's a friendship cake," she replied. "To thank you for chasing those boys away and for what you said when Master Courtenay and Lady Florilyn were laughing at me at Grannie's. Here, Percy."

"This is an unexpected pleasure!" he said as he took it from her hand. "I shall look forward to it—thank you!"

Slowly they left the road and began walking across the plateau toward the sea. In a few moments, they came to the stream that flowed down from the mountains westward across the moor and tumbled over Mochras Head into the sea. It had not much water in it now and was of no great depth, though was five or six feet in width. Percy paused, set the cake on the grass, then placed his hands on the sides of Gwyneth's little waist, plunged his feet into the water, and whisked her over to the other side.

"O–o–o–h!" she squealed with delight, "that was fun! But you've gotten your boots and trousers all wet."

"They will dry soon enough," laughed Percy. He recovered his gift and rejoined her.

Gwyneth led farther up the slope, and Percy was happy to follow.

"Come," said Gwyneth. "I want to show you the view from the top of the cliff."

They continued two or three hundred yards along the inland edge of the promontory.

"I have to stay back from the edge," said Gwyneth as they walked. "Papa knows I am careful. But he says I must always be cautious near the sea."

At length Gwyneth stopped, then threw herself on the grass and pointed her face out over the cliff edge. "Come, Percy," she said, "lay down beside me."

Percy laid his cake-gift on the grass beside him and did as she said.

"Scoot forward," she said. "Now, put your hands under your chin... like this. Look out—isn't the sea beautiful like this, so high above it?"

"Is this another of your special places?" asked Percy.

"Yes."

"So now I know about three. How many do you have?"

"I don't know. I've never counted. Probably six or eight."

They lay motionless for five or six minutes, drinking in the sea air. It was mingled with earthy aromas from the grass and moorland around them. Below, the waves splashed against the shoreline though the bluff-edge obscured the sight. In front of them, gulls played in the cliff-breezes.

"Papa says he will take me back to Ireland one day," said Gwyneth. "He wants to show me where my mother lived and where I was born."

They remained quiet as they stared out across the ancient waters.

At length Percy rose to a sitting position. "All this salt air has made me hungry," he said. "How would you like to join me for some tea cake?"

"Oh, but I couldn't, Percy. I made it for you!"

"So it's mine, is it?"

"Yes. I gave it to you."

"Then I can do anything I want with it?"

"Of course."

"Even share it with my friends?"

Gwyneth nodded with a smile.

"Then I want to share it with you!" Percy tore off a chunk of the soft white cake, split it in half, handed one portion to Gwyneth, then took a bite out of the other. "Delicious!" he exclaimed.

"It is supposed to be eaten with tea," said Gwyneth.

"I'll save the rest—I promise. Uh-oh!" he exclaimed, looking up. "I think I felt rain."

Within seconds huge raindrops were pelting them.

"O–ow—you were right!" cried Gwyneth. "Come, Percy! We'll run to my house. We'll have a fire and tea and dry out."

"And eat the rest of my cake!" Percy laughed.

They leaped to their feet and dashed across the moor as the downpour engulfed them. By the time they reached the stone cottage, though Percy had done his best to protect the tea cake inside his shirt, both were dripping wet.

With the promise to come back the next day if the rain cleared for another riding lesson, Percy returned to the manor late that afternoon. He was not yet quite dry but was happier than he had been in years. The humblest pleasures in life, simply lying on the ground looking out across the sea or getting caught in a rainstorm, gave him more joy than he ever could have imagined.

FORTY

Remote Cottage

With the basic principles of riding clearer in his mind and becoming more natural as he felt increasingly comfortable on the back of a horse, Percy had been out riding almost every day for the past several weeks. On several of those, his uncle had accompanied him. They had spoken of many things.

He often rode south through the gentle terrain of the coast and occasionally east. He was learning his way along the trails and roads in every direction. He had tried to replicate his lengthy precarious ride with Florilyn but turned back when he realized that he was in danger of losing his way. Whenever he wanted to practice his galloping technique, however, he went to the shore where it was level and the footing secure.

He knew he must eventually also learn to ride fast over bumpy grassland, even through wooded regions. It was for that reason that he had requested another lesson with his diminutive instructor.

The day after the downpour dawned fair though chilly. Percy waited until after lunch when he knew Florilyn usually went to her room. They had not spoken again about the incident at Madame Fleming's. After her strange friendliness of that day, he was afraid she might want to go riding with him again. But on the days of his lessons, he had to keep his riding secret. Once the door of her room closed behind her, Percy left the house for the stables to prepare for his afternoon's ride.

He set out down the drive and onto the main road. Instead of turning left on the village road, he continued north then veered onto the moor and through farmland until he was approaching the Barrie cottage.

Gwyneth saw him coming from behind the house. She ran excitedly to meet him. "Hi, Percy!" she cried.

"Hi, Gwyneth. . .are you ready to give me another lesson?"

"Let me just run inside and take the pot off the stove so it won't boil over."

She returned a minute later. "Shall I run to the beach?" she asked.

"Why don't you get up behind me and we'll ride together," said Percy. He reached down and took her hand. With a single motion as if he found her light as a feather, and with a high-pitched squeal of delight, Gwyneth flew up onto Grey Tide's back just behind the saddle. She stretched her arms around Percy's waist.

As Percy encouraged Grey Tide into motion, Gwyneth thought she had never been so happy in her life. Percy may have been only sixteen. But he was still a grown man in her eyes. She felt safer in his presence than with anyone other than her father.

"I would like to try galloping on grass instead of sand today," said Percy over his shoulder. "Florilyn will be sure to want to race someplace that won't be easy for me. Where can we go that is not *too* bumpy?"

"Go over there," said Gwyneth, "to the right and up the hill. I will show you."

They crossed the main road, continued through several fields full of grazing cattle. As the plateau rose away from the sea, the terrain of patchy moorland became less arable. They rode up and down several inclines, moving into the hills and toward the series of ridges they had been over together on the day he had lost his mount with Florilyn. On this day they were farther north than Percy had yet been.

"I thought you were going to take me someplace gentle and flat!" He laughed. "I wouldn't dare gallop here—I'd be thrown in no time."

"Don't worry, Percy," said Gwyneth behind him. "There is a flat meadow near the Muir cottage. I think you will like it. It is another of my special places."

"*Stevie* Muir?" said Percy.

"Yes, do you know Stevie?"

"I do indeed. I saw him shear a sheep in the market day contest. I didn't know you knew him—though I suppose you know everyone."

"Stevie is my cousin."

"Is he! What a coincidence! Well, it probably isn't that much of a coincidence. I suppose many of the families around here are related in one way or another."

"There is my aunt's house...just there. Can you see it?" said Gwyneth.

"I think so. . . . Ah, yes, there in the little hollow between the slopes."

They continued toward it. As they came closer, all at once a clustering mass of sheep came bounding toward them. Without waiting for Percy to stop, Gwyneth leaped to the ground and went running toward them. They baaed in a frenzy, nudging and sniffing and waddling around her. Gwyneth giggled in delight as she ran her hands through their woolly, greasy, dirty, matted coats while they pressed close around her. Percy reined in and stopped, his way blocked by the mass of sheep.

A minute later Stevie Muir appeared behind them. He waved and called out in greeting. "Hoy, Gwyneth!"

"Hi, Stevie. I brought Percy Drummond."

"So I see. Welcome to you, Mr. Drummond. So you came for your visit along with a wee friend!"

"I had no idea the two of you knew one another," said Percy. "Gwyneth tells me you're cousins."

"We are indeed. Let me run back and tell my mum to put the kettle on. It's not many visitors we get out here. She will be eager to show you the hospitality of the Welsh. She's heard about you, you see." He turned and ran toward the cottage.

"Come with me, Percy," said Gwyneth, leading the way slowly through the sheep. "They will stay out of Grey Tide's way."

Percy followed. As they came near the cottage, several barking dogs bounded to greet Gwyneth. The sheep did not seem concerned. Percy dismounted, and Gwyneth led him inside.

A woman of some fifty years stood at a black cookstove. Her partially graying dark hair fell down over a forehead and cheeks dappled with perspiration. In a word, her countenance looked *tired*. Stevie was nowhere in sight.

She turned toward them as they entered. In spite of her fatigue, her eyes lit up. "Ah, Gwyneth, my dear. How are ye the day?"

"Well, Auntie. This is Mr. Drummond."

"Welcome to ye, young man," said the woman, drying her hands on the apron tied around her waist. She extended a strong hand whose appearance indicated close acquaintance with hard work.

"Thank you, Mrs. Muir," said Percy. "Your son invited me for a visit several weeks ago. I am sorry to say I have been negligent. But Gwyneth finally got me up here. She says you are related."

"Ay. Her daddy's my brother."

Just then Stevie reappeared.

"Daddy's fine," he said to his mother then glanced at Percy. "My daddy's sick, you see, Mr. Drummond," he said. "He's forgotten most things and gets agitated when there's a commotion. I was just in telling him we had a guest so he wouldn't be confused. Come. . .I'll take you to him."

Percy followed into the adjacent room. There sat a man by appearance at least a decade older than Mrs. Muir. What thin hair he had left was pure white. His face was pale and drawn as he sat in an overstuffed chair staring vacantly ahead out of sunken eyes. A blanket of faded red wool lay over his knees and legs.

"I've brought you our visitor, Daddy," said Stevie. "This is Mr. Drummond."

Percy bent down with a smile. "Hello, Mr. Muir," he said. "I am happy to make your acquaintance." He took the man's hand where it lay in his lap and shook it gently. Stevie's father did not seem aware of Percy's presence.

Stevie led him across the room, and they sat down. A few minutes later, Gwyneth and Mrs. Muir appeared with a tray of tea things.

"I'm sorry I didn't know you were coming, Mr. Drummond," said his hostess. "I would have baked some scones. I'm afraid I have nothing to offer you other than buttered bread."

"And nothing goes quite so well with tea, Mrs. Muir," rejoined Percy cheerfully. "That is. . .would it be *laver bread* you are speaking of?"

"No," she said, laughing. "Not quite to your taste, I take it?"

"I have to admit, the idea of eating seaweed has been difficult to get accustomed to."

"Have no fear—my bread is nothing but thick dark rye and wheat."

"Then I will enjoy it heartily!"

"Ye be an easy young man to please. 'Tis not every day we get a visitor from the manor in our wee cottage. What am I saying? We have *never* had anyone from the manor set foot past our door, much less sit down with us for tea. We are right honored, sir."

Percy laughed. "I doubt my presence is worthy of such praise, Mrs. Muir. I am but a friend of Stevie's and Gwyneth's who is answering a long overdue invitation. But I thank you for your hospitality and kind words."

"We get the viscount's factor calling, Mum," said Stevie.

"Ay. Every six months like clockwork coming for his rents. Yet he never darkens the inside of my door, but just waits outside for me to bring it to him."

"Manor. . .what's that you say about the manor?" suddenly said the old man from across the room. "I worked at the manor, you know. The viscount treated me right well when I was a lad. Did odd jobs and ran errands for him, I did."

"Yes, Daddy," said Stevie. "We have a visitor from the manor."

"The viscount's come, you say? He'll be wanting me." He folded back a corner of the wool blanket, though it seemed too heavy for him to get off his knees, and struggled to rise.

"Nay, Daddy," now interposed Mrs. Muir. "The viscount's not here."

Bewildered and disappointed, her husband relaxed back into his chair. He continued to glance about the room, as if looking for someone. Slowly by degrees, he drifted again into silence.

"I can hardly imagine him working for the viscount," said Percy. "I would guess him to be quite a bit older than my uncle."

"He is speaking of the old viscount, Mr. Drummond," said Mrs. Muir. "It's your uncle's father he's thinking of. His mind's about gone, ye see, but his memory of his early years is as clear as the water in the lake up yonder on the far slopes of Rhinog Fawr. Much of the time he doesn't even know who I am, poor man. I have to watch that he doesn't wander off. He won't know how to get back home."

"I am sorry, Mrs. Muir," said Percy. "I had no idea. Can nothing be done for him?"

"Nothing but what the good Lord Himself can do. My dear man is in His hands now."

A few moments of reflective silence fell as they sipped at their tea.

"Is there anything he needs?" asked Percy at length. "Medications or the like, anything I might be able to obtain for you?"

"That is very kind of ye, Mr. Drummond," replied Stevie's mother. "With my man the way he is, we do struggle a bit to keep up with the garden and what things we are able to grow. The work's a little much for just the two of us now, and Stevie's got his hands full with the sheep and cows and chickens. But my brother helps us now and then, as he is able. That's Gwyneth's papa. With my daughter gone, Gwyneth comes and helps me clean the house. Don't you, darling?" she said, turning to Gwyneth with a smile. "We do right well, don't we, Stevie? We are more blessed than we can imagine. Stevie's sister, ye see, is a servant at Burrenchobay Hall. It isn't much Sir Armond can pay her, ye see, for he isn't of old money like Lord Snowdon. But what my Gracie gets she brings home to us, and we've mostly got all we need."

"If there ever is anything I can do," said Percy, then glanced toward Stevie, "you come to the manor, Stevie. You find me."

Stevie nodded. They chatted for another fifteen or twenty minutes.

At length they finished their tea and Percy glanced at Gwyneth. "Actually," he said, "Gwyneth and I came up here for what I must confess is an ulterior motive. Gwyneth has been giving me riding lessons."

"Has she now?" said Mrs. Muir.

"Galloping lessons, actually. I'm not so good on the back of a horse. Florilyn took me out a few weeks ago and succeeded in getting me both thrown and lost. Gwyneth told me she could teach me to ride fast enough that I could beat my cousin in a race. She said there is a place nearby where she wants me to practice."

"The meadow on the way to the lake, Stevie," said Gwyneth.

"Are you really going to race Miss Florilyn again?" asked Stevie enthusiastically.

"That is my plan," answered Percy. "She doesn't know it yet."

"I would love to see that!"

"Then you will definitely be notified of time and place!" Percy laughed. "But bring your bandages and smelling salts in case I end up on the ground again."

"You will win, Percy," said Gwyneth confidently.

"How can you be so certain?"

"I have seen you both ride. You are almost as fast already. You will win."

"I didn't know you were such an expert teacher, Gwyneth," said Stevie. "May I go with you? I might learn something myself."

The three young people rose.

"Thank you for the tea and bread, Auntie," said Gwyneth.

"Yes, thank you," added Percy, shaking the hand of Gwyneth's aunt. He walked across the room and again took Mr. Muir's limp hand. "Good-bye, Mr. Muir," he said.

"Are you the one from the manor?" asked the old man faintly. He glanced up but could not quite focus on Percy where he stood before him.

"Yes, sir."

"Did the viscount send you?"

"No, sir. I came to visit your son and wife."

"I have a son?"

"Yes, sir. Stevie."

He mumbled a few unintelligible words, and then his eyes glazed over again.

The three young people left the cottage.

"I will run ahead," said Stevie. "It's only about a mile." He turned and broke into a gentle loping stride away from the cottage.

Percy and Gwyneth remounted Grey Tide and set off at a leisurely pace after him. They arrived at the meadow ten minutes later.

For the next hour, both Stevie and Gwyneth coached Percy as he galloped back and forth over the grassy terrain. He was eventually comfortable enough to try jumping a tiny stream and did so several times without incident. Whenever he glanced over at Gwyneth, she reminded him, by extending her elbows and gently rocking them up and down, to feel the motion of the horse beneath him and to move in oneness with it.

When they were through, Gwyneth pronounced him ready, though Percy was still not altogether convinced.

FORTY-ONE

Picnic in the Hills

Rhawn Lorimer had not been pleased with Percy's rebuff on market day. She had been stewing and scheming ever since how she might try her wiles on him again. That Courtenay's sister was so obviously uninterested left the field wide open for her to pursue him.

There remained the mystery of the strange floral bouquets to get to the bottom of. She still had not made the connection in her mind between Percy's bouquet in the shop and the village witch-child. But whoever the secret girl was for whom Percy had bought the ribbon, Rhawn had no doubt that he could be enticed to forget her. But she had to get him *alone*.

And she couldn't help it—she was jealous of Florilyn. After what he had done in the village, what a goose not to see that he was crazy about her. Percy's words still annoyed her that he wouldn't risk a fight for *her*. It made Rhawn all the more determined to win him over.

She did not lose much sleep speculating on what would be the result to Percy from Courtenay if she was successful, *Boys had to be able to take care of themselves* about summed up her thoughts on the matter. Alongside Courtenay's view that girls ought to come to him, the two were ideally matched for one another in conceit.

Thus Rhawn Lorimer's machinations continued. Every time she

went near the manor, however, ostensibly to see Florilyn but keeping an eagle eye out for her cousin, there was no sign of him. And Courtenay always insisted on hanging around.

One day late in July, with high summer abroad throughout North Wales, Rhawn Lorimer decided that she would lure the rivals out for a ride. She would use Florilyn as the pawn for her stratagems. From certain comments from her friend, she gathered that the animosity between she and Percy had begun to wane. That fact concerned her more than a little. She had to act before it went too far and Florilyn took it into her head to return Percy's attentions.

Rhawn appeared at Westbrooke Manor midway through the morning. "Florilyn," she said excitedly, "it is a gorgeous warm day. I'm going to ask Courtenay to go for a ride toward the mountains. I haven't been into the hills for longer than I can remember. Do you want to go? Let's take a picnic lunch!"

"Why would I want to go with you and Courtenay?" replied Florilyn. "I don't want to tag along with the two of you. Haven't you heard about three's a crowd? Courtenay would hate me."

"It would be more fun with you along."

"Maybe for you!"

"Well. . .perhaps it wasn't such a good idea," sulked Rhawn.

"Why don't you just go without me?"

"I don't know," rejoined Rhawn hesitantly. "Courtenay's been, I don't know. . .a little funny lately. I don't know if he would be such good company by himself."

They were silent a moment. Rhawn was clearly disappointed.

"I've got an idea," said Florilyn. "I could see if Percy wants to go. . . that is, if you don't mind."

"Oh. . .okay—that sounds all right. Then we would each have someone to ride with. Do you think he would?"

"I'll ask him. He went to his room after breakfast. I think he's still there. He reads a lot," she added, as if the idea of reading a book was repulsive. Florilyn bounded out of the room and ran down the hall.

Percy's initial reaction when Florilyn appeared at his door was not promising.

"Courtenay and Rhawn are going for a ride—do you want to go?" Florilyn asked.

He met her words with a blank stare. "Why would I want to go riding with *them*?" he asked.

"You'll go with me. I'm going, too."

Percy shook his head. Rhawn Lorimer was dangerous. He wanted nothing to do with her. . .especially with Courtenay watching him like a hawk. "I'm sorry," he said, "but the book I'm in the middle of will be better company than those two."

"Please, Percy," said Florilyn. "It will be fun."

"Look, Florilyn, I don't want to do anything to irritate your brother. When it comes to Rhawn Lorimer, Courtenay is very edgy. Believe me, he *won't* want me around."

"I won't let him do anything to you."

"How will you stop him?" smiled Percy sardonically.

"He's not going to beat you up again with the two of us there."

"You're probably right."

"Come on. . .please!"

"All right." He nodded. "But you'd better keep Courtenay off me!" he added with a laugh.

It was soon arranged. Within half an hour, the four horses were saddled, Mrs. Drynwydd had packed a lunch and they set off.

Rhawn was in high spirits. It was obvious from the beginning that she intended to pay as much attention to Percy as to Courtenay.

Percy regretted his decision before the roof of the manor was out of sight behind them. He did his best to keep as far away from her as possible. He was hampered in this effort in that he was still not as skilled on uneven ground as the other three. But his skills had improved sufficiently that he mostly managed to keep one of his cousins between himself and Rhawn as they made their way eastward into the hills. The girls chatted away. Courtenay remained silent. Percy was content to follow his example.

As they went, he recalled a rumor that had come within his hearing in the village of a strange creature that haunted the lake regions of Snowdonia. It was said to walk on two legs and be the terror even of wolves and bears. He could not deny that he was curious to see what substance there was to the stories. He had no reason to trust what the village urchins said. Yet the fact that the younger of them, from reports pressed with great exaggeration upon the ears of their imaginations by older brothers and sisters, were terrified to venture much beyond the north-south road made him wonder what truth might exist in the tales.

A narrowing forced the girls to ride ahead. Percy found himself side by side with Courtenay.

"Is there any truth to the rumors of a lake monster in the mountains?" he asked his cousin.

Courtenay glanced to his side without much expression. "There is talk of it," he replied. "I've not heard it called a *monster*. Most of the people who claim to have seen it say that the thing is tiny."

"People have seen it?"

"People have *claimed* to see it."

"What do you think?"

"That it's nonsense. Colville and I have been riding in these hills since we were so high. We've never seen anything. That reminds me. . . we were supposed to take you hunting."

"No thanks!" Percy laughed. "I don't think your friend much cares for me. I'm not sure I want to go out in the mountains with him toting a rifle."

Courtenay smiled wryly. "I see what you mean," he said. "Yeah, he's not too fond of you. But I still think the creature talk is rubbish."

The girls ahead had been listening.

"Don't be so sure, Courtenay," said Florilyn over her shoulder. "What about Gwberr-niog?"

"What's *that*?" said Percy.

"A water-kelpie who lives in the mountain lakes," replied Florilyn.

"We all grew up hearing about it."

"Come on, Florilyn," insisted Courtenay, "you know as well as I do that it's all nonsense."

"Who says? I would never ride out here alone at night."

"I would," said Rhawn, making sport of the whole thing. "That is. . . if I could get someone to come with me."

Neither of the young men was inclined to take the bait.

"You'd be safe enough around here," said Courtenay. "Gwberr-niog only lives in the lakes farther north."

"I thought you didn't believe in him."

"I don't. I'm only saying that's where he is *supposed* to live."

"He eats humans, you know," said Rhawn. "And only comes out at night. That's when his hunger for human flesh is greatest."

"Rhawn—ugh," said Florilyn. "Don't talk so! You're going to make me afraid. You'll ruin our picnic."

"Nothing can hurt *us*, Florilyn," said Rhawn, turning to smile over her shoulder at Courtenay. "We have two brave men to take care of us." As she turned her head slowly around, she allowed her eyes to linger on Percy's face with an expression whose meaning was impossible to miss.

Percy glanced hurriedly away and did his best to ignore it.

The route before them widened again. The girls eased back. Again the horses continued along four abreast. They came to a long level pasture.

Suddenly Rhawn bolted. "Race you to the far side!" she cried galloping ahead.

Florilyn on Red Rhud was after her like a flash, with Courtenay, who did *not* like to be bested on the back of a horse by any girl, at her side.

Percy urged Grey Tide into an easy gallop. Even after his time with Gwyneth near the Muir cottage, he did not care about trying to keep up with the others. In seconds they were thirty yards ahead.

It was exactly as Rhawn had planned it. She knew what the other three were likely to do. As quickly as she bolted, she now abruptly reined in. Florilyn and Courtenay sped by, not immediately apprehending her intent. They were too caught up racing each other to look back.

Rhawn slowed, and Percy drew alongside. She cleverly kept Grey Tide at her side, gradually easing back until both horses had slowed to a trot and finally resumed a comfortable walk. Ahead, the other two sped on.

"So here we are," said Rhawn, "alone at last."

"I don't want us to be alone," said Percy.

"But I do."

"I thought you were going for a ride with Courtenay."

"That was only so I could be with you."

"You don't care what Courtenay thinks?"

"No. Why should I? Courtenay's a bore."

"That may be," laughed Percy, though without humor in his tone. "But he's a bore with a temper."

Percy realized that it was time he put into practice everything Gwyneth had told him a few days earlier. He dug his heels into Grey Tide's sides, leaned as far forward as he could, and eased into a gallop.

Rhawn laughed merrily and caught him within seconds. Percy saw he was not about to outrun her. But at least he could make a pretense of trying to keep up with his cousins. They rode up side by side two minutes later to where Courtenay and Florilyn sat waiting.

"I guess I'm not ready for that rematch quite yet, eh, Florilyn!" laughed Percy, trying to divert attention from Courtenay's suspicious glances.

"You kept in the saddle at least," she said. "That is an improvement!"

"What's this about a rematch?" asked Rhawn.

"Nothing," replied Percy. "Just a private little contest between Florilyn and me, isn't that right, Florilyn?"

"Percy has challenged me to a race," said Florilyn in fun, never one to keep anything to herself.

"Which I am obviously not yet ready for!" rejoined Percy.

For the rest of the day, as they ate their picnic lunch, and throughout the entire ride back, Percy remained more on his guard than ever. It was now he who watched Rhawn's every move like a hawk. She knew what he was doing and enjoyed the cat-and-mouse game immensely. As a result of it, Percy was forced to attempt more conversation with Courtenay. He kept to his side like a twin.

"Is it true that you were in trouble with the police?" Courtenay asked as they rode along.

"I'm afraid so," replied Percy.

"What was it for?"

"Nothing serious. Petty theft. I was stupid. I broke into shops and stole things."

"Why—I thought your parents were well off."

"They are. Like I said, I was stupid. It was just for the adventure of it. But it was to the point where my father couldn't protect me any longer. I was close to getting thrown into jail."

"You were actually. . .arrested?"

"Not exactly. Most of the policemen knew my father. They usually brought me home with stern words and warnings. But for my father's sake, they let me off. You know how it is. I imagine if you got in trouble, Rhawn's father wouldn't send you up for a stretch in Dartmoor."

Another smile creased Courtenay's lips. "Don't be too sure," he said.

Percy laughed. "What do you mean?"

"You know fathers—no young man is ever good enough for their little girls."

"I see," chuckled Percy. "Well, I suppose it is to your advantage that your fathers are friends."

"Maybe. . . Now all I have to do is keep her away from you!" said Courtenay with a significant smile.

"Believe me, you have nothing to worry about."

"So *you* say."

"It's true!" Percy laughed. "Besides, I'll be gone in a couple of weeks."

From high in a tree, the four riders were being watched as they went. Gwyneth had in truth been following for some time, running ahead, circling around, taking shortcuts up the steepest of the hills while they rode around them. She could not keep from curiously wondering what Percy was like when with the three older youths. It felt funny in her stomach to see her friend with them. Was he really the same person with them? As the afternoon progressed, she crept ever closer, hoping to catch sight of his face or hear his voice as they passed.

Suddenly Rhawn Lorimer looked up and let out an ear-piercing shriek. "Look, it's the witch-girl!" she cried, pointing up in the tree ahead of them. "She's right there. She's spying on us!"

Courtenay followed her gaze and saw the little miscreant. Filled with rage and immediately assuming his role as presumptive heir and future viscount, he kicked his horse forward. "Come down from there this instant!" he yelled up into the tree.

Trembling to have been discovered, Gwyneth did not move.

"I demand that you come down."

Still Gwyneth did not flinch.

He realized that she was calling his bluff. Unless he was prepared to climb up the tree after her, he would come off looking impotent. So Courtenay changed his tactic. "This is my property," he said. "You are on the Westbrooke Manor estate. You are not allowed here. Perhaps you wandered here by mistake, so I will let it go this time. But if I find you trespassing again, I will not be so lenient. I hope I have made myself understood."

"Watch yourself, Courtenay," said Florilyn. "You don't want to get any more bouquets."

Rhawn's ears perked up at the mention of the mystery of the flowers.

"It's all right. Let's go," said Courtenay, still a little ruffled. "The sooner we get away from here the better."

The others continued on their way.

Percy rode toward the tree, stopped, and glanced up. "Hello, Gwyneth," he said. "What are you doing so far from home? You're not lost?"

The merry laugh that met his ears rang out louder than he had imagined her voice capable of.

"Come down and join us. I'll give you a ride home."

Gwyneth scampered down through the branches as if she were a tree lizard. In less than a minute, she was standing beside Percy's mount.

He reached down with his hand and again pulled her up and behind him on Grey Tide's rump as if she were weightless.

The other three watched with mixed reactions to see their foursome suddenly turned into a fivesome, and an unwelcome one at that. For the rest of the way back, they kept their distance.

The remainder of the ride was subdued. Had he dared, Courtenay would have given Percy a tongue lashing for interfering. The two girls kept their own counsel as well, but for very different reasons.

Gradually Percy's horse, with Gwyneth hanging on behind him, moved farther ahead. Their companions could hear Gwyneth and Percy laughing and talking. The very sound of it irritated two of them almost to distraction.

Courtenay's brief thaw toward Percy had thoroughly frozen over. He was profoundly annoyed to have his rebuke of Gwyneth so completely ignored.

The incident had also seriously tarnished the luster in which Percy stood in Rhawn Lorimer's eyes. She had done everything but kiss him, and he had as good as laughed at her. Yet now he was falling all over himself to give the little witch a ride home. She was more jealous of Gwyneth than she had ever been of Florilyn.

How could she be jealous of a mere child? The whole thing made her furious. She was more than a little afraid of Gwyneth, too. She knew the rumors as well as everyone else. But there was nothing she could do.

As they rode, however, Florilyn found herself filled with odd and unexpected reactions that were strangely sympathetic toward Percy. She didn't dare say anything to the other two. But as she listened to Courtenay and Rhawn grumbling angrily, she found herself wondering just what was so despicable about his being nice to one of the village children.

Not so very long ago she had been intentionally cruel to him, trying to bait him and make him angry. Yet he had been stubbornly insistent on being nice to her, too. She didn't deserve it, but he had persistently paid back her meanness with kindness. How could she fault him for being nice to someone else?

Percy treated everyone the same, whether rich or poor, boy or girl, young or old. After a summer in his presence, she had begun to realize what an unusual, and perhaps even wonderful, quality that was.

FORTY-TWO

Lake Creature of Gwynedd

*T*he first days of his summer had been so tedious and slow. Suddenly Percy realized that his summer in Wales was flying by so rapidly that it would soon be at an end. What had begun as an incarceration had turned into the experience of a lifetime. It was with a poignant sense of melancholy that he realized he would soon be saying good-bye to all this.

Late in the morning of a brilliant warm day of early August, Percy set out on horseback for the hilly region northeast of Westbrooke Manor. After his ride with the other three, it had come into his mind to venture even farther into the mountainous inland region, where Stuart Wykeham, the gardener, told him several small, high, cold crystal lakes lay tucked between the peaks and offered a spectacular sight of the sort one never forgets.

Percy made his way through the east gate of the estate in high spirits, continued in the same direction through an ascending valley between two flanking ridges, then cut northward into the high hills. No trail marked his way underfoot, but he had been given rough directions by Wykeham and Hollin Radnor. He was confident enough in his sense of direction by this time that he almost wanted to get lost for the sheer pleasure of finding his way back out of the mountains.

A tremendous downpour had drenched the whole of Gwynedd the night before. Today's sun made the earth shine as though it had been sprinkled with diamonds. From its grasses and shrubs and trees gently rose a fragrance sweeter than the most costly perfume. The melody of Wales infected Percy as he rode happily along. He found himself occasionally breaking into some song or other he had heard in town, though he didn't even know the meaning of half the words he tried to sing.

The climb steepened steadily the farther inland he progressed. In two hours, Grey Tide was breathing heavily. As they descended into valley or dell, losing sight temporarily of mountains ahead, a quiet sense of isolation stole over him. Percy felt that he was entering a fairy-tale world disconnected from Wales and England altogether. Scarce breeze could be felt, no sound heard other than the occasional call of a hawk high overhead.

Rising out of these fairy hollows as he pursued his trek upward, the eastern mountains rose again into view. Once more Percy felt the gentle winds on his face. Pausing at the highest of each successive summit, he turned to behold the coastline spread out in the distance behind him, the deep blue of the sea stretched as to the very horizon. Then again he descended down the eastern slope, and all sense of being near the sea again vanished.

Midway through the afternoon, growing tired but with the weary pride of accomplishment, Percy approached what he hoped, if he had followed the landmarks indicated by the manor's two men correctly, would be the first of several lakes. He was leading Grey Tide through a wooded region of pine and fir. On his left rose a steep, rocky hillside, almost cliff-like and impassible, the opposite slope of which was supposed to overlook the tiny body of blue.

Making certain of his bearings, he worked his mount around the base of this small mountain as he continued to move gradually upward. At length he came to a jagged opening to his left where the shoulder of a projecting ridge opened between this hill and the next, extending down almost to Percy's level. Turning into this pass, Grey Tide scrambled with some difficulty up the rocky surface. Around several large boulders, Percy arrived at the overlook he sought.

Cresting the summit of the narrow opening between the higher hills, Percy saw below him, surrounded on all sides by jagged rocky hills and peaks, a tiny lake of the most gorgeous blue imaginable. Not a ripple disturbed its surface. In size it could not have been more than three or four hundred feet across. The blue of its surface shimmered with the richest shade he had ever seen, growing almost black at the center, indicating great depth. Around the edges, the hues lightened to pale shades of turquoise, so still and pure as to make what could be seen of the bottom near the shoreline absolutely sparkling in clarity.

Percy dismounted and stood as one transfixed. Trees surrounded most of the lake's circumference, broken on one side by cliffs and boulders rising straight up from the glistening surface in the direction of the overlooking peaks. Directly across from this cliff face, among the trees, a grassy meadow stretched away from the water's edge perhaps a hundred and fifty feet before giving way to the slopes of granite. Near the water's edge stood a dozen or more deer gently drinking from the lake and nibbling at the grass.

As he gazed, a sound began to invade Percy's ears. Faint at first, it gradually increased. He realized he was listening to some faint, strange, far-off kind of music. It did not sound human. But he had never heard bird or other animal make such a call. The crooning tone was melancholy, like the lamenting howl of wild dog or wolf. A faint hint of melody could be detected in the repetition of its ethereal notes, hovering ever and about some unknown minor key, never quite resolving itself, yet mysteriously satisfying and peaceful.

Suddenly Percy remembered the rumored lake creature of the mountains.

The strange, otherworldly, melodic crooning grew. Was this how the beast lured its victims into its lair, with sweet spells that wove a seductive enchantment over the senses, bewitching the unsuspecting to their eventual death? Was it perhaps a great bird of prey? The sound almost resembled the lonely cry of a hawk—peaceful, mesmerizing, terrifying. He knew great mountain birds existed, capable of killing animals many times their own size. Was it trying to lure him closer with the hypnotic beguilement of its music?

The sight below him was truly lovely. Was that part of the bedevilment itself? Yet the sound floating over mountains and forest was not one he could fear.

The strange crooning kept him riveted where he stood. It now seemed to be coming from the lake itself. He felt his feet moving forward, down the incline before him. . .toward the sound.

Suddenly from behind the trees beyond the meadow, a figure appeared, a white-clad child-figure from whom the haunting melody came.

Percy stopped and stood motionless.

Here was no mountain bird, nor lake creature nor kelpie. It was *Gwyneth* singing to the animals!

Even from this distance, under the crown that appeared reddish gold in the sunlight, he could almost see the two eyes of heaven's blue, behind which dwelt something whose light and life came from another world altogether, and from Him who made heaven and earth together.

A great joy rose in his heart as a smile rushed to Percy's lips. His first instinct was to call out and rush down to her. Yet some power restrained both feet and tongue.

Gwyneth held out her hand. Several deer slowly approached to nibble something from it. Around her feet scurried squirrels and chipmunks and rabbits and what looked to be a family of quail. Overhead swooped sparrows and robins. The melancholy crooning continued. Percy knew it was not meant for him.

By and by the melody ceased.

Gwyneth turned and retreated into the wood beyond the meadow. The rest of the small herd of deer lifted their heads from water and grass and followed her. So, too, did the smaller creatures.

Knowing that he had been chosen to witness something holy, with careful step Percy returned up to the overlook. He took Grey Tide's reins and led her on foot for five or ten minutes, then remounted and quietly retreated the way he had come.

He had been to Gwyneth's most special place of all. But it was one he could never tell her he had seen. This secluded corner of heaven had to remain hers alone.

FORTY-THREE

Cousins and Friends

*I*t was early August. In two weeks, Percy would return to Glasgow. He had been revolving many things in his mind, especially about his future, about his father and what he would say to him when he saw him again. He knew there was much he needed to make right.

Before that time came, however, he had one thing he had to take care of *here.*

After several more days of intense riding, he judged himself as ready as he would ever be. He found an opportunity when Florilyn was alone outside. "Hey," he called, running to catch her.

She turned. "Hi, Percy," she said, greeting him with a pleasant smile.

"I'll be returning to Glasgow before much longer," he said, falling into stride beside her.

"Is it that soon already?"

"I'm afraid so."

"It won't be the same here without you."

"Glad to get rid of me at last, eh!" Percy laughed good-naturedly.

"That's not what I meant."

"I know. Just teasing. You have to admit that your brother will be happy to see me go."

"Maybe so—but Courtenay can be an old poop. He didn't learn

to—" Florilyn hesitated. "I've. . .I have enjoyed having you here," she said after a moment, glancing toward him with an awkward smile. "I know I wasn't very nice at first—"

"Aw, forget it," said Percy. "No harm done. You know what Bill Shakespeare says."

"I remember," she smiled. " 'All's well that ends well.' Do you really know your Shakespeare that well?"

"Are you kidding?" Percy laughed. "I was a terrible student in school. I'm sure you know more Shakespeare than I do."

"I doubt that. I wasn't the shiniest apple in the barrel either."

Percy laughed again. "That's a good one! No—I just throw around a quote or two once in a while to pretend I know what I'm talking about."

Florilyn laughed. "You are too funny, Percy! You've always got a comeback. Is there *anything* in life you take seriously?"

"Probing the Drummond psyche, are you now?"

Florilyn smiled. "I suppose I'm interested in what makes you tick."

"That's a switch."

"You've got to give a girl a chance to change, to see things more clearly. That's only fair, don't you think?"

"You're right. I suppose we've both done some changing this summer. Why are you interested in what makes me tick?"

"I don't know. Isn't it natural for people to be interested in one another?"

"Maybe so. But I don't think anyone's ever said something like that to me before. I'm not sure I know what makes me tick myself!" Percy laughed.

"There you go making a joke again!"

"It wasn't really a joke. It's the truth," rejoined Percy, then grew quiet. "Yes—there are things I take seriously. Knowing that I will see my father in a couple weeks is enough to make me somber in a hurry."

"Why?"

"My father and I haven't exactly been on the best of terms for the last several years."

"You're not eager to see him?"

"That's not it exactly. It's more. . ." Percy paused and drew in a thoughtful breath. He remained quiet for several long seconds. "I'm not sure I want it to continue the way it's been," he went on at length. "You say you've changed. I'm changing, too. I am beginning to realize that my father is a good man, an honorable man, a man of character and principle. Maybe it's time I owned up to that fact. I *want* to own up to it. I want to know him man-to-man, not as a pouty, spoiled, self-centered boy."

Florilyn took in Percy's words without reply. They struck a chord in her heart as well.

"But I didn't come out here to talk about all that," Percy added with a smile.

"What then?"

"You and I have some unfinished business."

Florilyn returned his look with a confused expression. "What do you mean?"

"Our rematch," said Percy, eyes gleaming in fun. "I want another chance to race you."

"Ah!" exclaimed Florilyn, her eyes now also lighting up. "A glutton for punishment, are you?"

"You are assuming the outcome before we saddle the horses," chided Percy playfully.

"It's *your* pride on the line," rejoined Florilyn with equal humor.

"I will risk it. My pride is equal to the task."

"Then you're on, cousin!" Floriyn laughed. "Just name the time and place."

"You are going to let *me* pick the place?"

"Why not? I'm so much faster than you, I ought to give you *some* advantage."

Percy roared with delight. "You wouldn't care to place a small wager on the outcome?" he asked.

Now it was Florilyn's turn to break out in a peal of laughter. Her merriment could be heard throughout the manor grounds. "If you are so anxious to lose your money," she said.

"I wasn't thinking of money."

"What then?"

"I don't know—what about the loser waits on the winner for a day. She obeys his every command and wish with good humor and without complaint."

Florilyn could not stop laughing at the delicious prospect. "Don't you mean—*he* obeys *her* every command?"

"My dear cousin Florilyn, I fear you seriously underestimate your opponent."

"You are on!" giggled Florilyn again.

"Then I propose as our appointed venue," said Percy, "the harbor beach at low tide."

"Why there?" said Florilyn.

"That would make it a race of pure speed," replied Percy. "It is flat, straight, no streams or logs or obstacles for you to trick me with."

Florilyn smiled. Her mood grew subdued. "That was mean of me, wasn't it? I won't do that again. All right then, the beach it is."

"Tomorrow?"

"Agreed."

"And horses?"

"Obviously, as you are the serious underdog, it is only right of me to let you select your mount."

"Then I will ride Grey Tide. And you?"

"I will have to think about it. But probably Red Rhud."

"I will check with one of my fisherman friends this afternoon," said Percy. "I will let you know the exact time of low tide."

FORTY-FOUR

The Race

*A*t two o'clock on the following afternoon, just south of the Llanfryniog harbor, a strange scene had begun to unfold. A small gathering had formed on the wide glistening sand comprised of what might be considered an odd assortment of individuals. That Lord Snowdon's son and daughter and nephew appeared at the center of the commotion might seem to indicate some kind of aristocratic sport in progress. But that the shepherd from the inland hills, Stevie Muir, stood talking to Percy Drummond, while his tiny cousin, Gwyneth Barrie, held the reins of one of the prized horses from the manor's stables, spoke of wider involvement than merely the region's blue bloods.

Somehow through that mysterious osmosis by which news and gossip circulates about a small community, word had spread that there was to be a horse race that afternoon when the tide of Tremadog Bay reached its lowest. It did not take long for the news to become the chief topic of conversation.

Thus, from the village a steady stream was now walking toward the beach. It was comprised mostly of the younger element, led by Eardley White and Chandos Gwarthegydd, who, presuming upon their encounter with Percy, let it be known to their friends that they were now personal acquaintances of the young Scot and that he had taken them into his confidence. Whatever may have been his stern words to them, they could not help liking a man of the people such as Percy had proved himself to be.

Rhawn Lorimer was, of course, on hand with Courtenay as Florilyn's moral support. After what had happened a few days before in the hills, Rhawn hadn't quite made up her mind about Percy. But on this day, owing to her fear of Gwyneth, she kept close to Courtenay's side.

A few fishermen wandered in from the harbor. The bluff at the outskirts of the village was lined with spectators who, from a higher vantage point, would command the clearest view of the proceedings.

When everything was ready, Percy gestured to Florilyn. The two walked down the beach side by side apart from the others.

"This has turned out to be a bigger shindig than I imagined," chuckled Percy. "So much for our private little race."

"How did they all find out?" asked Florilyn.

"I thought you must have told them."

"Me?" Florilyn laughed. "I thought it was you!"

"Well, no matter. They're here now. So. . .are we agreed? We'll ride south and around the stake Stevie drove into the sand at the end of the beach where the rocks begin and back here. . .then again. Down and back twice."

"Agreed." Florilyn nodded.

Percy looked his cousin in the eye then gave her a wink and a smile and extended his hand. "Good luck," he said.

"And to you," rejoined Florilyn as she shook it. "You'll need it!"

"My, but you are confident!" Percy laughed. "So. . .shall we get under way and give these people what they came for?"

They turned and walked back. While they were talking, Stevie had run a long line in the sand with his staff, stretching from water's edge up to the soft sand.

"Well done, Stevie," said Percy. "Our start and finish line—impossible to miss."

The two contestants took the reins of their horses from Gwyneth and Courtenay and mounted.

"All right, then," said Percy, "from this line down the beach and back twice. We will each have someone stand here on the line as our turning points to begin the second leg. Gwyneth, would you stand on the line for me?"

"Yes, Percy," she replied.

"Courtenay?" said Florilyn.

Her brother looked with disgust toward Gwyneth but nodded.

The contestants gently eased their mounts to the line about ten yards apart. Both horses sensed the air of excitement. Percy and Florilyn looked over and smiled at each other.

"Ready?" said Percy.

"I'm ready," replied Florilyn.

"Courtenay," said Percy, "why don't you do the honors and start us off?"

"All right," said Courtenay. "To the line then. All right. Set. . .*go!*"

The shout of his voice and Percy's excitable kick in her flanks sent Grey Tide rearing slightly. Percy barely managed to keep his seat. By the time he had Grey Tide up to a gallop, amid frantic yelling and shouting from every side, Florilyn was twenty yards ahead and flying down the beach away from him.

He bolted after her, trying desperately to remember everything Gwyneth had taught him. He raised himself in the saddle, tried to feel Grey Tide's side with his knees, and leaned forward and stroked her neck.

Florilyn glanced behind, hair flying, eyes on fire. A great laugh sounded. Percy saw the gleam in her eyes and couldn't help laughing himself to see his cousin so full of joy.

Within seconds the cries and cheers from behind them were gone. The only sound remaining was of two sets of thundering hooves flying down the hard-packed sand, throwing great wet clods up behind them.

The distance to the stake and the first turn was some six hundred yards. Florilyn reached it first. As she turned Red Rhud sharply around, she was surprised to see Percy so close behind her that Grey Tide's nose was in danger of being brushed by her rival's out-flying tail and wicked feet. Florilyn had assumed herself pulling away. But so close was she to her twin that Grey Tide needed no guidance from Percy, mud splattering his face, to negotiate the tricky turnaround. She kept her position and spun sharply around.

They emerged from the turn with but a single length separating them. Florilyn glanced around a second time as they flew back toward the harbor, filled with the exciting terror of knowing that her cousin had learned his skills well. For the first time she realized that it would take all her prowess to keep him at bay.

By the time they were halfway back to the harbor and the shouts and yells came again into their ears, Grey Tide, her front splotched with wet sand from following so long, had drawn alongside Red Rhud's midsection. The twin mares and rivals matched each other stride for stride, sharp short gasps of white air pulsing from their flared nostrils, hooves thudding in perfect rhythm, a hurricane of sand flying behind them.

On they came. Slowly the spectators backed away. As the riders came more clearly into view, with Florilyn's long auburn hair flying in a tumult around her head on the bay mare beneath her, visible on the high side of the beach, with Percy on the gray toward the sea, Gwyneth and Courtenay took up positions on the finish line some twenty yards away from each other. Still no one, save those villagers lining the bluff above, could tell who was in the lead as the two riders slowly separated and made for their human turning posts.

With the yelling and cheering at a frenzy, they reached the line in a dead heat.

But Florilyn's experience told in the turn. She wheeled Red Rhud so tightly around Courtenay where he stood that he gave the mare's rump a swat as his sister flew back the way she had come.

Percy came in too tight to Gwyneth and could not hold the turn. This time Grey Tide had no one to follow and swung much too wide.

Unable to correct his error, Percy and his mount drifted many yards past Gwyneth and toward the water line. By the time he recovered and was bearing again southward, Florilyn had widened her lead again to fifteen yards.

As he circled around to straight, Percy glanced back to where Gwyneth stood unmoved. Her face was calm, placid, serene in the midst of the roar around her.

His eyes met hers. The sounds around him ceased. Though a hundred shouting spectators were screaming and exhorting him on, Percy heard nothing.

With Grey Tide thundering beneath him, he entered a dream world. . .a world of silence. Out of its center, two tiny orbs of deepest blue drew him into themselves.

The lips of his tiny friend were moving. And he knew what she was saying to him. *"Be one with Grey Tide. . .feel her rhythm. . .relax and let her run."*

She brought her hands together and held out her elbows as she had shown him a dozen times. Gently she rocked up and down with the fluid motion she had explained to him so often.

He had forgotten the most important principle of all—be one with the horse, let the rhythm of his body flow into hers. The movement of her arms and elbows reminded him that Grey Tide must feel nothing.

Then he saw on Gwyneth's lips the words, *"You will win."*

He glanced to the front. Suddenly his brain was again assaulted by the urgency of the race. There was Florilyn increasing her lead!

His instincts were to kick and yell and try all the harder. But Gwyneth's words remained. He forced himself to remain calm. He leaned forward, relaxed, and felt himself beginning to rise and fall in harmony with the powerful beast beneath him.

Moving lightly and rhythmically, immediately Percy saw the gap between them begin to shrink. Grey Tide again came even with Red Rhud's tail.

Percy had learned the lesson from his ill-fated turn around Gwyneth.

He glanced ahead. The stake was some two hundred yards away and slightly up the beach from their present heading. He guided Grey Tide gently to the left then urged her alongside Red Rhud's flank.

Florilyn glanced to her left with a grin full of competitive fire. But intent merely to keep ahead, she did not perceive Percy's strategy until it was too late.

The two horses reached the stake side by side. This time, however, it was Percy who clung to the post. Having thoughtlessly allowed him to overtake on the inside, Florilyn was forced to swing wide.

Keeping some reserve of power for the last, Grey Tide came out of the turn and thundered for home with Percy half a length in the lead. He did not relinquish it.

To exultant cries from the watching throng, Percy crossed Stevie's line two and a half lengths in front of his cousin.

FORTY-FIVE

The Accident

*E*xultant and smiling, Percy reined in and wheeled around as Gwyneth, Stevie, Eardley White, and Chandos Gwarthegydd, and half the youth population of Llanfryniog came running in jubilation to surround him with congratulatory shouts and cries. Whatever some may have thought of him two months before, he had reached exalted status now. Suddenly the young Scot, who had so recently come into their midst as a stranger, had, in a few exciting minutes, become a folk hero who had bested the daughter of the viscount.

No one was left to console Florilyn in her defeat but Courtenay and Rhawn Lorimer. And it was true that Florilyn had begun to change. It was equally true that such a beginning was admirable. Those of the village who considered her snooty and arrogant would in time come to alter their opinion.

Alas, it would not be on this day they would do so. For the demon of pride is neither easily nor permanently exorcised. As long as one remains in the flesh, it may rear its head, and violently, at a moment's notice.

The instant Florilyn realized that Percy had stolen a march on her at the far end of the beach, grabbing the post and forcing her wide, all the former antagonism toward him surged back upon her in a wave.

Seeing the back of Grey Tide's powerful haunches pulling away down the beach had enraged her. The pleasant banter between cousins and friends from minutes earlier vanished in the wind.

Crossing the line and realizing that she had been soundly trounced in full view of the entire community, the rage of her brother came rushing to the fore as if it were a familial curse. It possessed her with the evil spirit of anger and revenge.

By now a considerable crowd had gathered on the beach in a tumult over the exciting finish. Hardly slowing as she flew into its midst, Florilyn wheeled recklessly around. Heedless of whoever might get in her way, she powered her way toward Percy, breathing fire and shrieking irrational accusations. Men, women, and boys scurried from her path, for the glint in her eyes was dangerous.

A moment later, only Percy and Gwyneth remained on the sand ahead of her. Stevie was leading Grey Tide away, sweat pouring from her flanks, to calm her down.

Percy was gazing down with a tender smile of affection for his teacher. He had just thanked her for the reminder at the halfway point.

Florilyn saw the look that passed between them and apprehended all. The treachery against her had been Gwyneth's doing!

She flew toward them in a white fury. "You little urchin!" she cried. "What business is it of yours to interfere?"

Startled and shocked, Percy leaped aside.

Thinking Percy in danger, and for once in a position to help *him*, Gwyneth stepped in front of the horse's path. What had she to fear? All the horses at the manor were her friends. She stood calmly then lifted her hand to the charging animal. "Hello, Red Rhud," she said in a quiet voice. "It's your friend, Gwyneth. You don't need to be afraid."

Seeing the tiny girl in its path, the horse reared. Florilyn screamed and pulled back on the reins. She managed to keep herself in the saddle, but not without a frantic rearing and pawing and whinnying from the excitable and terrified horse.

When Florilyn found herself again secure on Red Rhud's back,

Gwyneth lay unconscious on the sand, blood dripping down the side of her forehead onto her cheek where one of the flailing hooves had grazed her above the ear. Staring down at what she had done, Florilyn's eyes widened in shock.

Percy came yelling toward her and pulled her from the horse in a rage. She hardly heard a word of the dreadful things he screamed in her face. He could only be kept from hitting her by Courtenay hurrying forward and pulling him away.

Meanwhile, Stevie rushed in, scooped Gwyneth into his arms, and ran for Grannie's cottage. She would know best what was to be done.

FORTY-SIX

Grannie's Cottage

*T*he crowd, so recently jubilant, was dead silent. No sound was heard as they watched Stevie bear the limp form in his arms, the white-haired head drooped bleeding over his elbow.

When Percy came to himself in a cold sweat, tears streaming from his eyes, the crowd was slowly moving away from the scene. Courtenay had had the presence of mind to secure both horses and was leading them away with Florilyn clinging to him like a child.

Percy staggered away to Grannie's. Stevie was already inside when he arrived. Gwyneth lay on Grannie's bed and was being tended by the only hands in the village to which the imperative ministration of love would be added to whatever physical succor they could provide. Someone had gone to the doctor's, but he was away and his wife did not expect him till after tea that evening. Someone had also run to the mine to find the girl's father.

The crowd slowly and silently followed through the streets, with many quiet murmurings and shaking of heads and clicking of tongues. None dared venture too close, though the cluster of curious onlookers gradually filled the lanes nearest Grannie's.

A pall set in over the entire village. Talk gradually resumed. Much quiet conversation hinted that something like this had been bound to happen to the girl because of her peculiar ways. No good came to those who dabbled in witchcraft.

On the other side were abundant speculations on the part of those who said that the viscount's two offspring had never been any good and that this was the inevitable result. *Would his daughter hang?* wondered not a few. Not with Styles Lorimer as magistrate, shook the heads of others. As everyone knew, he and the viscount cared more about their reputations than the law.

Eventually even Courtenay and Rhawn, with Florilyn stumbling between them in a daze, followed, though the talk about their fathers did not come within their hearing. They did their best to keep Courtenay's disconsolate sister from breaking down altogether. As they passed, the crowd parted noiselessly. Whatever may have been little Gwyneth's acquaintance with the forces of evil, there were a hundred eyewitnesses to what Florilyn had done. She was suddenly a pariah in their midst. They backed away with looks of revulsion, as if she were a leper.

In truth, it is doubtful that Florilyn meant to harm anyone. She was full of mischief and petty jealousies. But she was not an evil girl, only an immature and feisty one. It now remained to be determined what her outburst of temper was capable of making of her.

After some time, Grannie had Gwyneth comfortable and was wiping her face with a wet cloth. The wound was bandaged and the bleeding stopped. Grannie was speaking and singing softly to her with unintelligible words. Percy and Stevie sat at the bedside.

The time since the accident had calmed Percy from his fierce explosion on the beach. With Gwyneth's life hanging by a thread, in a vicarious sense, sixteen-year-old Percival Drummond's brief existence had also passed before the inner eyes of his soul. In the short time that had elapsed, he had grown still inside. Inexplicably, again the image of his father rose before his mind's eye. He knew his father's profession often required him to sit as he was sitting now, beside bedsides where death approached.

How did his father handle it? What did he say? What did he do?

Percy knew the answer. His father would pray. His father would speak to the grieving loved ones about God's fatherhood, about God's goodness, telling them that God's love covered all, even those things they could not understand. One of his favorite sayings was, "God is immeasurably more the lover of our loved ones than we are. And because He is their Father, He sometimes takes one of His children into His heart before we think it is time."

Some impulse caused Percy to glance toward the door where it stood open to the street.

There stood Florilyn in the light of the doorway. A look of abject horror was on her face. Tears stained her pale cheeks. As if in a trance, she slowly stumbled into the darkened cottage where none of the other villagers would have dared venture.

At the sight of her eyes, again rose the image of his father in Percy's mind. His father not only spoke of God's love, God's fatherhood, God's goodness, but he spoke of God's *forgiveness* and healing. He was always talking about reconciliation, between mankind and God, between friends, between parents and children. Reconciliation and healing—they were his father's constant themes. "If God's forgiveness is total," he had heard his father say, "can our forgiveness toward one another be less?"

In the second or two that passed as Percy stared into Florilyn's forlorn, desperate, tormented eyes, he knew that *this* was a moment for the healing and forgiveness his father spoke of. He knew exactly what his father would do at such a time. It was a moment to let the fatherhood of God bathe the wounds of a broken humanity with the balm of its forgiving love. Slowly he rose.

"Percy," whimpered Florilyn like a lost child, beginning to crumble. "I am so sorry. . . . I didn't mean—" She began to collapse.

Percy hurried to her as she fell into his arms. She burst into sobs of bitter remorse. Percy held her tight, and she wept like a baby.

FORTY-SEVEN

The Vigil

Codnor Barrie arrived an hour later.

By then, much of the crowd had returned to their homes. Percy went outside to see if Courtenay was anywhere about. Finding him, he asked him to bring a buggy from the manor for his sister. She was resting, he said, but he doubted she would be able to walk farther than to the cottage door.

Barrie went back to his home to get a few things then returned to spend the night on Grannie's floor. Stevie also returned home. The way was considerably longer and the dusk was well advanced by the time he again walked into Grannie's where he also intended to remain for the night.

It was nearly dark by the time Percy and Florilyn were again at last in their beds at Westbrooke Manor.

Percy slept but fitfully and was on his way back to the village the next morning shortly after dawn. He arrived at Grannie's cottage to find no change.

Under the circumstances, it was the best news they could hope for.

Florilyn did not leave her room for three days.

Dr. Rotherham examined Gwyneth and said that there was not much he could do for her beyond wait. He did not exactly couch it in such words, but the gist of his report to Codnor Barrie was essentially that his daughter would eventually wake up in the presence of her earthly father or her heavenly Father. No one at this point could tell which.

The bedside vigil of the small praying family continued.

On the fourth day, eyes drawn in spite of so much sleep, Florilyn accompanied Percy to Llanfryniog. She had hardly eaten since the race. Her cheeks were sunken, her whole face haggard and pale. The others received her kindly. Like true Christians, they knew that Florilyn's suffering was even greater than their own. Their compassion went out to her, and they took the suffering, foolish, immature girl to their hearts. When Codnor Barrie took her in his arms and stroked her hair as if she were his own daughter, Florilyn wept great tears of cleansing such as had never flowed from her eyes all the days of her life.

Thereafter, Florilyn insisted on sitting as much as she could at Gwyneth's side with the tiny white limp hand resting in hers. On and off she wept. At first her tears rose out of the well of her own guilt. As time went on, however, they became tears of repentance. The change may not seem like much to those who understand neither guilt nor repentance. But there is all the difference in the world in the eyes of Him who would have people's tears turn them to Him, that they might grow into His humble sons and daughters.

In a strange way, being at Gwyneth's side gave Florilyn hope. She began to eat and drink and regain her strength.

Then came a day when Percy could think of nothing but that he was soon scheduled to leave on the northbound coach. All day he and Florilyn took turns at Gwyneth's side, helping Grannie with tea and food for the small band, for Gwyneth's father and Stevie remained with them when not at their work.

A few of the more stouthearted and compassionate villagers began coming by, reminded of old friendship and at last laying aside foolish aversions. They remembered how Gwyneth always returned good for evil and how often Grannie had come to the aid of one or another in time of sickness. Some of these, as women do, brought food. Before many days, there was more on hand than would have been needed to feed twenty people.

As the day came closer, the burden of his impending departure weighed heavier and heavier on Percy's heart. How could he leave without knowing whether Gwyneth would live or die?

Evening came. Still there was no change.

After a simple supper, knowing that Gwyneth was well looked after, Percy went out into the warm evening. He walked through the village, up the plateau, and slowly made his way along the promontory toward Mochras Head.

How quickly the two months had flown by, he thought. He had changed more than he would ever have dreamed possible. What different thoughts and emotions floated through his brain as the still and peaceful evening settled over him.

He recalled his first night here, how angry the peacefulness of the country had made him. Even the crickets had angered him, he recalled with a smile. It was earlier now than on that night. The multitude of crickets had not yet taken over the moonglow of the countryside, though a few could be heard warming up for their nightly concert.

The sky over the sea showed radiant from horizon to apex in the fiery shades of gold, magenta, and violet he had come to associate with the Welsh coast. Perhaps the same colors radiated over the slate rooftops of Glasgow, but he had never noticed them. Never again would he look at a sunset and not recall this place with longing reminders of these weeks now drawing to a close.

Thinking of Gwyneth, he continued over the stream and to her special place at the edge of the bluff. Forgetting her father's three-foot rule, he sat down and let his legs dangle over the edge of the promontory as he stared out to sea. Slowly but inexorably, the giant yellow orb sank into the distant waters then sent up its flaming aftershoots far into the fading blue of the sky. He was still sitting unmoved half an hour later, until all shades of the gorgeous display had turned to purples and blacks and the rising moon began to exert its strength over the coming darkness.

At first he thought the changes had been caused by his new appreciation for the natural world that Gwyneth had helped him to see. Then he wondered if it was simply being away from the city, away from his parents and the unspoken pressures of youth and school and peers. Then he found himself thinking it must be the country itself. Everything was different here, the people, customs, sights, smells, foods, language, song.

Slowly a deeper truth began to dawn on his consciousness. He saw that the changes did not originate from any of these. Nature and the country and Gwyneth and new experiences were all but echos of *another* Voice speaking into his heart.

At last he knew whose that voice was. All these influences had come speaking to him from the voice of his father's God. And he knew by his father's example how to approach the Father of them both.

Percy backed away from the edge of the bluff and slowly sank to his knees in the soft grass.

Thank You, God, he prayed silently, *for bringing me here that You might speak into my heart. Thank You for the many ways You revealed Yourself and for opening my ears to hear. Thank You for Gwyneth,* he added as his voice choked, *and for all the ways she helped open my eyes to see You.*

He paused. *And thank You for my father, too,* he added. *Thank You that he did not give up on me either. I know now that he loves me. Give me the courage to keep growing, even back home, where it may be most difficult of all.*

Slowly he rose and set off back down toward the village.

He was at peace with himself. But he knew he could not leave Wales with Gwyneth's condition in doubt.

FORTY-EIGHT

A Dream and a Prayer

*B*y the time Percy returned to the cottage, it was nearly dark. Stevie had gone home to be with his mother for the night. Grannie and Gwyneth's father were sitting at the table in the kitchen. Florilyn dozed in the chair beside the bed.

All the way down from Mochras Head, Percy's thoughts revolved around little Gwyneth Barrie. He recalled every conversation he had had with her through the summer. He remembered fondly all her special places. Over all hovered the ghostly, mystical, otherworldly image of her singing to the animals beside the lake in the mountains.

He had not put it into so many words before this night. Suddenly it occurred to him that her peculiarities, her mysterious origins, her utter simplicity and humility—did they all have an astounding yet somehow plausible explanation? Perhaps she truly *wasn't* of this world....

Might she actually be...an *angel*?

Had she always been an angel? Perhaps she was now simply being called back to the true home of her origin.

With such thoughts swirling through his brain, Percy entered the cottage. He walked through the kitchen, nodded with a smile to Codnor and Grannie, then continued to the bedside.

Florilyn heard his step, woke, and looked up with a wan smile.

"Any change?"

Florilyn shook her head.

Percy sat down in the empty chair beside her. With the mood from his walk still imbuing him with a peaceful sense of presence, Florilyn glanced over in astonishment as he broke into audible prayer. "Oh God," he said aloud, "wherever she is right now. . .bring Gwyneth back. If she is truly one of Your angels, let us have her yet for a little while longer."

Florilyn saw that he was weeping. One of her hands still on the bed with Gwyneth's, she reached across and gently laid the other on Percy's arm.

A few minutes more they sat in silence. Percy recovered himself and breathed in deeply. He glanced at Florilyn and smiled an embarrassed smile.

"I've never heard you pray before," she said.

"I never have prayed out loud before." Percy smiled. "Well, except when I was a boy at bedtime. I've never done anything like that in my life."

He grew thoughtful. "Do you remember that first night when I was with your family at dinner, when you asked me if I believed in heaven and hell?"

Florilyn nodded.

"I don't know about that," said Percy. "But I think maybe I believe in God more than I realized at the time."

Slowly he rose and stood at the bedside gazing down at the pale face that was even whiter than the pillow it rested upon. All at once the features did not look so young or childlike. The expression on the face was ageless. . .like an angel's. Percy bent down and gently kissed the white forehead.

A moment more. . .

A gasp sounded from Florilyn's lips.

"*Percy!*" she breathed, her voice soft, hopeful, frightened, and full of wonder. She began to rise from her chair.

He saw it now. A tiny movement around the eyes. . .then a fluttering.

Slowly the lids began to open. Out from between them again peeped the eyes of heaven's blue!

"Percy," whispered the tiny lips from the bed as Gwyneth gazed up at the face staring down at her. "I hoped it would be you I saw when I woke up."

Heart pounding, head exploding for joy, Percy struggled desperately to remain calm. "You knew you would wake up?" he said with great effort, his voice husky and blinking hard.

"Of course," replied Gwyneth simply.

"Were you dreaming?"

"No, I was with my mother. She is everything I knew she would be, Percy. But I couldn't wake up until you prayed for me."

"You were waiting. . .for me to pray for you?"

"I'm not sure. It was dreamy. Maybe I was dreaming, because it was like being surrounded by a cloud of white. I think God was waiting for you to pray for me so I could wake up. But He was waiting so that your praying for me could wake *you* up, too."

For the first time, she now saw Florilyn standing at Percy's side. "Hello, Miss Florilyn," she said. "What are you doing here? I thought you were afraid of Grannie."

"Not anymore," Florilyn sobbed, sniffly and teary.

"I am sorry I made your horse rear," said Gwyneth. "I hope you were not hurt."

"Oh, you dear girl!" exclaimed Florilyn, able to contain herself no longer. She bent down and kissed Gwyneth on the cheek.

"Why are you crying, Miss Florilyn?"

"I am just happy that you are awake."

The voices from the bedside had been soft, but gradually their increasing volume and animation drifted into the hearing of the father and great-aunt in the kitchen. They realized that three voices were coming from the adjacent room, not two. They jumped up and rushed to the bedside.

FORTY-NINE

End of the Summer

*T*he morning came early.

Percy readied himself, said good-bye to all the servants, then, in as cheerful a manner as he could manage, to Courtenay.

Florilyn had been hanging back.

Percy walked toward her. "You will check on Gwyneth?" he said.

"I promise—every day."

"Let me know if there is any change. I think she will be fine. She already seems her normal self again."

Florilyn nodded. She smiled at her cousin with an expression that contained a world of meaning then stepped forward to hug him.

He returned her embrace affectionately.

"Good-bye, Percy," said Florilyn. "There is too much to try to say, so I will say nothing. I will never forget this summer."

"Nor I," rejoined Percy.

His aunt Katherine gave Percy a tender hug. "I hope you will visit us again," she whispered softly in his ear.

"I would like that," replied Percy, stepping back with a smile.

To his astonishment, he saw tears in the woman's eyes. She smiled, but it was a smile tinged with sadness.

"Well, let us be off, my boy!" boomed the viscount, trying with a little too much effort to counter the emotionally dense atmosphere of the occasion threatened by the faces of his wife and daughter and two or three of the servants. "We don't want that coach leaving without you, or you'll miss your train!"

The two left the manor for Llanfryniog. By the time they arrived, the thrice-weekly coach stood in front of the small inn, its four horses snorting and prancing impatiently.

There also stood Gwyneth, hanging back in the shadows of the building. She looked none the worse for wear. The only lasting reminder of recent events was a bandage between her ear and forehead, mostly covered by her wild crop of white hair.

Percy caught her eye.

Her lips parted in a radiant smile of innocent love. She would cry, too, but not until he was out of sight. In the event he never saw her again, her friend from Glasgow must remember her with a look of happiness on her face.

Percy's two bags were hoisted above. He and his uncle shook hands. The viscount managed some stiff words about his being welcome any time.

Percy climbed inside the coach and closed the door.

Only after the viscount stood back did Gwyneth now run forward.

"Get back, girl!" yelled the driver as he climbed up onto his box. "Don't you see these great horses? They'll trample you to death!"

"They won't hurt *me*, sir," she said sweetly.

Even at the sound of her voice, the agitated horses calmed. The driver muttered something and grabbed the reins.

Gwyneth walked calmly to the side of the coach where Percy sat looking out the window. She held up a small parcel wrapped in paper. "I baked you another tea cake, Percy," she said. "I didn't want you to get hungry."

"Thank you, Gwyneth," he said. "I shall think of you with every bite. If we stop for tea," he added, "I shall eat it with tea. . .as it is supposed to be eaten."

"Good-bye, Percy," she said. Her eyes seemed bluer than he had ever seen them.

"Good-bye, Gwyneth."

She stepped slowly back.

The driver gave a shout, and the coach lurched forward. Percy continued to wave through the open window.

There stood the receding forms of the great man of the region with his hand in the air. Several paces in front of him a girl with hair of white waved her own tiny hand. Slowly the coach disappeared from their view.

Viscount Lord Snowdon cast on the child a curious look.

Gwyneth smiled at him then walked away along the street as Westbrooke returned to his buggy.

Now at last came tears. Gwyneth did not even stop at Grannie's but continued the slow walk up the moor to her home, alone with her thoughts. She spent the afternoon with her animals.

Gwyneth's friends felt her sadness. Their mood remained subdued for two days.

FIFTY

Home in Glasgow

*E*dward and Mary Drummond saw a different look on their son's face the moment he stepped off the train when they greeted him on the platform of the Glasgow station. They little suspected the cause. They had to admit, however, that his pleasant and cheerful manner was a welcome surprise.

Percy had been due home for the fall session of school. It would be the last session expected of him. What would become of their son when it was completed, neither mother nor father had any idea. When his plans began to become more apparent, they would be in for the shock of their lives.

They had received but one curious note during their son's absence, from Edward's sister, saying that Percy's presence was full of unexpected surprises. What exactly Katherine meant by the odd phrase, they had no idea.

Being a few days later to arrive than previously planned, as he had notified them by telegram, Percy set about his studies in earnest almost the next day. He subsequently remained home every evening buried in his books. No mention was ever made of his former friendships or activities on the streets.

About two months later, shortly after his seventeenth birthday,

Percy sought his father in his study. He had been thinking through the interview ever since arriving home. But it had taken time to collect his thoughts and summon the courage to do what he knew he had to do. . .and *wanted* to do. He also had wanted to wait long enough to be certain he would not fall into old patterns.

"May I talk with you, Father?" he asked. His voice betrayed anxiety. Gone entirely was the arrogance he might have displayed a short time earlier.

"Of course, Percy," replied his father. "Come in. . .have a seat."

"If you don't mind, what I have to say I think is best said on my feet."

The vicar nodded.

Percy glanced toward the ground, then looked up again and drew in a deep breath. "I, uh. . .I don't exactly know how to say this," he began. "It's not an easy thing to do, but. . .well, I've come to apologize."

Still his father waited, listening patiently and with deep love in his eyes for this son who was about to become a man.

"I, uh. . .I've been nothing more than a fool these past couple of years," Percy went on. "Now that I look back on it, I can't imagine what I was thinking. You once asked me what kind of evil spirit had taken over inside me, and I can't think of any other explanation. When I try to recall exactly *why* I was so angry and full of resentment, I cannot think of a single good reason. You and Mother are the best and kindest and most loving parents I could hope to have. You gave me everything. You trained me well. You are good and godly people. What I was thinking to allow myself to become so alienated from you, I cannot imagine. I am embarrassed and sorrier than I can say for what I must have put you through. Yet you kept loving me, even in your occasional outbursts. You were only angry for what I was doing to myself. I see that now. You would have been wrong not to be angry for what I was doing. You saw how destructive it was to me."

The father's eyes filled. His breath grew shaky.

"When you sent me to Wales," Percy continued, "I began looking at things differently. A new set of eyes opened inside me—maybe a little like the second sight Uncle Roderick would tell me about on our rides together," he added, chuckling briefly. "I suppose being around Courtenay and Florilyn caused me to think about what kind of person I was becoming. In all honesty, Father, Courtenay just isn't very nice. He wasn't nice to me. He isn't nice to his mother. Maybe I saw more of myself reflected in him than I wanted to admit. Florilyn was the same at first. But the most curious thing happened. It was almost as if she began to change along with me. I still don't quite understand it exactly. But by the end of the summer, we had actually begun to form a friendship. We had an unfortunate row at the end. But that got patched up before I left. I actually think I miss her."

He paused, and his lips parted in a thin, reflective smile. "I had my ups and downs," he said. "At first I hated the country. I vowed not to let myself change. But in the end, the summer helped wake me up to the fact that I was making myself into a person of a certain sort, too, just like Courtenay, and that maybe I ought to give the matter more serious attention."

Again he paused. Another smile came across his face. "And I met a precious little girl there who helped me notice things I hadn't been in the habit of seeing before, a girl who loved animals and loved nature. She was tiny, almost fairylike, yet completely normal in every other way. Actually she wasn't so very much younger than me—three or four years, something like that. But her size made her appear younger than she really was. And she possessed such an astonishing maturity to see God's world in wondrous ways. I almost thought at times that she might be an angel."

"She sounds like a remarkable girl," said his father softly.

"She was. She cared about me, too. I know you and Mother care about me. But I suppose it sometimes takes somebody new to make you see what a wonderful thing that is and how grateful we should be when we are loved. She helped me see God's creation in new ways. I know you have taught me many of the same things through the years. I am embarrassed now to realize that it took somebody else to open my eyes to them, but. . .well, I suppose that's how it was."

He paused and exhaled a deep sigh then resumed. "Anyway, one of the things I feel I need especially to say to you, Father," Percy continued, "is that I respect and honor you for the man you are, for what you give to the people of the church, and for what you gave to me all those years that I was too blind to see until now. I am sorry. I ask you to forgive me. I don't think I will be quite so blind ever again."

Before Percy finished speaking, the poor vicar was on his feet, tears streaming down his face, covering the distance between them in two great strides. The next instant, father and son were in one another's arms, Percy weeping freely and without shame.

"I'm so sorry, Father. Do you forgive me?"

"You have *always* been forgiven, Percy, my son," whispered Edward. "The forgiveness has existed within my heart all along. Yet to complete the transaction, it was necessary for you to *ask*, that I might give it to you. So I *do* give it to you now. Of course you are forgiven for anything and everything. I love you."

"Thank you, Father," said Percy softly. "I love you, too."

A moment more they stood then gradually fell away.

"There is one more thing I need to say," said Percy. "Or, I should say, something I want to ask."

"Anything," replied the father, taking his chair again as he fumbled with his handkerchief at his eyes.

Percy took the seat his father had previously offered. He leaned forward then took a deep breath. "I have been thinking about my future," he began. "I have squandered the years when I should have been working and studying. I realize it is a great deal to ask. . .but might you be willing to help me catch back up on my studies and make up for my poor marks and help me prepare for the university? When we were out on our last ride together, Uncle Roderick suggested I try to make a go of it. I think I'd like to try."

"Of course, Percy. Nothing could delight me more."

"I know I will be a year, maybe two behind others my age. As it stands now, I could not even get into the university—"

"I know people that might be able to make a difference in that regard."

"I don't want strings pulled for me, Father," said Percy. "I want to work hard and improve my marks—"

"We shall find you a tutor."

"Perhaps I might enroll in one of the grammar schools to prepare for the bursary competition. I do not want to attend university until I have earned that right and until I am ready."

"What is it you think you want to study toward?" asked the vicar, having no idea what was coming.

"I haven't really settled on anything definite yet," replied Percy. "I don't have to make any hasty decisions."

He paused. An almost sheepish expression came over his face. "I know it may be hard for you to believe," Percy added after a moment, "but actually. . .I have been thinking of possibly following *your* own footsteps."

"Well, Percy," replied Drummond, whose heart swelled with pride and his eyes filled with tears to hear his son speak so, "in answer to your question—yes, I shall do all that is in my power to help you. . .if it means tutoring you myself!"

Part Two

Return Visit

1870

FIFTY-ONE

The University of the North

*T*ime is a curious commodity for the young. No clock's minute hand moves more slowly than one being watched by a bored and listless youth with time on his hands.

For the youth in love, however, or the young man filled with dreams and vision and energy and plans, time races by, and never a glance is sent toward the clock on the wall. The chimes of its hours seem to ring out every five minutes with the pressing reminder that there is not *enough* time. Caught up in the moment, hours, weeks, months race by in a blur.

Truly for the young at heart, a day is as a thousand years, a thousand years as a day. Youth's present stands as an eternal now of existence—there is no past, no future.

Percival Drummond's suddenly altered outlook on life was all-consuming. Quickly the eventful months in Wales receded as a dream into his memory. He did not *forget*. He would never forget. It was a good dream, a wondrous dream. Scarce an hour, certainly not a day passed that he did not think about Wales and smile with the reminder of those individuals who had made it such a pivotal time of new focus for him.

But as a result of those brief months, he now had new goals and dreams. Those ambitions drove him in a way he had never been driven before. He had no leisure to dwell on the past. The future beckoned.

Within a year of his return home from Snowdonia, he had applied himself so diligently to his studies that, with a little of his father's influence, but no more than Percy was comfortable with, he had so rapidly advanced ahead of his peers and beyond all expectations of his incredulous instructors, that shortly after his eighteenth birthday, having spent the summer of 1868 in an intensive preparatory program, he had been accepted to continue his studies at the University of Aberdeen the following year. His acceptance for the fall term, however, was predicated on yet another summer of hard work, in the great northern seaport itself, in a rigorous program for incoming Bajan, or first-year, students whose educational resumes were not quite as thorough as the university preferred to see.

Edward, Mary, and Percival Drummond traveled to Aberdeen together in May of that year to get Percy settled into his new lodgings for the summer and following term.

He still had not settled on a career. His initial enthusiasm for the pastorate had, if not waned, been tempered by the very practical question whether he would indeed be temperamentally suited, as he had said, to follow in his father's footsteps. Nothing could have pleased Edward Drummond more. Yet he desired the best for Percy over whatever gratification he might feel by having a son in the ministry. He therefore encouraged Percy to explore a wide range of options. He put to him the very questions he had forced upon himself at the same crossroads of his own life—*Is this truly what God wants me to do?* and *Is this how I can best serve Him with my life?*

Father and son continued to discuss the matter at length. Many thoughtful and personal letters passed between Aberdeen and Glasgow.

Percy's studies in the great northern university began in earnest in the fall of 1869. They remained so demanding that he hardly had time to think of anything else. By the end of the term, he and his father were discussing both law and engineering as alternate potential career choices. Percy found both possibilities intriguing ones.

As he began to contemplate his prospects for the upcoming summer prior to his second term, the first in two years in which he would not have required schooling to look forward to, reminders of Snowdonia drifted into his consciousness.

The song of Wales crept out of hiding and began singing again to his soul.

FIFTY-TWO

Westbrooke Manor Again

*I*t hardly seemed possible that three years had passed since Percy Drummond's eventful visit to North Wales. Life-changing it had indeed been.

At nineteen, as he now looked back on his existence leading up to that fateful time, his heart overflowed with gratitude for his father's courage to take such strong action on his behalf.

As he sat on the coach bouncing over the countryside toward Llanfryniog, how very different were the thoughts going through his brain from that day three years earlier when he and his father had jostled along this same road in chilly silence.

He remembered that first awkward encounter with his aunt Katherine and uncle Roderick. He thought he would be so bored in Wales. As it turned out, his memories of the coast of Gwynedd were among the most wonderful of his life.

He did not have as long this time as before—a mere three weeks. Then he would have to hurry north to begin a tutoring assignment in Aberdeen. But he determined to make the most of what time he had.

It would be interesting to see whether his cousins had changed. Reports had reached them that Courtenay had just completed his second year at Oxford and had not been home in all those two years. He had only preceded him to Wales by a couple of weeks. And Florilyn—he hardly knew what to expect from her. Would she be the old Florilyn or the new Florilyn, the tempestuous and self-centered girl of his first meeting three years ago or the girl who had begun to show signs of sensitivity and compassion?

Actually the invitation from his uncle a month ago, coinciding with Percy's own thoughts of another visit south, came as something of a surprise. He should think having his son home would be sufficient diversion for the viscount. As he fell to reflecting on his uncle Roderick, however, Percy realized what an enigma the man was. It was not until he was home in Glasgow after his previous visit—of course by then he was beginning to see *many* things differently—that he began to realize that he had grown genuinely fond of his uncle during his sojourn in his home.

Perhaps he felt sorry for him. It was not difficult to see that he was more or less alienated from many of those around him—wife, son, daughter, tenants. The origin of the tension that existed within the man was difficult to identify. At one moment he could be so impulsive, the next indecisive. Nor did closer inspection fail to reveal some lingering mystery that seemed to hover over his uncle's countenance like a far-off dream that nothing in his present circumstances appeared sufficient to account for.

Perhaps all these factors explained why Percy occasionally had the odd sensation, though he had been young at the time of his visit, that his uncle was attempting to reach out to him more than he was capable of to his own son or daughter.

Percy stepped from the coach in front of Mistress Chattan's inn and glanced around with an enormous feeling of satisfaction. It was all so familiar again!

He hardly had a chance to reflect on the sight of the main street or fill his lungs with the crisp, tangy sea air before a jubilant cry pierced his eardrums.

"Percy!"

He turned to see his cousin Florilyn rushing toward him from a waiting buggy across the street. She flew squealing to him, nearly knocking him over by her embrace.

"My, oh my!" laughed Percy, hugging her tight. He took a step back, placed his hands on her two shoulders, and looked her over from a considerably higher vantage point than before. "That is the most affectionate greeting I've had from anyone in years! Is it really you, my little Florilyn? When did you become a woman? Gosh, you are beautiful!"

Florilyn laughed in delight, though her face reddened with the compliment.

In truth, as Florilyn sat in the buggy with her mother and had seen the southbound coach roll up and stop in front of the inn, a sudden wave of timidity swept through her. What if Percy didn't remember her?

That was absurd, she told herself—of course he would remember! But what if he was. . .*different*. . .aloof. . .sophisticated? What if he had no use for her now? Courtenay had been *so* changed when he arrived two weeks ago. He hardly spoke to any of them, just sulked around moodily and acted as if he were better than everyone else. Being away at university had changed him. What if it had changed Percy? What if he—horrible thought!—was like Courtenay? She didn't think she could bear it.

As such reflections swirled through her brain, she saw a great lanky youth step onto the street. For a second or two she wasn't sure she recognized him. The young man was so tall! He appeared much older than she expected. He looked so dashing in the dark blue suit. Was it really. . .*him*?

Florilyn hesitated.

Then came a slight turn of the head. A breeze caught the corner of the light brown crop of hair in just the right way. It was all the recognition she needed.

Florilyn was out of the buggy bounding toward him the next moment. With the sound of his voice, all uncertainty vanished. He was still Percy!

True, the voice was deeper, more self-assured, no longer the voice of a boy on the threshold of manhood but of a youth well advanced toward it. But it was a voice that had lost none of its humor.

"I almost wasn't sure it was you," she said, "until I heard you speak. You're so tall!"

"What about you?" rejoined Percy. "You've put on two or three inches."

"You must have put on four or six! I think you're taller than Courtenay now. He will be so jealous."

"That's all I need!" Percy laughed.

"And you're just as funny as ever!"

"I'm still waiting for an answer to my question," said Percy.

"What question?"

"When did you become so stunningly beautiful?"

Again Florilyn laughed. This time she could not hide her embarrassment. "Maybe at the same time you became such a handsome man," she replied.

"Touché! A good one—you got me there." He laughed. "I can see that I had better not pester you about being beautiful, though I must say. . .you really are! Is that your mother with you?" he asked, glancing across the street.

"Yes, it's her."

Percy ran across and poked his head inside the covered buggy. "Aunt Katherine!" he said, leaning in and giving her a warm hug. "It is wonderful to see you again. You look well."

"And you, Percy," said his aunt. "Welcome again to Wales! Roderick would have come as well but got tied up with something or another. He will be so pleased to see you. He has been talking about your coming every day."

Inwardly Percy hoped his uncle wasn't doing so around Courtenay. "Just let me get my bags," he added and ran back to the coach.

Five minutes later they were bouncing out of town, Florilyn at the reins, Percy seated between her and her mother.

"I can't believe I am really here again!" said Percy. "Everything looks the same. I can't wait to explore everywhere—go riding and walk the beach. . .everything!"

Katherine laughed at his enthusiasm. "Are you sure three weeks will be enough?"

"No, it won't! Unfortunately, it's all I've got. The opportunity to tutor two young boys for the summer came up in Aberdeen. The pay was too good to turn down."

"Then we will go riding every day," said Florilyn.

"That sounds good to me."

"You will be interested in Roderick's latest project," said Katherine. "He is building new stables."

"*He* is building them?" asked Percy in surprise.

"He is having them built, I should say. He designed the structure and is supervising the construction."

"What is the purpose? Have you added more horses?"

"Daddy's going to raise race horses," said Florilyn enthusiastically.

"Really!"

"That is his dream," said Katherine. Her voice betrayed skepticism. She had been through too many of her husband's schemes to have much optimism concerning this latest one. . .especially as her husband's schemes could not budge an inch beyond the dream stage without *her* money. She was already beginning to regret allowing herself to be talked into funding the stables project. She would certainly think twice about letting him use any of her money to buy expensive thoroughbreds from Spain or Arabia. Let him find investors to go in on it with him. She had no desire to see her money go down a rat hole.

They rattled onto the cobblestones of the grounds and toward the great mansion. Behind the barns and stables, Percy immediately saw and heard banging and hammering from the work in progress. They had no sooner come to a stop than he was running off toward the scene.

"Percy, my boy!" boomed his uncle as he saw him running up. "You've become a big strapping fellow since I saw you!"

"Hello, Uncle Roderick!" said Percy as the two shook hands warmly. "Wow, this is some project you've undertaken."

"I plan to make them the finest stables in Wales," rejoined his uncle boisterously, "with horses capable of competing for the largest purses in Britain. Right now, as you can see, we're in the process of hoisting up the roof timbers."

"Do you need some help? I'll get into a different set of clothes and you'll have another set of arms." He hurried off.

His uncle watched him go with a fond yet wistful expression. Courtenay had shown not the slightest interest in the project, nor since his return even once offered to help. Percy hadn't been here two minutes and was already eager to pitch in with the laborers.

That evening the talk around the dinner table was more animated and spontaneous than the festive board at Westbrooke Manor had been in a very long time. That fact was due to two related but opposite facts—Percy's presence and Courtenay's absence.

"Do you remember when I was here before," Percy was saying, "on that first night? Florilyn, you were trying to bait your father and me into divulging ourselves closet atheists."

"I was not!" laughed Florilyn.

"You were, too," rejoined Percy. "You were chiding your father for not paying attention in church and trying to get me to say I didn't believe in heaven and hell. You were terrible! Aunt Katherine, you were having a fit."

By now Percy had his aunt and uncle and cousin in stitches at his depiction of a meal they all remembered very well.

"By the way," he went on, "as I recall, that whole conversation was prompted by the discovery of a body on the sand by the harbor. Was the murder ever solved?"

"Actually, no," replied the viscount. "The curious thing is that there continue to be occasional reports of strangers in the village asking about the man, unsavory characters by the sound of it, though I've never had occasion to be present at such times."

"Why don't you and I disguise ourselves and go down to Mistress Chattan's for a pint or two?" suggested Percy, looking at his aunt with a twinkle in his eye. "Maybe we could learn something."

"Goodness, Percy—what an idea!" she said, though she could not help smiling.

But her husband seemed to take the suggestion seriously. "Not a bad idea," he mused. "Though we would never pull it off. They would be certain to recognize me."

"We'll wait two or three weeks, of course," said Percy, feigning the utmost seriousness. "I didn't mean immediately. We'll grow beards and pull caps down to cover half our faces. . .and wear old grungy clothing, of course."

The viscount continued to mull the idea over as if seriously considering it. "I shall have to talk to Lorimer about it. He is baffled about the affair as well."

"Speaking of the magistrate, Florilyn," said Percy enthusiastically, anxious to get off the subject of an idea he had simply made in jest, "how is my old friend Rhawn Lorimer? Are she and Courtenay engaged yet?"

He was surprised as the atmosphere around the table went suddenly quiet. A few silent looks were exchanged.

"I must have stumbled into some uncharted waters," laughed Percy nervously.

"She and Courtenay have not exactly been on the best of terms since Courtenay got home," said Florilyn.

"Oh, yeah. . .why not?"

"Rhawn has been playing around," replied Florilyn bluntly.

"Goodness, Florilyn!" exclaimed her mother. "Must you be quite so outspoken?"

"It's true, Mother. Everyone knows it. When we were in London for the season last year," she went on, turning once more to Percy, "there were all kinds of stories. After we returned to Wales, the next thing we knew she had taken up with Colville."

"I thought it was you who had eyes for Burrenchobay," said Percy.

"Me?"

"You can't have forgotten the incident at market day where I got pummeled to save your honor."

"That was Colville's doing, you know that."

"And you told me that there was more to it."

"What's all this?" interjected the viscount. "Is there something about your row with Colville we haven't been told, Percy, my boy?"

"Oops, I forgot!" said Percy. "Sorry, Florilyn, old girl. It just slipped out."

"That's all right. Percy got into a fight with Colville that day, Daddy," she said, turning toward her father. "Colville tried to kiss me. I slapped him. And Percy came to my rescue. I later told Percy it was my fault, which it was."

"So you and Burrenchobay are no longer seeing each other?" said Percy.

"Good heavens, no. He and I parted brass rags ages ago, even before he began showing Rhawn his attention. Or, I should say, she began showing him hers."

"Ah. . .at last Courtenay's situation clarifies." Percy nodded significantly. "A little rivalry between friends! When the cat's away, eh? But I thought Burrenchobay was at university, too."

"He took a year off," said Florilyn. "He has been around for the past year, and Courtenay's been at Oxford. But. . . ," she added, then paused and gave Percy a wicked look of fun, "Rhawn is very anxious to see *you*."

"Oh boy! That's just great! Maybe I should just shoot myself now and get it over with. But after what you say about her escapades in London, what could she possibly see in a country bumpkin like me?"

"She has never lost her fascination for you. I think part of it is that you were the only boy in the world who didn't fall all over her."

Percy laughed briefly. His expression then faded into an odd smile. Quickly he recovered his aplomb. "So what about you, my dear Florilyn?" he said. "You are so beautiful—and I don't just say that to flatter my favorite cousin—after a glamorous coming out in London, where I'm sure you caught the eye of every eligible young bachelor between twenty and thirty. Surely you must have a stream of suitors lining up at the door outside to ask your father for your hand."

Florilyn threw her head back and laughed with abandon. "Percy, you *are* too funny!"

"I would wager ten gold sovereigns that you have had at least two marriage proposals since I saw you last. What about it, Uncle Roderick?" he added to his uncle.

"You will not find me taking your bet, Percy, my boy!" rejoined the viscount. "In truth, she has had three."

"*Three!* There—I knew it. Young men from all over England and Wales are no doubt asking one another even as we speak for directions to Westbrooke Manor in Snowdonia."

"And I will tell Papa to tell them the same thing he told the others," said Florilyn. "That is that I am not interested."

"You don't want to marry? What. . .is there something you are keeping from me, Florilyn? Are you considering taking holy orders and joining a convent?"

Florilyn could not help laughing again. "It's not that," she replied. "Of course I want to marry. I am just waiting for the right young man."

FIFTY-THREE

An Old Friend

Dinner concluded, Percy rose to excuse himself. "I am sorry not to be better company," he said. "But suddenly I realize that I am very tired. I suppose the trip—and that work on the stables, eh, Uncle Roderick!—took more of a toll than I realized. I may read for a while and get an early start on a good night's sleep. Oh, Aunt Katherine," he added, turning to his aunt, "my father and mother let me bring along their copy of the new MacDonald. I started it on the way down on the train."

"Which one?" asked his aunt eagerly.

"It's called *Robert Falconer*."

"Oh, I have it, too. I read it several months ago. I consider it his best so far. What masterful characterizations."

"I'm just at the part about the kite. What about you?"

"I am reading a new one of his called *A Seaboard Parish*. It's the sequel to *Annals of a Quiet Neighborhood*."

"I didn't know *Annals* had a sequel!" exclaimed Percy. "My dad *loves* that book. Ministers are alike, I suppose. He says, 'How could MacDonald know exactly what I am thinking?' I wonder if he knows there is a sequel."

"And now you are at Aberdeen," rejoined Katherine. "What is it like knowing you are walking the same cobbled streets and byways and halls that MacDonald probably walked twenty-five years ago?"

"I hadn't thought of that." Percy nodded. "It's rather an amazing thought. Well," he added, turning to his uncle and Florilyn, "good night to you all." He paused and smiled. "I cannot tell you how good it is to be here with you again," he said. "I have really missed you!"

The two women smiled in return.

The viscount seemed a little discomposed by the depth of Percy's sincerity. He offered a few awkward comments about the feeling being mutual and their being delighted to have him again.

Then Percy left them. As he crossed through the entryway hall on his way to the central staircase, he glanced absently down the corridor leading toward the east wing.

A girl he took for one of the servants was walking toward him, a stack of linens in her hands. Halfway down the corridor at a distance of some forty or fifty feet, at sight of him she stopped abruptly.

Percy arrested his movement at the same moment. He paused as his foot fell on the first step of the staircase. His eyes had just drifted up to the painting on the landing of his uncle's grandmother then back again. The lines of his forehead wrinkled as his head cocked in question. For two or three seconds he returned the girl's stare then slowly brought his foot back down to level. Something about the girl was oddly, wonderfully, confusingly familiar. His brain was racing.

Why was she standing so still? She had turned into a gold-haired statue.

Percy's eyes squinted imperceptibly. *Was* her hair gold? Or was the thin light of the corridor playing tricks on him? Was it actually a lighter shade of. . .nearly *white*!

The next moment his steps were hurrying along the tiles. "*Gwyneth?*" said Percy as he slowed and approached, in mingled recognition and disbelief.

She looked down shyly then up into his eyes.

The moment he saw their blue, all doubt vanished. There could be no mistaking the eyes he had once taken for those of an angel.

Her countenance was still timeless! And yet. . .she *had* aged. Hers was the ageless countenance of a child no longer, but the delicate agelessness of the woman-child that had grown up since he had last seen her.

"Is it really *you*?"

She smiled. "It is me, Percy," she replied in a bashful voice.

"But. . .but what are you doing *here*?" said Percy. "Oh, this is brilliant! It is terrific to see you!"

"And you, Percy," said Gwyneth. The voice had changed. If possible, it was yet more serene, slightly deeper of timbre, and surely no longer that of a child. "To answer your question," she said, "I am Lady Florilyn's maid."

"I can't believe it. That is wonderful!"

"Lady Florilyn has been very kind to me."

"I am so glad!"

"I knew you were coming," said Gwyneth. "But I did not know when. You have grown so tall. You are a man now, Percy."

Percy laughed with delight. Gwyneth had not changed! And now that he saw it close, her hair was indeed more tinged with hints of red and shades of gold. Her eyes were of yet deeper and more translucent blue. She had grown several inches, though that was hardly to be compared with what had been added to his stature. Though still very short, she was no longer abnormally tiny. Percival Drummond had indeed blossomed into a fine-looking young man. At the same time, young Gwyneth Barrie—though in all the village only her great-aunt and father beheld what was taking place before everyone's eyes—had become a girl poised on the threshold of becoming a young lady.

Gwyneth had arrived at that wonderful and delicate age hovering precariously between childhood and womanhood, showing one moment the past and, to the keen-eyed observer, the next instant the future. As yet her dawning personhood remained dormant except to the most discerning of eyes. In Percy's mind she would remain for yet a little while the simple, kindhearted girl who had handed him a humble nosegay and called him her friend. . .and through whose honest heart he had learned to appreciate the God of his fathers. In truth, the nymph of Wales was no more the child of his imagination. As his eyes had been opened to nature, they would soon open likewise to the mystery of womanhood. When they did, he would see all that he was meant to see.

Percy, however, did not appear a great deal different in Gwyneth's eyes, though she had to look up a little higher toward the sky to find his face. Because she had always seen inside the people she met, the changes that took place to their outside appearances meant less to her knowing of them than such externals meant to most people.

"Grannie will be so happy that you are back," said Gwyneth.

Percy smiled at the delightful thought of more cozy talks in front of Grannie's fire. "Will she remember me?" he asked.

"We talk of you often. But I should go, Percy," said Gwyneth, glancing around, Percy thought, a little nervously. Slowly she resumed her way along the corridor.

"Do you still. . .stay with your father?" asked Percy, falling into step beside her. "Or do you now live here at the manor?"

"I still live at home," she replied. "Only Mrs. Drynwydd and Mrs. Llewellyn, and Mr. Broakes and Mr. Radnor live in the servants' quarters. I work here three days a week, alternating with the other girls who come from the village. But we are not to talk to guests."

"I'm not a guest!" laughed Percy. "I'm just me."

"To Lord Snowdon and Lady Katherine, you are an *honored* guest, Percy."

"You must be joking!"

"No, Percy. The whole manor has been abuzz over your coming."

Percy laughed at the thought.

"As soon as I take these linens to the breakfast room," said Gwyneth, "I will walk home."

They reached the stairway. Gwyneth turned to the right, Percy toward the stairs.

"Good-bye, Percy," said Gwyneth.

"I will see you again soon, I promise," said Percy. "I will come visit you and Grannie tomorrow. Do you work tomorrow?"

"No, not tomorrow. Only Tuesday and Thursday and Saturday."

"Then I shall see you as early as I can get away."

FIFTY-FOUR

The Promontory

Percy returned to his room and sat down on the edge of his bed. The book he had intended to read sat on the desk. But his thoughts were too full of the changes in Gwyneth to think of Robert Falconer's kite. He rose again and strode to the window and gazed out over the countryside. It was about seven thirty. The sun was still high over Tremadog Bay to the west.

He stood for some time, absorbed in his thoughts. He had of course anticipated seeing little Gwyneth, as he still thought of her, probably more than anyone else other than Florilyn. But though logic told him that everyone aged at the same rate, somehow he had expected Gwyneth to remain the same. He had not actually said such to himself. Yet he had expected to find her still the tiny child he had known three years before. It was clear, however, that though she was still not yet five feet tall, she had *grown*. And not merely in stature. Her countenance was—there came the word again—ageless!

Was she an angel after all? He chuckled to himself at the thought.

Out the window, far below the manor toward the sea, a small figure was walking toward the promontory of Mochras Head.

He watched for some moments then turned and strode across the floor of his room. He did not pause until his hand was on the latch.

After having said his good nights and professed himself too tired for further company, he was hesitant to be seen going out again.

He crept from his room and glanced down the corridor toward Florilyn's door at the far end. He felt oddly like a sneak. It reminded him of his prodigal past, creeping furtively through the darkened streets of Glasgow. Those were unpleasant memories. Yet the compulsion to follow was too strong. But he did not want Florilyn to know he was leaving the house. . .or why.

He stole softly to the far end of the west wing, down the back stairway, and out by one of the side doors. Still conscious of not wanting to be seen, he made his way through the garden, around behind the stables, and onto the open moor leading down the slope toward the village and Mochras Head.

Probably when he reached the open plateau out from the cover of the wood surrounding the manor, he thought as he hurried along, the figure he had seen from his window would have disappeared farther in the direction of the village. If so, he would retrace his steps back to the manor and spend the rest of his evening with Falconer and Shargar. It was too late for a visit to the Barrie cottage. But if by chance he *should* meet someone out for an evening walk in that wonderful, quiet, fragrant, peaceful time of the evening his native Scots called "the gloamin'," that was a different matter altogether.

By the time he crossed the stream and was approaching the promontory, he knew he would not turn back. There she was, in her white maid's dress, seated two hundred yards ahead of him at the very tip of the cliff face. Her back was to him, as she sat staring out over the sea in the direction of the setting sun.

Percy continued on across the soft grass with noiseless step.

She did not turn her head.

He approached from behind.

"Hello, Percy," said Gwyneth softly without turning.

"So you *do* have the second sight after all," he said, easing to the ground beside her.

"Why do you say that?"

"Because you knew it was me without looking."

"I would know your step anywhere, Percy. Besides, no one else knows this place."

"Your special place," said Percy. "Do you have any new special places?"

"No. Some of them are just more special now because I once shared them with a friend. Those are now my *most* special places."

It fell quiet a few minutes. With a sunset, the sea, and miles of open moorland behind them, no words were needed. What was to be said, both felt without words.

"You've changed, Percy," said Gwyneth at length.

"In what way?"

"I haven't completely decided. You are older."

Percy broke out in a peal of laughter. "I am indeed. So are you, my dear Gwyneth."

"I know. But I meant older in a different way. It is a good older. I could see it in your eyes the moment I saw you at the manor. I hope my older is a good older, too."

"I am sure it is."

"Not everybody's older is a better older. I do not think Master Courtenay has become a better older."

"Does he still make fun of you?"

"He does not even speak to me. I think he disdains me. But Lady Florilyn is a better older. And she is *very* fond of you, Percy. She has been talking of nothing but your coming for weeks."

"I am fond of her, too. She has changed from the first time I came to Wales. And you are right, so have I. You did not know me before I first came here, Gwyneth. I was very foolish and wasn't very nice."

"I know, Percy. I heard Grannie's talk. She knew all about you. But I didn't care what anyone said. You were my friend, and you were kind to me."

"How long have you worked at the manor?" asked Percy.

"A year. Miss Florilyn was so nice to me after you left. She came to visit me, and even Grannie learned to like her. She came to our cottage once to see my animals. Then one of the maids at the manor left and she asked me if I would like to work for her mother and be paid. My father said he thought I should, so I did."

"Do you like it?"

"It is not so very hard work, though it is tedious. I do not have as much time with my father and my animals as I would like. But we have more money now. And Grannie says that I am not a little girl anymore and that when people get older their lives change. Grannie is very wise. I know that a girl like me must think of what she will do when she is older."

In that, Gwyneth's great-great-aunt was right—she was no longer a little girl. The quietness of Gwyneth's spirit was even deeper than before. One moment would the child burst into a laugh of glee, the next withdraw into her private solitary refuge of peace she shared only with those she loved. Because of the faraway gaze of her countenance, many of the villagers were now even more apprehensive of her than before.

Little did Percy realize how changed she was, and how beautiful she was on the verge of becoming. It takes far-seeing eyes to apprehend into what another is growing. Changed as he was, Percy had not yet become so wise as that. But the day of his own internal second sight was fast approaching.

"How old are you now, Gwyneth?" Percy asked.

"Sixteen," she replied.

"*Sixteen*—goodness, are you sure you didn't grow more years than me while I was gone?"

Gwyneth giggled, suddenly a girl again. "I was thirteen when you were here before. Some people thought I was young because I was so tiny. My father is a small man, and I am small, too."

"You are not so tiny now."

"Lady Florilyn is many inches taller than me."

"But her father and mother are both tall."

"How old are you, Percy? I forgot how old you were before. I have tried to remember because I know you told me."

"I was sixteen. I am nineteen now."

"You are a man, Percy," said Gwyneth softly. There was a world of meaning in the gentle expressiveness of her voice.

"Not quite, my dear Gwyneth! I am only on my way to becoming one, with a long way yet to go. I had the misfortune to have gotten a late start. How is Stevie?"

"You should ask him yourself."

"I intend to—very soon."

"His poor father is not well. Grannie says the Lord will take him before the summer is out. I hope she is right. It will be a relief to Auntie for her to know that he is healthy again."

"Perhaps you and I might ride up there for a visit tomorrow."

Gwyneth nodded. "Perhaps Lady Florilyn will want to ride with you somewhere else," she said.

"You might be right," said Percy. "We shall see. But I will definitely come to the village tomorrow. There are so many people I want to visit."

"Grannie is anxious to see you, too."

FIFTY-FIVE

Cottage in the Hills

*I*n spite of his long train ride followed by the southbound coach of the day before, and the fact that he lay reading in his bed by candlelight until past eleven, Percy awoke early and was downstairs to the breakfast room not long after seven. He knew Florilyn would not make an appearance for hours. Still, he was guiltily relieved to find the room empty.

To all appearance, Mrs. Drynwydd had only just brought out the covered silver pots from the kitchen, for they were steaming and fragrant. He ate in haste and was just finishing a second cup of tea with a last piece of toast when his aunt came in.

"Good morning, Percy," she said cheerily.

"Good morning, Aunt Katherine."

"Did you sleep well?"

"Very."

"How did Robert get on with his kite?"

A confused look met her question.

"Robert Falconer."

"Oh, right. . .of course!" Percy laughed. "Right—the kite. I moved a good way past that before falling asleep." He rose and began making his way toward the door.

"Where are you off to?" asked Katherine.

"I've been so anxious to ride in Wales again, I thought I would get an early start."

"Florilyn will be sorry to miss you."

"She and I will have many chances, I'm sure," laughed Percy.

As he left the house for the stables, he felt pangs of the same guilt that had come over him the previous evening—that he was being less than honest. Yet somehow he felt a gnawing uncertainty about what Florilyn would say to his being off so soon without her.

That Florilyn was changed, there could be no doubt. But the incident the day of the race three years before remained lodged in his memory. She had a temper; there was no denying that. He wanted to do nothing to rouse it again. But neither was he going to avoid visiting Gwyneth and Grannie and Stevie Muir and his other village friends for fear of her reaction.

Percy arrived at the Barrie cottage a little after eight. Codnor was already off for the mine. Gwyneth had not accompanied him. Percy saw her at the back of the cottage feeding her animals.

"Hey, Gwyneth!" Percy called out from atop Grey Tide while he was still a good way off.

She turned, waved, and waited for his approach.

"I thought I would ride in to see Grannie then out to Stevie's," he said as he cantered up. "Why don't you join me?"

"Do you want me to?"

"Of course! How could you even ask? Come on!" he said, reaching down and extending his hand. "Jump up behind me."

Though Gwyneth was at least four inches taller and fifteen pounds heavier than before, Percy was stronger in equal proportion. He took hold of her hand and whisked her up behind him as easily as before. Again sounded the girlish giggle Percy loved. She came to light behind him and stretched her arms around him.

Ten minutes later they were walking into the darkened kitchen of Grannie's cottage in Llanfryniog. A joyous reunion followed with hugs and exclamations of delight. Within moments the tea was on while Grannie continued to make over the giant of a man Percy had become in her eyes. In truth he did not quite yet measure a full six feet and was as slender as the trunk of a birch tree, though solid and strong.

"The last time I saw you here," said Percy to Gwyneth as they walked into the inner room of the cottage, "we were all praying for you. We didn't know if you would live."

"God was taking care of me," rejoined Gwyneth simply. "I was not afraid. And have you noticed, Percy—I do not stutter now."

"That's right! I hadn't stopped to think about it."

"I haven't stuttered since the accident on the sand. So you see, Lady Florilyn and Red Rhud did me a favor."

"I've often heard my father say that all things work for good. It must be true."

"My, oh my," said Grannie, turning toward Percy again, "you are tall for a Scot laddie! What your mama must be feeding you!"

Percy laughed again. "My dad still has an inch or two on me," he said. "And I've been away from home for a year, Grannie—at university in the north. But my landlady feeds me as well as my mother."

In Percy's eyes, Grannie, too, was much changed. A little shorter, he thought, stooped and more bowed in the back. Her eyes still sparkled with the vibrancy of what life remained. But it was clear that it would not be many years before Life itself would call her to the home of its origin. Now that Grannie was eighty-four, Percy could not but wonder how much longer she would be able to take care of herself, even with Gwyneth's help. And with Gwyneth now at the manor, the old woman was more on her own than ever.

Percy found himself thinking of his own grandparents. They were still spry, though they were probably a dozen years younger. But they were aging rapidly as well.

After tea and an hour's happy reminiscing, the bonds between the three were securely retightened as if no more than a day had passed, as is always the case when true friends meet again after an absence.

By ten o'clock, with the sun warming the earth beneath them, wooing from it the myriad fragrances the month of June is so uniquely capable of producing, Percy and Gwyneth were riding up into the hills on Grey Tide's back.

To sit so close to Percy, her arms around his great strong waist, knowing that he had not changed in three years except for the better, sent Gwyneth's spirits soaring. But her thoughts were for her alone. Like Mary of old, she kept them hidden where they would be safe and treasured them quietly in the depths of her heart.

Percy was in no hurry. For three years he had dreamed of being in Wales again. He did not rush Grey Tide along. Neither spoke much as they went. As much as their relationship was the same, both sensed, though differently, that much was new between them. They would never go back to how they were before.

There is a great difference between the motions within the heart of a thirteen-year-old girl and one who has reached sixteen and has arrived at the threshold of womanhood. Though she would always be childlike, Gwyneth would never be a child again.

They encountered Stevie and his flock of sheep well before reaching the house. Percy leaped from the saddle, leaving Gwyneth perched precariously on the back of Grey Tide's rump. The two young men ran forward and greeted each other like old friends, with sheep scattering and bleating in every direction around them.

"You've grown, Percy!" exclaimed Stevie. "Suddenly you're half a head taller than me!"

"But not half so strong!" rejoined Percy. "Look at you—you've added inches to your arms and shoulders. Goodness man, you look like the blacksmith!"

Stevie laughed. "I'm not quite so burly as that. Kyvwlch Gwarthegydd is the strongest man in two counties. His young Chandos shows signs of being the same one day."

"Your sheep look fine, Stevie," said Percy. "How's your mum?"

"Middlin'," replied Stevie. "Papa's doing poorly. It's nearly taken the life out of the poor woman."

"We are on our way to see her."

"She will be happy to see you. But I must get these lads and lassies up to their pasture, so I'll not be joining you."

"I shall see you again, then," said Percy, returning to Gwyneth where she sat waiting patiently on Grey Tide.

They reached the Muir cottage ten or fifteen minutes later. One look at Adela Muir told the story. She was worn and haggard. It appeared she had hardly slept in weeks.

"My poor Glythvyr's in a bad way, Mr. Drummond," she replied to Percy's inquiry about her husband. "He won't know you. He won't even know you're here. He doesn't know me or Stevie now either. That's the heartbreak of it. We're strangers to him, you see."

Percy nodded. "I would still like to see him, Mrs. Muir."

She led them inside.

Percy could smell the change even before his eyes adjusted to the dim light of the sick chamber. It was the stale stench of life slipping away.

He approached the makeshift bed. The thin form on it lay motionless and pale. The face staring up off the pillow was gaunt, almost as if its skin had been stretched over a skeleton's skull. That life remained was clear from the faint mumbling of the lips and the fumbling of fingers with the edge of the blanket. Percy could make out nothing of what he was saying. He glanced at the man's wife.

She shook her head. "It's just nonsense, you see," she said. "No one can make out a word of it."

Percy stooped down and gently laid a hand on the bony white arm. "Hello, Mr. Muir," he said. "It's Percy Drummond again. I'm here from the manor. I'm Lord Snowdon's nephew."

He thought he detected a faint increase of the man's muttering and a flicker of the eyes. But there was no other response.

After a moment, he pulled away, stood, and smiled sadly. "I am so sorry, Mrs. Muir," he said. "I cannot imagine how difficult it must be for you."

Gwyneth's aunt nodded. "I won't deny it," she said. "But it's the way of womanhood, isn't it, you see? I am just praying the Lord will take him soon, for his sake not mine, though Stevie will sorely miss him. He loves his daddy, you see."

They returned to the kitchen. After another hour, with tea and a few simple oatcakes, they said their good-byes.

They returned to Grey Tide, who had been waiting patiently and refreshing herself with grass and water and a few oats. Percy and Gwyneth began the ride back in silence.

Glythvyr Muir's condition sobered Percy. He thought of his father and realized anew the important role he played in so many lives. His only regret was that he had not begun to see his father for who he truly was while he had been at home. It was now too late to be part of it with his mother and father. The memory of his youthful blindness stung him anew with regret.

Absorbed in his thoughts, suddenly at a distance of three or four hundred yards, Percy saw six or eight horses of varying color gallop into sight, crest a small ridge, then disappear over the other side. "What was that?" he exclaimed. "Did you see it, Gwyneth?" he cried, turning around where he sat. "It was a band of horses. There was nobody with them!"

"It's the wild horses of Snowdonia," said Gwyneth calmly.

"*Wild* horses! There are wild horses here?"

"Oh yes, many more than that."

"Who do they belong to?"

"Nobody. They belong to themselves."

"Where do they live?"

"In the hills."

"Do you know where?"

"Yes."

"You know *exactly* where?"

"Of course. I know all the animals."

"Are the wild horses your friends, too?"

Gwyneth hesitated. "Not really my friends," she said after a moment. "They know me. But they are a little wary of me. They don't let me get close like the other animals do. Do you want to see where they live, Percy?"

"*Yes!*" exclaimed Percy.

"Then ride that way," said Gwyneth, pointing to her right and away from the direction they had been going."

"That's not where I saw them running."

"I thought you wanted to see where they lived."

Percy nodded and led Grey Tide to the right. He should know better by now, he smiled to himself, than to doubt Gwyneth!

She directed him back toward the hills, bearing north from the Muir cottage. Gradually they moved eastward in the direction of Rhinog Fawr where it loomed ahead of them. Not once again did Percy see any sign of the horses. He had begun to doubt whether he would see them again. But his trust in Gwyneth was so great that he said nothing.

They kept on. Gradually the strange sensation came over Percy that he recognized some of the terrain and landmarks about them. They continued to climb steadily into yet higher hills.

All at once as they came around the shoulder of a hill, before him rose a great cliff face of granite. He knew beyond any doubt that he had been here before. Gwyneth was leading him near the blue lake where he had seen her singing to the animals.

Almost the same moment, as if she had been reading his mind, Gwyneth's voice interrupted his thoughts. "We are close to the place now, Percy," she said. "But we must go very quietly. Horses frighten easily, you know. This is a very quiet place. It is one of my special places. I think I should lead the way now."

Percy stopped Grey Tide and climbed to the ground. Gwyneth scooted forward into the saddle. Percy placed his foot in the stirrup and, with a little more difficulty than getting Gwyneth behind *him*, managed to climb up behind her. Now it was his turn to stretch his hands around her waist. She was small enough that he could reach all the way around and take hold of the front of the saddle. Sitting tall, he could see straight over the top of her blond head.

Feeling his chest against her back and his arms around her midsection gave Gwyneth a feeling of happy power as she took the reins. She urged Grey Tide forward. Within minutes they were descending steeply. Percy still caught no glimpse of the lake.

Gwyneth led down through a rocky narrow wooded ravine. The cliff of granite loomed higher and higher above them as they descended into what was obviously a deep valley, though the trees and boulders surrounded them so closely on all sides that they could not see the bottom of it.

Finally Gwyneth stopped. "We must go no closer," she whispered. "They will hear Grey Tide's hooves and will know she is not one of them. We will walk the rest of the way."

Carefully they dismounted. Percy tied the reins to a tree. Gwyneth crept forward, making not a sound. Percy followed. After eight or ten minutes, the trees began to thin in front of them. Finally Gwyneth stopped. Percy drew alongside.

In the distance, some fifty yards away in a clearing beyond the trees, spread over with a carpet of lush green grass, ten or fifteen horses grazed peacefully. A few deer were also about. Rabbits occasionally scurried by. In the distance, Percy could just make out a glistening surface of translucent blue.

Neither said a word. They watched in silence for ten minutes.

Percy knew that alone, and crooning the otherworldly melody he had heard before, Gwyneth would have been able to make a closer approach. But he would never see these magnificent beasts closer than he was beholding them now.

It was a holy moment of oneness with creation that comes for most but once or twice in a lifetime. Yet Gwyneth Barrie seemed to live within that oneness all the days of her life.

FIFTY-SIX

Invitation and Ride

*P*ercy did not arrive back at the manor until midafternoon.

By the time lunch was concluded and still with no sign of him, Florilyn had retired to her room, a little perturbed, it is true, for she suspected that Percy had gone to the village. Every hour that went by demonstrated more clearly than ever that he was more eager to visit his peasant friends after three years than spend time with her. She had tried to read but was agitated. With the afternoon sun streaming through the west-facing window of her room, she had finally dozed.

When she went downstairs and outside again some time later, she found Percy atop her father's new stables, bare-chested and perspiring freely, holding one end of a massive roof timber in place while two laborers secured it at the ends.

She approached and looked up, shielding her eyes from the sun with her hand. "Percy, what are you doing up there?" she called out.

"What does it look like?" Percy yelled down. "We're putting the roof on."

"But why you? You're not a laborer. You don't get paid."

"I'm not doing it to get paid but to help your father. Besides, this is great fun! I haven't enjoyed myself so much in years."

"But. . .your hands—what if you get hurt or something?"

311

"A few blisters and a scrape or two—who wants lily-white hands that don't know how to work? Not me!"

"Where were you all morning?"

"I went for a ride."

"Where?"

"Up to see Stevie Muir," said Percy. In the time since he had left that morning, he had decided to be completely straightforward. "Gwyneth told me that his father is seriously ill. I wanted to visit them without delay. . .just in case, you know."

"When did you see Gwyneth?"

"Last night as she was leaving. I was amazed to find her working here! That was so kind of you to arrange for her to have a job, Florilyn. I am proud of you! She and I rode up to see the Muirs this morning."

"Oh. . .I was hoping to have a ride with you."

"So was I," said Percy. "But I thought it important to go to the Muirs as soon as possible. Now we've got to get these roof timbers set today. Maybe we could go with lunch tomorrow. Let's take that same ride from last time. . .you know, our first long ride together—but with me staying in the saddle this time!"

His enthusiasm mollified Florilyn's feelings that might, had the conversation gone differently, produced an outcome more reminiscent of the Florilyn of former days. No one had ever said the words "I am proud of you" to Florilyn Westbrooke in her life. She didn't know how to react, whether to receive them with quiet gratitude or take offense that one whom the pride of her past might have considered her social inferior could be proud of *her*. To her credit, she swallowed her perplexity, agreed to Percy's suggestion, and returned to the house.

On the following morning, as Percy and Florilyn were getting ready for their ride, a messenger arrived from Burrenchobay Hall.

Florilyn recognized the man on horseback as Richard Hawarden, Sir Armond's groom. Seeing an envelope in his hand, her natural curiosity was aroused, and she walked toward him as he dismounted. "Hello, Mr. Hawarden," she said, approaching from behind.

The groom turned. "Good mornin' tae ye, Miss Florilyn."

"What do you have there?"

"An invitation, my leddy—tae Mistress Davina's birthday party." He handed the envelope to Florilyn.

"Thank you," she said.

"Very good, Miss Florilyn," he said and returned to his horse.

Florilyn opened the envelope and read the engraved card inside. Percy walked up behind her.

"It seems we've all been invited to an event at Burrenchobay Hall," she said. "You are specifically included. If I didn't know better, I would think that scheming little Davina has eyes for you, Percy."

"What are you talking about?" he asked.

"You are quite the topic of conversation around here, you know. . . the handsome mysterious stranger from the north. Davina must have asked me ten times when you would be back."

Percy laughed again. "She's just a kid."

"Not anymore! She's sixteen next week. Believe me, she could go to London next season, no questions asked, and easily pass for eighteen. You talk about marriage proposals—she could scoop them in like flies to honey."

"Then maybe I should turn down my portion of the invitation," said Percy. "That family and yours. . .it's too complicated! I don't want to get in the middle of it. I'm not much for high society stuff anyway. I'll leave all that to you aristocrats."

Now it was Florilyn's turn to laugh. "We'll worry about Davina later. Let me take this invitation inside to my mother," she said. "Then we can be off."

Two hours later, the cousins arrived at the same level meadow that Percy recognized from their ill-fated ride three years earlier.

"I would never have found my way here alone," he said. "But I know this place well enough now that I see it. Ah, the memories come flooding back! Maybe it's my turn to challenge *you* to a race to the top," said Percy playfully.

"No, thank you. My racing days are over," said Florilyn in a quieter tone. "After what happened on the beach, the memory is too painful. I wouldn't mind if we rode *together* to the top. Then we can have lunch there."

"Sounds good to me. Let's go!"

Percy dug in his heels and galloped off across the grass. Florilyn followed and soon drew alongside. She looked across at him with a happy smile, eyes filled with fun, but without the twinkle of challenge she might have thrown him before. Both were content to ride beside each other. For the rest of the distance across the flat, they pushed their mounts but remained side by side.

"When we reach the wood," Percy called out, "you take the lead. I'm not sure I know the way."

Florilyn nodded.

Five or ten minutes later, stopping briefly at the stream to water the horses, and after navigating the woods and steep incline without incident, they crested the ridge.

"That was great!" exclaimed Percy as they eased the two mares to a gentle walk, looking about at the familiar sight. "It is nice still to be aboard after that climb."

Though the ridge was mostly rocky, they found a patch of tolerably soft grass where the twin mares could graze. They dismounted, tied the horses to the nearby shrubbery, and set out the simple lunch things they had brought.

"It is so quiet here," said Percy as they sat together. "I wouldn't know which direction the sea lay. In fact. . .I *don't* know!" He laughed.

"It's there," said Florilyn pointing, "straight west."

"How would I know which way is west?"

"I don't know. I've been out riding these hills for so long, I just know."

"It must have been wonderful to grow up here," said Percy, taking a bite out of an apple. "Not that I'm complaining. But the city—especially a place like Glasgow—it's nothing like this."

"And now you've traded one city for another."

"I suppose you're right. Unfortunately that's where they put the universities. So if you want an education, to the city you must go."

"How many years do you have left in Aberdeen?" asked Florilyn.

"Three. I've only got one year under my belt so far."

"Do you like it?"

"It's hard work, but yes—I do. I love studying and learning."

"What will you do. . .I mean when you've graduated?"

"I'm not sure yet. I am looking into engineering. I had thought about being a minister, too, like my dad."

"The *Reverend* Percy Drummund," said Florilyn slowly, trying out the sound of it. "Somehow it doesn't quite have the right ring. I think it would have to be the Reverend *Percival* Drummond."

"You're right." He laughed. "*Percy* isn't exactly right. What about for a solicitor? I'm also thinking of studying law, if God doesn't lead me into the ministry."

"I think you'll definitely need the *Percival* on the door of a solicitor's office."

"What about you, my dear Florilyn?" asked Percy.

"What about me?"

"You've turned into such a lady since I saw you. What are your plans?"

"Women don't have *plans*."

"Some do. Women making their mark in the world are all the rage these days. At university, some are saying that women will even vote in the not too distant future."

"*Vote*. . .women?"

"That's what they say."

"I can hardly believe that."

"Maybe you're right. It may never go that far. Nobody can see the future. Still, don't you have any plans?"

"There we are back to what I said before—women don't have plans. Men have plans, women get married."

"Bluntly put!" Percy laughed. "I guess you're right. So what does a pretty young woman like you do—just wait around until, like you said at dinner the other evening, the right man comes calling at your door?"

"I suppose that's about it."

"What if the right man never comes along?"

"Then a girl's got a big problem. She either gets more desperate as the years go by, or eventually she settles for second best."

"I was under the impression three years ago that you had every young man for miles wrapped around your little finger."

Florilyn smiled almost wistfully. "Maybe I did." She nodded reflectively. "I probably could marry several of them even now. But I've changed since then. I'm not so anxious to see a ring on my finger."

"You *are* changed. I saw it immediately. There is a quietness about you now. You seem content with yourself."

"I suppose I am. . .mostly. But aren't all girls a little insecure deep inside, wondering what people think of them?"

"I don't know. I'm not a girl."

"That is undeniably true!" Florilyn laughed. She paused and seemed to be thinking whether to say what had come to her mind. She glanced away.

Percy could tell she was embarrassed. He waited.

"Percy," she said after a moment, "do you—what you said before—do you really think I'm pretty?"

"Yes, I do. You are very attractive. Why?"

"I don't know. A girl never *really* knows what she looks like to people. You can look in a mirror for hours, but you don't really know. Everyone *wants* to be pretty. But you can't really trust what boys tell you. Half of them are such liars, and the other half are so shy they're afraid of their own shadows."

Percy laughed to hear such a characterization of his sex.

"All those young men you said had eyes for me. . .they were just trying to get me to like them and pay attention to them. Colville Burrenchobay—what a big oaf. All he wanted was to touch me and kiss me. Ugh! It makes me sick to think of it! How can I believe anything someone like that tells me?"

"So why did you ask me?"

"Because you're different, Percy. You say what you mean and mean what you say. You would never toy with a girl. I don't think you would even know how to. You're too real, too honest."

"I guess I never thought about it one way or another."

"Once I began to see you for who you were, you know. . .once I was through being nasty to you, I realized how shallow all the other young men were. I got tired of the games, of them trying to impress me and telling me I was pretty. I got tired of trying to impress them, too. Their words meant nothing. But coming from *you*. . .it means a lot. Thank you."

"Sure." Percy smiled.

"It was your coming here that changed me, you know, Percy. Like it or not, it's all your fault!" she added with a grin.

"That's quite a burden to put on a chap! So. . .you said you were waiting for the right kind of young man. How will you know?"

"I don't know." Florilyn smiled thoughtfully. "Do you ever really know ahead of time?"

"Probably not. I see what you mean."

"It's not as if you can prepare a form and ask them to tick all the boxes. It's not so cut-and-dried as all that."

"What *are* you looking for, then?"

Florilyn hesitated before answering. "Honestly?" she said at length.

"Of course."

"Say what I mean and mean what I say?"

Percy nodded.

"I suppose I am looking for someone. . .not so very different from you, Percy."

Now it was Percy's turn to grow thoughtful.

"You are considerate and fun to be around," Florilyn went on. "But you have a serious side, too. I can talk to you *and* laugh with you. You can't do that with everyone. No matter what happens, I know that you will be a gentleman."

"No one has ever called me a gentleman before."

"Well, you are. You can take it from a young woman who has met dozens of young men who aren't."

Again it grew silent.

"So, I will turn the question around—what about *you*?" said Florilyn. "Do you see lots of young women in Aberdeen—bonnie Scots lassies... parties and socializing every night?"

"I'm afraid not," replied Percy. "There are a few young ladies in the church I attend."

"Anyone special?"

Percy smiled. "No," he answered. "They're nice enough. But no one special."

FIFTY-SEVEN

Interlude

Several days had passed since Percy's arrival.

He had gone to the village every day, visited with the men at the harbor, been in all the shops, gone into Mistress Chattan's for several pints, and talked and laughed with the local fishermen and farmers and miners. He never went to Llanfryniog without tea with Grannie.

He ran into Chandos Gwarthegydd at his father's blacksmith's shop. As Stevie had said, Chandos showed signs of becoming as muscular as his father. The lad, now fifteen, was well capable of wielding his tools and keeping the fire in the forge glowing hot with coal. He could fashion a shoe for a horse as well as any blacksmith in Wales. He and Percy quickly formed a great friendship.

Seeing Gwyneth, however, was not so easy as before. Percy longed to walk and ride with her out on the hills and along the beach and to listen to her delightful, simple, humble talk about nature and God and animals and her special places.

But that became more difficult now that she was working at the manor. He couldn't simply drop in on her anytime as he had before. Nor did he so often find her at Grannie's. Neither could he interrupt her in the midst of her work. She had responsibilities now. He was on holiday. Gwyneth was not.

Even so, there were other demands on his time, too—as he quickly became one of the regular workers on the new stables. He was not obligated to maintain the work schedule of the hired men. But he enjoyed the project. Besides learning new skills, he was enjoying enormously working beside the humble Welshmen. He had only seen Courtenay two or three times, and then briefly.

He encountered Gwyneth from time to time as she went about her duties. She always glanced shyly away or greeted him simply as she passed.

Finally toward the end of one day, Percy saw her carrying a stack of towels on her way up to the family living quarters.

He had been lingering on the landing of the first floor, absently staring at the dozen or so portraits lining the walls of the main staircase. His eyes had again been arrested by the compelling expression and penetrating eyes of the woman his uncle had commented on during the first week of his previous visit. Every time he looked up at the image of her face, the woman's gaze drew him as if she were veritably *alive*. He found her gazing down at him every time he ascended or descended the stairs.

Hearing a step on the ground floor below, even as he was looking at the face of Lord Snowdon's grandmother, Percy glanced toward the sound. There was Gwyneth walking up the stairs. She was staring straight into his eyes.

For a moment, Percy gazed back stunned, then quickly looked back at the portrait. His face drained of color. The next moment the shocking revelation of what he had seen was interrupted by Gwyneth's voice.

He turned toward her as she approached with a smile. The brief expression was gone from her face. The trance that had come over him was instantly broken.

"Hello, Percy," she said. "You are standing there looking like you just saw a ghost!"

"Oh. . .yeah, sorry!" He laughed, shaking his head. "I was just. . .But, Gwyneth—I was hoping to run into you."

She reached the landing.

"I've hardly seen you at all," Percy went on. "I miss our talks."

"So do I, Percy," she said softly.

"Do you work tomorrow?"

Gwyneth shook her head.

"Then let's meet for the day."

"What about your work at the stables?" said Gwyneth. "All the rest of the servants are talking about what a big help you are. They say they have never seen Master Courtenay dirty his hands like you do."

"Just so long as they don't say it around him!" laughed Percy. "But the workers can get by without me. The roof is nearly done. They are just humoring me anyway. I don't really know what I am doing."

"That's not what Mr. Radnor says."

"Well, he has always been very nice. So what do you say about tomorrow?"

"If you really want to, Percy."

"Want to? I've been waiting for the chance."

"Would you like to come to Grannie's for breakfast tea?"

"That would be great!"

"Then I will walk my father to the mine at seven and be to Grannie's by eight."

"I'll be there."

The next morning, Percy left the manor on foot at seven thirty, just about the time Gwyneth was saying good-bye to her father for the day and returning to walk back to the village from the mine.

After breakfast tea with Grannie, Percy and Gwyneth left the cottage and walked through the village toward the harbor.

"Do the village people bother you much anymore?" asked Percy.

"Not so much," replied Gwyneth. "They don't talk to me, but at least they don't say cruel things. It is a great relief not to go to school. Grannie always taught me to return evil with kindness, and I tried to. One of my earliest memories is of Grannie's voice saying, 'Good returns fivefold. Secret good returns tenfold. Return good for evil—God never forgets.' But it is not so pleasant to have people make fun of you. I am glad not to be taking so many bouquets around as I once did."

They reached the beach. Percy paused to untie his shoes and take them off along with his socks. Gwyneth did the same. Before she was through, Percy had gone running off, yelling and laughing as he darted in and out of the incoming tide like a frolicksome dog. Gwyneth laughed with delight. Out of breath after a few minutes, he came running back to where she stood, still giggling to see him having so much fun.

"There is nothing like walking and running barefoot in the sand," he said as he picked up his shoes and they walked away from the harbor. I think this beach is one of my favorite places in the whole world. I think I will claim it as *my* special place! I wonder if you can see Ireland from here, too."

"Only on a very clear day, I think," said Gwyneth.

"The tide is out today," Percy went on. "Have you found any more spooky skeletons in the cave?"

"No," laughed Gwyneth. "I am still a little afraid to go there by myself."

"I've got it! You wait here," said Percy excitedly. "I'll run back to Grannie's and borrow a candle and matches. We'll explore it!"

He dashed off. As soon as he left the sand, he remembered his bare feet. He sat down and began to put his shoes and socks back on.

Almost the next instant Gwyneth ran past him. "*You* wait here!" she laughed. "I don't need shoes. I will get the candle and matches."

She was back almost in less time than it would have taken him to tie up his laces. Soon they were scampering over the rocky end of the beach toward the cave. Five minutes later they were inside.

Percy struck a match and lit the candle. With the flame flickering and sending its light and shadows dancing off the walls and roof of the perpetually wet rock, they ventured slowly inside.

"I've never seen the cave so bright," said Gwyneth, gazing all about. "It looks so different."

The cave was larger than Percy expected, easily forty or fifty feet to the far end where the downward slope of the roof met the walls at the sand. No dangerous protrusions or hidden stones were visible, and the sandy floor was smooth. The bottom sloped up markedly from the cave's mouth. If one did happen to get trapped inside by a sudden incoming tide, it would indeed be difficult to get out.

"Where did you see the skeleton?" asked Percy.

"I think about here," said Gwyneth, glancing about. "It is hard to tell. But it was only the head."

"You've never seen anything since?"

Gwyneth shook her head.

They reached the far end. Percy knelt down in the wet sand, feeling about with his free hand as he sent the light from the candle into every crevice and recess of the irregular rock of the walls. "It almost seems that it might go farther back," he said. "Look here, the rock angles farther in except that it is blocked up by sand. Waves must have constantly pushed the sand farther in and up against the rock. I wonder if there is another small chamber behind this pile of sand."

"I would be afraid to find out," said Gwyneth. "There might be spiders and crabs and scary little creatures. I would never come in here again if I thought there was a place where things like that were hiding!"

Percy laughed. "I thought you loved animals!"

"I do. But not spiders and bats and beetles that live where it's dark."

"Well, if there is more to this cave, we're not going to find it without a spade."

They crawled back away from the inner end of the cave until they could stand again, then left through the cave mouth and continued along the south portion of sandy beach. Soon they had their shoes on again and were climbing the trail up to the promontory of Mochras Head. They sat down at the top, gazing across the water.

"Can you see Ireland today?" asked Percy.

Gwyneth squinted. "I don't think so. Maybe. I can't be sure. Are you going to the party at Burrenchobay Hall, Percy?" asked Gwyneth abruptly.

"You heard about it, did you? I don't know. . . . I suppose. Though I would rather not."

"Why, Percy?"

"Oh, you know. . .all those highfalutin society people. I'm not cut out for all that. I'd rather be having a pint with the fishermen than get dressed up for a party."

"But you have to go."

"Why do you say that?"

"Because Miss Florilyn is expecting you to be her escort."

"Is she? Hmm, well I suppose I shall have to go, then."

"I saw you and Miss Florilyn leaving for a ride yesterday. Did you have fun?"

"Yes, we had a good time catching up since seeing one another during my last visit."

"She likes being with you, doesn't she?"

"I suppose."

"Where did you ride?"

"Where you met me three years ago way out in the hills, remember? You had to lead me home."

Gwyneth smiled but then grew quiet, even a little withdrawn.

They sat awhile in silence.

"Do you have any new animals?" he asked at length.

"A few."

"I would like to see them."

They rose and walked slowly away from the promontory and toward Gwyneth's home. The mood that had come over her passed. She was soon herself again.

FIFTY-EIGHT

Burrenchobay Hall

*T*he big day of the party finally came.

Florilyn spent all afternoon getting ready. Gwyneth and one of the other maids spent most of the day waiting on her. By five o'clock she was ready, every hair in place, her long lavender dress perfect. Mother and daughter had at last attached the final ribbon at the waist to the expensive dress they had purchased in London some months before.

"You look lovely, dear," said Katherine as she adjusted the bow in her daughter's glistening black hair.

"Do you think Percy will like the dress?" asked Florilyn.

"I am sure he will."

Outside a large brougham with Deaken Trenchard at the reins stood ready to transport Lord and Lady Snowdon, Florilyn, and Percy the four miles to Burrenchobay Hall. Courtenay had made his own arrangements and had left some time before.

Percy came down the central staircase looking stunning in a dark blue suit with a white shirt, vest, and red tie. Florilyn stood waiting at the bottom of the stairs. The sight nearly took her breath away. It was the same suit he had been wearing on the day of his arrival. Yet something about it on this day was especially stunning.

Gwyneth, too, had been watching for Percy's appearance. She stood out of sight along one of the corridors, hidden around a corner of the wall. She knew she was neglecting her work. But she could not help herself. The compulsion was too strong to set eyes on him before a grand event the likes of which she had been listening to Florilyn describe all day.

Her reaction was exactly like Florilyn's. At sight of Percy as she peeped around the corner, Gwyneth felt a tightening in her chest. Could that really be *her* Percy. . .her friend of the seashore and hills. . .the same Percy who sat in Grannie's cottage day after day as if he were a simple villager. . .her sharer of the special places? She could hardly believe it!

Then the familiar laugh echoed down the hall in response to something Florilyn had said. The sound fell into Gwyneth's ear with a pang even as it sent her heart leaping. It was Percy!

Yet how could Percy be two such different people? How could he walk and talk with her like a friend, run along with bare feet on the sand, laughing as he dashed in and out of the incoming waves like a jubilant boy, and now be so dazzling and handsome?

As she crept away and returned to her final duties of the day, many confusing thoughts rushed through the brain of Gwyneth Barrie. How could one like her, so small, so slow of speech, a simple peasant girl who kept animals and took care of her Grannie and her papa, ever be worthy of one like Percy Drummond?

The sight of him had been a revelation, a wonder. Yet it was also a crushing blow. In that moment, Gwyneth had also seen herself. She knew she had allowed herself to build foolish castles in the sky and to dream dreams that could never be.

The brougham with its four passengers left Westbrooke Manor and arrived at its destination forty minutes later.

The scene at the Burrenchobay estate as they approached was bright and festive. In the distance could be heard strains of music.

A servant led them in at the front door with the stream of guests who had been arriving for some time from the best homes throughout North Wales. The sounds grew louder, accompanied by laughter from behind the house. The butler continued before them through a wide hall decorated with medieval replicas, not unlike those in Westbrooke Manor, and out to the garden. There a hastily assembled choir of male voices was raised in resonant harmony to the strains of "God Save the Queen."

Always singing in Wales! Percy laughed to himself. He heard music coming from every cottage in Llanfryniog. Fishermen at their nets might spontaneously burst into song without warning, two or three together, and within minutes be joined by voices from boats out on the water. The servants around the house were constantly humming or singing to themselves.

The anthem ended with rousing applause from every quarter as the fifty or so guests broke into smaller groups.

The young lady for whom the occasion had been planned had purposefully delayed her appearance for maximum effect. . .and, most important, until the contingent from Westbrooke Manor arrived.

Davina Burrenchobay reached the bottom of the stairs, slowed and tried to calm herself, pinched both cheeks to make sure they were pink, then continued through the central hall and toward the gathering outside.

Several of her friends scurried to meet her.

"Has anyone seen Percy?" asked Davina.

"He's here!" said one of her friends excitedly. "He's over there with his uncle and your parents. . .*and* that Florilyn Westbrooke."

"Don't worry about her," said Davina. "Once he sets eyes on me, he will forget his cousin."

"Do you think he'll ask you to dance?" asked one of Davina's fawning friends.

"I intend to make sure of it, Iola. If he doesn't, I shall ask him!"

She continued through the crowd spread out on the expansive lawns to the side of the house, an entourage of four or five young ladies following her about just as she had once followed Florilyn.

"Ah, Lord Snowdon," said a distinguished-looking gentleman approaching the viscount and Katherine with outstretched hand, "how good of you to come."

"Thank you, Armond," replied Westbrooke. "And greetings to you, Lady Arial," he added, smiling to the woman at Burrenchobay's side.

The wives exchanged greetings along with their husbands.

Sir Armond Burrenchobay and Roderick Westbrooke had virtually grown up together on the north coast of Wales, both from old Welsh families. They had pursued different interests through the years, with the result that Burrenchobay had risen through the political ranks into its highest echelons.

"I would like you both to meet my nephew, Percival Drummond," said Westbrooke. "Percy is in Wales for a few weeks."

Handshakes followed.

"I've heard about your visit," said Burrenchobay to Percy. "You were here some years back, were you not? I believe my eldest son knows you."

"Yes, we. . .uh, ran into one another during my previous visit," replied Percy.

"That's fine—good. Perhaps you shall have a chance to renew your friendship."

The adults gradually moved away, talking among themselves.

"Hello, Percy," said Burrenchobay's daughter, slinking forward in the wake of her father's departure, dropping her eyes for just the right effect.

"Hello, Davina," replied Percy with the humorous poise of an adult speaking to a child. "Finally leaving the awkward age of fifteen behind, eh. Happy birthday."

At his side, Florilyn smiled inwardly at Percy's wit. She could not help enjoying the chagrin she saw in Davina's eyes at the reminder of how young Percy considered her.

"Thank you," said Davina recovering herself. "I'm so glad you could come. I am hoping you will dance with me. It *is* my birthday, you know."

"If Florilyn will allow me," rejoined Percy, casting a grin to his side, "I suppose it might be arranged. Wouldn't be right to disappoint the birthday girl!"

At the far end of the garden, Colville Burrenchobay came out of the house with Rhawn Lorimer at his side. Neither appeared happy. A perceptive observer would have seen that they had been arguing.

Percy was stunned by the change that had taken place. Both looked older than three short years could account for. If possible, Rhawn was even more beautiful than before, yet her face had a hard look, and she had done considerable filling out. Though her profile would still have been capable of making grown men swoon, she no longer boasted that willowy figure of youth that was still evident in Florilyn and young Davina.

As for Colville Burrenchobay, his expression and demeanor was, for lack of a better word, threatening. To call it evil might have been going too far. Still, Percy shuddered at the sight. He would not need to be reminded to keep well clear of Davina's older brother.

Soon the dancing was in full swing to the sound of a string sextet. Thinking it best to get the inevitable over with as quickly as possible, Percy had consented to Davina's entreaties. She was thus enjoying a second waltz with the young man, as she supposed, that she was about to steal from Florilyn Westbrooke. A few of the other girls, following Davina's example, had succeeded in enticing a handful of single youths in the direction of the music. Gradually the dance area filled with couples of all ages.

As dancing and discussions continued, servants moved silently among the guests bearing trays laden with tea, coffee, and for the most special of guests, samples from Burrenchobay's private reserve of thirty-year-old whiskey imported from the Scottish highlands. Several tables at one end would be heavily laden with a lavish spread of food within the hour and were now set with cups and saucers, milk and sugar, and additional steaming pots of tea.

Wives from twenty to sixty clustered about the grounds chatting about husbands and children and everything else wives and mothers talk about. These included several newly married young ladies, suddenly transformed from girls to matrons. One or two of these cast about distracted glances toward the dancers, accompanied by inward twinges of envy to think that they had married so young and would never more know the gaiety and freedom that Davina Burrenchobay and their former friends still enjoyed.

But the vortex of the gathering, as in all such events from London to Inverness, was reserved for the unmarried young men and young women who had been fortunate enough to receive invitations. Among them stirred budding affections to pluck a hundred invisible heartstrings that would result in many individual dramas of hope and heartbreak, triumph and disappointment.

Swirling and twirling with flourish, those young women were engaged in the wily art practiced since time began, of attempting to attract the eye of every young man on the premises. Some flirtations were modest, others bold, a few outright brazen. But all had the same end in view—to be *noticed*. . .then to draw a lingering shy smile, from some handsome boy, to be followed, whether in ten minutes or an hour, by the bashful invitation to the dance floor.

The most eligible of the young men, on their parts, carried out with exquisite perfection their own portion of the timeless rite, which was pretending *not* to notice. All the while they spoke of hunting and horses and guns, to all appearances oblivious to the giggles and fluttering eyelashes of the fairer sex.

The older and more handsome among them knew well enough that every smile, every laugh, every gesture was capable of causing one or another of the girls to go weak at the knees. Young men knew how to flirt, too. Thus, they chose exactly when to allow a grin, how wide to make their smiles, and where to direct them toward some vulnerable heart.

This was the centuries-old ritual of the British "coming out," practiced on the yearly stage of London's social season. Tonight's event had been planned merely as Davina Burrenchobay's warmup for the main event a year hence.

To have seen this undercurrent of coquetry on the part of the young ladies and roguery on the part of the young men and to have witnessed the self-preoccupied interplay among the youthful generation would have made the skin crawl on the arms and neck of Edward and Mary Drummond of Glasgow. That many of today's charms from the girl who swirled at the center of attention had been specifically designed in this case to lure and fascinate their own son would have broken their hearts. But they would have been proud to know that his reaction, after ten minutes at Burrenchobay Hall, was substantially the same as theirs would have been. None of the wiles directed at him exercised the slightest movement of either his heart or his ego. Already Percy was anxious to have the evening done with. For the sake of his aunt and uncle, however, he tried to enjoy himself.

At long last, having observed the machinations of the younger girls long enough, Rhawn Lorimer decided to show them how it was done. She left Davina's brother and prepared to move in for the kill.

As the drama of the social elite of Snowdonia was playing out its subtleties, on a hill overlooking Burrenchobay Hall, a lonely figure sat watching from a distance of some four hundred yards. The lights gleamed, and the music drifted up from afar and stung her young heart with longings she had never felt in the brief span of her sixteen years. After reaching home, consumed by thoughts of the celebration someone like her would never attend, Gwyneth had run over the hills, like a moth to the flame, and now sat watching and listening in silence as the dusk of evening closed around her.

"So, young Drummond," purred Rhawn Lorimer, sidling through the group of juveniles and squeezing Davina aside, "it would appear that you are the hit of the evening with the *younger* crowd."

Her emphasis of the word was lost neither on Percy nor the listening girls. But they had idolized Rhawn for a long time and were in truth a little afraid of her.

As she spoke, Rhawn gradually steered Percy away from the others. Unconsciously he followed, glancing about as if looking for Florilyn. A tingle of excited terror surged through him as he felt Rhawn's hand slip through his arm. Soon they were alone.

"I've been hurt that you haven't come to see me," she said seductively. "I hear you have been back for weeks."

"Not that long, really." Percy laughed, trying to make light of it. "I just arrived."

"Don't lie to me, Percy. You've been here almost two weeks. I keep track of you."

"I'm only here for a short visit anyway."

"All the more reason you should have come to see me. You will be leaving in a matter of days. We have much to catch up on."

Again Percy laughed, but nervously. He was feeling like a fly caught in the web of a very clever spider.

"Come, Percy. . .let's dance."

"I would really rather not, Rhawn," replied Percy. "I heard that you traded Courtenay for Colville, and I don't want to make *either* of them angry. I saw you with Colville, and he doesn't like me. Surely you know that. I think it would be best if I—"

"Percy, *please*," Rhawn interrupted. Her tone could hardly be mistaken. "I *want* to dance with you. If you don't, I will make a scene and tell Colville that you tried to get too friendly with me. I don't think you want that, do you, Percy? Whereas. . .if you give me what I want, I will make sure he keeps away from you."

Percy sighed. He knew when he was beaten. "I guess you win," he said. "So. . .may I have the honor of this dance?"

Rhawn smiled with her victory, gave a slight curtsy, and extended her hand. As if he were reaching for a cobra, Percy took it. They moved toward the rest of the dancers while Davina Burrenchobay looked on with helpless envy.

If Percy had hoped to placate Rhawn Lorimer in whatever game she was playing with a single inauspicious dance, he soon realized how mistaken he was. He found himself flying about among the other couples, wondering who was leading and who was following. Rhawn was loud and boisterous, laughing gaily as if intentionally trying to draw attention to herself. Percy wondered if she had been drinking.

The first dance was followed by a second, then a third. Between dances Rhawn clung to him like wallpaper. She continued to laugh and talk loudly. The eyes of everyone in the place followed them about. Mercifully, Colville Burrenchobay was nowhere to be seen. Percy had not seen Courtenay the whole evening.

After five dances, to Percy's profound relief, Rhawn excused herself, saying she was suddenly not feeling well. She disappeared inside the house.

Percy immediately glanced about for his cousin. He located her by the refreshment table almost the same instant he saw Davina Burrenchobay making a beeline toward him. He hurried toward Florilyn.

She saw him approaching and waited, a humorous smile on her lips. If she had been bothered that Percy had been thus far monopolized by her two former friends, she showed no sign of it.

Percy raised his eyebrows and shook his head as if overwhelmed and bewildered by what had taken place with Rhawn Lorimer. "I fear I have been neglecting you, my dear cousin," he said for the benefit of those standing nearby. "I hope you have been having a good time." He led her away, one eye roving to keep out of the way of the birthday girl, then put his arm around Florilyn's waist as the music to the next dance began.

As they moved together, he bent to her ear. "Why didn't you come rescue me? That Rhawn is too much!"

Florilyn's tinkling laughter sounded over the music. "It didn't appear to me that you needed rescuing," she said. "Besides, I've learned not to tangle with Rhawn."

"Do you think she's tipsy? She was acting really weird!"

"I don't know," replied Florilyn more seriously. "She is so changed, I hardly know her anymore."

"All I know is that I was in over my head. You just stay on my arm and don't let any of these conniving girls near me! And that includes little Davina. What is with her anyway?"

"She has a crush on you, Percy," laughed Florilyn. "She and all her friends. Isn't it obvious?"

"I thought I was supposed to be *your* escort. Fight them off with a stick if you have to! I'm yours for the rest of this evening—no one else's."

"If you say so." Florilyn laughed. "But if Rhawn comes back, you're on your own. I'm fond of you, Percy—but not fond enough to fight Rhawn for you."

"Hey—I fought for you once. Remember?"

"How could I forget? But Rhawn Lorimer is more dangerous than Colville Burrenchobay."

Meanwhile, the conversation between the two most powerful men in the region was progressing along different lines.

"I must say, Roderick," remarked the host, "what do you think of all this new money flooding into Wales on the heels of industry?"

"Good for the economy, I suppose," replied Westbrooke.

"Yes, but is it good for Wales?" rejoined Burrenenchobay. "Everywhere we've got *nouveau riche* industrialists buying up land, pretending they're something they're not."

"Where's the harm, Armond?" queried his neighbor.

"It's the idea of it I resent. I can't but think they're going to ruin the country in the end."

"You don't deny that the money is good for Wales."

"It may be her ruin as well. Look at what the slate mine has done to the land between our two estates."

"It gives people work."

"Perhaps, but I don't like to see the land cut to pieces. And if coal ever comes north, I hate the thought of it. Men like you and me must do our best to preserve the land of our heritage from such development."

"Men like *you*, don't you mean. I have no power to change the march of events. You do."

"I am but a humble back bencher, Roderick. I've got no more power in parliament than a fly on the wall."

Taking a break after several dances with Florilyn, and still keeping his eyes roving for any sign of danger, Percy wandered in the direction of his uncle and host.

"Ah, Percy, my boy, enjoying yourself?" said the viscount as he approached.

"All this dancing is a bit much for me, Uncle Roderick."

"You're young—enjoy it while you can. My friend Sir Armond here is a MP. Any complaints you have about the country, just bring them to him."

Burrenchobay laughed. "It is not quite so simple as that, young Drummond, I fear," he said. "So, you're a Scotsman, eh?"

"Yes, sir. My father is a vicar in Glasgow."

"A vicar. . .I see. Are all Scots as religious as they say?"

"I really don't know. What *do* they say?"

"That you Scots are all canting revivalists."

"I hope I am not a canting revivalist, as you say, Sir Armond. I thought it was you Welsh who were famous for revivals. In any event, my father is not a revivalist, I can assure you."

"Do you follow his ideals in matters of religion?"

"I would say so, yes. More than that, however, I hope I am simply a young man who tries to do what God gives him to do."

Burrenchobay stared at him blankly. "What exactly do you mean?" he asked after a moment. "I am not aware of ever being given anything by God to do myself. The phrase is new to me. I assume you mean something by it."

"Only that I try to order my life by the commands of Him who said He came from God to show us how to live."

Again, a stupefied stare met Percy's words. "I must say, if I didn't know better, I would think you were drunk. I know you Scots love whiskey and religion. Have you been partaking from my stock of Glen Grant over there at the refreshment table?"

"No, sir. I never touch it."

"Then I cannot imagine where a young man like you came by such notions. I've never heard the like from someone so young, nor from *anyone* outside the pulpit. Is that where you got it, from your father's pulpit?"

"Not from his pulpit, but from his character," replied Percy. "I wasn't a very good learner for most of my life. I am finally remembering much that my father taught me, the foremost teaching of which is to obey God and let Him order my steps so far as it lies within my power to do so."

"You'll have to excuse my nephew," laughed the viscount. "As he told you, his father, my brother-in-law, is a minister. Runs in families, I suppose." Even though his natural inclination was to explain away Percy's outspokenness to his friend, as he listened, the viscount could not help feeling a strange respect for his nephew. He had never considered himself a religious man and had always tended to look down on Katherine's brother. Yet what father would not be proud of a young man of such principle and moral character as Edward Drummond's son?

Gradually the dusk of the June evening enveloped the Wales countryside. Dancing and music, eating and drinking continued. As a chill slowly descended, some of the party moved inside to the parlors and drawing rooms of Burrenchobay Hall.

When Gwyneth finally rose to walk home from where she had been watching on the hill overlooking the hall, it was after ten and growing dark. She would almost have been able to find the way back to her cottage with her eyes closed. But the occasional tears that rose in her eyes made it more difficult to see the path beneath her feet. She had never cried for herself in her life. She knew she was crying for herself now, and she was ashamed.

Most of the guests who were not spending the night were gone from Burrenchobay Hall by eleven fifteen, aided in their homegoing by a near full moon and the dying remnants of a spectacular sunset in the west.

The carriage bearing the Westbrooke and Drummond contingent passed through the gates of Westbrooke Manor a few minutes before midnight.

Several days later it was all over the region that Rhawn Lorimer was in a young woman's worst trouble and that Percy was the cause of it.

FIFTY-NINE

Death Visits Snowdonia

*T*hree days after the party, Gwyneth was due for work at Westbrooke Manor. By ten o'clock she had still not made her appearance.

The rumors regarding Percy Drummond and Rhawn Lorimer did not drift so quickly up from Llanfryniog to Westbrooke Manor as they had circulated through the village. A few whispers, however, had begun to circulate among the servants and staff. As Lady Florilyn's best friend for many years and a frequent visitor to the manor, and then for a time as Courtenay's young lady, every one of them knew Rhawn Lorimer. Most had formed some opinion about her in recent years. They were only too happy to voice them in the servants' quarters or when Mrs. Drynwydd poured out eleven o'clock tea for the staff.

When Olwyn Gwlwlwyd finally carried the fully formed report from the village that Rhawn Lorimer was in a family way, whispering to Mrs. Drynwydd and Mrs. Llewellyn that their own Percy, whom they loved as if he were one of them, was the father-to-be, the women went into a flurry of denial, demanding where she had heard such a scandalous lie.

It happened that Florilyn chanced by the open door of the laundry room at that very moment looking for Gwyneth. She retreated swiftly and noiselessly along the hall, ears burning and eyes stinging from what she had heard.

It could not possibly be true, she told herself in a frenzy of girlish emotion. Percy wouldn't do that to her. Percy *couldn't* do that to her!

Yet in that irrational reaction to which youth is especially vulnerable, as her thoughts swirled in a turmoil of confusion, she took her vexation out on the nearest target.

Her emotions furious at Percy for stringing her along when he had been in love with Rhawn from the beginning—though she still didn't believe a word of it!—Florilyn stormed into Percy's room without benefit of announcing herself. "Where is she?" she exclaimed angrily.

Percy glanced up from the desk where he was writing to his father. There stood Florilyn, red-faced, eyes full of an expression he had never seen in them before. He gazed at her with a confused expression. "Where is. . . ? I'm not sure what you mean," he said.

"That little Gwyneth is late—two hours late! I've a good mind to tell her not to come back."

Percy rose and walked toward her. "Calm down, Florilyn," he said. "I'm sure there is a reasonable explanation."

He was shocked by the look on her face. She backed away as he approached, as if he had the plague.

"Tell you what," he said. "I'll ride down and find out what is going on."

Ten minutes later Percy was on Grey Tide's back galloping across the moor.

Florilyn watched him go from the window in her room. She then fell on her bed, crying in earnest at how ridiculously she had just behaved. She was frightened and furious and hurt all at once by the dreadful rumor. She was angry at Percy for being so nice to everyone, including Gwyneth and Rhawn and everyone. At the same time, she was angry at herself for acting like a featherbrain.

Percy reached the cottage of Codnor Barrie and found it empty. He remounted and rode in haste into town. There he found Grannie agitated. Percy said he had come looking for Gwyneth because she hadn't turned up for work at the manor and he was concerned.

"They won't find her at the manor today," said Grannie. "She's up at her auntie Adela's."

"Why there?" asked Percy.

"Little Gwyneth, bless her, awoke in the night with premonitions. She couldn't sleep. Thinking I was in danger, she came to me while it was yet dark, the dear girl. I was already awake, for I had been roused by the same fears. I felt death all around me. I was trembling, wondering if it was coming to me. But Gwyneth said that it was her uncle, not me. She crept into bed with me, but neither of us slept another wink. At dawn she set out for Adela's. Oh, if only I was there myself!"

"Do you think the old man is dying?" asked Percy.

"I have no doubt in my mind," replied Grannie.

"Could you ride that far, Grannie?" asked Percy. "That is, if I had a buggy?"

"Aye, I could, though it's been many a year since I was so far into the hills."

"Then wait for me and be ready. I will return as soon as I am able."

Percy left the cottage and raced back to the manor. He went in immediate search of his uncle. He found him in his study. "Uncle Roderick," he said, "I have a favor to ask."

"Anything, Percy, my boy."

"May I borrow one of your smaller buggies for the day?"

"Of course. What's the occasion?"

"I want to take Grannie Barrie up to the Muir cottage. It appears that Mr. Muir is dying."

"I cannot have that old witch in one of my buggies," said his uncle.

"It would mean a great deal to me, Uncle Roderick."

"Simply out of the question, Percy," said his uncle, shaking his head. "When I said anything, of course, I meant nothing like *that*. Anything else I can do for you?"

More annoyed than disappointed to see how widespread the nonsense about Grannie truly was, and still having no idea what mischief was circling ever closer to his own reputation, Percy left the house. Without hesitating, he went to the barn and immediately set about hitching the oldest buggy in the place to one of the most reliable horses, an old mare of some twelve years. It was a buggy that, to his knowledge, had not been used in years and a horse that was not taken out but once in six months, if that.

Fifteen minutes later he was on his way with both into the village. He found Grannie on pins and needles with excitement at the thought of a ride into the beloved hills that she had never expected to set eyes on again. Percy helped her up into the seat with the grace of one taking a young lady to a ball then climbed up beside her.

The way was rough, for the road, if such it could be called, had not been repaired in years. No buggy had traversed it in more years than anyone could remember, as Grannie told Percy while they bounced along. Percy found himself wondering if they would make it at all. If so, would he be able to return his uncle's buggy in one piece without the wheels being reduced to splinters?

Gwyneth heard their approach. She and Adela and Stevie Muir ran from the cottage, unable to imagine what could possibly bring a buggy to their door. They were amazed to see Grannie seated on the open bench beside Percy.

"Grannie!" exclaimed Adela. "How do you come here?"

"See for yourself, Adela. Gwyneth's friend Percy. How's the laddie?"

"He's fading, I'm thinking," replied Stevie's mother. "But it's the Lord's mercy to be taking him home at last."

Percy leaped down, then offered Grannie his hand and helped her to the ground as if she were a young woman again. Then they all went into the cottage together.

SIXTY

The Charge and Its Answer

*I*t was well after dinner that evening when Percy rode slowly back into the precincts of Westbrooke Manor, still having no premonition of the vortex of sordid controversy that was soon to engulf him.

He was weary from the long day, and his heart was full of its events. He had never witnessed death in his life. The experience had sobered him, not for the least of reasons the peace of those involved as they watched their beloved father and husband and uncle and friend go to his waking on the other side of the eternal sunrise.

Far from being sad, the experience was beautiful to behold. Tears had accompanied it. But they were tears of fullness not emptiness, tears of gratitude for a life well lived rather than those of sadness and regret. It was a day that would remain in his memory forever.

By now the last thing on his mind were the circumstances of the early morning. He had almost forgotten that he had taken the buggy without his uncle's permission. Nor had he an idea that, since learning of it, his uncle had been watching for his return all day, his anger seething hotter with every passing hour.

Percy was completely unprepared for his uncle's reaction as he stormed out of the house. Percy had just climbed down and was leading the horse into the barn when his uncle strode up behind him.

"What do you mean by stealing my buggy and taking it for the day?" said the viscount in a loud voice.

Percy turned. "I'm sorry, Uncle Roderick," he said. "I really needed to use a buggy, and I had no time to explain. I didn't think you would mind my using this old thing."

"Its age has nothing to do with it. That happens to be my buggy, and you stole it."

At last realizing that his uncle was truly angry, though still perplexed as to what could be the cause, Percy shook his head in confusion. "I don't quite know what to say, Uncle Roderick," he said. "It wasn't like that. Surely you aren't seriously thinking I *stole* it?"

"What else would you call it?"

"I would say that I borrowed it. I hoped you wouldn't mind."

"Well, I do mind! I specifically told you no."

"I didn't think it would be that serious to you. I apologize."

"And you expect me to accept your apology, just like that? Pretend it never happened, is that it?"

"I don't know, Uncle Roderick," sighed Percy, tired and in truth growing a little exasperated. "I am confused, that's all. I must say I did not expect this kind of reaction from you. Do whatever you want— throw me out. . .charge me a day's rent on buggy and horse and I will gladly pay it. . .send me home if you want. All I am saying is that I am sorry to have upset you. Again, I offer my apology."

Still huffing, but with the wind taken out of his sails by Percy's soft tongue, the viscount turned and strode back to the house.

Under the circumstances, when he had the buggy put away and Hollin Radnor had taken charge of the horse, Percy slipped into the house through the servants' entrance and went straight to his room without seeing any of the family.

He met only his aunt at breakfast the next morning. She was quieter than usual and seemed behaving oddly. The servants, too, throughout the day looked at him with peculiar expressions. He saw nothing of Florilyn.

By early afternoon, great black clouds were rolling in from the north, accompanied by a precipitous drop in temperature. Having by then judged that he would surely have cooled off, Percy again sought his uncle. He found him subdued and not particularly talkative. Whether he was embarrassed by what had taken place or still angry, Percy could not tell.

"Could I talk to you, Uncle Roderick?" asked Percy, standing at the open door.

An affirmative wave of the hand beckoned him in.

"I am sorry about the buggy incident," Percy began, "mostly for taking it behind your back. That was wrong of me. But it has occurred to me to wonder whether you are at all curious about my reasons."

"You told me you wished to take that old woman in the village to visit some peasants in the hills."

"Yes. If I recollect, you called her a witch."

"What of it?"

"She is not a witch, Uncle Roderick," rejoined Percy. "I happen to be on very friendly terms with Mrs. Barrie, as, I am happy to say, your daughter is also. She is one of the finest women in all Llanfryniog. You would know that yourself if you took more interest in your tenants."

"How dare you accuse me of. . .of. . ." The viscount hesitated. He didn't quite know *what* he was being accused of.

"Of not being interested in the lives of your people," added Percy, finishing the thought for him. "What would *you* call it, then?" he went on. "*Are* you interested in them, Uncle Roderick? One of them lay dying in his bed yesterday. One of his closest relatives wanted to see him before the end. Yet all you could think of was a dilapidated old buggy that was gathering dust in your barn that you will never ride in again as long as you live. Your people would love you if you gave them half a chance, Uncle Roderick. But you never go near them."

A heavy silence hung in the air. Percy's words stung all the more in that his uncle knew they were true. His anger of the day before had sufficiently spent itself so that whatever defense might have risen from his old Adam died before it reached his lips. "And. . .what of the old man?" he asked after a moment, making a stab at expressing a modicum of concern.

"He died late yesterday afternoon," replied Percy. "His family was around him. His hand rested in Grannie's as she prayed right up until the moment God took him. His wife and son were at his side, as were Gwyneth and myself. His passing was peaceful. It was one of the most extraordinary days I have ever spent, and I will never forget it. So while I am sorry to have upset you and for acting behind your back, I cannot be sorry that I was there or for making it possible for Mrs. Barrie to be there. When I last saw her, Florilyn was angry with Gwyneth for not coming to work. If you have any influence with your daughter in the matter, I hope you might speak a word to her on Gwyneth's behalf. I think she was perturbed at me as well. She was behaving irritably and strangely. I am not sure why. I doubt my influence will carry very far with her just now."

"Don't be too sure, Percy, my boy. You may discover that you carry *great* weight with Florilyn, more than you know. However, you're right—she tends to be impulsive. Family trait, you know. I will see what I can do."

"Thank you, sir."

"However, there may be reasons having nothing to do with what happened yesterday to account for my daughter's change of mood," the viscount said. "She has been devastated by the news, as we all have. She spent much of the day yesterday crying, as my wife tells me. For her brother's sake, your aunt shed a good many tears of her own as well. I did not hear of the affair until a short time ago. Maybe they tried to keep it from me, knowing that I was already angry with you. They probably thought I would send you away, which I may have to do anyway."

"I am sorry, Uncle Roderick," said Percy, "but I must confess I have no idea what you are talking about. What reason does Florilyn have to be angry with me and cry all day? And why would you send me away? Is it really over my use of that old buggy?"

"Tut, tut, my boy. It is more serious than that. I am talking about you and Miss Lorimer."

"What about us—that I danced with her the other night? Gosh, I am sorry if that hurt Florilyn's feelings. But the girl was most insistent. She threatened to make a scene if I did not dance with her. Under the circumstances, I thought it best—"

"By heavens, man!" thundered Lord Snowdon as his fist slammed down on his desk with a sudden resurfacing of his anger. "Stop playing innocent with me. Out with it! Is it true? That's all I want to know."

Percy stared back at his uncle dumbfounded.

"I told you. . .yes, I danced with the girl. I have never denied it. Everyone saw us. *You* saw us."

"Are you intentionally trying to act like an imbecile? I don't mean the dancing. I mean the rumor—is it true?"

"What rumor?"

"About you and the Lorimer girl! Her father came to see me this morning demanding to know what I intended to do. Are you or are you not the father of her child?"

Percy stared back speechless again. The words slammed into his brain like an ongoing locomotive. "Her. . .*child*!" he repeated slowly.

"She says you are the father."

Percy broke out laughing. "I know I'm not the most worldly wise young man in the world," he said, still chuckling, "but, Uncle Roderick. . . I've only been here three weeks."

"Stop making light of it, you young fool. This is a serious matter with grave consequences. She claims that you and she had a liaison in Glasgow."

At last his uncle's words silenced him. Percy exhaled slowly and stood for some time in silence. "I see," he said at length. "Yes, you're right, it is serious. I am sorry for seeming to take it lightly. I had no idea what was being said."

Again he drew in a deep breath and let it out slowly. No wonder Florilyn had been so strange yesterday morning. Then came an even more horrifying thought—what if the rumors had reached Gwyneth's ears?

His uncle's voice interrupted his reflections. "You still have not answered me," he said. "I must know. Is it true?"

Percy stood in silence. He was thinking hard. He was remembering many things he had heard and been taught through the years.

"I think, Uncle Roderick," he said at last, "that I would prefer not to answer."

"That is as good as admitting it is true!"

"Only in the mind of one who does not understand silence."

"I demand that you answer the charges!" the viscount shrieked.

"I am sorry, Uncle Roderick."

"Do you refuse me?"

"If you demand that I answer. . .yes."

"Then at least tell me *why* you refuse," rejoined his uncle, calming slightly.

"Jesus says not to worry about how to defend yourself. When accused, He did not defend Himself."

"What does that have to do with anything?"

"I try to follow His example."

"There you go preaching at me again!"

"I am sorry. Nothing was further from my mind."

"What was on your mind then?" asked the viscount sarcastically.

"That you are going to have to decide for youself whether you think I am capable of such a heinous thing as is being said. You have to decide what you think of my character. But I will not defend myself. Nor will I stoop to answer the charges."

At last the viscount was silenced, even if momentarily. "A noble sentiment," he said after a few seconds. "Idealistic, though naive. Would it not be easier to put all doubt about the matter to rest and simply to say yea or nay?"

"It would not put the matter to rest," said Percy.

"What makes you say that?"

"Because those inclined to believe the rumor would go on believing it even if I denied it. The stronger my denials, the surer they would be I was lying. One of the few Shakespeare quotes I happen to know concerns protesting too much. There are certain kinds of charges, Uncle Roderick, that can *only* be countered by silence—and those are charges against one's character and veracity as a man. I am not much of a man yet. But I am enough one to know that this is such a time. The only way you will be able to arrive at the truth in this matter, as you say, is for you to arrive at that truth within your *own* heart. Nothing I say will help you or convince you one way or the other. I alone must bear the burden of the doubts that may hound me as a result of this. But the burden of proof, for *you*, Uncle Roderick, must rest with you."

Percy turned and left him. Even as he walked down the corridor to the stairway, hoping he would encounter no one before reaching the sanctuary of his own room, his eyes filled. How many people would be hurt before this was over he could not begin to imagine. He hoped it could be kept from his parents. He had hurt them enough already. He also prayed the ugliness would not reach Gwyneth. Yet he saw no way she could not be drawn into a knowledge of it.

In his study, Lord Snowdon rose and walked to the window and stared out at the turbulent gray sky, alone with his thoughts. The young fool was made of stern stuff, he thought. Better stuff than his own son, he sighed wistfully. The boy had courage—courage to confront an ugly rumor calmly like a man. . .and courage as well to confront him to his face about his treatment of his tenants.

By jove if the young son of a minister wasn't right. He *did* avoid his tenants. He couldn't help it. Poverty made him uncomfortable.

If only he could find a young man like *that* to marry his daughter! That is, if the thing wasn't true. Young men like Percy Drummond didn't grow on trees, thought the viscount as he continued to reflect on the interview that had just taken place.

Already Percy's silence in the face of the accusation was beginning to accomplish its work. In his heart of hearts, Roderick Westbrooke was all but convinced of the falsehood of it.

By day's end, almost as a judgment against all of North Wales for the ease with which its gossipmongers were able to spread a lie, and the readiness of its inhabitants to believe it, a tremendous storm broke over the region. The wind battered the coastline. Rain poured down in sheets. No one who did not have business outside ventured into it.

SIXTY-ONE

The Power of Mistress Chattan's Brew

*T*he fishermen of North Wales were an independent breed who kept both friendships and compliments close to the vest. Young Percival Drummond had cultivated an association with several of the more liberal-minded among them. Whether he would even now be considered a *friend*, however, was doubtful. That he had come closer to it in a shorter time than any other visitor to Llanfryniog in memory, especially one so young, was certain. As far as compliments went, about the best that could be hoped for was a nod of the head as he walked away from the harbor and a mumbled aside, "Not a bad sort. . .for a Scots laddie."

They made their living in the hardest of all possible ways—at sea. They did not give the hand of friendship to one who was not worthy of the honor.

There was one consumable item of commerce, however, capable of lubricating geniality and accelerating the bonds, if not of true friendship at least of the laughter and free-flowing conversation that often passed for it among men who knew no better. That one thing was Mistress Chattan's ale. Everyone knew that she did not brew it herself. Yet to a man, the male inhabitants of Llanfryniog swore that it was unlike any beer in the world—light or dark, Irish or English, lager or ale.

And thus when a man such as Rupert Wilkes stood beers at Mistress Chattan's, he was a man granted unusual privileges of access and conversation. None of the locals knew anything about him or where he came from. He appeared periodically, was generous to one and all at the inn, and always seemed particularly interested in the old times. He was most curious about those who had been alive before the turn of the present century. His questions always got around eventually to old Sean Drindod and his friends who might have known one another in those bygone days.

After Drindod's death, the fellow had disappeared for a long while. The fishermen of Llanfryniog began to think they had seen the last of him. Then he began showing up again and gradually with increasing regularity. From Drindod he had heard the mysterious name "Bryn." Since that time, Mistress Chattan's ale had not sufficiently loosened the tongues of the village's oldest citizens to reveal more. Whether anyone knew who it was, he had not been able to discover. And he had to make his inquiries with care.

It took three years. But at last the drunken tongue of an old fisherman, long retired, who rarely frequented Mistress Chattan's establishment, divulged a name—Branwenn Myfanawy, as she was known as a child.

Wilkes took in the name with greater interest than he allowed himself to show, bought the man another pint, and continued to shrewdly ply him with questions that eventually led him to a description of the location of Grannie's cottage. Whether she was the same woman, he didn't know. But he would search the place and find out. If the old woman caused him trouble, she could join her friend Drindod.

SIXTY-TWO

Grannie's Tale

$\mathcal{M}$ ortified about what was being said about him, Percy kept to himself. He found the writings of MacDonald a great solace in his trouble. But his aunt and uncle were distant. The servants avoided him. He did not see Florilyn for an entire day. She did not appear at dinner. The greatest humiliation, however, was having to imagine what Gwyneth must think.

Gwyneth had indeed heard the rumors. She could scarcely avoid it among the other servants. Gwyneth Barrie had rarely known anger in her life. But what she heard filled her with righteous indignation. She kept her thoughts to herself but went about her duties with smoke coming out her ears. She may have been small, but this was enough to ignite the fire of indignation in her young heart. It would not have gone well for the magistrate's daughter had she dared pay a visit to the manor and encountered the righteous wrath of Codnor Barrie's daughter.

Gwyneth saw Percy from a distance two or three times. She could tell from the way he walked that he was downcast. She knew he was avoiding her. He was avoiding everyone. And she knew the reason. As furious as she was at the snake Rhawn Lorimer, she knew that Percy's pain must be far deeper to be falsely accused of something so disgusting.

She was burdened for Grannie, too. The old woman had not been herself since Glythvyr Muir's death. She had been talking to herself and behaving strangely ever since the simple funeral, which had been attended by less than a dozen people. Percy had been one of them, though he left quickly afterward. Gwyneth's heart was sore for her two best friends in the world besides her papa.

She asked her father if they could invite Percy and Grannie for supper at their cottage the next evening. It would be a good-bye supper for Percy. Maybe it would make Grannie feel better as well.

And so it was arranged. As she did not have to work, she spent the whole next day in preparations. She bundled up tightly and went out that morning in the driving rain. Her first visit was to the manor, where she left a brief note of invitation for Percy. Then she walked to Grannie's in town, telling her that her father would come for her with their cart after work. At last she went home, chilled to the bone, changed out of her wet clothes, added new coal to the fire, and got busy with preparations for the evening's meal.

Percy was delighted for a reason to miss another silent meal at the manor. He was eager to get away, storm or no storm.

Thankfully, the rain temporarily spent itself by midafternoon. Percy left the manor, bundled against the wind but not thinking that the rain might resume by the time he was on his way home. When he arrived at the Barrie Cottage about six o'clock that evening, Grannie and Codnor were just clattering up the lane. Above them the sky was black and menacing. Percy and Codnor helped Grannie to the ground, and they hurried inside amid a tumultuous wind.

"You will be leaving soon, Percy," said Gwyneth as the three walked in.

"Yes, tomorrow is my last day," he replied. He was relieved to find no one any different toward him. In truth, the rumors had not come within hearing of either Grannie or Codnor Barrie.

"My little girl will miss you, Percy," said Gwyneth's father, helping Grannie to a chair at the table.

"I know," sighed Percy. "I will miss everyone here, too. I almost feel that this is my home now."

The conversation between the four friends flowed freely. For the first time in two days, Percy managed to forget the weight hanging over him.

When supper was over and they retired to the sitting room, Grannie seemed to grow quiet.

"How is Mrs. Muir?" asked Percy, addressing them all. "And Stevie?"

"I have seen them only once since the funeral," said Gwyneth. "They are sad but relieved. The house seems empty without Uncle Glythvyr. But they know he is in a better place."

The reminder of Glythvyr Muir's death plunged Grannie deep into thought. "It is the way of all flesh," she said, leaning back in the rocking chair where she sat. "My own time is not far off, I'm thinking."

"What are you talking about, Grannie?" asked Gwyneth.

"The good man's passing has made me thoughtful, Gwyneth, dear. I am old. I cannot wait longer to tell what I know. The Lord could take me any time. I must tell my tale to them I can trust."

"What tale, Grannie?"

"Get your tea and sit with me. You, Gwyneth child. . .you, my dear Codnor. And you, too, Percy, for you are a good young man, and Grannie knows she can trust you."

In a few minutes they had gathered round her.

"It was like this," Grannie began. "I was walking on the beach as a child." The moment she began, her voice took on an ancient and mysterious tone. The time of which she spoke was seventy-nine years before, in the previous century. "I was out on the white sand below the bluff," she went on, "white and as pretty to a child then as it is now. It was early in the morning. Most of the village still slept. But there'd been a fierce storm all the previous day and most of the night, worse than this one around us now, worse than any storm I've ever seen. I'd felt forebodings in my young heart all night. I heard voices calling out of the wind, wailing in the midst of the storm. I didn't know what I know now, that I had been both blessed and cursed with the ancient eyes that see what a body sometimes wished she hadn't seen.

"I rose early. It was a still dawn. The wind had died down. All about outside was deathly calm, yet still I thought I heard voices, eventually only one voice. I don't mean with my ears, but I heard it inside. And with that voice wailing somewhere in the wind, I couldn't sleep. I'd always been a free kind of child, like yourself, Gwyneth, and my mama and papa seldom worried about me.

"I set out in the morning light. There was a chill over the coast where my feet were leading me—straight to the sea, for throughout the storm I knew the wailing was coming from its waves. I climbed down the path. By the time I reached the sand, the sun was creeping up from behind the mountains in the east, though the promontory kept the beach in darkness for many hours. There was no breath of wind. But the waves still pounded the shore as if reminding me what business they had been about the night before. The tide was brown and gray from the storm, menacing with the color of evil tidings.

"I glanced about, then began walking along the shore like I had a hundred times before. Only this time there was fear in my heart for what I might see. Above me two eyes were watching me. They were the eyes of another youngster in the village, though no friend of mine. He was on top of the cliff. I didn't see him yet. But I would see him before long.

"Halfway down the beach, what should I see but the very thing I knew I'd half expected—the body of a man lying at the water's edge. I ran toward him trembling and knelt down. He looked dead. I reached my hand slowly out to touch his arm.

"Then suddenly it moved! A groan sounded. My heart leaped to my throat in terror. I'd never seen a pirate, but that was surely what the man was. He was fearsome as any man I'd laid eyes on. That he had just come back, as I thought, from the dead made him all the more terrifying. Sensing that I was near, he rolled over. Slowly he opened his eyes and gazed into my face. He tried to speak but couldn't. Then he seemed to gain strength. Finally he spoke." Grannie stopped and took a sip of her tea.

Gwyneth's eyes were huge as she listened. "What did he say?" she asked.

"He said they'd been shipwrecked by the storm, that the great and mighty *Rhodri Mawr* had gone down with all its treasure aboard."

By now Percy's eyes were wide as well.

Grannie's voice took on an eerie sound as she relived the scene from days long gone by. " 'It's all there,' " she went on. " 'It's all out there,' the dying man said, trying to point behind him to the sea. 'The fools wouldn't listen to me. I told them to put in. But they wouldn't listen. Lifeboats no better than sticks in them waves. When the lifeboat broke up and the others went down, I laid hold of a piece of the keel that was floating nearby. It kept me afloat long enough, just long enough. I made it, I tell you. I made it here…and I'm giving it to you, little girl,' he said, now grabbing hold of my arm, 'I'm giving it all to you—the treasure of Dolau Cothi.'

"I stood listening in terror. I hardly heard what he was saying. 'Don't believe me, little girl? I tell you, I saw it…saw it all, helped dig it out of the ruins, a whole chestful—and it's all out there now. It's yours. Look, I'll prove it,' he said. He let go of my arm that he'd kept clutching. I was too terrified to run away. He tried to sit up but fell back into the shallow water, fumbling about in some pocket of his water-soaked clothes. Then his eyes lit up as with fire, and he exclaimed triumphantly. He turned toward me again and thrust in front of my eyes a round gold coin he had pinched between his thumb and forefinger. 'There, little girl—you see! I tell you the whole treasure's there…and it's *yours*.'

"Then a spasm seized him. He coughed and choked and fell backward. His eyes rolled back into his head. Now I was certain he was dead. But then he groaned again, and tried to get up, but still lay on the sand. He opened his eyes and motioned me closer. 'Little girl,' he said, 'you take this coin. It's valuable enough, but I tell you there's thousands of them—down there.' Again he pointed out to sea. 'You take it. You never know what fate your steps will lead you to. Yours led you to me. It's yours now.' He grabbed my hand and pressed the coin into it."

As the three listened to Grannie's spooky tale, suddenly the heavens erupted, and the rain again poured down. They had no idea that at that very moment, had she been at home, Grannie's premonitions about her own fate might well have come to pass.

For as the wild and stormy night advanced, Rupert Wilkes crept to her cottage. No light shown inside. There was no sign of life. He tried the latch on the door. It was not locked. He went inside.

But fate did not order Grannie to die that night by the hand that had murdered the very youngster of her story. And she went on with the tale. "Suddenly I heard footsteps running up behind me," Grannie continued. "I turned, and there was a little boy named Sean Drindod, a little village troublemaker, as I thought. And I was right, for he caused me trouble all his life till his untimely end three years ago."

"'What's that?' he cried, for he had seen the old pirate give me something. He grabbed at my hand and caught a glimpse of the gold. Seeing it, he struggled all the harder to take it from me. 'Give it to me, Bryn!' he cried.

"'The man gave it to me,' I said, squeezing my fingers tight. I knew that if once little Sean got his greedy hands on it, that was the last I would see of it. He fussed and ranted, but being four and I was five, I was stronger and faster than him, and he could do nothing to get it from me.

"I ran back to the village, little Sean on my heels still trying to get his hands on the coin. I told my father everything that had happened. He and some of the men went down to the beach. They found the poor old sailor on shore and pulled him up out of the water and buried him in the town cemetery where you see the marker to this day.

"Word spread quickly up and down the coast. Bits of wood and rope and sail and rigging were gradually found over the next few weeks, confirming that there had indeed been a shipwreck that night. I told everyone what the man had said about the treasure that had gone down with it, though most of the grown-ups laughed because they were already finding out that I saw things other people didn't see. Most of them didn't believe half my stories. And Sean Drindod was known as a mischief maker and liar throughout Llanfryniog. So his tale about the coin, which I repeated to no one, not a soul believed.

"All the rest of his life, Sean tried everything he could to get his hands on that coin. I think he thought it would lead him to the *Rhodri Mawr's* treasure where it had gone down with the ship. But I kept it where no other person ever saw it, though I know he told people of it, and I think he died because of it. And now my own life's in danger just like his."

"How do you know that, Grannie?" asked Codnor Barrie. His voice was serious.

"I can feel it, my boy," she replied. "I can *feel* it. There's those that are looking for me—I can feel their eyes upon me. Maybe it's only death itself that's stalking me. Whatever it be, it is time I passed the coin on, as it was passed on to me. Whether there ever was any box of treasure that went down with that ship, I don't know. But there is this one coin. And it shall be mine no longer." Slowly she untied the gold coin from the inside of her dress. She held it a moment in her hand.

None of the others had ever seen actual gold in their lives. Their eyes widened as they saw the gleam from the ancient coin glitter in the light of the room's lanterns.

She looked at each of the three in turn. "But who is meant to watch over it now?" she said. "I would give it to you, Codnor, for you're a good man, but trouble is bound to follow it, and whoever would find me could find you. But none would think to look for it from a child. So you, Gwyneth—you will take it and keep it safe. It shall be yours, for maybe you will need whatever it might bring you sometime in your life." Grannie handed the coin to Gwyneth.

Gwyneth stared in awe at the bright shiny thing in her palm.

"But be careful," Grannie said. "I fear more than one's been killed for it already. Put it somewhere it will be safe. Tell not a soul about it."

"Was the man who gave you this the same man I saw in the cave, Grannie?" asked Gwyneth.

"It couldn't have been him, Gwyneth, dear. The old pirate who gave me the coin was hauled up and buried with his head still attached to him."

A deep silence fell. The hour had grown late, and dusk was descending. It was nearly dark, and Percy knew he needed to be on his way. It had already been arranged that Grannie would spend the night in the cottage because of the weather.

"It doesn't appear the storm is going to let up," said Percy, glancing out the window. "If I am going to run back to the manor in the rain, I had better get started. Thank you for an enjoyable evening. And, Mr. Barrie, if I do not see you again before I go, good-bye until next time." The two shook hands.

Gwyneth walked with him to the door. When they were alone, she handed Percy the coin. "I want no part of it," she said. "It frightens me. You take it, Percy. You keep it."

"It is yours, Gwyneth."

"Then you keep it for me. Please," she said, with pleading in her eyes.

"I will keep it for *you*, then. But it will always be yours."

Finally launching himself through the door and out into the storm, Percy sprinted for the road then up the hill. When he arrived at the manor ten minutes later, he was drenched to the skin.

SIXTY-THREE

Uncle and Nephew

*T*he stormy night passed fitfully for Roderick Westbrooke, viscount Lord Snowdon.

The previous night he had slept like a baby, relieved as he grew more and more convinced in his mind that Percy was innocent of Rhawn Lorimer's charges. But gradually the other topic of the conversation that had taken place in his study returned to haunt him.

Percy's words from a day before played themselves over and over all night in his brain. *"Your people would love you if you gave them half a chance. . . . But you never go near them."*

The young blackguard had put his finger exactly on the nub of his discomfort with his position. He avoided the very people who depended on him, and upon whom he was likewise dependent for what meager income their rents provided.

The boy's manliness in refusing to defend himself. . .it had enraged him. Yet what a stout show of character!

In spite of his sleeplessness, yet also because of it, the viscount rose early. He felt that it was a day of new beginnings. He made an unexpectedly early appearance in the breakfast room.

The storm had passed and the day dawned cloudless and bright. The danger to Grannie's life had passed, and with it so had the tumult.

Percy and his aunt were the only others present, chatting over their tea and eggs and toast. Things seemed to be gradually returning to their former ways. There was still no sign of Florilyn.

"Ah, Percy, my boy. . .your last day in Wales, what?" said the viscount as he entered with unusual bounce to his step.

"Yes, sir. I am already feeling the sadness of departure coming over me."

"What do you have planned for the day?"

"I don't know—say my farewells, I suppose."

"How about you and I going for a ride together?"

"I would like that, Uncle Roderick."

"And, er. . .about that matter we discussed—the Lorimer girl. I told Katherine what you said. We are both in agreement—we *do* know you are innocent. You have proved yourself, and we know what mettle you are made of. You are right—sometimes silence is the best defense. I am sorry I doubted you."

"Thank you, Uncle Roderick. I appreciate that very much."

"After lunch, then?"

"I will look forward to it."

The ride that afternoon was not what Percy had expected. The apology seemed to have filled his uncle with new energy. He was in a rambunctious mood in the saddle, galloping with abandon, jumping streams recklessly. He was a skilled horseman, and Percy could hardly keep up with him.

"Easy, Uncle Roderick!" Percy laughed more than once as his uncle wobbled and nearly lost his seat. "Now I know where Florilyn gets her nerve in the saddle."

"I never felt better in my life, Percy, my boy. I feel like a young man again!"

On their way back, the viscount slowed, and they rode side by side together. They were still a good distance northeast of the manor.

"You know, Percy, my boy," said his uncle, "it has been a genuine pleasure to have you here this summer. Even more so than last time."

"Thank you, Uncle Roderick. I have enjoyed it, too. I appreciate your hospitality."

"I know my daughter has taken most of your time, but I have greatly enjoyed your company. I would say that I got the better half of the bargain—all your help with the stables—wouldn't you?"

"I had a great time. I wish I could stay longer. But I have a job waiting for me in Aberdeen."

"You are a responsible young man. I'm sure your father is very proud. And," he went on, clearing his throat, "I must repeat my apology for doubting you in the matter of that unfortunate business with the Lorimer girl. I knew better, of course. I was far too hasty to judge you."

"Think nothing of it, Uncle Roderick."

"But I feel bad about it. I had no right. Nevertheless, 'all's well that ends well,' as you are fond of saying."

"One of the two quotes from Shakespeare I know!" Percy laughed.

"What do you think of my daughter, Percy, my boy?" asked the viscount abruptly.

"I don't know, Uncle Roderick. In what way?"

"As a girl, you know—a young woman."

"I am very fond of her. We got off to a bit of a rocky start three years ago. But she and I have become the best of friends. I think a great deal of her."

The viscount took in his words thoughtfully.

Again they rode for a while in silence.

"You were right, too, Percy, my boy," the viscount began again, "about what you said about my contacts with the local peasantry. I have been far too distant. It took courage for you to look me in the eye and tell me that. You have helped me see the thing clearly. Isn't the Muir place around here somewhere?"

"Why yes, Uncle Roderick. It's probably a mile or two."

"Will you take me there and introduce me to the woman, the widow. I would like to see her."

"You will hardly need an introduction."

"Still, it might be awkward. I would feel better if you eased the way into it for me."

"Then I will be happy to." Percy veered off slightly to the left from the course they had been pursuing and led the rest of the way until the familiar cottage came into view.

They rode up. Stevie did not appear to be about, though two dogs ran barking toward them. The viscount appeared concerned.

"Don't worry, Uncle Roderick," said Percy, jumping down. "These lads know me…don't you, boys?" he said, stooping and roughing up the backs and heads of the tail-waggers with his hands. "Of course they'll have to take a little sniff of you," he said as his uncle dismounted. "It's their way of introducing themselves."

Moments later they were approaching the open door of the humble cottage.

As he began to duck down and walk inside, Gwyneth's aunt appeared.

"Why, Percy," she exclaimed, "what brings you—" Her words died on her lips as she saw the man walking up behind him.

"I've brought you a visitor, Mrs. Muir," said Percy. "He wanted to meet you. This is—"

"I know well enough who it is," interrupted Adela. "Welcome to you, sir…Lord Snowdon, sir."

"Percy has told me about your husband, Mrs. Muir," said the viscount a little nervously but with genuine feeling. He removed his riding cap and attempted an awkward smile. "I am sorry."

"Thank you, sir," replied Adela, her initial shock now giving way to her natural hospitality. "Won't you come in for a cup of tea?"

"We, uh…I don't think—" began the viscount.

"We would love to," said Percy.

"I'm sorry I don't have any fancy cakes or the like to offer you, sir," said Adela, leading them through the door into her kitchen.

"Mrs. Muir, your oatcakes are the best in Wales," said Percy. "I would have nothing else with tea even if you offered it to me."

They sat down at the table. Adela bustled about in a veritable panic of excitement to have the viscount under her roof. "How I wish my Glythvyr could have been here. He would have loved to see you, sir."

"I am sorry," replied the viscount. "I should not have waited so long to pay you a visit."

"Bless you, sir. He used to work at the manor as a lad, you know. For your father. He was fond of your father, he was." She poured out tea.

Stevie arrived a few minutes later, with equal astonishment to see who was sitting in his kitchen. The conversation continued to flow pleasantly.

After about thirty minutes, Percy judged that sufficient initial spadework had been done in his uncle's heart for one day. He rose and said that it was time they were leaving. He had much to do to prepare for his departure on the morrow. Hugs, handshakes, and tearful farewells followed. Who knew when Percy would visit the beloved cottage in the hills again?

"I know it will be difficult for you, losing your husband," said the viscount as they prepared to return to their horses. "You may consider your rent for the following term canceled, Mrs. Muir. I shall notify my factor."

"Bless you, sir!"

They mounted and rode off. Percy glanced back with a final wave to Stevie and his mother where they stood beside their cottage.

They rode most of the way back to the manor in silence. The brief encounter had penetrated deep into the soul of Roderick Westbrooke.

"That was a very kind gesture of you, Uncle Roderick," said Percy at length. "I know it meant the world to her. I honor you for it."

SIXTY-FOUR

Final Evening

Percy had just finished dressing for dinner when a soft knock came to his door. He answered it and was surprised to see Gwyneth standing in the corridor. "Hi, Gwyneth!" he said.

"I know you are a guest and I am a servant—" she began.

"*Gwyneth!*" He laughed. "I'm me, remember?"

She smiled and glanced briefly at the floor before looking up into his face. "I know you are leaving tomorrow," she said a little bashfully. "Everyone's been talking about it. Since you'll be at dinner when I leave tonight, I wanted to say good-bye."

"Oh, right," said Percy. "Yeah—it's come up faster than I expected... much too short a visit."

"But you will be back to Wales," said Gwyneth, trying to sound cheerful.

"Of course...absolutely. Actually, I had planned to come down to see you this evening after dinner."

"You did?"

"You didn't think I would leave without seeing you?"

"I knew you wouldn't do that. But I heard Lady Katherine saying they were having a special dinner tonight. I thought I should come see you...in case you were busy."

"Oh...right, I see. I didn't know Aunt Katherine had plans." Percy

365

thought a moment. "I've got an idea—let's meet tomorrow morning!"

"But you are leaving!"

"I mean early. The coach comes through at nine. That's when I have to be at the inn. Meet me before breakfast. I'll get there as soon after sunrise as I can."

"Where, Percy?"

"At our special place. . .where the sea and land meet and the waves crash, and we look across to see the sun set at the horizon, and if we are lucky all the way to the land of your birth. It will always be the most special of all the special places."

Gwyneth nodded. "When the sun comes up?"

"Right. I'll see you there!"

"But if for some reason you can't, Percy—"

"I will be there. I promise."

Though the dinner was lavish, and even Courtenay was relatively friendly, there was still no sign of Florilyn. It was hard for Percy to enter into the spirit of the evening knowing that he was the cause, even if indirectly, of Florilyn's not wanting to see him. It was at least gratifying that Courtenay extended his hand when he departed for the evening. It had come late in the game, but he hoped that at long last his cousin might be warming to him.

"I guess I haven't seen much of you this time, old man," said Courtenay, shaking Percy's hand. "But best of luck, and all that."

"To you as well, Courtenay. When do you return to Oxford?"

"August."

Percy nodded. "Right, well. . .hope it goes well. It's a lot of work, isn't it?"

"You know it! So. . .cheers then!" added Courtenay and left the sitting room where the four of them had been chatting since dinner.

Percy turned back into the room where his aunt and uncle sat.

"I am sorry about Florilyn, Percy," said his aunt for probably the fifth time. "I just don't know what's got into her. I know she is dreadfully embarrassed."

"She was angry with me," said Percy. "I understand that. Really, it's all right. She will get over it. When she does, you can assure her there are no hard feelings. All's forgiven and fine."

"I told her what you said to Roderick about not defending yourself. I'm sure she will come around and understand in the end."

"I know she will." Percy smiled. "Please don't worry about it, Aunt Katherine."

At length the conversation flagged. Everything that was to be said had been said two or three times. Percy excused himself, saying he would see them in the morning, and retired to his room.

SIXTY-FIVE

Where Land Meets Sea

G wyneth did not sleep well.

Her mental anxiety was caused by no premonition such as had awakened her during the night prior to her uncle's death, nor even anxiety about what had happened to Grannie's cottage. But she was anxious lest she oversleep and miss her farewell rendezvous with Percy. Every time she fell asleep, her subconscious brain jolted itself awake, and she looked toward the window to see if there was yet any sign of light.

Thus it went, on and off fitfully all night, until the faint imperceptible gray of first light began to hint that the sun was creeping slowly back around the earth in the direction of Snowdonia.

Gwyneth lay with her face to the window, watching the dawn approach slower than any watched pot that never boiled. There comes a moment, however, when all pots eventually boil. But with the coming of dawn, no such moment exists. *When* does dawn arrive is a question as much for the world's philosophers as for girls in love.

When at last Gwyneth could stand it no longer and judged that the morning had sufficiently arrived for her purposes, she crept quietly from between the blankets and dressed in silence. With nearly as many layers on as she would have donned had it been snowing, she found the bouquet of flowers she had picked last evening then stole noiselessly from the house into a morning heavy laden along the coast with a chill white mist.

⊷❧⊶

Percy slipped out of the manor shortly before six o'clock.

He was ready for the journey. His bag sat on the floor of his room.

Hoping to disturb no one, he left as he often did by the side entrance, walked around the house and down the drive through the main gate and to the moor. Twenty minutes later he was approaching the promontory of Mochras Head.

It was a cold morning. A thick fog had settled over all of Tremadog Bay during the night. The white mist seemed clinging to the promontory itself, rising two hundred feet in the air. But it had not drifted inland from the water.

As Percy approached, he entered a world of whiteness. He could scarcely see the edge of the promontory in front of him. When he reached Gwyneth's special place, though there would be no sight of the ancient waters below on this day, he was surprised to find himself alone. There was no sign of she whom he had come to meet.

Percy sat down at the familiar place where he and Gwyneth had enjoyed the view so many times. The ground was wet. He would have to change into another pair of trousers before leaving for the coach. He heard the waves, muted by the thick fog, beating against the rocks far below.

He waited for twenty minutes, then forty. When an hour had passed, he began to grow concerned. He checked his watch and continued his wait. Why hadn't she come?

Suddenly a horrible thought occurred to him. Was it possible that she had only just now heard of the rumor? Was she, like Florilyn, unable to face him?

⊷❧⊶

Gwyneth had not actually expected Percy to be at the shore at such an early hour.

But she did not mind arriving first nor waiting for hours if she had to. She only did not want to miss him. So she would be at the beach early.

It was, in fact, a few minutes before five when she passed Grannie's through a fog so thick she could scarcely see across the narrow lane. After the discovery that her home had been ransacked, Grannie was staying with her great-nephew. Nevertheless, Gwyneth said a brief prayer for her and continued on. It was the first time in memory she had not stopped in at the beloved cottage now sitting silent and cold and empty.

She walked down to the harbor in the white cloudy soup. She was all but certain Percy would come to the beach through town, not along the promontory path. The tide was coming in. To climb across the rocks by the cave, especially as he might be wearing his traveling clothes, would be all but impossible. He would have to come through town and pass close by her to reach the sandy beach that he called his *favorite place*.

She sat down on the concrete quay of the harbor and set the bouquet she had labored over with such care in her lap. It was tied with two pieces of the colored ribbon Percy had given her. This was no forgiveness bouquet but a gift from the depths of one human soul to another, speaking as flowers were created to speak, in the language of the heart.

There she waited. It was cold. But Gwyneth was warmly dressed, and the incoming and outgoing waves were of endless fascination.

An hour passed.

A few fishermen began to be about but paid her no heed.

Another slow hour went by. Still there was no sign of Percy.

By eight o'clock Percy could delay no longer. He looked at his watch one final time and let out a long sigh. They would be waiting for him at the manor to take him to the coach, no doubt wondering where he had disappeared to.

He stood, walked carefully to the edge, and gazed over the promontory. Still he could see nothing but white. "Gwyneth!" he yelled. His voice seemed lost in the fog.

The only reply was the sound of the tide far below.

"Gwyneth!" he cried a second time, louder than before. Sadly he turned, chilled to the bone, and ran across the moor in the direction of the manor.

By now he realized he had waited too long. He should have left the promontory sooner. Now he had no time to run by the cottage to see her. He pulled out his watch and glanced down as he ran, suddenly annoyed with himself. He should have left sooner!

He hurried up the hill and along the entryway, into the house, and to the breakfast room. He gulped down a hasty cup of tea and egg, then ran up to his room to fetch his bag and change his clothes, and returned along the corridor. He paused at Florilyn's door. It was closed. He hesitated a moment but then continued to the stairway.

He found his aunt and uncle downstairs with a buggy waiting.

"Don't want to be late, Percy, my boy," said his uncle with watch in hand, twiddling the chain nervously. "It's coming on to quarter till the hour."

SIXTY-SIX

When Young Hearts Part

Florilyn Westbrooke had cried more in the last two days than she ever remembered crying in her life. Certainly she had never cried so much for being hurt by a boy. She had never cared enough for anyone to be this hurt.

A *boy!*

What was she thinking? Percy was a *man*...and a wonderful young man. What had possessed her even to *think* he could be involved with Rhawn Lorimer? She knew it was another of Rhawn's lies. Why Rhawn had blamed Percy for her troubles, Florilyn couldn't imagine.

She had behaved like such an absolute fool. She didn't deserve someone like Percy. She had been too embarrassed to face him. Like a baby she had kept to her room, unable to look him in the face. Yet with every day that passed, desperately longing to see him, the impossibility of looking into those honest, strong eyes mounted. Finally she had created for herself an imaginary barrier too great to overcome.

And now he was gone!

She stood at her window and watched the buggy leaving for town with her father and mother. They were taking Percy away. If she ever saw him again, it would be with a Scottish wife on his arm. He would never know what he had meant to her, never know how much she had loved him.

Tears filled her eyes at her childish foolishness. She would, as she had said to him, have to settle for second best and marry some boring, unmanly youth from North Wales.

Suddenly Florilyn's eyes shot open. *Why* was it too late? Why could she not put an end to her idiocy. . .and right now?

The next moment she was bolting from her room and down the stairs. She flew outside and across the stones to the stables.

"Hollin. . .Hollin!" she cried. "Saddle Grey Tide. Saddle her faster than you have ever saddled a horse in your life!"

⁂

Gwyneth had no watch. But she could tell from the activity at the harbor and the sounds from the village that the day was coming to life. The fog was still thick, and she was chilled. Surely it was well past eight o'clock by now. Her father would already be at the mine wielding his hammer against the stones.

Where was Percy? Had she dozed without knowing it? Had she missed seeing him in the fog? *Why hadn't he come?*

Could the horrible rumor be true? Had he gone to spend his last hours with Rhawn Lorimer? She could hardly bear the thought.

What was she to do? It was too late to go looking for him at the manor.

In the distance, the vague sounds of galloping horses, with jingling and clanging and bouncing and an occasional yell of driver, intruded into her hearing. But she was too absorbed in her thoughts. The sounds did not register in her brain.

⁂

The coach bounded to a jostling stop in front of Mistress Chattan's inn. Percy took his bag from his uncle's buggy and walked across and set it on the ground beside it.

He returned to his aunt and uncle. "Well. . .thank you again," he said. "For everything. This is truly a second home for me."

"Percy. . .," began Katherine, then for lack of words stepped forward and hugged her nephew with tender feeling.

Percy stepped back and smiled. The affection between them was mutual.

"Well, Percy, my boy," said the viscount, never at his best at such moments, "looks like the coach is about ready for you. You're welcome anytime, of course—goes without saying, what? Give your father my best."

The two men shook hands. Percy turned and walked toward the coach.

Suddenly Gwyneth realized what she had heard. It was the northbound coach on its way into Llanfryniog!

Something must have detained Percy from coming to the beach. But she could at least say good-bye to him and give him her gift.

She leaped from the quay and dashed for Mistress Chattan's inn.

As Percy's foot reached for the step to climb inside, at the far end of the street between the two churches, the sound of galloping hooves thundered toward them. He paused and looked toward it.

A smile crept over his face as they came into view from out of the mist. It was a horse and rider, hair flying behind her, that he knew well.

Florilyn reined in dangerously and jumped to the ground and ran to him. He turned away from the coach door to meet her as she threw her arms around him.

"Percy, Percy!" she blubbered, beginning to cry all over again. "I am so sorry! I knew it wasn't true, what they were saying. Can you ever forgive me? I am so sorry!"

Percy returned her embrace and whispered a few words into her ear.

At the opposite end of the street, hurrying past the chapel and church from the harbor, Gwyneth sprinted into view of the inn.

Suddenly her feet came to a stop, and she stared in horror. Through the fog she saw Florilyn stepping back from Percy's arms. Then she quickly leaned forward again, tiptoed high, and kissed him.

A gasp escaped Gwyneth's lips. She turned away. The bouquet of a broken heart fell from her hand. Her eyes burned with hot tears as she ran into the nearest lane to keep from being seen. The moment she was out of sight, Gwyneth stopped, crumbled against the stones of a windowless wall, and wept.

When at last she was able to continue on her way, out of sight through the back alleys and lanes of the village to the safety of the moor, the tears continued to flow.

A few minutes later, the coach bounded into motion. His face at the open window, waving back to his aunt, uncle, and Florilyn where they stood together, Percy's eyes fell on a smattering of color lying in the dirt of the street. It was a small bouquet of flowers. . .tied with red and blue ribbon!

A pang seized his heart. Frantically he leaned from the window of the coach and hastily turned his head about in every direction. "Gwyneth!" he called. "Gwyneth!"

But his voice was lost in the thundering of hooves along the hard-packed dirt street. The coach clattered past the chapel, turned toward the harbor, and disappeared in the morning mist.

☙

Far behind her as she sped across the grass outside the village, the rumbling of the coach and four receded in the distance as it returned to the main road north of town.

Gwyneth paused in her flight and turned toward it. She could hear it but saw nothing. Her eyes were swimming in a blur of liquid, and the fog still lay thick all about her.

"Good-bye, Percy," she whispered.

PART THREE

Changes
1872

SIXTY-SEVEN

Changes

*A*gain time sped and crawled by, depending on who was looking at the clock.

In Glasgow, the ministry of Edward Drummond thrived, in large measure, though indirectly, because of his son. Estrangement between any of the human family acts like a great dam preventing the rivers of God being able to flow. Reconciliation demolishes those obstructions, and those waters again gush through their channels, and God is able to work.

Meanwhile, the vicar and his wife, Mary, kept careful watch in Glasgow's bookstores for every new title to land on their shelves by Aberdeenshire native George MacDonald. These they passed back and forth by mail and discussed in letters with Edward's sister. Of the three MacDonald devotees, however, only Edward had the appetite for the weighty volume entitled *Unspoken Sermons* that was released. The sisters-in-law confessed themselves more fond of the Scotsman's novels than his theological works.

In Llanfryniog, Kyvwlch Gwarthegydd continued to pound his anvil against religiosity every Sunday morning, while his son Chandos became burlier and wielded the blacksmith's hammer with increasing authority. In one thing, however, the son did not take after the father.

Through a friendship with the man's son, young Chandos fell under the influence of the new minister of the Methodist chapel at the north end of town. He had in consequence taken to reading with great interest a New Testament the minister had given him.

Mistress Chattan continued to do a brisk trade on the reputation of her ale.

Madame Fleming had *not* made closer approach to the Bible that sat with the books on her bookshelves. She kept it almost as a talisman to insure that no aspect of the spiritual and occult was omitted from her repertoire of hidden knowledge. In truth, she was a little afraid of it. She had not opened it in fifty years. But she was terrified at the thought of discarding it. With every year that passed her soul grew darker.

When things were put back in order, Grannie eventually returned to her cottage in the village. She still sensed that her end was near.

Codnor Barrie made slates and prospered in the greatest commodity of life, his own character.

Rhawn Lorimer, who had *not* paid sufficient attention to the growth of her character, continued to decline. The soil was being tilled, however, in preparation for that greatest of all invisible seed-birthings deep within the human garden. She gave birth to a baby boy. Though speculation ran rampant about whom the father might be, none was man enough to step forward to claim either a wife or a son. She remained under the roof of her parents. The magistrate and his wife were mortified at the disgrace that had befallen them.

At Westbrooke Manor, Roderick Westbrooke, viscount Lord Snowdon, completed his stables but quickly grew restless again. His dream of racing horses withered for lack of funds. His wife remained unwilling to finance the venture. Her tenderness toward her husband grew as she observed many changes that seemed taking place within him, including an increased attentiveness toward the people of the region and a new warmth and affection toward her. Neverheless, she did not feel it right to allow him to squander money on vain pursuits like yachts and race horses. It would do him no good to pamper such indulgences.

She had always known that he was running away from something, that there were memories haunting him from his life before she knew him. She had sensed it even when, as a young woman, she had fallen in love with the sensitive and quiet Welsh aristocrat eight years her senior. His grandiose schemes through the years, she was certain, were but attempts to flee from that past. She hoped that his new awareness and tenderness toward those around him signaled that at last he was finding the peace within himself that had so long eluded him.

Meanwhile, Katherine Westbrooke, like her brother and sister-in-law, continued to read every new book released from the pen of the Scotsman. Her recent readings had included the otherworldly tale *At the Back of the North Wind* and a new fantasy called *The Princess and the Goblin.*

The viscount and his wife took to visiting a few of the villagers. They also rekindled their love of riding together in the hills. On one such ride, the viscount led his wife to the cottage he had visited with Percy and introduced Katherine to Mrs. Muir and young Stevie. A warm and unexpected friendship sprouted between Katherine and Adela Muir, with whom Lady Snowdon began sharing her MacDonald books. The two women found within each other kindred spirits of the heart that completely transcended differences of station.

The viscount also took to walking in the village, visiting with the villagers as he went, even enjoying an occasional pint of Mistress Chattan's ale. More and more in consequence his wife accompanied him to town and visited the shops and made as many of her purchases for the manor as she was able to from them.

Courtenay Westbrooke returned to Oxford. His studies interested him less and less. He managed to struggle through another year. As he began his fourth year in the fall of 1871, however, knowledgeable parties questioned how much longer he would last.

In the hills, Stevie Muir tended his sheep and other animals, cared for his mother, took seconds in the next two shearing contests, and was touted as the young man to watch in coming years. In consequence of their occasional visits, both Lord and Lady Snowdon took a liking and developed a great fondness for Stevie's gentle spirit. The viscount was especially taken with his skill with animals. The result was the offer of a job at the manor—for two days a week only owing to the distance he had to travel and the extra work required in the matter of his own animals—as an assistant and apprentice to Hollin Radnor, whose step had begun to slow.

At Burrenchobay Hall, unable to land the Scot of her dreams, young Davina Burrenchobay was now engaged to the eldest son of Baronet Rasmussen of Blaenau Ffestiniog, a devilishly good-looking youth of twenty-two years, rich and as full of himself as Davina was of herself and destined for triumphant mediocrity in all things to which he set his hand.

Not much was heard about Colville Burrenchobay. He was still unmarried, though rumors about his entanglements continued. He returned to university, graduated without distinction, and had taken to traveling a good deal.

Young Ainsworth Burrenchobay took his brother's place in the gossip registers, was reportedly even better with a gun and with young women than his brother, and was preparing to enter Cambridge. To what purpose, however, would have been interesting to inquire.

Rupert Wilkes, the occasional visitor to Mistress Chattan's inn, was still no nearer the discovery of the treasure of Dolau Cothi.

And on the moor rising behind the village, Gwyneth Barrie took care of her father, Grannie, and her animals, in that order, while continuing to work three days a week at Westbrooke Manor. Her outward growth continued, albeit slowly. If she would never attain the stature of her peers, her late start had the advantage of keeping her adding an inch a year long after most of them had reached their final height. In that far more important kind of growth, that of *inner* stature, the life of grace and quiet peace within her continued to deepen and expand, adding not mere inches but cubits to her character.

Walking in Llanfryniog one day, the viscount saw approaching him a young woman of indeterminate age. She was short enough to be a child, but her countenance and the features of her face were those of a woman. He was arrested by the sight.

He grew more transfixed as she came closer. His steps came to a halt. He continued to stare at the face and snowy white hair as she walked toward him.

Slowly his face went pale. It was almost as if. . .but it could not be. . . not here! He shook his head, as if trying to wake from a dream as she stopped in front of him.

"Good morning, Lord Snowdon," she said sweetly.

The voice brought him once more awake to the present. But the smile that accompanied it nearly undid what little equanimity remained in the man's carriage. "Yes, uh. . .hello, er. . .what are, I mean. . ." He fumbled, as if he were the stutterer and she some princess that had stepped out of his dreams—as well she might be. "You, uh. . .I believe. . . that is, I know you, don't I? Your face is unaccountably familiar."

"Yes, sir," smiled Gwyneth. "I work for you, at the manor, Lord Snowdon. For your wife and daughter, that is."

"Ah, yes, of course. . .that explains it," he said. His voice revealed profound relief. "For a moment my brain was playing tricks on me. I knew there had to be some reason why. . .that is—but it is not important. So how are you this fine day?"

"Well, sir. . .very well."

"You are not working today?"

"No, sir. I work three days a week."

"Ah, right. . .I see. . .very good, then. What is your name, young lady?"

"Gwyneth Barrie, Lord Snowdon."

"Barrie. . .ah, right. Capital! Barrie, is it, then?" he replied. Again he appeared relieved. "Well then, Miss Barrie, good day to you." The two parted, though the viscount glanced back a time or two as he continued down the street.

Gwyneth stood staring after him for a few moments. She had found the interview almost as strange as he found it unnerving.

For days after, the incident haunted Roderick Westbrooke.

From his factor he discovered what he could about the name and learned all he could about Codnor Barrie, the girl's father. Barrie was a local man who had gone to Ireland seeking work as a young man. No one knew other than that when he returned to his native Snowdonia some years later, he had a daughter with him. It was rumored that the girl's mother had been tragically lost at sea, but no one knew more than that. There had at one time been suspicions about the girl, Heygate added, associating her with nature's darker side, rumors that had possibly originated with an old woman in the village, Barrie's great-aunt. They had largely died down in recent years, the factor said. No one had any charge to bring against any of the three.

The viscount took in the information with interest. Eventually came a day when he knew he must pay a confidential visit to the Barrie home.

All this time, Florilyn Westbrooke grew quieter, if possible more beautiful and stately. She seemed oddly content with the domestic life of the manor. She took on the increasing countenance of a woman, resembling her mother more and more. She mixed with the maids and staff far more than she ever had early in her life, even helping them with their duties from time to time.

The relationship between her and Gwyneth blossomed into a full, rich friendship, such as only two young women can share. That they once loved the same young man—the one openly, the other secretively—in no way interferred with their friendship. Their affection for each other was too selfless to let anything come between them, even a man.

The alternate days when Gwyneth did not come to the manor seemed drab and dull to Florilyn. The tedium had this benefit, however, that those were the days she learned for the first time in her life to love books. Many afternoons found her in the library. She had even begun to discover the stories of MacDonald, a fact that delighted her mother and gave mother and daughter endless opportunity for lively talk together.

In Aberdeen, meanwhile, after a rewarding remainder of the summer of 1870 tutoring two young boys, Percival Drummond was soon caught up again in his university studies. By the end of the school term, he and his father had all but settled on law as the profession most suited to his temperament and interests. When an opportunity arose the following summer to apprentice as a clerk in one of Abereen's prestigious law firms, he leaped at the chance to get a foot into the door of the legal community of Scotland.

Thus it was, as before, that he was prevented from returning to Wales as soon as he might have liked. The same position was made available again the following year, his Semi and Tertian terms behind him as he prepared to embark on his fourth and final Magistrand year at the university. But, he told the solicitor who had taken such an interest in him, he could not let the summer pass without a visit to Wales. If it meant giving up the opportunity, it was a price he would have to pay. There were friends he simply had to see, and one or two personal situations he had to resolve in his own mind, before any more time went by.

The man understood. He said his post would be waiting for him when he returned.

And so it was, in late June of 1872, after three weeks with his parents in Glasgow, that once again Percival Drummond prepared to travel south to Wales for a visit of undetermined length.

For reasons of his own, he told no one in Llanfryniog of his plans.

Sixty-Eight

Inns, Anvils, and Special Places

*P*ercy Drummond again returned to North Wales by train, followed by the southbound coach to the small coastal village of Llanfryniog on Tremadog Bay.

Three years in the university were behind him. At the age of twenty-one he was preparing to embark on a career in law. It was his hope to follow in the footsteps of his father, though with different letters behind his name and through distinctive professional means but with the same end in view—to open the eyes of his fellows to the love of their Father-Creator.

A flooded stream caused several hours' delay in his journey. Wales, like his homeland farther north, could have *weather* any time of the year!

By the time he arrived in Llanfryniog, the afternoon was well advanced toward evening. He could walk to the manor and easily be there in time for dinner. One of the reasons he had decided to come unannounced, however, and had enjoined his parents to hint at nothing by letter, was in hopes of getting the lay of the land, as it were, with regard to how things stood in the community. If there was information it would be well for him to possess, he hoped he might get wind of it at the inn or with a visit either to Grannie or Chandos Gwarthegydd.

He chastised himself the entire journey for not keeping in closer touch with those he loved. But his studies and apprenticeship at the law firm had proved so demanding that even the deep spiritual correspondence with his father, which he treasured, had suffered. And he still had at least two, perhaps three more years ahead of him before certification as a solicitor would be possible.

In spite of this, however, he had in recent months begun to ponder and pray about his personal future, not merely his professional career. With such thoughts making themselves more importune on his heart, how could Wales not beckon him again? He knew this was where that personal future must begin. He had not been in a position to declare himself openly before. It would still be a good while before he would be capable of supporting a wife and family. But at last he was ready to begin making plans, even if still distantly. . ._if_ she would have him. Before that, however, he must know how things stood.

He walked into the inn with his bags, wondering if he would be recognized. He now stood a full inch over six feet, with all the features of a man, lanky but filled out in shoulders and chest, his face showing strong lines above a firm chin, with a forehead overlooking both that spoke of wisdom developing behind it. If anything, his brown hair had lightened a shade and was full and thick as it fell around his ears. His smile was just as eager to brighten a room and his laughter no less spontaneous, though perhaps slightly more bass when it exploded from his mouth. His eyes were the same hazel, but their visage shone with a far-seeing light that had only been foreshadowed in his youth but whose potential was now becoming fully realized in his young manhood. His study of law and justice, along with mercy, had done much to deepen the intensity of his eyes.

A few heads glanced toward the door as he entered. Most paid him little heed. In truth he only recognized about half the men gathered for their late afternoon pint. But Mistress Chattan knew every customer who walked through the doors of her establishment, if not by name certainly by sight. And Percy had been in often enough that, notwithstanding the changes that had taken place upon his outer man, she knew him instantly. "Well, young Drummond," she said. "You're back, are you?"

"Hello, Mistress Chattan," said Percy with a smile. "I don't suppose there's any slipping into town unrecognized by you!"

"I heard nothing about your coming."

"No one knew."

"You didn't let those up at the manor know?"

Percy shook his head.

Mistress Chattan nodded with significant expression but revealed nothing.

"Why. . . ?" said Percy slowly. "Is there something I should know?"

"Nothing to speak of. Nothing for *me* to speak of. So you don't know about your cousin?"

"Florilyn?"

"The young man—Master Courtenay."

"No, what about him?"

"Came home from the university in midyear. There was talk of a scandal. Expelled is what I heard."

"What is he doing?"

"The same thing rich young men always do, sponging off his father waiting until his time comes to inherit."

"He will have a long wait!" laughed Percy.

"Not as long as most young men in his position," said Mistress Chattan in a cryptic tone.

"How do you mean?"

"Just that his father's older than most fathers of twenty-three-year-olds."

"Ah, I see. . .but not *that* old. My uncle is still in the prime of his life."

"It all depends on what you mean by the prime of life," remarked Mistress Chattan. "I'll warrant you'll notice more gray on his crown than you expect. And his shoulders are starting to sag. He's not far off from sixty, I'm thinking."

"What are you talking about!" laughed Percy. "My own father is only forty-five."

"That's as well may be," rejoined the innkeeper. "But I'm telling you that Lord Snowdon is nearly old enough to be your grandfather rather than your uncle."

She paused, glanced about, then leaned over the bar separating them and reached out with a fleshy hand and pulled Percy toward her. "You do know, don't you?" she whispered in a conspiratorial tone.

"Know what?"

"About your uncle's past."

"No, what about it?" said Percy, unconsciously lowering his voice in response to Mistress Chattan's suddenly peculiar manner.

"Just that the sins of the fathers follow the sons, as the Book says."

"What sins? What are you talking about?"

"Sins of the *flesh*, young Drummond. What other kinds of sins do young men commit? There was another woman. . .before your aunt."

"You have been drinking too much of your own ale, Mistress Chattan," said Percy, though suddenly he felt very cold.

"I'm only telling you what they *say*, though I never laid eyes on her," the woman went on. "No one around here ever laid eyes on her, for it wasn't here that it happened. Across the sea, they say. When he came back, he was lovesick but alone. There was a child, they say. Now do you see why I say that the sins of the sons follow the sins of the fathers?"

"Why are you telling me all this, Mistress Chattan?" asked Percy. "Not that I believe a word of it," he added with a laugh that betrayed more anxiety than humor. "You are the most tight-lipped woman in Llanfryniog. Why suddenly confide in me?"

"I don't know, young Drummond. Maybe because I like you. Maybe because your fortunes may be more linked to that family on the hill than you realize, and you ought to know who you are involved with. *Someone* ought to know the truth because none of them do except the man himself, and *he'll* never tell. Maybe because I figure that you will do right by me one day. Maybe because I've taken a liking to the old blighter since he began coming around. Maybe because I figure he deserves a better friend watching over him than that no-good son of his. I don't know why I told you, young Drummond. There's your answer."

"Fair enough." Percy nodded. "Are you saying that my uncle has been in here?"

"He has indeed. After you left last time, something peculiar seemed to get into him. He comes to the village now, visits with people, comes in and buys pints for the fishermen and talks to them just like you always did. If I didn't know better, I'd think he'd got religion. He talks to me like we're old friends."

"I am glad to hear it. And speaking of the manor, do you mind if I leave my bags with you for a few hours?" Percy asked. "I'll walk up to the manor and be back for them this evening or tomorrow morning."

"Not at all."

"But I will have a pint of your special ale first."

Carrying his glass, Percy walked toward a table where a few of his fishermen acquaintances were seated. They greeted him *almost* as they might a friend. He visited with them for half an hour or so and caught up on village news. He learned nothing of note other than confirming that they, too, had seen a change in his uncle. At length he bade them good afternoon.

Without his bags, Percy walked briefly about the village and looked in at several shops, always receiving the same warm greeting from the shopkeepers. Two or three made the same comment. "Oh, won't Lady Florilyn be excited to see you!"

At length he approached the smithy. The familiar pounding of hammer on anvil could be heard from a long way off. He saw the father at the forge and the son at the anvil as he walked toward them. The sight brought a sharp intake of breath to his lips. The two were nearly the same size!

"What ho, Percy!" cried Chandos as Percy came into sight. He dropped his hammer and bounded forward with outstretched hand. The great hulking seventeen-year-old nearly crushed his hand in his grip.

"My, oh my, Chandos!" exclaimed Percy. "What a brute of a fellow you've become. It wouldn't go well for me *now* if I tried to order you around like I once did. You would thrash me!"

"No worry of that, Percy. You did me a great favor that day."

"How so?"

"You made me see what I was becoming. I didn't like what I saw. I wanted to be like you—a *good* young man. You helped set me on that road."

"I am more than a little amazed to hear you say it," rejoined Percy. "But pleased, nonetheless. Hello, Mr. Gwarthegydd," he said as the blacksmith came toward him with a smile and a black outstretched hand.

"So you're back, are you, laddie?"

"For a while—just a visit. I am still at the university. I've a year to go, then law school after that."

"I always said you would make something of yourself. Too bad the same can't be said for that high and mighty cousin of yours."

"I heard he had some trouble at school. What about Florilyn?" he asked. "I've been out of touch with everyone. Is she married yet. . .or engaged?"

He spoke matter-of-factly, though in truth he knew the answer to his own question. His mother kept him closely enough informed that if a change of that magnitude had come along, he would know about it. But he hoped to get Chandos talking.

Both father and son stared at Percy with odd expressions.

"She's not married, Percy," said Chandos at length. "Why would you think that?"

"Well, she's twenty now. Many young women are married by twenty."

"She's waiting."

"For what?"

"What do you think, man?" exclaimed Chandos. "For you! There's not a bloke in two counties who even looks at her now. Everyone knows how things stand."

"Everyone, it would appear, but me," said Percy. He had hoped for news. But this was more than he had bargained for.

By the time Percy set out from Llanfryniog, with much on his mind, it was a few minutes before seven o'clock. As he left town, he cast a glance inland to the cottage he longed to visit more than any other. But it was late. That was a visit that could not be rushed. To try to see Gwyneth now would delay him beyond a reasonable hour to arrive at the manor. They had much to talk about, not the least of which was why she had not come to meet him on the morning of his previous parting. He had been haunted ever since by unknown fears of what might have been the cause. The greatest of these had blossomed into the fear that she might no longer even be with her father, but that it might be *she* who had married during his absence, not Florilyn. He also had to find out what days Gwyneth was working now, *if* she was still at the manor. No brief visit would suffice. He would visit the Barrie cottage tomorrow, when he hoped to learn all.

In the meantime, however, as he made his way out of the village, breathing in deeply of the coastal air, he took a brief detour along the promontory of Mochras Head. Notwithstanding his perplexity about the last time he had been here, he took time to walk to Gwyneth's special place. He sat down and gazed out over the azure sea as it prepared a few hours hence to receive the golden orb into itself in its nightly burial, that the earth and its inhabitants might have their daily season of rest. There was no fog on this day. He only prayed that an explanation presented itself about the events of that day two years before and the meaning of the bouquet he had seen on the street—some explanation that did not break his heart.

After ten or fifteen minutes of quiet reflection, as he allowed the peace of the "special place" to fill him again, Percy rose and continued on to Westbrooke Manor. He walked up the drive, keeping his eyes moving. He did not want to encounter Gwyneth like this, with a chance meeting as she was leaving the manor for home. But all was quiet, and he saw no one.

He walked toward the great house. There were the new stables, completed now though mostly unoccupied. His feet echoed softly over the flagged paving stones of the entryway. He paused at the front door. Even after an absence of two years, he felt no duty to ring the bell. This was home.

He turned the latch and went inside. The only voices he heard came from the kitchen in the distance, where the staff would be having their dinner. He walked through the entryway, along the corridor, and toward the dining room. At last he heard soft voices from the family. He paused, smiled to himself, then opened the door and walked into the room.

Four heads turned toward him at once. A stunned silence followed. In their shock at seeing him in their midst, aunt, uncle, and both cousins all seemed for the briefest of instants not to know him.

The silence did not last long. A great shriek sounded as Florilyn leaped from her chair, knocking it backward onto the floor behind her. "Percy!" she cried as she ran across the room to him and flung her arms about him.

SIXTY-NINE

Sonship

Later that evening, when they had returned with the buggy after retrieving Percy's bags from town, Percy and Florilyn left the house as a warm dusk descended. Without conscious intent, their steps led them toward the garden east of the manor.

"So, it's law, is it?" said Florilyn. "When you were here last you were talking about engineering and the church as potential professions as well."

"You have a good memory!"

"I was paying attention." Florilyn smiled. "I also had the benefit of an occasional letter from your mother to mine. Otherwise I would know nothing about how you had spent the last two years. So I really must thank you for all those long, newsy letters."

Percy laughed. "I know, I know," he said. "I am sorry. I've been terrible."

"Yes, you have!"

"You have no idea how demanding school is."

"It takes every minute of your time?"

"Well, maybe not *every* minute. I admit that as a letter writer I am a failure."

"You write to your father, I hear."

"That's different."

"How so?"

"We don't talk about ourselves or what we are doing."

"What do you write each other about, then?"

"Ideas. . .theology."

"Sounds boring."

"Are you kidding? I love dialoguing back and forth with my father about the ideas of faith. What could be more exciting than that? But I apologize for not keeping in touch better. I thought about you all a lot, if that is any consolation."

"Well. . .maybe it makes up for it a little," said Florilyn playfully. "But *just* a little. A girl gets lonely, you know. She looks for letters in the post. Still. . .now that you're here, I *may* decide to forgive you. So what made you decide that you wanted to be a solicitor instead of a minister?"

"My father encouraged me in that direction."

"I would think he would have wanted you to follow him into the church."

"My father is too selfless for that."

"What do you mean?"

"He is trying to help me discover what is best for *me*, not what *he* might prefer. In the end, we both felt that my personality would be better suited for law."

"How did you come to that conclusion?"

Percy thought a moment. "It wasn't anything specific," he said. "We sought God's guidance, of course. But there were no telegrams from heaven. God doesn't reveal His will that way. My father says that the Lord speaks with a soft voice into our senses, with nudges into our hearts and brains, not shouts, with subtle pressures in one direction or another. He simply suggested we pray and see what we sensed, to see if we felt any of those gentle inward nudgings toward either ministry or law. By then we had pretty much omitted engineering."

"And did you. . .feel the nudging, I mean?"

"Gradually, yes. I can't say exactly how. Like my father says, it was subtle. I found myself thinking more about law and becoming enthusiastic about it. Then the offer of an internship came last summer from a solicitor's firm in Aberdeen. That was the confirmation of circumstance."

"What's that?"

"My father says that God makes His will in our lives known by the subtle inner nudges in response to our prayers, and He confirms that leading by circumstance. He says that the Lord uses circumstances to confirm His leading, even occasionally to change the direction of His leading. As long as we're not in a hurry and willing to wait, the two always line up at some point—the direction of the leading and the circumstances that make it possible to follow that leading. When the two line up, you can be confident that God might indeed be indicating a certain direction."

"*Might* be. That doesn't sound very definite."

"You never know 100 percent. There's a certain amount of guesswork involved in following the Lord's leading. My father says that our own desires can interfere and make us think God is leading when we are really just following what we want to do ourselves. It is also easy to *misinterpret* circumstances and think they're saying something they're not. That's why the most important thing in listening to God's voice is to set aside your own desires and ambitions. And then be willing to go *slow* in making decisions. That's another thing my father says, that God is never in a hurry."

"You make it sound like the decision of what you should pursue was your father's. Wasn't it ultimately your decision to make?"

"Sure. But I placed the decision before him and asked what he thought I should do. He is my father. My life is not entirely my own. It can never be."

"Your life is not your *own*?"

"I said not *entirely* my own. We are linked to those who came before. I believe we have a duty to them."

"You have a duty to do what your father wants you to do, even now that you are a grown man?"

"Not completely. Of course not. But to a degree, yes. The fact that he is paying for my education gives him the right to offer his input. And I genuinely want it. The generations of families is very important in God's economy. We have a duty to our ancestors, to live faithfully and to honor their names. It is not an idea that is much in vogue today when most perceive that they have no duty to anyone but themselves. But we *do* have duties that extend wider than that. In that lineage, my father is the one God placed immediately over me. That fact carries great weight. It carries the assumption that my father perceives it as his duty to help me find what God wants me to do. He does so not to please himself but to help me fulfill *my* place in God's plan."

"Do you think your father really thinks of all that every time you ask for his advice?"

"Absolutely. I know it for a fact. He seeks my best, not his own. He always seeks the best of others, not himself."

"He sounds like a remarkable man."

"He is. That's why I know I can place my uncertainties in his hands and that he will seek only my absolute best. That is the whole basis of the thing—my assurance that my father wants the very *best* for me. Even if he didn't, I would still consider it my duty to heed him, even to obey him if he made it a matter of obedience. But hey—you know all this. My mother says you have been reading MacDonald. My father is like David Elginbrod to me. I realize that not all fathers are as wise as mine. I can imagine it being very difficult to obey if you did not have the assurance that your father or mother was seeking your best. In a way, I suppose, I have it easy. I know that about my parents. It makes it easy to heed their advice, even to obey them on the rare occasions now when it might still come to that."

"Most people our age would laugh to hear you say such things," said Florilyn. "They would consider you loony. But you're right. It does sound like the sort of father-son relationship MacDonald talks about. I can hardly imagine what Courtenay would say!"

"I am sure that is true," smiled Percy. "But for the first time in my life I am at peace being the son of my father. I do not intend to lose out on what being a son can teach me. I am not anxious to be independent of him. And since I am still young, and since I spent some years in rebellion, my father is in a position to know what is best for me better than I am myself. That's what it means to trust his wisdom. It means trusting *him* to know my best even above my own desires, trusting him, in a sense, to speak for God in my life."

"You make it sound as though he makes all your decisions."

"Not at all. Every individual grows into an autonomy and independence as a man or woman in their own right. That is exactly what every parent ought to be working toward. My father wants that very thing for me. He doesn't tell me what to do. But I *want* his advice and counsel. He gives me his impressions, helps me focus on spiritual principles, points out factors I may not have considered. And he will sometimes urge me very strongly in one direction or another. But in the end, he always encourages me to make my own decisions. *Now*, at least that's what he does. Five years ago he *made* me come here. I had no choice then because I was incapable of wise choices. I was sixteen and rebellious. I had been in trouble with the police. It's different now. Part of that process is his trust of me, too."

"I think I begin to see. . .a little," said Florilyn thoughtfully.

"It's really a wonderful thing—the more I trust him, the more he trusts me. That's why our dialogue is based not on either of us trying to convince the other to any particular point of view but about mutually trying to figure out what is best. In that my father's vote, you might say, weighs very heavily, even though the ultimate decision rests with me. That probably sounds contradictory, but that is sort of how the mechanics of the thing work in practice."

"Will you ever consider yourself fully on your own, so that you *don't* think about what your father says?"

"I hope not. My father is a wise man. Why would I *ever* not want to glean as much of that wisdom as possible? As long as I live, he will always be ahead of me spiritually simply because he is older and has been listening to God's voice longer. And he still wants the wisdom of his father, even though, as you know, Grandpa has been in China for ten years. In the same way, I will always be spiritually ahead of *my* children, if I have any, in the same way. That's the way the generations are supposed to work. I will go to my grave, long after my father is dead, *still* doing my best to learn from his wisdom. I think that's the way God intended it to be with sons and fathers."

"I doubt that's the way Courtenay looks at it!" laughed Florilyn.

"Courtenay has not spent his life developing spiritual eyesight. It grieves me to say that for most of my life I didn't either. I have only been learning to see my father in this way for five years. That's why I am trying so hard to listen to him and learn from him now, even though I am no longer under his roof and technically, I suppose you might say, on my own. And as I said, my father still sees himself learning from his father, where *he* is the son. Of course, Grandpa recognizes him as a man of God in his own right, because that's what he prepared him to be. But my father looks up to him just as I look up to my father."

"It must be remarkable to be part of something like that," said Florilyn. "I knew that Grandfather and Grandmother Drummond had gone to China, but sad to say, Mother has learned not to talk about spiritual things around the rest of us. I feel bad about that now. I had no idea all that was at work between. . .well, all three of you, I guess."

"I admit that it is not very common. But as I said, I believe it is God's pattern."

They sat down on one of the garden's stone benches. Dusk was closing heavily around them. It was now after ten o'clock. The sounds of evening drifted toward them from the nearby trees. They sat for several minutes.

"What about. . .your future?" asked Florilyn, at length voicing the question that had been on her mind for two years. As she spoke, her voice betrayed a slight quiver.

"That's one of the things I hope to resolve while I am here," replied Percy.

As much hopefulness as Florilyn might have hoped to take from his answer, his expression revealed nothing. "What does your father think. . .about us?"

"He is pleased that we have become so close," replied Percy, again revealing nothing.

Once more it was quiet.

Percy drew in a deep breath. "It is getting late," he said. "Suddenly I am very tired. It's been a long day." Slowly he rose. "Shall we go in?" he asked.

"I think I will sit a little longer," replied Florilyn. "You've given me so much to think about. I have never heard anything like what you have described between you and your father. . .and even your grandfather's role in it. It sounds both wonderful and frightening. I've never considered that a father and son, or a daughter I suppose as well, could trust one another like that and be such. . . It sounds like your father is actually your best friend."

"He really is. That's exactly right. I know there would be many who would think me out of my mind to talk about my father this way. Others would think me a fool. I don't know, perhaps this is not a road everyone can walk. I don't even say everyone should. I don't know. I am still young. I am probably guilty of the common hubris of youth of thinking I know more than I really do. All I can say is that this is the way I have chosen to obey the command to honor my father and mother."

Florilyn smiled. "Well, I don't think you a fool. But I need time to absorb it all."

"All right. Well then, I'll leave you to your thoughts. How about a ride tomorrow afternoon? After we both sleep in!"

"I would like that," said Florilyn with a smile.

Percy turned to go.

"Oh, Percy," said Florilyn after him, "did you stop by to see anyone else in the village or on your way up here this evening?"

"I stopped in at the inn, then by the smithy, then I came straight here. Why?"

"Oh, nothing. It's just that there is something you need to know, something you ought to be prepared for. I've been trying to find a way to tell you all evening."

"What?"

Florilyn hesitated. "Come to think of it," she added with a smile, "there's no sense ruining your evening. I'll tell you in the morning. Though not too early!"

"I know. You like to sleep in. But now I will worry about what it might be. My night's ruined either way."

"I'm sorry," rejoined Florilyn. "I shouldn't have said anything. It will keep until tomorrow. If I know you, you won't worry about it for long. I'll tell you everything in the morning. Well, everything I know, which isn't much."

Assuming she had something to tell him about Rhawn Lorimer or one of the Burrenchobays, or possibly something to do with her brother and the university scandal Mistress Chattan had mentioned, Percy consented to wait. "Sure. . .okay. Good night, Florilyn."

"Good night, Percy. It's really nice to have you back."

SEVENTY

Old Wounds, New Beginnings

Expecting to sleep till at least eight or nine, Percy was wide awake the next morning before seven. After a spirited visit with his aunt in the breakfast room, he decided to walk to the village. It was hours before Florilyn would make an appearance for the day after the late evening. With a ride planned for the afternoon, he wanted to wait no longer before visiting Grannie and Gwyneth.

Walking past the draper's shop on the afternoon of his arrival, Percy was reminded of the first time he had set eyes on Rhawn Lorimer. The momentary exchange that fateful day had seemed innocent enough. But even then, the flirtatious mischief had been evident in her eye.

He knew it well might stir up the old rumor, but he needed to see her. He had unfinished business with her, too, just as he did with Gwyneth—though of a much different nature. He had to look Rhawn in the eye and ask her *why*. If Florilyn's news concerned Rhawn, he might just as well find it out for himself.

While they ate breakfast, he asked his aunt about Rhawn.

"We have hardly seen her in the last two years," replied Katherine. "She and Florilyn never visit anymore."

"I would like to drop in on her this morning."

"Goodness, Percy. . .why?"

"It's just something I need to do. I am concerned about her, for one thing. I want to ask her why she did it."

"I wouldn't want to have anything to do with her. Aren't you afraid of stirring everything up again? People will talk."

"Who cares? And why would people talk? Are you saying. . . ? Is she not married? Did the father not come forward?"

"No to both," answered his aunt. "She is still living with her parents. She has a baby boy."

"No one ever owned up to it?"

Katherine shook her head.

"And Rhawn never divulged the truth?"

"No."

"Did she ever absolve me?" asked Percy.

"Yes, eventually she came clean and said she had lied about you."

Percy took in the information thoughtfully.

"*Must* you see her, Percy?" asked Katherine.

He thought about her question a moment. "I don't know if I *have* to, but I want to. Things need to be brought to resolution. It's something my dad's always talking about—reconciliation and healing. I *have* to see if there might be an opening with Rhawn. If not, at least I will have tried."

His aunt nodded then her lips broke into a smile. "That's your father, all right," she said. "Even as a teen he could not tolerate conflict. He was always trying to resolve differences between people. Why should I expect Edward's son to be any different? Like father, like son, I suppose."

"That's a great compliment coming from you, Aunt Katherine."

Percy left her and set out for Llanfryniog about eight thirty. He left Florilyn a brief note saying he would be back by noon. Whatever she had to tell him would have to wait for later in the day.

He walked straight to the village. He wanted to get that visit out of the way first. Then he would have plenty of time with Gwyneth afterward.

He made no attempt to hide his movements. He went directly to the magistrate's home. A woman whom he had never seen answered the door.

"Mrs. Lorimer?" said Percy.

"Yes," she answered, looking him over with a questioning eye.

"Is Rhawn here?" Percy asked. "I am a friend of hers."

"Do I know you?"

"No, ma'am. I've not been in Llanfryniog for two years."

Whatever suspicions Percy's statement might have aroused in Mrs. Lorimer's mind, she kept to herself. She disappeared into the house, leaving the door open and Percy standing outside.

A minute later Rhawn appeared.

"Hello, Rhawn," said Percy with a smile.

She stared back at him blankly, not believing her eyes. In the distance Percy heard the sounds of a child.

"Percy!" she said in a soft, almost questioning voice. Her eyes began to fill. The change that had come over her was remarkable. On her face was the look of a sad and broken young woman.

Percy stepped forward and embraced her.

She began to weep in earnest, though softly.

"Why have you come here, Percy?" she asked at length, stepping back and wiping her eyes. "Aren't you afraid of being seen. . .of what people will say?"

"No, I am not concerned."

"Are you. . .angry with me?" she asked, forcing a sad, almost frightened smile.

"No, not that either. I do have to say that I was surprised and disappointed."

"Have you come to rub salt in the wounds?"

"Rhawn! I would never do that."

"Why, then? Why would you want to see me?"

"I had to ask you *why*. . .why you did it. Why did you, Rhawn?"

She smiled again more sadly than before. "Can't you guess?"

"No, honestly I can't. What did I ever do to hurt you?"

"Nothing, Percy," she said, starting to cry again. "Nothing at all. That is the reason."

"I don't follow you."

"I knew the real father would never acknowledge his child. He had already turned his back on me. I knew he would never marry me. You were the nicest boy I had ever met. I suppose I hoped that maybe. . . But it was stupid and selfish of me. I was not in the habit back then of thinking of anyone but myself. I didn't think of the consequences to you. I am sorry for what I must have put you through. I just thought. . ."

She looked away and began to cry again. "I did it because I was selfish, Percy," she went on in a halting voice. "I kept trying to convince myself that you were smitten with me. All my life I had been able to make any boy I wanted fall all over me. You were the first boy who didn't. It made me crazy to conquer you. I told myself that you were playing hard to get, that you really loved me. But everyone knew how it was between you and Florilyn. I knew well enough that she was in love with you."

She was looking down as she spoke and did not see Percy's expression of surprise at her words.

"That made me angry, too," Rhawn went on, "that she might succeed where I had failed. I suppose I was trying to get back at you both, and at the same time I hoped that you might. . . I suppose I still hadn't given up on the idea that you might actually care for me in some way. I see now how foolish. . .that you never—" Rhawn glanced away, crying again.

She started a moment later when she felt two strong hands on her shoulders. She looked up. Percy was staring straight into her eyes with a more peaceful look of love and compassion than she had ever seen from anyone in her life.

"Rhawn," he said, smiling tenderly. "You were right. I did not love you in that way. I hope you do not mistake my visit today in thinking that has changed. I cannot love you as a man would. I cannot be a father to your child. But I want to be a friend to you. I would like us to make a new beginning, if you are willing. I think Florilyn is ready to be your friend again, as well."

"Oh, Percy. . .I don't know. Why would you treat me this way? After all I. . .I mean, why would you be so good to me?"

Percy smiled.

It was the old smile she remembered!

"Isn't that what friends are for?" he said.

Rhawn could hardly believe how kind and generous he was. "Would you. . .could you come in for a cup of tea?" she asked. "I would like you to meet my mother. . .and my son."

SEVENTY-ONE

Gone

Percy left the Lorimer home thirty minutes later, full of many thoughts. Mostly he felt compassion for Rhawn. She was now reaping the fruit of the foolishness of her younger years. But all beginnings offer hope for new life. Perhaps this might be such a day for her.

He turned into the lane toward Grannie's. He hoped he might find Gwyneth there. After tea with Grannie, they could walk along the beach together.

It was great to be back, he thought. Just walking through the streets of Llanfryniog made him happy.

He couldn't wait to see Gwyneth again. He was nearly running by the time he reached Grannie's. He tried to calm himself, reminding himself how changed Gwyneth was last time. He had *almost* not recognized her that day he had first seen her working at the manor. In his eyes she would always be the nymph of the Snowdonian hills, the lake creature out of whose hands deer came to eat. Yet she was bound to be changed again. And still the question dogged him why she had not met him two years before.

He slowed. *Would she be taller?* he wondered with a smile. She would never be as tall as Florilyn. But she *might* grow to five feet, and then be not much more than a foot shorter than he.

She would be eighteen now. Would the same thing happen as before? Would he gaze upon the face beneath the head of white and wonder, *Is it really her?*

As he went, he also tried to prepare himself for the possibility that there could be a young man in her life...*if* she wasn't engaged or married already. He had *tried* to prepare himself for it. But he knew he wasn't *really* prepared for such news.

He reached Grannie's cottage. Strange, thought Percy, there was no smoke drifting out of the chimney. He went to the familiar door and knocked. There was no response from inside. A second knock, then a third produced the same result. He tried the latch. It was locked. Grannie *never* locked her door. Something felt wrong.

He thought a moment, then turned and quickly broke into a run in the direction of the cottage outside the village. He hoped the explanation was as simple as that Grannie was with them. With the premonition growing that something wasn't right, he ran across the moorland plateau. He ran straight to the door of the cottage and knocked.

It opened a minute later. A rough-looking man, unshaven for several days and with a scowl on his face, opened the door and stared at him. "What do you want, mate?" he growled.

"I came to see the Barries," said Percy, glancing into the house behind the man in perplexity.

"Ain't nobody by that name here."

"Codnor Barrie? He has a daughter by the name of Gwyneth?"

"Look, mate—this is my place. I ain't heard of no Barrie."

"How long have you lived here?"

"Seven months. Came from Australia to work in the mines. Now they ain't giving me the work they promised. Now beat it!" The door slammed in Percy's face.

He walked to the side of the house. Not a creature nor pen was to be seen behind it. In bewilderment Percy hurried back to the village. He went straight to Grannie's again. This time he knocked on the door of the house next to it. It opened, and he was met by Grannie's neighbor, a woman Percy had seen a few times in the past. "Good morning," he said.

"It's Mr. Drummond, isn't it?" she said.

"Yes, and I'm hoping you can tell me where Grannie is, and Gwyneth and her father. I just returned and found a stranger living in the cottage on the moor, and not a very friendly one. Grannie's door is locked up tight."

"I'm sorry to be the bearer of such tidings, Mr. Drummond," said the old woman, "but they're gone."

"*Gone. . .where?*"

"I don't know, Mr. Drummond."

"Why did they leave?"

"Nobody knows. It's a mystery. One day Mr. Barrie appeared with his cart at Grannie's and picked up a few things. I figured she was going up to live with them. She was ailing, Grannie was, and the lass had been coming down every day. But then I never saw her again. Next thing I knew folks were saying they'd disappeared—all three of them."

"*Disappeared!*" exclaimed Percy. "It makes no sense."

The woman shook her head, as if to say that she agreed with him but had no other answer to give.

"Grannie's place has been vacant ever since," she said. "But like you say, a fellow from the mines is living in Codnor's place, honest man, though he's a surly one."

"So I discovered. But how can it be that no one knows where they went? Did he have work elsewhere? Was he fired from the mine? There must be *some* explanation."

"That's why it's a mystery, Mr. Drummond."

Percy thanked the woman and left.

Not a young man prone to downcast moods, this was as shattering a blow as Percy had ever known in his life. He half stumbled out of town in the direction of the harbor in a stupor of desolation. A few fishermen were about, but he did not pause to speak with them. Unaware that Gwyneth had been sitting at that very spot waiting for him two years earlier, while he had been sitting on the promontory waiting for her, he passed the corner of the concrete quay and continued onto the beach.

He made his way slowly, memories flooding him as he went—his talks with Gwyneth, playing in the tide, the race with Florilyn—so many memories. He was in no playful mood today and plodded along heedless of his steps.

The tide was about halfway in, which made climbing over the rocks and boulders and tidepools at the end of the north beach more difficult. By the time he reached the south beach with the promontory rising high on his left, his boots and trousers were wet to the knees. He hardly noticed.

He glanced toward the cave, water almost to its mouth. He had no appetite to explore without Gwyneth. On he walked. He reached the base of the promontory path then slowly climbed up to the plateau of Mochras Head. Sighing dejectedly, he again sought Gwyneth's special place.

He sat down on the wet grass, just as he had on that misty morning two years before. It was clear today. He stared out across the blue sea, trying to imagine the Irish coastline, though he was never sure whether he *really* saw it.

"Oh. . .Gwyneth, Gwyneth," he whispered. "Where have you gone?"

SEVENTY-TWO

The Viscount and His Factor

Percy arrived back at Westbrooke Manor about ten thirty. He found Florilyn in the breakfast room. She had just read his note.

"Oh, Percy!" she said. "I had hoped to talk to you before you went into town. I can see from your face that you know."

He nodded, slumped into a chair, and buried his face in his hands.

"I am sorry, Percy," said Florilyn. "I know what Gwyneth meant to you. I wanted to find a way to tell you last night, but it just—I don't know. . . . I couldn't find a way. She was my friend, too. I'm sorry."

Percy looked toward her and smiled sadly. "It's all right," he said. "As you said, you didn't want to ruin my evening. And it would have." He drew in a long breath and exhaled slowly. "I talked to Grannie's neighbor," he said. "The story she recounts is almost incomprehensible. . . that they left without a word to anyone."

"That is exactly how it was," rejoined Florilyn. "One day Gwyneth was working here and everything was fine. Two days later my father told me she would not be returning. I asked why. He said that she and her father had left Llanfryniog. I was stunned. She'd not said a word to me. There wasn't a hint of it ahead of time. Immediately I rode down to the cottage, but they were already gone. I never saw Gwyneth again. I am still completely bewildered."

411

"Your father must know *something*."

"He said his factor informed him that Barrie had given notice and told him he would not be renewing his rental of the cottage."

"Then I need to talk to Mr. Heygate. Someone *has* to know something."

"I tried," said Florilyn. "I finally gave up. I asked everyone in the village, every one of Grannie's neighbors. I rode up to the Muirs. Even they didn't know. Stevie and his mother were as surprised as I was. They didn't say good-bye to them either. I have done my best for eight months to find out something. Gwyneth and I had become very close. But they seem to have wanted no one to know where they had gone."

Percy listened in stunned disbelief. "Then maybe I need to hear it for myself," he said. Percy left Florilyn with her late breakfast and went upstairs.

He found Lord Snowdon in his study. Even more than on the previous evening, he noticed what Mistress Chattan had warned him of—that his uncle appeared to have aged more than a mere two years would account for. He was shocked at how gray he had become.

"Ah, Percy, my boy!" said his uncle. "Out for a ride so early on your first morning back with us, I see."

"No, sir," replied Percy. "I walked to town and then to visit my friends Codnor Barrie and his daughter."

"I, uh. . .am not familiar with the name," rejoined the viscount, who stood when Percy entered. In fact he knew the name better than that of any of his tenants, former or present.

"The girl worked here as a servant in the manor, Uncle Roderick. I don't see how you could not have known her."

"Well, er. . .of course, that is, you can hardly expect me to be on intimate terms with all my wife's maids," said his uncle as he sat down again. As he did, he winced visibly. "Blasted knee!" he muttered. "Don't ever get old, Percy, my boy. It plays havoc with your knees. I just hope I die before I get so decrepit I can't walk. But where were we? Ah, yes, some girl you mentioned that you say worked here. Perhaps. . .that is to say, perhaps I might recognize her face if I were to see her."

"Unfortunately, that is impossible."

"Why is that?"

"Because their cottage is now occupied by someone else," Percy answered. "The Barries have moved, up and gone without a trace. Florilyn tells me your factor was the one who spoke with Mr. Barrie. I would like to know what you know, Uncle Roderick. It is a matter of great personal urgency to me. Whatever it takes, I *have* to find them."

"What are these people to you, Percy, my boy. . .if you don't mind my asking?" said his uncle.

"They are close and dear friends. The girl, Gwyneth is her name, helped me more than anyone other than my own father, to see God's handiwork about me, as well as inside me. She is one of the most remarkable individuals I have ever met. She was also very close to Florilyn. I have to find her. . .for both our sakes."

"She, uh. . .sounds like an extraordinary young girl, you say. Yes, quite—and a peasant, the daughter of a miner, you say. Most extraordinary. How would, uh. . .such a one come to possess this vast knowledge about the church?"

"You mistake me, Uncle Roderick. It would not surprise me if the girl had never set foot inside a church in her life. What I said was that she had helped me to see God in His creation and within myself. Unless a man like my father is in the pulpit, judging by its success rate, church seems to me singularly ill equipped for the transmission of that revelation into human hearts."

"Ah, yes. . .I see. . .of course, of course. So then, er. . .Barrie is the name, you say. Hmm, yes, I seem to recall something about it. Yes, a very sudden departure it was, I believe."

"What exactly did your factor tell you?"

"Just that. . .if I recall, let me think. . .that the man told him he was leaving Llanfryniog and the slate mine."

"There was nothing else?"

"Not that I, uh. . .not that I recall."

Percy turned to go. "Do you know where I might find your factor?" he said.

"I could not say with certainty, though you might try his office. I believe he had business in Penrhyndeudraeth later. If I am not mistaken, he planned to spend the night there and take the train up to Llanfairpwllgwyngyllgogerychwyrndrobwllllantysiliogogogoch."

"To where?" exclaimed Percy.

His uncle chuckled. "It's a village in Anglesey," he said. "Translated it means, 'St. Mary's Church in the hollow of white hazel near the rushing whirlpool and Tysilio of the Red Cave's Church.' I thought I might get you with that one, Percy, my boy."

"What do people in a hurry call it?" asked Percy.

"Llanfair Pwllgwyngell, or just Llanfair. Tilman plans to visit his son's family on the peninsula for a day or two. Whether he has left yet I do not know."

"Then I had better try to catch him before he leaves."

Percy hastened downstairs and to the south wing. His knock at the factor's door was answered by a summons to enter.

"Ah, young Drummond!" said Tilman Heygate, rising to meet him and shaking his hand warmly.

"Hello, Mr. Heygate."

"I heard you were back. You're looking very well—healthy and with another inch or two to your credit."

"I've just come from the viscount," said Percy. "I hope you might be able to shed some light on the sudden disappearance of Codnor Barrie and his daughter."

"Barrie—he was the slate miner?" replied the factor, resuming his seat behind his desk.

"Yes, sir," said Percy, taking the chair opposite him.

"Rented a cottage from us out on the moor, about a mile east of the village, wasn't it?"

"That's right."

"Yes, I recall it now. I found it very strange," nodded Heygate thoughtfully.

"What exactly did Mr. Barrie say?" asked Percy.

"A note came here to the manor from him asking to see me," replied Heygate.

"Did you think that strange?"

"Not at all. I handle matters for all the viscount's tenants. They pay their rents to me. They bring their complaints to me."

"He didn't say what it was about?"

"Just that he wanted to see me. I knew he worked in the slates, so I rode down there the next evening. His daughter was with him and greeted me pleasantly. A nice girl, she struck me. . .worked at the manor as well, I believe."

"That's right." Percy nodded.

"The man said he needed to talk to me in private. The girl left the cottage. She kept a number of animals in pens and a fenced area behind the house. When we were alone, Barrie told me that a change had come to his situation. He and his daughter would be leaving Llanfryniog and quitting their tenancy. He said that they would be moving soon, adding that the viscount had been very kind to him. He asked me to thank him. Then he handed me three one pound notes for the rent that was due. He asked me to say nothing to anyone but the viscount. His daughter did not know of his plans yet, he said, nor another soul."

"Did you ask him why he was leaving?"

"I did. He merely said that an opportunity had arisen that would prove of great benefit to his daughter, that he hoped thereby perhaps even to secure for her an education beyond what was available here and give her opportunities she would never otherwise have. It was not an opportunity he could afford to pass up."

"Was it a more lucrative job somewhere?"

"I don't know, Percy," replied Heygate. "I had the idea that he might have come into money. Not wealth, mind you, but enough to make the move he was talking about and live comfortably. He said nothing specifically. It was simply the sense I had. He was vague. I asked when they were leaving. He said they would be gone the following day. I asked where they were going. He said he could not say. Again he adjured me to secrecy. But it was hardly necessary. I knew nothing anyway."

"And that was it?"

"I'm afraid so. We shook hands. I took the three pounds and returned to the manor and told the viscount what had transpired. He received the information without comment or overmuch curiosity. And that was it. A month later I rented the cottage to a man new to the mines. To my knowledge, no one has heard from the Barrie fellow or the girl since."

SEVENTY-THREE

Cousins Facing the Future

For the rest of the day, Percy kept mostly to himself. Florilyn knew he needed time to adjust to the sudden shock of finding Gwyneth gone. They did not ride that afternoon.

There exist few better antidotes to the mental and emotional doldrums, however, than demanding physical exertion. After an afternoon watching him wander aimlessly about the manor, inspecting the stables he had helped build two years before, rekindling his friendships with Grey Tide and Red Rhud and several other horses, and chatting with Hollin Radnor and Stuart Wyckham, Florilyn determined that she would get her cousin away from the house the next morning.

Percy spent the evening with a George MacDonald title he had not seen, *Ranald Bannerman's Boyhood*. His aunt had handed it to him after dinner, telling him it had just come out that year, and that she had only recently finished it. However, he had a difficult time concentrating on the words on the page.

Florilyn appeared surprisingly early in the breakfast room the next morning. She was upbeat and cheerful, ready to do her best to bring life back to Percy's spirit. "It's a beautiful day, Percy," she said as they ate. "I am going for a ride. I hope you will join me."

"Sure," said Percy, though without his customary enthusiasm. "I guess I haven't been very good company. Sorry. . .but life goes on, as they say."

"That's the way I felt for weeks after Gwyneth disappeared," said Florilyn.

They agreed to meet at the stables at ten. Percy was already there when Florilyn arrived in her riding habit.

"Hollin has just been telling me about this beautiful black stallion," said Percy. He was standing at the stall of a jet-black powerful horse he had never seen before.

"A nasty brute," said Florilyn. "His name is Demon, and for good reason. He's a four-year-old. I'm surprised he hasn't snapped at you standing there. My father bought him hoping to race him. After getting him here, it became obvious why my father got him at the price he did. He's altogether unmanageable. What did Hollin tell you?"

"Exactly the same," replied Percy, "that he counseled your father against the purchase, but that Uncle Roderick had his heart set on a thoroughbred, and here was one to be had at a price he could afford."

"That about sums it up."

"Have you ridden him?" asked Percy.

Florilyn laughed, though the sound erupting from her mouth more resembled a snort. "I wouldn't be caught dead on that horse's back!"

"Does *anyone* ride him?"

"Courtenay can. Papa *thinks* he can. But it makes me nervous whenever he takes him out. We all pray he will come back alive! Mother has begged Papa to cut his losses and give the horse to Padrig Gwlwlwyd. My father is a good horseman. But he isn't as strong as he once was. He's not steady enough in the saddle for a dangerous horse like that. But he is a proud man. He doesn't want to admit that the horse is too much for him."

"Then I shall certainly keep my distance," said Percy. "Are Grey Tide and Red Rhud still the best choices for me?"

"That depends on what kind of mount you want."

"You know me—I'm a beginner, remember."

"Hardly!" rejoined Florilyn. "You can claim to be faster than me."

Even as she said the words, a flash of pain crossed Florilyn's face. "To answer your question, they are probably more reliable than ever. They are nine years old and not as fast as they once were but still the best two mounts in our stables. I think I will take out Crimson Sun."

"Who's that?"

"Red Rhud's foal. He's only a year and a half. We're still training him. But he is a gentle young stallion. I'll take him today, and he can get to know your voice and smell. Perhaps you can try him later."

"Sound's good. I'll stick with Grey Tide then."

Half an hour later, they left the grounds.

"Have you seen Harlech Castle?" asked Florilyn.

"No. North of here, isn't it?"

"Yes, about three or four miles. It's worth the ride."

They set out down the hill. Florilyn led along the main road, bypassing the village. They came in sight of what had for so long been the Barrie cottage, though neither mentioned it.

"How long will you be staying?" asked Florilyn as they clomped slowly along side by side. "Will you be here all summer?"

"You have no objection?" said Percy, a hint of fun returning to his tone.

"Goodness, no! I hope you do."

"Well that's good, because I still have a score to settle with you from five years ago."

"With me? What are you talking about?" Florilyn laughed.

"Our bet. . .on the race. . .that day on the beach. You *owe* me! The loser has to wait on the winner for a day."

"Hmm. . .I'd hoped you had forgotten that!" She smiled.

"I am simply biding my time, waiting for just the right moment to claim my winnings," rejoined Percy. "But to answer your question, I have no timetable. I have a good apprenticeship with a solicitor's firm in Aberdeen. Mr. Snyder, the man who's taken me under his wing, didn't want me to come south at all. I am supposed to be working for him right now. But I told him I had to take time to come to Wales again."

"He is expecting you back?"

Percy nodded. "But I gave no promises when that would be. There are things I wanted to settle before I return north."

"*Things?* About. . .what?"

"Just. . .things, you know. The future and all that. Sometimes you need to get away from your normal routine to put your life in perspective. I will graduate in a year. Then I plan to enter law school. There is much to consider."

"And after that?" probed Florilyn.

"I don't know—the practice of law, I suppose. I probably don't sound very enthusiastic. But I love law. It's fascinating to wrap your mind around all sides of a dilemma. But there are so many types of law. I haven't settled on an area of specialization yet. There are times I think nothing would be as rewarding as being a country solicitor in some small, out-of-the-way village where you would know everyone and be part of the community. You would have the chance to help people and be involved in their lives."

"Someplace like. . .Llanfryniog?" queried Florilyn.

"I suppose. Though I doubt the need for a solicitor's services is felt often enough in a village *this* small to make a poor lawyer much of a living." Percy chuckled. "But then I waver to the opposite extreme and think about the opportunities in a large city like Aberdeen or Edinburgh or Glasgow."

"I cannot imagine you as the big-city type." Florilyn smiled.

"I've been a city boy all my life except for my brief times here."

"Which is the real you?"

"Hmm. . .a good question. I'm not sure I know yet. Maybe that's one of those things I need to resolve. What about you?"

"What about me?"

"What are your plans?"

"You asked me that once before. I told you that women don't have plans. I am a country girl—I don't think there's any doubt about that. I once thought I would love the big city. London is exciting and vibrant and all that, but it's not for me. I could never live anywhere I couldn't ride for an hour without seeing another human being."

"I never took you for a loner."

Florilyn smiled. "I'm not sure that's the word I would use. I just like being out in the country, with nature all about me and with no sounds of bustle and activity."

They rode on in silence. In former years they would have been galloping and laughing and bantering and racing. On this day, however, their hearts were full of the thoughts that young men and young women often have who are not sure what the future holds. Theirs was an uncertain time in life. Adulthood beckoned, but the perplexities of youth remained. Those perplexities hung heavy on the hearts of the two cousins as they contemplated what lay ahead for them.

"I think a lot of you, Florilyn," said Percy at length. "I hope you know that."

"I think I do," replied Florilyn. "The feeling is mutual."

Again it was quiet. Both were thinking. Yet neither could divulge the full nature of their thoughts. The rest of the ride passed uneventfully.

Percy's mind was busier than he let on.

SEVENTY-FOUR

The Familiar Hills

*P*ercy's ride with Florilyn helped clarify his thoughts. It also added new complexities to his speculations.

There was much to think about, much to pray about. If ever he needed his father, that time was now. Unfortunately his father was three hundred miles away. Something also told him that the decision before him was one he needed to resolve on his own. If he was not sure enough to make up his own mind, then he was not sure *enough*. He had to be sure within *himself*.

He did not ride with Florilyn again for the rest of the week. He saw little of her. But he was watching. More and more, she filled his thoughts and prayers.

Roderick, Katherine, and Florilyn went to church on Sunday. Courtenay never accompanied them now. His aunt and uncle assumed Percy would go with them. But after comments he had heard in the village, Percy knew that sufficient speculation existed about his intentions toward his cousin without fueling it further by allowing half the town to see them together.

From his manner on their ride, Florilyn understood that it was time for her to wait. She accompanied her parents with a quiet, hopeful, patient heart.

Once they were on their way, Percy went to the stables, saddled Grey Tide, and set out northeastward into the Snowdonian hills. The moment he left the manor, he knew his destination.

Percy arrived at the overlook high above the translucent mountain lake an hour and a half later. At this place he had heard Gwyneth's wonderfully strange crooning voice beckoning to the animals that they could come to her without fear. He now knew the way down to the meadow as well. But he would never take that path again. The sights to which it led could be shared with only one person in the world.

Up here, however, this overlook was *his* private special place. Not even Gwyneth knew of that day he had watched her until the holiness of the moment had overwhelmed him.

This was another day like that one. Though Gwyneth would never know of it, his heart must again somehow connect with hers. He would give anything to know what she was thinking at this moment. The questions filling his mind were not merely about why she had left. She could not remain in Llanfryniog without her father and Grannie. Wherever they went, she would always go. They were her chief responsibility. He would never question that.

But why had there been no word to anyone? Not to Florilyn. . .no message left for him. Her leaving also left unanswered the nagging question why she had not met him on the promontory two years earlier. The unexpected turmoil of recent days left *too* much unanswered.

Why should he not be happy for Gwyneth? Whatever had taken place, wherever they had gone, Codnor Barrie would do nothing that was not for her best. He knew the man well enough to know that. According to Tilman Heygate, Gwyneth's future was the primary reason for the move. Perhaps they had inherited money from a distant relative.

Then why the mystery? Or had Codnor been offered a lucrative job elsewhere that would enable him to pay for further education for Gwyneth? Was it even possible that she had been betrothed to a man of means somewhere? Could *that* be the opportunity Barrie spoke of?

Whatever it was, how could he be sad for himself? Gwyneth was being given opportunities that Barrie could not have reason to expect from any other quarter. It was time for him to be *glad* for them, to rejoice for whatever future Gwyneth's father was now in a position to give her.

What, then, did this sudden change mean for him? Where did it leave his personal reasons for coming to Wales this summer? Had he become too anxious for God to reveal His will?

If Gwyneth was truly *gone*. . .forever. . .if he had no way to find her and would never see her again. . .what would she want him to do now? He could almost hear her voice as he recalled his previous visit: *"Miss Florilyn is expecting you to be her escort."*

At last the question that had been stirring and bubbling in the emotional confusion of his subconscious for days rose to the surface. The words were simple. But the implication was enormous: Would she want him to give his love to another? To one whom she herself loved as selflessly as he knew Gwyneth loved Florilyn?

Percy smiled. He knew the answer well enough. Gwyneth was so selfless, she would *never* think of herself. She would only think of him and those she loved. He knew beyond a doubt that he would have her blessing.

Could that perhaps be the reason she had not come to meet him at the promontory? Had she been trying to tell him two years ago that she knew Florilyn loved him and that ultimately he would have to choose between them? Had she been trying to make that choice easier for him even then?

And yet. . .he still had Florilyn's best to think of. Was it right. . .for *her*?

Percy had left Glasgow for Wales a week ago knowing that love beat in his heart. But was *love* the same as *affection*? And where did friendship between two young people fit into the kind of love that would last a lifetime? He had come here to find out the answers to such questions. But then immediately upon his arrival, so suddenly, circumstances had changed.

Pausing in his thoughts, Percy reflected on that word—*circumstances.* Was this an example of what his father so often said, that the Lord used circumstances to confirm His leading. . .occasionally even to *change* the direction of his leading?

"What are You trying to say to me, Lord?" Percy whispered aloud. "Are these *Your* circumstances speaking to me?"

Even his own soft voice seemed an intrusion upon the solemnity of the place where he sat.

Percy's thoughts filled with Florilyn. He knew that she loved him. Whether she was actually expecting a proposal he had no way of knowing. But if what Chandos said was universally known, she must have been *waiting* for one.

Could he love her as she deserved to be loved? Could he give her of his very best without a divided heart?

Then came a startling question: Were he and Florilyn being drawn together all along?

The question sent him into a new round of reflection. He had once told her he was proud of her. But it went far deeper than that. She had become a young woman of character. She had been a bratty girl during his first visit. She and Courtenay had been birds of a feather. But then who was *he* to be talking? He had been a bratty kid, too. He chuckled to himself at the thought.

It took a special kind of person, and genuine depth of character, to change. . .really *change.* Florilyn had done so. He admired her for it. He did not love her for that reason alone, but that depth of character certainly deepened his regard for her.

He had changed. Florilyn had changed. Perhaps *they* were now birds of a feather. . .a young man and young woman who had been on the same spiritual journey all along. Was it perhaps even a journey, because she had always been good, in some strange way, that it was *impossible* for Gwyneth fully to share?

Had he and Florilyn been meant for each other from the beginning? If God was indeed leading them together, could he trust Him, even trust Him for himself, that he *could* be the best for Florilyn? To accept God's leading also implied trusting Him enough to follow that leading.

Over the next few days, Percy continued to walk and ride alone. He visited many of his old haunts. He walked the hills praying and contemplating the future.

Over the coming days the sense—was it the divine nudging?— slowly grew on him that the answer to the big question was *yes*. He had come seeking resolution. Even more. . .a life companion. It seemed that God had now given him the answer he had been praying for.

After another week, he knew it was time to talk to Florilyn. This time about their future together.

SEVENTY-FIVE

Florilyn

By the sound of the knock, Florilyn knew who it was. She went to the door. There stood Percy. His look was unlike any expression she had seen on his countenance. He looked embarrassed, almost bashful.

"I need to talk to you, Florilyn," he said, glancing down at the floor. "I would *like* to talk to you, I should say. . .if you have time. . .or should I come back—"

"Goodness, no. Of course I have time, Percy."

He waited in the corridor.

She dashed into the room a moment then joined him and closed the door behind her.

They walked downstairs and left the house. It was silent for some time.

Percy led the way toward the garden. He was uncharacteristically agitated.

Florilyn waited.

"You have really changed, Florilyn," he said. "You are a different person than when I first came."

"You know why, don't you, Percy?" she asked softly.

"I suppose you grew up and began to see things differently. We all did. Remember what a jerk I was that first summer?"

"You were never a jerk, Percy."

"I made a pretty good impression of one! Maybe I should just say that I had a lot of growing up to do. So I changed, too. But so did you, and I am impressed and proud of you."

"You said that to me once before," rejoined Florilyn. "I wasn't quite sure what to think. I do now. . .at least I think so. It makes me happy to know you feel that way about me." Florilyn paused. "There's more to the changes in me than just being twenty now," she went on after a moment. "It's because of you, Percy. *You* helped me see things. You helped me grow up. You helped me see myself and helped me grow into someone better. Everything you told me about your father. . .that's how you have been to me. I learned to trust you in the same way that you trust your father."

"That is high praise," said Percy. His voice was soft and thoughtful. "That is a remarkable thing for one person to say to another."

"I mean every word."

"I know you do. That's what makes it remarkable. Thank you."

They walked on, descending more deeply into the depths of the garden. As they spoke softly together, Percy shared what was on his heart and the decision he had come to, which was to ask her to be his wife.

Florilyn's heart swelled. Slowly her eyes began to fill. "Do you really mean it, Percy?" she said.

He looked at her and smiled. "Of course I mean it."

"Oh, Percy," she said softly, her voice full of the tears that were flowing from her eyes, "you have made me the happiest girl in the world." She slipped her hand through his arm, and they continued to walk slowly through the garden.

"There is a question I have to ask, Percy," said Florilyn as they returned in the direction of the house some time later.

He waited.

"What about Gwyneth?"

Percy drew in a long sigh. "Nothing gets past you," he said with a smile.

"I know you loved her. At first I didn't realize it. But I grew to know it as I grew to love her, too."

"It's no secret," said Percy. "I loved you both. I love you for how you changed and for who you have become. I loved her with a sort of deep gratitude for helping me learn to see God. But I believe the circumstances as they developed were God's way of leading you and me together."

"Like what you told me your father talks about."

Percy nodded. Slowly a smile spread over his face. "Have I ever told you how I once wondered if Gwyneth was an angel?" he asked.

"No!" said Florilyn. "An *angel*?"

"I really did, at first. She was so different, so otherworldly. She would appear when you least expected it. And she helped me to change—like you said that I helped you."

Florilyn listened as Percy went on.

"Now I am wondering," he said. "I know it sounds crazy, but with her disappearing like this, maybe she really *was* an angel, sent in some strange way to lead us together. Then when her job was over, she left us."

"You don't *really* think so?"

"I don't know." Percy chuckled. "But it's a nice thought."

"She helped teach us *both* about God." Florilyn nodded. "That's what angels do, isn't it?"

"And about each other as well," agreed Percy. "I wonder if we would have come together without her. She will always be part of us."

"My only regret is that she cannot be at our wedding. I wish she could stand beside me. I will never forget her."

Later that afternoon, a knock came on the viscount's door.

"Might I talk to you, Uncle Roderick?" said Percy when his uncle opened the door. "There is a personal matter I would like to discuss and an important question I need to ask you."

"Certainly, Percy, my boy! Come in and sit down. Was that you and

Florilyn I saw in the garden earlier?"

"Yes, sir. Actually that is what I would like to talk to you about." He closed the door behind him and took a seat with his uncle.

They remained in close conference for thirty minutes.

Feeling as if a great weight had been lifted from his shoulders, on the following morning Percy rode into Llanfryniog. He was in high spirits. At last he was ready to walk the streets and lanes and visit in the shops and walk to the harbor and beach. He was astonished to find people looking at him differently.

He was puzzled by the smiles until one woman stopped as he approached and extended her hand. "I hear congratulations are in order, Mr. Percy," she said. "May I offer my hand and wish you and Miss Florilyn all the best."

Percy shook her hand. "Does word really spread so fast?" He laughed. "All this only happened yesterday."

"The whole village knows, Mr. Percy," said the woman. "It doesn't take long for this kind of news to pass along. Good day to you, sir."

Percy watched her amble off, still amazed by the exchange. He didn't even know the woman's name, but she seemed to know everything about him.

SEVENTY-SIX

Joy Comes to the Manor

Though some might have attributed his ebullient spirits to the relief of a father having a daughter off his hands, the viscount's joy went far deeper. He knew that Florilyn was engaged to a worthy young man whom he already loved as a son. His was a double portion of happiness.

Katherine's spirits and those of the entire staff of Westbrooke Manor were equally celebratory.

Stevie Muir had not been to work for two days. When he next appeared, therefore, he had heard nothing. Word of the engagement was the first news out of Hollin Radnor's mouth. Immediately Stevie went in search of Percy.

He encountered Florilyn on his way toward the house. "Miss Florilyn," he said excitedly, "I just heard the news about you and Percy. Congratulations!"

"Thank you, Stevie. I am very happy."

"You deserve it, Miss Florilyn."

She looked at him with a puzzled expression. "I don't. . . How do you mean?" she said.

"Just that you are a young lady of quality and character," replied Stevie.

"What a nice thing to say!"

431

"I have been watching you for years. I have come to have great admiration for you. Not many girls in your position—from wealth and privilege, you know—not many grow to be the kind of young lady you have become. I know your parents are proud of you. You deserve a fine man like Percy. And he is lucky to have someone like you."

"Thank you, Stevie. No one has ever said something like that to me before except Percy."

"I mean it. I am happy for you both." Stevie continued in search of Percy.

Florilyn stared after him a moment with an odd expression. She had never paid much attention to Stevie Muir before. There was obviously more to him than met the eye.

❦

"Percy, my boy," said the viscount as he and Percy walked down the main staircase together, "and at last I can legitimately call you that, eh!—how about father and prospective bridegroom going for a ride together? We need to talk about your future, yours and mine and my daughter's."

"I would like that, Uncle Roderick."

"That brings up another point of protocol to be decided. What will you call me after you are my son-in-law? Bit of a perplexity, what?"

"I'm sure we will be able to come to an amenable solution, *Uncle* Roderick!" laughed Percy.

They met Stevie in the entryway.

"Hello, Lord Snowdon," he said. "Percy, I was on my way to find you and offer my congratulations. I only heard this morning."

"Thank you, Stevie," smiled Percy as the two friends shook hands.

The three continued outside toward the stables.

"Stevie, my good man, Percy and I fancy a ride today. Saddle me the black demon. What is your fancy, Percy, my boy?"

"Red Rhud, I think," replied Percy. "But are you sure the stallion is wise, Uncle Roderick? Florilyn tells me he's dangerous."

"Bah! Women's talk. I can master any horse. I am in such high spirits I am ready to take on the world. You have made me a happy man, Percy, my boy."

Percy glanced toward Stevie with concern. Stevie's face registered the same anxiety. He was well acquainted with the dangerous temperament of the stallion.

But the viscount was insistent. Stevie therefore set about saddling him, while keeping a wary eye on the beast's eyes and ears.

SEVENTY-SEVEN

The River between the Ridges

Percy and Lord Snowdon left the grounds eastward. Without intending it but with little choice, Percy's uncle led out at a reckless pace. The stallion had not been aired for days and was fierce with energy. It was all Percy could do to keep up.

This was his first ride this summer on Red Rhud's back. As he had noticed with Grey Tide, she had lost a step from previous visits. He was not able to draw alongside his uncle until they were a mile from the manor and the stallion's initial burst of fiery energy was somewhat dissipated.

"That is some spunky animal!" shouted Percy as he tried to catch up.

"A noble beast," rejoined his uncle over his shoulder. "As soon as I have the chance, I hope to race him in Manchester."

"Who will ride him?"

"I'll get someone. Maybe Courtenay. He can handle him."

"Are you sure racing a horse like that is a good idea?"

"Have you been talking to my wife and daughter?" laughed Westbrooke. "Horse racing is a man's business, Percy, my boy. You can't make money without risk. Perhaps we shall be partners."

As Percy at last drew even, the stallion Demon suddenly lurched sideways and snapped with great sharp teeth at Red Rhud's neck.

Percy swerved to the right with a startled cry, nearly toppling out of the saddle.

"Now I am sure that racing that animal is not a good idea."

"Nonsense, Percy, my boy!" rejoined the viscount. "Spirit, that's what's wanted in a champion thoroughbred. This Demon has it, and to spare. He is full of energy, that's all. He needs to be given the rein, the freedom to run. Let him go at top speed, and he is as easy to handle as any of my wife's mares."

With the words he dug in his heels and did just as he said, and again gave Demon the rein. Horse and rider shot off with a speed marvelous to behold had Percy not been terrified for his uncle's life.

Again he urged Red Rhud on as fast as he dared. But it was not enough to keep pace with his uncle. In spite of the lessons Gwyneth had given him, he was still not completely confident as a horseman. Within moments his uncle was out of sight.

Percy continued up the incline. As he crested the ridge, he gazed frantically for any sign of him. Halfway down the opposite slope far ahead, the black maniacal creature was tearing up great clods. His uncle appeared out of control, jostling about in the saddle.

In the distance, the stallion suddenly stopped abruptly and reared. As far away as he was, Percy heard great whinnying cries. They were not horse sounds of fright but of wrath. Percy galloped on.

His uncle had taken out his riding whip and was shouting and wielding it freely. In the contest of wills between man and enraged beast, however, the whip was not a wise instrument of mediation.

Suddenly Demon reared again and rose nearly erect. He was clearly trying to unseat his rider. His front hooves pawed violently at the air. The viscount only barely held to the saddle.

Demon crashed down on his forelegs, jumping and bucking wildly. Then without warning he broke into another furious gallop. Percy had still not reached them when the two receded again into the distance.

At the bottom of the valley between the two ridges flowed a small river, hardly worthy of the name but of more size than a mere stream.

It wound through a rocky channel of uneven terrain strewn with rocks of many sizes and some large boulders. It was a much different course than that of the stream through Gwyneth's special meadow. It was no place for a wild horse.

But there was no stopping Demon now. Some four hundred yards ahead, he reached the water and launched himself into the air.

Percy heard a great cry. A moment later he saw the black stallion flying up the hill on the opposite side of the river.

No rider was in the saddle.

He shouted to Red Rhud and hurried toward the scene. Gradually he slowed as the footing became treacherous. Reaching the stream, Percy reined in, jumped to the ground, and sloshed through the water.

He found his uncle lying motionless on the far side.

He ran to him and knelt down. A nasty gash was visible on the top of his head where he had crashed into a rock. Wet blood from it flowed into his hair. His hat was yards away. A huge welt rose from his skull.

"Ah, Percy, my boy," he said weakly, gasping for breath. "The brute threw me. You were right. . .a dangerous creature. I was a fool to think—"

"Just rest easy, Uncle Roderick," said Percy. "Don't try to talk. I saw the whole thing. The horse went wild."

"I can't. I'm cold, Percy, my boy."

Percy flung his riding jacket from him and laid it over his uncle's chest. The viscount's legs from the knees down lay wet in the streambed.

"I can't feel my legs, Percy, my boy. . .don't think I can ride. . .if that confounded horse. . .could ride back together. . .but I. . .don't think I have the strength. . .to climb up."

"Don't worry, Uncle Roderick," said Percy. "I'll ride back to the manor. We'll bring a cart. You just rest."

"Sorry to be a bother. . .Percy. . .my boy."

"Think nothing of it, Uncle Roderick."

Percy saw that he had begun to shiver. He yanked off his shirt and laid it under the jacket. He then splashed back through the water where Red Rhud waited patiently, mounted quickly, and galloped bare-chested in the direction of the manor.

There was no sign of Demon anywhere.

SEVENTY-EIGHT

The Ambulance Cart

Percy galloped recklessly into the grounds shouting for Stevie and Hollin. By the time they had a small flatbed cart hitched to one of the sturdier horses and Percy had run inside for another shirt and jacket, the commotion had emptied the house with word that their master had had a serious fall.

"Where is he, Percy?" asked Florilyn as Percy mounted Red Rhud.

"Where the river runs through the valley, between the ridges on the path we took three days ago, you know, where the ford is so rocky."

"What where you doing there?"

"I'm not sure your uncle intended it. Demon was out of control."

"We'll be right behind you," said Katherine. She and Florilyn ran to the stables to saddle two more horses.

Seconds later Percy was flying eastward away from the manor. Stevie knew the place exactly from Percy's description. He and Hollin followed with the cart.

By the time Katherine and Florilyn arrived, Percy was seated beside the viscount. There was little he could do. His uncle was barely conscious.

The cart was only ten minutes behind, bumping down the rocks. They pulled it through the water then set about lifting the viscount onto it.

"Gently, gently!" exhorted Stevie. "Hollin, you and Percy lift by each shoulder. Lady Katherine and Lady Florilyn, you lift at his waist. I fear his right leg is broken. We must keep him flat."

Katherine's face had gone as pale as her husband's when she saw him lying broken among the rocks. "Will he. . . What do you think, Steven?" she asked.

"I cannot say, Lady Katherine," replied Stevie. "His head has been injured. We must get him to Dr. Rotherham with all the haste we dare."

The others stood by to follow Stevie's orders. None questioned his taking charge.

Katherine hesitated then knelt close to the viscount's face. It was ghostly white. "Oh, Roderick. . .Roderick," she said softly. "Be brave. . . be strong. We will get him home." She bent forward and kissed him.

His lips quivered and his eyelids fluttered. But he was unable to speak.

"Oh, dear Roderick—"

"Please, Lady Katherine," urged Stevie. "We must delay no longer." She stood.

"Place your hands under his waist, Lady Katherine," said Stevie, "just as Lady Florilyn is doing."

How much help she could provide in her condition was doubtful.

When he was in position beside the viscount's legs, Stevie nodded to the other two men. "All right, then," he said, "everyone lift. . .slowly, gently. . ."

He was not so heavy for five of them. But being dead weight and limp as a wet rag, he made an exceedingly awkward burden. A groan sounded from the viscount's mouth as they lifted him. They managed to get him high enough to lie on the blankets and pillows they had gathered to cushion the bed of the cart.

Even under the best of conditions, without a road, it would not be a comfortable ride. They had to bump their way over open fields, up and down the ridge, through woodland and across several streams. It took considerably longer than Stevie would have liked. But he chose to err on the side of caution and not add to the viscount's injuries.

Meanwhile, Katherine and Florilyn rode ahead. Florilyn galloped straight to town. Luckily she found Dr. Rotherham at home.

Katherine went on to the manor to prepare a sickroom on the ground floor. By the time the ambulance cart bearing her husband arrived, she had recovered from her initial shock and was again the strong matron of her home.

A bed was ready and a blazing fire roared in the hearth. Dry clothes were waiting. The entire staff was gathered at Katherine's side, anxious and ready to obey the slightest command. Florilyn and Dr. Rotherham had arrived only minutes before the cart clattered into the entryway.

Everyone ran outside. They looked on as Dr. Rotherham now took charge. With the men, he helped get the viscount, completely unconscious, inside and to bed. After giving what instructions were necessary, Dr. Rotherham left the manor to return to his surgery for the required supplies and tools to set the leg.

The bedside vigil began.

SEVENTY-NINE

At the Bedside

*I*n spite of his distant manner, the viscount was loved by his staff. His tenderness toward Katherine of late had had its effect on his overall demeanor.

The increase of smiles and kind words had spread among the rest of them as well. He grew appreciative of little things. He became free in expressing his gratitude, even plucked an occasional rose from the garden for Mrs. Drynwydd or Mrs. Llewellyn. This caused the two women to blush and babble a good deal but warmed their hearts more than the viscount ever knew. The accident, therefore, cast a cloud of gloom over the house.

Word quickly spread through Llanfryniog. The pall of hushed voices and tiptoed step extended throughout the whole village. On the following Sunday, prayers in all three churches were heavy of heart on the viscount's behalf.

All that day Kyvwlch Gwarthegydd's hammer was silent. The blacksmith would never have called the thoughts rising from his mind *prayers*. But God's heart is more open-minded than man's. He received the good man's compassion for the viscount and his family into His eternal bosom, nonetheless that the man denied His existence. God is the Father of Christians and atheists alike, though only the former get the full benefit of that Fatherhood by acknowledging their childness. But Gwarthegydd was *concerned*, and in his own way his unacknowledged Father in heaven received that concern on the viscount's behalf.

Dr. Rotherham set the leg but doubted, even if the patient recovered, whether it would ever be much use again. He was far more worried about the injury to the head and neck. The extremeties continued cold, the broken leg like a chunk of ice. He knew what dreadful danger that fact portended. There was little to be done but wait and see how rapidly and how far recovery spread through the viscount's body.

Courtenay, who had been away a few days, returned and was civil and courteous to all. He seemed genuinely shaken by the turn of events. He was horseman enough to know how dangerous a fall such as his father had taken could be. He was also perceptive enough to read on the doctor's face what he was not saying. Courtenay still knew nothing about how matters stood between Percy and his sister.

Eventually the murderer Demon wandered back to the manor. Hunger had somewhat quieted him, and Stevie was able to secure and return him to the stables. He immediately sought Katherine with his recommendation that the beast either be sold or put down. "You can never reform a bad-tempered horse," said Stevie. "If you are in agreement, with your permission, I would like to talk to Padrig Gwlwlwyd to see if he might have use for him. If he does, how much would you want for him, Lady Katherine?"

"If he wants him, Steven," she replied, "he may have him. I want nothing for him. I don't want a dangerous animal like that on my conscience. I would give him to Mr. Gwlwlwyd only on the condition that he never put the animal into the hands of one whom he might harm."

"A wise stipulation, Lady Katherine," Stevie nodded. "If Padrig does not think he can be reformed, I will put him down."

"Thank you, Steven."

Hearing of his mother's decision, Courtenay was furious. His anger stemmed not so much from the fact that the horse would be lost to him but that his mother had consulted Stevie Muir instead of him.

Hours went by and turned into days. Though the viscount did not regain consciousness, he was never alone. Someone sat at the bedside around the clock. Dr. Rotherham came every morning to see if there had been a change.

When the viscount awoke on the sixth day, Courtenay rode immediately for Llanfryniog and returned with the doctor. Great was the rejoicing of the entire community.

Though he kept his concerns to himself, Dr. Rotherham knew the joyous mood to be premature. Though the viscount appeared to have some of his strength back, circulation remained poor. The extremities were not warming as they should. The left leg was as numb to a poke of the needle as the right.

To Courtenay's great annoyance, as often as he was awake, his father seemed more to desire Percy near him than his own flesh and blood. In truth, the sickroom made Courtenay uncomfortable, and he was only too happy to yield his place. Nor did he feel any great filial affection toward his father. But the idea that Percy was so close to him rekindled his former antagonism toward his cousin.

At last Dr. Rotherham's professional ethics demanded that he tell someone what he feared. He shrank from making a full revelation to Lady Snowdon for fear of an emotional reaction that would ripple through the house and do no one any good. To tell the children and not the wife would hardly do. In the end, he realized he had no alternative but to speak to the viscount himself.

He went into the sick chamber, requested of Lady Florilyn that he be left alone for a few minutes with the patient, closed the door behind her, and then sat down in the chair beside the bed.

"Come to deliver the bad news in person, eh, doctor?" said the viscount, attempting with humor to mask his concern. He had seen the look on Rotherham's face the moment he entered.

"You are not so far wrong, Lord Snowdon," replied the doctor. "I would be remiss not to disclose the nature of your injuries to someone.

I hesitate to speak frankly with your wife. I am here to ask your will in the matter. Would you like your wife and son and daughter present?"

"Present for what?"

"For what I have to say."

"No, confound you," snapped the viscount, fear overpowering courtesy. "Just say it."

"You are certain you wouldn't like your family—"

"No, blast you—get on with it!"

The doctor sat patiently until the viscount calmed.

"Your leg is not recovering as I had hoped," said Rotherham after a few moments.

"Nonsense. I feel fine. Merely a little faintness."

"Your right leg is broken below the knee," Rotherham went on, ignoring the viscount's protestations. "The injury to both knee and leg are so severe it is unlikely you will walk normally again. Though I cannot be absolutely certain at this point, it may be that amputation will be necessary to save your life."

At the word, the viscount turned his face to the wall. The positive horror of the thought filled him with such dread that he was trembling like a child.

"I am yet more concerned about the injury to your head and neck, Lord Snowdon," Dr. Rotherham went on. "Your left leg, though to all appearances sound, does not respond to stimulation. I fear paralysis."

"Is there nothing you can do?"

"I fear not, my lord."

"Am I dying, then?"

"Absent a miracle from on high, sir, I fear. . ."

"Confounded doctors—can't give a man a straight answer," growled the viscount. "Blackguards, all of you! I'm dying—why can't you just say it? I'm man enough to take it. No one lives forever."

Again Dr. Rotherham waited. "What would you like me to do, my lord?" he asked at length.

"About what?" said the viscount testily.

"Your leg."

"Pooh—don't think I am going to give you leave to saw the thing off!" said the viscount, trembling again at the thought. "Where's the use if it's not going to save me? Let my head recover, and we'll talk about it then."

"By then it may be too late."

"Then it will be too late and the consequences will be mine!" cried the viscount.

"Would you like me to discuss the matter with your wife?" asked the doctor calmly.

"Good heavens, no! The poor woman would wither and go to pieces at the very idea." The viscount paused and grew serious. "There is one thing you can do for me, doctor," he said at length.

"Anything, my lord."

"Is there anyone you can trust, who can hold his tongue? If you could get a message to Porthmadog, a telegram or send someone to fetch my solicitor here—Murray is his name."

"I know the man. Yes, I could arrange it."

"Good. I would appreciate it. Thank you, doctor."

Dr. Rotherham left the room.

Florilyn returned. "Is everything all right, Daddy?" she said.

"Yes, yes, of course. Everything's fine."

She knew from his tone that he was lying. But she did not press it.

Her father closed his eyes and pretended to doze. Suddenly there was little time to put right what he had neglected for too many years. He had tried to make some amends a few months ago. Now suddenly the past returned upon him with renewed pangs of guilt.

But what could he do? How could it be managed? Whom could he trust?

He had tried to keep from hurting Katherine. Now he wondered if he had done the right thing. So long lethargic and drowsy, his conscience was coming awake. And it stung him.

Mr. Murray arrived the following afternoon. He presented himself and asked to see viscount Lord Snowdon.

Broakes vaguely recognized the man but asked whom should he say was calling.

"Lord Snowdon's solicitor, Hamilton Murray," the man replied.

It did not take long thereafter for word to circulate through the house, supplied with minor emendations by Broakes, that the viscount was closeted with his solicitor for the purpose of changing his will.

When the rumor reached Lady Katherine's ears not many minutes later, she put an immediate stop to it. "Don't be absurd, Mrs. Drynwydd," she said, walking into the kitchen and overhearing what had not been intended for her ears. "The disposition of the estate and Westbrooke Manor is decreed by the terms of the original grant of land centuries ago. The title goes with the manor to the eldest child. My husband could not change those terms if he wanted to. I can tell you of a certainty that he is not writing a new will."

Despite her strong words, Katherine left the kitchen shaken. She paused in the corridor, light-headed, and took two or three deep breaths to steady herself. She then hurried directly to the sick chamber. She found her husband and Mr. Murray alone.

"Ah, Katherine," said the viscount weakly, "you remember Mr. Murray?"

"Yes. . .of course."

"Hello again, Lady Snowdon," said the solicitor, extending his hand.

Katherine shook it but went straight to the bedside. "What is this all about, Roderick?" she asked.

"A mere formality, my dear," he answered. "It is only a precaution. I am having Mr. Murray draw up a document—just in case—naming you trustee of the estate until Courtenay is twenty-five. You remember the terms—he will not inherit until his twenty-fifth birthday. But should I. . .that is, in the unlikely event. . .that is, should something happen before that time. . .it is one of the ambiguities of the terms of the inheritance. I never bothered with it before now. But I want you protected. . .just in case."

"I see. Of course. That makes perfect sense. Well then," she said, turning to go, "I will. . .uh, leave the two of you—"

"No, please stay, Katherine," said the viscount. "This concerns you as well as me. I simply did not want to upset you. As long as you are here. . . please stay."

EIGHTY

Eternal Uncertainties

*T*emporarily at his ease for having legalized Katherine's trustee-ship over the estate, the viscount rested comfortably for the remainder of the day. He even seemed slightly improved.

The next morning, during Courtenay's brief daily visit to the sick chamber, his father motioned for him to sit down beside him. "So, Courtenay, lad," said the viscount, "you ought to, uh. . .know the state of affairs. They don't give me much hope, you see. . . ."

Courtenay listened in silence. He was uncomfortable.

"It will soon be in your hands, you know," his father went on. "You know, I believe, how things stand. . .you will inherit when you are twenty-five. That time will be here before you know it. Only don't make the same mistakes I did, you know. . .foolishness of youth and all that. Keep a good head on your shoulders. . .take care of your mother and sister. . . ."

Courtenay nodded and mumbled a few words of consent. But tenderness had never been a virtue that had existed between them. Neither father nor son knew how to call upon it when it was needed the most.

They spoke stiffly and haltingly for two or three minutes more. At length the viscount confessed himself fatigued and needing a rest, at which time Courtenay left him.

The interview with the solicitor Murray had at last awakened Katherine to the dire nature of her husband's condition. Though he tried to put an optimistic face on it for her sake, she knew that *he* considered the affidavit more than a precautionary measure. He thought he was dying and was certain that the trusteeship would be enforced. . .and soon.

Now the stark reality of the thing began to overwhelm her. Her father was a free thinker and had taught her and her brother Edward to trust more in God than in the doctrines of men. Nevertheless, Katherine could not prevent the natural anxiety of the pervasive judgmental mind-set so prevalent in the mildewed air of the church from filling her with a vague sense of dread.

Regular church attendance notwithstanding, Roderick had never been a spiritual man. She now began to fear for his soul. Despite her upbringing, despite her brother's influence, and despite the gentle whisperings of an eternally loving fatherhood from the pen of the prophet MacDonald, the terrible burden of the wrath of God began to fill her with horrifying images of flames and her poor Roderick in the midst of them.

When Reverend Ramsey came to call, in response to her expressed concern conveyed by the confidential note she had asked Percy to deliver, the viscount more than half suspected who had put him up to it. He grumbled a good deal about having to entertain a parson at a time like this. But he consented to the interview.

It was a formal, strained, almost businesslike affair. Though Fatherhood was the only side of God's nature capable of offering a hopeful glimpse of eternity, in truth Reverend Ramsey knew as little about the fatherhood of God as did Roderick Westbrooke. Ramsey exited the room after thirty minutes with the viscount's soul unchanged. He offered Katherine a few platitudes then left the manor with a sigh of relief. Consoling the dying and grieving was the part of his job he hated most.

Meanwhile, in the sick chamber, the clerical visit had at least served the purpose of turning Roderick Westbrooke's eyes inward, where all have to look eventually. The fact that the fellow Ramsey had had no more spiritual food to offer him at the deathbed than he did from the pulpit only made the viscount hunger the more for one who might possibly be able to tell him where he stood with God. Not that it would do him much good, he thought, but he would like to have some idea what to expect when he went to sleep for the last time and woke up somewhere *else*.

He had always looked down on the fellow, but he would give a thousand pounds right now for twenty minutes with Katherine's brother, Edward Drummond, or her father for that matter. There were two men who seemed to know something about God that had escaped the rest of the cloth. What did they teach ministers in their seminaries anyway? The fool Ramsey was useless.

Unfortunately, he did not have a thousand pounds. And Edward was hundreds of miles away!

I wonder how much the son has gleaned from the father, he thought to himself.

When Katherine again appeared after seeing Reverend Ramsey to the door, her husband asked her to send Percy to see him.

EIGHTY-ONE

High Questions

"*A*h, Percy, my boy!" said the viscount when his nephew entered. "Come in, sit down, and offer some comfort to your uncle." His voice was weak and resigned, though surprisingly cheerful.

Percy had been in and out of the sickroom almost constantly since the accident. But he immediately sensed a change. He knew of neither the solicitor's visit nor the minister's. But he could tell something was different. He sat down beside the bedside.

"They tell me I am dying, Percy," said the viscount.

The bluntness of the statement stung Percy afresh. He was still a young man, not so well acquainted as his father with the cruel vicissitudes of life. "I am sorry, Uncle Roderick," he said.

"Ah, well, part of life they say, what?"

"I, uh. . . How long does the doctor think it will be?" asked Percy tentatively.

"Bah, who knows. You know what bunglers doctors are—can't save a man but won't give him a straight answer."

"And. . .there's nothing they can do?"

"The man wants to whack off my leg. Then he tells me my other is paralyzed, so what's the use? I'll never walk again with or without legs. Then he has the infernal cheek to tell me the problem is my head. . .something about the spine, whatever that's got to do with it. Can't make up his mind. No wonder he's got no cure for what ails a man. Tell me, Percy, my boy, do you believe in heaven?"

The abruptness of the question took Percy off guard. "Uh, yes. . .yes, I do, Uncle Roderick," he said.

"I recall our first dinner together, when my daughter was baiting you. You were uncertain."

"I've grown stronger in my beliefs these last five years."

"Ah, well. . .good for you. Back then we were discussing the eternal destination of the old salt found on the beach. Now it's my turn, eh? So what do you think, now that you are five years older, Percy—will I go to heaven?"

"I don't know, Uncle Roderick. You really, uh. . .ought to be talking to my dad."

"Your father's not here."

"Isn't there someone. . .your minister in town that you would rather—"

"Bah, what he knows about God wouldn't fit through the eye of a needle, as the old saying goes. You've shown yourself a young man whom I respect, Percy, my boy. I want to know what *you* think. It wouldn't surprise me if you told me just what your father would anyway. So I ask you again, do *you* think I will go to heaven?"

"All right then, I would still say I don't know. I don't really know how you and God stand with one another."

"I've been a faithful churchman all my life. Does that count for anything?"

"No, I don't think it does."

"What does, then?"

"How you and God stand with one another. Whether you have made yourself His child."

"What do you mean by that? He's God the Father, isn't He? That includes everyone."

"Indeed. But have you made Him *your* Father?"

"You're talking in circles, Percy, my boy."

"I would never do that with you, Uncle Roderick."

"Then what in blazes do you mean?"

"That even though God is our Father, we must become His children. That is not something that happens in church."

"An incredible statement coming from a vicar's son."

"I learned it from my father. I *do* know that to be something he would say to you."

"What? Your father preaches that people don't have to go to church?"

"I didn't say that, Uncle Roderick. Of course my father wants people to go to church. But when they do, he tells them that it is not in church that they become God's children."

"Where is it then?"

"In their hearts."

"Ah, yes. . .well, there is that of course."

"It is a truth not widely preached. Again, those are my father's very words."

"So, Percy, my boy, do you think I will wake up in *hell*, then, when all this is over?"

"I could not say, Uncle Roderick. I would not presume to speak for God."

"Then I repeat. . .I merely ask your opinion."

"Then I would say the same thing I did before—that I am not personally aware how things stand between you and God."

"That's everything to you, then, is it—how a man stands with God?"

"Yes, that is everything."

"Even I don't know how I stand with Him. There are things in my past that hang heavy upon me, Percy, my boy. How am I to know what God thinks of it all?"

"I am certain of one thing—that He is a good Father," rejoined Percy, "and that He will forgive anything He is able to forgive. I know I am young, and I have little right to speak of such high truths. But there are things in my past that weigh upon my conscience, too."

"What regrets could a young fellow like you possibly have?" asked the viscount, not pausing to consider that the actions harrying his memory at present had been committed when he was younger than Percy.

"The regret of foolishness and youthful hubris, Uncle Roderick," replied Percy. "For years I did not recognize my father's wisdom. I treated him contemptibly. I will feel the pangs of that stupidity all my life."

"All young people are immature. Can't be too hard on yourself, Percy, my boy."

"The young may be immature. I'm sure I still am in many ways. But that is no excuse for willful blindness. Young people *choose* their rebellious attitudes just as I chose mine. They are not a mere part of youth that cannot be avoided. Therefore, I am responsible for my rebellious attitudes. But though my father has forgiven me, the most difficult part is forgiving myself. When I asked my father to forgive me, he said, 'You have always been forgiven. The forgiveness has existed within my heart all along.' That wonderful expression of love has been with me ever since. The forgiveness of my father's heart strengthens me to believe in God's forgiveness. I know God is saying the same to you at this moment. I truly believe those are God's words to you. . .right now."

"That would be a remarkable thing. . .if you are right."

"I believe it with all my heart. I believe that God is more forgiving toward us than most of us are toward ourselves. Then my father added these words, which maybe God says to us as well. He said, 'To complete the transaction, it was necessary for you to ask, that I might give it to you.'"

The viscount was silent for several long minutes. "What should I do, then," he said at length, "now that I am lying on my deathbed? What should I do now that it is nearly too late?"

"It is never too late."

"It is jolly well close to it if one is dying. So what is a man to do?"

"The same thing that God wants us to do every day of our lives.

Facing death changes nothing. It is no different for you at this moment than it is for me."

"What should I do, then?" repeated the viscount.

"Repent of your sins, and be His child."

The words seemed to jolt him, as if Percy had dashed him in the face with a cup of cold water. They bit deep into the long-repressed guilt that had been gnawing away at his conscience.

"*Child*. . .child, you say. Repent of my sins," he added softly. "If you only knew. . .not so easy as you think when there are others involved. I tried to find her, but she was gone, I tell you. Makes repentance dashed difficult, I dare say."

"Repentance is always possible."

"But what of the *child*. . . ? It's too late for all that. So tell me, Percy," said his uncle, coming suddenly out of his mental wanderings, "what do you think of my daughter? She is my child, too, you know."

"I love her, Uncle Roderick."

"I am glad to hear it. I know you will take good care of her."

"I will."

"You will not let. . .that is to say, whatever happens. . .if she should. . . of course, her mother's money would still go to her, along with Courtenay, of course. . .but you would protect her? You would keep her from being hurt?"

"Of course. I will take care of her, Uncle Roderick. You may be assured of that."

The viscount paused. He thought for a long time. "There is another matter. . .of some delicacy, Percy, my boy," he resumed after a long silence. "I need to tell someone. You're right. It is not too late. Too late for *me*, I dare say, but perhaps not for you. You are a solicitor now, I understand."

"No, Uncle Roderick. I am merely studying toward that end."

"Perhaps it will be good enough. If I were to tell you something, would you be bound by confidentiality, a bit like the confessional, I dare say?"

"If you imposed it upon me, yes, I would honor your request."

"Well, it may be a little of the solicitor and priest together," said the viscount. "A confession and a legal document all rolled into one, eh? And here you are, a vicar's son and a future solicitor—I say you will do nicely, Percy, my boy. The perfect lawyer-priest. Go fetch paper and whatever else you need. I want you to take down a statement. Say nothing to anyone. Breathe not a word of it. Now go—get back here as soon as you can."

EIGHTY-TWO

Percy's Commission

Less than five minutes had elapsed when Percy reentered the sick chamber. During that time, the viscount continued to relive much that had remained buried for decades. Percy's words had stung him with the necessity to set right what had remained unresolved from long before.

"Ah, good. . .back so soon?" he said. "You can use that writing desk over there. Is the door closed? You told no one what I asked you to do?"

"I hurried to my room and back without encountering a soul, Uncle Roderick."

"Then sit down. I will dictate. This will be a legal affidavit, will it not?"

"If you sign it, I would assume so," replied Percy. "But are you sure you wouldn't rather have your own solicitor—"

"I want you, Percy. I know I can trust you. This matter may have widespread consequences after I am gone. There is something I need you to do for me. Everything hinges on whether you are successful or not. . .someone I need you to find. But *if* you cannot find her, this need never come out. I am loath to hurt Katherine. But even if it comes late, one must do one's duty. That's part of repentance, is it not?"

"So I would assume, Uncle Roderick. But," Percy added, "if the

457

estate is concerned, would you not rather speak to Courtenay? He is your heir, after all, and—"

"Bah—I could never trust *him* with this," said the viscount. "He would be consumed with self-interest. It is a terrible thing to have to say about one's own son, but in all candor, Percy, my boy, I don't trust the scoundrel. I half suspect him to be the father of the Lorimer girl's whelp, but he's not man enough to own up to it. No, I could not trust him to do the right thing."

Percy sat down across the room at a small table with paper, pen, and ink.

"You may disown me by the time I am through, Percy, my boy," said the viscount. "The story I have to tell is one I have never divulged to another soul. God forgive me, not even Katherine knows of it, though I kept it from her for her own sake. But I pray you will not take out your anger toward me on Florilyn."

"You need have no worry about that, Uncle Roderick. Nothing you could possibly say will change my affection for you."

"You are a good boy, Percy. After this, Florilyn may need you more than ever. So will Katherine. Be good to them, Percy."

"I will."

"You see, Percy, my boy. . ." his uncle began.

For the next thirty minutes, he told Percy of his early life, his travels, confessing alternate bouts of waywardness and repentance, of decisions made and decisions regretted. Soon he was rambling such that Percy could follow but portions of the disjointed narrative. He was not at all clear at every point who he was talking about.

"Promise me you will try to find her, Percy, my boy," he said several times.

"I will do all that is in my power."

"Tell her I'm sorry I didn't come back. . .didn't try harder. But she had disappeared, you see. . .had no idea. . .where she had gone. After a while. . .so long ago. . .couldn't go back. . .by then. . .your aunt, you see. I didn't want to hurt her."

After some time, the viscount was breathing heavily. He seemed spent. But he gathered himself once again, told Percy to start writing, and then began to dictate. He became lucid again. As the story unfolded, at last much of what he had said previously began to fit together.

The affidavit took an hour to compose. When it was completed, Percy took it to him to sign. It was with some difficulty that he was able to hold the pen to do so. By then he was exhausted.

"Keep it in a safe place, Percy, my boy," said the viscount. His voice was barely more than a whisper. "No one must see it unless your search is successful. Otherwise, Katherine need never know."

"I understand."

Within minutes his uncle was asleep, and Percy left him.

EIGHTY-THREE

Farewell Prayer

*T*he visits with his solicitor, minister, and nephew had taxed what remained of the viscount's strength to its limit.

Having conducted with the former and latter what remained of the final business burdening his heart, almost from the moment Percy left him he began to fade. He had remained strong long enough to do what needed to be done. There was no more need for strength. He had put his affairs in order. His spirit now seemed to relax and give in to the inevitable.

The next days passed drearily. Dr. Rotherham came and went but had nothing to report. He knew the end was not far off. The efforts of the ministering staff of family and servants were now for the sole purpose of making the viscount comfortable. He said less and less, stopped eating, and eventually was able to drink only what was poured into his mouth a few drops at a time by spoon.

Late in the afternoon of the fifth day since they had been closeted together for purposes of the affidavit, an urgent knock came to Percy's door. He rose to answer it.

There stood Mrs. Drynwydd. "You're wanted, Mr. Percy," she said. "Quickly, sir. It's the viscount."

Percy ran along the corridor, flew down the staircase, resumed a walk, and tried to calm himself as he walked into the sickroom. There sat Katherine and Florilyn on either side of the bed. The viscount's two hands rested between each of theirs.

Percy approached. His uncle's skin seemed to have been stretched over the bones, his eyes sunken and dark, his flesh a ghastly gray. Seeing Percy approach, the viscount's eyes drifted toward him. His lips quivered as if trying to smile.

Katherine glanced toward Percy with a smile. "His breathing was labored," said Percy's aunt. "His eyes were closed. I was afraid. . .but he seems comfortable again."

Percy nodded and took the chair from the writing table, carried it to the bedside, then sat down beside her.

There was nothing to do but wait. The afternoon waned. The viscount dozed, woke, glanced about, tried to speak though could only mumble incoherently, and then dozed again.

That evening smells from the kitchen drifted in and revived him. He had not eaten in days, but the mere aroma of food was strengthening. Florilyn managed to get several spoonfuls of water into his mouth, moistening his tongue sufficiently that he was able to summon a few final fragments of halting speech.

"Percy. . .my boy," he said wearily, "and there's my Katy. . .and Flory. Where's Courtenay?"

"Steven has ridden to Sir Armond's for him," said Katherine. "He will be home soon. The rest of us are here, Roderick."

"Ah. . . ," sighed the viscount. He closed his eyes briefly then drew in a breath. "You're all. . .you've been so—good to me—I need to—I'm going. . .I've got to—got to make. . .an apology to—forgive me, Katy—I never meant—you were a good wife—better than I deserved—"

He sighed weakly. "I'm ready," he said after another minute. "I don't know—if God. . .that is. . .one never knows, but—if He will have me. . .I'm ready—see what He can make of me now. . .if He—" He did not have the strength to continue.

"Would you like me to pray, Uncle Roderick?" said Percy.

An imperceptible nod of the head was the viscount's only response.

The room fell silent. Percy thought a moment then drew in a breath. "Oh heavenly Father," he began, "we know so little of this strange thing we call death, which You invested with the power to give us life. Now, our Father, breathe more life into the soul of Your dying son to give him the courage and power to face the dawn of his new life. Heal our loved one at this time of his great need—heal him with the strength to die."

The faintest "Amen" came from the bed.

Katherine and Florilyn were weeping. What a mighty prayer had come spontaneously from the mouth of the vicar's son!

"You sent dear Roderick Westbrooke," Percy continued, "our husband and father and uncle—You sent him into the world as a tiny babe, just as You did Your own dear Son. Now help him out of it as Your child again and birth him into the new life that comes of being in Your presence. We dying men are Your children, and You take us back again into Yourself, into the eternal home of Your heart, to be with You and to be with Jesus, our elder brother, who conquered death on our behalf. Give Your dying child peace to yield himself into Your arms. Amen."

"Amen," the viscount whispered again.

"Be good to her. . .Percy. . .my boy. . . ."

"I will."

"And find—"

"Have no worries about anything," said Percy.

He clutched for Katherine's hand, which still held his. "Katy!" he murmured then glanced toward Florilyn with a smile. "Flory, my dear. I'm going— Percy, be good to— Katy—"

The sentence remained unfinished. The light went out of his eyes as his lids slowly closed. His head sank back into the pillow as a faint breath of air expired from his lungs.

He was dead.

Florilyn cried out and broke into heaving sobs as she turned faint. Katherine wept quietly. Percy saw Florilyn's eyes going back into her head. He jumped up and ran around the bed in time to catch her as she collapsed. He carried her limp in his arms toward the door.

As he walked from the room, he turned to see Katherine lay her head on her husband's chest. He hurried out with Florilyn, leaving his aunt to whisper in private her final good-byes to the man she had loved.

EIGHTY-FOUR

End or Beginning?

$\mathcal{E}$dward and Mary Drummond had been receiving regular updates on their brother-in-law's condition. Plans were already in place to leave Glasgow for Wales the moment a telegram arrived announcing his passing. When it came, Katherine asked her brother to conduct the service. Percy's parents planned to stay as long as needed for Edward's sister's sake.

The whole village turned out for the funeral. Dignitaries from throughout Wales were present.

Llanfryniog's three ministers had the sadly unusual experience of being under the same roof at the same time, sharing the benches and stalls of the largest of their churches with parishioners from their three congregations. One could only conjecture whether they were too deeply entrenched in the learned doctrines of their denominations to receive Vicar Edward Drummond's triumphant assertion of the fatherhood of God as manna for their religiously trained intellects.

Percy's father took as text his favorite passage of scripture save one, the parable of the prodigal son, emphasizing on the occasion of his brother-in-law's passing the father's implied words, "Welcome home, son!"

Time would tell whether the ministries of his three colleagues would change as a result of this new word spoken about the loving Father whom

Jesus called Abba. One thing was certain—such words had never been proclaimed prior to this day from any of Llanfryniog's pulpits.

Whether the clergymen would be or not, there was one seated among them who *would* forever be changed by what he heard. He had decided to attend the funeral at the last minute. He walked into the building he had so long despised with no little trepidation at what his fellow villagers were thinking to see him present. As he listened beside wife and great hulking son, Kyvwlch Gwarthegydd sat as one stunned. He walked out of the church fifty minutes later in a stupor. He had never heard the like before.

If God was like *this* man represented him, an actual Father…a good and loving *Father*…that changed everything!

Kyvwlch Gwarthegydd saw nothing in religion he liked or wanted. He never had. He hated the religious spirit with a passion. But one thing he knew as much about as he did the smithy's art was fatherhood. He was himself a father. He knew what love beat in his heart for Chandos. He would do *anything* for his son. He would give his very life for him.

If God was like *that*, then it meant the Creator was like *him*…just a Father! Could it be…was it possible that it was true after all?

What all the doctrines and sermons and persuasive arguments in the world would never achieve if the man lived to be two hundred had been accomplished in a few short minutes. The simple vision of the prodigal's open-hearted father, waiting to receive his son into his arms with a great smile on his face, had opened a window of lovely truth into the honest soul of the Welsh blacksmith.

Those who maintain that the threat of hell is the Christian's most effective tool for evangelism little understand the deepest rhythms of the human soul. Still less do they understand the heart of the Father of Jesus Christ.

The assembly walked quietly from the church to the surrounding cemetery where the viscount was laid to rest with the generations of Westbrookes who had gone before. One by one they greeted Katherine and Florilyn and Courtenay respectfully then slowly returned to their homes. The visitors who had come great distances returned in hired buggies to Dolgellau and Blaenau Ffestiniog, where most spent the night in the hotels and inns of North Wales before catching the train north or south on the following day. Among the last to leave the churchyard were Stevie and Adela Muir, both of whom hugged Katherine and Florilyn warmly.

The day after the funeral, Tilman Heygate sought Katherine in the parlor where she and Edward and Mary were seated together. "I am sorry to disturb you, Lady Katherine," he said. "But if I might have a minute of your time."

"Of course, Tilman," she said. "You can speak freely in front of my brother and sister-in-law."

"Yes, ma'am. Well, you see, it's like this. My son, he and his wife have been urging me to come up to the peninsula to be near them. The grandchildren are growing fast, you see. I've stayed on out of loyalty to your husband, but since there'll no doubt be changes coming, and I'm sorry for any inconvenience to yourself, Lady Katherine, but it's one of those things that can't be helped, you see. The long and the short of it is that I'm thinking that now is a good time." What the good man had not said was that he expected young Courtenay to be taking over general oversight of the manor, and he vowed that he would not spend a day in his employ.

"I understand, Tilman," said Katherine. "I will be sorry to lose you."

"Thank you, Lady Katherine. You and your husband have been very good to me."

"When is it you are thinking of making a change?"

"Maybe a month or two, Lady Katherine. As soon as you can find someone."

"I shall see what I can do."

"That doesn't sound good," said her brother when the factor had left them.

"I don't like to lose him," said Katherine. "He knows more about the estate than I do."

"Do you have anyone in mind?" asked Edward.

"Not that I can—" Suddenly Katherine stopped. A smile spread over her face. "What an intriguing idea!" she said, speaking almost to herself. "We have a young man here, a friend of Percy's actually, and about the same age. . . . I know he is young, but he has shown that he can take charge in a crisis. He is bright, good with numbers, intelligent, dependable, decisive, completely trustworthy. He knows everyone for miles and is universally liked and respected. Now that I think about it, he strikes me as the perfect choice to help me run things around here until Courtenay is twenty-five."

"What is the lad's name?" asked Mary.

"Steven. . .Steven Muir. I know his mother quite well. She's begun reading MacDonald, too!"

"What better to recommend her son than that!" laughed Mary. "You will have the whole region reading the Scotsman before long."

"Is that when Courtenay inherits," asked Edward, "at twenty-five?"

Katherine nodded. "What it will be like after that, I can only imagine."

Later that day, Katherine went to Percy in private. "I have just been informed by Tilman Heygate," she told him, "that he will be leaving the manor and moving to be near his son's family. What would you think if I made Steven Muir my new factor?"

"I think it is a brilliant idea, Aunt Katherine," replied Percy enthusiastically. "But where do things stand with Courtenay?"

"The estate will not be his for another year and a half. He will no doubt be annoyed that I don't turn it over to him now, but I know him too well. As long as I am trustee, I must do what I consider best for the estate."

EIGHTY-FIVE

Knotted Strands

*T*wo days after the funeral, from the window of her room, Florilyn saw Percy and his father walking away from the house in earnest conversation. She smiled to herself. She had no idea what they were saying. But at last she knew the nature of the discussion between them.

Watching the two for the last three days had been a revelation. She had never seen a father and son, or daughter and mother for that matter, talk so freely. . .like *friends*. They listened to each other, probed each other's thoughts, and mutually respected the other's ideas. They talked constantly. . .about *everything*!

She left her room and went downstairs to join her mother and aunt in the sitting room.

East of the house, Percy and his father continued slowly through the wood and up the gently rising slope east of the manor.

"There's something I need to ask you about, Dad," Percy said. "Before he died, Uncle Roderick made a request of me. It is extremely complicated and might require a good deal of time and travel, even expense. I'm not sure what I should do, how soon to begin, and where to place it in my considerations of school and the apprenticeship."

"What is it?" asked Percy's father.

"That's just it. I can't tell you. He asked that it remain confidential. Do you think the fact that he is dead changes that? I mean. . .is one still bound to a promise to a dead man?"

"An interesting question. It probably depends on the individual case. Are other people involved?"

Percy nodded.

"Could they be hurt if you divulged what you and Roderick talked about?"

"It's possible."

"Then it seems to me that you must honor your word as long as possible. It may in time become necessary to speak more openly. If it reaches a point where you absolutely have no idea what to do, we can rethink it. Perhaps you will need to tell me later. But for the immediate future, I think the safest policy is for you to keep your own counsel."

"I would give anything to tell you about it."

"The time may come when you will feel it right to do so. The Lord will show you what to do."

"Do you think I ought to begin immediately and take a leave of absence from school?"

"How urgent is the matter?"

"It didn't strike me as especially urgent. Actually, he never really said anything about *when*. Knowing he was dying, he simply wanted me to take care of it."

"Could it wait until you graduate?"

"I suppose. That would also give me time to consider how best to carry out Uncle Roderick's commission."

"And as well, if you are to be married, it seems in everyone's best interest for you to graduate first. That is another argument in favor of waiting."

"I see what you mean. Because of what's happened, though, I do think I ought to remain here for the summer. I wanted to ask your advice. . .what would you think of my writing to Mr. Snyder and telling him it will be impossible for me to apprentice with his firm this summer?"

"I think that is a wise decision," replied his father. "You are needed here. Florilyn and her mother are your primary responsibilities now. And I've heard Courtenay talking about taking a trip."

Father and son glanced up to see Florilyn, Mary, and Katherine approaching. They had come out of the house together.

"Hello, ladies!" said Edward, greeting them with a smile. "How are you managing, Katherine?" he said, walking toward her and embracing her affectionately.

His sister sighed and smiled sadly.

They all now turned and walked toward the garden.

"It will be hard for some time," said Katherine after a moment. "It was so sudden. But your message at the funeral helped more than you know. Sometimes I need to be reminded how good God really is. It is easy to forget. How do you do it, Edward—always put your finger on the exact point of truth needed?"

Her brother laughed.

Florilyn glanced toward him, struck suddenly at how very much like Percy's his laugh sounded.

"As I remember, you found that annoying when we were growing up!" Edward chuckled.

"Not anymore. Whenever I hear it now, it reminds me of Father."

"It is easy for us all to forget," said Edward after a moment. "I am trying to remember what our father taught us, too, Katherine. His vision of God is so much larger than mine. I am still learning. The natural human tendency is to doubt God rather than trust Him. I don't know why. I must constantly remind myself that God is on *our* side in this struggle we call life."

"That is just like what Father would say! At seventy-five, he is still hungry to know more about God."

"I hope you will be saying the same of me when I am seventy-five," rejoined Edward.

Florilyn walked between the men and slipped her hands into their two arms. "Percy speaks very highly of you, Uncle Edward," she said. "I have never seen a son honor a father as he does you. I feel that I know you almost as well as I know him."

"I am aware of it, Florilyn." The vicar smiled. "I am a man most fortunate to have such a son. *And* such a niece!"

"Now it looks as if you will be a father to me, as well as an uncle."

"It is an assignment I look forward to, my dear."

The five continued to walk about the grounds, speaking of many things. Not the least of which subjects that came up was the future of the two young people.

Percy shared with Katherine and Florilyn that he had decided not to return to Aberdeen for the summer apprenticeship, but to remain with them. . .with their permission, of course. Both were overjoyed and relieved beyond words. He then explained his conviction that he and his father felt it best that he return to complete his fourth year at the university so as to graduate before pursuing matrimonial plans.

Everyone agreed that it was a wise course of action. The other considerations that were on his mind, Percy kept to himself. Many questions remained.

Several days after the funeral, Rhawn Lorimer surprised everyone by appearing at Westbrooke Manor. Her son was with her, and a look of compassionate humility was on her face. She asked to see Florilyn and Katherine. She expressed her sympathies then added that she would like them to meet her son. Her tone was so gentle and her demeanor so changed, that they invited her to stay for tea—though it proved a somewhat rambunctious affair with a youngster about. From that day forward, she and Florilyn began a wonderful new friendship together.

Katherine consulted in private with Steven Muir, as she always called him. With quiet and humble gratitude, he accepted her offer. She added, however, that no announcement of it should be made until she made it herself. He must say nothing even to his mother.

After a few more days, Mary and Edward Drummond left on the

coach for Blaenau Ffestiniog where they caught the train that, after several connections, took them back to Scotland.

Two weeks later, declaring himself in need of a holiday, Courtenay Westbrooke left for the South of France, expecting at the end of his hiatus to find the weight of his father's responsibilities falling to his shoulders.

He did not return for three months. By then Percy had resumed his studies in Abereen. To Courtenay's great surprise and smoldering fury, Stevie Muir was confidently and capably in charge as Lady Katherine's factor at Westbrooke Manor.

No one quite knew why from the very day of the viscount's funeral the hammer and anvil of Kyvwlch Gwarthegydd's smithy were thereafter silent on Sundays. Nor did a soul ever know his dark secret—that when his wife and Chandos were occupied at church, he crept to his son's room to snatch peeks inside the Bible on the shelf, hoping to discover more about who God really was.

Percy's plans and what came of them will require another book.

The Treasure
of the
Celtic Triangle

Dedication

To the memory and legacy of
George MacDonald,
whose books and characters and spiritual vision still contain a
power undiminished by the passage of more than a century to
inspire hearts, change lives, and fill the soul with the wonders
of God's expansive fatherhood.

PART ONE

Changes at Westbrooke Manor

Late 1872

ONE

Factor and Heir

A clock of ancient date overlooking a stone-paved stable yard—originally rimmed with gold, fitted with brass ornamentation and shiny black hands, all now tarnished with the passage not merely of its circling minutes and hours but of centuries—had just struck the hour of one o'clock.

It was a chilly day in the second week of October. The sun was bravely doing its best to counter the effects of a biting wind blowing down through the Celtic triangle onto the coast of north Wales. Alas, it rose a little lower in the sky every day. Thus, with every successive revolution of the earth into darkness and back again into its light, the great glowing orb had less warmth to shed abroad in the land. Those offshore winds pierced to the bone. They originated far to the north in regions where glaciers and icebergs made their homes, birthplace of the winter, which even now had begun its inexorable yearly march southward into the lands of men.

Whatever happy memories remained of July and August had gone briefly into hiding. The sunlight seemed thin and not altogether up for the task. There would yet appear more exquisite reminders of the splendorous summer recently past. Autumn's delicious warmth and the fragrances of earth's slow, pleasant death into its yearly recreative slumber would return by tomorrow, perhaps the day after. It would hold winter at bay as long as it could.

But as today's chill breeze portended, it would eventually be forced to lay down the struggle and die a peaceful and quiet death. Beneath the ground its life must lie, while winter roared and blustered above, until such time as cousin spring rescued earth's life again from the grave.

A young man of twenty-two, stocky, strong, of medium height, shoulders broad and muscular, with light hair and a chiseled face, skin tough, leathery, and tan from exposure to the weather from the time he could walk emerged from the building. He was leading a gorgeous white stallion of three years, whose coat was gracefully highlighted by a few lines of gray, from its stall and through the back door of the stables. There a flat, grassy area suited his purpose more than the hard stones in front between stables and house. He was used to weather of any kind and laughed at cold and wind and rain. What were they to him when there was a world to enjoy?

The beautiful creature following him had only been wearing the bridle a week. The young man thought him ready for a saddle today. He planned to move slowly, however, and continue to wait if he displayed the slightest resistance.

He was one who knew animals *almost* as well as his diminutive cousin, who had mysteriously disappeared from Snowdonia with her father a year before. *No one* could communicate with the creatures of the animal kingdom like she did. But after a life with sheep in the nearby hills where he had made his home until recently, he found the intuitive connection between man and horse a wonder and joy. In the month since his mistress had purchased this Anglo-Arabian from Padrig Gwlwlwyd in the village, he had been talking to him and walking him daily, allowing the animal to know him and trust him before attempting to ride him.

Within a few weeks of her husband's funeral, Lady Snowdon had asked him to be on the lookout for a horse of equal or greater potential than the one they had recently lost. It would, she explained, be a way to remember her husband and perhaps in some small way mitigate her son's inevitable disappointment at finding the wild black gone. Nor could it be denied that Lady Snowdon herself loved horses no less than the two men of the family. During these recent months of loss, the solitary green hills of Snowdonia had been her frequent solace in companionship with one or another of the mounts in her well-stocked stables.

One look at the Anglo-Arabian and she had fallen in love instantly. There was no haggling about the price. She had settled the financial arrangements, and he was in his new home in the manor's stables the day after that. Surely there would be no lamenting the loss of the black now. Perhaps she would make the Anglo a homecoming gift for her son. . .whenever that might be.

Meanwhile, in spite of the brightness of the day, an autumn chill had begun. Fires had been lit throughout Westbrooke Manor, the proud and ancient house that stood at the center of the estate of the late Viscount Lord Snowdon some two miles inland from Cardigan Bay. Hours later, they were still doing their best to warm the living quarters of Lady Snowdon, Katherine Westbrooke, widowed three and a half months earlier by the sudden death of her husband, and her twenty-year-old daughter, Florilyn.

Lord and Lady Snowdon's eldest son and presumptive heir to title and property, twenty-three-year-old Courtenay, had unexpectedly returned without notice the night before, about dusk, from three months abroad. He had not appeared at breakfast and had made a mere token luncheon, with surprisingly little to say to either mother or sister after so long away.

In truth, his father's death from a riding accident the previous June had shaken Courtenay more than he wanted to admit. He had needed to get away from Wales. And he had done so.

Thinking himself recovered at last and prepared to confidently take up his mantle as the future viscount in his father's stead, he found his homecoming—forced upon him sooner than he had planned—plagued by uncertainty. After spending what money he had, he was confronted with the painful realization that he was not exactly certain how the finances were supposed to work during this awkward interim before the Westbrooke estate became legally his. He was in possession of his own bank account, of course, and had been since the age of sixteen. But where the money came from that appeared in it each month, he didn't know. He had had some vague idea that his father was responsible. He knew furthermore that his father and mother sometimes argued about money. He knew no details other than that his mother was rich and his father was less so. He had never given the matter much thought. The mechanics of finances in marital relationships lay miles outside his ken. As long as he was well provided for, that was all he cared about.

But his resources had dwindled during his sojourn on the continent, an eventuality he had neither anticipated nor made much effort to forestall. Finally the sobering reality began to hit him that his account was running dry and was not being replenished in its customary fashion. This unpleasant fact ultimately left him no alternative but to return home, irritably disposed toward the world in general for this inconvenience to himself. He assumed the matter due to a procedural glitch or legal delay in the affairs of the estate occasioned by his father's death and whatever stipulations superintended the months between now and his twenty-fifth birthday. Gnawing suspicions were at work, however, that made him uneasy.

His first order of business was to see the family lawyer and get his account beefed up. He planned to ride to Porthmadog this afternoon for that very purpose. After that, whether he would return to the continent for another month or two or perhaps spend the winter season in London, always a diverting prospect, he hadn't yet made up his mind.

After lunch, Courtenay wandered outside. He shivered and glanced about. Though not overly fond of riding as a means to interact with nature and the animal kingdom, he was enamored of it as sport. His father's dream of racing the black stallion Demon, possibly with Courtenay himself in the saddle, had remained with him, and even gone to his head. He was at least three stone too heavy to jockey a winning horse even at a backwater racetrack for the most miserly of purses. But he fancied himself an accomplished rider. In fact, his self-assessment was not far wrong. He was probably the fastest rider in Gwynedd.

That Demon had been responsible for his father's death caused him little concern. Courtenay attributed the accident as much to his father's recklessness and his Scottish cousin's presence on that fateful day as he did to the uncontrollable stallion.

But though Courtenay Westbrooke was aware that he must wait until his twenty-fifth birthday to inherit his father's title, he knew nothing of the trusteeship his father had set in motion on his deathbed giving his wife, Katherine, control of the estate for the next eighteen months. Neither was he aware of the retirement of his father's factor, Tilman Heygate, or that in his absence his mother had hired a replacement.

Ever since losing the majority of what remained of his assets two weeks before in a horse race in France, Courtenay had been revolving in his mind how he might put his father's plan into action and quickly raise some badly needed cash for himself in the event the legalities took time to sort out. He would enter Demon in a few races, possibly at Chester. He intended to begin immediately. With a few wins under his belt, and with his father's funds eventually transferred to his account, he would be able to afford to enter larger races and compete for more sizeable purses in some of the major handicap events in England.

He wandered into the old stables, seeing evidence neither of his father's groom, Hollin Radnor, nor of the black stallion whom he fancied to ride into Porthmadog. The place was virtually empty except for the old nags his mother and sister rode. He continued through to the back of the darkened building and toward the new stables where he assumed the powerful black thoroughbred now made its home.

On the grassy flat between the two stables, he saw the young man about his own age leading a graceful, almost elegant beast of white and light gray in a slow, wide circle. He stopped and watched a minute as the trainer now removed a lump of sugar from his pocket and held it toward the horse's big fleshy lips.

At length he approached, prepared to assert the rights of his position, especially over one whom he took for nothing more than a clodhopping herdsman of a ragamuffin flock of sheep. The two young men had grown up in close proximity to each other, and the scion of the region's aristocratic family looked down upon the other as contemptibly beneath him in every way. "You'll spoil that stallion, Muir," he said in a tone of command.

Steven Muir turned, though gently. The sound had startled the horse, and he sought by his demeanor to keep him calm at the intrusion of a stranger. "Master Courtenay!" he said with a wide smile. "I did not know you were back. Welcome home!"

"I arrived last night. I must admit I am surprised to find you still here."

"Your mother has been very kind."

"Yes, well. . .now that I have returned there will be a few changes. What are you trying to do with that horse?"

"He has never been ridden, Master Courtenay. I am preparing him for the saddle. I hope to ride him in another two weeks."

"Then it's the whip and spur he'll need, Muir, not sugar."

"That is not my preferred method."

"We shall see about that. In the future, you may address me as *my lord*, or *Mr. Westbrooke*. The *Lord Snowdon* will have to wait a year."

"Yes, sir. . .*my lord*," nodded Steven.

"Where is Radnor?" asked Courtenay.

"I could not say, my lord."

"I take it you are still helping him out around the place?"

"When I can, yes."

"Well then, you can help out now by saddling the black stallion for me. I take it he is being kept in the new stables?"

"Not exactly, my lord."

"Never mind, then. Wherever he is, saddle him. I will be taking him out."

"I fear that will not be possible, my lord."

"What the devil are you talking about?"

"I assume you were referring to the stallion Demon?"

"Of course that's who I'm talking about! Either tell me where he is or why you refuse to saddle him for me."

"Demon is no longer with us, my lord. Your mother instructed me to give him to Padrig Gwlwlwyd. . .or to get rid—"

"You let that fool sell him! Why *you?*"

"Lady Snowdon trusted my judgment. She left the matter in my hands."

"I can't imagine what she was thinking!"

"You will have to take that up with her, my lord."

"So you took the horse to Gwlwlwyd?"

Steven nodded.

"I hope you got a good price."

"Your mother did not want a good price."

"That's absurd. Why not?"

"She considered the animal dangerous. After what happened to your father, she simply wanted rid of him. She was fearful of endangering a new owner."

Courtenay burst out in a derisive laugh. "That's hardly sound policy in horse selling. 'Let the buyer beware' is the foundation of that business."

"Your mother did not want the breaking of the sixth commandment on her head."

"Good enough policy in the church but heresy in the horse market. A man buys a horse as he takes a wife—for better or worse."

"That is not the way a Christian ought to look at it."

"And what would be?" asked Courtenay sarcastically.

"If one knows the dangers of a horse, failing to reveal them to a new owner would also break the ninth commandment. We are told not to bear false witness against our neighbor."

A snort sounded from Courtenay's mouth. "There is one commandment you seem to find especially difficult, Muir, and that is to mind your own business. So what did you do?"

"Your mother instructed me, if he felt he could reform him, to give Demon to Mr. Gwlwlwyd at no charge."

"That is ridiculous! The horse was worth five hundred pounds!"

"Those were your mother's instructions."

"What did the man say?"

"He declined to take the animal. He said there was the curse of death on him."

"So what did you do?"

"I put him down, my lord."

Courtenay stared back as if he had not heard him correctly.

"You *what*?"

"I put him down," answered Steven calmly.

Stunned into speechless fury, Courtenay turned on his heels and stormed angrily back toward the house.

TWO

Mother and Son

Courtenay found his mother still in the luncheon room with a book.

Katherine Westbrooke glanced up. The thundercloud on Courtenay's brow was impossible to mistake.

He approached and glowered down at her. "I have just learned from that lout Stevie Muir that you instructed him to put Demon down!" he said angrily.

"That is true," replied Katherine calmly.

"You had no right."

"It seemed the best course of action under the circumstances."

"But you had no right."

"Why would I not? I am the one who bought him."

"He was my horse!"

"I believe he was your father's horse."

"Yes, and with Father dead, he was mine. How dare you presume—"

"You were gone," rejoined Katherine in a slightly peremptory tone. "I thought it best," she repeated.

"On what basis, if I may ask?"

"The beast was a murderer. He had already taken one life. I had no intention of his endangering another."

"That is ridiculous. He was only dangerous to one who did not know how to handle him. I had plans for that animal. I will never forgive you

485

for interfering in my plans."

The words hit Katherine as if they had been shot from a gun. She tried not to allow the pain to show. She knew what he perceived as her emotional weakness would only anger her son the more. "I am sorry, Courtenay," she said softly. "As I said, I thought it best. Perhaps I was wrong. Your father's death weighed heavily upon me. But while you were away, I bought another stallion, an Anglo-Arabian. I thought you might like—"

"Yes, I saw it," snapped Courtenay. "He's nothing like what I had with Demon, what I would have been able to do with him! And what is that simpleton Muir still doing around here? He says he is training the thing. He knows nothing about horses."

"Actually, he knows horses very well. He has a compelling way with them."

"I want to know what he is doing here."

"I decided to keep him. He is a big help."

"He is an idiot. I don't like him. I want him gone before the day is out."

Katherine drew in a deep breath, struggling between tears and rising indignation of her own. "And if I choose to keep him?" she said. Her tone contained a slight edge such as Courtenay had never heard from her before. It was the hint of a challenge.

"Then he will be working for you not me," he replied curtly. "Just tell him to keep out of my way. Make sure he knows that his duties here will not last one minute past the day I am in charge. I can't stand the sight of the ridiculous fellow. What is that solicitor's name. . .Father's man in Porthmadog?"

"Mr. Murray. . .Hamilton Murray," replied Katherine.

Courtenay turned to leave the room.

"Where are you going?" asked his mother behind him.

"To see Murray and get some money in the bank and get the problem with my account sorted out."

"Courtenay," said Katherine after him as he again moved toward the door, "before you see him, you ought to know—"

"All I need to know is where to find him. What's done with Demon is done. Now that I am here and prepared to take up my position, Mother, I will thank you not to interfere further in my affairs. I would not want things to become unpleasant for you. I will not be home for dinner."

THREE

Rude Awakening

*D*uring the long afternoon ride up the coast and around the Traeth Bach inlet, Courtenay's mood alternated between anger and a growing disquiet. His mother was different. It had unnerved him. She was more self-assured, confident, her manner calm but uncomfortably firm. She seemed altogether unruffled by what he said. He wasn't sure he liked the change.

All along he had assumed, though the estate was in legal limbo until he came of age, that he was de facto in charge. He tried to convince himself that all it would take was a visit to his father's solicitor to straighten out the confusion. He certainly had no intention of letting his mother throw her weight around.

Though concerned, Courtenay was still not yet cognizant of the painful reality of his position. As an indulgent father, the viscount had given him whatever he wanted and kept him well supplied with cash. Courtenay had not anticipated the least straitening of his financial security after his father's death. If anything, he assumed, notwithstanding the twenty-fifth birthday stipulation of the inheritance, that financially he would have the full benefit of his father's resources immediately at his command. Though confident the matter would quickly be resolved, an undefined angst whispered in his ear that his mother was up to something that did not bode well. In actual fact, he was about to reap the fruit of his father's financial status more speedily than he might have wished. He had no idea that without his wife's generosity, his father would have been what nearly amounted to a landed and titled pauper.

Three hours after setting out, the Gelderlander, his favorite mount before Demon, in a hot lather at the livery, Courtenay Westbrooke sat in a chair opposite the desk of Hamilton Murray in the solicitor's offices of Murray, Sidcup, and Murray. The jaw of the would-be heir hung open at what he had just heard. "A *trusteeship*. . . ," he repeated in disbelief. "And it makes no mention whatever of *my* role as the future viscount?"

"I am afraid that is the situation as it stands. . .yes," replied Murray.

The office fell quiet as Courtenay sat shaking his head in annoyance. He was doing his best to keep from exploding. But only with difficulty. "At whose behest was this so-called trusteeship drawn up?" Courtenay asked at length.

"Your father's, Mr. Westbrooke," replied Murray. "It was several days before his death. I took it down myself."

"Where was I?"

"I really couldn't say, Mr. Westbrooke."

"My father did not ask for me?"

"No, sir."

"And my mother was there?"

"That is correct."

"You are positive there was no coercion?"

"Of course not. Your father may have been weak, but he had all his mental faculties. This was how he wanted it."

"And you, as the family solicitor, did not intercede on my behalf?"

"That would not have been my place, Mr. Westbrooke. I represented your father, not you."

"Well you represent me now. It might have behooved you to think of that sooner. From where I sit, it appears that you have betrayed my interests."

"I am sorry you should see it like that."

Courtenay thought a moment. "I could contest it in court," he said at length.

"You would not prevail," replied Murray. "I fail to see what advantage you would hope to gain."

"To invalidate the trusteeship of my mother over me."

"It is not a trusteeship over *you*, Mr. Westbrooke. It is over the estate. Your father simply felt—"

"Don't split hairs with me, Murray," Courtenay shot back. "This effectively puts me under my mother's thumb for the next year and a half. I have no intention of allowing such a state of affairs to persist."

"Even if the trusteeship were somehow invalidated, you would still not inherit until your twenty-fifth birthday. The terms of inheritance of the viscountcy and estate are clear and irrevocable—the eldest child of the viscount or viscountess, or their issue, regardless of gender, succeeds to the title and inherits the property on his or her twenty-fifth birthday."

"Provision would yet be made for my financial needs."

"That is true. In that case the court would act as trustee. However, you would not have unfettered access to estate funds. Perhaps there would be a stipend, but other than that—"

"That would be an improvement upon my current predicament," rejoined Courtenay testily. "So what recourse do I have? How do I access my own funds?"

"As I say, Mr. Westbrooke, those funds are not yet yours. At present your mother controls everything. Have you spoken with her about it?"

A snort sounded from Courtenay's mouth. "My mother is a woman. Do you really expect her to be reasonable about it? I am sure she is enjoying her little power grab."

"I have found Lady Snowdon to be an intelligent and thoughtful woman."

"Yes, well you are entitled to your opinion. But unless you can come up with some way around it, once I do become viscount, I will be engaging a new solicitor to handle my affairs. I doubt the Westbrooke retainer is one you would be eager to lose, Mr. Murray, so I suggest you think of something."

"I am sorry, Mr. Westbrooke, but legally my hands are tied. I must abide by the terms of the trusteeship. At this point, I represent your mother."

Courtenay's long ride back to Llanfryniog was filled with smoldering anger and venomous thoughts.

The stark reality began to dawn on him that he was dependent upon his mother for everything. The same eye-opening reality had long been a thorn in the side of the marriage between Roderick and Katherine Westbrooke. The late viscount had been a man of dreams and schemes. But his wife, who with her brother Edward Drummond of Glasgow had inherited half a small fortune from Courtenay's grandfather, was of a more prudent temperament. With what little cash remained to accompany the title and property beyond what meager rents the homes and cottages of the nearby village of Llanfryniog provided, the viscount found himself in the humiliating position of having to rely on his wife for anything that might be considered of a speculative nature.

Now the viscount's son, still some months away from his twenty-fourth birthday, realized that he had no job, no prospects, no money. Having failed to complete his studies at Oxford, he found himself at loose ends. What was he to do until he was twenty-five?

It was a good thing Courtenay saw no one, and that the manor had mostly retired for the night before he left Mistress Chattan's pub, where he had moodily partaken of what passed for a supper and far more ale than was good for him.

The only conclusion the stringy beef, hard potatoes, and brussels sprouts that resembled rocks had left him with was that he had no intention of going cap in hand to his mother to beg for money. What a humiliating prospect!

FOUR

Letter to Aberdeen

*I*n the two rooms he occupied on the top floor of the Aberdeen boarding house, Percival Drummond, in his fourth year at the university in the great northern city of Scotland, eased into the comfortable overstuffed chair in his room with a cup of tea. His day's studies were done. In his hand he held a sealed letter that had been waiting for him when he arrived home.

He took a satisfying swallow, then set the cup down on the table beside him, slit open the envelope, and removed two blue handwritten sheets from inside it.

Dear Percy, he read in the familiar feminine hand.

> *At last it has happened. Mother and I were surprised two days ago when Courtenay appeared without warning. He has hardly said a word to either of us since returning home. We don't know where he has been. I thought he was distant and aloof before. But, goodness! It is terrible now. I can't imagine that he and I used to be close. But like you and I have talked about so many times, we have all changed since your first summer with us in Wales five years ago.*

> *What I cannot understand about Courtenay is why he is so irritable. He's twenty-three. Shouldn't he be acting more like a man? He seems angry at the whole world. Whatever he had hoped*

to accomplish during his three months away after Daddy's death, it
certainly has not improved his disposition.

But on to more cheerful topics! I'm sorry for beginning this
letter with my dreary news!

I hope all is well and that your studies are not too demanding.
I think of you constantly and cannot wait until we see one another
again. But I know it is wise for you to graduate before we think of
the future. Only I miss you so dreadfully!

Percy set the letter aside a moment with a smile. He missed her,
too. He could almost hear her voice as if she were speaking rather than
writing to him. He picked up his cup of tea with his free hand and
resumed.

I told you, I think, about the gorgeous new horse Mother bought,
an Anglo-Arabian stallion we have named Snowdonia. He is
the most exquisite blend of white and gray. The instant we saw
him, mother and I immediately thought of the snow on the gray
mountains of Gwynedd. He almost seemed to name himself. Steven
has been training him and thinks he will soon be comfortable with a
saddle. He hopes to ride him in another few weeks. Steven has a way
with horses that reminds me of Gwyneth. Maybe it runs in families!
There is still no word of her. Her disappearance remains a mystery.

Steven is such a dear. He is the most gracious and considerate
young man I have ever met—except for you, of course! He is so
nice to everyone, and everyone loves him—other than Courtenay.
Mother has not once regretted her decision to make him factor when
Mr. Heygate left. Everything is running as smoothly as before, even
with Daddy and Mr. Heygate gone. I can tell that Mother misses
Daddy terribly. She doesn't talk about it, but I can tell. I miss him,
too. Daddy was gruff and distant sometimes. But he loved us and
we knew it.

Speaking of Steven—I can't think of him as Stevie anymore.
Mother calls him Steven, and now that he walks about so

confidently and in charge of the estate for Mother, he seems so different. Mother and Mrs. Muir have become such good friends, especially with them both losing their husbands. And with Steven now living and working at the manor, Mother asked Mrs. Muir if she would like to work for her, too, as sort of a second housekeeper. Mrs. Llewellyn is not a young woman, and she had confessed to my mother that going up and down the stairs was becoming more difficult for her. She is relieved and happy to have Mrs. Muir's help. So now both Steven and Mrs. Muir are living at the manor and working for us. Steven is selling his flock and all their animals, though it's been difficult for him to arrange everything. Some of them he is giving to the poor families of the region. Mother says she will make up any losses. I don't know what is going to happen to their cottage in the hills. But his mother seems very happy here.

I have been trying to follow in your father's and mother's footsteps, and my mother's, too, and read some of Mr. MacDonald's books. I have to admit, they are very long and sometimes difficult. The Scottish dialect is hard to understand. Maybe not for you because you are Scottish. I could read them more easily if someone translated the Scots for me. But I am going slow and trying to absorb what I read. I am reading one of his novels called David Elginbrod, *which Mother says is his first realistic novel. She says before that he wrote poetry and fantasies and short stories. It is a story about three young people called Hugh and Margaret and Euphra. (What a funny name!) I am not too far into it yet.*

Rhawn Lorimer and I had a nice visit a few days ago, just before Courtenay came home. Her little son is spunky and full of energy. Poor Rhawn, she seems sad. But I think she is growing. She is thinking about God and life and about what kind of person she wants to be. We all have to think about those kinds of things eventually. You helped me think about them, just like Gwyneth helped you do so. Now perhaps it is Rhawn's turn. It is very humbling to realize that in some small way I am helping her, too. It makes me quiet and happy inside to realize that I am actually

helping another person. We talk about many things, and she asks
me questions about God and life and why I changed. It is an
extraordinary thing to have someone you grew up with ask you
those kinds of questions. I would rather you were here to talk to her.
But maybe God will be able to help Rhawn find peace regardless.
I hope so. I pray for her.

   I pray for you, too, and think of you, as I said, every day. I
am lonely for you, but I am not really lonely at all. Steven is a
wonderful friend, as is Mother of course, and now Steven's mother,
too. Even Mr. MacDonald is becoming a friend in his own way,
though I do not know him. I think he lives in London. Can you
imagine what it would be like to meet him! So I am not really
lonely, but I do miss you. I so hope that you and your family will be
able to come to Wales and spend Christmas with us.

   I know you are busy with your studies. But when you have
time, please write me back. I long for any word from you.

Yours,
Florilyn

Percy sat back in his chair and drew in a thoughtful breath, then
exhaled slowly. He glanced at his watch. It would be forty minutes
before Mrs. Treadway had his supper ready. If he didn't answer Florilyn's
letter now, the way things usually went, it might be days before he got
around to it. He rose with letter in hand, picked up his cup of tea, and
walked across the room to his desk.

FIVE

Brother and Sister

*D*ear *Florilyn,* Florilyn read.

I read your recent letter, as always, with great joy in the midst of my busy life here at the university. It is always such a happy event to find an envelope with your hand on it waiting for me after a day of classes and meetings with professors and library research and all the rest with which my life is consumed. I wait until I have a hot cup of tea beside me and can sit down and relax, sharing the peaceful moments with you and imagining that we are enjoying tea together at the end of a long day.

Hearing you talk about the manor. . .it sounds like such life is there. How could you possibly be lonely? Now I feel homesick for you all—if one can feel homesick about a place that has never been his home. . .though Llanfryniog and the manor and all the surrounding region will always feel like home to me!

After receiving your letter, I decided to find a copy of the book by MacDonald you mentioned. I know my parents have it—they have all his books. But I will buy a copy and read it with you. It will be a way to share together even though so many miles separate us— knowing that we are reading the same book, getting to know the same characters. There are any number of bookshops in Aberdeen, and MacDonald is a great favorite. Everyone at the university is

very proud of him, and many professors still remember his student
days here.

    My parents and I are talking about our Christmas plans.
Weather is always a factor to consider so far north. As long as
snowdrifts are not blocking the tracks, I will take the train from
Aberdeen to Glasgow. Then my parents and I will travel together
by train down to Wales. It will not be like one of my former summer
visits—I will only have a week to spend with you. But it will be
a joy!

Florilyn continued to read of Percy's studies, about his friends and
acquaintances and humorous incidents involving one or two of his
professors. She relished every word, laughed more than once, and was
near tears when she finally set the pages aside, remembering again how
Percy could always make her laugh.

She wiped her eyes, stood, and walked to the window of her room.
There she gazed out on the scene spread out before her. The sea in the
distance to the west, but partially visible through the trees surrounding
most of the house, stretched north and south along Tremadog Bay. Sails
of a few fishing boats could be seen off the coast in the direction of the
peninsula of Lleyn, faintly visible on the clearest of days stretching far
west until it faded from sight.

Sheep and cattle were plentiful in the surrounding fields and
pastures. As the terrain rose inland toward the mountainous slopes of
Snowdonia's peaks, the population of cattle dwindled noticeably, except
for here and there a family cow whose provision of milk kept many of
the poor crofters alive. Mostly what remained, as grassy pastures and
meadows increasingly gave way to the rocks and boulders of the higher
elevations, were woolly dots of white. Sheep could survive almost
anywhere.

West of her vantage point, the promontory known as Mochras
Head rose above the sea. From it a wide plateau, bordered by the abrupt
cliff-edge of the headland, descended to the village and harbor of
Llanfryniog, a small but bustling center of activity. Many of the region's

men were employed in the nearby slate mine, while others eked out a meager living from the sea or the land itself.

A single main street ran through the center of Llanfryniog. From it smaller streets, lanes, walkways, and cottages spread out in both directions in random disorder toward the sea to the west, and inland and up the plateau in the other.

Several shops along the town's main street were supplemented by homes whose windows offered an assorted miscellany of goods. Most of their offerings cost no more than a penny or two, certainly not more than a few shillings. There were also a variety of services available from a blacksmith, a cobbler, and a doctor from their homes on the outskirts of the village.

Llanfryniog boasted three churches, one school, a harbor, and an inn and pub that served the best ale for miles and in front of which a north-south coach stopped daily, connecting the coastal villages of the region with the larger towns of north Wales, where train service might take them throughout all Britain.

Near the top of the Mochras slope, a private avenue led off the main road east and inland. An imposing iron gate across it, with gatehouse beside, stood fifty yards off the main road. From this impressive entryway, the approach led for half a mile along a winding tree-lined course up a continuing incline to Westbrooke Manor, at the second-floor window of which the late viscount's daughter, Florilyn Westbrooke, still stood. It was the largest mansion for fifty miles and was situated in the foothills of the Cambrian range, which led farther inland to the southern peaks of Snowdonia.

At length Florilyn drew in a long sigh, melancholy but with a heart of contentment, and left her room. She glanced down the corridor toward what they still called "Percy's room" with a fond smile then turned in the opposite direction for the main staircase and continued downstairs. The letter from Percy put her in the mood for a ride. The cold front had passed, and glorious golden autumn again reigned in Wales.

She reached the ground floor and heard voices engaged in heated exchange. One was raised in argument. The answering voice, however, was soft. She turned toward them. She had about lost her patience with Courtenay. She wasn't about to stand by and let him berate their mother without coming to her defense.

She walked through the door of the sitting room and saw Courtenay standing with his back turned. He was facing his mother who was seated.

"Why didn't you tell me about the trusteeship?" he had just said. His tone was demanding. Florilyn could hardly believe the change that had come over him.

"I tried to, Courtenay," said Katherine calmly. "You weren't listening. You interrupted me and stormed off in a huff."

"You should have tried harder. You put me in an awkward position with Murray."

"What would you have me do, restrain you forcibly as if you were a child?"

"All this begs the question why you cut off deposits into my bank account," said Courtenay, ignoring his mother's question.

"I did not cut off deposits into your account."

"Someone did. Nothing has gone into it since Father's death."

"I did not know the status of your account," said Katherine. "I still know nothing about it. I have done nothing at all about your account. For all I knew, you might have had ten thousand pounds. Your father never shared with me what his accommodations were with you."

"He made no arrangement in the trusteeship for my financial well being?"

"There was no mention of finances whatever. It was simply a matter of legal administration of the affairs of the estate."

"Be that as it may, now that you know that I have no money, what do you intend to do about it?"

"I shall have to think about it," answered Katherine. "I would be glad to provide you and your sister an allowance for your personal needs. I will be fair."

"Like you gave us when we were children?"

"That is not what I meant. Perhaps you and I could sit down and look at your plans and what you consider a reasonable—"

"I have no intention of discussing my *plans* with you," interrupted Courtenay. "I am telling you that I have financial needs. I have a right to what is mine. I intend to return to the continent."

"That is, of course, up to you. But I do not intend to finance with *my* money travels that have no purpose."

"It is my money, not yours."

"I was speaking of my own funds," rejoined Katherine. "The income from estate properties will indeed be yours soon enough. But I will not see you squander it now. It would be a different matter if you were to return to the university—"

"You actually intend to dictate my future!"

Katherine let out a lengthy sigh. "I have tried to be patient and understanding, Courtenay," she said after a moment. "I know this all must be a shock to you. But until you are twenty-five, the estate is mine to manage as I feel is best. I am doing so for you. . .for *your* best. . . maybe to protect you from yourself, from doing something hastily and foolishly."

"It is nice to hear what trust you have in me," said Courtenay in a mocking tone.

"You are young, that is all. It will take time for you to grow into your role. Believe me, I am doing what I consider best for you and for the estate. I believe you will thank me one day. And during this time when I am in charge, Steven Muir is helping me."

"You trust him above me?"

"I did not say that. It would really make this easier if you did not misinterpret and overreact to my words. You were gone. I heard nothing from you. I had no idea when you would be back or what your plans were. Steven has shown himself to be reliable and trustworthy and capable of handling my business affairs."

"What do you mean, handling your *business* affairs?" asked Courtenay almost mockingly. "I knew he was helping out Radnor as an assistant groom. But how could a groom know anything about business?"

"He is more than my groom, Courtenay. Tilman Heygate is gone. I am depending on Steven Muir now."

"He's nothing but a shepherd."

"He *is* more than that, Courtenay. Not that there is anything demeaning about being a shepherd. I believe kings occasionally come from shepherd stock. Steven is more educated and knowledgeable than you realize. He has proved himself capable even beyond what I anticipated. The people love him. That is good for everyone. When your father was gone, and after you left, I had to make a decision. You asked me if I trust him above you—during these past three months, the answer is *yes*. Where were you if I needed you? You left almost without a word. How was I to know if and when I would see you again? There was much to do in your father's absence. Therefore, I made the decision not only to keep Steven on at the manor but to hire him as my factor."

"Your *factor*!" exclaimed Courtenay, incredulous at the very idea. "That is the most preposterous thing I have heard in my life. He's a complete nincompoop!"

"Nevertheless, I have no intention of changing my mind."

"Well, unless you do change your mind, things will not go well with you, Mother, once I am in control—no, and not well for the fool, Stevie Muir, either. Don't forget, in a year and a half, I will be sitting where you are sitting now. I will be in control, and you will have nothing to say about any of it. My first order of business will be to evict Muir from that cottage of his."

"He and his mother are living at the manor now."

"Good! That will make them the easier to evict! You will pay for your interference in my affairs, Mother."

Courtenay spun around, his face red, and strode toward the door. He saw Florilyn standing just inside it. "And *you*!" he spat. "You knew all about this and said nothing to me? I thought you were my friend!"

"I thought so, too, Courtenay," Florilyn shot back. Her face, too, was red, though from a much different kind of anger. "It has been a great grief to me to see how changed you are. No friend of mine would speak so rudely to my mother," she added heatedly. "Only a bounder would speak so to his *own* mother."

A suppressed oath escaped Courtenay's lips of such nature as the mother and sister of a gentleman should never hear. He continued on his way, brushed past Florilyn with a look of contempt and scorn, and left the house with his temper at the boiling point.

Florilyn walked to her mother, who was by now in tears, and sat down beside her. "I'm sorry, Mother," she said softly.

Katherine forced a smile as she wiped at her eyes then sighed again. "He is right, you know," she said. "Courtenay could make our lives miserable. A dowager viscountess and her unmarried daughter do not command a great deal of status in this world. I can hardly imagine how changed everything will be around here when Courtenay, as he so pointedly put it, is in control. If I refuse to give him whatever he wants, he would have no qualms about doubling the rents on everyone for miles. Your father had compassion and cared for the people, though he often did not have money to do everything he might have wished. Beneath his impersonal exterior, he was a good man. I doubt Courtenay will think twice about his tenants."

"Don't forget, Mother," said Florilyn, "by the time Courtenay accedes to the title, Percy and I will be married. If Courtenay is troublesome, you will come live with us."

Katherine smiled.

"You would have me leave Westbrooke Manor, my dear?"

"Rather than have Courtenay make your life miserable. You and Percy and I, and all the grandchildren we will give you. . .we will find a cottage in the hills, and we will raise horses and we will ride and all be happy together. Let Courtenay have his old title and this house. Don't get me wrong, Mother—I love it here. I would bring Percy here to live if I could. But Courtenay *will* inherit. There is nothing we can do to change that. So we will make the best of it and all be happy somewhere else."

"And what will become of Adela and Steven? Perhaps we should not be too anxious to let their cottage to new tenants. They may need it again."

"We shall take *two* cottages in the hills," said Florilyn gaily. "We shall build a second one to go with it. Steven shall continue as factor for our small little peasant community in the hills, with the dowager viscountess as our honored mistress."

Katherine laughed to hear her daughter talk so. She had a way of making the simplest things sound so wonderful.

SIX

Discussions in London

Lord Coloraine Litchfield rarely read obituaries in *The Times*. They were for the elderly, worried that they might find their *own* names among those who had departed the earth for better places. Death columns did not make up the regular reading program for mining magnates and captains of industry in the prime of their rush to expand their bank accounts and conquer the world for capitalism and commerce.

He had stumbled on the small notice quite by accident in an announcement concerning a vacancy in the House of Lords owing to the death of Gwynedd viscount Lord Snowdon, whose seat in the Lords would not be filled for eighteen months. Litchfield's eyes shot open.

Moments later he was seated in consultation with his private secretary, Palmer Sutcliffe.

"What we need to find out," Litchfield said once Sutcliffe had perused the announcement, "is who is now in control of Snowdon's affairs and his land."

"I assume, under the circumstances," said Sutcliffe thoughtfully, "that there would be a trusteeship in effect. The thing's probably in the hands of solicitors."

"But why this vacancy in the Lords? As I recall, the fellow had a son."

"Do you know when the peerage was created?" asked Sutcliffe.

"No, nothing. It is of ancient date, I believe."

"The inheritance stipulations can be unbelievably complex in some instances. Though perhaps this is straightforward enough. It may be no more than a case of the son coming of age."

"Find out what you can. This may move our Wales project back to the top of the list."

"I will make inquiries immediately—discreetly of course."

"What about the old rascal who claimed to know the exact location—that thieving Cardi who said he possessed chunks he had taken out of the ground?"

"What he showed me was real enough," nodded Sutcliffe. "Of course he might have taken it from anywhere. The question will be whether he is even still alive and whether we can locate him again. It's been, what. . .five years?"

Litchfield nodded. "I had all but given up on the thing," he said. "There was no way around Lord Snowdon's intractability after he called our bluff. I must admit, I underestimated the fellow. He was sharper than I gave him credit for. He would have owned half interest in the project before agreeing to sell. That was more than I was prepared to give. I would far rather simply purchase the land outright. Then one hundred percent of the proceeds would be ours."

"What makes you think the son is not cut from the same cloth?" asked Sutcliffe.

"I have no idea. Perhaps he is. But the thing is certainly worth exploring again," replied Litchfield. "Deaths these days often have unforeseen consequences on a man's heirs—financial difficulties, tax burdens, past debts that suddenly change the financial landscape. One never knows what might be possible. Perhaps we might find the wife or the son more amenable, shall we say, to an attractive offer to purchase a small portion of out-of-the-way acreage than we did the viscount. Find out what you can, and how we could most likely make a successful approach."

SEVEN

A Reflective Ride

Florilyn rode into Llanfryniog still upset at her brother. She passed between the Catholic and Church of England houses of worship at the south end of town, continued along the main street past the post, the inn, and several shops.

The familiar ubiquitous clanking of hammer against anvil from the smithy where Kyvwlch and Chandos Gwarthegydd now worked together unconsciously drew her glance to the right. Between an irregular row of cottages and buildings, through a narrow lane, she caught a brief glimpse of a steeply slanted purple roof. She shuddered briefly at the reminder of the day she and her cousin had visited the creepy home of the fortune-teller of dubious reputation. Florilyn had never forgotten Madame Fleming's spooky words.

"A great change will come to you," the mysterious woman had said. *"An inheritance that is yours will be taken away. But you will find love, and one will be faithful to you, though he is the least in your eyes. He will be your protector, and you will gain a greater inheritance in the end."*

As repulsive as was the old hag, Florilyn reflected, had her weird prediction already come true? Perhaps the inheritance she said would be taken away was her father. Now he *was* gone. He had been taken away from them all. And she had indeed found love. She didn't believe in Madame Fleming's hocus-pocus, but she had to admit that her words seemed eerily prophetic.

She continued to the far end of town, past the white Methodist chapel and school, following the road left and down to the shore and the harbor, where she arrived at length on the long stretch of sandy beach south of the harbor. There she let her favorite mare, Red Rhud, go for a good gallop the full length of the flat, sandy expanse at the water's edge.

For over a year after her race here with Percy, she had not been able to come to this beach at all. Finally she had come to terms with the past, with what she had been, and with what she was now becoming. This beach would always fill her with sad thoughts, especially with Gwyneth now gone from Llanfryniog, nobody knew where. At last she was able to let that melancholy turn her heart toward prayer for the tiny enigmatic angel, as Percy sometimes called her, rather than inward with self-recrimination for how cruel she had once been to the girl who had later become her friend.

Though today's ride was prompted by Percy's letter and her brother's insufferable behavior, she found her thoughts turning toward dear Gwyneth Barrie, the mysterious nymph of Llanfryniog.

Gwyneth's diminutive stature, kind and soft-spoken nature, and unruly head of white hair would have been enough in themselves to invite taunts from other children. Along with these visible peculiarities, however, was the fact that she had no mother—at least no one knew who her mother was—and that her father, hard-working slate miner Codnor Barrie, was himself so short as to be considered by many a dwarf. To these was added the affiliation of father and daughter with Codnor Barrie's great-aunt, christened Branwenn Myfanawy but simply known as "Grannie" to those few who claimed acquaintance with her. Though as kindhearted a woman as any in the region, she had been considered a witch by many in the village for what were considered her eccentric ways. There was not a grain of truth to the rumors. But that did not prevent them. The final and perhaps most serious charge against poor little Gwyneth was a serious impediment of speech. She stuttered, all the more so when nervous or agitated. It was all the excuse the cruel-minded children of the village had needed to torment her endlessly in her younger years. It was also the only justification the gossipmongers and old women needed to brand her a witch-child along with her great-great-aunt.

But Gwyneth and Grannie had tried to return the evil of the community with good, often in the form of anonymous floral bouquets left on one door or another about town after an offense or rude word. The general antipathy toward Gwyneth and Grannie was all the more illogical in light of the general esteem in which Gwyneth's cousin, Steven Muir, now factor at the manor, and his mother, Barrie's sister, were held. But prejudice and suspicion are rarely guided by logic.

Gwyneth's fortunes had begun to change five years before. It was then that Florilyn's Scottish cousin Percival Drummond, after a string of reckless incidents threatened to land him in a Glasgow jail, had been sent to Wales for the purpose of passing the summer with aunt and uncle and family.

She and Percy had not hit it off at first, Florilyn remembered with a smile. But Percy made little Gwyneth's acquaintance almost his first day in Wales. Knowing nothing of how she was viewed by others in the community, assuming her an odd but delightful child, and having no idea that a mere three years in age separated them, Percy was immediately enchanted. His friendship with the little blond nymph had changed Percy from a rebellious teen into a sensitive young man, newly awakened to God's presence in the world and more importantly within himself. A new relationship with his father had followed subsequent to his return home to Glasgow at summer's end.

To her own great surprise, Florilyn reflected, the change in Percy had also wrought changes in her. She, too, had begun to look up and ask how God fit into her life. . .and how she fit into His. Indeed, little Gwyneth Barrie's innocent, trusting, loving, forgiving outlook on life had influenced many—she and Percy perhaps most of all. Remarkably, Gwyneth's stuttering had ceased abruptly after the accident at the end of that same summer.

Percy, son of Florilyn's mother's brother Edward, a vicar of the Church of Scotland in Glasgow, and wife, Mary, had eventually passed a good portion of three summers of his youth with them in Wales. Now he was in his fourth and final year at Aberdeen University, planning to continue his studies toward a future in law.

When she first began to love Percy, Florilyn had asked herself many times. It had come upon her slowly. Had it begun as long ago as his first summer in Wales when he was sixteen and she fifteen?

There was no doubt that she had missed him after he was gone and thought about him far more than she would have admitted either to herself or to him. By the time he returned for a second visit, she was eighteen and in grave danger of falling in love with the tall, dashing nineteen-year-old. The moment she saw him step off the coach, her heart had leaped within her. But *his* feelings remained a mystery. Even though nothing had been said, their friendship had deepened into what seemed like more. How much more she had been afraid to ask herself even then. She knew, too, that Percy remained captivated with Gwyneth, who was also growing rapidly into a young woman.

By then she and Gwyneth had become the best of friends. Gwyneth was working at the manor as a lady's maid to Florilyn and her mother. Nothing, not even a man, not even Percy, would come between them. But it was no secret that they both cherished more than a passing affection for the good-looking and chivalrous young Scot.

Then suddenly without warning, about a year ago, the enigmatic little family of outcasts had disappeared from Llanfryniog without a trace—Codnor and Gwyneth Barrie and Grannie "Bryn" Myfanawy. Not a word had been heard from them since. No one knew a thing, not even Adela Muir, Codnor's sister and Gwyneth's aunt.

Florilyn halfway expected her father to have more information concerning the mysterious affair than he let on. But he had revealed nothing, and now he was dead. Whatever secrets he may have possessed he had taken with him to his grave.

Percy had returned to Wales last summer knowing nothing of the strange turn of events. The shock of finding Gwyneth gone had unsettled him more than anything Florilyn had ever seen. But out of the suddenly altered circumstances had come the decision that would change both their lives forever. She and Percy had been engaged since the final days of the previous June.

There was still no word, no trace, no hint of Gwyneth Barrie's whereabouts. Florilyn wondered if the mystery would ever be solved.

EIGHT

Schemes

A week after their initial discussion about the Wales situation, as they were now calling it, Palmer Sutcliffe found his employer in his office. "I have learned a few details concerning the Westbrooke affair," he said when he was seated. "I have a contact in Porthmadog who is acquainted with the solicitor for the late viscount's estate. He was able to learn that Lord Snowdon established a trusteeship for the estate in which he named his wife trustee. That is where it stands at present. The solicitor is involved of course, but effectively the man's widow is in complete control."

"And the son?" asked Lord Litchfield.

"He will not inherit until he is twenty-five."

"How old is he now?"

"Twenty-three."

"What do we know about the woman, Lady Snowdon?"

"She is the daughter of a Scottish earl—of good family, well respected, quite wealthy. Though apparently the earl, her father, has very peculiar notions."

"What kind of notions?"

"Religious. A fanatic, they say."

"Religious fanaticism is nothing unusual in Scotland. They breed preachers there like rabbits. What's so unusual about this earl? Do I know him? Does he sit in the House?"

"I don't think he has ever occupied his seat. He is known to completely eschew politics."

"What does he do then?"

"As I said, he is a man of substantial wealth. However, over the years he has given half his fortune away to various Christian mission organizations, particularly one in China. And then—get this—at sixty-four the man went off with his wife and joined the mission himself. They have been in China as some kind of missionaries ever since."

"That's the most absurd thing I've ever heard," laughed Litchfield. "What kind of missionaries could a doddering old earl and his wife make? What in the world are they doing, preaching to the natives, for God's sake! The thing's preposterous."

"I don't know. But that is the way things apparently stand."

"They gave all their money to this missions outfit?"

"About half as I understand it, to a number of missions and charities. They split what remained of their fortune between a son and the daughter in question. Lady Snowdon's brother is a vicar in Glasgow. Both are apparently as fanatical about religion as their parents."

"A family of fools."

"Perhaps, but wealthy fools," remarked Sutcliffe. "Money apparently means nothing to them. Lord Snowdon, whatever our difficulties with him, seems to have been the only sane one in the entire brood."

"In other words, he didn't marry the woman for her religion?"

"Very unlikely, I would say. More likely for her money. He had been strapped for years."

"Then money will be no inducement to his widow."

"Again, most unlikely."

"How do we approach them then? How will we induce the woman to sell if she is independently wealthy?"

"There may be no alternative but to await the son's ascension to the title."

"How long will that be, did you say?"

"A year and a half."

"We've already waited five years! Why not approach the son now?"

"He would have no legal authority to sell any of the estate."

"What would we have to lose? It may be that he has influence with the mother."

"Or it could be that we might make the preliminary arrangements with letters of intent. It could take us eighteen months to be ready to begin blasting as it is—with all the legalities required to draw up the papers, getting the equipment there, and so on. It is not too soon to begin."

"You're right. With an agreement in place, we could be ready to begin the day the sale is consummated."

"Let me see what more I can learn about the young man. If like his father he is financially straitened, we might attempt exactly the same line of approach with him. Youth is not always wise in the ways of the world. We may be able to use that to our advantage."

"Do you suppose he knows of our previous communications?"

"There is no way to know. We must simply choose our words with care."

"Then find out what you can."

"Would you like me again to draft a preliminary letter?" asked Sutcliffe.

Litchfield thought a moment. "Yes," he nodded slowly. "But in my own name, I think. We don't want to make the same mistake twice. We will have to hope the son is not so shrewd as his father. Word it to imply that Snowdon had already agreed and that all he must do to pocket a sizeable sum of cash is to agree to what his father had already set in motion."

NINE

A Different View in the Hills

*I*t had rained incessantly for three days. Florilyn walked out the front door of Westbrooke Manor just after lunch. She was weary of the dreary atmosphere. She had had her nose buried in the MacDonald novel she was reading for as long she could tolerate for one morning. She had never been a great reader. Though she was enjoying it, she was still, and always would be, an outdoor person. When the rain finally began to let up about eleven o'clock, she determined that one way or another she *would* spend the afternoon outside.

The clouds seemed at last to have emptied of their waterlogged floodgates and called a temporary halt to the deluge upon west Britain. The sun, however, gave no indication that it intended to battle the thick cloud cover for supremacy. A gray-white sky overspread the earth with a canopy of gloomy monotony. But it was relatively warm, pleasantly humid, refreshing in its own way with just enough bite in the moist air to keep it from being muggy. All in all it was a perfect autumn afternoon of late October.

As Florilyn meandered away from the house, she breathed in deeply of the liquid fragrant air. Three days of rain had made everything clean. The ground was wet beneath her feet. Puddles were scattered everywhere about the entryway. Drops still fell from the eaves of the house, from every branch of every tree, from fading flowers and rosebushes and shrubs. Droplets clung to every blade of grass. Water was everywhere. But at least the rain had stopped.

The air smelled *good*! It was the aroma of autumn, so different from that of its cousin spring. It was the smell of dirt, of peat, of wetness, of decay. . .of brown not green. Though it spoke of winter's approach, it was yet sweet and pleasant.

She had no plans in mind for the afternoon. It seemed too wet for a ride. She just wanted to be outside. Perhaps she would bundle up, bring out a warm cup of chocolate, and read in the summerhouse. Then let the rain come back and do its worst!

She wandered toward the stables. It was dark inside as she entered. It took a good while for her eyes to accustom themselves to the dim light, for it was not bright enough outside to help much. She heard sounds and squinted. She had not seen Courtenay all day. Perhaps he, too, planned to take advantage of the lapse in the rain and was preparing for a ride. She soon realized, however, that the sounds were coming not from her brother but from Steven Muir at the far end of the great barn. He was occupied with one of the horses. "Steven, is that you?" she called into the semidarkness.

"Miss Florilyn—yes," came the familiar voice in reply. "I am checking on Grey Tide."

"How is she?" asked Florilyn, approaching slowly.

"I would guess that she is perhaps two weeks away," replied Steven. "I am not sure she will be ready for Mr. Percy to ride if he comes for Christmas."

"He has ridden Red Rhud many times," said Florilyn. "I am not so worried about which horse he will ride as I am about snow and whether he and his parents will be able to get here at all."

"He will find a way. I am sure he is anxious to see you again." Steven turned and walked toward the back of the barn.

Florilyn followed him outside. There she saw Red Rhud saddled and apparently waiting for him. "Are you going out?" Florilyn asked.

"I am. I've been waiting for the rain to break."

"Where are you going?"

"Out to the Cnychwr croft. Their rent is due, but I haven't had the chance to get out there. I haven't seen them since Mr. Heygate left. Would you like to join me?"

"Oh. . .yes—I think I would. This rain has been making me crazy. A ride would be nice, but I didn't want to go out alone."

"Then I will saddle Black Flame. You may take your pick of mounts. But I should warn you," added Steven, "it is six miles at least. We will not be back until late. The rain may resume."

"As long as you promise to take care of me, I won't be worried."

Steven laughed. "You have my promise! It is not cold. Even if we should get wet, I don't think it will do us any harm."

"I will go change into my riding clothes and get my raincoat while you saddle Black Flame."

Twenty minutes later, Florilyn Westbrooke set out through the eastern gate beside her mother's young factor, who was only two years older than she. Accustomed to being in command and usually leading the way even when she rode with Percy, she found herself following, even occasionally along a few routes into the mountainous east she was not familiar with. Steven led the way almost due east toward the southern flank of Rhinog Fawr then veered south around the base of the mountain.

At length they came around its far slope, where he again took a northerly bearing toward their destination, which sat nearly under the shadow of the peak to its northwest. It was a strange place for a croft. But the stone cottage had been there as long as anyone could remember. One family after another had somehow managed to scrape together an existence on the five acres that surrounded it, with cows and sheep and chickens and potatoes and what vegetables they were able to grow during the summer and autumn months.

"Do you miss your father?" asked Florilyn as they rode.

"Of course," replied Steven. "But he was so unlike himself the last few years of his life, in another way it is a relief to have him released from all that. My mother misses him terribly. They spent their whole adult lives together. How about you?"

"I do miss my father," replied Florilyn. "He and I never really talked much together, though he was different the last few years. I suppose I miss his presence about the manor more than anything."

"In what way was he different?"

"He seemed to pay more attention to little things. We began to talk more often."

"What about your mother?"

"She doesn't talk about him. But I can tell she is sad. Did you and your father talk?" asked Florilyn.

"My papa wasn't a talkative man," replied Steven. "I loved him dearly, and he was a good man to one and all. But no, we didn't talk much. Sometimes we worked together for hours without saying a word. We simply enjoyed being together. But he was a quiet man."

"Percy says he and his father discuss whatever he is thinking about. He says he asks his father's advice about everything. When I listen to him, I find myself wishing I had enjoyed something like that with my father, even wondering if I could have if I had been less self-absorbed."

"I don't know whether that is true," said Steven. "People are different. Not all men are capable of that kind of thing. Percy is fortunate, but he might not have been able to talk in the same way to your father either. We take the fathers we are given. We have to find God in them as it expresses itself in their own individual ways. I learned to see God's fatherhood in my father, though I do not believe he once spoke a word about God to me in my life."

"It's amazing to hear you say that," rejoined Florilyn. "That's exactly like something Percy would say."

Steven laughed. "I take that as a great compliment. But look, there is the Cnychwr cottage ahead. We seem to have made it without rain."

As they approached the stone house, Steven looked over the flock of sheep in the field next to it with a curious expression. They were full of wool and ragged looking. They should have been shorn long before now.

Two dogs came bounding and barking out to greet them. Steven jumped down and let them get used to him before allowing Florilyn to dismount. "Wait for me just a minute," said Steven. "I'll go tell them we're here. Then I'll hold the dogs away for you."

He ran toward the cottage as a girl of eleven or twelve came outside to see what the barking was about. Steven spoke with her a minute then returned to Florilyn. "The girl says both her parents are sick in bed. I'm going in to talk to them. Do you want to wait here?"

"No, I'll go with you," said Florilyn. She dismounted, and the two walked to the cottage and inside.

They made their way through a large open kitchen into a dim sitting room. From there the girl led into the single small bedroom off the sitting room, which they all shared. There a man and woman lay in a large bed.

"Stevie Muir, so it's you, is it?" said a voice weakly from the darkness. "Arial said it was you."

"It's me, Kynwal," answered Steven. "She says you've been sick."

"It's laid us both on our backs," added a woman's voice in barely more than a whisper.

"Hello, Lilybet," said Steven. "I'm sorry to see you after so long under these circumstances."

"We heard you and your mum's gone to the manor now," said Mr. Cnychwr. "We hear that you've been made factor. I always said you was meant for bigger things. So it's Lady Snowdon's rent you'll be wanting, I'm thinking."

"That is why I came," said Steven. "And to tell you of the change. I wasn't sure you'd heard."

"We knew all about it, Stevie. But I'm afraid I've nothing to give you. I've been down near a month. Then Lilybet come down with the evil thing after me."

"He's just got weaker and weaker," said the woman. "I took care of him as best I could. But then came a day when I couldn't stand up myself. My legs just wouldn't hold me. We'd have surely died if Arial hadn't been here."

"I didn't have the strength to shear the sheep," said Kynwal. "Even if I had, I couldn't have got the fleece in to market."

"Don't you worry about it, Kynwal," said Steven. "Lady Snowdon will be more concerned for yourselves than your rent. We will see what we can do. What about food—do you have what you need?"

"Isn't much either of us can eat. No appetite, you see. No strength even to eat. But Arial's keeping the two cows milked, and there's always plenty of eggs. This time of year we've got apples and a few vegetables."

"Good. Well then, we will be on our way. We have a long ride back ahead of us. But I will send Dr. Rotherham out to see you as soon as possible."

"Don't bother the doctor, Stevie. We've got no money to—"

"We need to get you two back on your feet. Don't you worry about the doctor."

Seemingly for the first time, Mrs. Cnychwr noticed the figure standing behind Steven in the shadows. She was hardly able to lift her head off the pillow for a better look. "Who's that you brought with you, Steven?" she asked.

"It's Lady Florilyn from the manor, Lilybet—Lord and Lady Snowdon's daughter."

A gasp of astonishment left the woman's lips. "The saints preserve us!" she exclaimed. "My Lady Florilyn. . . I'm sorry for you to see us like this—but welcome to you. If only I could offer you something. You honor our poor cottage."

"Thank you, Mrs. Cnychwr," said Florilyn, stepping forward to the bedside. She reached out and laid a hand gently on the woman's arm. "I am sorry you are ill. But Steven is right. We will send the doctor out immediately."

"You are very kind, my lady."

"My mother will see to it, and anything else you need."

Ten minutes later, Florilyn and Steven began the ride back around the mountain and down to the coast.

"What would my father and Mr. Heygate do when someone could not pay the rent?" Florilyn asked.

"I don't know," replied Steven. "I'm sure under the circumstances they would have been lenient, as they were with us when my father was ill."

"Did my father ever evict people for not paying?"

"He did, yes—I knew of a few cases. But your father was an understanding man. In most cases, the people deserved to be evicted, and the town is better off without them."

"But you knew my mother would not be concerned that the Cnychwrs were unable to pay?"

"Oh, yes. . .of course. I know your mother's heart. Besides, there is money and to spare for their rent walking around on the backs of his flock of sheep."

"But if he cannot shear them. . ."

Steven chuckled as if her worry was absurd. "His sheep will all be shorn within the week," he said, "though not quite to the skin as winter is approaching."

"Who will shear them?"

"Me, of course!" laughed Steven.

They reached the manor, wet but laughing, for one brief dousing from above had nearly drenched them. They separated and went to their respective quarters for dry clothes. Then Steven sought Katherine to apprise her of the situation at the Cnychwr croft.

TEN

A Tempting Offer

*T*he letter that arrived at Westbrooke Manor for Courtenay bore no return address or indication who the sender might be. It therefore aroused no curiosity in Lady Katherine's mind as her eyes fell upon it along with the rest of the morning's mail.

Courtenay, however, immediately noticed the London postmark and slit open the envelope with a certain mild interest. Intrigued he withdrew the single sheet.

Mr. Westbrooke, he read,

My deepest condolences at the death of your father. He and I were colleagues in the House of Lords. However, I only recently learned of his passing. I look forward to meeting you as my colleague as well when you become eligible to sit with the Lords, which I understand will be in approximately a year and a half.

Your father and I were involved in discussions involving a business transaction, which I had every reason to believe would have been mutually beneficial to us both, and especially lucrative for your father. Unfortunately the thing did not reach fruition. Our correspondence lagged as other priorities consumed our attentions. Now sadly, just as I was about to contact him again, your father's untimely death came before we could resume our plans.

I am writing now in hopes that perhaps you might be able to carry forward what your father and I were not able to complete.

My discussions with your father were quite simple: It has been my hope to purchase a small portion of acreage from your father's estate—your estate now—far on the eastern boundary of the Westbrooke property. The reason is purely a sentimental one. I spent some of the happiest years of my life as a boy romping the walking trails and footpaths of those hills. It has been my desire at the later stages of my life to build a small cottage on a site I was especially fond of that is situated on the slopes of one of Gwynedd's smaller peaks. The property lies at the boundary of your estate. Your father felt that its remote location among his holdings would represent no great sacrifice to the overall Westbrooke estate and had in principle agreed to the sale.

I can assure you that my plans would in no way encroach on your future privacy as Viscount Lord Snowdon. My access would be gained by a right of way eastward through public lands from the road between Blaenau Ffestiniog and Dolgellau.

I would purchase whatever amount of land you would graciously consent to part with up to a thousand or more acres. However, if a transaction of such size is impossible, I could carry out the plans for my small cottage with as little as twenty. Your father and I had not yet settled on the number of acres of my purchase or a price per acre, though I am prepared to be as generous in an offer to you as I would have been to him.

As you and I will be colleagues and will enjoy a long future together, it strikes me as best under the circumstances if I conduct these arrangements with yourself in confidentiality without involving your mother, whom I understand is at present trustee over your father's estate. I am hoping you and I might come to some arrangement relatively soon, even perhaps before you officially inherit your father's title. If we could come to a mutually beneficial agreement, being a wealthy man, I can assure you that I would make it worth your while. I would be in a position to forward you

*a sizeable advance payment as an earnest pledge toward the final
purchase price.*

*If you feel you would be interested in pursuing this matter in
your father's stead, I will put an offer together for your consideration,
which, as I say, would include a cash advance to yourself.*

I am, Mr. Westbrooke,

Faithfully yours,

Lord Coleraine Litchfield

Courtenay set the letter aside with a sigh filled with emotions it
would have been difficult to identify. His first impulse was to set pen to
paper immediately. His hand quivered to do so. But he realized it would
be foolish. He was no businessman, but he was certainly knowledgeable
enough in the ways of the world to know that one could not appear *too*
eager.

He tried to pretend he was spending the following days thinking
through the pros and cons of the thing before arriving at a well-
reasoned decision. In truth, he was simply waiting for enough time to
pass to make the fellow Litchfield, whoever he was, squirm just enough
anticipating a reply.

His mother and sister noted the difference in his countenance
instantly, the subtle smirk, as if he knew something he was not telling.
Katherine suspected him of having something up his sleeve, which he
did. But she was the last one to whom he would divulge what he was
thinking.

After six days, Courtenay judged that enough time had gone by. He
sat down at the writing table in his room and began to write the letter
he had been composing in his mind since the moment his eyes had
fallen on Litchfield's words, "cash advance to yourself."

Lord Coleraine Litchfield, he wrote.

My Lord,

*I am in receipt of your letter and have been giving the matter a
great deal of thought. Though as you note, I will not be in control of*

the estate's affairs for another year and a half, I would be amenable to the idea of setting in motion before that time the preliminaries for a transaction such as you have outlined.

I will entertain any reasonable offer you would make. The size of the acreage I would be willing to sell would entirely depend on the price per acre offered. The total sum would weigh most heavily in the balance as there have been inevitable strains placed upon my finances as a result of my father's death and my eventual assumption of his title and estate.

I will of course need to know the exact location in question. With that information and some idea of the specifics of the offer you are prepared to make, we will be in a position to speak more definitely about a timetable. Be assured that our discussions and negotiations will remain confidential.

> I am,
> Yours sincerely,
> Courtenay Westbrooke

Five days later, Courtenay received his reply.

Mr. Westbrooke,

I was delighted to receive your letter and hope that this may be the beginning of a rewarding business relationship that will benefit us both.

Enclosed you will see site drawings showing the northeastern portions of your estate boundaries, indicating the area of my interest. I have outlined four potential scenarios, any of which I would be willing to consider—a twenty-acre sale, another of one hundred acres, a third of five hundred, and a fourth of one thousand acres. The price offered per acre would of course be larger for the smaller plots.

My research tells me that such land in Gwynedd has been selling in recent years for approximately five pounds an acre. As a preliminary offer, I would commit to paying you eight pounds an acre for twenty acres, six for one hundred acres, five for five hundred, and four for one thousand acres. Furthermore, I will pay one-fourth immediately upon our signing a binding sales agreement, with the balance forthcoming at the consummation of the sale once you hold legal title to the land.

If you find these terms agreeable, perhaps it might be appropriate for me to plan a trip to North Wales for us to meet in person and finalize the arrangements. We will, of course, devise some plausible explanation for my visit.

I am,
Faithfully yours,
Lord Coleraine Litchfield

ELEVEN

Nugget

*W*ithin a week of Florilyn's and Steven's visit to the croft at the base of Rhinog Fawr, not only had Katherine and Adela Muir paid the two invalids a visit, so, too, had Dr. Rotherham. He prescribed a medication he was confident would help them begin eating again and get the husband and wife on their way to returning strength.

For several days thereafter, Adela and Steven Muir stayed at the Cnychwr cottage. They nursed the two patients, prepared food, saw to the animals, and gave young Arial a badly needed rest. When they left, mother and son clattered back to town behind the croft's single horse atop a wagonload of fresh wool, which, it being late in the season and no other wool being sold, Steven was confident would bring Kynwal Cnychwr a good price.

"Do you ever miss living out here, Mother?" Steven asked as they bounced along.

Adela thought a moment. "Being out in the hills like this brings back many memories," she said at length. "I miss your father, I miss the life we enjoyed, the animals, being so close to nature all the time. But living at the manor is more like I remember from my childhood. Of course, we lived in nothing so lavish—it was a simple home by manor standards. What I mean is. . . I don't know how to describe it—the way of life, I suppose. . .having people about, servants, stables, books, gardens. My mother only had one servant, and she only came to the house three days a week. Still, reading MacDonald's books brings it all back to me now."

"In what way?"

"His stories mostly have to do with gentle folk, people of means. It's just the way he writes about them. We were certainly not wealthy by any standards. But my father and grandfather had roots among the gentility."

"You didn't miss that when you married Father?"

"Aspects of it, of course. But there were many children, and times were hard. Even from such a background, one isn't always able to dictate the future. And love doesn't always fall according to station in life. I loved your father and wanted to be his wife. And we had a good life together. I regret not a minute of it. However, I do enjoy being at the manor now, especially having access to a library again. My grandfather had a marvelous library. I've often wondered what became of all his books. To answer your question, I have no regrets about the past, nor about the present."

~⁓~

A wonderful warm day dawned toward the end of the first week of November, several days after Steven's return to the manor. Most of the trees, like the sheep on the surrounding fields, had lost their summer adornment. Their leaves of yellow and red and orange were strewn on the ground everywhere and rapidly turning brown.

The moment Florilyn saw the sun streaming through her bedroom window, she knew it was a day for a long ride. One could never depend on the weather after November. This might be the last such day in North Wales for months.

After breakfast, she dressed in her riding clothes and left the house for the stables. Their aging groom, Hollin Radnor, was nowhere to be seen. From the depths of the darkness, however, Florilyn heard peculiar sounds, scuffling and low snorting, as from a horse in distress. She hurried inside the great barn.

The sounds were coming from Grey Tide's stall. She was walking about, obviously restless. Her tail was high and her hips distended. As Florilyn approached, she moved about in a circular motion and awkwardly slumped to her side on the floor. Her hind portions were quivering. Snorts and whines of discomfort continued.

She was ready to foal!

Florilyn hurried from the barn. She called out as she ran to the new stables. There was no sign of Radnor or Stuart Wyckham anywhere. At length she bolted for the house. She ran straight to the factor's office at the end of the ground floor of the west wing then ran inside without knocking.

Steven sat across the room, an open ledger on the desk in front of him. He looked up at the sound of his door crashing open.

"Steven!" cried Florilyn. "It's Grey Tide. I think she's ready! More than ready—I think it's started! But I couldn't find Hollin."

Already Steven was on his feet, sprinting from the room with Florilyn on his heels. By the time she followed him into the barn, Steven was kneeling behind Grey Tide in the stall.

"You're right," he said, glancing up as she tentatively entered. "Labor is well under way. But she is in pain. It may be a difficult birth. Something seems wrong."

Florilyn stood watching wide-eyed with a grimace of mingled disgust and awe as Steven plunged his hand inside Grey Tide and felt for the position of the foal.

"Just as I thought," he said. "I can't feel the legs."

"What does that mean?" asked Florilyn.

"The forelegs and head have to come out together. Otherwise we'll have real problems. . .uh, oh, look out—stand back!"

Steven withdrew his hand and leaped back as Grey Tide struggled again to her feet and began shuffling about the stall. She was obviously agitated.

"Easy, Grey Tide. . .easy, girl," said Steven softly, walking slowly to her head where he tried to stroke her nose and neck to calm her down. "Don't be afraid, girl. . . . You're having a baby. Just relax, Grey Tide."

"Oh no, ugh…Steven!" exclaimed Florilyn. "Something is happening back here. Oh, ick…Steven!"

"What is it?" said Steven, calmly leaving Grey Tide's head and returning to where Florilyn stood behind her.

"What's all that white?"

"Nothing to worry about. That's the birth sack. It's called the amnion. The foal is inside…but…yes, it's as I thought—the head is coming without the legs. The bag's already broken. Oops—she's trying to lay down again. Easy, Grey Tide…gently, big girl," he said, leaning against the mare's rump as she began to settle again to the floor. "Lady Florilyn!" he cried. "Come over here. We can't let her crush the foal's head. Here…push with me!"

Cautiously Florilyn stepped to Steven's side and shoved, though how much help she was under the circumstances was questionable. She had never witnessed anything like this in her life.

As Grey Tide struggled to ease herself to the ground, Steven pushed with all his might to make sure she came down on her side. Even as she did, the head of the foal was fully visible. The mare's contractions were coming steady and strong.

"I'll have to go inside to find the legs," said Steven when Grey Tide was lying comfortably on the ground. "Lady Florilyn, I'll need your help. I know this may be unpleasant—but can you be brave and help me?"

"I'll try, Steven."

"Kneel down here. Do you see—the head is out. Grasp the little torso just below the head with both your hands. Come—I'll help you." Steven took Florilyn's two hands and set them gently around the white mass. "Here, Lady Florilyn—we must move quickly. You can see the head and neck, can you not?"

"Yes…oh, ugh!"

"Now with your hand like this… Good—now very gently apply a little pressure and try to prevent the foal coming farther until I have the legs out…very gently. Can you do that?"

"I think so…. Oh, it's all wet and sticky…ick!"

"Be brave, Lady Florilyn. We have to try to save Grey Tide's foal.

Now I have to go back inside. I must get the forelegs out before the foal tries to get up. The minute she is breathing her instinct will be to stand. If her legs are still inside, she could damage Grey Tide's insides."

Again Steven reached inside. He felt along the length of the foal's slender body, now about half exposed. Gradually he managed to extricate first one tiny hoof and leg, then the other.

"The forelegs are out—good," he said at length. "Now, Lady Florilyn, very gently. . .pull. We can let her come the rest of the way."

Still grimacing but clutching firmly around the tiny form, Florilyn did as Steven said. Almost instantly the foal slid the rest of the way until only her back legs still rested inside.

Kneeling beside Florilyn, Steven set his hands atop Florilyn's. "Pull again. We must get the other two legs out."

Within seconds the tiny form lay motionless on the ground before them. The birth was over, but the foal was not breathing.

"Is. . .is it dead?" asked Florilyn as she gazed down at the wet, bloody mass in front of her.

"I don't know," said Steven, jumping to his feet. He grabbed several handfuls of clean straw from across the stall and tossed it in front of Florilyn. "Here, wipe it down with dry straw. Try to get the mouth open if you can."

"Where are you going?" she asked in sudden panic.

"Just over here," said Steven as he walked around the large form of the mother lying on her side recovering from the birth. "I need to get Grey Tide on her feet. We'll need her help to save her foal. While I'm doing that, tickle the foal's nose with a piece of straw and blow into its mouth and nose."

Tentatively Florilyn took some of the straw and began wiping at the wet, limp form.

"Oh. . .Steven—something's happening. Oh, ick. . . There's a lot of blood and icky-looking stuff coming out—ugh. I think Grey Tide's bleeding!"

"It's the afterbirth. Nothing to worry about. . .though it usually takes twenty minutes to an hour. This is fast. Come, Grey Tide. . .up!

Come, girl, you need to help us get your little foal breathing." Steven pushed and cajoled, but the poor mare was obviously spent. "Any sign of life?" he called out to Florilyn.

"No. I think he's dead."

"*Is* it a colt?"

"Oh, I. . .I don't know. I didn't actually. . .*look*." Florilyn was now stroking the lifeless little head gently with one hand. With two fingers inside its mouth, she blew at its nose and mouth and tried to coax life into being.

With a swaying and wriggling, Grey Tide struggled to her forelegs then up to her feet. Steven was careful to lead her a few steps forward before allowing her to turn around. As she turned, she gave a low snort then bent her long nose toward the newborn, nudged its head a time or two, but then turned toward the messy mass on the ground.

"Oh, no. . .ick. Goodness, Steven!" cried Florilyn. "She's trying to eat it! How disgusting!"

"She's just doing what instinct tells her. Come, Grey Tide," he said, trying to pull her back. "Time for all that later. Your little baby needs you. I'll get rid of it so you won't be distracted." He grabbed a shovel and scooped up the afterbirth and removed it from the stall.

Soon Grey Tide was bent down toward her little son, as confirmed by Steven, licking its head and nose where they lay on Florilyn's lap.

Steven bent down and began rubbing vigorously and gently squeezing the foal's ribs. Still there was no response. He lifted one of the tiny feet off the ground and dropped it. Then again.

Suddenly, the colt's head jerked on the side of Florilyn's leg. The same instant she felt a fierce sucking on her fingers. As if jolted by a bolt of lightning, suddenly the whole tiny body trembled.

"Steven. . .what should I do?" exclaimed Florilyn. "It's going to pull my fingers off."

"Nothing, just relax. You've done what you needed to do—you brought him back to life. Let his head rest on your lap another minute. He's got to get used to all this. Give him a minute."

Steven knelt beside her. "He seems to be breathing normally. That's good. I think he'll be fine. Good work, Grey Tide," he said, patting the mother's nose as she continued to lick the tiny face. "Remove your fingers from its mouth when you can," said Steven. "He needs to smell Grey Tide."

Slowly Florilyn did so.

"Now, very gently. . .ease yourself back and set the little head on the floor. We need to leave mother and foal together. He needs to get used to her smell."

Gradually Florilyn scooted away.

"Good," said Steven, smiling at her. "Now we wait."

"What will happen next?" asked Florilyn.

"He's only been breathing about a minute," replied Steven. "He'll get used to that, and then he'll lift his head. You see how he's just lying flat on his side? He'll be upright in a matter of minutes. Right from birth, horses have remarkably strong necks. After that, though he is still weak, instinct will make him try to get up."

Steven rose and glanced about the stall. "It looks like. . .yes, the cord has broken. That's good. I need to apply iodine to the stump so it will dry. Do you mind being alone a minute?"

"Where are you going?"

"Just over to the cabinet where Hollin keeps his supplies." Steven hurried away and returned quickly with the bottle of iodine. Florilyn watched in amazement as he checked the stump where the cord had broken and carefully doused it with iodine.

"How do you know how to do all this?" asked Florilyn.

"When you're a shepherd you grow up taking care of animals. It's part of the shepherd's life."

"You're not a shepherd anymore, Steven."

"I will always think of myself as one." When the procedure was complete, he knelt back.

"When will he be able to stand?" asked Florilyn.

"It will be soon," replied Steven. "Half an hour after he stands, we'll lead Grey Tide to the grass outside. The little foal will follow, somewhat wobbly. He will be walking and running before you know it. As soon as he's on his feet, he will try to suckle."

"How does he know. . .where to suck?" asked Florilyn.

"It takes some time. It's random at first. But Grey Tide will help him find the right place. It is instinctive. Both know what to do. By the way, what is his name?"

"What do you mean?"

"He's got to have a name. Grey Tide is your mare. You should be the one who names her foal."

"Oh. . . I suppose you're right. How exciting. Let me think."

It was quiet a few moments. Both sat watching mare and foal with their noses together. Grey Tide continued to lick and sniff at the tiny face and head.

"Oh look, Steven. . .it's just like you said!" exclaimed Florilyn. "Look—he's lifting his head and squirming about. Is he trying to stand?"

"Mostly just now to get his legs beneath his body. But he is feeling his legs, feeling their strength. He will try to stand up any minute now."

"I love his color. It's such a light golden hue. Will the color stay as it is?"

"Probably. It may darken in time, but it will always be tan or, as you say, golden."

"Then I think I have decided on a name. He shall be called Nugget."

"A brilliant name. I like it. Well done! And thank you for your help. You did very well. Was this your first birthing?"

"Couldn't you tell?" laughed Florilyn. "I was in a panic."

"I suppose I could," chuckled Steven. "You weren't exactly calm and collected."

"I was terrified!"

"I'm sorry to say it, but your riding clothes are a mess," said Steven. "I don't ever think I've seen you look quite so. . .earthy."

Suddenly Florilyn realized what she must look like. She glanced down at her hands and dress—covered with dirt and blood. "You're right—what a sight I must be!" she exclaimed. "I will definitely not be going for a ride in these clothes," she added, laughing.

"You look lovely—just like a farm girl! And I am glad you were here. You probably saved little Nugget's life."

"How could that be?"

"If you hadn't come for me when you did, there is no telling what might have happened. In just those first few seconds before Grey Tide got to him, touching him, stroking his head, making sure his mouth was open—those seconds may have made the difference between life and death."

Steven rose to his feet and extended his hand to Florilyn where she still knelt on the floor of the stall. "I think we can leave mother and son alone for a while now," he said.

Florilyn reached up. She took his hand, and he pulled her to her feet. "Then I think I will go inside and change my clothes," she said. "I'm afraid these may now be fit only for the rubbish bin."

"Well done again, Lady Florilyn," said Steven as Florilyn left the stall and walked toward the door of the barn.

She paused and turned back. "It sounds funny to have you call me that," she said with an odd smile. "I mean, after sharing something like this, why should I call you just Steven and you have to call me Lady Florilyn? I would rather you simply called me by name."

"But you are a lady," said Steven.

"That's not how I think of myself. If you can still think of yourself as a shepherd, why can't I just think of myself as an ordinary girl?"

"You're hardly a *girl*."

"Don't confuse me with the facts," laughed Florilyn. "If you have the right to think of yourself as you want to, why don't I?"

"Your logic has the parallel between you and me backward."

"Girls don't have to be logical, don't you know."

Steven laughed at the logic even of her illogical argument.

"Besides," Florilyn added with a smile, "look at me. As you pointed out, do I *look* like a lady?"

Again Steven chuckled. "You have a point. But you always will be a lady to me. However, I will address you any way you like."

"Then please call me Florilyn. If something like this doesn't make us equals, I don't know what does."

"All right. . .*Florilyn*," nodded Steven. "As you wish. I consider myself honored to be allowed the privilege."

Florilyn smiled then continued out of the barn and to the house.

By the time she returned twenty minutes later, along with her mother to see the new colt, Nugget had begun struggling to stand on his four slender, frail legs. She and Katherine and Steven watched, laughing a good deal at the humorous attempt.

"He's such a little dear!" said Florilyn. "There is nothing so cute as a baby animal. Just look at him, Steven!"

An hour later, mother and son were outside on the enclosed grass between the stables. By then Nugget had found his feet and had begun to scamper about, alternating between suckling from beneath Grey Tide and exploring his new environment. Seemingly uninterested in her foal's antics, Grey Tide munched away on the grass at her feet and from a bale of hay Steven had provided.

Florilyn spent most of the day sitting on a low bench on one side of the enclosure, watching every move the little foal made. Steven's words had plunged deep into her heart. If she had not actually saved the little colt's life, that she may have helped in a small way to do so gave her a feeling that she had never had before. She would always feel a special bond with this little horse. She imagined that perhaps Nugget felt it, too.

Many times throughout the day, as he became used to her sight and smell where she sat calmly watching, he wandered over for brief sniffing visits. He took one of several naps of the afternoon at Florilyn's side, sleeping peacefully as Florilyn gently stroked his neck and back.

TWELVE

Over His Head

Courtenay pondered Litchfield's offer for several days. The thought that with a mere signature on a piece of paper he could raise a sum of badly needed cash sent him into a near frenzy of anticipation to move the thing forward with all possible haste. Realistically, however, how much good would a paltry hundred and sixty pounds do him? It would only bring him forty pounds immediately, with the remainder not coming until he was twenty-five. Selling the man twenty acres was hardly the solution he needed.

Forty pounds! Courtenay thought. It was a laughable amount. He had burned through more than that in a week on the continent! It would do nothing to resolve his financial predicament.

Perhaps the man was making a fair offer. For all he knew, five pounds might be the going rate for acreage. But the language in the man's letters sounded as if money was the least of his problems. If he was a wealthy man, as he said, why not call his bluff and push him to the limit? There was no reason to part with a portion of the estate unless it put him in a significantly stronger financial position. He might be able to get double, perhaps triple, what Litchfield had put forward.

When he began his next letter to London, Courtenay knew he was running a risk. He might shove the man away. But in his gut, he doubted it. The fellow obviously wanted the land. Well then, let him jolly well pay for it. He could play the game, too. He would show the Londoner that he wasn't dealing with some country bumpkin.

Lord Litchfield, he began,

While I appreciate the offer set out in your last letter, I really could not possibly entertain the thought of selling land that has been in our family for centuries for less than ten pounds an acre for one thousand acres. I would not want you to interpret this as a commitment to that figure. But that is certainly the minimum I would look at.

If you are interested in submitting a more realistic offer, I will entertain it. Otherwise, I will consult my financial advisors with the aim of presenting you a counter proposal.

Should you choose to submit an alternative offer, I would also want to receive no less than one-third in payment up front, with two-thirds to be paid at the finalization of the sale.

Yours faithfully,
Courtenay Westbrooke

Litchfield read the communication and smiled. His ploy had worked to perfection. He doubted the boy even had any financial advisors. He was in over his head and had no idea who he was dealing with.

Litchfield knew he would probably have gone as high as fifty pounds an acre to the boy's father. Now here they were quibbling about price in the vicinity of ten!

The five-year wait appeared to have been well spent. It looked like he might get his land for a fraction of what he might have laid out for the project earlier.

Mr. Westbrooke,

I see that your father raised his son to be as shrewd as he was himself. You are an able negotiator and, as the saying goes, drive a hard bargain. As you have me at a disadvantage, since it is your land I desire to purchase and no other, it would seem that I have no alternative but to yield to your terms.

*The amount you speak of is admittedly very high. It would
take me some time to raise such capital. I assume, as you mention
a minimum figure of ten pounds for a thousand acres that your
acceptable terms for lesser acreage would be correspondingly higher.*

*Let me propose the following: sixteen pounds an acre for five
hundred acres, a total of £8,000; or thirteen pounds an acre for one
thousand acres, or £13,000.*

*If those terms are acceptable to you, I will have the preliminary
papers drawn up. That will take some time, and winter will soon be
upon us. But if you find my offer satisfactory, I will set the process
in motion. Then we can arrange a time that is mutually acceptable
for me to visit you in Wales, perhaps in the spring. At that time we
can formalize our intentions. I will also agree to your stipulation
of one-third down. When I come, upon receipt of your signature on
the documents, I will place a check for either £2,700 or £4,400 into
your hands.*

I am,

Sincerely yours,

Lord Coleraine Litchfield

Courtenay's eyes nearly popped out of his head as he read Litchfield's letter. He had done it! He had successfully extracted from
Litchfield a commitment for more than *triple* his original offer. This
would definitely get him out of his financial straits and keep him flush
until his twenty-fifth birthday.

He wouldn't need his mother's money now. Let her eat cake!

Thirteen

Reflections

Percy Drummond had not forgotten his uncle Roderick's mysterious deathbed commission of the previous June that had enjoined him to secrecy on an assignment he little understood.

The viscount had been fond of Percy. The lad's engagement to his daughter had put the viscount in an exuberant, even reckless mood. He and Percy had gone riding the next day. For their ride he took out the dangerous black stallion Demon. It was a decision that cost him his life. The tempestuous horse had thrown him while leaping an uneven and rocky stream. The viscount's fall proved mortal. He had broken several bones and badly injured his neck. Both paralysis and gangrene soon became apparent.

As he lay on his deathbed, after consulting with his solicitor and after a probing talk with Percy about eternal matters and the destiny of his own soul, Lord Snowdon had requested his nephew to go through his files and put in order what he could, take care of anything it might be best that Katherine not see, and then to take down the private affidavit that now occupied Percy's thoughts.

He withdrew the document from where he kept it among his personal papers. No one, not even his Aunt Katherine nor his father or mother, knew of it. No one else in the world knew of the secrets this affidavit divulged concerning the viscount's past.

Slowly Percy unfolded the paper and began reading again the words, written in his own hand, that stunned him as much now as they had that day the previous June when he first heard them from his uncle's mouth.

To whom it may concern, especially to my dear wife, Katherine, my family, and to Hamilton Murray, our faithful solicitor of many years:

I make this affidavit on the 27ᵗʰ day of June, in the year 1872, in the presence of my nephew, Percival Drummond, son of Edward and Mary Drummond of Glasgow. I am of sound mind, but failing body. Those matters I here disclose, I have kept to myself more than thirty years for the sake of you whom I love so dearly. It was never my intention to speak of them. But conscience now compels me to make a clean breast of it. I earnestly pray that doing so will not cause undo pain, especially to you, my dear Katherine. I pray the truth, though painful, will be its own reward. I do not want to die with secrets on my conscience. May God forgive me if it is wrong to divulge what I could never tell another soul. But if truth matters, then may God heal whatever wounds it may cause. He knows better than anyone that I have not always lived by the dictates and demands of truth. It is admittedly a late time to start. But as my nephew reminds me, it is never too late to make a beginning. I hope therefore that I can die having taken a few faltering steps in the direction of becoming a man of truth.

At sixteen years of age, as a spoiled son of what I thought was wealth, I left Wales on a youthful grand tour, as we called it in those days—to see the world and spend money and generally squander my youth on the altar of irresponsibility. It turned out that my father was not the wealthy man I took him for. Before my travels were over, I was nearly out of money. I found myself in Ireland chasing the fleeting dream of riches in the rivers of Wicklow, though what remained to be found was doubtful. There my heart was smitten with a young Irish lass of working, though not peasant stock. Her name was Avonmara O'Sullivan.

Several months later we were married in a small parish church in County Wicklow. We were both children, she a mere eighteen years of age and myself nineteen. Whether it was wise or ill fated from the beginning, who can say. But it was done, though our brief happiness would not last. . . .

Percy continued on to the conclusion of the sad tale that had been meant for his ears alone.

Not a moment went by that he was not keenly aware of the burden his uncle had placed upon him. On his shoulders alone rested the decision whether Katherine and Courtenay and Florilyn, or anyone else for that matter, would ever know of Roderick Westbrooke's first marriage. If he judged it best that they never know, then the secret of his past would go to the grave with the former viscount.

His uncle's words had never left him. *"No one must see it unless your search is successful. Otherwise, Katherine need never know."*

Percy had not exactly given his promise. But if he kept it to himself, even out of respect for his uncle, what kind of man of truth did that make *him*? Would he be justified in keeping the matter secret in order to protect the feelings of his aunt? The demand of truth had borne heavily upon his uncle's heart at the end of his life. But what was now the demand of truth that *he* must heed? If a full revelation did no one any discernable *good*, what would be its purpose? Even truth could injure. Was it right to injure for some abstract commitment to truth, if there was no good to anyone to be gained? Thus far, Percy had arrived at no resolution to the complex conundrum.

After talking the matter over in vague terms with his father, without divulging specifics, Percy's conclusion had been that the investigation demanded no serious urgency on his part. It could wait until his graduation from the university the following May. Then he would devote the summer to seeing what he could learn. Perhaps by then more clarity might present itself about how to balance the scales between full disclosure and faithfulness to his uncle's wish that Katherine be protected from pain if his search proved unsuccessful.

Even so, his uncle's dying words gnawed at him. Percy could not escape the feeling that perhaps the matter of the affidavit was more urgent than he might realize. Yet what could he do. . .so far away. . .in Aberdeen? For that matter, what could he do even in Wales? He had no idea how to carry out his uncle's request. To make any beginning at all would require being at Westbrooke Manor.

Obviously that would have to wait. But the more time that passed, the more uneasy he became.

Even as Percy was reading her father's words, in Wales Florilyn was engrossed in the novel by Percy's fellow Scot, George MacDonald.

As she neared the end of the book, she was reminded of its opening where the characters Hugh Sutherland and Margaret Elginbrod first met. She flipped back to the beginning of the volume and read it again.

> *"It was, of course, quite by accident that Sutherland had met Margaret in the fir-wood. The wind had changed during the night, and swept all the clouds from the face of the sky; and when he looked out in the morning, he saw the fir-tops waving in the sunlight, and heard the sound of a south-west wind sweeping through them with the tune of running waters in its course. Sutherland's heart began to be joyful at the sight of the genial motions of Nature, telling of warmth and blessedness at hand. He dressed in haste, and went out to meet the Spring. He wandered into the heart of the wood. The wind blew cool, but not cold; and was filled with a delicious odour from the earth, which Sutherland took as a sign that she was coming alive at last. And the Spring he went out to meet, met him. For, first, at the foot of a tree, he spied a tiny primrose, peeping out of its rough, careful leaves. As he passed on with the primrose in his hand, thinking it was almost cruel to pluck it, the Spring met him, as if in her own shape, in the person of Margaret, whom he spied a little way off, leaning against the stem*

of a Scotch fir. He went up to her with some shyness; for the presence
of even a child-maiden was enough to make Sutherland shy. But
she, when she heard his footsteps, dropped her eyes slowly from
the tree-top, and waited his approach. He said nothing at first,
but offered her, instead of speech, the primrose he had just plucked,
which she received with a smile of the eyes only, and the sweetest
'thank you, sir,' he had ever heard. . .a lovely girl, with the woman
waking in her eyes."

Florilyn had not been present when Percy and Gwyneth first met on the slopes of the Snowdonian hills, though she had heard about it from both of them. As she read again of this fictional meeting between MacDonald's two characters, she was suddenly struck with the similarity between the two. Percy's meeting of Gwyneth that day had also been accidental, prompted, Florilyn hardly needed to be reminded, by her own deceit toward her cousin on their first ride together. Even then, as Percy had described her, he had begun "to be joyful at the sight of the genial motions of Nature." His meeting with Gwyneth that day had also involved an exchange of flowers, though in their case from the girl to the young man. And could more apt words than MacDonald's of Margaret be chosen to describe Gwyneth during those years when everyone thought her still a "child-maiden," but when in fact womanhood was slowly "waking in her eyes"? The similarities between the fictional characters of the novel and Percy's first summer in Wales were remarkable.

Florilyn set the book aside and drew in a long, reflective sigh. So much had changed since then. Percy had indeed become nature's friend. Gwyneth had grown from the child-maiden into a woman. She had become their maid for a season at the manor but was now gone from their lives. In Gwyneth's absence, Florilyn herself had become engaged to Percy. Who could have foreseen any of it five years ago?

With a deep breath, Florilyn returned to her place toward the end of the book and resumed her reading.

FOURTEEN

Contingency Plans

$\mathcal{E}$ver since her daughter's lighthearted banter about what they would do if Courtenay proved troublesome after acceding to the title, Katherine Westbrooke had been revolving an idea in her mind. The notion of living in a cottage in the hills may have sounded romantic to Florilyn, but it was not Katherine's idea of an attractive prospect. She needed no luxury—she could be happy even in a humble cottage. But she did not relish the idea of being so isolated and remote as they would be at the former Muir cottage. Especially with Roderick now gone, she needed to stay in contact with people, not only locally but with her brother and Mary in Glasgow. She needed the daily post and the option of easy travel that being near the coach and rail lines afforded.

On a day when she was certain that Courtenay would not learn of her movements, neither mentioning her plans to Florilyn or Steven or Adela, she requested of Steven a ride into the village to meet the northbound coach. She would be back the following day, she explained, when he could meet her again. She only told them that she must pay a visit to someone on the peninsula. She divulged nothing more.

Later that afternoon, she was seated in the office of Hamilton Murray, of Murray, Sidcup, and Murray. She came straight to the point. "I realize that you and I do not know one another extremely well, Mr. Murray," she began. "You were faithful to my husband, and I know he considered you a friend as well. However, as our son will himself be viscount in eighteen months, I realize that you are in a somewhat delicate position. Technically, for the present you represent me according to the terms of the trusteeship my husband established. In less than two years, however, you will be my son's solicitor. It may be that my son's interests and mine are not in harmony. He has, I believe, been to see you about finances."

"He has," nodded Murray.

"My question, then," Katherine went on, "is a simple one. How far may I trust you, Mr. Murray? If my present wishes were at odds with what might be considered my son's future best interest—or let me say, his most *lucrative* future interest—where would your loyalties lie?"

"I am the estate's solicitor," replied Murray. "At present I represent you. I will be faithful to carry out your wishes in whatever—"

"Please, Mr. Murray," interrupted Katherine. "I know a little at least about legal obfuscation. I need advice, and I need to know which side of the fence you are standing on. I need to know if I can trust you to give me advice that is in my best interest, despite the fact that doing so may prove awkward for you in the future when you find yourself representing my son. If not, I will seek that advice from an objective third party. I am asking you, as a man of integrity, to tell me candidly if you would be looking to your future professional relations with my son and the estate when he is viscount in how you advised *me* during this interim."

Murray took in her statement thoughtfully. The hint of a smile creased his lips. "Your husband knew what he was doing in making you trustee," he said at length. "You are very plain spoken, and I admire that. So I will be as well. I do not mean to offend you, Lady Snowdon, and please forgive my bluntness. . .but the fact is, I do not like your son. He may turn out to be wonderfully gracious and selfless, but at present I do not see such qualities manifesting themselves. It would grieve me to see him take actions that would hurt the estate or the people of the surrounding region. It thus behooves me to remain the solicitor for the Westbrooke estate if possible so that I might exert what influence lies open to me to keep that from happening. On the other hand, if I should offend him and should he choose to retain other counsel, I would not grieve overmuch. Though such is not always possible, I prefer to represent individuals whom I respect. I will not intentionally cross your son, but neither will I attempt to curry his favor. I hope my meaning is clear. My loyalties at present are entirely and un-equivocally to yourself and your late husband. I would not give a second's thought to whether your son would approve or disapprove of either your actions or my own."

"Very well," rejoined Katherine, "then I will lay out my predicament to you. I think it entirely possible that Courtenay will make life difficult for me once he inherits. It is not for myself alone that I am concerned but also for my daughter, and for my factor, the young man Steven Muir, and his mother, who also recently lost her husband. I have money, of course. Courtenay could do nothing to render me destitute, but he could make my life extremely unpleasant. It is not my desire to leave Westbrooke Manor. But I have to realize that such may become almost an inevitability once he is in control of everything. He is already angry with me at finding himself financially strapped—a condition which he lays at my feet rather than his own. He has essentially demanded money under threat of doing exactly what I said—making my life unbearable in the future. It breaks my heart to be at odds with him. He is my son, after all, and I love him. But I must also be realistic about my own future and make plans for myself should remaining at Westbrooke Manor become impossible."

"You do not seriously believe that he would throw you out?" said Murray. "I am not certain whether he even could do so legally. I shall have to look into the matter."

"I doubt he would try anything so drastic," said Katherine. "But he could make it a miserable place for me to live, especially after Florilyn is married and possibly gone. I could not remain where I was scorned and looked down upon. The awkwardness of it would be extreme."

"What do you have in mind?" asked the solicitor.

Katherine drew in a long breath. "I have been revolving in my mind a plan about which I would need your counsel and help," she went on after a moment. "I would like to secure a property, or perhaps several properties, that I could own in my own name, free and unencumbered by the estate. Would this be possible, such that they would be unassailable by Courtenay?"

"You could of course purchase any form of property you like in your own name," replied Murray.

"But all the land for miles in every direction is owned by the estate?"

"You are, I take it, planning to stay in the Llanfryniog region?"

"Such would be my intention. It is my home. Much, I suppose, would depend on Florilyn's future. If there were grandchildren, naturally I would want to be near her family. I confess it is my hope that Florilyn and her husband may remain in the area as well. As I said, I am thinking of trying to make provision for us all that will be free from Courtenay's potential interference."

"I see. So you are asking me how you might acquire land near your present home?"

Katherine nodded.

"As long as you are in control of the trusteeship, you can sell estate lands."

"Are you saying that I could sell land or a property owned by the estate. . .to myself?"

"That would be the simplest way. I see nothing legally that would stop you."

"And if I purchased a house in the village, say, or bought a parcel of acreage and built a new house upon it, with my own money, Courtenay could do nothing to evict me?"

"Provided we attend to all the proper legalities to be certain the deed is drawn up and registered to you, he would have no power over it whatever. The property would be yours."

"He would be furious, no doubt. He would see it as my having stolen a portion of his inheritance."

"There would be nothing he could do about it. And he would benefit from such a transaction. Essentially you would be buying the property from your son. As you know, the estate does not bring in a great income, a fact that was something of a trial for your late husband. Perhaps your son would be grateful."

Katherine nodded. "Somehow I doubt it," she said. "In any event, I think you have answered my question, Mr. Murray. I shall begin looking for suitable property where, if worse comes to worst, I may live out my years. You could, I assume, draw up all the necessary legal documents?"

"Certainly. The only stipulation in any such transaction is that you would have to pay the estate a fair market price so that your son could not later contest the sale in court. But that is easily managed. We would bring in an outside appraiser for just such a purpose."

"Then I will pay *more* than market price."

Katherine spent the night at a boardinghouse and returned on the southbound coach the next day. Even as she bounced through Llanfryniog beside Steven Muir on her way back to the manor, Katherine glanced about with new eyes, wondering where among the homes of the region she might make her future.

That same afternoon she went out for a long and thoughtful ride of several hours, through the streets of Llanfryniog and back along the plateau up to Mochras Head before returning inland to Westbrooke Manor. Her mind was full of many things.

FIFTEEN

David Elginbrod

florilyn was about four-fifths of the way through the novel, *David Elginbrod*. The title character was now dead. As she read, reminded of the death of her own father, Florilyn felt a fleeting bond with David's daughter, Margaret Elginbrod. But they were from such different stations. Margaret was a peasant. Try as she would, Florilyn could not quite put herself in Margaret's shoes.

Suddenly as she began reading the chapter entitled "The Lady's Maid," Florilyn realized, if she was going to place herself in the story at all, she was not the character of Margaret; she was *Euphra Cameron*—the spoiled aristocratic young woman Hugh Sutherland was enchanted with.

The realization was far from pleasant. Fictional though she was, Euphra was mean, self-centered, and petty. Hugh's fascination with her was one of the mysteries of the story.

With suddenly heightened interest, Florilyn read of Euphra's treatment of Margaret upon discovery of the personal letter she had written to David Elginbrod, not yet knowing him to be Margaret's father.

"Margaret had sought Euphra's room, with the intention
of restoring to her the letter which she had written. Hopes of
ministration filled Margaret's heart; but she expected, from what
she knew of her, that anger would be Miss Cameron's first feeling.

549

'What do you want?' she said angrily.

'This is your letter, Miss Cameron, is it not?' said Margaret, advancing with it in her hand.

Euphra took it, glanced at the direction, started up in a passion, and let loose the whole gathered irritability of contempt, weariness, disappointment, and suffering, upon Margaret. Her dark eyes flashed with rage.

'What right have you, pray, to handle my letters? How did you get this! And open, too. I declare! I suppose you have read it?'

Margaret was afraid of exciting more wrath before she had an opportunity of explaining; but Euphra gave her no time to think of a reply.

'You have read it, you shameless woman! Impudent prying! Pray, did you hope to find a secret worth a bribe?'

She advanced on Margaret till within a foot of her.

'Why don't you answer, you hussy?'

Margaret stood quietly, waiting for an opportunity to speak. Her face was very pale, but perfectly still, and her eyes did not quail.

'You do not know my name, Miss Cameron; of course you could not.'

'Your name! What is that to me?'

'That,' said Margaret, pointing to the letter, 'is my father's name.'

Euphra looked at her own direction again, and then looked at Margaret. She was so bewildered, that if she had any thoughts, she did not know them. Margaret went on:

'My father is dead. My mother sent the letter to me.'

'What is it to you? Do you think I am going to make a confidante of you?'"

Florilyn's heart smote her, and she could read no more. She put the book aside as tears filled her eyes.

She had been just like Euphra. She had treated poor Gwyneth the same way—rudely and angrily. If parallels with the story were to be drawn, Gwyneth was the saintly Margaret, and she was the unlovely Euphra.

She had changed, thought Florilyn to herself, and she thanked God for it. But there were times when the memory of what she had once been still made her cry. She had been shameful toward Gwyneth. Maybe she *was* Euphra after all!

Once the parallels with the story were clear, Florilyn saw them everywhere. It might as well have been a story set in Westbrooke Manor! On every page as she read over the ensuing days, as Margaret became Euphra's maid, as their friendship blossomed, as Euphra began to grow and change, and as it became clear that both girls were smitten with Hugh Sutherland, Florilyn was no longer reading about Margaret and Euphra. . .she was reading about herself and Gwyneth and Percy!

She was drawn into the story so deeply that she was living in it. What intrigue the love triangle took on in her mind! Of course Margaret and Euphra shared their feelings about Hugh far more openly than she and Gwyneth ever had about Percy.

> *"Margaret could not proceed very far in the story of her life without making some reference to Hugh Sutherland. But she carefully avoided mentioning his name.*
>
> *'Ah!' said Euphra, one day, 'your history is a little like mine there; a tutor comes into them both. Did you not fall dreadfully in love with him?'*
>
> *'I loved him very much.'*
>
> *'Do you never see him?'*
>
> *Margaret was silent. Euphra knew her well enough not to repeat the question.*
>
> *'I should have been in love with him, I know. . .Mr. Sutherland did me some good, Margaret.'*
>
> *'Mr. Sutherland loved you very much, Miss Cameron.'"*

It was exactly what dear Gwyneth might have said! Florilyn remembered when Gwyneth had urged Percy to go to the party at Burrenchobay Hall with her. Even as she continued her reading, the names on the page might have been Percival Drummond, Florilyn Westbrooke, and Gwyneth Barrie.

> "'He loved me once,' said poor Euphra, with a sigh.
> 'I saw he did. That was why I began to love you too.'
> Margaret had at last unwittingly opened the door of her secret. But Euphra could not understand what she meant.
> 'What do you mean, Margaret?'
> Margaret both blushed and laughed outright.
> 'I must confess it,' said she, at once; 'it cannot hurt him now: my tutor and yours are the same.'
> 'And you never spoke all the time he was here!'
> 'Not once. He never knew I was in the house.'
> 'How strange! And you saw he loved me?'
> 'Yes.'
> 'And you were not jealous?'
> 'I did not say that. But I soon found that the only way to escape from my jealousy, if the feeling I had was jealousy, was to love you too. I did.'
> 'You beautiful creature! But you could not have loved him much.'
> 'I loved him enough to love you for his sake.'
> It would have been unendurable to Euphra, a little while before, to find that she had a rival in a servant. Now she scarcely regarded that aspect of her position."

Again Florilyn put the book down thoughtfully. *Had* Gwyneth been in love with Percy? If so, she would never have divulged it.

SIXTEEN

Surveying the Landscape

Katherine Westbrooke's brain had been busy. She knew that time passed quickly. She must not unnecessarily delay whatever planned changes she hoped to make. She would have to complete all necessary legalities before Courtenay's twenty-fifth birthday or he would move to stop her in the courts. She hoped, as Hamilton Murray had suggested, that he might be grateful for the infusion of cash into the estate's coffers. However, she knew she mustn't bank on the unpredictable responses of a self-motivated and, as things presently stood, angry young man.

She therefore made a number of visits to the village and its environs, but thus far without inspiration coming to her.

The only home within miles that might have been considered large enough and suitable for the extended household of an aristocratic dowager viscountess was that occupied by Styles Lorimer and his wife and daughter, Rhawn, and her son. There were rumors that Mr. and Mrs. Lorimer were considering a move to southern England. But nothing was known for certain. It was doubtful they would make a decision anytime soon.

There were several sizeable farms within a mile or two of Llanfryniog. All were occupied, however, and she had no intention of evicting one of her tenants for the sake of her own potential future need.

Gradually the idea floated out of the mists to the surface of Katherine's thoughts. What was to prevent her building a new home instead? Florilyn's words returned to her memory: *"We shall build a second cottage to go with it."* If they could build a cottage, they could just as well build a house sizeable enough to suit all her needs, with stables and paddocks and pastures and meadows for whatever animals she wanted to raise, as well as quarters for Adela and Steven, and perhaps, she dared only hope, also for her daughter and family. Nothing so imposing or on the grand scale of the manor itself—her funds were not unlimited, nor were her tastes of an extravagant nature—but something large enough to be functional and comfortable for two or three families.

At length Katherine realized it was time she spoke with Florilyn, divulged what was on her mind, and canvassed her thoughts on the matter. A decision could possibly affect her future as well.

She waited until Courtenay was at Burrenchobay Hall visiting Colville Burrenchobay then sought Florilyn in her room. "I would like to talk to you, dear," she said, poking her head through the open doorway.

Florilyn glanced up from her book then laid it aside. "Of course, Mother," she said. "Come in. Your expression looks serious. Is something wrong?"

Katherine sat down in one of several chairs about the expansive room and drew in a long sigh. "It shows that plainly, does it?" she said with a melancholy smile.

"I don't always know *what* you are thinking," rejoined Florilyn. "But I can tell when you are downcast."

"It's about your brother," said Katherine. "He's much changed since your father's death."

"I know it only too well. I used to think we were friends. He's too snooty and full of himself to bother with the likes of me now. I hate the way he treats you, Mother."

"It's obvious he resents not being able to lord it over us. He thinks he should have been made viscount immediately. He also blames me for his present financial straits."

"It's not your fault that Daddy's not here to indulge him."

"He thinks it is my duty to continue doing so. The anger that is stewing inside him is worrisome to me. Honestly, Florilyn, I am very concerned for our future. You, of course, will be married. But I fear Courtenay may make my life so intolerable here that I may have no alternative but to find another place to live. We spoke about it almost jokingly before. I now fear it may be more likely than we thought. Leaving the manor may become a practical necessity."

"But the manor is *yours*, Mother."

"It won't be once Courtenay turns twenty-five."

"Where would you go?"

"I have been reflecting on what you said before, about us living in a cottage in the hills."

"I was just thinking out loud, Mother!" laughed Florilyn. "I didn't *really* think you would leave the manor."

"What if I have to? What would you think if I built a new house that would not be under Courtenay's control?"

Florilyn stared back at her mother without expression. "You mean. . . Where, Mother. . .on the grounds somewhere?" she said at length.

"I don't know. . .somewhere near the village, yet far enough from the manor where we could live our own lives."

Florilyn rose and wandered to her window. She stood with her back to her mother, looking out toward the hills of Snowdonia to the east and the plateau overlooking the waters of Tremadog Bay to the west. "You said *we*," she said at length.

"I know you will be married," rejoined Katherine. "But that may not take place before Courtenay's twenty-fifth birthday. . . . I don't know what your plans are. But do *you* relish the idea of being here after that?"

"We could live our own lives, Mother."

"What if he took it into his head to charge you rent?"

Florilyn spun around from the window. "He wouldn't dare!" she said.

"He might not be able to evict me because of my position, but I doubt there would be any restrictions on what he could do to you."

The two women were quiet for several moments.

"Then let's go for a ride, Mother," said Florilyn at length. "We shall look for a perfect place for your new home!"

An hour later, mother and daughter set out from Westbrooke Manor on Red Rhud and Crimson Son. They rode east, up the rising slope to the top of the inland ridge, then bore northward. From the height they had gained, the entire plateau below, stretching down to the village of Llanfryniog, and the blue waters of Tremadog Bay were visible, with their own Westbrooke Manor and its grounds and gardens below and to their left.

"What a beautiful site this would be for a home!" exclaimed Katherine as they rode, with the sea and coastline all spread out below.

"You would have to build a road all the way up here, Mother."

"A road would be more easily managed than building a house! If it were to be *your* home, Florilyn—and who is to say that it wouldn't be one day—and if you could live anywhere in the entire region, where would *you* choose?"

Florilyn reined in and gazed all about. "That is a hard question, Mother," she said. "But. . .let me see. . . I do love the mountains. But then there is snow in the winter when you get too far inland. And the sight of the sea is spectacular. Just think what it would be to have all your windows overlooking the ocean."

Florilyn's thoughts drifted back to an hour earlier when she and her mother had been talking in her room, and the view as she was standing at the window. "Probably down there, Mother," she said after a minute. She pointed from their high vantage point to the plateau of Mochras Head. "On the headland overlooking the sea."

Katherine followed her daughter's outstretched arm. Slowly she began to nod. "Yes, I see. . .it would be a spectacular site for a home. Closer to the manor," she added, "but also near to the village and main road. Shall we go have a closer look? I may like your idea."

She turned Crimson Son down the slope in the direction of the sea, and Florilyn followed.

SEVENTEEN

The Revelation of the Fir Wood

Florilyn reached the last chapter of her book. As she began reading, her eyes grew wide.

It wasn't only that two girls both loved Hugh Sutherland. Hugh had to discover which of the two *he* really loved. . .and had loved all along.

A sudden pang seized Florilyn's heart. It was *not* the aristocratic Euphra that in the end took possession of Hugh's heart, but the peasant girl Margaret!

"*She was the angel herself,*" she read on the page.

Percy often called Gwyneth an angel.

Hugh at length discovered that he had loved Margaret from the first day in the fir wood. Was her own fate, Florilyn mused, destined to be the same as Euphra's? Loving. . .would *she*, too, have to let him go?

> "*It was with a mingling of strange emotions that Hugh approached the scene of those not very old, and yet, to his feeling, quite early memories. The dusk was beginning to gather. The hoar-frost lay thick on the ground. The pine-trees stood up in the cold.*
>
> *Here and there amongst them, rose the Titans of the little forest—the huge, old, contorted, wizard-like, yet benevolent*

beings—the Scotch firs. Towards one of these he bent his way. It was the one under which he had seen Margaret, when he met her first in the wood. To think that the young girl to whom he had given the primrose he had just found should now be the queen of his heart! Her childish dream of the angel haunting the wood had been true, only she was the angel herself. He drew near the place. How well he knew it! He seated himself, cold as it was in the February of Scotland, at the foot of the blessed tree.

While he sat with his eyes fixed on the ground, a light rustle in the fallen leaves made him raise them suddenly. It was all winter and fallen leaves about him; but he lifted his eyes, and in his soul it was summer: Margaret stood before him. She looked just the same—at home everywhere; most at home in Nature's secret chamber.

She came nearer.

'Margaret!' he murmured.

She came close to him. He rose, trembling.

'Margaret, dare I love you?' he faltered.

She looked at him with wide-open eyes.

'Me?' exclaimed Margaret, and her eyes did not move from his. A slight rose-flush bloomed out on her motionless face.

She looked at him with parted lips.

'Do you remember this?' she said, taking from her pocket a little book, and from the book a withered flower.

Hugh saw that it was like a primrose, and hoped against hope that it was the one which he had given to her, on the spring morning in the fir-wood.

'Why did you keep that?' he said.

'Because I loved you.'

'Loved me?'

'Yes. Didn't you know?'

'Why did you say, then, that you didn't care if—if—?'

'Because love is enough, Hugh.—That was why.'"

Tears flooded Florilyn's eyes. The deepest love had not come as Hugh had expected it. He *thought* he had loved Euphra. But his heart had belonged to Margaret all along. In the same way, Percy *thought* he was in love with her.

But from the beginning. . .since his first days in Wales. . .had his heart always belonged—?

Florilyn burst into sobs. She could not complete the thought. She closed the book, rose, and went to her window. She stood for several minutes but could not stop the flow of tears.

At length she left her room and walked down the corridor away from the main staircase, seeking the back stairs and door to the outside that Percy had himself used many times. The cool air felt good on her hot face. But it could not still the turmoil in her heart.

With the weather turning increasingly cold and damp, for the next several weeks Florilyn made the approaching winter her companion in melancholy. For hours she walked along the Mochras promontory staring down at the gray sea below or along the chilly misty beach beneath the headland or in the gardens of the manor or woods nearer home. Daily she visited little Nugget, who recognized her voice and came scampering at her call.

Not having been a great reader, Florilyn had never before experienced the power of a book to move the human heart so deeply. But this story, and the interwoven lives of its two young women loving the same young man, along with the fictional fir wood, which in her mind had become the fields and hills of North Wales, pressed heavily upon her heart.

At length she knew what she had to do.

She must let Percy discover his own fir wood. . .and who was the angel awaiting him there.

Eighteen

Wales Again

*A*s Percy and his mother and father sat clattering south in the train from Glasgow, Percy could not escape the feeling that something beyond a festive Christmas celebration awaited him in Wales. It would be going too far to call it a sense of impending doom. Yet perhaps something a little like it.

"You're uncommonly quiet, Percy," said his mother on the afternoon of their first day of the journey.

"Sorry, Mother," smiled Percy. "A lot on my mind I suppose."

"School?"

"No, not really. It's going well, though I am anticipating graduating in May with more than a little eagerness."

"You still haven't said what you will do after you and Florilyn are married—go to work for Mr. Snyder or begin law school."

"That's because I haven't decided myself. Actually, I may do neither. There's something. . .I have to take care of—a personal matter. I don't know how long it will take."

"What is it?" asked Mrs. Drummond.

"I can't say, Mother," answered Percy. He glanced toward his father. "I told Dad about it last summer and said the same thing—that I couldn't tell him the specifics. It's something I promised Uncle Roderick I would look into before he died. I have no idea what will be involved or how long it will take. Beyond that, I can say nothing. I promised it would remain between him and me."

It was quiet a few minutes. Percy stared out the window at the passing countryside and at last let out a long sigh. "But it's more than that," he said, turning again toward his mother. "Something seems to have changed with Florilyn in recent weeks."

"How do you mean, Percy?" asked Mary.

"I don't know. It's hard to put my finger on. Her letters have just been. . .different—distant, detached, almost formal in a way. We were writing back and forth regularly, sharing about everything—it was like talking with each other in person. We've both been reading the same MacDonald novel—I told you about that—and discussing it in our letters. All of a sudden last month I didn't hear from her for two weeks. When at last another letter came, like I said, it was different. It's been that way ever since. She's not mentioned the book again. She says almost nothing personal. It's altogether strange."

"She is probably just nervous about getting married."

"Why would she be, Mother? I thought all young women longed to be married."

Mary laughed. "You are probably right. I was just trying to find a logical explanation."

"I know it's pointless to worry about it," said Percy. "I'm sure it will all come clear soon enough. She says she has something important to talk to me about. Whatever it is, I know she will tell me in her own way. But the change in her letters has been disconcerting."

The three Christmas travelers in the southbound coach bounded to a stop in front of Mistress Chattan's inn on the following day. The main street through Llanfryniog lay in mud from one side to the other. A chill wind swept up from the sea, bending the smoke from every chimney in the village horizontal toward the inland mountains, by now all covered with snow.

Percy's previous visits to Snowdonia had come in summer, when the land and air were rich and full of warmth and growth and life. As he stepped out of the coach onto the muddy street and glanced about, a drearier prospect could hardly be imagined. As a Scot, he knew well enough what winter could be like. He had left Aberdeen four days earlier with snowdrifts piled three feet high along the sides of the streets. He had somehow hoped, this far south, that it might be warmer. One look up and down the familiar street, however, told him instantly how wrong he had been. Even snowdrifts would be preferable to mud.

A two-seat carriage from the manor sat just up the street waiting for them. Inside, bundled in coats and hats and scarves and blankets, sat Katherine and Florilyn.

As Edward climbed down from one side of the coach, and Percy emerged out the door of the other, Steven Muir ran along the walkway beside the inn to meet them.

"Stevie!" exclaimed Percy as the two shook hands.

"Welcome back to Wales, Percy," said Steven. "And to you, Mr. Drummond," he added to Edward.

"It is good to see you once again, Steven," said Edward. "I understand congratulations are in order for your new position at the manor."

"Thank you," replied Steven. "Your sister has been very kind to me. Hello, Mrs. Drummond," he added as Edward helped Percy's mother to the ground. "Lady Katherine and Lady Florilyn are there in the carriage," he said, pointing ahead. "I told them to stay bundled up. You may go get settled with them if you like. We brought extra blankets. I will see to your bags."

The three made their way along the walkway to the waiting carriage. As they approached, the two women set aside the blankets that had been spread over their knees and stepped to the ground.

"Mary. . .Edward!" said Katherine, approaching with open arms. "I'm sorry we aren't able to welcome you with a more pleasant day."

"Winter in Britain is a universal trial to us all!" laughed Edward. "We Scots are used to it, you know as well as I do. We both grew up in worse than this."

Behind her mother, Florilyn shook hands with her aunt and uncle then glanced toward Percy where he waited at their side.

"Florilyn!" he said, bounding forward and wrapping her in his arms.

She said nothing, slowly stretching her arms around his back, though without corresponding pressure to answer his embrace. They stepped back. Florilyn smiled, though somewhat awkwardly, then turned toward the carriage. The others followed. Whether it was by design or accident, Florilyn scrambled onto the rear bench between her mother and aunt, seemingly by intent to avoid finding herself at Percy's side, while father and son took their places in front.

A moment later Steven jumped up to join them, sat down between the two men, grabbed the reins, and they were off. The ride of a mile and a half passed quickly. Before they knew it, the gray stones of Westbrooke Manor were looming through the bare trees before them.

NINETEEN

A Conversation in the Library

The three Drummonds had arrived at Westbrooke Manor on the morning before Christmas Eve. Percy returned to town with Steven to retrieve their bags. By the time they returned and were safely back inside, it had begun to rain and the temperature had dropped several degrees. There was no talk of walks or rides outside for the rest of the day.

The company remained indoors and mostly together after lunch and for most of the afternoon. Courtenay, however, did not grace their Scottish guests with the honor of his presence.

Even though they were together nearly the entire rest of the day, Percy and Florilyn were never alone, and their conversation remained light. Florilyn was friendly though subdued. By day's end, Percy was more convinced than ever that something was amiss.

Florilyn made no appearance on Christmas Eve morning in the breakfast room. She had never been an early riser. Nevertheless, Percy was surprised. As much as they had anticipated seeing each other, it was almost—though how could that be—as if she were avoiding him. Her exuberance after his arrival on his previous two visits was nowhere in evidence.

Early in the afternoon, Percy wandered to the library. The familiar sights and smells greeted him with a wave of pleasant nostalgia. He smiled as he breathed in deeply then began absently wandering through the rows of tall shelves, glancing up and down and sideways at the spines of the old volumes. He was in no frame of mind at the moment to sit down and read, though he recalled fondly his first excursion into this bookish wonderland more than five years before when his aunt had first introduced him to author George MacDonald.

He turned a corner at the end of the row of shelves and saw a figure in an alcove with her back turned. She stood staring out the tall bay window. This time it was not his aunt but the young woman whose quiet behavior had been occupying his thoughts. Slowly he approached from behind. "A penny for your thoughts," said Percy softly.

Florilyn heard his step and was not startled by his voice. She remained still as a statue.

Percy came to her side and stood looking out upon the wet, dreary winter's day. It was an altogether depressing outlook. It was nothing, however, compared to the desolation at that moment in Florilyn Westbrooke's heart.

They stood for a long while in silence.

Finally Percy turned toward her. His movement at last broke the pent-up dam in Florilyn's heart. She turned to face him with the most forlorn expression he had ever seen on her face. The look in her eyes was pleading. . .fearful for what she knew she must do.

"Oh, Percy!" she said as she broke into tears.

Still with no idea what was the cause of her dismay, Percy said nothing. He merely opened his arms and received her into his embrace. Florilyn laid her head on his chest and softly wept.

They stood thus for several minutes until the initial storm passed. After some time Percy led her to a small couch in one of the library's several reading nooks. They sat down together. He waited.

"There is something I must talk to you about," said Florilyn at length. Her voice was shaky and halting.

"I know," said Percy, smiling.

"You know?"

"I knew *something* was on your mind. Your letters changed. I knew you would tell me when you were ready."

"Oh Percy, I'm sorry. I should have told you sooner. I didn't know what to say. I wanted to wait until I saw you. But once I did see you yesterday I was filled with so many doubts and fears and I didn't want to hurt you. I didn't know what to do."

"You have nothing to fear from me," he said. "Surely you know that."

"I know, Percy," rejoined Florilyn. "You are so good to me. You were always better to me than I deserved."

"Now don't let's get started on that again!" said Percy with a light laugh. "We've been over all that before."

"You know what I mean. I'm just grateful, that's all."

"So what is it you have to tell me? Let's get it out. It's Christmas Eve, you know. Big dinner planned tonight. We don't want to cast a pall over the festivities."

"It's not so easy," said Florilyn with a sad smile. She drew in a deep breath and exhaled slowly. "Oh, Percy. . . I love you so much. You know that, don't you?"

"I do," replied Percy. "The feeling is mutual."

"That's what makes it so hard. Percy. . . How much of the MacDonald novel have you read? You haven't finished it, have you?"

"I'm afraid not. I bogged down probably about halfway. There's always a big push with papers and assignments before the Christmas break. Why? What does the book have to do with it?"

"Everything. Didn't you see the similarities in it. . .you know, with us. . .between you and Hugh and everything?"

"Hmm. . .actually, no," said Percy thoughtfully. "You think I am like Hugh?"

"You aren't *like* him—but the circumstances. . .his going to university in Aberdeen just like you. . .his meeting Margaret."

"I, uh. . .I didn't think about that. And you see a parallel between you and Margaret?"

"Not me. . .Gwyneth."

He stared back at her, confused at the point she was trying to make. "In the story, Hugh. . . ," Percy began. "Hugh is in love with Euphra," he said. "What does Margaret have to do with it?"

"He *thinks* he is in love with Euphra," rejoined Florilyn. "Oh Percy, this would be so much simpler if you had read the ending. It's all in the book."

"All what?"

"Oh, Percy!" Florilyn blurted out. "I think we may have made a mistake!"

Percy looked at her in disbelief.

Again Florilyn began to cry.

"You. . .don't think we should marry?"

"That's not it! I can't imagine anything more wonderful than being your wife. Who wouldn't want to be your wife? But I think maybe we rushed into it too quickly. Perhaps we *are* meant to be husband and wife. But I think we decided too fast. I suppose that. . . Well, I'm not *completely* sure I'm in love with you, Percy. I mean. . .I *do* love you, but. . .I think I may have been, I don't know, so flattered that you asked me to marry you, that maybe I was too caught up with the *idea* of being in love that I never stopped to ask myself if I was *actually* in love with you. I thought I was, all those years after your first visit. But once we were engaged, and after finishing the book. . .I just wasn't sure anymore. I'm so sorry. And then. . .I also cannot help asking. . .whether you are truly in love with me." She paused.

Percy waited, still reeling from what he had heard.

"Do you remember telling me about you and your father talking about how God uses circumstances to lead us in making decisions?"

Percy nodded. "Of course," he replied softly.

"What I have been sensing," Florilyn went on, "is that perhaps we rushed too quickly into it last July. Perhaps we misinterpreted what the changing circumstances were supposed to mean."

"What changing circumstances?" asked Percy.

"Gwyneth's leaving," answered Florilyn. "You told me then that you had to wrestle through what it meant."

"I remember. And I did wrestle through it," said Percy. "What does Gwyneth have to do with it now?"

"Percy!" said Florilyn almost in frustration. "She has everything to do with it. *She* is the reason we have to wait. I should say she is the reason *you* have to wait. I have to wait to be sure of my *own* heart. We both have to wait for different reasons. Don't you see? You *think* you wrestled it through, but it was only a week. Then the decision was made. I'm not sure that was enough time for either of us to fully know our hearts."

Percy exhaled a long sigh. "I think I see what you mean. . .in principle at least. The idea is going to take some getting used to. I still don't see what you mean about Gwyneth and the MacDonald book."

"Gwyneth is Margaret in the book, Percy! Hugh thought he was in love with Euphra. . .but all along he was meant to discover his love for *Margaret*. Don't you see? In the same way, what if part of your heart still belongs to Gwyneth? You have to find out. You have to discover what is deep in your heart, just as I have to discover what is in mine."

Percy sat staring back at Florilyn dumbfounded. Slowly he began shaking his head. "I—I don't know what to say," he said softly.

"Finish reading the book, Percy," said Florilyn. "Then you will understand."

"What do you want to do then?"

"I think you should talk it over with your father," replied Florilyn. "Then I think we should simply call off the engagement. . .for now at least. Please understand, this doesn't mean that my feelings for you have changed. But I have to be sure about those feelings. I have to be *certain* I am in love with you. And I want you to discover your own fir wood."

"My. . .fir wood?"

"Finish the book, Percy. You have to find out who is the angel waiting for you in the fir wood."

"I will talk to my father," he said, nodding. "He will probably want to talk to us both. I'm sure he will want to hear what you are thinking from your own lips." Percy rose and walked again to the window. "It looks like the rain may be letting up," he said. "Perhaps we shall get a ride in eventually."

"It's still chilly out," rejoined Florilyn. "It was so cold yesterday I was surprised to wake up this morning and not see snow on the ground. I was certain snow was in the air."

Percy turned and walked back to the couch. He extended his hand. Florilyn took it, and he pulled her to her feet. "We're still friends, right?" he said, trying to sound upbeat, though still more than a little confused by this sudden turn of events.

"Oh Percy, we will always be much more than just friends! It is only that I want to be sure that we read God's leading in the right way. Marriage is too important to rush into."

"Then we will continue to talk and pray. . .and talk to my father. In the meantime, why don't we bundle up and go outside, and you can introduce me to this new colt of Grey Tide's that you are so fond of."

TWENTY

Edward Drummond

*H*aving disclosed the burdens that were pressing upon her, Florilyn's spirits immediately lifted. She was gay and lively again. After dressing for it, they went outside to visit Percy's old friends in the stables, as well as little Nugget who was growing rapidly. It took Percy an hour or two, however, to absorb and readjust to the suddenly altered outlook on his future.

Midway through the afternoon, as the women were busy with Adela Muir and Mrs. Drenwydd and Mrs. Llewellyn in the kitchen and dining room with Christmas food preparation and decorating, Percy sought his father. "Dad," he said, "there's something important I need to talk to you about. Could we go for a walk outside? It's not raining at the minute. I need your advice."

As she had once before, Florilyn watched from one of the windows as Percy and his father, bundled up against the cold, walked away from the house in earnest conversation. A fresh wave of sadness enveloped her. A few rapid misty blinks of her eyes followed. She could not prevent a nagging fear that she had relinquished her best and only chance to be married at all. But mostly she was relieved to have at last released the anxiety that had consumed her for weeks. Whatever the future held, she knew she had done the *right* thing. She was content now to leave the matter in the hands of the two men and God.

She turned away and tried to distract herself with candles and ribbons and the Christmas tree and a few last gifts to wrap. But it was no use. She could think of nothing but the conversation taking place outside.

At length she went upstairs to her room. In her present frame of mind, she would rather be alone. Absently she picked up a book and sat down in her favorite chair and tried to read. But she could not concentrate.

She started at the sound of a knock on her door twenty minutes later. She jumped up and ran to it.

There stood Percy. "Hi," he said with an almost embarrassed expression. "My dad would like to talk to you. . .both of us, actually."

"Sure," nodded Florilyn and left the room with him.

They walked in silence together. Florilyn's spirits were subdued. She felt awkward beside Percy's somber silence. It was so unlike him. She feared for what he might be thinking. He led her into the small sitting room adjoining the guest room where his parents were staying.

Edward Drummond stood at the window, his back to them as they entered. It was a big afternoon for staring out of windows. He turned at the sound of the door and strode across the floor. Whatever Florilyn might have been expecting, an affectionate greeting from Percy's father was not it. A warm smile spread over his face, and he embraced her with genuine feeling. "My dear!" he said, holding her tightly. As he released her and stepped back, Florilyn saw tears in his eyes. He smiled again as he blinked hard. "Shall we sit down?" he said. "We have important matters to talk and pray about."

They took seats on the couch and two chairs, and Edward resumed. "Percy has told me a little of your predicament, shall we call it," he said. "Out of faithfulness to you, he did not want to divulge too much. He felt I ought to hear whatever you were comfortable telling me yourself. I realize you do not know me so intimately—I have probably always just been a distant uncle to you. But I hope you will be able to trust me. My only desire is to help the two of you discover what is God's will. I will say or do nothing stemming from any motives of my own other than to help you know what is in your hearts and know what is best for you to do. Do you think you can trust me?"

"I will try, Uncle Edward," replied Florilyn. "I believe I can. I trust Percy, and he trusts you. So how can I not trust you, also?"

"Then why don't you explain to me what you have been thinking?"

Florilyn took a deep breath. It was quiet a few moments as she composed her thoughts. "In a way," she began, casting a half-nervous, half-humorous smile toward Percy's father, "it's your fault, Uncle Edward. . .and my mother's. It all began with a George MacDonald novel I read, which I would never have done if you two weren't talking about him all the time."

"Ah, yes," smiled the vicar. "Which one of his books was it?"

"*David Elginbrod.*"

The vicar nodded. "One of my favorites. MacDonald does have a way of probing the heart through his characters, does he not?"

"I've never read a book that drew me into it so completely," said Florilyn. "By the time I was finished, I wasn't reading about MacDonald's characters at all but about Percy and me." She paused and again drew in a thoughtful breath. "Percy told me about a conversation you and he had about circumstances," she began again. "He said you talked about going slow, about how God uses circumstances to make his will clear but that you have to be careful not to imbue circumstances with *too* much significance, either, because you never know for *certain* whether God is speaking through them. That's why, Percy said, you always told him that God is never in a hurry, that we must give God as much time as possible to clarify what the circumstances are supposed to mean."

"Very eloquently put, my dear," said Edward. "I doubt if I said it so clearly myself."

"It has remained with me ever since," Florilyn went on. "Then as I read the MacDonald novel, the sense grew upon me that perhaps Percy and I had been hastier than we should have been and perhaps *hadn't* given God enough time. I knew I had to talk to him, though it was one of the hardest things I have ever done." She cast Percy an apologetic smile. She then went on to tell her uncle about Gwyneth's leaving and of the similarities she had seen in the story with their own circumstances.

At length the room fell silent. Florilyn was in tears. But they were good tears.

"My first response," said Edward after a minute or two, "is to commend you for your honesty and fortitude. What you have done in voicing your reservation is not something most young people have the courage to do. I know Percy feels the same. As painful as this time may be for both of you, he admires what you have done."

Florilyn glanced with an expression of question toward Percy where he sat. "Is that really true, Percy?" she said.

"Absolutely."

"I thought you were angry with me."

"Not for a second. Like Dad says, sure it is painful. But how could I not admire you? He's right—it took courage. It shows that you were trying to listen to God's voice."

Florilyn smiled, though almost bashfully. She was not accustomed to being praised for spiritual virtue—especially by a vicar and his son!

"However God leads in the end," Edward went on, "slowing down the process is always a good thing. There is never a disadvantage to going slow if there is the slightest doubt about a course of action. It is fearfully easy to run ahead of God. But he is never in a rush. Even should it turn out that it is indeed God's will for the two of you to marry, this pause for prayerful reevaluation will only make that decision stronger in the end."

TWENTY-ONE

Boxing Day in Llanfryniog

*T*he three left the room a short time later. Edward told his wife and sister that he and the young people had an important matter to discuss with them. Meal preparations and decorating was suspended. When at last everything was out in the open, Florilyn's tears had passed. She was at last ready to join in the revelry of the Christmas spirit.

The reaction of the two mothers at the news that the engagement of their son and daughter had been called off, however, was one of melancholy and a good many tears. In light of Florilyn's near gaiety, and that neither did Percy seem shattered by the turn of events, they did not ask too many questions. Both secretly hoped to get more enlightenment privately from Edward later.

The afternoon progressed. The mood of Katherine Westbrooke and Mary Drummond remained subdued. But gradually the festive spirit returned to the household. By the time they sat down with their guests and members of the household for a lavish Christmas Eve dinner, all hints of the low spirits from earlier in the day were gone.

Around the table in the formal dining room sat Katherine, Courtenay, and Florilyn Westbrooke; Edward, Mary, and Percy Drummond; Adela and Steven Muir, with Hollin Radnor; Mrs. Drynwydd, Katherine's cook; Mrs. Llewellyn, the housekeeper; and Jeremiah Broakes, the Westbrooke butler. The only one of the number who did not seem to be entering into the spirit of the season was Courtenay. He had finally made a belated appearance but was annoyed in the extreme to be seated at the same table with staff and servants.

The women pitched in to clean up after dinner. The assembly then retired to the formal sitting room. The remainder of Christmas Eve was spent in lively conversation, singing carols, and exchanging a few gifts. Once the dinner had time to settle, Christmas cake and warm mulled wine punch were brought in from the kitchen to cap off the pleasant evening.

After the early morning church services and celebrations of song, Christmas day for most households in Wales was a family affair. It was a quiet day to enjoy the giving of simple gifts along with good food, warm fires, hot tea, here and there a toddy, and usually an afternoon nap to make up for the sleep lost to the early morning. By the end of the day, no one was actually hungry for an evening meal, though most went through the ritual of nibbling at the platters of ham or roast turkey or pheasant, with perhaps a fresh mince pie or plum pudding added to what was left of the fruit cake from the day before.

A thoughtful mood settled over the manor as its inhabitants returned from the village in the cold shortly after daybreak. Most climbed back upstairs to their rooms, some to sleep, some to read, some to ponder what the day represented. Edward's prayer and words of the night before had given them much to consider. But mostly they were thinking of loved ones—of what was, what had been, and what never would be again. It was after a quiet, and for some a melancholy, morning that brought sad reminders of hidden heartaches to tinge the day's glories with invisible pain.

Katherine was full of the remembrance of Christmases past—with a family of four. Now that family had dwindled to three, and for all Courtenay's grumpiness it might as well be only two.

As she sat alone in her sitting room, a distant sound caused her heart to leap. She was reminded of the happy shouts of a boy's excited voice. Memories flooded her mind. . .of the Christmas morning she and Roderick had taken nine-year-old Courtenay outside and presented him his very own first pony. It was one of the happiest Christmases ever.

The sound came again. With a wistful sigh, she realized it was only a door closing somewhere. No sounds of children would enliven this day and bring joy to her mother's heart. Those days were gone. Courtenay was no longer nine. He was an angry young man of twenty-three who cherished no fond or loving thoughts toward her.

There had been many strains in their family over the years. But they had always enjoyed Christmas as a happy time. Now she was a widow. She was estranged from her son. Though surrounded by many who loved her, she could not help feeling isolated. . .even alone. She knew she should be happy. But she could not help feeling stabs of loneliness.

Florilyn had been relieved the previous afternoon after unburdening herself to Percy and his father. When she awoke on Christmas morning, however, a wave of melancholy swept into her heart like an incoming tide. Her feelings were more fragile than she realized. Percy's reaction to their talk, and his demeanor through the rest of the day and evening, had unsettled her.

What she had expected, she could not have said. Perhaps she was surprised at how quickly he had accepted her decision. Had she wanted him to protest with more vigor? Had she hoped he would try to talk her out of suspending the engagement? Had she wanted Percy to protest and say that he was desperately in love with her and that nothing would dissuade him from marrying her?

On the other hand, if he had seemed more devastated, she might have steeled herself to be strong and supportive. But now less than a day later, he was behaving as if nothing had happened. For all she had said about God's will and knowing what they were doing was right, why hadn't he fought a little harder against it? Didn't Percy know how hard this was for her? If she didn't know better, she would think that he was *glad* to have the engagement called off!

So sure of herself yesterday, suddenly her emotions were playing tricks on her, turning themselves upside down and inside out with no logic or rhyme or reason. She didn't know what she thought or what she felt.

On his part, Percy likewise woke on Christmas morning to an inrush of confusion. He had spent half the night tossing and turning and trying to come to grips with Florilyn's decision. He had done his best to hide his turmoil by acting normal. He would need to come to terms with the sudden change in his own way. He would go for rides and walks and spend time alone, thinking and praying on his own. In the meantime, having no idea that doing so only made her think he cared less than he did, he determined to put Florilyn at ease by being as cheerful as possible. He would not add to her burden by being downcast himself.

In her own room in another part of the house, Mrs. Drynwydd prepared for her own private Christmas ritual. Alone and with her door closed, she removed from her bureau a wooden box whose red paint was worn and dulled by the passage of years. She carried it to her rocking chair, sat down, and, with lips already quivering, unlatched and lifted off its top.

Her eyes began to moisten the moment they fell on the familiar contents—love letters from a time long ago, when she was young and the hopes and dreams of life all lay ahead, the envelopes containing them brittle and yellowed with age; a few trinkets of jewelry, Christmas gifts from her husband; two or three tree ornaments; a pair of baby shoes; and finally a tiny white china doll. She had labored over the dress of yellow and red for months before the Christmas when her daughter was six. Never had a girl loved a doll so much! She carried it with her nearly every moment for the next year and slept with it cuddled beside her under her blankets every night for the rest of her brief life.

Before her twelfth birthday, her daughter was dead, and her husband with her. Whether Christmas was celebrated in heaven, Elvira Drynwydd didn't know. But she tried to comfort herself with the thought that at least they were together.

Laying the doll in her lap, she reached across to the table at her right and picked up a small silver music box. It had also been a gift from her husband. Slowly she wound its key then again set it beside her. Listening to its haunting strains on Christmas morning did not make her happy. Every year the pain of memories brought fresh tears. But she had to remember. Love never forgets.

With her daughter's doll pressed to her breast, the wife and mother who now celebrated Christmas alone rocked gently back and forth. Softly she mouthed the words, *"Silent night, holy night. . .all is calm, all is bright,"* to the simple melody that for many brought joy but caused her heart to ache more deeply than at any other time of year. . .and quietly wept.

All through the great house, others of the extended manor family found themselves similarly reflecting on the hopes and disappointments the season inevitably brings—homesickness not for a place, but for the innocent world of childhood. Family sorrows and broken relationships and bittersweet reminders of lost loved ones, all intruded minor chords into the carols of Bethlehem, reminding one and all that in the midst of its celebration, Christmas brings pangs of regret. . .and yearnings for what can never be again. The great house was still. No children's voices, no happy shouts, no scampering footsteps reverberated within its rooms and corridors. Only memories echoing with silent nostalgic dissonance against the empty walls of longing hearts.

As they gathered in midafternoon for the Christmas meal, Katherine bowed her head and herself led them in prayer. "Father God," she prayed, "we come to You with hearts full of gratitude for the gift of Your Son and the gift of Yourself You have provided for us. We thank You for this day and for all it represents in our lives. Yet some of us also come to You on this day with heavy hearts for the sorrow of losses of those we love and even with uncertainties for the future. We ask that You will enable us to grow through these heartaches and allow our fears and unknowns and our silent burdens make us into the people You want us to be." She paused.

The dining room was silent.

"Make us into Your people, heavenly Father," she added softly. "Amen."

Beside her, Adela reached over and took her hand. She smiled and mouthed a silent, *Thank you.* The two women understood each other.

The loss of a husband or wife is never so difficult as on the special days of the year. Though many avoid speaking of those who are gone, those who loved them hunger to hear their names spoken aloud. Mrs. Llewellyn, too, was also thinking of her departed husband. Even Hollin Radnor and stoic Jeremiah Broakes experienced twinges of melancholy to be reminded again of life's joys and sorrows and of mothers and fathers now passed from the earth.

"I'm sorry, Edward," said Katherine. "I didn't mean to usurp your role as head of the family, not to mention as a minister. But I felt I needed to pray."

"It was a beautiful prayer, Katherine," said Edward. "It must be hard for you to celebrate Christmas with Roderick gone. And you, Adela—I'm sorry, I've forgotten how to pronounce your husband's name."

"Glythvyr," said Adela with a quiet smile.

"Ah yes," nodded Edward. "Well, God bless them both and bless their memories in your hearts."

Both housekeeper and cook were also thinking of their husbands but said nothing.

Katherine had been taught by her parents, and had learned from her own experience, that the best antidote for personal sorrow is service to others. Midway through the meal she explained her scheme for the remainder of the day, and the day that would follow—a day when those of means traditionally boxed up gifts and food to share with those less fortunate. "Tomorrow is Boxing Day," she began. "I have plans for us all. I want us to visit every home in the village, and the surrounding crofts, with gifts of good cheer. I have been ordering food and drink and gifts from purveyors throughout Wales and northern England. Regular shipments have been arriving at the manor for two months in preparation. I have also been keeping our ladies busy in the kitchen baking Christmas cakes and puddings. They probably thought I was preparing for seven years of famine!" She looked at Mrs. Llewellyn with a smile.

The housekeeper glanced toward Mrs. Drynwydd, and both ladies nodded their heads and returned her smile.

"So we will all pitch in this afternoon and tomorrow, preparing the hampers, and then tomorrow deliver them. I want someone from the manor to visit every house and cottage in Llanfryniog with a gift in remembrance of the season. We will take Christmas hampers to those most in need and a bottle of sherry or port to the rest. Hollin knows every man, woman, and child for miles around. He has been helping me with this. In addition, each household will receive ten pounds and a note personally from me."

She paused. A far-off look came into her eye, followed by the rising of a few tears. "I've not told any of you this," she said, "but several months after Roderick's death, Mr. Murray surprised me by delivering to me a check for £1,000. He said it was from a life insurance policy Roderick had taken out. I had never heard of such a thing. I asked him what life insurance meant. He told me that Roderick had paid to have his life insured, such that if anything happened to him I would receive the amount in question. I still did not entirely understand. Roderick knew that I would not be in need. Yet for whatever reason, he chose to do it. I can only believe that he would be pleased if I were to use it, not for myself, but for our people. Therefore, I determined that I would use this money in some way that would reflect the love he had come to have late in his life for our community."

Her voice became husky, and she brushed at her eyes. "Sometimes it is not until a person is gone," she went on, "that we reflect on who they really were. We come perhaps to know them better in death in some ways even than we did in life. I want to honor the good that was in Roderick by telling the people that the gifts of these ten pound notes are from him, from money he left for me to use for the village he loved."

When dinner was completed, the extended family of Westbrooke Manor, the three families of Westbrookes, Drummonds, and Muirs, along with those of the staff who lived at the manor, gathered in Katherine's sitting room. In the last month it had become a warehouse of goods and wrapping supplies, with boxes of food and cases of sherry and port stacked everywhere. There they began the happy work of assembling and filling some fifty wicker hampers with cured hams, cheeses, crackers, biscuits, Christmas cakes and puddings, and other assorted edible treats to be enjoyed on New Year's Day, a day of yet greater feasting and celebration, with many of its own unique traditions, even than Christmas itself. After she set the work in motion, Katherine sat down at a writing table on one side of the room and continued the task she had begun some days before of writing out nearly a hundred brief notes of Christmas greeting to be included with each gift along with a ten-pound note.

Conversation and laughter in the room was lively. Once Katherine had enlisted everyone, except Courtenay, in her plan, there was no more time for the intrusion of sadness. Occasionally Edward broke into song. He was immediately joined by the rest, usually in three- or four-part harmony, such that by nightfall, weary and content with their day's work, they had sung nearly every Christmas hymn or carol in the hymnary.

Early in the evening, Mrs. Drynwydd and Mrs. Llewellyn slipped away. Half an hour later the rest took a break and went downstairs to enjoy the brief repast the two faithful ladies had set out—meats, breads, pies, cakes, and cheeses. Then again they returned upstairs and went back to work.

Conversation lasted late into the evening. Gradually sleepiness overtook the company. One after another rose, said good night, and retired in anticipation of the big day ahead of them on the morrow.

Steven and Hollin were in the barn by ten on the morning of Boxing Day hitching all available means of transport, which included the large and small carriages and two buggies. Percy soon joined them. By eleven the four horse-drawn vehicles stood outside the manor's front door. Soon a processional was in progress between the upper room of preparation and the front of the house, while two or three of the men loaded the buggies. Several boxes were also loaded containing bottles of sherry and port, each tied with a ribbon. Knowing that most of the villagers would take the opportunity to sleep as long into the morning as possible, they did not begin their first excursions down the drive until just before one.

They reached town and split in four directions. With hampers or bottles in hand, each member of Katherine's immediate family—herself, Edward, Mary, Percy, and Florilyn—began knocking on the doors of the cottages to personally deliver their gifts. Within an hour, the whole village was abuzz. No longer were knocks required. Doors were thrown wide in greeting before they reached them. At each home they found themselves enthusiastically invited in for drinks, sometimes for tea, occasionally for something stronger. With every visit their progress slowed. The villagers were beside themselves with eager gratitude to reciprocate with whatever means of hospitality were available to them. Had they allowed it, every home would have kept their visitors for an hour!

Meanwhile, Hollin, who had accompanied them to town, returned to the manor with the largest carriage, where Mrs. Drynwydd, Mrs. Llewellyn, Steven, Adela, and Broakes were all ready to load it with the second round of provisions. It was a bone-chilling day of gray skies that portended snow. But never are human hearts warmed more than when engaged in service, ministry, or goodness to others of their kind.

The busy transport and delivery of hampers and drink and monetary gifts continued all afternoon. Few at the manor or in the homes of the village even noticed the cold. Those homes Katherine visited personally considered themselves as honored as if the queen herself had appeared on their doorsteps. When the last hamper was delivered, and she, Edward, Mary, Florilyn, and Percy rode back up the hill to the manor in the deepening dusk, all five were exhausted from constant visiting with exuberant villagers.

The only difficulty presented by the day was the question of whom to deliver bottles of sherry to Madame Fleming and Mistress Chattan. None of the three women felt comfortable entering either of their two establishments. Edward therefore paid a brief call on the enigmatic Fleming, while Percy, confessing a begrudging fondness for her, delivered a bottle and the best wishes of the viscountess to the proprietress of the inn.

Late that evening, the vicar and his wife retired to their own room. Edward slipped his nightshirt over his head. "A long and tiring but satisfying Boxing Day, wouldn't you say, my dear?" he said.

"Extraordinary is how I would describe it," rejoined Mary. "The humble gratitude and hospitality of the people in town was like nothing I have ever seen. It's not something one witnesses with regularity in Glasgow. They truly *love* your sister."

"It warms my heart to realize it," nodded Edward. "Especially after the loss of her husband."

"I'm certain the holidays were difficult for her. She was probably thinking of Roderick. I noticed a quiet about the place this morning on the part of others as well. I felt that there was much sadness mingled with the joy of the day."

"Christmas always brings memories and often disappointments. As blessed as we are now to be able to share the holiday one in heart with our son, I remember the pain of those Christmases when he was estranged from us. I ache for those who find Christmas a sad and lonely time. Katherine is now facing a double sorrow. Courtenay is certainly not being a true son to her in her time of need."

"On Christmas Eve, he was rolling his eyes and had a sour look on his face when you were talking about Christmas and God's fatherhood. Poor Katherine—how it must grieve her heart."

"Yet in spite of it, she was thinking of what she could do to make the season special for others."

Mary nodded thoughtfully. "I was thinking that very thing all afternoon," she said. "I admire your sister more than I can say. She did not let her own feelings keep her from reaching out to the community. She may not have *felt* the joy of Christmas in her own heart, but she *lived* what Christmas means—giving life and love to those around us. It was a memorable day. Katherine is indeed an amazing woman."

It began to snow about midnight. By the first light of the following morning, all Gwynedd lay under a blanket of white.

TWENTY-TWO

Farewell

$\mathcal{E}$dward, Mary, and Percy Drummond prepared to depart Westbrooke Manor for their return to Scotland on the second of January of the new year, 1873.

Percy found Florilyn alone in the sitting room after breakfast.

"So you'll soon be off," she said. She tried to sound cheery, but without much success. "It will be dreary when you're gone. Of course it always seems dreary after you leave."

"You always manage to survive," rejoined Percy. "Just think of me—far north under piles of snow, with papers to write and endless lectures to sit through."

"You'll be through, when is it—in May?"

"May it is," he said, exhaling a long sigh. "It seems too good to be true that I will actually graduate from the university! Who would have imagined it back when I was running through the streets of Glasgow trying to keep from being arrested!"

"You've changed."

"As have you."

"Then what will you do?" asked Florilyn.

"My first order of business will definitely be a return to Wales."

"Really?" exclaimed Florilyn. "Oh, that's wonderful. I didn't know if you—"

"No worries. I will be back as soon as I graduate. Or possibly June. There is something I have to do for your father. . .and I'll want to see you, of course."

"For my father?" said Florilyn.

"I will tell you all about it when I can. And we have our own future to decide on, too, you know."

Florilyn looked away. The subject was still painful to her.

"I *do* admire you for your courage," he added. "What my dad said is true."

"Thank you," nodded Florilyn. Her voice was shaky.

"I am still uncertain what I am supposed to be trying to figure out," Percy went on. "Gwyneth is gone. There is no way to find her. Even if I may have had more feelings for her once than I realized, what difference does it make now?"

"Like I said before," replied Florilyn, "we both have to know what is in our hearts."

Percy nodded then took Florilyn in his arms. Neither spoke as they embraced affectionately. After several seconds they stepped back.

"Your decision has made me admire you as a godly woman," said Percy. "Whatever happens in the future, you are my dear cousin and friend."

"And we'll both keep reading MacDonald," said Florilyn, forcing a smile.

"I don't know!" laughed Percy. "I don't want him to get me into any more trouble."

He detected momentary chagrin on Florilyn's face.

"Hey, only joking!" he added quickly. "I don't have as much time to read as you do. But I shall try."

They gazed into each other's eyes. Florilyn's were misty. Percy stepped forward and kissed her lightly on the cheek, then stepped back and smiled. Though they could not see what the future held, both knew they were doing the right thing.

As Percy climbed the stairs one last time to fetch his bag from his room a few minutes later, he paused on the landing to gaze at the portraits of the Westbrooke lineage. His eyes came to rest once again, as they often did when he was here, on the compelling face of his uncle Roderick's grandmother. The penetrating expression of her eyes was so mesmerizing that Percy felt that he *knew* her, that he had actually seen her. Yet he knew that was impossible. She had been dead decades before he was even born.

He shook his head in perplexity then continued up the stairs.

TWENTY-THREE

Plans and Schemes

Katherine did not bring up the subject of property or a new home to Florilyn again. She did not want to risk loose talk or overheard conversations. But she did not remain idle.

She made several more visits to Hamilton Murray's office, riding to Porthmadog by buggy and keeping her destination to herself. It did not take long after her ride with Florilyn to decide on the Mochras Head plateau as the ideal site for a future home. She knew that Courtenay had no great love of the sea. She had never seen him walking or riding along the coastline. She doubted he would miss the land in question. But she had long since given up trying to anticipate his reactions to anything. Whether he would be angry at her intentions, once they became known, or grateful for the extra sum in his account when he became viscount, she would hazard no guess.

Keeping his name out of it, under Murray's supervision an engineering firm from Shrewsbury was hired. It was far enough away, both he and Katherine thought, to keep local speculation from being able to dig too deeply into the matter. When the surveyors arrived on the scene, not only would they have no idea who had hired them, in all likelihood they would never have heard of Westbrooke Manor or the Viscount Lord Snowdon or his widow.

Courtenay, meanwhile, had replied to Lord Litchfield, agreeing to the terms he had outlined for sale of one thousand acres of land on the eastern boundary on the northern quadrant of the Westbrooke estate. Now all he had to do was wait.

Thus, both mother and son kept busy on their private schemes aimed to circumvent the difficulties posed to each by the other. Neither knew what the other was up to. But both saw an expression in the other's eyes that spoke of secrets. Courtenay had instructed the postman in Llanfryniog to keep mail addressed to him separate from what came to the manor and to hold it for him until he called for it personally. Katherine thus remained unaware of the correspondence between her son and London.

The two met but infrequently. Courtenay did not take his meals with his mother or sister. He regarded his present straitened circumstances as little more than house arrest in enemy-occupied territory. But he bore it with stoicism, knowing that his ship was on the horizon and was coming closer every day.

How Courtenay occupied his time was a mystery. He rode as much as the weather would permit. Though he looked down on the villagers and miners and farmers, he was frequently seen in Mistress Chattan's pub. In view of his future position among them, the men were deferential and friendly. The pleasure Courtenay took in hearing himself addressed as "my lord" no doubt contributed its share to his increasingly regular visits to the place. When he felt his meager supply of funds could afford it, he stood everyone a round of Mistress Chattan's best ale. He thus gradually gained the approbation of men who had been accustomed for years to regard him as a spoiled wastrel. All the while they remained unaware that one of his first planned ordinances as viscount would be to double most of their rents.

The friend of Courtenay's youth, Colville Burrenchobay, eldest son of parliamentarian Armand Burrenchobay, himself a wastrel of yet greater reputation than Courtenay, had recently returned to the family seat of Burrenchobay Hall. His return was not due to financial considerations—his father kept him well supplied with funds—but simply from the boredom of travel. He had sown his wild oats in their season, but now, as he reached his middle twenties, he had begun to think of his future. How great were his political aspirations, even he could not have said. If he had thoughts of following his father's footsteps to Westminster, however, the settled life of a gentleman would provide a more suitable basis from which to do so.

When Courtenay and Colville were together now, therefore, they were no longer two rowdy youths but the eldest scions of two of North Wales' oldest families. They drank expensive brandy and went shooting for pheasants and roe, not rabbits.

Riding back from Llanfryniog to the manor one day in late February, a strange sight met Courtenay's eyes. Five or six men with surveying equipment were spread out between the main road and the promontory. His first reaction was bewilderment, his second anger. He dug his heels into the sides of his mount and galloped off the road and over the wide plateau toward the scene.

"What is the meaning of this?" he said in a demanding tone. "Who are you people? Who's in charge here?"

The man closest to him, who did not take kindly to his tone, nodded toward a group of men across the grass.

Courtenay kicked at his horse's flanks and galloped toward them. "Which one of you is in charge here?" Courtenay asked as he rode up.

"I am," one of the men replied, turning toward him.

"What's going on here? What are you doing?"

"I would think it is obvious," said the man. "We are surveying the site."

"What for?"

"I really could not say. I am a surveyor not a planner."

"Who hired you?"

"The job came through a solicitor in Shrewsbury."

"Shrewsbury!" exclaimed Courtenay. "That's impossible. There has obviously been some mistake. So I am ordering you and your men off this land."

"And who are you to be giving such an order?"

"I own this land, you fool. I am the future viscount, Lord Snowdon."

"Ah yes, we were specifically told about you, that you might be troublesome."

"What were you told?"

"That you might try to throw your weight around, but that you had no legal standing in the matter. We were told to ignore whatever you might say."

In a white fury, Courtenay stared back at the plainspoken man a moment, then wheeled his mount around and made for home. He burst in upon his mother, making no attempt to hide his anger. "Mother, what is going on down at the promontory? There are surveyors everywhere. Are you behind it?"

"I am."

"I demand to know what it is all about."

"Just a little project of mine."

"What kind of project?"

"Nothing you need worry about. I am having some of the estate boundary lines looked into."

"There are no boundaries down there. Our land extends for miles along the coast and inland to the north-south road. I demand to know what's going on."

"That tone will get nowhere with me, Courtenay."

"Do you refuse to tell me what it is about?"

"I have told you, I am having some boundary lines looked into. That is all I intend to divulge about it."

Far from satisfied, Courtenay left the room more determined than ever to accelerate his own plans. He did not like this new tone of determination he had noticed in his mother of late. She was becoming too independent for her own good.

TWENTY-FOUR

Visitor from England

Lord Coleraine Litchfield stepped gingerly from the tipsy dinghy that had brought him from the anchored yacht out in the bay and onto the concrete pier. He glanced up the street and at the poor-looking stone buildings comprising the Welsh village of Llanfryniog. He did his best not to grimace at the thought of where he would be forced to spend the next several days. Only one thing could bring him this far away from civilization. That was the thought of making money. For that he would endure it with as much good humor as was possible under the circumstances.

Several more communications had gone back and forth between Westbrooke Manor and London, leading eventually to an invitation to the north. Commitments in London and the horrible winter's weather had delayed his meeting with the young scion of the Westbrooke estate until early March. But he was in Wales at last.

Before the Englishman could speculate further on the locale or his own personal fortunes, a lanky and well-dressed, though obviously rustic man approached. "Lord Litchfield," he said with an accent so unintelligibly thick the Englishman scarcely recognized his own name, "I am Deakin Trenchard, former footman at Westbrooke Manor. I am retired now and living in the village, but Mr. Courtenay asked me to meet you and take you to the manor, where he is awaiting you."

"Ah, yes. . .uh, Trenchard. Lead on, then," replied Litchfield.

The man turned, and the newcomer followed him from the pier to a waiting carriage. Fifteen minutes later they were winding their way up the tree-lined drive where Lord Litchfield beheld his first sight of the estate known as Westbrooke Manor.

A tolerable looking sort of place, he thought to himself—interesting mixture of brick and stone, although it was a bit severe to his taste. *It will no doubt be a dreary time of it, but—*

Further reflections were cut short. As the carriage slowed to a crunching stop on the gravel drive, his host came from the wide front doors and bounded ebulliently toward his guest.

"Lord Litchfield," he said, "I am Courtenay Westbrooke. I am happy you have been able to come."

"I am pleased to meet you at last, young Westbrooke," rejoined Litchfield, shaking the other's hand as he stepped down.

"Come in. We shall have tea," said Courtenay. "You have had a pleasant voyage I trust?"

"I am not altogether a man of the sea," replied Litchfield. "But we enjoyed calm seas and clear skies. Actually," he added, "I prefer the train, but a passing fancy of nostalgia turned my thoughts to the ancient mode of transport. It was not so bad as I expected. I may buy the yacht when I return to Bristol."

As they entered the house, Litchfield was still speaking. "Tell me," he was saying, "is the property—"

A quick glance from his host, accompanied by an imperceptible movement of finger to lips, communicated its message well enough. He fell silent as a stately lady who appeared about fifty approached.

Courtenay presented his mother. Lord Litchfield greeted Katherine with a smile and extended his hand. She returned the greeting with a hint of question in her eyes. Katherine was certain this visit was more than a mere social call. But she had not been able to discover what her son was up to.

Litchfield detected caution in the touch of her palm as she allowed him to shake it.

"Thank you for your hospitality, Lady Snowdon," he said. "And my belated condolences at the loss of your husband."

"Thank you. You knew my husband then?"

"We were acquaintances in the House of Lords."

Katherine nodded. "And now you have business with my son?"

"As he will be filling your husband's seat himself in a matter of months, I wanted to take the opportunity of seeing how I might be able to be of service to him."

"I see. Well, if there is anything you need during your stay, do not hesitate to make it known."

"Thank you, Lady Snowdon. You are most kind."

Courtenay led his guest upstairs to his room. He left him to refresh himself, adding that he would join him downstairs in the drawing room for tea at his convenience.

Descending the stairway a few minutes later, Litchfield saw an attractive girl whom he judged in her early twenties watching him from the end of the corridor. He nodded, but neither spoke. She, too, like the woman he had just met, appeared on her guard. He wondered what kind of place he had stepped into.

After stiff conversation with son and mother at tea, during which the purpose of his visit did not arise, Courtenay invited his guest for a stroll about the grounds. Alone they would be able more freely to discuss the matter that had brought the Englishman here.

"To answer the question you began to pose earlier," said Courtenay after they had left the house behind them, "yes, we shall have the opportunity to view the property. I beg your patience, however. Let us wait a day or two. Then we shall have a ride into the hills. We must be prudent and not discuss the matter around my mother or sister."

"Your sister?"

"She is younger than myself by two years. She would be no more favorably inclined toward my plans than my mother."

"I believe I saw her in the corridor a short time ago. She looked as if she were eyeing me cautiously."

"That's her."

"Your mother does not favor the sale?" said Litchfield.

"That is precisely the case. Of course, she knows nothing about it, which is why we have to be prudent in what we say."

"Why does it matter? We cannot finalize the transaction until you become viscount anyway."

"Technically, I don't suppose it does matter. And it certainly won't after I come of age. But I would rather not upset her unnecessarily. Unfortunately until that time she still controls the estate's finances, and thus my own. I have the feeling that she may be attempting to sell off a portion of estate lands behind my back. Whatever she is up to, I do not want her meddling in our agreement. There would be no telling what trouble she might cause us."

"I was led to understand—"

"I assure you," interrupted Courtenay, "there will be no problem. I simply want us to keep my mother out of it. She has strange notions about money. Her brother is a priest, you see, and the family, though wealthy, has passed down to its present scions—my mother and uncle— an inordinate fear of what they call mammon."

Two days passed. Lord Litchfield had done his best, without success, to amuse himself with cards, boring walks, even more boring conversation, and two or three visits to the village, ostensibly to see to the yacht that had brought him here but in reality merely for something to do.

On the third day, Courtenay suggested a ride. He gave orders for Radnor to saddle his two favorite mounts now that the stallion Demon was gone, a four-year-old gelding of extremely dark gray, though not dapple, with patches of pure black, and a rich chestnut stallion with white mane and tail. They were known as Night Fire and Cymru Gold.

The two men set out for the hills northeast of the estate within the hour. From the window of the second-floor library, Katherine watched them go. Their gay mood when they returned four hours later confirmed what she had been thinking since the day of Litchfield's arrival—Courtenay was definitely up to something.

TWENTY-FIVE

High Words

Courtenay Westbrooke left Llanfryniog, riding north to meet the main road on his way to Porthmadog. He was in jubilant spirits. In the pocket of his coat was a check, signed by Lord Coleraine Litchfield, for the unbelievable sum of £4,400. It had come in this morning's post. Litchfield had not *quite* delivered it into his hands during his visit of a month earlier as promised. But that hardly mattered now! Courtenay intended to waste no time depositing it into his account. His money problems were over at last!

He could take *ten* trips to the continent between today and his twenty-fifth birthday and hardly make a dent in his suddenly acquired fortune. And double this would be waiting for him when the transaction was consummated eleven months from now. His ordeal under his mother's thumb was over! He would buy the most expensive bottle of brandy Porthmadog had to offer then stop by Burrenchobay Hall on his return and allow his friend to share in his good fortune.

As he passed the Methodist Chapel, a woman emerged from one of the fishermen's cottages alongside the road and began walking toward the center of town. When she saw who was approaching along the road, her face brightened. She stepped into the street to meet him.

"Mr. Courtenay, my lord," she said, curtseying slightly and smiling nervously.

Courtenay reined in the gray-black gelding and stared down at her.

"I want to thank you, sir," she added, "in the matter of the rent."

"What are you talking about?" said Courtenay brusquely.

"The rent, sir. . .your forgiving our rent until my man is able to work again."

"Forgiving your rent?" repeated Courtenay. "You mean to tell me you are paying no rent?"

"My man, sir—he broke his arm from a fall in the boat during that big storm back in January, sir. Dr. Rotherham fixed him up real good, but he ain't been able to work all this time."

"What's that got to do with your rent?" asked Courtenay.

"Your man, your factor, Stevie Muir, my lord," replied the woman with growing trepidation, "he said he forgave our rent till my man was back to work."

"He did not talk to me about it," rejoined Courtenay. "But he will soon enough! As for your rent, you will pay up everything you owe or you will be evicted within the month. What is your name?"

"Naughtie, my lord," said the woman, trembling from Courtenay's sudden outburst.

With a vicious yank of the reins, Courtenay wheeled his mount away from the woman and galloped out of town as she stared after him in tears. The poor horse beneath him paid a dear price for Steven Muir's gesture of kindness. The creature was in a lather of exhaustion before Courtenay was halfway to Porthmadog, its hindquarters nearly raw from the whip.

"You can't give these people too much," he said to himself as he rode. "They will get the idea you are weak. They will take advantage at every turn." They had to know he intended to rule firmly. How much more damage was that lout of a so-called factor going to do before he was able to get rid of him! He didn't know whether to be angrier at his mother or Muir.

By the time he reached the bank, his fury had receded. He was once again aglow in the knowledge that he was in possession of more money than he had ever had in his life. When his fortune was safely deposited in his account, he lunched at the Lleyn Arms while his horse was fed and watered then purchased his brandy and started for home.

❧

Three weeks later, toward the end of April, Steven Muir was at the harbor unloading a shipment of provisions that had come for Lady Snowdon from London. When his wagon was full, he made the rounds of the harbor visiting what fishermen were present, with the result that by the time he started back for the manor he had purchased several nice cod to deliver to Mrs. Llewellyn.

He climbed up, flicked the reins, and urged the aging but faithful cob into motion. As he left the harbor behind and approached the chapel, he saw a cart in the street ahead of him being loaded with what appeared to be household possessions. He came nearer, drew rein, and jumped down.

"Let me give you a hand with that, Jamie," he said to the woman beside the cart who was attempting to hoist a chair up into it. He took hold of the chair himself and swung it high into the air and onto the flat bed of the cart. "Where are you bound with all this?"

"Just to my sister's down in Barmouth, Stevie."

"Is she so sorely in need that you must empty your own house to help furnish hers?"

"She's in no need, Stevie. 'Tis she that's taking us in. We're going to 'bide with her."

Mr. Naughtie, his arm still in a sling, now emerged from the stone cottage.

Steven looked back and forth between the man and his wife in confusion. "But why?" he asked. "You'll surely be back to the fishing in another month, Jock. If it's food you're needing, I'll have a sack of oats and a bushel of potatoes on your doorstep within an hour."

"It's no food, Stevie," said Jock Naughtie as he walked toward them. " 'Tis money we're in need of. . .for the rent, you know. We got none."

"I told you, Jock, you'll be paying no more rent till you're healthy and strong and you're back to work on McKinnon's boat."

The man looked down to the ground but said nothing.

Steven looked toward his wife.

An embarrassed expression came over her face. "Meaning no disrespect to yourself, Stevie," she said. "We know you meant well. But you're not the laird, you know."

"Of course not. But I don't know what you mean."

"The laird, the young viscount, Stevie—he said we must pay all the rent we owe or quit."

"What?" exclaimed Steven. "When did this happen?"

"About three weeks ago."

"Why didn't you tell me?"

"We ain't seen you since."

"Why didn't you come find me at the manor?"

"The likes of us couldn't well show ourselves at the big house. We didn't want to anger the young viscount."

"He's not the viscount yet," replied Steven. "And he's got no right to pretend to be. His mother still sets the rents and collects them, and I work for her not Courtenay." Steven was brimming with anger like a pot rising to a slow boil. He stood thinking for a moment. "Jock, Jamie. . . the two of you go back inside and have a cup of tea," he said. "Don't take another thing from your house until I get back. Lady Snowdon will know of this. I can promise you that she will not hear of your leaving unless that is your wish. But it will not be over money." He turned, jumped back onto his wagon, and sent old Dusty up the street in front of his burden with as much speed as the aging cob could muster.

Steven arrived at the manor twenty or twenty-five minutes later, his anger with Courtenay's presumption greater than ever. He jumped from the wagon and strode toward the front door, intending to seek an immediate interview with his mistress. Halfway across the gravel entry, a movement caught his eye.

Courtenay had just left the house by a side entrance and was striding toward the new stables.

Steven turned and hurried after him. He rounded the wall of the barn just as Courtenay, whip in hand, was leading Cymru Gold, already saddled, out onto the grass. "A moment of your time, *your lordship*," said Steven with emphasis, "if you please."

Courtenay detected challenge in the tone. He turned haughtily to face him as Steven came forward. One look at the young shepherd's face brought all the latent anger in his own soul immediately to the surface. Courtenay's eyes flashed dangerously.

Steven stopped ten feet away. He did not want to get too close, not for fear of Courtenay but in respect of his own strength and what he might do if aroused. "I have just come from town," he said. "There I was informed by Jock and Jamie Naughtie that you gave them notice to pay their back rents or quit."

"I don't keep track of the names of the village peasantry. But yes, I spoke to a woman some time back who told me you had taken the liberty of forgiving their rents. I set her straight soon enough."

"You had no right to interfere," said Steven, forcing himself to speak softly.

"I had no right to interfere!" sneered Courtenay. "Just whose tenants do you suppose those people are?"

"At present they are your mother's. She has given me responsibility over their well-being."

"*Their* well-being! What about the well-being of the estate?"

"They are one and the same."

"Perhaps in the eyes of a fool. A businessman would see it differently."

"Fortunately, I am no businessman. I am the Westbrooke Manor factor."

"Yes, and a notable farce you have made the office. But you won't be for long. You would be advised to begin making plans for your future, Muir. You will rent no cottage or house from me anywhere within miles of here. I won't have these blackguards taking their problems to you and thinking me a cad because I don't have the heart of an old woman like you."

"Only a cad would throw a man and woman out of their home at the very time fortune turns against them."

"How dare you!" cried Courtenay. His pent-up fury at last exploded. Before Steven could protect himself, a stinging blow from Courtenay's whip lashed across Steven's midsection and shoulder. Luckily for all concerned, the thong did not find skin.

Taken completely by surprise, all Steven could do as the whip was withdrawn and sent at him again was turn away and protect his head and face. He bolted for cover as several more lashes snapped across his back.

Courtenay sprinted after him, hardly aware of Florilyn's screams as she ran from the house. She had witnessed the argument from one of the library windows. Knowing what Courtenay was capable of she had dashed for the stairs. Running straight at him, she threw herself against Courtenay with the full force of her body as he coiled his arm for another blow.

"Stop it. . .stop it, Courtenay!" she shrieked.

Courtenay swore violently and spun toward her. With his free hand, he grasped her arm and shoved her from him. "This doesn't concern you!" he shouted.

He raised the whip, but Florilyn attacked again with the viciousness of a wildcat, yelling and pummeling Courtenay's face with surprisingly accurate blows from her two fists.

The blood of his rage now reached its heights. Courtenay retaliated with a whack across Florilyn's cheek. She screamed in pain. He shoved her back, and she stumbled and fell to the ground. Courtenay advanced with the coiled whip in his hand and raised it to strike her again. In fairness, he only intended to use it as a blunt instrument, not as the lethal weapon a horsewhip could be in the hand of an expert.

More fortunately for him than for her, Florilyn's attack gave Steven time to recover. As Courtenay raised the coiled leather above his ear, he felt it suddenly wrested from his hand. He spun around to find Steven holding it and standing three feet from him. "And only a scoundrel would strike a woman, Courtenay!" said Steven, loudly yet with surprising calm. "You are both a cad *and* a scoundrel. Now get away before it goes worse for you."

With marvelous speed, Courtenay's only reply was a lightning blow with his right fist in the direction of Steven's jaw. But he underestimated

Steven's dexterity. A quick step to the side and Courtney's fist found only air. He lost his balance momentarily but quickly recovered. "Stand and face me like a man, Muir!" he shouted, adding a string of imprecations. "Defend yourself or receive the beating you deserve."

"I will not defend myself," said Steven, backing slowly away. "But I assure you that you will not lay another hand on your sister. She is the finest young woman for miles, both beautiful and honorable. You shame yourself as the lowest of men by treating her with anything less than the respect she deserves, and by speaking with such a foul tongue in her presence. I will not defend myself, but I will defend her if you touch her again. And if one more vile word leaves your lips in her hearing, you will have to answer to me, Courtenay Westbrooke—and I promise you, it will not go well for you."

A tense silence filled the small courtyard. Katherine, who had heard Florilyn's screams, now ran out the front door.

Courtenay glared at Steven through clenched teeth. It did not take more than a second or two for him to realize he did not like his chances now that he had relinquished the advantage of the whip. "I'll kill you for this, Muir," he spat. "No one makes me look like a fool. You might as well pack your bags now if you know what's good for you. Your future here is finished."

Courtenay turned, strode toward his mount, who had waited patiently through the ruckus, mounted, then galloped off. It was a mercy for the horse that Steven was still holding the whip.

TWENTY-SIX

Threats

Steven stooped down, offered his hand, and helped Florilyn to her feet.

Katherine hurried toward them. "What is. . . Oh, Steven—your back and shoulder are bleeding! Florilyn, what's—"

"Courtenay attacked Steven with his horsewhip, Mother!" said Florilyn angrily. "It was horrible! Then he hit me and knocked me down."

"Courtenay *hit* you?" exclaimed Katherine in disbelief. Now she noticed that one of Florilyn's cheeks was bright red. "Oh, my. . .Florilyn, dear. . .how could he. . .that. . .that—"

"I am sorry, Lady Katherine," said Steven, turning toward his mistress. "I fear it was my fault."

"Steven, how can you say that!" said Florilyn. "I saw what he did. He was whipping you!"

"I should not have confronted him," rejoined Steven. "I precipitated the argument and made him angry. I should have spoken with you first, Lady Katherine. I am afraid I let my own anger get the better of me."

"*Anger*, Steven! I watched the whole thing," said Florilyn. "You were so calm I wondered what you were doing. You didn't even raise your voice when Courtenay was swearing at you. Why didn't you give him what he deserved? Anyone could see that you weren't afraid of him."

"No, I wasn't afraid."

"Why then?"

"There are those who think it is a disgrace for a man to be struck by another man. I happen to believe the opposite. I consider it a disgrace to strike another."

Florilyn stared at him, wondering if she had heard him correctly.

"I would have struck him to protect you," Steven went on, "but not to defend myself. I am twice as strong as your brother. And I was *very* angry. That's why I was trying hard to remain calm. Anger and strength—the two do not go well together. I might have hurt him very badly. That would have done him no good at all."

"Steven," now said Katherine, "you must tell me what this was all about. Courtenay is my son, and you are my factor. If there are differences so serious as this, I must know of them. Why do you say it was your fault?"

"There was a dispute about one of your tenants, Lady Katherine," replied Steven. "You remember the Naughties, from the village—Jock Naughtie is the fisherman who broke his arm rather badly in that January storm?"

"I remember."

"I found out today that Jamie, that's Jock's wife, encountered Courtenay a few weeks ago. Courtenay learned that we had forgiven their rents until Jock was back at the fishing. Courtenay told them they must pay all back rents or quit."

"He didn't!"

"I fear so, my lady," said Steven. "I learned of it when I was in the village just now. Jamie and Jock were packing their belongings to leave."

"We must stop them. I won't have Courtenay meddling while the estate remains in my hands. Especially I am not about to allow him to evict them!"

"I told them to do nothing more," said Steven.

"I will go see them myself. I want to apologize personally. Will you take me to them, Steven?"

"Of course, Lady Katherine."

"After we get you cleaned and bandaged, that is," said Katherine. "And Florilyn," she added, turning again to her daughter, "are you badly hurt?"

"No, Mother. I will be sore. But I am more furious than hurt."

"Then let us go inside and see to Steven's injuries."

With the help of Steven's mother, who seemed less concerned about a few scrapes and bruises and cuts than the two Westbrooke women, Steven's two or three bleeding wounds were cleaned and bandaged. With a fresh shirt, he was soon himself again, though he, too, would be sore for a week.

Within the hour, he and Katherine set out for the village in one of the manor's small buggies. When they knocked and were admitted to the Naughtie cottage, with the cart still sitting in the street half full of a miscellany of possessions, the humble fisherman and his wife were beside themselves to show what hospitality they were capable of to the former viscount's wife. As hospitality is a matter of the heart more than luxury of provision, Katherine felt as welcomed as she would have in any castle in Wales. Probably more so. The good man and his wife were profuse in their gratitude. Jamie cried. Steven added as a final condition that they must tell no one of the altercation with Courtenay or what he had tried to do. He *would* be viscount one day. They must all give him the chance to become a caring landlord to his people. Toward this end, they must prejudice no one against him.

Katherine, however, moved as she was by Steven's simple speech of forgiveness, returned to the manor determined to prevent any recurrence of the incident or any further interference from her son. She was waiting for him when he returned from his ride. She met him at the foot of the stairs. "I would like to talk to you, Courtenay," she said without preamble. "Would you please meet me in your father's study in five minutes?"

"Perhaps I am not inclined to talk to you, Mother," he retorted. "After the way you took that Stevie Muir's side earlier, I have nothing to say to you."

"It may be I who have something to say to you. If you will not come to the study, then I will say it here for the whole household to hear."

Courtenay returned his mother a look of daggers then continued up the stairs.

Katherine tried to compose herself. She walked calmly to her late husband's study, sat down in the chair behind his desk, and waited. This was not an interview she was looking forward to.

Courtenay walked in ten minutes later without knocking. If his behavior from earlier or his lengthy ride had subdued or shamed him in his own estimation, he displayed no sign of it. His eyes glowed with the fire of indignation. His was not a character easily humbled. It was doubtful he had ever felt the twinge of self-mortification in his life.

"Please sit down," said Katherine matter-of-factly.

"I prefer to stand," rejoined Courtenay. It was not true. But in his present frame of mind, he would have countered *any* request or command from his mother for no reason other than to set himself against her will.

"Suit yourself," she said. "What I have to say will not take long. I have been apprised of your interference in my affairs in the matter of one of our tenants in the village by the name of Naughtie. You apparently gave them notice to quit unless they paid all their back rents, directly contradicting what my factor had told them."

Courtenay burst out laughing with disdain. "Your *factor*! Ha, ha! You continue to play this ridiculous charade with the clodhopper Muir. Ha, ha, ha!"

"He *is* my factor," said Katherine firmly. "And he is in charge of my affairs at present, not you. Fortunately he and I have been able to undo the mischief you caused the poor people. But I will thank you not to interfere with my tenants again."

The laughter on Courtenay's face died out as quickly as it had come. "*Your* tenants?" he said.

"For the present, yes."

"You haven't forgotten whose tenants they will be in a year's time?"

"You are not likely to let me forget, are you? But though I cannot control what you will do then, I can prevent your interfering now. And if you again threaten or so much as lay a hand on Steven Muir—"

"The fool deserved the thrashing I gave him."

"Nevertheless, if you lay a hand on him, or on your sister, I will take steps—"

"You will take *steps*!" Courtenay spat back. "Pray, what kind of steps would you take against me, Mother!"

"A man who strikes a woman, a brother who strikes his sister, is a rogue and a villain, and I will not have such in my house. If I have to, I will take steps to have you removed to keep you from such an attack again."

"Have me *removed*!" cried Courtenay, his rage mounting. "*Your* house! You forget yourself, Mother. This is *my* house. The entire Westbrooke estate is *mine*. You are a mere temporary trustee. But none of it belongs to you or ever will. So do not threaten me. You cannot have me removed. I will not have you make me look like a weak child in the eyes of my tenants. If you persist with such threats, you will leave me no alternative but to have *you* removed."

"You would not dare evict a former viscountess in full view of all of North Wales. Your father may be dead, but I am still Lady Snowdon. Even London would be rocked by the scandal you would bring upon yourself. Do not think too highly of yourself, Courtenay. You would be despised for such arrogance."

But Courtenay was nowise cowed. He did not know what it was to recognize that he had gone too far and back down. "In that case," he said, "I give you formal notice here and now, Mother, that neither you nor your daughter will be welcome to call this your home after next March. You will receive written notification of your eviction in due course."

He turned and strode from the study, leaving Katherine staring after him in horrified silence. Slowly her eyes filled. How could her own son have come to this? Her mother's heart broke at the thought of what he had become.

TWENTY-SEVEN

Summer Plans

No more incidents or outbursts marred the slow dawning of spring in the gardens of Westbrooke Manor. After the high words they had exchanged in her husband's study, Katherine had not so much as spoken another word to Courtenay again. Nor had she had the opportunity. She scarcely saw him. If Courtenay had kept out of the way of the household before, he was now little more than a ghost whose occasional presence was assumed but whom no one had actually *seen*.

He came and went by one of the seldom-used back stairways, and his footsteps were heard but now and then. The echo of horses' hooves from the stables also gave evidence of his movements and his daily comings and goings. The only one of the staff who maintained regular contact with the late viscount's son was Mrs. Drenwydd. Somehow Courtenay contrived to make his wishes known. For a month she had been delivering his tea and meals, on schedule, to his private apartment of two rooms. Adela kept his quarters clean, the bed made and supplied with fresh linens, but rarely saw its occupant. Sometimes, she reported, the bed was not slept in for days at a time. At such times, the cook was not notified in advance, only learning that the young master, as they still called him, had not touched his food when she came to take away the tray. But she continued to bring tea and cakes and the next meal at their appointed times, for one never knew when he might be in residence again, and she was terrified of angering him. How he occupied his time was a mystery.

He was certainly not missed. Absent though he was, however, the bitter argument between Katherine and Courtenay cast an ongoing pall over Westbrooke Manor. Though Katherine did not divulge the specifics of their exchange, the heated shouts had been heard by Florilyn in her room and Adela Muir in hers, as well as two or three of the staff.

Katherine had not been herself since. There was no doubt what was the cause of her gloom. Her own future did not concern her. She grieved for what her son had become. She did, however, accelerate her plans for Mochras Head. She wrote to solicitor Murray with the request that he discreetly retain a suitable architect and arrange a meeting at the manor to begin the process of designing what she was now confident would be her new home. It was already too late to hope to complete construction before Courtenay's birthday. But she and Florilyn could spend a month, even a year if need be, with Edward and Mary in Glasgow. She had no intention of waiting for the ignominy of being cast adrift by her son. She and Florilyn would be packed and gone the day before Courtenay acquired the title. She still had not resolved how best to care for Adela and Steven and the rest of her staff. Those who wanted to remain in Courtenay's employ, if he chose to keep them, could certainly remain. Those he did not plan to keep, she would employ at the new house. What to do in the interim, however, before construction was complete, weighed upon her as an unknown yet to be resolved.

Courtenay, meanwhile, bided his time with useless and vain distractions—traveling, eating, visiting, drinking, hunting. While Lord Litchfield in London was busily engaged in making plans for his new acquisition in Wales, the sale could not have been further from Courtenay's mind. With Litchfield's money in the bank, he felt again the exuberant freedom of wealth. The only hint that he planned to sail for the continent for the summer and possibly longer were a few words to Mrs. Drenwydd around the first of May, telling her that he would be traveling abroad and would not require meals for some time, adding that he would apprise her further when his plans became definite.

He and Colville Burrenchobay were returning from a pheasant hunt one afternoon, on their way through Llanfryniog from the north, where they intended to slake their thirst with however many tankards of Mistress Chattan's ale it took to accomplish the job. Courtenay had been trying to persuade his friend to accompany him to France in two weeks.

The figure of a woman came toward them along the walkway beside the street, a boy of two to three years at her side.

"Is that. . .by the saints—is that Rhawn Lorimer?" exclaimed Courtenay in a low voice.

"I can hardly tell," chuckled Colville. "I haven't seen her in years."

"She must have put on two stone. To think that I once fancied *that*!"

Rhawn saw them as they approached. Her eyes narrowed as she glanced from one to the other.

As they rode by, both young men nodded slightly. No words were exchanged.

"If looks could kill, eh?" said Courtenay softly.

"That expression she cast you was the look of a woman spurned, old man," said Colville. "When are you going to own up to being the father of her brat there?"

"What are you talking about?" Courtenay shot back irritably.

"Everyone knows it."

"Don't talk rubbish. They know no such thing."

"If not you, who else could the father be?"

"Some might think it was you."

"Bah. I wasn't even around at the time. I heard she met several no-goods when she was in London. You know the English! None of them would own up to it. With the reputation she had, I doubt she even knows who the father is."

Both burst out laughing. Their speculations went no further as they reined up in front of the inn, dismounted, and went inside.

༺༻

Farther to the north, Edward and Mary Drummond sat in a second-class coach of the Aberdeen Express, bound for the great northern seaport and the graduation of their son from Aberdeen University. Their enthusiasm for the trip had been heightened two days before by a letter from Edward's cousin Henry in Stirling with the news that he and his son of the same name, Percy's junior by six months, had decided to accept their invitation to Percy's graduation. That same afternoon, they would take the train north from Edinburgh, where young Henry was studying for the ministry of the Free Church at New College. They would meet them at their boardinghouse after their arrival.

Though the families of Edward and the elder Henry Drummond had been much together as the two had grown into adulthood, Edward's eventual settling in Glasgow had greatly reduced their contact in recent years. In spite of the reasonable proximity of Stirling to Glasgow, the two younger Drummond cousins had met but two or three times during their boyhood. As both boys had grown into fine young men with hearts for God, it seemed a shame to Edward that they were not more intimately acquainted. He was thus delighted with his cousin's acceptance of the invitation.

The five Drummonds sat together at a celebratory dinner two evenings later in the restaurant of one of Aberdeen's finer hotels. The two second cousins hit it off immediately. They would have been taken by an observer to be lifelong friends.

"So it's law next, is it, Percy?" young Henry had just asked.

"No decision yet," replied Percy. "Actually, for a time I was considering the ministry, like my father. . .and like you now, too. But after much prayer, I am sensing a leading in the direction of law. I have to tell you, though, at the moment the thought of more schooling is not especially appealing. I just want to put it behind me."

"I know what you mean," rejoined Henry. "After I graduated, I considered taking a break from my studies. But," he added, casting a glance across the table, "my father encouraged me to keep the momentum strong. If I wanted my divinity degree, he said, it would be best to continue in pursuit of the goal."

"No doubt wise advice. I have the advantage of having worked for a law firm here in Aberdeen for several summers. They will hire me full-time as an intern if I want to postpone law school."

"Is that what you're going to do?"

"Again. . .no decision yet. There is something I have to do first, before I embark on any career plans—a promise that I must fulfill."

"Sounds mysterious."

"It is mysterious!" now laughed Edward. "Neither Mary nor I know what it is. Percy has been very tight lipped."

"I promised to tell no one," said Percy. "That's part of it, too—confidentiality. The first thing I need to do is return to Wales in a few weeks to attempt to fulfill my promise."

"Wales?" asked the elder Henry.

"To visit my aunt," said Percy.

"Ah, right. . .Katherine. She's the one who married into the aristocracy, is she not?"

"The Viscount Lord Snowdon," nodded Edward. "My sister, your cousin, is none other than the Viscountess Lady Snowdon. The viscount died a year ago. Percy was there at the time and made a deathbed promise to Katherine's husband, which is the source of his perplexity and our mystery."

The eyes of the others around the table all came to rest on Percy. He drew in a long breath and sighed. "That's about it," he said. "It is indeed a perplexity because I am not sure how to carry out my uncle's dying wish. But I promised him I would try. So I will go to Wales and hope to be given direction on what to do next."

"I have an idea for you," said young Henry. "Actually, I haven't talked to you about this yet, Father," he added, glancing toward his father. "I just learned of it a few days ago. D. L. Moody and Ira Sankey are coming to Scotland on an evangelistic mission in the fall. I would like to take a leave from New College and work with them. . .with your permission, Father." He turned again to Percy. "Why don't you join me, Percy?" he said enthusiastically. "Can you imagine what an experience—to work alongside Moody! It's an opportunity that may never come again. I want to be part of it."

Percy took in the suggestion with obvious interest. "I will have to see how it goes in Wales," he said. "It sounds like an intriguing possibility. What will you do?"

"They enlist local support wherever they travel to help with organization and crowds and in counseling people after the services. I suppose it will be personal evangelism with those who have shown interest or have given their hearts to Christ."

The conversation and dinner continued late into the evening. When they finally retired for the night, the two young cousins agreed to stay in touch and keep each other apprised of their future plans.

Parting the next day, as the two Henry Drummonds prepared to board their train for Edinburgh, young Henry approached his father's cousin as they waited in the station.

"Cousin Edward," he said. "I have a request to make of you, if you don't mind."

"Certainly, Henry," replied Edward.

"My mother and father have always spoken highly of your spiritual insights—how you see things in the spiritual world differently from most Christians. I am embarrassed to ask, but would you look at some writings I am working on? My father has read most of them and offered a few ideas. I would like to hear what you think as well."

"I would be happy to, Henry," replied Edward. "What's it about?"

"It's a series of devotional talks based on First Corinthians 13. I am occasionally called on to address my fellow students at chapel. I would appreciate any thoughts you might have."

"It would be my pleasure," replied Edward.

His cousin's son handed him a small sheaf of handwritten pages.

"You don't mind if I read it, too?" asked Percy.

"Of course not, Percy," replied Henry. "I would appreciate your thoughts as well—as someone my own age."

"This is not your only copy?" asked Edward.

"No, I copied out a clean draft for you. My own is too filled with notes and scratchings from my pen. No one could possibly make sense of it!"

With final handshakes and promises to write, the two Henrys, father and son, boarded their train.

The three Glaswegians departed for Glasgow the following morning, with all Percy's belongings from four years at the university.

TWENTY-EIGHT

Wales through New Eyes

*P*ercival Drummond, M.A., arrived at Llanfryniog in North Wales in the last week of May, 1873. As he alighted from the coach in front of the inn, he thought to himself how the progression of his life seemed inexorably linked to his periodic sojourns in this rural seat of his aunt and uncle and cousins. Westbrooke Manor had come to feel more like his true home even than the parsonage in Glasgow in which he had been raised.

While the coachman took down his bags and set them beside the inn, he glanced up and down the familiar street. How many times had he been here, he wondered. His first visit as a rebellious sixteen-year-old in 1867 had been filled with so many discoveries about God and nature and himself. Then his return visit as a nineteen-year-old university student in 1870. . .and again two years later. That was the fateful visit of a year ago, when the accident had occurred that had taken his uncle's life. Finally the short stay last Christmas. Now here he was again, a university graduate of twenty-two, with an uncertain future ahead of him.

Almost simultaneous to the departure of the coach and four that had brought him down the coast from the train at Blaenau Ffestiniog, the Westbrooke Manor buggy appeared at the end of the street to the south of town, coming between the two churches and making good speed. As he approached, Percy saw Steven Muir at the reins.

He waited as the carriage slowed and drew alongside the inn. Steven jumped down and ran toward him with outstretched hand. He seemed to Percy's eyes to have aged two years. Being in a position of responsibility obviously agreed with him.

"Hello, Stevie!" said Percy, reverting to the nickname by which he had first known him.

"Welcome back to Wales, Percy!" said Steven. "As always, the whole manor is anxiously awaiting you."

"The *whole* manor?" laughed Percy.

"Ah, if you're meaning Mister Courtenay. . .he's away to the continent."

Behind Steven, Percy now saw Florilyn alight from the carriage. She smiled and walked toward him. The two cousins embraced affectionately, then stepped back and gazed a moment into each other's eyes. If anything since the ending of their engagement, Florilyn had grown quieter and more beautiful, reminding all who saw her of Katherine.

After the initial heartache from what she had done, the months since had been good ones for Florilyn's soul. She participated in the domestic life of the manor and spent much of her free time in the library. There her newfound love for reading blossomed into a passion. She and her mother grew closer than ever, talked often about Percy and what Florilyn had done, and had even begun to pray together. As rare as such a thing might be in the world, mother and daughter truly became the best of friends and confidantes.

In the second or two as she gazed into Percy's eyes, a strange and unexpected sensation filled Florilyn's heart. How she *loved* him! Yet in that instant, she realized that her love for Percy was the love of a sister for a brother. . .the natural love for a brother that Courtenay had never allowed to flourish within her.

"You look well, Florilyn," said Percy. "You seem at peace."

"Perhaps I am," said Florilyn. "You look good, too, Percy. I can see from your face that you are relieved that the stress of school is behind you."

Percy nodded. "It is a great relief, I will admit. If I go to law school eventually, it will probably be far more rigorous. But I'm not thinking about that now."

Steven already had Percy's bags loaded. The three climbed into the buggy.

Florilyn sat down between the two young men and slipped her hands through their two arms. "I don't know that I have ever felt so safe and secure and happy as to have two such wonderful men beside me!" she exclaimed as they set off.

Percy roared with laughter.

"Oh Percy, it is always so good when you come home, isn't it, Steven? Your laughter brings the sun out!"

"I am glad to be of service!" said Percy, laughing again. "So, Steven," he went on, "how does the life of a gentleman suit you?"

"I am hardly that, Percy!" laughed Steven. "Merely a humble factor."

"A factor is *almost* a gentleman, is it not?"

"I will always be a sheepherder at heart."

"Don't let him tell you stories, Percy," said Florilyn. "Steven knows everything about the estate. Mother says he manages it all. The business of the estate would be impossible without him, she says."

"Good for you, Steven! I am happy it has worked out well for everyone. What does Courtenay think of having you for his—" Percy stopped abruptly as they passed a young woman from behind. "Wait a minute—hold on, Steven!" he said. "Isn't that. . . Yes, it is!" He leaped down from the carriage as Steven pulled to a stop. He ran around the horse to the side of the street. "Rhawn!" he cried. "I thought it was you!"

Before Rhawn Lorimer had a chance even to greet him, she found herself embraced by the last person she had expected to see. "Percy!" she exclaimed as he stepped back. "You're back in Wales!"

"I only just arrived. Florilyn and Steven came to collect me from the coach," he added, glancing toward the two where they sat in the buggy.

Rhawn smiled up at them.

"You're looking well. Being a mother must be a good influence on you."

"Thank you," said Rhawn a little shyly, glancing away.

"Are you still living at your parents' home?" asked Percy.

Rhawn nodded.

"And your son?"

"He is well. He's two and a half now—rambunctious and talkative."

"I can't wait to see him. I'll come visit. We'll go for a ride together!" Percy turned and walked back to the carriage and climbed up.

Steven flicked the reins and they bounded into motion as Rhawn stood a moment staring after them.

It was quiet in the carriage for a minute or two.

"Is there still no. . . ," Percy began. "I mean. . .the boy still has no father, I take it?"

"No *acknowledged* father," said Florilyn.

"Do you and she still see one another?"

"We get together from time to time," nodded Florilyn. "I've actually gotten her started reading MacDonald's books."

"She's said nothing to you about who the father is?"

"She would never do that. It's never come up between us."

They left Llanfryniog behind them, joined the main road, and continued southward.

"What is happening over there?" said Percy as they rode up the plateau and he looked toward the promontory of Mochras Head.

"Actually," said Florilyn, "my mother is building a new house."

"What?"

"She and I will be leaving the manor when Courtenay becomes viscount."

"You're kidding! Voluntarily, or is he forcing you out?"

"A little of both!" laughed Florilyn. "Now that the new house is begun, Mother is excited. Just wait till you see the drawings. It will be beautiful, overlooking the sea with the most spectacular views imaginable."

"So how is my old friend and nemesis doing?" asked Percy.

"Courtenay you mean?"

"Who else? Can't wait to see me, what?"

"Actually, Courtenay's gone," replied Florilyn. "He left for France about a month ago. How he found the money for a trip has Mother baffled," she went on. "To all accounts he was basically penniless except for what Mother occasionally gave him. Then all of a sudden something seemed to change. The next thing we knew, he was gone again. We've not heard a word from him."

"But he becomes viscount. . .when?"

"He turns twenty-five next March."

On the continent, Courtenay's newfound wealth was in fact evaporating rather more quickly than he would have hoped, largely from unwise investments at Europe's racetracks. He seemed neither concerned nor inclined to moderate his expensive addiction. There was more waiting for him in a few months' time. Once he was viscount, he would raise rents across the board sufficient to keep from finding himself in the same boat as had his father.

His father's dream of owning a stable of thoroughbred racehorses of his own had taken possession of Courtenay. His travels also served the ostensible purpose of giving him the opportunity to make several purchases. He was not a wise judge of horseflesh, far too impetuous and given to the lure of externals. But as is often the case with such young men, his confidence in his decision-making prowess was of inverse proportion to its wisdom. The *last* thing he would think to do was seek the counsel of those older and wiser than himself. His hubris was well developed in the extreme.

The thought never now entered his mind of resuming his studies at Oxford. What did he need a degree for? By this time next year, he would be sitting in the House of Lords!

Steven and Florilyn continued with their Scots passenger through the gate into the precincts of Westbrooke Manor.

Katherine was watching for their arrival from the window of the study. The moment the buggy came into view, she was on her way down the stairs. The entire household staff was also aware of their honored guest's impending arrival and had contrived to be at or near the front door with their mistress to greet him.

Katherine walked outside and hurried toward the carriage. She embraced Percy almost the moment his feet touched the ground. "Welcome home, Percy!" she whispered into his ears.

Percy stepped back and looked into his aunt's eyes. He saw a new light of assurance, poise, and calm in her countenance.

In the six months since Christmas, the viscount's widow had added more than a few strands of gray now that the milestone of fifty had come and gone. The grief of finding herself without a husband while still a relatively young woman caused her, even now, occasional tears when alone at night. But that she had grown within herself was obvious from one look deep into her eyes. Notwithstanding the tussles with Courtenay, she was more confident and self-assured. Many decisions had been forced upon her. She had risen to meet them with a maturity and grace that would have made her late husband proud. She continued what she and her husband had begun during the final year or two of his life, visiting the homes and shops of the villagers who were, even if but temporarily, her tenants and making sure their needs were being met.

Even with the prospect looming of having to leave her home, she was looking to the future not with defeat but as a challenge to be met with zestful optimism. She had successfully concluded the purchase from the estate of one hundred sixty acres stretching inland from the promontory of Mochras Head approximately a quarter mile at its narrowest up to three-quarters of a mile at the point of the promontory, bounded to the east by the village road and main road south to Barmouth. Now that Courtenay had laid his cards on the table, she was almost looking forward to the inevitable move to the new home of her design. Nevertheless, she was greatly relieved to be able to embark on the project in his absence.

Mostly, however, Katherine Westbrooke had grown spiritually. The sensitivities of her youth, nurtured in the home of a godly mother and father, had been so thoroughly stifled during the years of her marriage as to almost have receded into dormancy. The strong roots of that spiritual legacy had now revived and sent new life throughout the entire plant of her being. Not only was she now reading every new MacDonald novel as it came off the press, she was venturing into the deep waters of his sermons as well and had begun her own inquiry through daily Bible reading into the true nature and character of God.

Truly had she allowed the tragedies that had come to her to work together for good in her life.

TWENTY-NINE

Reflections Past and Future

*I*n the warm soft-scented twilight, Percy Drummond stood at the open window of his familiar room in Westbrooke Manor. It was late. Though tired from his journey and the emotionally draining day of visiting and laughter and rekindling old friendships, his brain was too occupied for sleep.

He was here at last. The moment of truth had finally arrived when he would have to decide how to carry out his uncle's dying commission. He had put off the *how* of that mystery for almost a year. The future had arrived.

After today, learning of Courtenay's intolerable actions, the urgency of his mission was suddenly borne upon him with new force. Perhaps it had been a mistake to wait so long. With Katherine involved in the construction of a new home on the assumption that Courtenay would be viscount in nine or ten months, there wasn't a moment to lose. The perplexity, and seeming impossibility of his mission, again pressed with great weight upon Percy's mind.

Slowly the words rose unbidden from his subconscious. Yet they were words his subconscious was training itself to pray with every inward breath and exhaling of his spiritual lungs. "Lord," he whispered, "show me what to do."

This visit was unlike any previous. He was, if not quite, *almost* a grown man. Florilyn was a grown woman. He had completed his studies at the university. This was no mere summer holiday between school terms. Eventually he would have to explain himself—what he was doing here. If he disclosed that he was on a mission for his uncle, questions would immediately arise. He must keep his purpose to himself. Yet he must also have some pretext for being here.

Still without a clear picture of what he would do, Percy turned from the window and blew out the candle to end the long day.

The next morning dawned warm and bright. Percy slept till after nine and found Florilyn and Katherine in the breakfast room awaiting him. "That's as late as I have slept for a long time!" he said. "I have to say, it felt good."

After a friendly visit with his aunt and cousin, Percy found the question he had been hoping to avoid suddenly staring him in the face.

"I had been under the impression you were thinking of law school, Percy," said Katherine. "Listening to you yesterday, it sounds as though your plans are indefinite. I was actually surprised to learn that you would be visiting us again. Delighted, of course! Merely surprised. How long will you be with us? What *are* your plans?"

Katherine saw him glance down at the cup of tea in his hand with an uncertain expression. "Please," she added quickly, "you are welcome as long as you like. You are always welcome—you know that! I am simply interested."

"Actually, Aunt Katherine," replied Percy, "my future is cloudy. I honestly don't know how to answer you. Yes, law school looms on the horizon as a possibility. And of course Florilyn and I have to talk," he added, glancing toward Florilyn with a smile, "and seek what is God's will for us."

"I understand."

"This has become like a second home to me," Percy went on. "As much as I love being with my mother and father, I am more at peace here in the country. With my future uncertain, I felt that this was where I should be to ask God about it. I hope you don't mind."

"Of course not. You are family. This *is* your home! At least," she added, "for another few months. Once Courtenay turns twenty-five, the manor may no longer be home to any of us! Florilyn and I may have to spend a few months or a year in Glasgow with *your* parents while our new home is being completed."

Percy realized that he may never have a more appropriate moment to hint at the most important reason he had returned to Wales. "There is another thing," he said, choosing his words with care. "Before he died, Uncle Roderick asked me to. . .well, sort through some of his old things, papers and so on." He hesitated.

His aunt was looking at him with an expression of perplexity.

"He, uh. . ." Percy went on, "he didn't feel he could trust Courtenay to do it, he said. I'm sorry to have to say that—"

"No, I understand completely," said Katherine. "Courtenay has not shown himself to be the young man of sterling character we had hoped he might be."

"He knew his death would be devastating for you," Percy continued. "So he asked me to put his things in order, I suppose is how one might put it. I think the fact that I was hoping to study law may have influenced him as well. He was under the impression that my being a *student* of law gave me a sort of legal standing if such became necessary—that while you were trustee for the estate, I would be able to act on his behalf as well. I assured him that I had no legal standing and suggested that he speak to his own solicitor. But he was insistent that he wanted me to dig into his past. . .that is. . .to see that legalities were being followed. I have the sense that he may have been concerned about Courtenay as well, afraid that he might try to manipulate affairs to his own advantage."

"Roderick had good reason to be concerned."

"Perhaps Courtenay was his chief concern. It may be that he preferred that I be the lightning rod for Courtenay's hostility rather than you, that is if it turned out that Courtenay attempted to exploit his position prematurely or in some manner inconsistent with his rights as presumptive heir." Percy drew in a long breath. He was having great difficulty avoiding the central issue of his uncle's secret affidavit.

"What exactly. . .did he want you to *do*?" asked Katherine.

"Actually, I am uncertain about that myself," replied Percy, thankful that the wording of his aunt's question allowed him to answer with complete candor. "I think simply to go through his papers and files, put things in order for you. He didn't want you to be burdened by anything. As I understand it—though as I say, I have been in some perplexity about it myself—he simply wanted to be certain that all the affairs of the estate were properly settled and in legal order. His main thoughts were of you. He wanted to protect you from any burden his death was likely to cause. Perhaps I should have undertaken the charge sooner. It now seems that Uncle Roderick's fears about Courtenay were indeed well founded. Now that I learn what he has done, I regret waiting until now. At the time there did not seem to be great urgency. After talking with my father, we determined that I should complete my studies and then return here. It may be that decision wasn't the best."

"Whatever he had in mind, he chose you for good reason, Percy. What's done is done. None of us can go back and rewrite the past."

It was silent momentarily.

"Well, the whole thing remains a mystery to me," said Katherine at length. "I have no idea what Roderick expected you to do. The affairs of the estate seem to be in good hands with our solicitor, Mr. Murray, and with Steven managing my daily affairs. But it sounds as though you have no more idea than I do what he had in mind."

Percy did not reply. Already he feared he had said too much. But it was too late to take his words back.

"I assume that you will want to start in Roderick's study," said his aunt, interrupting his reverie. "I have been using it for my office as well, but he was right in that I had no appetite for going through any old papers or files. I have not even looked in the safe. So consider the study yours for now, Percy. I will remove my few things while you are working. If there is anything you need, or any way I can help, of course you will tell me."

"I will, Aunt Katherine," nodded Percy.

"And if you unearth any deep, dark mysteries, I will be curious to learn of them!"

Again, Percy said nothing.

THIRTY

The Green Hills of Snowdonia

*I*t is a gorgeous day. How about a ride?" asked Percy as he and Florilyn left the breakfast room and wandered outside into the warm morning together.

"If everyone saw us riding off," said Florilyn with a smile, "there will be sure to be talk. All the servants are dying to know if we are going to resume our engagement."

"How do you know?"

"I overhear them," laughed Florilyn. "They're not so clever at hiding their curiosity as they think. Mrs. Drenwydd says that you have come to propose to me again!"

Percy chuckled. "Well then, it would be a shame for us not to keep them guessing. But we could go out as a threesome or a foursome instead."

"With whom?"

"I don't know—I thought with Stevie. . .I mean Steven. And maybe Rhawn Lorimer."

"Rhawn!" said Florilyn in surprise.

"I feel sorry for her. And I like her. She's lonely."

"She was awful to you."

"That was a long time ago. She's changed. You know that better than I do."

"How can you be so *good*, Percy?"

"I'm not. But my heart goes out to her."

"It might be fun at that. I know it would mean the world to her."

They walked toward the garden in silence. Florilyn slipped her hand through Percy's arm.

"Percy, Percy. . ." She sighed. "What does the future hold for us? Do you think there is an *us*?"

"I don't know. I'm in no hurry. And I can tell that you are content. You look *well*, Florilyn—prettier than ever and at peace with your life. The more time that passed after my Christmas visit, the more I saw the wisdom in what you did. I mean, I love you and always will. But now I am asking God if the love I have for you is the love of a brother, or a cousin I suppose I should say, or the love of a husband."

"That's exactly what I found myself thinking when I saw you yesterday!"

"It may be that what I have to do for your father will help us know what we are to do."

"How could that be?"

"I don't know. I am just taking one step at a time and seeing what comes of it."

A peculiar look of question came over Florilyn's face. "There's more to it than what you told Mother, isn't there?" she said. Percy glanced toward Florilyn to see if she was baiting him. But her expression was serious.

"Why would you say that?" he asked.

"Because I know you. I could tell that you were hemming and hawing, trying as hard to keep from saying what you wanted to avoid as to say what you did."

"Do you think your mother noticed?"

"I don't know. I doubt it."

They walked on in silence.

"So are you going to answer my question?" said Florilyn at length.

"Do I have to?"

"No. I won't coerce it out of you."

"Fair enough. Then. . .yes, there *may* be more to it. But there may not be. I was perfectly truthful in saying that your father's request is mostly a mystery to me, too. I may turn up nothing. I have no idea what to expect."

"I still think there's more to it even than that," said Florilyn with the hint of a twinkle in her eye. "But I will let that suffice. . .for now. As long as you promise to tell me if you discover anything interesting. . .especially about Courtenay. How I would love to turn the tables on him after how he has treated Mother."

"I'm sorry, I can make no promises. I will promise you this—I will tell you whatever I *can* tell you."

"Very cryptic!"

"So what do you think, shall we ask if Steven can tear himself away from his duties for a ride?"

"I will go see him right now," said Florilyn. "Why don't you ride into town and see if Rhawn can join us?"

The four young people set off from Westbrooke Manor shortly after midday with a picnic lunch packed by Mrs. Drenwydd. Rhawn Lorimer was quiet but happier than she had been in months to be on the back of a horse again with friends her own age. They rode into the hills eastward, four abreast, until they crested the first inland ridge. The trees thickened as they descended out of sight from the sea.

Florilyn and Rhawn took the lead, riding beside each other. Soon they were talking like the old friends they were as Percy and Steven lagged behind.

"It is so nice to have a break from mothering," said Rhawn. "I love little Aiden to death. . .but he is exhausting! Thank you so much for inviting me, Florilyn."

"It was Percy's idea."

"It was?"

"He is very fond of you."

"Are there any. . . I mean, have you and he—" Rhawn hesitated.

"Have we come to a decision yet? No. We are waiting to see what develops."

"Don't you. . . I mean, don't you still *want* to marry him?"

"Not if he's not the right one for me."

"How could he *not* be? Young men like Percy don't come along every day!"

"That's true. He's one in a million. But it still has to be right. Marriage is too important to rush into."

Rhawn did not reply. It was already too late for her to have a marriage that was *right*.

Their two squires rode briskly up beside them, cutting off further conversation.

"Take us to the meadow where we first raced, Florilyn," said Percy. "That will be a good place for lunch."

"I think I have heard that story," said Steven. "Didn't you come to an inglorious end?"

"I did indeed!" laughed Percy. "But I have learned a little about keeping the saddle beneath me since then. Perhaps I shall play a return engagement!"

"You and I've already done that!" laughed Florilyn. "You don't have to prove anything to me. I know you're as fast as I am now. Rhawn used to be the best horsewoman for miles," she added.

"That was a long time ago!" laughed Rhawn.

"Perhaps we should coax the men into a race, Rhawn," said Florilyn playfully.

"Steven and I are not competitive with each other," rejoined Percy. "Both of us would probably want the other one to win. If you're itching for a race, you'll have to lay down the challenge yourself, Florilyn, my dear!"

Florilyn cast Percy another smile that said, *Perhaps I will at that!*

They continued eastward down the ridge, through the valley at its back, across several streams, through woodland and meadow, and gradually up the next ridge until again they rose to its height and reached the parallel crest another two miles farther inland. There they reined in and gazed about. The regularly spaced peaks of Gwynedd running in a line north and south were clearly visible both to their right and left, their jagged peaks of granite dotted with snow.

"Look," said Steven, "you can faintly see Snowdonia there, far to the north beyond the other mountains."

"It's still covered in snow," said Percy. "I assumed it would be gone by now. This could be the Scottish Highlands."

"We had a good heavy snowfall only two weeks ago," said Steven. "It's early yet—not quite June. Snowdonia can keep its snow till July in a late spring."

"Have you ever climbed it, Steven?"

"My father took me up when I was a lad. It's not a rigorous climb. But it's certainly desolate up there—nothing but rock, gray and barren. It's a wasteland. But the view is spectacular. Personally, I prefer the green hills all around, with meadows and forests and rivers and pasturelands. A mountaintop, I have always thought, is a dead thing. A meadow with a brook running through it is a *living* thing—abundant with life. I would rather see *life* and *growth* about me, not death."

"Eloquently put, my friend," said Percy. "In people most of all."

Gradually they continued down the slope from the ridge toward the expansive meadow at its base, which was their objective.

"I have always considered green the color of growth and life and energy and hope," Steven said as they went. "It must be God's favorite color, don't you think, since so much of his creation he painted with so many interesting and varied shades of green."

"People are like mountains or meadows, too, don't you think, Steven," said Percy reflectively. "If they are not growing, then something is dead inside them. God's meadows, that's what he created us to be. We are intended to be live, growing, flourishing reflections of his creation."

"The vicar's son!" laughed Florilyn good naturedly. "Is a sermon coming on, Percy? Perhaps you are cut out for the pulpit after all."

"What's this?" said Steven.

Percy laughed. "I once asked Florilyn what she thought of my career options—law or the ministry."

"You were thinking seriously about the ministry?"

"I was," nodded Percy. "Once the Lord got hold of my life, everything changed. I wanted to be God's man in whatever vocation I was most suited. I wanted to be an effective spokesman for truth. Eventually I decided that would be law."

"But you're still not opposed to delivering the occasional short sermon, are you, Percy!" chided Florilyn in fun.

Percy laughed with delight. "One never knows when the occasion may call for it, my dear!"

"I rather like it," said Rhawn. "The others glanced at her and saw that she was serious. "I've never heard people talk about God like you three do. I always thought of God as so distant and far away. But you all bring him into everything. It's not easy to learn to grow when you've been a self-centered dead mountain of stone all your life."

Rhawn had not intended to bring an end to the conversation. But her words caused them all to become reflective. They rode on some distance in silence.

At length Florilyn urged Red Rhud ahead. A few minutes later, she led with a brief gallop into the meadow. "Here we are again, Percy!" she called out over her shoulder. "Are you sure you don't want to race me to the far end?"

"Maybe after lunch," he answered. "I'm hungry! I'm eager to see what Mrs. Drenwydd has prepared for us."

They reined in and dismounted. Soon the four horses were enjoying the grass and water from the living meadow, and the two young women and two young men were seated on the grass in the warmth of the sun enjoying the provisions provided by the Westbrooke Manor cook.

THIRTY-ONE

Growing Human Meadows

For individuals of any age, especially young people full of thoughts and experiences, to share with equal give-and-take in conversation with their peers is one of life's rare treasures. Most are so enamored with the sound of their own voices that listening becomes a lost art.

These were four friends, however, interested equally in one *another* as they were eager to orate at length from the storehouse of their own ideas and opinions. When one spoke, the others truly *listened*…listened to the heart, to the soul, listened to the *person*, because they were interested and cared. There was no debate of ideas, only sharing of thoughts and feelings and impressions. They were more intent to *know* one another truly than to be known themselves. The occasional silences that arose between them were part and parcel of the fabric of human intercourse.

It is not often in life that such conversations are allowed to take place. In most discussions, individuals have some ideas to put forward or some commentaries on life from their own experiences to share. The object in the former case is to bolster their own theses while disproving their neighbors'. The object in the latter is to hold the conversational floor for as long as their breath holds out. They may have originally adopted this particular viewpoint because of some sign of truth in it. But now this method of communicating is generally to block up every cranny in their minds where more truth might enter or to keep talking long enough that no alternate perspectives are able to squeeze a word in edgewise.

In the present case, unusual as it is for as many as four earnest, humble, truth-seeking, and listening young people to come together, here were four simply set on gaining what insights the *others* were able to offer. Thus it was that after an hour, they had partaken of two meals, both physical and relational. Each of the four knew the other three more deeply than before. They were no longer mere youths, but young adults embarking on life and desirous of knowing all that life could mean and should mean.

"I don't like to be the one to break this up," said Steven at last as he stood to stretch his legs, "but it is time I thought about returning to the manor. I promised your mother, Florilyn, that she could have her first ride on Snowdonia this afternoon. She has been waiting so long, I daren't disappoint her."

"That's the new white stallion?" asked Percy, rising to his feet also. He offered Rhawn his hand and helped her up from the grass.

Steven nodded. "I've been bringing him along very slowly. I've been riding him myself now for a few months, and he has at last settled down. Lady Katherine is a skilled horsewoman. But after what happened to the viscount, I will take no chances."

"You will accompany her, I take it?"

"For her first ride, absolutely."

Florilyn and Rhawn gathered up the lunch things and put them into the leather bag. Slowly the four walked to their waiting mounts.

"Are you ready for that race now, Percy?" said Florilyn with a twinkle in her eye.

"We shall see."

They mounted and set off slowly. Gradually Florilyn increased the pace, then broke into a gentle gallop and wheeled Red Rhud back the way they had come toward the edge of the meadow.

"Where are you going?" Percy called out.

"I'm giving you the advantage!" Florilyn called back, laughing.

"You'll need all the help you can to beat me to the far end!"

Percy laughed but did not seem inclined to take the bait.

Beside him, however, a grin spread across Steven's face. He was riding one of Courtenay's favorite mounts, the Chestnut stallion Cymru Gold. He well knew what the horse was capable of. He turned to Percy. "Watch this," he said. "We'll show the little lady a thing or two." Suddenly he bolted away from them with marvelous acceleration.

Behind them they heard Florilyn shriek. "Steven!" she cried. "I offered *you* no head start!" The next instant she was after him in a mad frenzy of shouts and pounding hooves across the grass.

Looking behind him, once Steven realized that she had taken his bait, he slowed to allow her to catch up. Side by side they rode for a few seconds, glancing back and forth at each other with the gleam of fun and challenge in their eyes, Florilyn's auburn hair trailing behind her.

Steven held Florilyn's eyes for a moment then winked in fun and shouted something in Gaelic Florilyn did not understand. Suddenly, though she was at nearly a full gallop, Cymru Gold began to pull steadily away from her.

"Steven!" she shouted again.

All she heard in reply was the sound of Steven's laughter receding away from her.

Florilyn dug in her heels and urged Red Rhud on with a mighty effort. But it was little use.

Behind them Percy and Rhawn watched and laughed in delight.

"I am afraid Florilyn has at last taken on a more worthy adversary than I ever was!" said Percy.

"Steven looks like he is loving every minute of it!" said Rhawn. "And so here we are together again, Percy—just like that other time, do you remember, when I was the one who baited Courtenay and Florilyn?"

"I remember!" laughed Percy. "Then you fell back so you could get me alone. You really were devious in your day."

A look of pain came over Rhawn's face.

Percy saw that he had touched a raw nerve. "Sorry," he said. "I meant nothing by it."

"I know, Percy. You couldn't hurt a fly if you wanted to. You're the most considerate person I've ever met. That's what makes it hurt so much to remember how I used to be."

"How so?"

"I had eyes for you for all the wrong reasons. I thought you were too cute for words. And I was tired of Colville and Courtenay. You were a challenge. But I never saw the real person you were. I didn't care about all that back then. I was shallow and selfish. I thought I could turn the head of any boy in the world. Then I met you. You were different. But I still had no eyes to see it. And look where it got me," she added with a ironic laugh in which the sadness was all too evident.

"I don't know, Rhawn," said Percy. "You are *growing*, like Steven was talking about. You are becoming God's live meadow. Maybe it took some heartbreak to get you there. Don't forget—or maybe you never knew, I don't know—I was sent to my Uncle Roderick and Aunt Katherine for the first time because my parents were desperate."

"Yes." Rhawn smiled. "Florilyn told me all about you back then. She didn't like you much at first."

Percy roared with laughter. "The feeling was mutual!" he said.

"Then five years later, the two of you were engaged."

"And now are un-engaged," said Percy. "An altogether strange sequence of events. But whatever you think you were, I was probably worse. You didn't know me then. I was a petty thief. I was in trouble with the Glasgow police. I had the best parents in the world, but I despised them. It still brings tears to my eyes to remember what I put them through. When my father finally put his foot down and sent me here, I thought he had sent me to prison. I was rebellious and conceited and self-centered. Yet somehow God used all that to wake me up inside. Look. . .they've reached the opposite side of the meadow! From here, I would say Steven had her by at least two lengths."

Neither spoke for a minute as their two horses walked gently across the grass.

"How does God wake people up, as you say?" asked Rhawn at length.

"By using the circumstances of their lives," answered Percy. "At least that's what he did with me. I found myself in new and strange—and at the time unpleasant—circumstances. Those circumstances forced me to start thinking about things."

"What kind of things?"

"I suppose mostly the kind of person I wanted to be. And about who God is and whether he had something to say about the way my life went."

Again Rhawn was silent. She was obviously thinking. "May I ask you something, Percy. . .something serious, I mean?"

"Of course. You know you can."

"There's really no one else I can talk to about. . .you know, about what happened. . .about my son. Everyone around here. . .even Florilyn—I know what they think. But you, Percy. . .I *think* that you don't care about all that. I think you accept me. . .just as a person who knows she made a mistake but who wants to be better."

"That is exactly how I see you."

"I want to wake up. I'm trying to wake up. Florilyn's given me some books to read where the people are thinking about God all the time. But it's hard to wake up. I don't know what to do. Maybe I was like a mountain of rock for too long. Maybe I can never become a growing meadow." She turned away, blinking hard trying to keep away the tears.

"Anyone can grow, Rhawn. Surely you know that. If you want to grow, you will. It's just that most people don't care about being different than they are. What they *are* is good enough. But for people like you and me, who have been through some scrapes in life, what we were *isn't* good enough. We want to be *better*. At least I did. And you're telling me that you do. So you *will* be. You *are* growing, Rhawn. I can see the change in you."

"Really?"

"Of course."

Rhawn wiped at her eyes and smiled a melancholy smile. "There were people who thought you were my son's father," she said at length.

"I know."

"I'm afraid I allowed them to think so. I'm sorry, Percy. It was an awful thing for me to do."

"All is forgiven."

"I wish you were Aiden's father. I mean. . .not because of—you know. . .not because of *that*. I just mean. . .you would be a good father, Percy. You wouldn't desert me and leave me alone."

Again Rhawn was quiet. "That's what I wanted to ask you, Percy," she said after a moment. "I don't know what to do."

"About what?"

"Whether to say something. . .whether to confront him. . .whether to force him to tell what happened."

"I hope you won't take this the wrong way," said Percy. "I mean, it is an awkward question to ask, but I'm sure you knew that there was talk. You *do* know who the father is?"

Rhawn nodded. "But I don't know how long to be silent. My son needs a father, a family, grandparents and cousins. But he would hate me if I told who he was. I want him to *want* to be a father."

"You are in a difficult position. You're right—to try to force him might make him all the more antagonistic."

"But how long do I wait, Percy? I've been waiting three years."

"Have you prayed about what to do?"

"Why would God listen to someone like me? You know what I've been."

"God doesn't care what we have been. He only cares what we are becoming. The growing meadow, remember?"

Rhawn forced a smile. "It's hard to believe that God cares about me," she said.

"He doesn't just care about you—he loves you. . .as his daughter. Just think how you love your little son. That is only the tiniest measure of how God feels about us. We are really and truly His children, and He is the best Father in the world."

"Do you really think God loves me?"

"Oh, Rhawn—He loves you more than you can imagine!"

Rhawn glanced away. This time the tears came. By the time she was herself again, Steven and Florilyn were riding back to join them, laughing and talking gaily.

THIRTY-TWO

The Search Begins

O n the morning following their ride into the hills, Percy sought his aunt after breakfast. "I think I would like to begin looking through Uncle Roderick's papers and things, Aunt Katherine," he said. "Whatever it is I am to do, it won't get done unless I make a beginning."

"Of course, Percy. What may I do to help?"

"I don't know. I suppose I should start in his study, if you don't mind."

"You may consider it your own office, for as long as you like," replied his aunt. "It's not locked. You may come and go as you please. There are a few keys on a ring. I don't even know what all of them are for. One I believe is to the safe I mentioned. Shall we go upstairs and have a look?"

Percy walked up the main staircase and followed his aunt into the late viscount's study. He glanced about fondly. It was just as he remembered it. The last time he had been in this office, his uncle had been giving him his blessing to marry his daughter.

"Here are the keys I told you about," said Katherine, taking a small ring from a hook on the wall behind the door. "There is the safe next to Roderick's gun cabinet. You will want to go through the desk, of course, and the file drawers over there in the cabinet on the far wall. I can't think what you will find. But perhaps it is as you say, just putting Roderick's papers in order."

She turned to leave, then hesitated and looked back to where Percy stood in the middle of the room. "I confess," she added with a smile, "I know this must be daunting for you, but I am relieved. I have little taste for paperwork. No one enjoys going through a loved one's personal effects after they're gone. But if you have questions or need my help, please ask."

Percy nodded, and his aunt left him.

He wandered about the small room, looking about thoughtfully, then sat down in his uncle's chair behind the large desk. What *was* he to do, he wondered.

Slowly he began to open one drawer of the desk at a time. Nothing of possible significance caught his eye—only the assorted paraphernalia of years. . .perhaps even centuries. How old was this desk? How many of these old tools, knives, fasteners, keys, pencils, pens, sealing wax, nails, screws, matches, tape, and the memorabiliac gadgetry and odds and ends that inevitably accumulate in a desk had preceded his uncle? As interesting as some of the old items might be, there was certainly nothing among this miscellany of flotsam and jetsam to offer any clues.

He opened the two larger bottom drawers. They were filled with files, folders, and envelopes, mostly yellowed with age and few displaying labels or the least hint of their contents. It would take forever to go through them all. And for what purpose? Surely his uncle had left nothing in plain view like this that would connect him to his brief former life in Ireland so long ago.

Percy rose and walked to the safe. His natural curiosity was aroused by the mere presence in the room of something that spoke so obviously of secrets. It sat on the floor to a height of approximately three feet, and in width about half that.

He knelt to one knee and tried several of the keys on the ring until he found one that turned in the lock. He grasped the handle and turned. A dull muffled clank sounded from within the mechanism. The mere sound sent a thrill of mystery through him. There was no safe in his parents' home in Glasgow. Who had safes but wealthy people for the purpose of protecting their riches? He had never actually looked inside a safe in his life.

Slowly he swung back the massive iron door. What he was expecting it would have been difficult to say. But gazing inside the small vault turned out to be a disappointment. The thing was half empty. A few large envelopes lay on the bottom. Shelves contained assorted papers. Several locked drawers were built into the lower quadrant of the right side. He tried the smaller keys of the key ring but none fit. Judging by the rest of the safe, they were probably empty. Whatever might be inside them, it would have to wait until a later time.

He had hoped perhaps to discover a stash of 100-pound notes or a silver-lined box full of diamond and pearl and ruby jewelry, or some other mysterious treasure. He cast a last look about the uninteresting contents then closed the door.

He rose, walked to the window, and stood staring out at the countryside below. From deep within the subconscious recesses of his brain, words from his grandfather drifted hazily up into his memory. He tried to remember the occasion. . .his father and grandfather had been talking seriously about spiritual things. He hadn't been interested himself. He was probably ten or eleven at the time.

Suddenly now from out of the past, as if bringing a message for this moment in his life, they returned with crystalline clarity.

"When you are uncertain of the course you are to pursue," he could hear his grandfather saying almost as if he were sitting in his uncle's chair behind him, *"get quiet before God. Center down, as our Quaker brethren like to say. Then listen. The still, small voice will speak. But you must learn to hear it. You must attune yourself to its soft and subtle rhythms within your spirit. The inner voice is never loud. You will not receive its promptings through the newspaper headlines, but as it were through some tiny printed message embedded deep in the paper. The Spirit speaks with nudges, not proclamations. These it takes years of practice to learn to hear. They emerge out of your own thoughts. . .yet they are distinct from your own thoughts. Even that distinction, however, is subtle, oh so very subtle. The enemy will seek with his wiles to ensnare you into thinking that your desires and ambitions, couched in the thoughts that come, are God's thoughts. They may be, though it takes great wisdom to know how to divine between them. Always be wary*

of justifying your own ambitions. The still, small voice most often nudges you to lay down your ambitions, not pursue them. Until the desires of your heart emerge out of the wellsprings of God's will, your own ambitions may be your enemy. It is only after they are laid on the altar of relinquishment, and there die into the will of God, that your ambitions become your strength. So lay aside your own ambitions, then listen. . .listen to the heavenly nudges. As they grow within you, move one step at a time into the light of their leading."

Percy found himself wondering how old his father was at the time. What had been the circumstances that had prompted the discussion with his grandfather? He could not imagine his father wrestling with personal ambition. Though it had taken him some years to recognize it, his father had been what seemed such a rock of spiritual wisdom. Yet some uncertainty in his life must have occasioned the conversation that he now found himself recalling.

But none of that mattered. The words had come today for *him*. Percy stepped back from the window and slipped slowly to his knees.

Spirit of God, he prayed quietly, *I am exactly at such a moment. I don't know what course to pursue. I do not even know if I have any ambition or will of my own in the matter. I simply don't know what I am to do or how I am to do it. I ask for Your help, Your guidance. Speak to me, Lord. Show me what You would have me do.*

He remained where he was, silent, listening, for perhaps five minutes. Finally he rose with a deep sigh of peace and again stood at the window. Far below in the distance, in the direction of the village, he could just make out the roof of the old Barrie cottage.

With the sight came an inner impulse to visit it again. Was this a quiet nudge in response to his prayer? What could the Barrie croft possibly have to do with his mission for his uncle?

Again his grandfather spoke from out of the past: *"Listen to the heavenly nudges and move one step at a time."*

Percy drew in a long breath then turned from the window and left the office in search of his aunt. If one step had been shown, he would take it.

Percy began to descend the main stairway, glancing about him. As he had been so many times in this house, he was again arrested by the gallery of portraits, some centuries old, of his uncle's ancestors. The compelling face of his uncle Roderick's grandmother above the landing halfway down the stairs was usually what drew the eyes and demanded attention, as if she were the matriarch presiding over the entire family legacy, past, present, and future. On this day, however, Percy found his eyes drifting to the other women, some young, some old, whose images hung between the ground and first floors. He stood staring at each, one at a time, for several seconds. Slowly began to dawn upon him a recognition of familiarity that all the women had in common. Was it the eyes. . .the nose. . .the forehead. . .the chin. . .the prominent cheekbones? He could not tell. The dresses were different, the styles of portraiture distinctive as having been painted in different eras. Yet some indescribable feature in every face was common between them.

Now rose before his mind's eye *another* face. Even as he stood staring at the wall, a voice sounded from the first-floor landing above him.

"What are you staring so intently at?"

He nearly jumped out of his skin and spun around.

"Percy. . .what!" laughed Florilyn. "You're face is white as a sheet. You look like you've seen a ghost."

"I. . .just—you startled me!" said Percy, joining her laughter. "Maybe it was a little like seeing a ghost. I had just realized how much you look like all these women."

"Those women!" exclaimed Florilyn. "Ugh—they're all ancient and dour!"

"You know what I mean—I noticed the family resemblance. Of course *you* are far more beautiful than any of them."

"That's better," smiled Florilyn gaily. She walked down to join him. "Why shouldn't I look like them? They *are* my ancestors, after all."

"I just hadn't seen it before. I was seeing your face, then suddenly you spoke, and there you were—not a ghost exactly. . .but you know what I mean."

"So have you finished your sleuthing in my father's study?" asked Florilyn as they continued down the stairs together.

"Finished!" laughed Percy. "I only started fifteen minutes ago."

"Did you find anything?"

"No. I don't even know what I expect to find."

"What are you doing now?"

"I'm looking for your mother. Then I'll probably ride in toward town."

"Would you like company?"

An awkward expression crossed Percy's face. "Actually. . .this is something I have to do alone, Florilyn," he said. "I hope you don't mind."

"No, that's fine. I shouldn't have asked."

Percy nodded and smiled, and Florilyn left him. He found Katherine in the kitchen with Mrs. Drenwydd.

"Aunt Katherine," he said, "when I was here last summer there was an Australian in the cottage where the Barries used to live—an unfriendly chap! Is he still there?"

"No, he didn't last long at the mine from what I understand. He's been gone for months. The place is vacant now."

"Would you mind if I went down there?"

"Not at all."

"I would like to see the place again. I spent some happy times there. Will I need a key?"

Katherine laughed. "I doubt if there are a half dozen cottages in all Llanfryniog that even have locks on the doors! No, you won't need a key."

THIRTY-THREE

The Cottage

I t was with a strange feeling almost of reverence an hour later that Percy opened the door and crept into the cottage that had once been filled with such life. It was so still and quiet. Even in Gwyneth's absence, the sense of her presence remained. Slowly Percy walked about through the two rooms of the cottage. He recognized a few pieces of furniture that were left. What clue he hoped to find here about his uncle, he could not imagine. Nor to answer the mystery of why Codnor Barrie, his daughter Gwyneth, and his great-aunt had disappeared from Llanfryniog without a trace, or where they might have gone.

As he walked about, Percy reflected further on the small family's strange disappearance. He gazed at the stone walls, the fireplace, the great beams overhead, the floor of thick wood planks. He stood in front of the hearth, now cold and lifeless. The mantel was embedded in the stonework, a massive beam of oak of obvious ancient date, gnarled and pitted.

At length Percy turned away and walked outside, closing the door behind him. He wandered behind the house where Gwyneth had kept her animals. The lifelessness here was even more profound than in the cottage. Most of the large enclosing fence where her menagerie of animals had made their home was still visible, though in poor repair. But the pens and animals were gone. Only one small enclosure was left, mostly in ruins, its thin roof partially collapsed upon the decaying boards of a wall. Percy walked toward it.

On the other side of the fence, a movement caught his eye. He turned and saw a small gray rabbit hopping slowly toward him across the grass. It slowed as it came closer. It did not seem afraid.

Percy knelt down and gently extended his hand through the fence.

Tentatively the small creature took a few more steps toward him and sniffed at his fingers.

"Is that you, Bunny White Tail?" said Percy, gently stroking the furry gray back.

Still the bunny did not shy away.

"I believe it is you. You miss your mistress, too, don't you? Have you been here all this time waiting for her?"

For some moments, the young man and the bunny held a magical communion, bound together by the one who was the reason they were both there but who was now gone. At length Bunny White Tail bounced away, and again Percy stood.

Turning from the fence, he ducked low and walked under the partially collapsed roof of the dilapidated pen where once hungry animals knew to come along with those who were injured. With a fond smile, he looked about.

What was that hanging from an end of rusted wire? It looked like a clump of dried flowers!

He took two quick steps toward it and gently took hold of it. It was one of Gwyneth's friendship bouquets!

Images and memories flooded him from that first day when he had been the recipient of a fresh bouquet of wildflowers not so very different from this.

"Grannie says always greet a stranger with flowers," he recalled her saying at their first meeting.

Full of the cockiness of youth, he had replied with the air of one more pleased with himself than he had a right to be. *"So you consider me a stranger, do you?"* he had said.

"I've never seen your face before."

"*Then what do you intend to do about it?*"

"*Give you the flowers I picked for you, of course.*"

Even now, so much later, Percy recalled how his sixteen-year-old rebel's heart had been suddenly touched by the kindness of the child-stranger.

"*Surely you meant these for someone else?*" he said.

"*I picked them for you,*" Gwyneth had answered simply, gazing into his face with wide, innocent eyes. "*Now that I have given you flowers, I must know who you are. What is your name, so I shall know whom to ask for when I go to Glasgow?*"

Percy had laughed with delight. She was charming beyond words!

"*My name is Percival. . .Percival Drummond, at your service,*" he had answered. "*My friends call me Percy.*"

"*What would you like me to call you, Mr. Drummond?*"

"*You must call me Percy. What is your name?*"

"*Gwyneth Barrie.*"

"*Then, Gwyneth Barrie, I am happy to make your acquaintance. But why did you pick these for me?*" Percy had asked about Gwyneth's simple gift of flowers on that day.

"*I saw you coming,*" she replied.

"*You didn't know me when you picked them. Surely you don't give flowers to every stranger you pass.*"

"*Only those who are going to become my friends.*"

"*You knew that about me?*"

"*Of course.*"

"*How did you know?*"

"*I saw on your face the look of a friend.*"

Percy's thoughts returned to the present. The quietness around him deepened. It was too quiet—the stillness of desolation.

He glanced down at the flowers in his hand, held together by a small piece of yellowed paper and tied around with a bit of blue ribbon.

The blue ribbon! Of course—he remembered now. . .the very ribbon he had given her!

Slowly he untied the ribbon, so as not to damage the fragile flowers, then unfolded the crinkled paper that had held them together. There was writing inside!

> *Dear Percy,* he read.
>
> *These flowers are for you. I hope you come here one day and find them. I will never forget you.*

A stab stung Percy's heart. He remembered the day he had waited for her so long on the edge of the bluff at Mochras Head. He had never seen her again.

"Oh, Gwyneth," he whispered, "where have you gone?"

THIRTY-FOUR

The Inn

*A*s he left the cottage and rode toward Llanfryniog, his mind and heart quiet and full of many things, Percy recalled his return to Wales a year ago when he had stopped in at Mistress Chattan's pub before continuing on to the manor. She had dropped several cryptic comments he had hardly understood, things about his uncle along with hints that she knew more than she was saying. Maybe it was time he paid the good Mistress Chattan another visit.

Percy walked into the thin light of Mistress Chattan's establishment. It was midafternoon. He was glad to find the place empty of patrons. Mistress Chattan was nowhere to be seen. Percy sat down at one of the tables and waited.

Presently the proprietress appeared from her quarters, walking out from behind the long wooden bar. Still large, still clad in the familiar white apron spread about with stains and splotches evidencing the day's work, she appeared to have shed a few pounds since he had last seen her. She still glided across the floor with the soft, stealthy step of a cat. Her hair was nearly entirely gray now, the wrinkles in her face and neck more pronounced.

For the first time since he had made her acquaintance, a fleeting tinge of sadness swept through Percy at the sight. She was aging and alone. What did her future hold?

"Well, young Drummond," she said as she saw her lone customer, "you're back, are you?"

"Hello, Mistress Chattan," said Percy, greeting her with a smile. "You probably already knew I was here."

"I did indeed."

"You know everything that goes on in this village."

"It pays for one like me to keep abreast of happenings."

"Is your ale still the best?"

"I've no cause to think otherwise. But you shall be the judge of that yourself."

"Then pour me a pint and we shall see!" laughed Percy. "Come join me, Mistress Chattan," he added.

She returned a moment later, set a tall glass in front of Percy, then eased into a chair opposite him. "So you're not going to marry the lass after all?" she said.

"You do know everything!" laughed Percy. "Are we so much the subject of the town's talk?"

"There's nothing quite like a broken engagement to set tongues wagging."

"It's not so much a broken engagement but a *postponed* one. We are simply waiting."

"Waiting for what?"

"To see if it is right."

Whether Percy's answer conveyed in any sense of the word an *accurate* view of the situation was doubtful. But she did not press her inquiry further. A student of the human condition in her own way, which she exploited through her position, aided by the liquid inventory of her stock-in-trade, Mistress Chattan was not by any stretch of the imagination a spiritual woman. What insight she possessed into human nature had been gleaned for one purpose alone—that she might gain power over those who came her way. She had come into more than her share of secrets. By subtle art, attentive ear, and skillfully placed sympathetic comment, she had through the years obtained much information that might be useful to possess. But to understand

the spiritual movements within the heart of one like Percy Drummond
lay completely outside her ken.

"So what do you know of Lord Snowdon's past, then?" asked Percy
abruptly.

Mistress Chattan's eyes narrowed. If the question took her by
surprise, she did not reveal it. "What makes you think I know anything?"
she said.

"You dropped many hints when I was here a year ago. You told me
there had been another woman before my Aunt Katherine."

"I only told you what I have heard. But no one around here knows
of it, for it all took place across the sea."

"You said there was a child?"

"There's children and there's children. That's why I asked you if you
knew about your uncle's past."

"I may know more than I once did," said Percy with an enigmatic
tone of his own.

It was not lost on Mistress Chattan. One of her dark eyebrows
curled up in question.

"But it's my opinion that you know more than you've said as well,"
Percy added. "Now it is time for me to know what you know."

It was silent for twenty or thirty seconds. Mistress Chattan was
thinking. "So the young man's about to become the new viscount, is he?"
she said at length.

"You seem well up on the affairs of the manor."

"I know things, young Drummond. I know when his twenty-fifth
birthday is and what might make him rue the fact that it didn't come
earlier."

"What do you mean?" asked Percy.

"Just that there may be others to consider."

Percy took in the whispered words without revealing anything.
Now he was thinking hard, wondering how much to reveal. He knew
one like Mistress Chattan *might* be dangerous. He had to walk with
care. "Others?" he repeated. "Who are you talking about?"

"I will say no more than that. There were rumors."

"What kind of rumors?"

"About what drew your uncle to Ireland in the first place."

"What was it then?"

"The lure, what else? What seduces all young men—and the lure of riches. . .the lust for gold."

THIRTY-FIVE

The Library

$\mathcal{P}$ercy left Mistress Chattan's with much to think about. From the inn he went to the Lorimer home, visited with Rhawn for an hour, then began the ride back up the plateau to Westbrooke Manor. When he arrived it was nearly time for dinner.

He took his mount to the stables, unsaddled it, and then made his way around to the side entrance of the manor. He hurried up to his room with the bouquet tied with the blue ribbon in his hand, clutching it as if it were a tiny baby bird, careful over every stem and petal, but strangely shy lest Florilyn see it. Depositing it in his room, he descended by the main stairway to the dining room where his aunt and Florilyn were about to begin the evening meal without him.

Later that evening, Percy went upstairs. Instead of returning to his room, he went to the library. He had not wanted to tell Florilyn that he had not even brought the MacDonald book she had been reading with him.

He sought the shelf where he knew his aunt kept her growing supply of MacDonald books. The collection had indeed grown since he was last here. He stepped closer and examined the spines where the titles stood side by side. Some were familiar. Some he had heard his parents mention. Some were altogether new to him: *Adela Cathcart, Alec Forbes of Howglen, Guild Court, Unspoken Sermons, Annals of a Quiet*

Neighbourhood, Ranald Bannerman's Boyhood, Robert Falconer, A Seaboard Parish, At the Back of the North Wind, The Princess and the Goblin, The Vicar's Daughter. . .

There was the one he was looking for—*David Elginbrod.* Percy removed it from the shelf, found his favorite chair in one of the window alcoves, flipped through the pages toward the end until he found his place, and began reading.

An hour later, as Percy began to get drowsy, the words on the page suddenly arrested his attention. *"He gathered together the few memorials of the old ship gone down in the quiet ocean of time; paid one visit of sorrowful gladness to Margaret's home. . ."*

It was just like his visit earlier in the day to the cottage on the moor—memorials of the passage of time from his visit to Gwyneth's former home. Even with the thought, he remembered what Florilyn had said when he was here for Christmas.

"Gwyneth is Margaret in the book, Percy!" she had said. *"Hugh thought he was in love with Euphra. . .but all along he was meant to discover his love for Margaret. Don't you see? In the same way, what if part of your heart still belongs to Gwyneth?"*

Wide awake now, Percy continued to read, remembering again how Gwyneth, when he was a "pilgrim" in Wales, had awakened him to nature, to God, to himself. And yet, through it all, it was the face of Gwyneth herself that rose, dawning within him like a crescent moon.

"Perhaps the greatest benefit that resulted to Hugh from being made a pilgrim on the earth," Percy read, *"was, that Nature herself saw him, and took him in. She spoke to him from the depths of air, from the winds that harp upon the boughs, and from the streams that sing as they go. It is no wonder that the form of Margaret, the gathering of the thousand forms of nature into one harmony of loveliness, should rise again upon the world of his imagination.*

She had dawned on him like a sweet crescent moon, hanging far-off in a cold and low horizon. Now, lifting his eyes, he saw that same moon nearly at the full, and high overhead. He knew that he loved her now. He knew that every place he went through caught a glimmer of romance the moment he thought of her. But the growth of these feelings had been gradual—so slow and gradual, that when he recognized them, it seemed to him as if he had felt them from the first. The fact was, that as soon as he began to be capable of loving Margaret, he had begun to love her. Now that Nature revealed herself to him full of Life, it was natural that he should recognize Margaret as greater than himself. She had been one with Nature from childhood, and when he began to be one with Nature too, he must become one with her."

Percy's hands were nearly trembling by now as he held the book. Florilyn's words were probing his brain, his heart, his whole being: *"Gwyneth is Margaret in the book, Percy! What if part of your heart still belongs to Gwyneth? You have to find out. You have to discover what is in your heart."*

He continued to read MacDonald's words about the fictional Hugh and Margaret. But he was no longer reading about Hugh Sutherland. He was reading about himself!

"But dared he think of loving her, a creature inspired with a presence of the Spirit of God, clothed with a garment of beauty which her spirit wove out of its own loveliness? She was a being to glorify any man. What, then, if she gave her love! She would bring with her the presence of God himself, for she walked ever in his light, and that light clung to her and radiated from her. True, many young maidens must be walking in the sunshine of God, else whence the light and loveliness and bloom, the smile and the laugh of their youth? But Margaret not only walked in this light: she knew it and whence it came. She looked up to its source, and it illuminated her face.

The silent girl of old days, whose countenance wore the stillness of an unsunned pool, had blossomed into the calm, stately woman, upon whose face lay slumbering thought, ever ready to wake into life and motion. Dared he love her?"

Percy drew in a deep breath, closed the book, then rose and stared out toward the sea in the distance. From the alcove he could also view the sea that Gwyneth loved so much. . .and to the east the hills where he had first met the nymph of Gwynedd when she was a mere thirteen and he was a sophisticated youth of sixteen.

How little he had known back then! All the wisdom had dwelt in *her*, not him. But he had had no eyes to see it at their first meeting.

He still stood at the window ten minutes later, absorbed in his thoughts. At length he turned. Taking the book with him, he left the library and returned to his room.

Night slowly closed in upon Westbrooke Manor. Two hours later Percy lay in his bed, awake and full of many thoughts.

Somehow he drifted to sleep. As occupied as his brain had been, he slept surprisingly sound—the gift given to youth—and awoke rested and refreshed with the sun streaming into his room.

Then rushed back upon him the torrent of thoughts from the previous night. Rather than overwhelming him, however, they poured over him as though he were standing beneath the waterfall of a bracing mountain stream, with its icy waters pounding over his head. He would meet the challenge of whatever the new day brought him with vigor.

Yes, he had loved Gwyneth. Oh, how difficult it must have been for Florilyn when she realized it—and how hard for her to tell him!

After breakfast he saddled Red Rhud and set off for the village. But again, his way led him to the Barrie cottage. Something was here, he mused as he rode up, something he was meant to find.

But where. . .but what?

He dismounted and again entered the cottage. Everything was just as it had been the day before. Yet in his mind's eye, it now glowed with the luster of the love blossoming in his heart. But alas, the bloom had flowered too late!

God, he prayed silently, *what do You have for me to see? Why have You led me here? Guide my steps, my thoughts, my eyes.*

Moving slowly through the rooms as he had the day before, a sense of anticipation, of something at hand, filled Percy's mind.

His thoughts full of Gwyneth and what he had read the night before, he left the cottage. As he prepared to mount Red Rhud, he turned back.

There, several yards to the right of the door, partially obscured by several overgrown rosebushes, stood a small stone sign or monument with words carved into it: MOR BHAIRNE A INBHEAR DÉ.

What could it mean? It was clearly Gaelic, that much he knew. But the words conveyed no hint of meaning.

He remembered seeing it many times before but had never thought to ask what the Gaelic words might mean or why that particular name had been given to the cottage. He must ask Steven.

With a new mystery added to all the rest, thoughtfully he rode away from the cottage.

THIRTY-SIX

The Meadow

I nstead of returning to the village as he had on the previous day, Percy found himself leading Red Rhud east into the hills and toward the peaks of Snowdonia. He hardly knew where he was bound at first. But gradually he knew. Would he be able to find the place without Gwyneth to guide him?

He rode up and inland for an hour, stopping many times to assess his position, often uncertain yet sure he was moving steadily closer to his destination.

At last he began to recognize the granite cliffs and the shape of several peaks. Certain of his bearings now, he led Red Rhud a short time later through the jagged opening to his left where the shoulder of a projecting ridge opened between one hill and the next, then up the rocky incline, round the large cluster of boulders, and finally to the overlook where he was again able to see the tiny lake of blue-green far below.

Its surface shone like glass. Near the water's edge, several deer were drinking from the lake and nibbling at the surrounding grasses of the meadow.

With a momentary pang of sadness, he realized that he would hear no haunting ethereal melody on this day from the lake creature of Gwynedd. He saw no sign of the wild horses. After a few moments, he urged Red Rhud on.

Soon he was descending steeply through a rocky ravine surrounded on both sides by fir and pine, with granite cliffs looming high above. When he judged he had come near the place beyond which Gwyneth would not let him go, he stopped, dismounted, tied the reins to a tree, and walked on gently and quietly.

In the clearing beyond the wood, a half dozen deer grazed upon the carpet of green while a dozen rabbits scurried among them. Behind lay the shimmering emerald surface.

He stood in silence for ten minutes. Quietness reigned in this place. Gwyneth's spirit surely hovered over it.

Suddenly a sound disturbed the hush of peace. Within seconds the deer and rabbits disappeared into the surrounding trees. Percy wondered if he had caused their flight.

Then it came again, from high above him on the other side of the valley…metallic noises and the sounds of horses. Then he heard voices… men's voices.

He looked all about. There they were, three or four men on horseback high above the lake on a projecting ledge on the far side. They were unloading equipment of some kind.

They were too far away to see clearly. But though he could not hear their words distinctly, their voices echoed off the rocks.

As he watched, one of the men now set up a surveyor's tripod and transit. Another pulled out a sketch pad and began to draw the lake and valley.

With stealthy and careful step, Percy retreated deeper into the safety of the pine and fir wood until he could retrace his steps to Red Rhud. If he had heard them, surely they would soon enough be alerted to his presence as well. He led Red Rhud back the way he had come as slowly and quietly as possible. Once on the high path again, he remounted. For several minutes he took great care to lead Red Rhud quietly, then increased his pace and made for the manor with greater speed than he had ridden up into the hills.

He tied Red Rhud in front of the house and went to find his aunt. "Aunt Katherine," he said, "do you know that small lake in the mountains to the northeast?"

"There are an abundance of small lakes in Snowdonia, Percy."

"It's between here and Burrenchobay Hall, but east and surrounded by high granite cliffs."

"It could be any of several—I really cannot say that I know for certain the one you are speaking of. Why, Percy?"

"I just came from there. It is a place I ride occasionally. I first heard about it from Florilyn and Courtenay. They said it was the home of a water kelpie."

Katherine laughed. "I have heard those stories as well. Gwberr-niog I believe he is called."

"That's him! I had forgotten the name. But after hearing about the lake, Stuart gave me directions so I could find it for myself. I rode up there again today. I saw some men there with surveying equipment—Englishmen as far as I could tell from their accents, though I couldn't make out what they were saying. I wondered if the lake was on Westbrooke property. Are you having surveying done?"

"No," answered Katherine with an expression of concern. "My surveying for the new house was completed months ago."

"They definitely had surveying equipment. I saw that much."

"I don't know that I like the sound of this," she said rising. "I will have a talk with Stuart to find out exactly where this lake is and if it is on our land."

Keenly aware that he had been neglecting Florilyn since his arrival and concerned for her feelings, Percy spent the afternoon with his cousin. They had a long ride and talk together. Percy even dared suggest a race on the beach with their two favorite mounts again, Grey Tide and Red Rhud, and was happy with Florilyn's acceptance. Her feelings of guilt over the accident involving Gwyneth seemed at last to have faded completely into the past.

The delightful afternoon reminded him why it had been easy to love her. That love had now turned to respect and admiration. He was now more certain than ever that she was right and that he must discover what might be the depths of his other love.

THIRTY-SEVEN

The Drawer

*T*he following morning found Percy again in his uncle's study.

On this occasion he took more care than had been possible with a mere cursory search. He spent the entire morning examining the contents of the desk drawers and cabinet and safe. Most of the papers he found were of little apparent use, many of the files predating his uncle altogether—personal correspondence, business records, journals and ledgers from the various factors who had worked for the estate dating back centuries.

He did, however, locate a brown envelope with the single word LITCHFIELD in ink on the flap. It appeared more recent than the others he had opened. The letters from one Lord Coleraine Litchfield contained no particular significance as he perused them. Yet they clearly concerned the potential sale of estate lands. He knew his aunt should be made aware of them, if she was not already.

Percy found his aunt reading in her private sitting room. "Aunt Katherine," he said, "I found an envelope containing some letters to Uncle Roderick from a few years ago. You might know all about it, but it seemed important enough to ask you about." He handed her the envelope.

Katherine removed the letters. As she read one after another, Percy saw her internal temperature beginning to rise. At length she began shaking her head. "I don't know whether to yell or cry," she said. "No. . .I had no idea Roderick was engaged in this correspondence. Apparently he was planning to sell some of the estate's land. I cannot say I am surprised," she added with a smile. "He was always short of cash, always trying to talk me into giving him money for one of his schemes. I am sorry to think that money came between us. But the sad fact of the matter is, it did."

"You don't know what came of this, then?"

Katherine shook her head. "I cannot imagine that anything did," she said. "Technically as viscount, Roderick could have sold estate lands without my permission. But surely I would have known. The fact that Hamilton Murray has never mentioned it convinces me that nothing came of it. These are all dated six years ago. However. . ." she added thoughtfully, "this man Litchfield was here visiting only a couple months ago—ostensibly because of Courtenay's eventual role in the House of Lords. I wonder. . ." Her voice faded away. She shook her head but did not complete the thought.

"Would you like me to leave the letters with you?" asked Percy after a moment.

Katherine sighed. "No, take them back to the study. I don't want them," she said. She returned the letters to the envelope and handed it to Percy. "Where did you find them?"

"In the cabinet of files."

"If I should need them, I'll know where to find them."

Percy returned upstairs to the study. Again he sat down at his uncle's desk. One at a time he opened its drawers. As he pulled out the bottom drawer, he heard a sound, as of something shifting. He stooped and peered all the way to the back but saw only the papers and envelopes he had looked through before. Puzzled, he gave the drawer a sharp jiggle. The sound came again. Examining the back of it more closely, he saw what now looked like a false back to the drawer.

He pulled it all the way out toward him. A thin block of wood had been wedged across the width of the drawer. He tried to dislodge it with his fingers, but it held fast.

The next moment he was outside and making for the workshop to find a small hammer. Five minutes later he sat down again, reached into the back of the drawer, and gave one edge of the piece of wood a light rap. Then again. The wedge of wood gave way. Percy removed it, set it aside, and reached all the way now into the true back of the drawer that had not been visible before.

His hand fell on something. He pulled it out and saw that he was holding a black lacquered box about eight inches by six inches and perhaps three inches deep. He lifted it out of the drawer and set it on the desk.

The latch for the lid had no lock. He unfastened the latch and lifted the lid back. Inside were a few five and ten pound notes—not exactly a fortune—several pens, a bottle of ink, and a few other odds and ends. Most interesting of all, however, was a key ring containing perhaps a dozen small keys.

Why had his uncle kept these keys here, nearly impossible to find unless one were looking for them, instead of with the others on the ring behind the door?

Percy looked them over. Suddenly he remembered. The drawers in the safe!

He was out of the chair and across the room in an instant. Quickly he unlocked the safe as before, threw back the door, and fumbled with the new set of small keys.

The first four accomplished nothing. The fifth, a small brass key scarcely two inches long, slid effortlessly into the lock of the bottom drawer to the right of the inside of the safe. Percy turned the key, heard a slight click, and then pulled the drawer toward him.

There sat a pile of letters, still in their envelopes. . .unopened.

He reached into the drawer and removed them. He did not immediately recognize the names to whom the letters were addressed. But he knew his uncle's hand well enough, as well as the return address: WESTBROOKE MANOR, LLANFRYNIOG, GWYNEDD, WALES. Every letter had been sent to a town in Ireland. Every one had been returned, unopened, stamped with the words, MOVED WITHOUT FORWARD.

The yellowed age of the envelopes indicated that they were old. Percy squinted and could faintly make out the postal stamps. All had been sent in 1842.

He drew in a long breath and exhaled thoughtfully. Letters in his uncle's hand that predated his 1847 marriage to Aunt Katherine.

He closed the safe and returned with the stack of envelopes to his uncle's desk. He sat down and set the letters in front of him. To read them seemed almost a sacrilege. But he could not show them to his aunt. There was no one else to read them but him.

He glanced through them all again. Folded between the envelopes was a newspaper clipping, the paper old and brittle. Carefully he unfolded it. The small headline read: GOLD FINDS ON INCREASE WEST OF WICKLOW.

He began to read the article.

> *"It has been assumed for years that the 1795 gold rush had spent itself well before 1820. But sporadic new finds continued to rekindle interest throughout the 1830s, and even more recently. Gold was first discovered in County Wicklow in what was subsequently named the Gold Mines River in 1795. The boom continued until 1830, during which time it is estimated that eight thousand ounces of gold were extracted from alluvial gravels of the region. Simultaneously, this period also witnessed the greatest coal mining and slate production episode in Ireland. All this activity also prompted a boom in shipbuilding in eastern Ireland, most notably in the seaport of Arklow, south of Wicklow. . . ."*

Percy continued to peruse the article. But the letters held far more interest. He glanced through them again. All bore the destination Laragh, County Wicklow, Ireland.

Wicklow. . .where they had been mining for gold!

He scanned the newspaper clipping again. He could find no mention of the date when the article was written. Was it gold that had taken his uncle there?

Along with Mistress Chattan's words, he now remembered, on his deathbed, his uncle's words, *"I was young and foolish and had dreams of making my fortune. There were rumors of gold, and that was enough to fire my imagination."*

Percy knew he had to read the letters. But he could take no chances of his aunt discovering them. Closing all the desk drawers, locking the safe again and keeping the small ring of keys with him, then carefully taking the stack of letters and slipping them beneath his shirt, he left the study and hastened up to the privacy of his own room.

Before he lay down to sleep that night, Percy knew that fulfilling his uncle's commission must next take him to Ireland. He must attempt to accomplish, even if it were thirty years later, what his uncle had not been able to with these letters.

If he failed, no one need ever know.

THIRTY-EIGHT

Departure

The next morning at breakfast, Percy broke the news to Florilyn and Katherine. "I am afraid I must take my departure sooner than I had planned," he said.

Mother and daughter looked at him with surprise.

"Why. . . Are you going home so soon?" asked Florilyn.

"I'm not going home. There is something I have to do."

"Where are you going, then?"

"I would rather not say."

Florilyn's face registered obvious disappointment. "But. . .you've only been here a few days," she said.

"I know. I am sorry," said Percy. "I can see that this has come out of the blue. I realize I haven't spent as much time with you as I had hoped. I will make it up to you when I return—I promise. But there is something I have to do. I don't think it can wait."

"Does this have to do with what Roderick asked you to do for him?" asked Katherine.

"It may, Aunt Katherine," replied Percy. "I can't be certain."

"Did you find something in his study?"

"I may have. Again, I cannot say for certain. I am sorry, but I just cannot say more. Actually, Uncle Roderick did not give me specifics. I am nearly as much in the dark as you. I hope you can trust me."

Again his aunt and cousin stared back with expressions of bewilderment.

"Of course we can, Percy," said Katherine after a moment. "When will you leave?"

"Tomorrow, I think."

The rest of the breakfast passed somewhat somberly. Percy knew that Florilyn was not merely disappointed. He could tell that her feelings were hurt, as much that he did not feel himself able to confide in her as that he was leaving.

He spent the rest of the morning in his room, again perusing the letters he had found as well as completing *David Elginbrod*.

After lunch, he invited Florilyn for another ride, this time into the hills. Her mood was obviously subdued.

"I was embarrassed to tell you when I came," he said after they were well away from the manor and climbing toward Rhinog Fawr, "but I hadn't yet finished the MacDonald book. I knew it was important to you, but school was just too hectic. I finally did so last night and this morning. I think I see everything you were saying to me last Christmas."

Florilyn nodded.

"It was hard to hear at the time," Percy went on, "but the wisdom of it is growing on me."

"Does your leaving have anything to do with Gwyneth?" asked Florilyn. "Mother said you went down to her cottage."

"Not really," answered Percy. "I just wanted to look around. There was nothing there."

"So you're not leaving because you have some new idea where she went to."

"Nothing like that. It has nothing to do with her."

"Does it have anything to do with *me*?"

"How do you mean?"

"Are you. . .disappointed with me?"

"No, not at all. Why would you think that?"

"I thought maybe that you. . .I don't know. . .that you found it awkward or didn't want to be with me anymore."

"Oh, Florilyn—that's not how I feel at all. I'm sorry if I—"

"It's not you, Percy," said Florilyn. "It's only that I feel. . . It is just hard sometimes. I miss you, that's all."

"I know. The feeling is mutual. I've had bouts of sadness, even depression, these last six months. . .you know. . .wondering about it all."

They rode on for several minutes in silence.

"What about the book?" asked Florilyn at length.

"I now understand about Hugh and Margaret," replied Percy. "Whether their story has to do with me. . .with *us*. . .that I still do not know." He paused a moment. "Are you. . . ," he began hesitantly, "are you still at peace with what you did?"

Florilyn smiled wistfully. "I think so," she replied slowly. "It makes me sad when I think about it. Doubts creep in. I wonder what it will be like if I one day have to watch you marry someone else." Her voice quivered slightly. "Then I worry that I may never marry at all. Girls always worry about such things. The worse thing I worry about is that I do not want to be like Euphra—like she was before, you know. But if and when we do marry, or *don't*. . .we will be stronger for having waited long enough to be sure. I know that in my head, but sometimes my heart forgets."

"You would never be like Euphra. You are too wonderful for that. But you don't know how much it relieves me to hear you say what you did," said Percy. "I think you've pretty well summed up how I feel as well."

Having cleared the air, the rest of the ride proved thoroughly enjoyable. They raced several times, explored a few new places, and spent the entire afternoon and most of the evening together.

The enjoyable day brought to Percy's remembrance that he had actually made *two* promises to his uncle. One of them, after he left, he would not be in a position to keep. He had not thought of it in practical terms during his final year in Aberdeen. But with so many changes bound to come to Westbrooke Manor in the coming months, he must perhaps be more attentive to it than ever. Late in the day he found Steven Muir in his office.

"So you are leaving us, eh, Percy?" said Steven where he sat behind his desk. "We've hardly had the chance to exchange two words, and now you are off again!"

"I am sorry about that," nodded Percy, easing himself into a chair opposite him. "It is actually quite unexpected but cannot be helped. I made a promise to my uncle that I have to attend to." Percy paused then drew in a thoughtful breath. "There is something I need to ask you to do for me, Steven," he said.

"Just name it."

"Before my uncle died, he asked me to take care of my aunt and Florilyn. Of course at the time he thought that Florilyn and I would marry. With those plans now uncertain, the situation is obviously changed. Nevertheless, I told him I would do my best to protect them and see that no harm came to them."

"He could not have left them in better hands," said Steven.

"Perhaps," rejoined Percy. "But now I am leaving. And with the strain caused by Courtenay's position looming larger every day, I cannot help being concerned. I don't know how long I will be away. . .and I would like to ask you to do your best for them in my absence and make sure no hurt of any kind comes to them."

"I would do so even without your request," said Steven solemnly. "I try to do so every day. But knowing I am standing in your stead, and indeed acting on behalf of the viscount himself, I will be especially diligent."

"Thank you. That will make my leaving easier," said Percy. "I know they are in good hands."

Percy was up early, and his two bags packed the following morning. He had breakfasted an hour before the northbound coach was scheduled to pass through town.

Florilyn and Steven took him in the small carriage into the village.

One last item of business remained. "I need to say good-bye to Rhawn," said Percy as Steven led the carriage into town. "Do you mind if we stop by her house?"

They drew up in front of the Lorimer home a minute or two later.

Percy jumped down and went to the door. Two minutes later, Rhawn returned to the carriage with him.

"Room for one more?" said Percy. "I think we can all squeeze in. Rhawn's going to the inn with us." He climbed back up, gave Rhawn his hand, and helped her up beside him.

Ten minutes later, the northbound coach bounded along the street and pulled to a noisy stop in front of Mistress Chattan's inn. Percy shook Steven's hand, then embraced Florilyn and kissed her on the cheek. She did her best to smile but was wiping at her eyes. Finally Percy turned to Rhawn. He opened his arms, and she walked into his embrace.

"Thank you for believing in me, Percy," she whispered. "I am going to keep coming awake. I will become a growing meadow, Percy."

"You already are, Rhawn. The flowers of spring are bursting out all over."

She smiled. "You are too nice to me, Percy! No one has every treated me like you have. And I am going to be better. I am going to keep growing. I will make you proud of me one day."

"I am already proud of you, Rhawn. Anyone who is growing is deserving of great respect."

She was blinking hard.

"And I will ask for God's help about what I should do," she added in a quivering voice, "like you said I should."

She stepped back and smiled again. In her moist eyes was the light of hope. She had begun to know that she was truly loved, both by God and by the faithful friends he had given her.

PART TWO

Ireland

Summer-Fall 1873

THIRTY-NINE

Across the Ancient Waters

Twenty-two-year-old Percival Drummond, third in the generations of godly Drummond men and who now prepared to take his place in the man's work of that lineage, stood at the prow of a passenger ferry plunging through the waters of the ancient Celtic Triangle. He was on a mission whose result he could not possibly foresee.

Not divulging to his aunt and cousin that his destination was Ireland, he had taken the coach north to Blaenau Ffestiniog then to Bangor and finally Holyhead on the island of Anglesey, where he had embarked the next day for Dublin. In the Irish capital, he had dispatched a telegram to his parents informing them briefly of his plans. From Dublin, led only by the newspaper clipping and letters he had found, he took a coach south along the Irish coast to the county seat of Wicklow.

A few days ago, the only possible clues he had to guide him in what his uncle had desired of him he had derived from the deathbed affidavit he had written out for him a year before. The entire thing had been mysterious, and many of his uncle's words cryptic and puzzling. At the time, he had himself been filled with the youthful emotions of feeling partially responsible for his uncle's mortal accident. He had been too overwhelmed to absorb what was happening and his role in it.

Now that a year had passed, he realized how ill prepared he was for the task his uncle had set before him. If only he had asked more questions, probed his uncle for more details. But the events of that fateful week had rushed by him like a blistering wind of uncertainty. The death and grief and funeral had consumed all else by their intensity. Now his uncle was gone. He had taken his secrets to the grave with him.

Suddenly, Percy had the newly discovered letters to accompany the affidavit. He still had no idea where they would lead. But at least he had *something* to shed additional light on his uncle's dying disclosure—the name of the town that had apparently been his first wife's home, or that of her relatives. It was a place to begin.

The day was fair, the ocean breezes light and fragrant with sea, salt, and sunshine. Percy turned from the bow of the vessel, walked to the passenger deck, and sat down in one of several vacant chairs. From inside his coat he pulled out the affidavit and again read, in his own hand, his uncle's words.

> *To whom it may concern, especially to my dear wife Katherine, my family, and to Hamilton Murray, our faithful solicitor of many years:*
>
> *I make this affidavit on the 27th day of June in the year 1872 in the presence of my nephew, Percival Drummond, son of Edward and Mary Drummond of Glasgow, whom, for reasons that will become clear, I have asked to set my final affairs in order. I am of sound mind, but failing body. . . .*

Even to read the words brought his uncle's familiar voice back into Percy's memory and tears rose in his eyes. Whatever his uncle had been, however he may have failed as a husband and father early in his life, Percy had grown to love him. The remembrance of their brief friendship would always be dear to him.

> *At sixteen years of age,* Percy continued, *as a spoiled son of what I thought was wealth, I left Wales on a youthful grand tour, as we called it in those days—to see the world and spend money*

and generally squander my youth on the altar of irresponsibility. It turned out that my father was not the wealthy man I took him for. Before my travels were over, I was nearly out of money. I found myself in Ireland chasing the fleeting dream of riches in the rivers of Wicklow, though what remained to be found was doubtful. There my heart was smitten with a young Irish lass of working, though not peasant stock. Her name was Avonmara O'Sullivan.

Several months later we were married in a small parish church in County Wicklow. We were both children, she a mere eighteen years of age and myself nineteen. Whether it was wise or ill fated from the beginning, who can say. But it was done, though our brief happiness would not last.

I can hardly recall what my plans were. The years have faded and my memory with them. I think I assumed that one day we would return to Wales as Lord and Lady Snowdon, after I inherited the title. But I was in no hurry to return after our marriage. The lure of the gold in eastern Ireland still possessed me, though most of the treasure had been unearthed decades earlier. Nor was I anxious to bring a new wife back to Llanfryniog where I would always be looked upon as a spendthrift son who had never amounted to much. Whatever I was, at least in Ireland I could be myself. People knew that I was of aristocratic stock, but they had no preconceptions formed against me. The thought even fleetingly occurred to me that I might find work—though I had never worked in my life—in the shipyards down the coast in Arklow. The husband of my sister-in-law had been involved in that trade before marrying my wife's sister.

So we remained in Ireland and the following months were some of the happiest of my life. A daughter was born to us a year later, but my dear Avonmara died in childbirth. I was devastated. I could not even think clearly enough to give her a name. I did not return to the house for days. It was Avonmara's mother who gave her the name Morvern and took charge of caring for her and saw that she was baptized in the Catholic church.

As I recovered from the shock of losing my young wife, I knew I was unfit to care for a child. I had married at nineteen and was now a mere twenty and without means. Without Avonmara, Ireland became suddenly desolate. The thought of remaining was odious to me. My life had been shattered. I decided to return at last to Wales, thinking, I suppose, to try to establish myself and prepare for my eventual role as viscount. My father was aging and not in the best of health by this time. Marriage and becoming a father had begun to sober me to my responsibilities but sadly had only begun to do so. I told Mrs. O'Sullivan that I would return for my daughter as soon as I was able and would provide a good life for her and, as my resources enabled me, to help all of the rest of them as well, for times then in Ireland were difficult not only for the poor but for everyone.

Alas, time went by more quickly than I anticipated. I became involved in two or three questionable business schemes—that was always my Achilles' heel—and before I knew it, years had passed. I was still a foolish young man. Finally I made plans to go back to Ireland after my father's death and my assumption to the title. Even then I was young, only twenty-eight, but I assumed on the strength of my new position that I would be capable of providing my daughter the life she deserved. I wrote to Mrs. O'Sullivan, telling her of my plans, but my letters were returned unopened. I wrote several times, then to her sister. But all the letters were returned. I assumed that Avonmara's family was angry with me for, as they saw it, deserting my child. So I sailed for Ireland myself. But what should I find but that they were all gone from the town where we had lived. The entire family had disappeared.

It was not perhaps altogether to be wondered at. Those were desperate times in Ireland. The worst of the potato famine was still a year or two away, but it had begun by that time. People were starving and fleeing Ireland in droves. Entire villages were sometimes abandoned. The country was in chaos, and it would get worse. I went to the home where Avonmara and I had lived, where

Mrs. O'Sullivan had lived, where her sister, Vanora Maloney, and her family had lived. Two were vacant, the third was occupied by a newcomer who had never heard of either the O'Sullivans or the Maloneys. It crossed my mind to wonder if they had left with the intent of keeping me from my daughter. They must have wondered what kind of father I would make after deserting her for so long. If that were true, I could hardly blame them.

I returned to Wales, disconsolate all over again. At last I wanted to be a father to my daughter, who would now have been eight. But I had no idea how to find her. I took to travel again, suffering great pangs of conscience and remorse. I met dear Katherine in Glasgow. At first I saw no reason to tell her of my past, but doing so became increasingly difficult with each passing year. We were married in 1847, and gradually my past faded away as a dream and I put the memory of that time behind me. Courtenay was born, then Florilyn, and I managed to convince myself, now that I was a father again, that my sin had not been so very great and tried to excuse it on the basis of youthful folly. For years, whenever I remembered, I was jealous of protecting the estate for Courtenay, my only son. But now I realize that right must be done. . .whatever it might mean. I must attempt to make my past right by my daughter Morvern. For if she can be found, she is my rightful firstborn and heir. . . .

Percy set the paper down and sighed deeply. Thoughts of Courtenay made him realize again what was at stake. Even if he did find the viscount's first daughter, Courtenay would surely challenge any threat to his position in the courts. In the hands of the right barrister, he would no doubt have a strong case. Percy knew well enough that a skilled barrister could twist the law into so many knots it could say anything. Sadly, there were many in the legal profession who were motivated by money more than truth or justice.

Not a moment went by that Percy was not aware of the consequences of his uncle's secret first marriage. He could still hear his uncle's voice imploring him to help him do what he had never been able to do himself.

"God forgive me, not even Katherine knows of it. . . . You are a good boy, Percy. Be good to them. They may need you now more than ever. Promise me you will try to find her, Percy my boy. . . . Everything hinges on whether you are successful or not. I tried to find her, but she was gone, I tell you. Makes repentance dashed difficult, I dare say. Tell her I'm sorry I didn't come back. But she had disappeared, you see. . . ."

He didn't like doing this behind his aunt's back. But he knew the pain such a revelation would cause her. And such had been his uncle's wish as well, that if at all possible she should be spared that pain.

"I am loath to hurt Katherine," his uncle had said. *"If you cannot find her, this need never come out. No one must know about what you have written unless you are successful."*

A year had passed since he had heard those words. Now suddenly everything was changing. His aunt was building a new home, his cousin Courtenay would be the new Lord Snowdon in less than a year, and he was on his way to Ireland to see what he could do to fulfill his uncle's dying wish to find the daughter he had never seen again.

FORTY

The Westbrooke Factor

The day after Percy's departure, Florilyn walked into the kitchen. There she saw Adela Muir, Mrs. Drenwydd, Mrs. Llewellyn, Stuart Wyckham, and Hollin Radnor talking to a man who had his back turned, dressed in an impeccable black suit who was holding a top hat in his hand. She hadn't known her mother was expecting a guest. This man looked like someone important, though she almost thought she recognized the back of his head and wild shock of light hair. And what was he doing talking among the servants?

Two or three of the heads turned at the sound of her entrance.

"Oh, I'm sorry," said Florilyn, "I didn't know you had a guest. I was looking for—" Her next words died on her lips.

The man in the black suit turned toward the sound of her voice.

"Steven!" she said softly, her eyes wide in astonishment. She stared at him another moment then suddenly became aware of the heat that was creeping up the back of her neck. Rarely one at a loss for words, she was unaccountably filled with embarrassment from the eyes resting upon her. She turned and walked quickly from the room.

Steven hurried after her. He came alongside her halfway along the corridor. "Sorry," he said. "Did I do something to—"

"No," laughed Florilyn, recovering herself. "The sight of you all dressed up. . .it just took me by surprise. I didn't know what to say.

Goodness, Steven—you are an aristocratic gentleman!"

Steven laughed. "I had the same reaction when I looked in the mirror this morning," he said. " 'Who's *that*!' I said."

"What's the occasion?"

"It's a suit of my father's. My mother thought I should wear it if I was to be in London on business for a respected woman like Lady Snowdon. She cleaned and pressed it and dressed me up like I was a boy again!"

"You're going to London?"

"I leave on the train this afternoon from Dolgellau."

"What for?"

"On business for your mother," replied Steven. "There are some papers she wants me to file with the proper agencies concerning the transfer of title on the land, as well as talk to an engineer about the window design on the west-facing walls of the house that look out to sea. She also wants me to find out what I can about a certain fellow in the House of Lords she is interested in."

"Who is that?"

"You should probably ask your mother," replied Steven. "She asked me to keep my inquiries confidential. I'm sure she wouldn't mind your knowing, but she ought to be the one to tell you. But," he added apologetically as his step slowed, "I have to be off or I will miss my train. I was just saying good-bye to the others and giving Hollin and Stuart some last-minute instructions for the days I will be gone."

"Then have a good trip, Steven," said Florilyn, turning toward him with a smile. "I hope you enjoy London."

"Is that possible?" he rejoined laughing. "I think I shall be anxious to get back to Wales."

They shook hands then Steven hastened back to the kitchen.

Florilyn watched him go with a curious expression.

Later that afternoon, as she wandered through the stables and outside, she found herself thinking about the young man whom she had always regarded as little more than a shepherd but in whom her mother had placed so much trust. More and more he carried himself as a young man of breeding, even education, as did Steven's mother Adela. Besides being thoughtful and considerate, Steven was well spoken and genteel. She wondered if there had been more education in his background than she was aware of.

She and her mother were alone at lunch several hours later.

"Do you and Adela Muir still talk about MacDonald?" Florilyn asked. "Does she still read his books?"

"As avidly as ever," answered Katherine with a light laugh. "Whenever I get a new one, she usually finishes it before I do."

"You let her read them first?"

"She is a much faster reader than I. Even with her work, she breezes through them in three or four days. It only makes sense for her to read them first rather than having to wait several weeks for me to finish what is often a five-hundred-page book."

"Then you discuss them?"

Katherine nodded. "Usually she sees more in the characters and in the spiritual truths MacDonald has woven into their life stories than I do. She is a very perceptive reader."

"That seems unusual for a domestic."

"Adela was never a domestic until she came here. She is more educated than most people realize."

"How do you mean?"

"Her father was a schoolteacher on the peninsula. She grew up in an environment of learning and education, with books everywhere she says."

"I had no idea. Did you know that when you hired her?"

"Not exactly, though I had an idea there must have been something in her background to account for her love of books and her fluency with the world of ideas after she began to work here. Finally I asked her about it, and she told me the whole story."

"Which is. . . ?"

"Just what I told you, that she is the daughter of a teacher who was the son of a curate. They were relatively poor, and she was the youngest of five. She had no opportunity to further her education beyond what her father and mother gave her. Her brother, Gwyneth's father, came to Llanfryniog to work in the slates at a young age, staying with their great-aunt, Mrs. Myfanawy, who was a native of Llanfryniog."

"That's Grannie?" said Florilyn.

Katherine nodded. "After the parents died," she went on, "Adela had no place to go. She followed Codnor here and also stayed with Mrs. Myfanawy awhile until she fell in love with Glythvyr Muir and became a shepherd's wife. But their father and grandfather—the teacher and the curate—were gentlemen and well educated."

"That would account for Steven, too."

"*Account* for him. . . ? What do you mean?"

"He seems so much more than just a shepherd boy, as if he had more education and gentlemanly training than he would have received at the village school."

"Adela tried to do as much for his education as she could. She says he was always a great reader and devoured whatever books they could get their hands on. I must say, I have never regretted making him factor. He has as much business sense and skill in managing things as Tilman Heygate ever had."

"And now he's off to London on your business. I saw him all dressed up before he left. He looked like a dandy!"

"That was a shock, I have to admit!" laughed Katherine.

It grew silent for a few moments as mother and daughter each finished her soup.

"Will the new house be finished when Courtenay turns twenty-five?" asked Florilyn at length.

"There is little chance of that, I'm afraid," replied Katherine. "The work will slow considerably once winter sets in."

"What will we do? Do you really think he will kick us out of the manor?"

Katherine sighed. "I have long since stopped trying to predict what your brother will do. I doubt he will be quite so brazen as that. But he has made abundantly clear that I will not be welcome here. Until the new house is completed, I have assumed that we will go to Edward and Mary's in Glasgow. They would make us more than welcome. I am going down to the site this afternoon. There are two or three points Steven wanted me to look at. Care to join me?"

"I would like that."

Later that evening, alone in her room, the conversation with her mother and visit to Mochras Head and the construction site of the new house left Florilyn in an agitated state about the future. Months before, she would have written to Percy and poured out her heart and frustrations and uncertainties. As she sat down at her writing desk to attempt to do so now, however, she suddenly realized that she didn't even know where he was.

Almost the same moment, the image of Steven, handsome in his suit and with the top hat in his hand, rose into her mind. With the image came a smile, and she found herself wishing that, in Percy's absence, Steven were here and that she could talk to him. Whenever they chanced to talk, whether about the weather or horses or sometimes when Florilyn had mentioned something she had read, his responses always surprised her. They were calm, deliberate, well thought out. It seemed that whatever she found herself thinking about, Steven had thought about it already himself. Now that she had learned that he was not merely a talented peasant-shepherd but was of educated, even gentlemanly lineage, she would value his responses even more.

FORTY-ONE

Laragh

Midway through his second day on the ancient Emerald Isle, Percy rode into the village of Laragh in the single-horse buggy he had rented in Wicklow. He had no idea what he would do here. But Laragh was his only lead. The addresses on the letters confirmed this as the home of his uncle's first wife.

What he hoped to find so many years later, Percy had no idea. If his uncle had not been able to find his daughter after an absence of only eight years, what could he hope to do after thirty? But perhaps the O'Sullivans had returned. He would try to find the addresses, perhaps inquire at the post for the people his uncle had written to. He would see what he could learn about the names on the envelopes. Surely there was someone here who knew them.

He found the town's only inn. After seeing to his horse's lodgings, he was soon comfortably laying out his few things in what would be his own accommodation until his next steps were shown him.

Again his grandfather's words returned to him.

"Listen to the heavenly nudges. As they grow within you, move one step at a time into the light of their leading."

Percy sat down at the small writing table in the room, took out his uncle's letters from his satchel, and set them before him. Now that he was here, he needed to read them again, slowly, quietly. He had to see what missing pieces they could provide of his uncle's story.

He withdrew the first and unfolded the yellowed sheet.

April 17, 1842
Pine Cottage
Laragh, County Wicklow

Dear Mrs. O'Sullivan,

I must first offer my profoundest apologies for being out of contact with you for so long. I have been attempting to set things in order in my life that will make it possible for me to be a responsible father and give young Morvern the life she deserves. She would be eight now, and my negligence in waiting so long to see her again weighs heavily upon my conscience. However, at last it is my hope to change that. I have not remarried, and the memory of dear Avonmara remains precious in my heart. My father died two years ago, and I have now come into his title in my own right. I did not fully divulge my position before. I wanted Avonmara to know me and love me as I was, not for any future title that might come to me. I am, however, now a viscount. I am not a wealthy man, but I can assure you that Morvern will have all the advantages of her position that I am able to give her.

I hope you and she and all your family are well. After hearing from you, I will make plans to come to Ireland personally so that Morvern might begin her life with me as her father.

I am,
Sincerely yours,
Your son-in-law,
Roderick Westbrooke, Viscount Lord Snowdon
Llanfryniog, Gwynedd, Wales

Percy refolded the letter and replaced it in the envelope then withdrew the next.

May 10, 1842
Pine Cottage
Laragh, County Wicklow

Dear Mrs. O'Sullivan,

I write again in hopes that my letter of last month, which came back to me unopened, was perhaps waylaid in the post and returned by mistake. I pray this letter will reach you. In it I expressed my sincere apologies for being out of contact with you so many years. In attempting to set things in order in my life, I believe that it is now possible for me to be a responsible father and give my daughter the life she deserves. My tardiness in being so long to contact you weighs heavily upon my conscience. However, my father died two years ago, and I have now come into a viscountcy in my own right. I am not wealthy, but I can assure you that I can give Morvern all the advantages of her position as the daughter of a viscount.

I pray you and she and your family are well. I would like to make plans to come to Ireland personally as soon as possible so that Morvern might begin her new life with me.

I am,
Sincerely yours,
Your son-in-law,
Roderick Westbrooke, Viscount Lord Snowdon
Llanfryniog, Gwynedd, Wales

Next he read the third, which followed yet a month later.

June 15, 1842
Pine Cottage
Laragh, County Wicklow

Dear Mrs. O'Sullivan,
This is my third attempt to establish contact with you. My

previous two letters have been returned unopened. If you by any
chance receive this, please forgive me for neglecting my duty for
so long. It would be perfectly understandable if you never wanted
to see me again; however, I hope you will find it in your heart to
allow me to make up for the past by providing Morvern a future
with the opportunities I can provide her as the daughter of a
viscount.

I hope you and Morvern are well. Please reply. I am longing to
see my daughter again.

I am, yet again,
Sincerely yours,
Your son-in-law,
Roderick Westbrooke, Viscount Lord Snowdon
Llanfryniog, Gwynedd, Wales

Finally Percy's uncle had written to his wife's sister.

July 21, 1842
Vanora Maloney
Dell Bank
Laragh, County Wicklow

Dear Vanora,
I have written to your mother three times, attempting to
establish contact again with you all, and especially with Morvern.
I realize it has been a long time, and my silence is inexcusable. I
can only beg the forgiveness of you all and say that I am at last in
a position to give my daughter every advantage I can afford her.
I would very much appreciate your speaking to your mother on
my behalf and assuring her of my good intentions. My letters are
returned labeled "Moved Without Forward." If your mother and
Morvern have indeed moved, perhaps you could put me in touch
with them.
I would like to come to Ireland as soon as possible so that

Morvern might begin her life with me as her father.

I hope you and Daibheid and your family are well.

I am,

Sincerely yours,

Your brother-in-law,

Roderick Westbrooke, Viscount Lord Snowdon

Llanfryniog, Gwynedd, Wales

Then had followed another half dozen letters to both Pine Cottage and Dell Bank in the same vein throughout the fall of 1842, after which, Percy assumed, had come his uncle's ill-fated return to Ireland.

FORTY-TWO

Market Day

 arket day in Llanfryniog in the year 1873 had been planned a week earlier than usual. Thus it was that on the Saturday of the last week of June, wagons and carts and carriages began to roll into the small coastal village of North Wales while the morning was early and a chill still hung in the air.

By midmorning, dozens of tables and booths and stands were spread out between the Methodist chapel and the village, displaying a great variety of homegrown and homemade wares. Of the former, because they were in season, strawberries and new potatoes were among the most prominent. They were supplemented by turnips, carrots, floral bouquets, bottles of elderberry and hedgerow wines, cheeses, and jams, as well as small trinkets and sweeties for the children. Handcrafts made through the winter and spring months by the women of Llanfryniog rounded out the inventory of stock in trade. And of course all the fisher wives arrived with baskets full of the previous day's or night's catch.

Indeed, describing their goods as for *trade* was not far from the truth. As hard as they worked to prepare for it, few actually expected to go home that evening with more money in their pockets than they came with. Everyone saved up their pennies and shillings for market day. But though the collection did not amount to much, spending was as greatly anticipated as selling. Money *circulated* between the villagers, but there was little *accumulation*. This was a day not for profit but for fun. What one received from selling goods was happily spent or traded at a neighbor's table. All the women knitted wool caps and socks and sweaters and scarves, and everyone grew potatoes and made cheese. They did not *need* to buy from one another—it was simply the accepted means of lubricating commerce in a small farming and fishing community. Where cash was in short supply, barter was as common as coin. It was not the economic profitability of the exercise that everyone looked forward to but the social tradition in the life of the community. If visitors from inland or along the coast north and south added to the general flow of commerce with an influx of cash, perhaps all would go home feeling that the day had been well spent.

By noon the town was full with bustle and activity. Singing could be heard and would continue all afternoon. All three churches boasted choirs that practiced months for this day. The children from the school came together to alternate their own choral numbers with the adult choirs from the three churches. Fiddlers and accordionists and dancers filled in at every opportunity. There was not a minute throughout the day when some music was not drifting through the air over the numerous activities. Aromas from fires and kettles tempted the hungry to part with a few coins for their lunch. A variety of games and amusements kept children scurrying about excitedly from one to another to another.

Nor would any market day be complete without a suitable offering of animal flesh for sale or trade. At one end of the field was tied an assortment of pigs, sheep, horses, and several bulls to see what offers might be made. By noon, Chandos and Kyvwlch Gwarthegydd, Padrig Gwlwlwyd, Holin Radnor from the manor, and a handful of men were clustered about examining teeth and legs, hooves and flanks, and talking of all things equine, bovine, and porcine.

It was not the sort of gathering that Colville Burrenchobay would normally have given a tuppence for now that he was a sophisticated young man of twenty-four. But his sixteen-year-old brother Ainsworth had arrived at that age where young ladies and mischief in general exercised great fascination. When their sister Davina and her fiancé,

William Rasmussen, son of Baronet Rasmussen of Blaenau Ffestiniog, decided to join him, Colville was hardly inclined to stay home alone.

The brothers Burrenchobay led the way into Llanfryniog about one o'clock. Colville was not expecting much from the afternoon. Ainsworth, however, recently returned from a first year at Cambridge as undistinguished as that of his brother several years before, was hungry for amusement and sport. He was also eager to survey what pretty new faces the new summer might have turned up. Behind them, though she was engaged to the handsome young man at her side, Davina glanced about with as lively an eye as her younger brother. She was still a month shy of her nineteenth birthday and not quite yet cured of the flirtatious demon that had so successfully enchanted young Rasmussen.

Heads turned as the young people rode slowly up the road on their horses from the harbor to the chapel then made their way toward the town and site of the day's festivities. The three Burrenchobays were used to commanding attention wherever they went. Their father being the parliamentary representative for coastal Gwynedd was enough in itself to draw looks from men and women alike. They were not aristocrats by birth, though their father had been knighted and was now known as Sir Armond. With Lord Snowdon dead and Courtenay, his presumptive heir, out of the country, the MP's two sons and daughter were as close to aristocracy as anyone living along the coast was likely to claim on this day. That rumors had followed the two Burrenchobay sons for years added curiosity and a hint of terrified excitement on the part of the young ladies whenever the two were present. Colville's amorous escapades had been a subject of local gossip for years. Ainsworth was anxious to follow in his brother's tradition. Both were known to be good with their fists and even better with their guns. They were handsome, hot tempered, and enjoyed being in the limelight—an irresistible, if dangerous, combination.

As for young Willy Rasmussen, some might have questioned whether a mere baronet's son from the inland regions of Snowdonia would qualify as an aristocrat at all. It was universally accepted that Willy, never known for his intellectual prowess, had made the best of the match. The moment Davina's engagement was announced, there had been great disappointment in Llanfryniog. Though Davina was five years younger than Courtenay Westbrooke, many had hoped to see the important families of the region joined by two marriages. Colville's with Florilyn had been accepted for years as a *fait accompli*. Now, with Lady Florilyn involved with her Scots cousin—though no one quite knew where the thing stood—neither of the Westbrooke-Burrenchobay marriages seemed likely to materialize.

By the time the foursome split apart, the sheep-shearing contest was about ready to get under way. Ainsworth quickly disappeared with three or four girls in tow hanging on his every exaggerated tale of life at the great English university. Willy Rasmussen followed Davina about like a well-trained puppy as she visited with the village girls too old to wilt from Ainsworth's smiles. The envious glances went curiously in both directions. With the foolishness of youth that judged by looks rather than character, every girl in the place hoped someday to be so lucky as Davina in landing a squire as handsome as young Willy Rasmussen. On her part, however, pangs of envy also stole unbidden into Davina's heart to realize that for her the game of fascination and conquest was done. In her quieter moments, she wondered if she had perhaps acted too hastily in accepting Willy's proposal. The result was an occasional wistful glance about the crowd to see what young men were in attendance. If Willy noticed her roving eyes, he remained oblivious to its cause.

Colville, meanwhile, seeing no eligible young women near his own age—by their midtwenties, the young women of rural North Wales were either married or such as to be of no interest to him—had wandered toward the gathering of men looking over several horses that Padrig Gwlwlwyd, one of those who *did* hope to profit from the day's sales, had brought in for the occasion.

"Looking for a new addition to your father's stable, young Burrenchobay?" said Gwlwlwyd as Colville approached the gathering. "I have two or three that would do him proud."

"My father does not buy his horseflesh from village fairs," rejoined

Colville with obvious condescension.

"For yourself, then?"

"Horses are not my game, Gwlwlwyd," said Colville. He glanced about with humorous disdain. "Neither are cows or pigs. I will leave the animals to you."

At the far end of the field, shouts and cheers rose from the first shearing contestant—a burly young fifteen-year-old cousin of Chandos Gwarthegydd who displayed every indication of being a future champion. He was followed by Eardley White, Chandos's best friend of childhood who had filled out in direct opposite proportion to the blacksmith's son. Chandos could now claim to top sixteen stone, every pebble of it muscle and mostly concentrated in his chest, arms, and shoulders. One look at Eardley, on the other hand, at barely ten stone and over six feet tall, would have greatly interested the mathematician Euclid when devising his theory of what comprised a straight line.

But deft, coordination, and an innate skill in keeping a sheep relaxed under the knife were more necessary to shearing speed than brawn, and Eardley trimmed eleven seconds from Kethtrwm Gwarthegydd's time. After several more local shepherds had their go, the crowd became frenzied as it cheered on its favorites. That a good deal of modest betting had taken place on the outcome always added to the keen interest in the competition.

Six more contestants came and went. Still Eardley's time of forty-seven seconds held, though now the margin to second place had dropped to a mere three seconds.

Finally a late entrant who had just arrived stepped forward. A cheer rose, for he was a great favorite with everyone for miles. He had shown great promise as a youth in being the likely heir apparent to his father's unmatched skill with the razor-sharp shearing scissors. However, he had not entered the contest for two years. His current occupation was one that had not kept him in practice. Yet discussion and new bets were feverish as he readied himself for the contest. The predictions of his chances were mixed.

The new contestant's dress, indeed his entire bearing, might have led a newcomer to the village to conclude that he was of aristocratic blood, for he carried himself with a stature and authority that belied his humble roots in the foothills of the Snowdonian mountains. But the moment Steven Muir pulled off his shirt, for the day was hot, and turned toward the throng with a grin, they all knew the manor's young factor to whom they now paid their rent was still their own beloved Stevie.

Few noticed the young woman who had gradually worked her way closer to the front of the noisy commotion. Slowly she squeezed through until she was standing near the front, staring at the sight of his bare chest and rippling shoulders.

"We'll see what the work of a dandy's made of you now, Stevie!" shouted a man from amid the crowd.

"I can outshear you with my eyes closed, Dirmyg!" laughed Steven.

"But can you best young White?" said another above the din.

"There's only one way to find out, Fflergant," rejoined Steven. "I'm ready," he added, turning toward the judges. "Bring me the wiggliest one of the batch!"

The crowd quieted as Steven took hold of the sheep between his knees, gripped a fistful of thick wool with his left hand and held the scissors at the ready in his right, and awaited the command from Ehangwen Pugh who held the watch.

"Ready yourself, Stevie!" he shouted. "Five seconds. . .four. . .three. . . two. . .one. . .go!"

With lightning agility, Steven's hand tore into the mass of wool with the scissors with such speed that it seemed impossible to prevent its two sharp points from puncturing the animal's skin. Instantly the yelling and shouts resumed at a frantic pitch. Within seconds the back was bare. Steven flopped the sheep onto its back, keeping tight hold of the writhing legs.

Amid the din, a young woman's voice rose above the rest. It was not just who she was that suddenly turned all eyes toward her. She was also the only one in the crowd cheering Stevie on with his formal name. Most of the gathering had never heard it used of Glythvyr Muir's son in his life. "Go, Steven!" cried Florilyn. "Faster. . .you can do it—come on, Steven. . .Steven. Go. . .go!"

Caught up in the excitement of the moment, Florilyn did not notice that everyone's eyes were resting on her. That the viscount's daughter would take such interest in sheepshearing was unusual in itself. That she was so excitedly cheering on her mother's young factor was enough to spark more than idle curiosity.

With a last great effort, Steven flung the coat of wool in a single piece away from the tiny white body that emerged from beneath. Not a scratch of blood was showing. He turned expectantly toward Ehangwen Pugh.

"Forty-seven seconds!" called out the timekeeper. "It's a tie with Eardley."

Another rousing cheer rose, Florilyn's voice as loud as the rest. As she glanced about with a great smile on her face, Florilyn suddenly realized that everyone was staring at her. Her mouth hung open a moment longer. Her face reddened as she realized what she had done. Unaccountably embarrassed, quickly she turned and ran through the crowd and away from the scene.

Steven, who had heard her cheering voice, saw her go. He had no time to think about it further.

Lanky Eardley White now stepped forward and shook Steven's hand vigorously. "Well done, Stevie!" he said. "The factoring seems to agree with you. You've lost nothing of your touch."

The two turned together toward the crowd, which applauded them as the apparent victors. After five more contestants, the tie between the two young men still held.

Meanwhile, Florilyn hurried away, doing her best to avoid the stares that followed her. She ran between booths and tables and children and dogs and merrymakers to where she had tied her mount. Unaware from where he had been milling about the horse selling that Colville Burrenchobay had heard the commotion at the sheepshearing and had observed her strange flight, Florilyn mounted Red Rhud and made for the road.

The crowd thinned as she approached the harbor. The tide was low. Reaching the wide expanse of hard-packed wet sand, she encouraged her mount to a brief gallop. Once she was well alone, she reined back and continued on more slowly to the end of the beach.

She was thinking about many new and unexpected things.

FORTY-THREE

Aspirations Personal and Political

Colville Burrenchobay had been tempted to accompany Courtenay to the continent six weeks earlier. But what was to be gained by forever acting the part of a rich ne'er-do-well son? He was a university graduate with nothing else to show for his life. He had little interest in gallivanting about Europe with Courtenay Westbrooke, pretending they were still eighteen-year-olds.

As much as friendship, the relationship between the two best friends had always been one of competition and rivalry. Either would go to any length to best the other. That rivalry now took an unexpected turn in the brain of the MP's son.

In the year since the tragic accident, the viscount's death had exercised a strange and subtle effect on Colville Burrenchobay. The knowledge that his friend, younger by a year, was soon to become Viscount Lord Snowdon, occupant of a seat in the House of Lords, and overnight regarded as the most important man in the region, turned Colville's thoughts toward his own future. He did not like the idea of being suddenly forced to walk in the shadow of one to whom he had always felt superior.

If his reflections did not actually begin to revolve around the thought of "settling down," as was the custom for young men in their twenties, something akin to such motions of his brain became more active than before. He had rarely given much thought to his future. He assumed that his inheritance would be more than adequate for whatever life he chose for himself. A better entrée into the world of politics, however, could hardly be imagined than his father's reputation as a member of the House of Commons of long standing. It was like handing him an engraved invitation to Westminster on a plate with watercress around it. And in this modern age, Commons trumped the Lords in prestige by a mile. A viscount was nothing alongside a member of Commons.

The idea of a stand for parliament himself, whenever his father decided to step aside, thus began to take root in his thoughts. And with these slow-building reflections and shifting priorities, thoughts of marriage also began to intrude into the gray cells of his mind. As they did, the face of the most beautiful and eligible young lady in Snowdonia rose out of the mists of the past. That she would one day be rich besides, for her mother was known to be of independent wealth, was also a fact that did not escape Colville Burrenchobay's notice. Sight of her in the village during market day a week or two earlier had not left him. He had to admit. . .the little vixen was more beautiful than he remembered her. She would make heads turn in Westminster. He would be noticed instantly with a woman like that on his arm!

Thus it was, one warm day in mid-July, that Colville Burrenchobay presented himself at the door of Westbrooke Manor. He had come, he said to Broakes, to pay his respects to Lady Florilyn.

Florilyn's first thought was to turn around and retreat to the safety of her room. But it was a grand day, and Colville's smile and invitation for a ride seemed genuine enough. She accepted.

By day's end, she was delightfully surprised at the change that had come over him. He had behaved as a perfect gentleman.

"I must say, Colville," said Florilyn as they parted, "you have changed since we last rode together."

"I am a reformed young man," he said. "My foolish ways are behind me. I may even resume my studies and secure an advanced degree."

"My, oh my!" exclaimed Florilyn laughing. "Colville Burrenchobay, the scholar and academic."

"I doubt I would go that far."

"In any case—I enjoyed myself today. Thank you."

"The summer appears a fine one. Perhaps we could see one another again."

Florilyn nodded with a smile, and Colville left her.

Elsewhere on the grounds of Westbrooke Manor, Steven Muir continued his supervision of the construction of Katherine's new home on the promontory. Stone masons and carpenters had all been employed, some from Chester, others from Shrewsbury, still others from as far away as Cardiff. Their presence was straining the limits of Mistress Chattan's inn, though some of the workers were also put up in the servants' quarters at the manor. Huge wagons of stone and mortar and other supplies rumbled past Llanfryniog almost daily from all over England and Wales. The outer walls of granite had begun not merely to rise but to significantly alter the landscape. Slowly but surely the formidable outline of the house moved from drawings to reality.

Steven was at the site every day and reported progress to Katherine. Mistress and factor consulted together almost daily about whatever situations happened to arise. Katherine rode or walked down to the site, sometimes several times a day, as her enthusiasm mounted daily to see her house taking shape before her eyes. Her enthusiasm, however, was bittersweet. She loved the manor, and thoughts of the new house could not fail to be accompanied by reminders of the reason for its necessity.

Thinking little more about the ride with Colville than that two childhood friends had renewed their acquaintance for a day, and certainly anticipating nothing more coming of it, Florilyn was altogether unprepared for the invitation to Burrenchobay Hall for dinner that arrived several days later. Her own reaction surprised her almost as much as the invitation itself.

She showed her mother the letter that had come in the post. "It sounds like fun," said Florilyn.

"I have never cared for Colville Burrenchobay," rejoined Katherine. "I don't like your seeing him, Florilyn, especially after a young man as nice as Percy."

"Percy's not here, Mother," rejoined Florilyn a little testily. "What do you expect me to do, sit around and become a spinster?"

"I thought you and Percy—"

"It's over between Percy and me, Mother," said Florilyn. The frustration that had been fermenting in her subconscious that even she was unaware of at last bubbled to the surface. "He stayed all of three days and didn't even tell me where he was going," she went on. "That ought to show well enough what he thinks of me."

"His leaving had nothing to do with you."

"Maybe, but even when he was here, we hardly saw one another. I'm sure it is a relief to him to be away from me."

"Florilyn—goodness! What has put such thoughts in your head? You know better than that."

"Do I, Mother? Do I *really* know what Percy thinks of me? Sometimes I wonder if I ever did." She turned and walked away.

Katherine stared perplexed after her.

Alone later, Florilyn regretted her words. She knew well enough that she had broken it off with Percy, not him with her. Why had she taken her own uneasiness over what *she* had done out on her mother? She had been agitated ever since market day, for reasons she could not identify. For some peculiar reason, Colville's invitation came almost as a relief. It gave her an excuse to recall the childish attraction she once thought she had for him. Maybe he *had* changed. At any rate, it gave her something else to think about.

There was no denying that Florilyn had begun to worry about her future. The invitation sent a tingle of renewed hope through her. She would not think for an instant of actually marrying Colville Burrenchobay. But it was nice to have someone show some interest in her.

In the days following, Florilyn anticipated the evening more than she dared let on. When the day came, Colville presented himself in his father's finest buggy.

Steven watched them go with mixed thoughts of his own. Neither did he, any more than Katherine, like this new trend events were taking.

"So, Florilyn, my dear," said Sir Armond Burrenchobay as they sat at the exquisitely appointed table in the formal dining room two hours later, "tell me about this cousin of yours. You were engaged for a time, I understand, but now it is off?"

"That's pretty much it," replied Florilyn.

"What happened? Did the two of you come to blows?"

"Nothing like that. We just decided, after Daddy's accident, that perhaps we had rushed into it."

"Who is the fellow, anyway?"

"You met him right here, at Davina's birthday party—Percy Drummond."

"Ah yes, the Scottish chap. Your father seemed inordinately fond of him."

"Percy and my father were very close."

"Struck me as a trifle too religious for my blood. Wasn't his father a priest or some such? A twenty-year-old going about preaching. . .a bit much, what? Ah well, no harm done. Now you and Colville can get to know one another again, now that you're no longer children. See what comes of it, eh, Colville, my boy?" he added with a wink to his son. "Someone's got to start giving us some grandchildren before long, what? Young Davina's hopeless."

An awkward silence followed Sir Armond's candid rambling. Florilyn hoped no one noticed the redness she felt in her neck and face as she glanced down at her plate.

FORTY-FOUR

Dead Ends in Laragh

$\mathcal{F}$or more than a week, Percy had been trying to locate the mysterious names to whom his uncle had written in 1842. He had discovered, however, that the name O'Sullivan in eastern Ireland was as common as MacDonald or Gordon or Campbell in his native Scotland. He met several O'Sullivans but none who had heard of Avonmara or Vanora O'Sullivan or their parents who might have lived at Pine Cottage or Dell Bank in the 1830s or 1840s.

Learning the locations of the two homes from the postmistress, he paid visits to both houses. The current residents knew nothing. The lady at the post told him to expect as much. At least six different families had lived in both places in the last twenty years, she said. To find anyone from three decades or more before was like the proverbial needle in a haystack.

Everyone said the same thing. The potato famine of 1845–48 had altered everything. Most had left. Few remained from the old times. Those who stayed saw faces and families come and go in a blur. All Ireland had been turned upside down. Thousands packed up and left without telling anyone where they were going. Most of the time they didn't know themselves. . .for England, for the United States if they were lucky enough to scrape together money for the passage. . .*anywhere* they might find work. . .anywhere there was someone who might take them in.

But 1842. . .wasn't that *before* the famine, Percy asked several times. Where had these people gone? Why had these letters not been delivered?

The postmistress, a woman in her forties, was too young to remember. She gave Percy the name of her predecessor, one Danny McNeil. Percy paid him a visit.

Yes, he remembered the O'Sullivans, he said. They had a lass who married an Englishman, he thought, or some foreigner.

"Do you remember her marriage?" Percy asked enthusiastically.

"Now that you mention it, I recollect something about it. She was too young to be marrying, folks said, a mere child herself, they said. But the laddie from England, or wherever it was, swept her off her feet, folks said. Then she had a child but died giving birth."

"After that, they left Laragh? And the baby with them?"

"Must have, now that you bring my mind back to it. Wasn't long after—can't remember exactly—that they were gone."

"Do you remember these?" said Percy, showing him the envelopes of his uncle's letters.

McNeil looked them over and shook his head. "Can't say as I do. But aye, that's my stamp."

"You have no idea where they went?"

"I wouldn't have stamped it 'Unknown' if I'd known where they were, would I now, laddie?"

"I suppose not. Do you remember who lived in these two cottages after Mrs. O'Sullivan and Avonmara's sister Vanora left?"

"Can't say I do. People come and people go. Even a postmaster can't keep track of them all, laddie. They were terrible times. They lasted three years. . .five years, in some places eight or ten. The potato crops gradually came back and life went on. But by then all Ireland had been changed, decimated some would say—so many people gone and dead. The whole country had to start over."

"Was there work to be had?"

"Aye, in time. There was always the shipbuilding down in Arklow if a man was willing to work hard. Decent pay in the shipyards, too, they say, though I was happy enough in the post and never did that kind of work myself."

McNeil paused a moment. "Now that you get my mind thinking on those times," he went on, "seems I recall that some of the men from here went down to the shipyards when the famine hit. It was a way to keep their families alive. Men would do anything for that."

FORTY-FIVE

Dubious Scion

$\mathcal{E}$ver since Percy had seen the men in the mountains northeast of the manor, Katherine had been silently pondering the matter. Her disquiet had grown. Lord Litchfield's visit to Wales also preyed upon her mind. She could not prevent the foreboding sense that somehow the two events were related. She had done some investigating of her own since Percy's departure and had discovered more about Lord Litchfield than that he had been her husband's colleague in the House of Lords. He was also one of England's leading mining magnates. It was no secret that Wales contained some of the richest mineral deposits in all Britain—not slate merely, but also coal and gold.

She had retrieved the letters from Litchfield to her husband that Percy had discovered in the files in the study and perused them several times. But without seeing her husband's half of the correspondence, she could tell nothing definite. Yet more importantly, how had Courtenay's recent contact with the man begun. . .and for what purpose? One thing was clear—there had been discussions about the sale of estate lands.

As if materializing out of her thoughts, Courtenay Westbrooke returned from the continent no worse for wear and with less than £500 left in his account at Porthmadog. The dramatic shrinkage of his funds was in part explained by the fact that he was leading two one-year-old thoroughbreds and a two-year-old for which he had paid at least twice what they were worth. He had transported them by train across France, by ship across the channel, and by train the rest of the way, then led them himself overland for the final ten miles of their journey. He was in high spirits and well confident that the three speedsters would make him rich within five years.

His optimism over the future was short lived. As he passed along the main road south of Llanfryniog on his way to the manor, he observed more to alarm him than mere surveying on his land—a full-fledged building project of massive scale was under way on Mochras Head! Walls of stone had grown ten feet high. He had no idea his mother was planning anything so preposterously enormous. And there was the imbecile Muir walking about with papers in his hand as if he was in charge of the thing.

Courtenay reached home in a white fury and saw his prize new purchases into their new quarters. Though his father's aging groom knew more about horses than anyone in Gwynedd other than Padrig Gwlwlwyd, Courtenay would never trust his expensive new acquisitions with one like Hollin Radnor.

The moment the three horses were safely in their new stalls and provided with oats and water, he went angrily in search of his mother. He burst into the ground-floor sitting room like an enraged bull. "What is the meaning of this, Mother?" he demanded without word of greeting.

"It is nice to see you again, too, Courtenay," she said, not without a little bite in her tone.

"I want to know what is going on over on Mochras Head!"

"You told me that I would no longer be welcome at the manor after you inherit. You left me no alternative but to build a new home for myself."

"But it is on my land!"

"Not yet yours, Courtenay."

"It will be soon enough. I can evict you from there just as well as from the manor."

"I fear not, Courtenay. The parcel where my home is being

constructed is no longer part of the estate."

"What are you talking about? Of course it is."

"That portion of land has been sold."

"Sold! To whom?"

"To me. I purchased it from the estate in my own name. You can be assured that it is perfectly legal. Hamilton Murray has seen to that."

"I will stop you. I will have the sale invalidated."

"I'm afraid there is nothing you can do, Courtenay. It has been finalized for months. Before you complain too highly, I paid the estate more than market value for the land. Those funds will be yours once you are viscount. The whole thing will actually prove profitable to you. And while we are on the subject of land sales, I want to know what is going on between you and Lord Litchfield."

"That is none of your affair," answered Courtenay testily.

"It is my affair until you are twenty-five. Some men I suspect as being in his employ were seen in the mountains at the northeast of the estate. I want to know what they were doing there."

"As you have your secrets, Mother, perhaps I have mine."

"Are you planning to sell land to Lord Litchfield?"

"If I were, what business would it be of yours?"

"It is my business until next March. I do not like the idea of men trespassing on the estate. I want to know what business you have with Lord Litchfield."

"It is for the good of the estate that I invited Lord Litchfield to come," replied Courtenay, not directly addressing his mother's question. "I will not spend my life as a landed pauper like Father did. My means are none of your concern."

"I am trustee of the estate. All estate business is my concern."

"Nothing will be finalized until I am twenty-five. My business affairs at that point will be of no interest to you."

"Are you planning to sell him estate lands?" asked Katherine bluntly.

"I am considering it."

"I will not allow it. I will not allow you to tear up this land for coal, if that is the nature of whatever scheme you are hatching."

"Coal has nothing to do with it, Mother."

"I don't know whether to believe you or not."

"Believe what you like, Mother."

"Then why was Lord Litchfield here? Certainly not merely to welcome you to the House of Lords. Come, Courtenay, he is well known for his mining investments."

Able to contain himself no longer, Courtenay burst out in a laugh of derision. "There is really nothing so pitiful as a woman trying to exert power when she has none. You are pathetic, Mother. There is nothing you can do to prevent me doing whatever I like. All this will be mine in March. If I choose to sell a portion of land to Litchfield, I will do so. You can do nothing to stop me."

Courtenay turned and walked from the room, leaving his mother in tears.

FORTY-SIX

The Parish Church

*A*ll Percy's attempts to locate the apparent relations of his uncle's first wife had turned up nothing. Whether Mrs. O'Sullivan was even still alive was doubtful. She would probably be in her seventies or eighties by now. His uncle's affidavit stated that Avonmara had been eighteen at the time of their marriage. Forty years had passed since.

Besides the old postmaster, Percy knew that the person he most needed to speak with was the parish priest, and if possible examine the parish record books. Visiting the ancient Catholic church was not an easy task, however. Day after day he found it locked up like a drum, and the rectory behind it dark and to all appearances uninhabited.

On his fifth day to visit the place, an elderly woman saw him turning to leave, yet again, unsuccessfully. She ambled across the street. "Is it something you'll be wanting in the church, laddie?" she said to him.

"Yes, actually—I had hoped to speak with the priest," replied Percy. "But every day it is locked, and the place seems vacant."

"Aye, Father Halliday is down in Cork, you see. Won't be back till next week."

"He is coming back, then?"

"Oh, aye. But if it's mass you're wanting, the priest from Wicklow will be here tomorrow."

"No, I need to see your own priest. What was his name you said?"

"Father Halliday."

"Father Halliday—right. When do you think he will be back?"

"Tuesday or Wednesday is likely."

"Good—thank you very much."

"Where are you from, laddie?"

"Scotland."

"Oh, aye," said the woman, nodding knowingly, then walked off toward the center of the village.

The following Tuesday afternoon, at last Percy found the church and rectory occupied. His knock on the rectory door was answered by a man wearing a priest's robe who appeared in his midforties. Percy explained that he had been trying to see him and told him the reason for his visit. Father Halliday, like many Percy had spoken with, was too young to remember the events of the 1830s and 1840s. But he agreed to give Percy access to the record books of the church.

He led Percy from the rectory into the church and to the vestry. "Here we are," he said at length, opening the record of marriages. What was the year you said you were interested in?"

"The early 1830s, I believe," replied Percy. "My uncle was nineteen at the time. He died last year. I believe he was fifty-seven or fifty-eight. So that would be thirty-nine or forty years ago."

"I see," replied the priest. "Here are the listings for 1832. There were apparently nine marriages performed that year. What did you say was your uncle's name?"

"Westbrooke. . .Roderick Westbrooke."

Father Halliday scanned down the list of entries. "None here by that name." He turned over the large leaf of the book to the following year. "1833. . . ," he said, tracing down the list with his finger. "Ah, yes. . . It would appear that you are right. Here is a marriage listed on April 11 between one Roderick Westbrook and Avonmara O'Sullivan."

"That's it!" exclaimed Percy. "So my uncle *was* married here, just like he said. Right here in this church. Is there any further information?"

"Only that the marriage was performed by my predecessor, Father O'Leary."

"Is he still living?"

"Yes, but he is very old."

"Is he still in Laragh?"

"He is. He lives in a small cottage provided him by the church."

"I would like to talk to him. What about the record of births?"

"That would be in another book. It should be over here. . . ," said Father Halliday, closing the marriage book and taking down another from the shelf.

"What year?"

"A year later. . .1834."

"I see. . .all right," he said, laying the large book open on the desk and flipping through the pages. "There would seem to have been quite a number of births that year. . .scanning down. . .it would have to have been after, let me see. . .sometime after January. . . Here we are, January. . .February. . .March. . .ah yes, March 18—the birth of a daughter, Morvern, to Roderick and Avonmara Westbrooke. She was baptized one week later. Oh, but this is odd—the father does not appear to have been present."

"She is the woman I am looking for!" said Percy excitedly. "Morvern Westbrooke. . .although it is likely that she might be known as Morvern O'Sullivan. . .and of course, she would no doubt be married now. That would make her now, let me see, thirty-nine years old."

"Why would she be called O'Sullivan?"

"I don't know that," replied Percy. "But she was raised by her grandmother, Mrs. O'Sullivan. My uncle returned to Wales. When he came back for her, Mrs. O'Sullivan and his daughter were gone. He never saw them again."

"As you say, she would probably be married now."

"Do you think I would be able to speak with the priest who married them?" asked Percy. "You say he is still in the village?"

"Yes, but how much help he will be, I cannot say. He is elderly, and the past is fading from his mind. But I will take you to him. We can ask if he has the information you seek."

They left the church. After a five-minute walk through the village,

Percy found himself following the priest toward the rear of a small stone cottage into a small but obviously well-kept garden.

"If the sun is shining," said Father Halliday, "we will be sure to find Father O'Leary in his garden. . .and indeed, there he is. Father Bernard!" he said, approaching with outstretched hand. "I have a young man here who would like to meet you."

An aging man, still wearing the black robe of his profession, turned from the rosebush that had been commanding his attention, clippers in hand, to meet them.

"This is Percival Drummond, Father Bernard," said the priest. "He has come from Wales searching for a long-lost relation."

"Not exactly a relation of mine—not directly at least," said Percy, shaking the older man's hand. "I am looking for a daughter of my uncle. I am his nephew by his second marriage. My uncle died last year. He lost track of his daughter shortly after her birth. I promised him I would try to find her."

The old priest appeared confused as Percy related his brief story. "I see. How may I help you then?" said Father O'Leary.

"We managed to locate the marriage and the girl's birth in the parish books," said Father Halliday. "The girl was born Morvern Westbrooke in 1834. It is likely, however, that she was raised by her maternal grand-mother, Mrs. O'Sullivan."

"O'Sullivan. . .O'Sullivan. . .yes, I remember—the mother died in childbirth. Not altogether uncommon, yet a tragedy nevertheless."

"Do you remember what happened to the family. . .especially to the baby?" asked Percy.

"O'Sullivan you say the name was?"

Percy nodded.

"I cannot say. I lost track of them, I think. I believe they left some time later. Times became hard when the blight hit. It was impossible to remember them all."

"What about the relatives? Avonmara had a sister?"

"Avonmara. . .Who is Avonmara?"

"Avonmara O'Sullivan. . .my uncle's wife, the mother of the child."

"A sister, you say? What was her name?"

"Vanora. Her married name was Maloney, I believe."

"I really could not say. Hmm, Maloney. . .Maloney. . . It does seem that I remember. . .but no, it's gone now. Everyone was leaving, you see. They had to follow the work as best they could. Not that there was much work to be found. Some went to Arklow, as I recall."

"Is that where they went, do you think?"

"I am sorry, young man—I really cannot say. My memory, you see. . . it is not what it once was."

FORTY-SEVEN

A Promise Kept and a Promise Scorned

During Percy's absence, Colville Burrenchobay was busy. For the next few weeks of the summer, he and Florilyn were nearly inseparable.

Katherine was beside herself over where it might lead. She saw the look in Colville's eye. It was not an expression she liked.

Suddenly Florilyn was reverting to her old ways. But what could a mother do? Daily she prayed for Percy's return. He had always had a good influence on Florilyn.

Meanwhile, Colville had so skillfully worked his magic that Florilyn was completely seduced by his charms. They rode together nearly every day—at the shore, in the mountains, to the nearby towns and villages for lunch or tea. Florilyn spent as much time at Burrenchobay Hall as at the manor. Sir Armond and Lady Burrenchobay had gone so far as to make up a special room for her use to stay over when she and Colville were together late in the evenings.

The changes in Florilyn had not gone unnoticed by Steven Muir. He saw his mistress's concern and shared it.

Hoping to revive something of the former friendship that had blossomed between them, one day he seized the opportunity he had been waiting for. Seeing Florilyn walking toward the stables, he hurried after her. "Good morning, Florilyn," he said.

She glanced toward him, seemingly affronted now by the familiar address that had once passed between them as easily as if they were brother and sister. She kept on without a reply.

"Little Nugget misses you," said Steven. "You spend little time with him now, unlike you did after he was born. I have been thinking of training him with the saddle. Would you like to help? You might like to ride him and teach him to know your seat and the commands of your voice."

"I don't think so, Steven," replied Florilyn. "Colville says I need a powerful mount beneath me."

"I do not like to see you spending so much time with him, Florilyn."

She spun around and shot him a piercing look.

"You may address me as *Lady* Florilyn, if you please!" she said.

"Forgive me, Lady Florilyn," said Steven calmly. "I still do not like to see you so much with Colville Burrenchobay."

"And why not, pray tell?" she shot back haughtily.

"Because he is not worthy of you. I have known him all my life."

"So have I."

"I do not trust him."

"He has changed."

"I doubt that, my lady. The expression in his eye when he looks at you is one of opportunism, not love."

"You presume to know the difference?" said Florilyn with disdain.

"I believe I do."

"And what gives you the right to interfere in my affairs?" she retorted angrily.

"The right of one who cares about you, my lady, who wants only the best for you, and who promised to protect you from harm."

"*Promised*. . . What makes you think I need your protection? Whom did you promise?"

"In a manner of speaking, your father."

"My father is dead. I do not recall his placing me in *your* charge."

"I promised one to whom he did entrust your well-being."

"Ah, my mother you mean. And you somehow assume that being her factor gives you the right—"

"I meant Percy, Lady Florilyn," said Steven.

"*Percy!* What does he have to do with me now?"

"I promised him that I would look after you, for his sake as well as my own."

"Percy can keep his nose out of my business! If he doesn't want to marry me, then he has nothing to say about it. He never liked Colville. He is just jealous."

"Percy knows nothing about Colville. I am merely telling you what I think he would say if he were here, that Colville Burrenchobay is not worthy of you."

"Well, you can tell Percy, when you happen to see him again, that I care not a straw for what he may think, and that if Colville proposes to me, I intend to accept him."

She turned and walked away, leaving Steven staring after her, heartbroken at how quickly her former teenage conceit had returned in the form of aristocratic womanly hauteur.

FORTY-EIGHT

A Delicate Communiqué

*B*y early August, Percy realized there was nothing left for him to do in Ireland.

He had confirmed his uncle's marriage to Avonmara O'Sullivan and the birth of their daughter, Morvern, and that the O'Sullivans were gone by the time of the viscount's return to Wales. Beyond those sketchy facts, he had come to a dead end. What point was there in trying to continue? He hadn't learned anything that his uncle didn't know. He shrank from returning to Westbrooke Manor just now, with nothing definite to tell anyone, nothing to account for his absence, no resolution to his future with Florilyn. Knowing nothing of the danger in which Florilyn stood, nor did he feel any urgency to do so. It would be best now to begin thinking through his own prospects in Glasgow.

Leaving the address of his parents with Father Halliday, he returned to Dublin, from where he set sail for Glasgow. Perhaps it was time to make plans for law school.

When he arrived home, Percy had a long talk with his mother and father. Then followed prayer between the three about Percy's future and especially about Florilyn.

"As you are weighing your options," said Edward as the evening drew to a close, "I have something I think you might like to read. Whether it will help focus your thoughts and prayers, I cannot say. But it is truly

715

one of the most remarkable expositions of scripture I have ever read. It has had a profound impact on me."

"Don't tell me," laughed Percy, "a new book by George MacDonald."

Edward joined him in laughter. "A good guess. But I'm afraid not. My friends at Henry King publishers, however, tell me that one of his best novels yet is in the works but won't be out for a couple of years."

"What's it about?"

"A fisherman," they say. "It's set in a fishing village up in your neck of the woods northwest of Aberdeen."

"Where's that?" asked Percy.

"Cullen."

"I've heard of it. One of my classmates was from there. As I recall also, some of the students went up there on holiday. So MacDonald's next novel takes place there?"

"The next one they will be publishing. MacDonald was there a year ago researching for it. But then a lecture tour in America set the schedule back. Apparently the MacDonalds are planning another visit to Cullen next month. In any event, it sounds like something to look forward to."

"But that's not what you were telling me about?"

"No. Actually I was referring to the manuscript young cousin Henry gave me to look at when he and his father came to Aberdeen for your graduation. I know he's a young man, but it is truly remarkable. I believe our cousin may have quite a future ahead of him. He may become the most famous Drummond of all."

"Then I would definitely like to read it," said Percy. "Have you spoken with him about it? Didn't he ask for your thoughts?"

"I wrote him a letter of lavish praise for his insights," replied Edward. "I told him it was the greatest thing in the world I have ever read on First Corinthians 13. I said he ought to publish it."

"What did Henry say?"

"He was flattered and appreciative. He said his father had also encouraged him to have it published but that he was not completely satisfied with it yet. He liked my phrase though. He said, if I had no objection, he might use that for the title."

"What phrase?"

"The greatest thing in the world. It is an exposition of love, as set forth by Paul in First Corinthians 13. What could be a greater thing in the world than love?"

"I will definitely look forward to reading it. Have you heard more about his hope to be involved with the Moody mission?"

"As far as I know he is still planning to join as a student volunteer."

"Now that I am more or less at loose ends," mused Percy, "perhaps I should join him after all."

Later in his room, it was not his cousin Henry Drummond's treatise on 1 Corinthians 13 that first drew Percy's attention, however, but rather the beginning of a long overdue letter to his aunt. Somehow he had to try to explain himself and, to the degree he was able, put the matter to rest in both his mind and hers. He would have to walk a tightrope to do so. Now that he had told his father a little more, he would let him read his words first, to avoid saying either too much or too little.

He set aside the manuscript of his cousin's that his father had given him and took out a fresh sheet of writing paper and pen.

Dear Aunt Katherine, he began.

　My greetings both to you and Florilyn and everyone at Westbrooke Manor. I am back in Glasgow with my parents. I felt I needed to see them and talk some things over with my father. I have just arrived.

　I know I left Wales hastily, and I apologize for that, also for not being able to explain more about my sudden departure and subsequent silence. I hope that you will understand my reasons for leaving abruptly when I tell you that the request Uncle Roderick made of me involved more than merely sorting through the papers and files in his study. There were certain delicate matters on his mind that he had too long neglected and which he felt might be of consequence to Courtenay, and indeed his entire family, concerning his legacy and the inheritance of his title and the estate should they come out.

I don't know how much of his life before your marriage you are familiar with, no doubt far more than me. You surely know that he spent time in Ireland during the latter years of his youth. He told me few details other than that while there he had been consumed by the lust for gold in that region of Ireland, which had experienced a gold rush in the early years of the century. During that time, he said, there were several associations with certain individuals he had not seen since and with whom he had lost touch. He asked me to see if I could locate among his papers any connections to those persons by which—

Percy paused, struggling desperately to find the right words. His position would be much easier had he never said a word to his aunt about his promise to his uncle. But it had come out, and now he must make the best of it.

He read over what he had just written then continued.

He asked me to see if I could locate among his papers any connections to those persons by which. . .they could be located, or that would give me reason to believe that they might one day jeopardize his or Courtenay's position as viscount, or make demands upon Courtenay that he would be unable to accede to.

I realize my words are dreadfully vague. I am sorry again. It was vague to me also when Uncle Roderick spoke to me of these things. He asked me specifically not to burden you with it if nothing came of it. Simply know that all his thoughts as he spoke to me were of you and the family he loved so dearly. He wanted no hurt or anxiety to come to any of you. He asked me to take care of this last request specifically for that reason, so that you would not be unnecessarily burdened with it.

Having found among his papers what I thought might lead me to the individuals involved, I went to Ireland to attempt to carry out this final request. However, all my attempts were unsuccessful. I discovered nothing untoward. Actually, I discovered nothing at

all. There is no record that I was able to find of anyone who knew
Uncle Roderick when he was there. I believe I can safely say that
no associations or obligations from the past need be of concern to
yourself or to Courtenay.

> *If there is anything that I can do for you, I hope you will not*
hesitate to call on me.

Percy paused, then added:

> *Please give my loving best to Florilyn. Tell her I will write soon.*
> *All the best, and with deep affection,*
>
> > *Percy*

He set down the pen and exhaled deeply, then undressed, blew out his candle, and fell sleepily onto his bed.

The following morning Percy found his father in his office preparing to leave for his office at the church. "Dad," said Percy, "I have a favor to ask."

"Anything, Percy."

"I wrote a letter to Aunt Katherine last night after I talked with you and Mom. Would you read it and tell me what you think?"

"Sure...absolutely."

"I need to know if you think I have said too much or too little, or have been too ambiguous or not ambiguous enough. I know you don't know what Uncle Roderick asked me to do any more than Aunt Katherine does. But I need to know what you think she will think. She is your sister. No one would know better than you." He handed his father the paper.

Edward read it slowly then set the letter aside.

"Knowing Roderick as I did," he began after a moment, "I would conclude from this that he was involved in something perhaps not altogether aboveboard—a scheme perhaps, probably with wealth at the bottom of it, that did not turn out as he had hoped. What that would possibly have to do with Courtenay's inheritance, I have no idea. Perhaps

Roderick still had debts from years before, and he was afraid of it coming back to haunt Courtenay. Perhaps he pledged Westbrooke Manor against the scheme. He was always a schemer. This rings true to what I knew of him. I could see any of a number of options. He might have bought into an old gold mine, for all I know. When he and Katherine first became involved, he was veiled about his past. We knew he had been in Ireland, but nothing more. Financial trouble would certainly explain it."

Percy nodded as he listened. He was both satisfied and dissatisfied with his father's answer. How could he know if he was doing the right thing, leading his aunt to believe, as his father had, something that *wasn't* true? It was either that or say nothing at all. He must *somehow* account for his actions. If only he had said nothing about his pledge to his uncle.

FORTY-NINE

Subtle Innuendos

*T*hat same afternoon Percy sat down to write an equally difficult letter to his cousin.

Dear Florilyn, he began.

As I am sure your mother has told you, I am back in Glasgow with my parents after a generally uneventful time in Ireland.

I realize that the future is unsettled for us both. If my handling of my own uncertainties has contributed to your anxieties, I sincerely apologize. My focus was so entirely occupied last term with completion of my studies. Then our plans were turned upside down by the MacDonald novel we read and what you felt we were to do in consequence. As time went on, my promise to your father weighed more and more heavily upon me.

With all that at last behind me, I feel as if I am breathing a great sigh of relief!

He set aside the pen for a moment and drew in a breath. Ever since his father's mention the previous evening of his cousin Henry, an idea had been floating about in his subconscious. As he wrote, it began to take more definite form.

Naturally, Percy resumed, *my thoughts turn often to you and to the predicament, it might be called, of our situation. We were both agreed, as I am certain we still are, that what we want above all is God's will. We want to do what He wants us to do. I continue to ask Him to reveal that will. I know you are praying that prayer with me. It is hard at times, as I know it must be for you, that our plans remain nebulous. But I am confident that God will show us what we are to do in His time. We will both be stronger for it. As I think I once told you, my father says that God is never in a hurry. That is a difficult lesson for we who are young, but I realize the wisdom of such a truth.*

As we continue waiting for Him to reveal His will, and as I contemplate my own future and the possibility of law school, an exciting idea has come to me. I am certain you have heard of the American evangelist D. L. Moody. The newspapers are full of him and news of so many giving their lives to the Lord as a result of his powerful preaching. He is scheduling his first mission to Scotland in a few months. As one of Glasgow's leading ministers, my father will be involved to the extent he is able. In all his missions, Rev. Moody calls upon local Christian volunteers, many of them students, to help in his missions—with crowd control, organization, ushering, counseling, and distribution of literature and material, follow-up, and so on. If I decide to apply to law school, it will be a year or more before I would begin.

Therefore, I am seriously considering joining my cousin Henry, who shares my family name of Drummond, in becoming a volunteer for the Scotland Moody mission. He is about our age, and I know you would like him. They need women volunteers as well as men. It has occurred to me that it would provide a good opportunity for you and me to grow together in our spiritual lives, while participating in a worthy endeavor for the kingdom of God. By working side by side in such an environment, we would strengthen our spiritual bonds and perhaps be in a stronger position to discern His will for our future together.

*As I went to the home of my aunt and uncle at a time of
uncertainty in my life, what would you think of coming to
Glasgow, where you would be welcome with my parents for as long
as you liked, and joining me in working in the Moody mission? I
think it would be. . .*

Florilyn set the letter aside without reading further. She had read
the whole thing once. But now on her second time through, she had
had enough.

The day was a warm one. She had come outside to read the letter
on one of the garden benches. She glanced up from where she sat to see
Colville Burrenchobay riding up the drive. She had been expecting him.

He dismounted, tied his mount, and walked forward and sat down
beside her. "A serious expression," he said, glancing at the handwritten
sheets in her hand. "Bad news?"

"No," answered Florilyn with a light laugh. Her tone carried a hint
of lingering annoyance from what she had been reading. "Just a letter
from Percy."

"Ah, right. . .your Scottish cousin. So how goes the engagement?"
probed Colville.

"It's off. You knew that. Why else would I be seeing you?"

"I thought. . .his writing you a letter. . .that perhaps the two of you
had kissed and made up."

Something resembling a snort sounded from Florilyn's lips.
"Hardly," she said without trying to hide her sarcasm. "I don't think
Percy is interested in making up." She handed Colville the letter then
rose and walked about the garden to work off her agitation.

Colville could hardly believe his good fortune. He had been subtly
trying for weeks to learn how things stood between Florilyn and her
erstwhile fiancé in order to more shrewdly plan his own strategy. All at
once a letter from the young Scot had unexpectedly fallen into his lap.
He read in haste lest she change her mind about wanting him to see it.
"Sounds like a bit of a religious fanatic, what?" said Colville after two
or three minutes, tentatively feeling which way the wind of Florilyn's

reaction might be blowing.

Florilyn did not reply.

"Is that true," he added, "what he says about you and he trying to find, what did he call it. . .God's will?"

"That was the idea," replied Florilyn noncommittedly.

"About what?"

"Whether He wanted us to get married."

"What about what *you* want?" asked Colville.

"We're supposed to want what God wants."

"Well, I don't!" laughed Colville. "I want what I want. Life would be no fun if everyone went around trying to think what God wanted them to do."

Florilyn shrugged.

"You don't really go along with all that, do you?" he asked.

"I thought I did," sighed Florilyn.

"Where does your cousin get those ideas anyway?"

"His father's a minister."

"I guess I heard something about that. Still, he seems pretty young to be so religious. You don't really want to marry a fellow who's going to be a gray-haired old church mouse by the time he's forty. What if after you were married he decided to become a minister?"

"Actually he was thinking about that very thing."

"There, you see. I would keep clear of a bloke like that."

"Not to worry. He's decided to study law instead."

"Hmm. . .a lawyer with religion—an interesting combination. Still, what's this mission thing all about? Who's the fellow Moody?"

"Just what he says—an American evangelist."

"A hellfire preacher?"

"I suppose."

"And he wants you to join him in helping get people saved. Ha, ha, ha!" laughed Colville. "That's priceless. Florilyn Westbrooke, evangelist. Ha, ha!"

Colville's laughter grated on Florilyn and made her uncomfortable. But she said nothing further and quickly changed the subject.

FIFTY

The Announcement

$\mathcal{W}$hen Percy had not heard from Florilyn for two weeks, he began to grow concerned. Several more letters followed from Glasgow to Llanfryniog with the same result.

In north Wales, Percy's letter to her sent Katherine into a fresh round of anxiety. She realized that in all likelihood Percy would not be returning to Westbrooke Manor anytime soon. Everything in her cried out to write him to implore him to come. But how could she? As things stood between Percy and Florilyn, Percy was hardly the one to tell Florilyn to stop seeing Colville unless he planned to marry her himself. She had not even told Edward and Mary about the change in Florilyn. From two or three comments Florilyn had made, she knew that at present Percy's stock had dropped considerably in her daughter's estimation. She more than half suspected the cause.

Meanwhile, events moved inexorably toward their inevitable conclusion. Katherine Westbrooke's house continued to rise on the plateau overlooking Mochras Head. Colville Burrenchobay and Florilyn Westbrooke continued to spend most days together. It was only a matter of time before their engagement would be announced.

Christmas was approaching. Edward and Mary invited Katherine and Florilyn north for the holidays. Florilyn said she was not interested in seeing Percy, or any of them for that matter. Katherine did not want to leave her alone to spend Christmas at Burrenchobay Hall. She silently feared she would come back to discover that her daughter was engaged or, worse, had married Colville hastily in her absence.

Christmas was a strained affair at Westbrooke Manor, certainly nothing like the gay celebration of giving of a year before. Courtenay was gone. Florilyn was moody and anxious to be off to Burrenchobay Hall. Colville called for her shortly after eleven. Christmas dinner at the manor began quietly. Katherine's immediate family had now dwindled to one—herself. The thanksgiving in her heart, however, though tinged with sadness, was genuine. She had around her a staff that loved her, and Adela and Steven now seemed truly like her own family. She asked Steven to pray.

Florilyn spent the rest of Christmas day with Colville's family. A great feast was held at the hall in honor of the occasion. As she did frequently these days, Florilyn stayed over in what the whole family now called "Florilyn's room."

On the following morning, even before Florilyn had returned to Westbrooke Manor to tell her mother in person, the great Boxing Day news was all over Llanfryniog that on the previous evening at Burrenchobay Hall, the engagement had been announced of Florilyn Westbrooke to Colville Burrenchobay.

PART THREE

Treasure of the Celtic Triangle

1874

FIFTY-ONE

News from Ireland

D. L. Moody had arrived in England in June of 1873. He was unable to generate much interest in his evangelistic method by the local clergy. In his first meeting in York, he spoke to a congregation of eight. Over the following weeks, gradually attendance increased. However, the numbers remained small. The ministers of York continued cool and unsupportive toward the American.

From York, at the invitation of two interested ministers, Moody and his musical partner, Ira Sankey, traveled to Sunderland then to Newcastle. Though criticism continued from the English clergy, in Newcastle five ministers offered their chapels for meetings. Gradually a groundswell of interest began to grow.

But it was not until Moody and Sankey crossed into Scotland that Moody's evangelistic messages exploded upon the public. Scotland's centuries-old spiritual vitality immediately responded to Moody's challenge. From the first meetings held in Edinburgh in November, no building in the city was sufficient to hold the enormous crowds. The watch-night service on the last day of the year continued for five hours. Moody's farewell address to Edinburgh was held in early January of 1874 on the slopes of Arthur's Seat. From Edinburgh, Moody traveled to Dundee then to Glasgow where the story was much the same. Hundreds of local volunteers were kept busy with the thousands who responded to Moody's evangelistic call.

After working for a Glasgow law firm through the winter, Percy joined his cousin Henry to participate with the Moody mission when the evangelist arrived in Glasgow.

From Glasgow, Moody's meetings continued in Scotland as he traveled to Perth, Montrose, Aberdeen, Inverness, and finally all the way north to John o' Groats. In Aberdeen, it was estimated that up to twenty thousand attended the meetings.

Though Percy volunteered only for the Glasgow meetings, his cousin traveled with Moody for several months, during which time a lifelong friendship between young Drummond and the American was formed. During all this time, Percy did not visit Wales again.

A day at length came when Katherine could keep silent no longer. She finally asked Florilyn when she intended to tell Percy of her engagement to Colville Burrenchobay.

"I don't know, Mother," replied Florilyn testily. "Why would Percy care? He had the chance to marry me, didn't he? I'm twenty-three. I need to get on with my life and stop waiting for him to figure out what God wants him to do. What about what I want? I probably won't tell him at all."

"I was twenty-five when your father and I were married," rejoined Katherine. "It's not such a bad thing to wait a few years."

"I've waited long enough, Mother. I intend to marry Colville and maybe be the wife of a parliamentarian one day. That's what he says. It's better than being the wife of a roving evangelist. I can't think of anything worse! Percy's so changed from the man I thought I was in love with."

Katherine knew further expostulation was useless. It pained her to hear Florilyn speak so. Percy was not the only one who had changed. Colville's influence on Florilyn had been anything but healthy. Katherine shrank from telling Percy of the engagement herself. If only he were in Wales. Yet with Florilyn's attitude toward him so soured, what could even Percy do now? She only hoped something happened to intervene between now and the lavish summer wedding being planned for Burrenchobay Hall.

Steven was no less concerned than Katherine. He had considered writing Percy in Glasgow so that he would at least know how far Florilyn had sunk. His conclusion, however, was that his interference would probably only make the situation worse. Whatever change was to come had to come from within Florilyn herself.

What a grief it was to these two who loved her—the viscountess and her young factor—to see what the evil influence of one who did not love the truth had been able to work within Florilyn's heart and mind.

And thus as the weeks lengthened into months, the Drummond household in Glasgow had no inkling of the developments in North Wales. While uncertainty reigned at Westbrooke Manor, a letter arrived at the vicarage in Glasgow in late February with Percy's name on the envelope. Percy did not recognize the hand. The postmark was from Ireland. Motivated as much from curiosity concerning his failed quest as from the knowledge that Courtenay Westbrooke's twenty-fifth birthday was only three weeks away, he tore at the envelope with fumbling fingers, pulled out two blue sheets, and read:

> *My dear Mr. Drummond,*
>
> *Though we have not spoken since you were in Laragh last summer inquiring after the O'Sullivan and Maloney families in your search for your uncle's antecedents in Ireland, I hope you will forgive my presumption in writing you and, for lack of a better phrase, taking matters into my own hands.*
>
> *Your plight remained on my mind after you left me. Perhaps it was the earnestness of your desire to find the truth and do the right thing. It has been my experience that there are many who claim to love truth but are not quite so committed to doing the right thing— to following truth even when to do so becomes uncomfortable. Truth can be but an intellectual exercise if it is not empowered by an obedient heart determined to do the right thing. I knew that your heart hungered not only for truth, but also for right.*
>
> *At length I took it upon myself to send out a brief letter through the priestly grapevine of eastern Ireland to inquire whether my*

*brothers of nearby parishes were acquainted in their congregations
with the names O'Sullivan or Maloney, or even Westbrooke, the
other name you mentioned. That was before Christmas. I heard
nothing until recently. Then I received a reply from a priest in
Arklow who has a woman named Vanora Maloney in his church
whose husband works in the shipyards. I told him briefly the reason
for my inquiry and asked him to make discreet inquiries. It turns
out that these Maloneys indeed at one time lived in Laragh and
relocated with his family and mother-in-law, one Maighdlin
O'Sullivan who is no longer living.*

*The names would hardly seem to be coincidental. Perhaps these
are indeed the people you are looking for.*

Hurriedly Percy scanned the remainder of the second sheet.

*I wonder if you are following the work in your country of
Rev. Moody. I believe he is planning to visit Ireland after leaving
Scotland. The "Camp Meeting Revival" style is not what most
Catholics are drawn to. I must admit, however, that I admire the
man, and he is certainly a positive force for the kingdom of God
in the world. Perhaps it would not be an altogether bad thing if
more Catholics took their faith with the same personal ardor that
evangelicals do. I have considered writing a book, trying to urge my
fellow Catholics in that direction. The title* Catholicism Renewed
continues to reverberate in my brain.

*But all that is a matter left for another discussion in the event
we have the opportunity to meet again. But if we do not meet
again in this world, perhaps we shall have that discussion in the
next!*

*I am,
Sincerely yours,
Father Robert James Halliday,
Laragh Parish, Wicklow
Ireland*

Excitedly Percy ran into the breakfast room where his parents were enjoying a last cup of tea together. "Mom. . .Dad," he said still holding the letter, "I have to go back to Ireland!"

"I take it there have been developments?" said his father.

"Possibly huge ones! I will tell you everything when I am able. But for now, as I told you before, I can say no more than you already know." He turned to leave the room.

"Where are you. . .You're not leaving now?" said his mother after him.

"I'll go down to the P & O office to see when there is a sailing for Dublin," replied Percy. "But yes, I will be on the first available ship. I'll stop by the law firm. They won't have a problem doing without me for a week."

FIFTY-TWO

Arklow

*P*ercy did not write to tell Father Halliday of his plans. A letter would in all probability reach him no sooner than he would in person. When he walked into the small, dimly lit church, however, the priest did not seem surprised to see him.

"Ah, Mr. Drummond," he said with a warm smile. He strode toward Percy with outstretched hand. The two shook hands affectionately. "I had a feeling I would see you again! You must have left the instant you received my letter."

"I sailed a day later," said Percy. "It was the first ship I could make."

"I take it you think it possible the people I mentioned are the ones you are looking for?"

"There is no way to know for certain. I hope it will be possible to speak with them."

"I was so sure that you would want to investigate further that I wrote to Father Abban to expect us."

"*Us?*"

"I thought I would take you down, and we could both meet him together. I asked him if he might be able to discover whether there was a young girl in the family of his parish. Where are you staying?"

"Nowhere," laughed Percy. "I just arrived."

"Then you shall stay here with me tonight," said Father Halliday.

"I have a small guest room next to my quarters. We shall ride down to Arklow tomorrow."

The ride of fifteen miles south through the hills from Laragh in Father Halliday's one-horse buggy took most of the following morning. They arrived in the shipbuilding port of Arklow about midday. Even had Father Halliday not been familiar with the town, the church would not have been difficult to find. Its spire rose prominently over the stone buildings of the place. They found Father Abban in the rectory behind the church eating lunch.

"Robert!" he exclaimed when he opened the door to their knock. "How good to see you again!"

"And you, John," replied Father Halliday as the two priests embraced. "It has been too long. We must keep closer in touch. But may I introduce you to Mr. Drummond," he said, turning and drawing Percy forward. "He is the young man who has been looking for the people I mentioned."

"I am happy to meet you, Mr. Drummond," said the priest, who was himself a young man not more than six or eight years older than Percy.

"Thank you. The pleasure is mine," said Percy, shaking his hand.

"Come in, please. . . . You must have had a long ride. I just sat down to lunch, and my housekeeper prepared enough for an army. You can join me. The teapot is still steaming."

The three went inside and were soon sitting at the table.

"After your letter, Robert," said Father Abban, "last Sunday I tentatively spoke to Mrs. Maloney. I broached the subject of whether a girl had accompanied them from Laragh when they left with Mrs. O'Sullivan. She nodded and said that it was her sister's daughter. They had helped her mother care for the girl after her sister's unexpected death."

"Then she must be the girl I am looking for!" said Percy with obvious enthusiasm.

"You are assuming that they are the same people."

"The coincidences seem too remarkable to be otherwise. What else did you learn?"

"Nothing really. Daibheid walked up then, the woman's husband. He told her to say nothing more. He seemed agitated. I probed a bit and asked if my sermon had somehow upset him. He is a tempestuous man. I have had to confront him about his temper on several occasions. He said he did not want people asking about a past they were trying to forget. I glanced at Vanora. She gave me a helpless look that said she would tell me more if she could."

"What is it all about, John?" now asked Father Halliday.

"I really don't know," replied Father Abban. "There are things from the past he does not want talked about. I think they must concern their niece."

"Do you think Mrs. Maloney would talk to me?" asked Percy.

"If she was alone. . .perhaps. If her husband found out, he could be furious. I would have to think long and hard before I allowed myself to be party to going behind his back. Is the matter truly of such importance?"

"I believe that the girl, the Maloneys' niece, may be the rightful heir to a sizeable estate, as well as a title, in North Wales," replied Percy. "The task of finding his daughter was entrusted to me by the late viscount, Lord Snowdon, shortly before his death."

"What is your personal interest?"

"Lord Snowdon was my uncle. For reasons of his own, he entrusted to me the facts of his first marriage, and the birth of a daughter, to one Avonmara O'Sullivan of Laragh, who died in childbirth. He told no one else of these things before he died. He asked me to do what I could to find his daughter."

"And if progeny could be proven, she would inherit. . .as a woman?"

"As far as I understand it, yes," replied Percy. "The terms of the original viscountcy were established such that the eldest, or his or her offspring or their issue, would inherit both estate and title irrespective of gender."

Both priests pondered his words a moment.

"I see," nodded Father Abban at length. "Your quest is based on no idle curiosity. Much indeed is at stake." He paused and drew in a thoughtful breath. "Under the circumstances," he nodded after a moment, "it would seem that we have no alternative but to see what we can learn further. I will arrange a visit with Vanora Maloney when her husband is at work. If the facts seem to warrant it, we will of course have to confide the nature of our inquiry to him as well."

FIFTY-THREE

A Family Grief

Percy and Father Halliday waited at the church while Father Abban paid a visit to the Maloney home. He returned within the hour to say that his request had been crowned with success—Vanora Maloney agreed to meet with Percy. Only they must be gone well before evening when her husband returned from work.

"What are we waiting for!" said Percy, jumping to his feet.

"After your long journey, I thought you might find it best to wait a day and rest?"

"I need to find the girl as soon as possible."

The two priests and their new young Welsh friend left the rectory by foot a short time later. Ten minutes later they approached a stone house set in the middle of a long row of attached dwellings. Father Abban led the way to the door. The other two stepped back as he knocked.

Moments later the door opened, revealing a woman who appeared in her middle to late fifties. Percy's eyes immediately went to her head of bright orange hair in which was mingled evidence of the approach of white.

"Hello again, Vanora," said Father Abban. "As you can see, we decided to come soon. We thought it best to get this behind us."

The woman smiled, though nervously as she glanced behind her own priest toward Percy and Father Halliday, then opened the door

738

and gestured for them to enter. She led them inside. They sat down in a small but comfortable sitting room.

"Thank you for agreeing to speak with us, Vanora," began Father Abban. "I realize this is awkward as long as Daibheid does not want these things talked about. But Mr. Drummond here has convinced me that the matter is of great importance. When the time comes, I will speak with Daibheid. He will know that you only agreed upon my urging."

Mrs. Maloney nodded, again glancing uneasily toward the other two.

"So let me introduce my two friends," he said. "This is Father Halliday, priest in Laragh, where you were born I believe, isn't that correct?"

She nodded.

"Father, this is Vanora Maloney."

"I am pleased to meet you, Mrs. Maloney," said Father Halliday.

"Is Father O'Leary still living?" she asked.

"Yes, he is," replied Father Halliday.

"If you see him," said Mrs. Maloney, attempting another smile, "would you give him my greeting. We should have told him where we were going and why we were leaving."

"I will indeed. I am certain it will make him happy to know that you remember him."

"And this young man is Mr. Percival Drummond," Father Abban added, now turning toward Percy. "He is from Wales and came to Ireland last year hoping to locate your sister's daughter. At last finding where you are living, with Father Halliday's help, he hopes that you will not mind answering his questions. Mr. Drummond believes that he is the nephew of your sister's husband."

"Hello, Mrs. Maloney," said Percy, rising from his chair and extending his hand. "I very much appreciate your agreeing to see me."

She nodded, again forcing a nervous smile.

Percy resumed his seat.

"I don't know what I can tell you," said Mrs. Maloney. "It's been years since we left Laragh."

"The first thing is simply to confirm that your sister was indeed Avonmara O'Sullivan?" asked Percy.

Mrs. Maloney nodded.

"The same Avonmara O'Sullivan who married Roderick Westbrooke?"

"I believe that was the man's name."

"And they had a daughter?"

Again she nodded. "Her name was Morvern," she said. "But whatever happiness there might have been at her birth was short lived. My mother and I both knew, for we were at her side through the birthing, that Avonmara was weak. She had never been strong, you see. All her life she was not sickly exactly, but not strong. Though she was two years older, I was bigger and taller and stronger and faster from the time we were wee lassies. We both had bright carroty hair just like our mum, though mine's starting to fade, you see," she added, running a hand over her head. "All the O'Sullivan women had bright red crops, you see. But Avonmara was a beauty. Even frail like she was, there was a mystery about her. She was a quiet girl. When she looked at you, and smiled her mysterious smile, her eyes went straight through you. When the young Welshman came, he was smitten with her. And she was taken with his good looks and flair. She was too young to marry. Mother warned her. But Avonmara was in love, and she said that when love comes, you couldn't wait. You couldn't think that love would come again if you didn't take it when you had the chance.

"Those were hard times in Ireland. Our family wasn't poor, you see. We weren't of peasant stock, but times were hard for everyone. I don't know what the man told her about himself or if he thought he would take her away somewhere, but we all thought he had money and he told her that she would never want for a thing. So she didn't listen to anyone's cautions. She married the man, though she was but eighteen. He didn't take her away, and we were happy about that. They stayed there in Laragh, though I don't know what he did. He never seemed to work, but they had all they needed. When Avonmara knew that she was to be a mother, she was so happy. For a year she was happier than we'd ever seen her. Mother and Father began to think perhaps they had misjudged the man. He seemed to be a good enough husband. But then as her time drew near, I knew she was weakening. Her face was pale, and she did not put on the weight she should. Her face and cheeks were thin. I knew Mother was worried, too. She never spoke about it, but I could see it in her face. Then little Morvern was born, with a healthy crop of O'Sullivan orange hair, but within a day poor Avonmara was gone." Mrs. Maloney took a deep breath and looked down. She blinked hard, and her hand went to her eyes.

The three men waited.

"It didn't take long for us to know that Mum had been right about her husband," she went on after a moment. "For all his dash and good looks and all the rest, he fell apart. He hardly kept control of himself at the funeral. Maybe it showed how much he loved her, but he wasn't much of a man about it. Naturally Mum and I took care of the baby. That went without saying. She was Mum's granddaughter and my own niece, and Avonmara's husband was just a boy of twenty himself. What could *he* do to take care of a child? He didn't even give her her name, didn't attend the christening at the church. We would not see him for days at a time. Then came a day when he came to the house and told my mum that he was leaving Ireland, that he had to go home to see about his father. He promised to return when he was able to take care of the baby. But we never saw him again. That was the last time any of us ever saw him." Again she stopped, her hands folded and her eyes in her lap. Reliving the grief from the past had clearly not been easy.

"I am very sorry for the pain you and your family suffered," said Percy after a moment. "As Father Abban told you, Roderick Westbrooke was my uncle. He died a year ago. Among his last thoughts were reminders of your sister, his first wife, Avonmara—"

"So he remarried, did he?"

"Yes, ma'am," nodded Percy. "I am his nephew by his second marriage."

"What is his wife's name. . .his second wife?"

"Katherine, Mrs. Maloney. She is my aunt. But as I say, he was thinking, too, of your sister, for she was the love of his youth. He asked me to try to find her family—you and your mother, though I understand she is now gone, and of course his daughter. He hoped I would be able to convey something of his sorrow at having deserted you all after Avonmara's death. He was full of remorse for leaving as he did. I realize that is small consolation, but he wanted you to know. He also wanted you to know that he eventually returned to Laragh and made considerable effort to locate his daughter. But he could not find where you had gone." Percy pulled from his pocket the envelopes addressed in his uncle's hand both to her mother, Mrs. O'Sullivan, as well as to herself. He handed them to her.

Slowly she looked at them one by one then smiled sadly. "So he came back after all, did he?" she said. "I am surprised...but maybe not altogether surprised. He *did* love her—that much was plain. But it came too late to do his daughter much good. She never saw her father in her life."

"I know, Mrs. Maloney," said Percy. "I feel the sadness with you. But perhaps it is not completely too late for him to be a father to her...in a manner of speaking. I don't know how much of my uncle's background your family knew. I don't know what he told Avonmara and your parents. But my uncle was an important man. There is not a great deal of money involved. But more than money is at stake. Your niece Morvern, if we can prove that she was indeed his daughter, would be my uncle's firstborn. The terms of the inheritance are independent of gender. A daughter can inherit as well as a son. That is why I must find her. She is in all likelihood the heir of my uncle's estate."

Mrs. Maloney stared back at Percy with a blank expression.

"That is why I urged Father Abban to ask you to allow me to speak with you. So where is the girl now?" asked Percy. "I realize by now that she is a grown woman. Does she live around here?"

"Mr. Drummond...I thought you knew."

"Knew what?"

"I am afraid Morvern is dead."

FIFTY-FOUR

A Bargain Struck

*E*arly that same morning, Courtenay Westbrooke saddled his mount and set off on the northern road to meet his future colleague and business associate at a small hotel in Bronaber on the north-south inland road through the region of Gwynedd. It was a ride of fifteen to eighteen miles. Though Bronaber was a small and out-of-the-way village, Litchfield had wanted to stay in close proximity to his upcoming acquisition.

In two weeks, thought Courtenay with satisfaction, he would finally and officially be known as the Viscount Lord Snowdon. There was no need to pretend any longer or play what petty games had been necessary to keep his plans from his mother. His sale of the land to Lord Litchfield would be finalized the day following his birthday. He had therefore given Litchfield leave to begin moving equipment into the area in order to begin constructing the road into his new property. His mother could do nothing to stop them now.

Thus it was, as Percy Drummond sat in the home of Vanora Maloney in the shipbuilding center of Arklow on the eastern coast of Ireland, that on a remote corner of his late uncle's estate in North Wales, his cousin and the mining entrepreneur, Lord Coleraine Litchfield, along with several assembled experts from near London, made their way through the remote hills of Snowdonia. Courtenay still had no idea of Litchfield's ultimate ambitions. Litchfield merely identified his colleagues as construction consultants.

It was the prior-arranged responsibility of Litchfield's assistant, Palmer Sutcliffe, to engage Courtenay sufficiently in conversation, drawing him away from the rest, that Litchfield and his "consultants" might confer more easily with the scruffy man beside him, most of whose teeth were gone and who had apparently made no acquaintance with a razor or a bar of soap in a good while. As they went, Litchfield made pretext of looking about as though with nostalgic thoughts of his boyhood while considering the best potential location for a home in the Snowdonian mountains. He was not, however, thinking of the scenery but rather about the fortune that lay beneath it.

As yet, young Westbrooke had no idea of the exact location where his surveyors had been seen several months before. He preferred to keep it that way. The less the young fool knew, the better.

Coming into the grassy valley that lay in the hollows of the ridge adjacent to the lake, which was his object of interest, Litchfield reined in and dismounted. The others of the party followed his lead.

"Ah, yes," he exclaimed, "it is just as I remember it!" He began walking about, to all appearances considering the most suitable options for a building site.

In the distance, the sudden sound of many hooves interrupted the tranquility of the scene. They turned to see a dozen or fifteen horses galloping up the far ridge and out of sight.

"What are those?" exclaimed Litchfield.

"There are wild horses all throughout Snowdonia," replied Courtenay.

"Who do they belong to? They were magnificent!"

"Don't get any ideas," rejoined Courtenay. "The horses on any of this land are mine. They roam everywhere, but that gives you no rights if they come onto your thousand acres."

"Whatever you say," laughed Litchfield. "Horses are not my business."

"Mr. Westbrooke," said Sutcliffe, walking up to Courtenay's side, "I realize you were interested in seeing the proposed site for Lord Litchfield's mountain retreat. However, might I propose that you and

I now return to the hotel and go over the final documents together?"

"I thought the documents were finalized," said Courtenay.

"To be sure. . .yes, mostly they are. There remain just one or two details to be ironed out."

"Can't they wait until the final transfer is to take effect?"

"I fear not, Mr. Westbrooke," said Sutcliffe. "Everything must be in perfect order so that the transfer occurs the day after your assumption of the title. There is also," he added, "the matter of an additional payment."

"What additional payment?" asked Courtenay.

"Since we are so close to the final date of closing the transaction, Lord Litchfield thought that he might advance you an additional payment toward the agreed-upon sum. I have a check for one thousand pounds made out to you at the hotel."

"I see. . . . Well, in that case," said Courtenay enthusiastically, "I suggest we get back and iron out those details you mentioned. . .and perhaps add a clause that excludes rights of horseflesh."

Litchfield smiled to himself as the two returned to their mounts. There were times, he mused, when Palmer Sutcliffe was worth every penny he paid him!

The moment they were out of sight, he walked back to his own horse. "All right," he shouted. "Let's get on with it."

Twenty minutes later, the party of four men arrived at the high overlook. Below them the waters of a small green mountain lake glistened in the sunlight.

"All right, Bagge," said Litchfield, inching his mount beside his scruffy crony, "it's time for you to keep up your half of the bargain. I want to know exactly where that gold came from that you showed us in Cardiff."

"There was some mention in our recent negotiations," said Bagge in a gravelly voice, "of two hundred pounds."

Litchfield smiled. "You are a sly one, Bagge. What? Don't you trust me?"

"I trust nobody. *Would* you pay me if you knew what I know without needing me no more?"

"Of course, Bagge. I am a man of my word."

"That may be, or not—I don't really care. But you get nothing more from me until I see the two hundred pounds."

Litchfield nodded, smiled again with condescending humor, then reached inside his coat. He pulled out ten crisp new twenty-pound notes—more money than Foulis Bagge had ever laid eyes on in one place in his life. He handed it to him.

With wide, greedy eyes, Bagge clutched the notes in his fist then held them to his leathery, hairy lips and kissed them. "You'll get what you paid for all right," he said. "It's down there, under the lake."

"What do you mean *under* it?"

"There's a cave. Nobody knows the entrance but me. It's where the gold came from. It was the year of the big draught, in '57. I used to know these hills like the back of my own hand. I found the cave when the water was low and the lake was nearly empty. That's when I found the gold. When I came back for more, the rains had begun again, and the lake had filled the cave. I've been coming back for years. But it's no use for the likes of me—I'm no fish. The gold's there, but the lower parts of the cave are filled with water."

Litchfield nodded and glanced at the two men who had been listening behind him.

"It's plausible enough," said one of them to his expression of question. "Of course it means we'll have to drain the lake or stop up its entry into the cave. But it's possible."

"All right then, Bagge," said Litchfield. "Lead the way. I want to see the entrance to this cave of gold. Once I am satisfied, you can keep the two hundred pounds and go to the devil for all I care."

FIFTY-FIVE

End of the Quest. . .or Perhaps Not

Percy stared back dumbstruck at the sister of his uncle's first wife. "*Dead?*" he repeated, hoping he had not heard her correctly.

Mrs. Maloney nodded.

Slowly Percy shook his head dejectedly. "I guess that's it then," he said. He let out a long sigh then glanced at the two priests. "I suppose my search has suddenly come to an end," he said. "I had hoped that I was about to find my uncle's daughter. At least now I know. . .and I can put my uncle's past to rest once and for all."

Again he turned to Mrs. Maloney. "I hope you won't mind telling me what happened," he said. "After that I promise I will pester you with no more questions. You have been most kind, but I would like to know what happened."

"I see no reason not to tell you," she replied. "You have come a long way. Even if we had no use for your uncle, that is not your fault. I suppose you deserve to know."

She took a breath, again remembering the past, and resumed her story. "As I told you, we never saw Morvern's father, your uncle, again. Morvern grew up. Eventually I married my husband Daibheid. My father died, but my mother continued to keep Morvern with her, though we lived nearby and I helped with her on most days when she was young. But my Daibheid, you see, he wanted children of his own.

747

He said it was no business of ours to take her in. So she remained with my mum. We had a son. He was born when Morvern was five. Then the famine hit, and my husband was out of work. My papa was gone by then, and my mother had nothing. Daibheid had worked in the shipyards for a time, before we were married, you see. So we all left Laragh, Mum and Morvern and Daibheid and me and our little Nigel, and we came here to Arklow. We had to do something to keep from starving. Daibheid found good work again, and we've been here ever since."

Again she paused. "It wasn't until Morvern was eighteen that the trouble started again."

"Trouble? How do you mean. . .*again*?"

"She seemed fated to go the same way as her own mother. She was beautiful, you see, just like her mother, only tall and with the same bright red hair. But then she met a Welshman just like Avonmara. He was a good man, I suppose, and a hard worker, but we all hated to see our Morvern involved with a man when she was still so young. Morvern was all my mother had by then, you see, and she was just like Mum's own daughter. Mum never let her use your uncle's name. She was just Morvern O'Sullivan. My poor mum, God rest her soul, she cursed your uncle for deserting his daughter, though maybe that wasn't right now that you tell me he tried to find her. But she died hating him, which is a sad thing to say about any two people in this world."

She glanced again at the letters she still held in her hand, again smiling sadly to see her name and her mother's name on the envelopes. "We never knew, you see—never knew he was trying to find us. . .that he wanted to be a good father to her after all. How could we know? We were gone by then, you see. It might have been different had we known. But we didn't know. Then Morvern met the other Welshman, you see, come over for the work in the shipyards, just like my Daibheid. They met at work, you see, and were friends for a time. But when he took a fancy to young Morvern, my mum said it boded no good. But young Morvern was determined to marry him, just like her mother had been to marry your uncle. The mother and daughter were just alike, you see, young and beautiful and swept off their feet, you might say. So Morvern married the man, and my mum was terrified for what would happen. My mum was always one for premonitions, you might say. By then Mum's red hair had turned as white as snow, as mine's doing now, you see. And when Morvern came to be with child just like her own mother, Mum was dreadfully afraid the same fate would befall her as had poor Avonmara. There was a midwife in Arklow at that time. She was a strange woman, too acquainted with evil some said. Mrs. Faoiltiarna was her name. Whether that was her real name or not, no one knew, but it could not have suited her more perfectly."

"Why do you say that?" asked Percy.

"The name means Wolf Lady, and that's what she was. She made it her business to know other people's secrets, and she parlayed them into power over them, and she listened to such folk that other people would have nothing to do with. My mum was one, as she got older, who was too much taken with the peculiarities of life, you might say. My Daibheid said no good would come of it, but Mum insisted that the midwife attend the birth of Morvern's baby. She thought maybe the woman's strange powers would be able to fight off the power of death she was convinced was hovering over our family, trying to destroy us. My Daibheid and Mum argued fiercely over it and yelled at one another like mortal enemies, though one was my own mother and the other was my husband. Daibheid insisted the woman was evil. He said that to bring her into the house would portend no good. And Morvern's young husband, he agreed with Daibheid. But in the end, Morvern let her grandmother decide the matter, for she was the only mother she had ever known, you see, and she could do no other than to trust her. So the midwife was called in, and Morvern gave birth to a daughter."

"A daughter!" exclaimed Percy, his hopes suddenly revived.

"Aye, but not one you'll be wanting to find, I'm thinking."

"Why do you say that?"

"The instant Daibheid laid eyes on her, the first words out of his mouth were that the curse of the Wolf Lady's evil had come to the family. He was more furious at my mother than ever. After that he wouldn't let me or our Nigel see Morvern or her baby or her husband or my mother.

He was a devout man, you see, my Daibheid. He was certain there was evil afoot. He wanted nothing to do with the little girl or any of them anymore. As the weeks passed, then months, his words seemed to be confirmed."

"In what way?" asked Percy.

"The baby was strange from the start. In her eyes was a look from another world. Daibheid didn't want me to have anything to do with any of them. He called the midwife a witch. He said she had passed her evil into the family. But when he was at work, I couldn't help myself, you see, for I am a woman, and they were my family, you see—my mum and Morvern and her child. But Daibheid told people about her otherworldly look and her strange ways, and before long, you see, there was talk and dreadful things began being said about us. All at once Morvern's husband told my mum he was taking his wife and child and they were leaving Arklow. My mum was both heartbroken and furious at once, but she had brought it on herself with all the talk of evil forebodings and bringing in the midwife to the birth. The little man was a good man, you see, and he knew the evil such rumors about his child could work. He didn't want our family hurt by them either. So he took Morvern and the child away, and we never saw Morvern again. A year later, my mum received a letter from him telling her that Morvern was dead. Mum never recovered. It was a family curse, Daibheid said. Mum lived no more than a year after that. It was the midwife, Daibheid said. She was the cause of it. She was an evil that would mean the death of us all."

"Why did people call on her services?"

"She knew every birthing that was coming and wormed her way into their homes. People were afraid of her, that she would put a curse on them or work some other devilry. But eventually her evil ways caught up with her."

"What happened?"

"There was a man whose wife was about to give birth—you remember, Father," she said, glancing toward Father Abban, "Mr. Keefe, from the shipyards."

The priest nodded.

"When the woman came oiling around, he would have none of it,"
Mrs. Maloney went on. "He told her never to show her face around his
house. There were threats and high words. She was enraged. No one had
dared refuse her so publicly. He was an important man, you see, and
everyone knew that he had rebuked her to her face. She shouted some
incantation back at him then said that a gruesome and premature death
would come to him. He laughed back in her face. No fat purple witch
could tell the future, he said."

"She claimed to be able to see into the future?"

"It was one of the ways she made people fear her."

"Why did he call her a *purple* witch?"

"She always wore purple, and with horrid earrings of snakes and
ugly creatures. But their argument, you see, took place outside the
man's home. She shrieked terrible curses at him as she stormed off.
The whole neighborhood heard her. Within days, what had happened
was all over town, that he had called her a witch. Rumors began to
circulate that her strange ways had all along been rooted in close
connections to the dark forces of the underworld. And when poor
Mr. Keefe died suddenly a year later, the charge of witch confirmed
for all to see, some of the men of the community began devising a way
to get rid of her."

"You mean kill her?"

"That may have been what they intended. Daibheid would never tell
me. But she got wind of it and suddenly disappeared, fled for her life.
Nobody ever saw her again, and no one was sorry. Morvern's daughter
was the last child she delivered in Ireland. Daibheid said a curse was on
the girl because of it. Even when she came back, though she was our
own kin and my own sister's granddaughter, he wouldn't let us have
anything to do with her."

"What do you mean, when she came back? Who came back?"

"Morvern's baby, my own niece—though she's grown into a woman
now, of course. I haven't laid eyes on her myself, but I've spoken with
them who have."

"She is back in Arklow?" said Percy.

"Not in the town. In the hills to the west, I believe. I don't know her exact whereabouts."

"I need to find her."

"She is not of this world. She is not one your uncle would want to claim as his own."

"But if she is his heir, as Morvern's daughter, then I must find her. She must know it."

"They say she is one of strange ways. There is truth to what Daibheid has always said, that evil has followed her because a witch brought her into the world. But when she is married, I hope to see her again. She is to be married soon, you see. There are those who know, and they tell me about her because I am her aunt."

"Do you know when the marriage is to take place?"

"In a week, I believe, though her husband-to-be is an older man in his thirties and she is still young."

"I must talk to this girl."

"I can't tell you where to find her even if I dared. All I can tell you is what I hear, that every Sunday morning, rain or shine, her habit is to climb to the top of Lugnaquilla, unless it is covered in snow. No one knows why."

"Lugnaquilla—what is that?"

"It is the highest mountain in County Wicklow. It is inland and north, about fifteen miles from here. It is easily visible on a clear day. As she goes, they say the girl plucks wildflowers along the path. They say she gathers them into a bouquet and leaves them at the top."

"There would not be many flowers at this time of the year."

"They say if there are no flowers, she makes her bouquets of weeds and grasses."

"What is the name of the mountain again?"

"Lugnaquilla. It is most often known by the name given to its peak."

"What is that?"

"It is called Percy's Table."

Percy smiled. *An interesting coincidence,* he thought. He had not known that he had a mountain named after him in Ireland!

The room fell silent.

"It seems that perhaps it is time for us to take our leave, Vanora," said Father Abban. "We do not want to presume on your kindness. I know you are concerned for the time."

Mrs. Maloney smiled, again nervously, and nodded.

"Thank you very much, Mrs. Maloney," said Percy as they rose. "I appreciate everything you have told me. You have been most helpful."

"And have no worries, Vanora," added Father Abban. "When the time comes, I will speak with Daibheid."

"Thank you, Father."

The three men walked toward the door.

"Oh," said Percy, pausing and turning back to Mrs. Maloney, "I meant to ask about this before when you mentioned it, but it slipped my mind. What did you mean when you said that the instant your husband laid eyes on Morvern's baby, his first words were that the curse of the woman's evil had come upon the family? Was it because of what you said about the look in her eyes?"

"No, not her eyes. That couldn't be seen until later, until she began to look about and you had the uncanny feeling she was seeing into you."

"What was it then?"

"It was her hair, you see."

"What about it?"

"All the O'Sullivan girls that anyone can remember had red hair, the girl's mother and grandmother, my sister and myself, and her great-grandmother."

"But Morvern's baby did not?"

"That's why the sight of it struck fear into my Daibheid's very soul. The moment she was born, the child's hair was white as my Mum's, you see."

FIFTY-SIX

The Heart of the Factor

Steven Muir was beside himself.

The primary source of his anxiety was not Courtenay's imminent assumption to the viscountcy and the loss of his job. He was worried neither for himself nor his mother. The house on Mochras Head, Katherine had already assured him, would contain quarters for them both, and their employment was assured. If Lady Katherine went to her brother's in Glasgow until its completion, a dozen or more homes in Llanfryniog or the surrounding hills would happily take him in, and his mother, until that time.

His anxiety was rather for Lady Florilyn. The thought of her marrying Colville Burrenchobay was so odious in his mind as to have rendered him physically sick for two weeks.

Steven's feelings were born in no petty human jealousy but rather in a lifelong acquaintance with the eldest son of Gwynedd's parliamentarian. He knew something of what Burrenchobay was. He had also gained more than a passing glimpse of what Florilyn *could be* and was on her way to becoming. That *was* and that *becoming* could not be united without one of the two destroying the other.

Light and darkness cannot coexist. One must be extinguished in the triumph of its opposite. God will triumph. Sin will be extinguished from the universe.

But the light that had been newly growing in Florilyn was not strong enough to illuminate a soul so consumed with itself as that of Colville Burrenchobay. A tender growing human plant can too easily wither in the overpowering presence of one who is far too pleased with himself. Nothing is so lethal to the need to "become" as self-satisfaction. Falling under the spell of his alluring blandishments, Florilyn was not even aware of the thousand subtleties by which he encouraged her to nourish the self rather than kill it. Like her ancient Mother of Life, she had eaten of the fruit, so pleasing to the eye. And it had done its work.

Though he had not been an intellectual standout at Cambridge, Colville Burrenchobay was bright enough instinctively to know that to control her he must divide Florilyn from her past. Nothing accomplishes that end so readily as feeding pride, while offering tantalizing innuendos of derogation against any and all who were part of that past.

Steven hoped, however, that what he thought of as the "new Florilyn" was not altogether dead yet.

But what could *he* do to reawaken her? He had again become as nothing in her eyes. What had seemed a genuine friendship blossoming between them had evaporated as if it had never been. To all appearances, she despised him. Whether this was due to Colville's whispered lies into her willing ear or from a deeper change in her own heart. . .he had not inquired too deeply. Indeed, perhaps the two were not so very different. That her ear had proved willing to listen to his subtle disseverations and gradually accept them as her own, perhaps revealed as much about her own insecurity as it did Colville's motives to lure her away from all former affections.

The evening was late as Steven stood at his window. The countryside of Wales glowed in the pale light of a full moon coming in and out from behind turbulent clouds in the night sky. It had rained most of the afternoon. Though the storm had passed inland toward England, its windy retreat was still evident overhead. The tumultuous sky mirrored the turmoil in Steven's own soul.

He had never paused to analyze his feelings for Florilyn to their depths. As a youth he had merely noticed her from afar and felt a strange sense of protectiveness over her. Hired by her father, then her mother, and brought into sudden and daily proximity to the family, his devotion had been as a servant who desired her best and sought to serve. That deeper feelings occasionally stirred within him, he took as merely a natural response of the human animal. He attached no great significance to them. That she had begun to reciprocate his friendship, that they had been able to laugh and talk together, these moments he treasured as among the manifold privileges of his job, but little more.

All the feelings—had he been another sort of young man, or from a higher social standing, that he might have looked at more closely and questioned where they might possibly lead—were subserved in his consciousness to the love that Florilyn had once carried toward his friend, Percy Drummond. Even the suspension of their engagement he assumed was but temporary. He considered nothing to be gained by it for himself other than the continued opportunity to serve his young mistress.

From the very day Florilyn began seeing Colville Burrenchobay, however, something new awoke in the heart of Steven Muir. A giant was born in the gentle young man. He knew what it was. He loved her more deeply than he had allowed himself to admit. But with the realization came the horrifying thought that his love might be born in jealousy toward Colville. If such were true, he would give Lady Katherine his notice and leave this place and never lay eyes on Florilyn again. Nothing was more hateful to him than even the merest possibility that he might succumb to such an evil emotion as jealousy.

And yet. . .was his concern for her future only for *himself*?

No, he knew it was not. He cared for *her* and desired her *best*. For her best, he would turn and walk away. Likewise. . .for her best he would come against any threat to her well-being. Not to possess her, but that the true Florilyn might emerge victorious over the Florilyn that Colville would attempt to control. Though she never laid eyes on him again, though she might hate him, he must still do his *best* for her and try to prevent her making a terrible mistake.

But how? What was his responsibility? How was he to do right for her, to do his best for her? How could things be set right again in Florilyn's life? Could *he*, such as he was in her eyes, assist in such a setting-right? What was he to *do*?

For several more minutes he stood gazing out upon the windy night. He was too agitated to sleep. At length he turned, lit a small candle, and left his room. With quiet step he crept through the darkened corridors of the great house. A few minutes later, he found himself at the doors of the library. However strange it may seem for the hired servants in a house of ancient title and property to have full access to such regions, it was Lady Katherine's will that everyone connected with Westbrooke Manor, from lowest to highest, consider the library his or her own personal region of dreams, rest, escape, retreat, learning, study, and imagination. Anyone might borrow any book or use the library at any time a schedule permitted.

As quietly as he could, he opened the double doors and swung them back wide enough to enter. His mother and Lady Katherine were forever talking about the author MacDonald. He was an avid reader himself, but his tastes in recent years had tended to run in different currents than were found in fiction. He knew what they all said, that MacDonald's fiction was unlike any other. The only thing of MacDonald's he had yet read himself was his volume of *Unspoken Sermons*.

He went to the shelf and stood before it. Everyone in the house by now knew where the MacDonald books were located. It was the most frequently used part of the library, and its contents grew yearly. Randomly he pulled out one volume after another, flipping through each, allowing his eyes to rest on one passage or another, hoping perhaps to discover some nugget of written gold buried within the pages between the decorated boards. . .something that would illuminate his way in this dark hour of his soul.

For half an hour he tried one book, then another, then another, returning to several a second, even a third time, also flipping slowly through his own favorite book of MacDonald's sermons.

He had nearly begun to despair when suddenly his eyes fell on a passage whose words seemed to compel him, even as they spoke of the compulsion of God's love toward the setting right of wrong in human life.

> " *He will set it right, my lord,'* " he read, " *'but probably in a way your lordship will not like. He is compelled to do terrible things sometimes.'* "

The words arrested Steven's attention as if he had been struck in the face. That God would be *compelled* to do terrible things toward those he loves was a concept altogether new. He continued on.

> " *'Compelled!—what should compel him?'*
> *'The love that is in him, the love that he is. He cannot let us have our own way to the ruin of everything in us he cares for!'* "

The words perfectly described exactly what he had been thinking about Florilyn—that she must not be allowed to have her own way to the ruin of everything good that had been growing in her.

Steven's eyes continued down the page.

> *"Then the spirit awoke in Donal—or came upon him—and he spoke.*
> *'My lord,' he said, 'anything I can do, watching with you night and day, giving myself to help you, I am ready for. It will be very hard, I know. I will do all that lies in me to deliver you. I will give my life to strengthen yours, and count it well spent and myself honoured. I shall have lived a life worth living! Resolve, my lord— in God's name resolve at once to be free. But one thing you may not have, my lord, is your own will. You will never be free by seeking your own will, until you make your will his.'* "

With a finger between the pages, Steven took the book and candle to one of the library's reading chairs and sat down. He turned to the beginning of the chapter and read it in its entirety in order to gain more of the context of the passage that had drawn his attention. Before he retired for the night two hours later, the book lay on the table in his own room. He had completed its first fifty pages before sleep overtook him.

The single word *compel* remained with him in sleep. By the time he awoke the following morning, his way had begun to become clear. If love required *compulsion* to do what was best for the beloved and set things right, then he would not shy away from it.

FIFTY-SEVEN

Lugnaquilla

Percy was at the base of the mountain called Lugnaquilla shortly
after daybreak on the following Sunday morning. He had been given
directions and a map by Father Abban, along with precautions of the
mountain treacheries if a thick morning fog or afternoon mist off the
sea obscured his way.

The priest invited Percy to remain with him in Arklow as his guest
for as long as his business made it necessary. He had been with him
for three days, during which time the two young men had had many
lively and informative discussions on matters of faith—discovering
more points of commonality and brotherhood than either would have
anticipated. In the meantime, Father Halliday returned to Laragh.

According to Father Abban, any of a half dozen sheep tracks and
walking paths led to the summit of Lugnaquilla. Bogs and boulders and
cliffs and ravines, however, were everywhere, and one must be attentive
and vigilant. Having not the remotest idea from which direction
the mystery girl he had heard about from Vanora Maloney came up the
mountain on her weekly trek or when, Percy resolved to be at the top
as early in the day as possible. He would remain until sunset if need be
so as not to miss her.

He dressed warm and, at Father Abban's insistence, had packed
food and water. Father Abban took him to the base of the mountain

by buggy shortly after sunrise then returned to town for his weekly priestly duties presiding over Sunday's scheduled masses. As he began the assent, in his right hand Percy clutched one of his new friend's stout walking staffs.

The way gradually steepened as he went. He made his way across boggy fields and meadows, through light woodlands bordered by a few thickly forested glades and hillsides, up and down dells and valleys, jumping a dozen small brooks and watercourses, and sloshing through several chilly, frothing streams whose waters plunged down to meet the Avonbeg River where it flowed around the base of the mountain toward the sea.

Next to one of these, his step was arrested by an unexpected sight. It reminded him that death was slowly relinquishing the earth from its temporary prison, and that the Son of liberating spring was on its way to set the captives free. So near his foot that his step nearly crushed it, in the shadow of a large stone, the tiny yellow face of a new spring primrose peeped up at him from amid its rough cabbage-like leaves.

The sight of the simple blossom stung him with nostalgic reminders of many things—both conscious and subconscious. . .of Hugh Sutherland and Margaret Elginbrod and the fir wood of their story, of Florilyn and Snowdonia's green hills, of sunrises and sunsets and high overlooks above the sea, of angels and mysteries and floral bouquets. He paused, set down his staff, and stooped to pluck it. He stood again, drew in a deep breath of satisfaction, and slowly continued on his way.

It was not an especially steep or arduous climb. As he had been forewarned, however, he found his way long and circuitous and filled with many tracks and paths that appeared promising but that led nowhere or ended abruptly at the edge of some ravine or cliff. Thankfully, though the ground was wet, the day was relatively clear. No thick fog topped the mountain, though clusters of mist clung here and there to some of its low-lying valleys. Thus, it was after many retracings of his steps, as the spring sun rose high in the sky and began to send down what warmth it possessed in this first week of March, perspiring freely in spite of the chilly morning air, that Percy at last approached

Lugnaquilla's expansive flat summit that had been given his own name, "Percy's Table."

What he had expected, Percy himself could not have said. Reaching the top of the three-thousand-foot hill and finding it desolate and empty, without hint that another human being was within miles, filled him with a vague sense of disappointment.

He stopped and gazed about. Slowly he turned in every direction until he had peered into the distance toward all the 360 degrees of the compass. A few clouds of mists obscured visibility here and there. But the sea, east toward Wicklow fifteen miles distant, was easily visible stretching out to his right and left.

He strolled aimlessly about for a few minutes then found a dry bit of grass and sat down. He began his wait with an apple, a hunk of cheese, a piece of bread, and water from the canvas bag of provisions provided him by Father Abban. For the first time he now regretted that he had not thought to bring a book from the well-stocked library at the rectory.

He had arisen for his day's quest while it was yet dark. The walk had been easy enough, but the cumulative effect had fatigued him. After his brief breakfast, with the sun beating down and warming earth and humanity as one, it was not long before sleepiness began to overtake him.

Percy stretched out on the grass and began to doze.

FIFTY-EIGHT

Percy's Table

*T*he walker whose weekly habit for two years had been to make this solitary trek did not often encounter fellow sojourners at this time of year. Heart and mind were free to wander where they would without distraction or interruption.

Her thoughts on this day, as always, were of the one she came here to remember with the tiny bouquets that would be meaningless to any other. Her mind was filled, too, with the great change that was soon to come upon her. She would not long be able to continue this weekly habit. She had set out this morning knowing that today's journey would likely be her last. She would be married in two weeks. As another man's wife, she could not continue paying tribute to one from her past whom she would never see again.

The one to whom she had been pledged was a good man, and she must be a good wife to him. Love found easy reception in her heart toward all of God's creation. She could love, and therefore she *would* love. Her father had chosen him for her, in spite of the difference in their ages, because he knew he would be a caring husband for his daughter. She honored her father. And thus she would learn to love.

But on this day, one last time, her love would look back, not forward...and she would remember.

There came a breath of something in the west.

Percy stirred from where he lay, half rose, and looked about.

What had awakened him? No hint of wind caressed his face, unusual on such a peak as this. But some rustling, some far-off sound, some *presence* had intruded into his brain.

He sat. . .listening intently. It seemed that all the world was waiting in stillness for something at hand.

It came again.

Percy froze. A chill swept through his body.

A faint, far-off tune came floating up the mountain from somewhere. Someone was singing, but in no voice of this world. The sound was of some melancholy lament. . .haunting, mysterious, as from some ancient Celtic love ballad whose ethereal melody remained forever unresolved.

Slowly he rose to his feet, searching to detect from which direction it came.

As she softly sang, the walker stooped to grasp a handful of spring grasses and added them to the earthy bouquet clutched in her other hand. If this was indeed the last bouquet she would leave in memory of the one who lived in her heart, she was sorry it contained no flowers. But spring was still early, and she had seen none today.

She rose again to continue to the summit. As she did, she saw a figure ahead. The sight startled her.

A man stood in the distance staring at her.

Abruptly her singing stopped. It must be a vision, born in her imagination. She gazed at the figure in disbelief then slowly walked toward it.

A gasp escaped Percy's lips.

The rays of the sun, falling on the girl's head from behind, gave it a radiant golden hue. But as she came nearer, he saw that the wild crop of luxuriant hair was of purest white.

He stood transfixed. He could not move. He could only stare in wonder.

Closer she moved, gliding noiseless over the ground. Every line of her countenance came into focus, and he knew he was gazing at no mirage.

The *eyes*...deep blue-green...eyes that spoke of the sea! Changeable...depthless...radiant...liquid...alive with the light of life.

The *face*...the same, yet new...older, wiser, if possible more beautiful, full of mystery...and at peace.

The angel of his dreams had materialized as from out of Lugnaquilla's mists. Was she indeed, as he once said, an angel from on high? Had she always been an angel?

As he beheld her features, seeing them for the first time in more than three and a half years and now contained in a woman's face, suddenly all the eyes from the portraits on the landing at Westbrooke Manor leaped out at him. The truth had been in plain view all along. How could they not have seen it!

She slowed then stood before him.

"*Gwyneth!*" he breathed in a reverent whisper. "Is it...can it be...is it really *you* I have been searching for?"

For answer, she merely took another step forward, the smile on her face saying that somehow she did not find it incredible that the weekly vision she cherished in her heart had become real.

Percy opened his arms and swallowed her into his embrace. "I cannot believe that you are here," he whispered.

"I am always here, Percy," Gwyneth said. "In my heart, I am always with you."

They stood long minutes in silence. Or perhaps it was an hour. On the top of Percy's Table, for these two, time would nevermore have meaning. They were swallowed up in eternity.

"Until you spoke, I did not know if you were real," said Gwyneth at length. "I always see you when I come here. But the real you is older than the you of my imagination."

The spell was undone. She was the same Gwyneth of old!

Percy stepped back and broke into the laughter of pure joy. The sound of his happiness ringing out over the hilltop was as enchanting to Gwyneth as her mysterious voice of song was to him. She broke out in a giggle of delighted girlish pleasure.

"Here, Percy," she said, handing him the bouquet of weeds and grasses. "I picked these for you."

"Surely you meant them for someone else?" said Percy with a humorous smile.

"I come here every week and leave you a bouquet, Percy."

"Surely you don't give flowers to every stranger you meet."

"Only those who are going to become my friends," rejoined Gwyneth with a smile of her own.

"You knew that about me?"

"Of course."

"How did you know?"

"I saw on your face the look of a friend."

Again Percy laughed with delight to be reminded of their first meeting on the hills of Snowdonia. He turned and stooped to find the faded primrose where it had slipped from between his fingers when he had fallen asleep. "And I have something for you," he said, handing it to her.

"A new spring primrose! Oh, thank you, Percy!"

"Gwyneth, Gwyneth... I cannot believe it! But it really *is* you, isn't it?"

"I think so, Percy. I think I am me. Have you been in Wales?"

"Several times since you left. I visited your cottage. No one is living in it now. You will never guess who I saw—Bunny White Tail!"

Gwyneth smiled. "It was hard to leave the animals. I still do not understand why we had to leave. But my father said there was no other way. I know there was something he did not tell me. But I trust him to know best."

She glanced away. An expression crossed her face that Percy had never seen before. Then she looked earnestly back into his face. "Are you and Florilyn...," she began then hesitated.

"No, we are not married, if that's what you were about to ask," said Percy. "But I hear *you* are to be."

Gwyneth smiled and nodded. She had tried to hide it, but Percy saw that her heart was filled with complex emotions at the prospect. "My father thinks it best," she said. "He wants me well taken care of when he is gone. Oh, my father!" Gwyneth exclaimed as if suddenly remembering. "He will be so happy to see you!"

"Yes, and there are things I must talk over with him as well," nodded Percy. "Where do you live?"

"Just down the slope, in one of the dells along the side of the mountain. My father raises sheep now. We have a fine house, and he has a large flock. I think he is happier now than when he worked in the slates. Come, Percy," she said excitedly, taking his hand and beginning to run off down the mountain, "I will take you to him!"

"Wait, let me get my things!" laughed Percy. He quickly returned a few steps for the knapsack and staff then hurried after her.

FIFTY-NINE

Factor and Son

$\mathcal{A}$s Gwyneth skipped merrily down the slope with Percy chasing after her, back at Westbrooke Manor, Steven Muir had sent through one of the housemaids in his mother's charge the request to Courtenay in his apartment, where he knew him to be at present, that he would be grateful to see him in his office at his earliest convenience.

Steven knew it would rankle Courtenay thus to be summoned as if *he* were the servant and Steven his master. In all likelihood it would ensure that the ensuing interview began in a combative tone. But he had done so intentionally. It was necessary to establish his authority, even if but briefly, to demand from Courtenay what the viscount's son would never condescend to give him by simple request—a straight and honest answer to a direct question. In other words, the truth.

Courtenay walked through the open door of the factor's office without benefit of knocking or announcing himself. He was breathing fire. "What is the meaning of this, Muir!" he demanded, striding angrily across the floor where he stood glaring down at Steven behind his desk. "Let us get one thing clear—you do not summon *me*! If you have business with me, then you come find me. I am not your lackey. I had been considering keeping you on after I am viscount. But if there are more incidents of this kind, I will turn you out on your ear without notice, and your mother with you. Do I make myself clear?"

Steven sat calmly staring into Courtenay's eyes until he had finished his rant. Slowly he rose, walked from behind the desk and across the floor, closed the door of the office, then returned where he stopped and faced Courtenay. "Please sit down, Courtenay," he said in a soft voice, gesturing toward one of two chairs.

"Did I not make myself understood?" rejoined Courtenay. "I will not have you telling me what to do!"

"Courtenay, please," repeated Steven. "Just sit down. I would like to speak with you about a serious matter."

"I have no intention of speaking to you about anything, Muir!" Courtenay shot back. "Now get out of my way before I dismiss you on the spot."

He took two steps toward the door. But he did not take a third. With a swiftness and strength of which he scarcely guessed the other capable, he found his shoulders clasped helplessly between Steven's two huge hands. As if he were a rag doll, he was unceremoniously thrown back and shoved down into the chair he had a moment earlier been invited to take under his own power.

Courtenay's face glowed crimson. "How dare you lay a hand on me, Muir!" he cried, his eyes flashing fire as he leaped to his feet. "You will pay for that!"

Even as a clenched fist shot toward Steven's face, his arm was arrested in mid-flight by the vice-grip of Steven's right hand. Courtenay stood glowering, though obviously powerless. Steven squeezed his arm then slowly twisted it and pushed backward until, with a cry of pain, Courtenay fell back again into the chair.

"You could have broken my arm!"

"I would have been sorry had you forced matters that far," said Steven. "I told you I wanted to talk to you. You and I *will* talk, with or without your cooperation. You took the whip to me once, and I did not defend myself. I had my reasons. But do not mistake me, Courtenay. I know something of your strength, for I have been watching you for years. I also know my own. I could put you on the ground without raising so much as a bead of sweat. You fancy yourself a powerful man, but I fear you no more than I would a ten-year-old. So I suggest we have our talk, that you answer my question, and that you go your way. It will be simpler for us both if you cooperate."

"What do you want, Muir?" said Courtenay in sulking fury.

"I have a simple question to ask, and I want a simple answer. Are you the father of Rhawn Lorimer's child?"

"Go to the devil, Muir."

"I will have to ask you for directions. Now I put you the question again—are you the father?"

"And I give you the same answer I gave you before. I will tell you nothing."

Standing before him, Steven drew in a breath then turned and paced about a few moments.

Courtenay's eyes darted toward the door. For a brief instant he considered trying to end this humiliation by making a dash for it. But he did not relish the consequences if he failed. Nor was his pride fond of the notion of running away like a frightened child.

"You will be viscount in what, nine or ten days," said Steven, turning again toward him. "Not that you may care about your reputation either in the community or the House of Lords, but there may come a time when what is said of you will be of some consequence. If you do not tell me, I will let it be known that you refused to answer me. You know what people will assume."

"I will tell them that *you* are the father of the Lorimer brat."

A smile spread across Steven's face. "Do you seriously think anyone would believe that?" he said. "To make such a charge would only convince everyone all the more that you are the guilty party. On the other hand, if you deny it and I learn you are lying, and if that is the case I *will* find out. . .I promise you that it will go worse for you than had you confessed honorably to the truth from the beginning. You have only one choice, Courtenay. That is to tell me the truth. If you are the father, and you tell me plainly, I will respect your honesty and pursue the matter no further."

Even in his fury at finding himself powerless before this clod-hopping interloper of a factor, Courtenay was yet in sufficient awe of his calm demeanor and measured tone that he did not for a moment doubt that he would do exactly as he said. He knew something of the esteem in which Steven was held throughout the community. He was practical enough to realize the consequences of crossing him. "I am not the father," he answered after a moment.

Steven nodded then walked back behind his desk and sat down.

"I presume that is all, Muir?"

"Yes. Thank you, Courtenay."

Courtenay rose and stood a moment. "You may consider this your notice, Muir," he said. "You are hereby terminated. I want you and your mother gone from the manor by six o'clock on the morning of the seventeenth, which is my birthday. Is that understood?"

"Very clearly."

Steven watched Courtenay go, more sad than angry, then took out a sheet of writing paper, set it before him, and took pen in hand.

Dear Percy, he began,

We are only days from Courtenay's birthday and his assumption of the viscountcy. However, that is not the reason I am writing, but rather about a crisis concerning Florilyn. I do not know if you have been apprised of recent events—her engagement to Colville Burrenchobay. My own concern for her well-being and future mounts daily. She is much changed—and I am heartbroken to have to say, not for the better. The spiritual being that had begun to blossom, under Burrenchobay's influence, is fast becoming a withered flower and a mere memory of happier times. I am writing to implore you to return for the purpose of speaking to her and warning her of the danger of being joined for life with such a one.

We are two men who love her. We cannot allow this to happen without speaking forthrightly to her. I do not want to act without you, but I fear time is critical. Every day that passes she seems to slip deeper into what I am convinced is a deceptive attempt to woo her affections and distance her from her mother and the rest of us.

Please consider my request seriously. The matter is urgent. Please come.

Your friend and servant,
Steven Muir

SIXTY

The Viscount, the Miner, and the Scot

*A*s they approached down one of Lugnaquilla's projecting ridges, Percy saw that the new Barrie home was indeed a fine one, easily twice the size of their former cottage in Wales. In the distance, the diminutive figure of Codnor Barrie was surrounded by several sheepdogs and a huge, moving mass of white.

They walked toward the shepherd and his flock. He saw them coming and turned to meet them.

"Look who I found on the mountain, Papa!" exclaimed Gwyneth, as they made their way into the midst of the flock.

Barrie's face held its perplexed expression but a moment then brightened into a huge smile as recognition dawned.

"Mr. Drummond!" he cried. "How do you come to be here?"

"It's a miracle, Papa," said Gwyneth simply. "I think an angel led him to us."

"Gwyneth may not be far wrong, Mr. Barrie," said Percy as the two shook hands. "I would rather say that God led my steps, and I *found* an angel."

Gwyneth glanced away shyly.

Barrie looked back and forth between the two and understood. "Do you and I need to have a talk, Mr. Drummond?" he said.

"We do indeed, sir," replied Percy.

Beside herself with curiosity about what the two were saying, Gwyneth's sense of the propriety of things kept her from intruding. She walked quietly toward the house, pausing once at the door to glance back.

The two men, the younger towering over the older, walked slowly away across the field, heads as close as their difference in height would allow. They were obviously engaged in earnest conversation.

Her heart full of many things she dared not think, she watched them a few moments more then went inside.

An hour later, from where she stood at the window, Gwyneth saw the two returning.

Her father's face wore a serious expression. He nodded occasionally as Percy spoke.

She stepped back from the window.

As they came nearer the house, Percy noticed above the door a beam of oak into which were carved two words in Gaelic—the house name, he presumed. Though he could not read them, they seemed somehow familiar. He had no leisure to think about it, for a moment later Barrie led him through the door and into the spacious sitting room.

"Grannie!" Percy exclaimed as he saw the old woman sitting across the room in a positive fever of anticipation for whom Gwyneth had told her was coming.

She scarcely had time to pull herself up before finding her aging frame nearly crushed by Percy's embrace. "Aye, laddie," she said, "you're as big and strong and handsome as I knew you must be!" she said. She pulled his head down toward her and kissed him on the cheek.

"And you, Grannie!" said Percy exuberantly. "You look well indeed."

"For an old woman of eighty-eight years, I'm just grateful enough to the Lord for keeping me here long enough to feast my eyes on your face one more time."

"Oh, but Grannie," said Percy excitedly as he released her, "I just remembered. I have something of yours!" He reached into his pocket and pulled from it the gold coin she had been given on the sands of Llanfryniog more than eighty years before. He held it toward her.

"No, no, laddie!" she said. "That night when I told you how I came by it, and the evil that had stalked me because of it, I said I wanted it no more. I gave it to another to keep. But I'm thinking it wasn't you."

"You're right," smiled Percy. "Perhaps it is time I returned it to her." He turned toward Gwyneth where she stood watching. "You gave me this for safekeeping," said Percy. "I told you at the time that I would always consider it yours. I have carried it with me every day since. Not a day went by that I did not think of you. It remained with me as an unspoken pledge of our. . .of a friendship that I treasured. You are a grown woman now. It is time I returned it." He held the coin to Gwyneth.

Her hand reached out, and he placed it in her palm. His fingers lingered briefly upon hers. She felt a sudden heat rising in her cheeks. She pulled her hand away as it closed over the coin and glanced away.

"But why have you come, laddie?" said Grannie as she eased back into her chair. "How did you find us?"

"It is a long and intricate story, Grannie," replied Percy as he and Codnor also took seats.

Gwyneth moved toward the kitchen at the far end of the room and put a kettle on the stove for tea.

"It concerns my uncle, the viscount," began Percy. "He had a riding accident a year ago, and his injuries were mortal. He died a week later."

"God bless the man—I am sorry to hear it."

"On his deathbed he asked me to do something," Percy continued. "He asked me to find someone that no one else in his family, not even my Aunt Katherine or Florilyn or Courtenay, knew about. Then he told me a story he had told no other living person in more than thirty years." Percy paused and drew in a breath.

By now Gwyneth was seated with the rest of them. She and Grannie listened intently as Percy told them what he had already told Gwyneth's father—of his uncle's sojourn in Ireland as a young man, of his marriage to Avonmara O'Sullivan, and of the tragic circumstances that had followed in which he lost track of the daughter that had been born to him. "It was this daughter, whom he had never seen again," said

Percy, "whom I thought he wanted me to find."

"But if he was dying," said Gwyneth, "why would it matter so much to him?"

"Because according to the terms of his viscountcy, she would be his legal heir, not Courtenay."

"But she was a girl, laddie," said Grannie. "How could that be?"

"Every peerage is unique," explained Percy. "They are established according to terms that must be legally followed in perpetuity unless the peerage is abolished. The particular viscountcy my uncle inherited from his father must originally have been established by a progressive and far-seeing man who determined that a firstborn daughter, and her own children who followed, was equally deserving of the rights and privileges of the title as a son. I have been studying law, you see, Grannie, and I looked into it as much as I was able. It is extremely unusual, but those are the terms. No doubt it will ultimately have to be decided in court. But my uncle was certain enough of the legality of the terms to commission me, as I thought, to find his daughter. He knew she was the rightful heir by his first marriage."

"Did you find her, laddie?"

"I am afraid not, Grannie," replied Percy. He turned toward Codnor Barrie. "Perhaps you should explain the rest of it, Codnor," he said.

Barrie nodded. The others waited as he collected his thoughts then turned toward Gwyneth. "I always told you, lassie," he began, "that you were born across the water from where we lived—that you were born here in Ireland. But you never knew why I was here. There came a time, you see, when the mine in Wales had to close. Parliament was trying to improve on safety everywhere, and the labor movement was gaining strength. So they closed the mine to make changes and make working conditions safer than before. I was a young man at the time, not as adventurous as some but with my own share of the adventurous spirit. There was talk of work in the shipyards of Arklow on Ireland's east coast. So I came here for the work. In the shipyards, I met an Irishman who had come south to the town for the same reason when his family fell on hard times in the years before the famine. He had brought his family with him, though that was years before I met him, which included his mother-in-law and her granddaughter. The girl was the man's niece. She was a beauty, with bright red hair and white skin that looked like an angel's face, tall and slender. She stood five inches above me, and I fell in love with her. She was your mother, lassie, and she was the best woman in the world. Her name was Morvern." He paused and smiled sadly as he remembered. Slowly he sighed as he allowed his thoughts to linger fondly over the memory. Then he continued. "But Morvern's grandmother didn't like me," he said. "She did not want us to marry."

"Why, Papa?" said Gwyneth with the simplicity of a devoted daughter. "Who would not like you?"

"It was because I was a Welshman," Codnor replied. "Morvern's father, you see, was also a Welshman, and he had deserted them after she was born. That's why Morvern lived with her grandmother, because her own mother died when giving birth, and her father promised to come back to provide for her and take care of her but never did. Then they fell on desperate times, and she became yet more bitter at the father for leaving them in such straits."

"What did you do, Papa, if Mama's mother didn't like you?"

"Morvern and I married in spite of her," Barrie replied. "Maybe it was wrong. Perhaps we should have waited. I was young, and sometimes the young are not as wise as they think. But I determined to be the best husband and father a man could be and to win Morvern's grandmother over. I would prove to her that I was a good man and wasn't like the man who had married her daughter. I would provide for her granddaughter, and for her, too, if she would let me. A year later you were born, Gwyneth. But your white hair frightened people. They thought a curse was on you. It was only the curse of goodness, though that was the last thing they could understand. They began to say cruel things about you and about me. Even my friend, Morvern's own uncle, said that I had brought evil to their family. I couldn't let my wife and daughter be spoken of in that way. By then the mines were operating again in Wales. Morvern and I made plans to sail from Ireland and begin a new life in my own country where we would be free from people thinking evil of us. So you and I and your mother sailed for Wales. But a terrible storm came up in the Celtic triangle on the day of our sailing, and your mother was swept overboard—"

He drew in a shaky breath and looked away, wiping at his eyes. "I never forgave myself for sailing that night." He struggled to go on. "I was only twenty-five at the time, heartbroken with grief and left alone with an infant daughter. When we arrived in Wales, there was nothing I could do but try to make the best of it for you. If I had gone back to your Irish kinfolk, they would have hated me all the more for bringing Morvern's death upon her. The poor family—they lost two daughters who married Welshmen. What else could they do but hate the Welsh? So I stayed where we were. I tried to be a good father—"

"You were the best father a girl ever had, Papa," said Gwyneth, rising and going to him. She knelt beside him and took his hands in hers.

He gazed down upon her, his eyes full of tears. "That's all I knew of it, lassie," said Barrie after a moment. "I tried to be a faithful man, and I sent what money I could to Mrs. O'Sullivan, who was your great-grandmother, until I was sent word that she had died. But I never heard anything from her or the rest of the family after that. You grew up into a fine girl. The other children were cruel to you, but you made the best of it, with Grannie's help. I doubt it's done you any harm. For the sticks and stones of hurtful words injure us no more than we let them. And like Grannie always told you, they make us into better people if we use them to learn to forgive."

"They did not hurt me, Papa."

"Then came a day," Barrie continued, "when I received a surprise visitor at the cottage. It was the viscount, Lord Snowdon himself. He asked if he could speak with me privately."

"I think I remember it," said Gwyneth. "I was with my animals behind the cottage. I thought he had come for his rent."

"The rent was the last thing on his mind that day," her father went on. "I invited him inside, and we had a long talk. He was curious, he said, about my past. I didn't know why. He asked if I had ever been in

Ireland. I told him about my time there, that I had gone looking for work and had married there. He asked about you, Gwyneth. I told him you were born in Ireland. He asked my wife's name. I replied that it was Morvern O'Sullivan. He seemed taken aback but then asked me where she was now. I told him she was dead. He was silent for a time, then rose, thanked me, and left.

"I thought the thing strange but could make nothing of it. Then came another visit, three or four years later. Gwyneth, by then you were growing into a beautiful young woman and you were working at the manor for his wife and daughter. That's when the viscount came to me again when you were away from the cottage. He was more serious now. He spoke to me like we were old friends. He told me he had been thinking much about our earlier conversation. He now had something to confide in me that I must never tell another soul. I replied that I would agree so long as my conscience allowed. He nodded and added that he did not think what he had to say would place a constraint on my conscience. Then he proceeded to tell me about his own past, how he, too, like me, had gone to Ireland as a young man and had fallen in love with a red-haired Irish beauty. Her name was Avonmara O'Sullivan."

Now for the first time, both Gwyneth and Grannie recognized the name O'Sullivan. Their eyes widened as Barrie continued.

He saw their reaction and smiled. "I see that you remember the name," he said, nodding. "I was shocked as well. In what seems a remarkable coincidence, the child that was born to the viscount and Avonmara O'Sullivan was a girl called Morvern. She was, in fact, the very same Morvern O'Sullivan I had fallen in love with and married. . . my own wife. . .and your mother, Gwyneth."

The room was silent as Gwyneth sat absorbing the stunning fact.

"You cannot be saying. . .but does that mean," she said slowly, "that Avonmara O'Sullivan was *my* grandmother. . ." She paused, hardly able to bring herself to complete the thought. Unable to believe she was saying the words, she slowly added, "And Lord Snowdon was my grandfather?"

"That is exactly what it means, my child," said Barrie tenderly.

Again the room was silent as Gwyneth struggled to take in what he had just said. "I always thought he looked at me strangely," she said after a moment. "There were times I saw him in the village, and he simply stared at me."

"It was one of those occasions," rejoined her father, "that prompted his first visit to me. He suddenly recognized in your face the very face of his young love. It was after that he came to talk to me. As you grew older, and after you were at the manor and he saw more of you, the conviction grew on him all the more that her eyes, the eyes of Avonmara O'Sullivan, had been passed on to you."

"What happened to her?" asked Gwyneth seriously.

"She died when your mother was born. After her death, the viscount returned to Wales. He planned to come back for his daughter. But by the time he returned, she was gone from the village where her family had lived, and he never saw his daughter again. He was devastated over the guilt he felt at having waited too long. And then, when you were older, as I say, he came to me again. He had reason to believe, he said, that you were his granddaughter. That had been the reason for his curiosity about my past. Now he realized that he wanted to do something for you. But he could not openly acknowledge that he had had a child before meeting his wife, Lady Snowdon. He did not want to hurt her or jeopardize her standing in the community. He saw no need for his past to come out. If he was to do something for you, provide for you, in acknowledgment of his love for your grandmother and mother, he must do so in secret. He was not a wealthy man, he said, but he would give us what money he could. Only I must agree to leave Llanfryniog in secret, telling not a soul the reason or where we were going. He did not even want to know himself, he said. We must simply disappear. If I would agree, then he would provide the means for us to have a good life."

He paused briefly. "Some might say that he was trying to cover up a youthful indiscretion. There would even be some who would say that he was trying to blackmail me into silence about something he had kept hushed up for over thirty years. But I honestly felt the man to be sincere. He had no reason to confess all this to me otherwise. His heart was genuine. He wanted to do good for you."

He drew in a breath. "For better or worse," he sighed, "I agreed. I knew that he was offering what I could never give you. I knew also that none of us would outlive the occasional persecutions that came to us in Llanfryniog, though they had lessened over the years. I felt it my responsibility to give you both—you, Grannie, as well," he added, glancing at his great-aunt, "a life free of that if I could. And I had to think of your future when I was gone, Gwyneth," he continued, turning again toward his daughter. "Before he was through, the poor viscount was in tears. His grief was more than he could bear not to have seen his daughter again. By then the poignant reality was borne in upon me that I was in the presence of my own father-in-law. I was watching him weep at the memory of his first love and the daughter they had together. . .the very woman I had loved myself. He told me how he had gone back and tried to find his daughter. So I agreed to the terms of his offer. That's when I told the two of you that we were leaving Llanfryniog, but that we must do so without telling a soul. If I was wrong, may God forgive me, and may you forgive me, Grannie, and you, Gwyneth dear. I did what I thought was best for us all. So we set sail and returned to the land of my former happiness. It was the only place outside North Wales I had ever lived, the only other place where I felt I could make a home."

Barrie let out a long emotional sigh.

SIXTY-ONE

Unexpected Weight of Duty

*A*t length, unable to say more, Codnor Barrie glanced toward Percy.

"But then," said Percy, picking up the story again from the viscount's side, "when my uncle knew he was dying, apparently he changed his mind about keeping his connection with you secret." He paused as he looked at Gwyneth. "He wanted me to find you," said Percy. "If I could, he wanted the truth to come out at last and for right to be done."

"Find *me*?" said Gwyneth. "You said before that he asked you to find his daughter."

"I said I *thought* he wanted me to find his daughter," rejoined Percy. "His mind was wandering by then. He was occasionally confused. He seemed to have forgotten what your father told him, that your mother was dead. He confused you with your mother. All this time, I thought he wanted me to find his daughter, when actually it was you he wanted me to find, Gwyneth. It was *you* he was thinking of on his deathbed."

"Why would Lord Snowdon care about me?"

"For the same reason he came to talk to your father about you. For the same reason he wanted to provide for you."

"But he had already done so, and we were gone. Why did he want you to find me then?"

"Because when he spoke to your father, he did not tell him

782

everything," answered Percy. "There was one vital bit of information he kept from him."

"What was that?"

"He did not tell his daughter's *real* name," answered Percy.

"It wasn't O'Sullivan?"

"Avonmara's *maiden* name was O'Sullivan. But when she married, she became Avonmara Westbrooke. Your mother's real name was Morvern Westbrooke."

Grannie had been intently following the conversation. "They were married!" she now exclaimed.

Percy nodded. "In Laragh, north of here. The marriage is listed in the parish record book for 1833. . .between Roderick Westbrooke, the future Lord Snowdon, and Avonmara O'Sullivan. Their marriage made your mother my uncle's rightful heir."

"The Lord be praised!" exclaimed Grannie.

Gwyneth glanced back and forth in bewilderment between Percy and her father.

"Gwyneth, lassie," said Barrie, "that's why young Percy came looking for you. You are not only Lord Snowdon's granddaughter. . .you are also his heir."

"Your father is right," nodded Percy. "Your mother, Morvern, whom your father married as Morvern O'Sullivan but who was really Morvern Westbrooke, was the daughter of Avonmara O'Sullivan and Roderick Westbrooke. You are the daughter of his firstborn and his heir. So we have to get back to Wales without delay."

"Back to Wales. . .why?"

"Courtenay's birthday is in a matter of days. He is about to inherit the title and the entire estate. Once he does, it will be too late. It may have been to prevent Courtenay from becoming viscount, seeing what sort of man he was becoming, that prompted my uncle to tell me of his past and send me on a quest to find his rightful heir. Having found you, I must complete that quest."

"But I have no desire to take it from Courtenay," said Gwyneth hesitantly. "I am happy where I am."

"Of course you are," said Percy. "But there is your duty to consider. If this is indeed the fate that has fallen to you, can you neglect it? You little know to what Courtenay has sunk. He has threatened to turn my Aunt Katherine out of the manor. I believe you have a responsibility to your grandfather's wish. That was simply that you as his true heir, if you could be found, should inherit in place of Courtenay. I think he knew that you would do right for everyone, for the village, and especially for his wife. I do not think he believed that would be true if Courtenay became viscount."

Gwyneth was quiet several long minutes. At length she rose, walked slowly across the room, and left the house.

"The lassie's suddenly got much for her mind to weigh," said Grannie when she was gone. "She was always a thoughtful lassie. But she's never had a worry or care in her life. Now there's a great burden on her shoulders. She's got to be a grown-up woman. It's likely a fearsome thing for her innocent heart."

"What should I do, Grannie?" said Codnor, still not pausing to reflect what change Percy's revelation might bring to his own life.

"Let her be, laddie. She's been building strength into her soul for twenty years. It strikes me as likely that it's all been preparing her for this moment. She's a strong lassie and getting stronger, I'll warrant, even as we speak. She'll see her way through to what the Lord would have of her. When that time comes, nothing will stop her from the doing of it."

Though the water in the kettle had been boiling for twenty minutes, tea had long been forgotten in the rush of the conversation and Percy's startling words about the viscount's first marriage. As it now grew quiet, the practicalities of the corporeal man began to make themselves felt. The man of the house realized that for some time he had been aware of the aroma of mutton roasting in the oven. Grannie, too, seemed to notice it. Slowly she rose and walked to the stove. From the bin she took two handfuls of potatoes and plopped them into a steaming kettle of water.

"Where are you staying, Percy, lad?" asked Barrie.

"With the young Catholic priest in Arklow, Father Abban."

"When were you to return to him?"

"I made no arrangements. I said I would walk back into town."

"It is a long way. You have come down on the far side of the mountain. I will take you back when the time comes. So you must join us for Sunday dinner and the afternoon."

"Nothing could delight me more."

"Then come," said Barrie rising, "I will introduce you to my sheep and dogs while the potatoes are boiling."

They left the cottage. In the distance, Percy saw Gwyneth walking away from the house. She entered a small wood near their home and disappeared from sight. The two men continued toward the sheep.

Thirty minutes later, Codnor Barrie began a walk down the hill on an unexpected mission. As he did, Percy made his way toward the wood.

It was with a mingling of strange emotions that he felt himself closed up in the shadows of the tall firs and pines a few minutes later. He hardly considered the significance of the moment, for it was not at all by accident that Percival Drummond now sought Gwyneth Barrie in the fir wood. Deeper into its depths he went.

She seemed to sense his presence behind her, even before she heard his footsteps behind her. She stopped and turned.

Her heart leaped at the sight. But she was not surprised. For how could she wonder to see before her eyes the form of which her soul was full? She stood watching. . .and waiting.

Percy approached slowly. "Gwyneth!" he whispered then held out his hand to her.

She took it. They walked on amid the tall trees in silence.

"Are you in love with him?" Percy asked at length.

"He is the man my father chose for me to marry," replied Gwyneth.

"But are you in love with him?"

"I will learn to love him."

"But. . .if there was someone else. . ."

She dared not glance at him.

"Gwyneth," he persisted, "*if* there was someone else. . .someone who loved you with all his heart. . ."

Tears began to rise in her eyes.

"Gwyneth. . .*must* you marry him?"

"It is what my father—"

"I *do* love you, Gwyneth," said Percy. "I think perhaps I always loved you, though it took me some years to know it. I have spoken with your father," he added. "He is on his way now to your betrothed with a request to relinquish you. . .if such is your wish. He has given me permission to ask. . .if you would be *my* wife instead."

SIXTY-TWO

New Friends

*H*aving written his urgent request to Percy, Steven Muir's anxiety was only temporarily relieved.

An unintentionally overheard argument between Florilyn and Lady Katherine, during which he heard the words, in a rude and angry voice, "old enough to marry without your permission. . .Colville says. . . perhaps not even wait until summer," was enough to convince him that he must delay no longer. To act was imperative. He might not hear back from Percy for a week, maybe two. It could be months before he was actually in a position to return to Wales. By then it would be too late.

After two more days, therefore, Steven sought his mistress in her quarters. "Lady Katherine," he said, "I have what might seem a strange request. Before I make it, I must ask you a question."

"Of course, Steven," said Katherine.

"I apologize if I am interfering in your personal affairs, but I would very much like to know if you are in favor of Lady Florilyn's marriage to Colville Burrenchobay."

"Need you ask, Steven?"

"I have some idea how you feel, Lady Katherine, but I must be certain nothing has changed."

"Nothing has changed. I abhor the very idea. As much as it is possible for a Christian to say such a thing, I fear I loathe that young

787

man. The thought of Florilyn marrying him is disgusting to me."

Steven listened somberly. It was as he suspected.

"Sadly, she no longer listens to me," Katherine went on. "She cares not a feather what I think. There was a time when young people sought their parents' wisdom and counsel in the matter of marriage. Apparently that time, at least in this family, is long past. I cannot prevent the sense that Colville has been subtly prejudicing her against me."

"I think it is entirely likely," nodded Steven.

"Why do you ask?" said Katherine.

"Because with your permission, I would like to speak with Lady Florilyn."

"Do you think it would do any good?"

"Perhaps not. She is entirely changed toward me as well. But I must try. I am considering speaking to her with another whom she was also once close to. I would rather not divulge more."

"You have my blessing, Steven," said Katherine. "I will be deeply grateful for anything you are able to do."

Steven left his mistress and walked briskly to the stables. Within minutes he was on his way in the two-seater buggy into Llanfryniog. Fifteen minutes after that, the buggy sat on the street in front of the Lorimer home, and Steven was walking toward the door. Ten minutes after that, Steven was guiding the horse out of town with Rhawn Lorimer seated at his side, her son in the care of her mother. The question he must put to Florilyn's onetime friend required quiet and solitude.

He led about a mile inland, on the dirt track that led in the direction of his former home in the hills, then reined in. They sat a few moments in silence, taking in the view of the sea in the distance.

"I realize you do not know me well, Rhawn," Steven began. "There have been few occasions through the years where our paths have crossed. But it is my sincere hope that you will consider me a friend and will be able to trust me."

"Everyone thinks well of you, Stevie," said Rhawn. "If I did not know better, I would think you were the viscount now."

Steven laughed. "Hardly that! It is merely my wish to serve Lady

Katherine faithfully. I hope you will know that it is from that same heart of service that I requested to speak with you."

"I know that, Stevie. Even though you and I have never been close friends, I know there is not a selfish bone in your body. What do you want to talk to me about?"

"Your son, Rhawn," replied Steven. "I need to know who the father is."

The bluntness of his statement took Rhawn off guard. She sat for a moment in silence. "I trust you enough to know that you would not ask unless you had a good reason," she said at length. "But I made a vow to myself three years ago that I would not divulge his name. I would rather my son have no father at all than to have a reluctant father who is unwilling to acknowledge him."

"I understand, and I respect you for that," said Steven. "But there are others involved. It may now be that you have to consider your silence in light of wider considerations than your son alone. I am thinking of Florilyn and our responsibility to her."

They continued to talk. Steven explained the burden that had been growing on his heart and what had come into his mind to do about it. His request coincided with a great longing that had arisen in Rhawn's heart in recent weeks for the father of her son to acknowledge the boy—even if it should be only to herself. By now she had all but given up hope that there would ever be more.

It was not long before Rhawn was in tears. Soon Steven knew the whole story. Steven's great arm around her as she wept quietly gave Rhawn a comfort she had never experienced in her life—the comfort of a caring, loving brother.

Steven pulled up in front of the Lorimer home an hour later.

Rhawn turned to look at him and smiled through eyes still moist and glistening. "It feels good to have told someone," she said.

"I hope it was not too hard for you."

"Good things are sometimes hard. No, it was not too hard."

Steven jumped out of the buggy and helped Rhawn to the ground. "Be ready at a moment's notice," he said. "I will look for an opportunity. When it comes, we may have to act quickly."

SIXTY-THREE

Confrontation

*I*t was a rare day that Florilyn Westbrooke and Colville Burrenchobay did not see each other, if not spend most of the day together. Colville had been so successful in subtly creating division between Florilyn and her mother that Florilyn no longer apprised Katherine of her movements or plans. She came and went as she pleased, ordered the servants about with the same hauteur that had been characteristic of her young teen years, and in general carried herself as if *she* rather than her brother were about to come into the title and property.

It is hardly surprising under these circumstances that she and Courtenay resumed their former bonds. There was no more talk of Florilyn leaving the manor after Courtenay's birthday. They openly laughed about their mother building a grand new home and living in it by herself. They were equally mocking of Steven Muir, Courtenay counting the days when he could order him to pack his bags and they would never see him again.

Though both Katherine and Steven shrank from small stratagems, they were nonetheless enough convinced of the rightness of what must be done that they were watching and waiting together. Without divulging the secret he had learned, Steven had taken Katherine into his confidence sufficiently to gain her approval a second time. Thus it was that she came to him about one o'clock one day upon learning from

Mrs. Drynwydd that Florilyn had ordered afternoon tea to be served for herself and a guest at four o'clock in the sunroom. None had any doubt who that guest would be.

Steven was on his way into town within a quarter hour.

Their tea, with cakes and scones and biscuits, was well under way, Mrs. Drynwydd having departed a few minutes earlier, when the sunroom door opened. Florilyn and Colville glanced toward it, and the laughter died on their lips.

Rhawn Lorimer and Katherine walked in with a young boy between them who had just turned three.

Not having seen Rhawn for months and constrained by her presence from flying off the handle at her mother, for a few seconds Florilyn was merely flustered at the unexpected interruption. "Rhawn!" she said, "What are you. . .I mean, it is nice to see you, but. . .you can see that I am—"

Struggling to regain her poise, Florilyn's eyes darted back and forth between the two. Rhawn and her mother had not accidentally barged in upon her tête-à-tête with Colville. Something sinister was afoot.

The next moment, Katherine took the youngster by the hand and led him from the room. Florilyn's eyes flashed with suspicion. Rhawn's lips quivered then flitted toward Colville with an expression of silent entreaty.

He had been so thoroughly taken by surprise that nervousness overcame him. Hardly knowing what he said, he fell back on trying to make light of the awkward encounter. "So. . .Rhawn"—he half laughed, affecting cheerfulness—"I don't recall that we sent for a child. Nice-looking fellow, though."

Rhawn turned white at the rebuff.

Not one to lose her equanimity for long, Florilyn drew herself up to her full height. "What is going on here, Rhawn?" she said in a demanding tone. "Something tells me this is no coincidence. You came in here knowing full well that Colville and I were having tea. Did my mother—"

"Your mother had nothing to do with it," said Rhawn.

"Then what is she doing with. . .with—"

"He is my son, Florilyn," said Rhawn, recovering herself a little. "I told her I wanted to speak with you in private."

"Then come back another time. As you can see," added Florilyn haughtily, "I have a previous engagement."

The words seemed to wake Rhawn again to the business at hand. "Florilyn," she said, "I *want* to talk to you, and I want to talk to you now."

"What you have to say, then, you can say in front of Colville."

"What I have to say is for your ears alone. *Mister* Burrenchobay," she added, turning to Colville, "perhaps you would be so kind as to excuse us."

Seeing that Florilyn was taking his part, Colville had also recovered himself and was in no temper to be ordered about. "I believe that Lady Florilyn has made it clear enough," he replied coolly, "that she wishes me to stay."

Rhawn stood helplessly silent as the two stared daggers into her eyes.

The next moment, from where he had been listening outside on the terrace, Steven Muir opened the french doors and strode into the room.

SIXTY-FOUR

Return of the Heiress

*A*bout the time Colville Burrenchobay had set out from his home for afternoon tea at the manor, the southbound coach from Blaenau Ffestiniog left the main road, turned toward the sea, and bounced along toward its next stop in front of Mistress Chattan's inn on the main street of the coastal village of Llanfryniog.

As much as her calm demeanor was capable of yielding to girlish excitement, Gwyneth Barrie was looking out through the window with an exuberant smile on her face, taking in with eager anticipation the sights she had not known whether she would ever see again. Even the muddy main street of a town that had never extended its kindness to her was a sight imbued with nostalgic happiness.

At her side, having no idea that Steven's urgent letter to him was just arriving at his parents' home in Glasgow, Percival Drummond was filled with far different emotions than he had ever felt when returning to this beloved coastline of North Wales. Momentous changes were coming. One of them had already come. When he stepped onto the street a few minutes later and reached back up into the coach, it was to help to the ground his new fiancée.

It was the twelfth of March in the year 1874, five days before Courtenay Westbrooke's twenty-fifth birthday. Percy and Gwyneth had said good-bye to Gwyneth's father two days earlier in Dublin, promising to get word to him and Grannie the moment there were any developments to report.

Whenever Percy came to Llanfryniog, word quickly spread that "young Mr. Drummond" was back in town. On this occasion, however, the rumors surrounding his arrival quickly filled with additional fodder for gossip. A few eyes turned as the two waited for their bags, a few more as Percy left Gwyneth on the walkway and took their bags inside for a brief talk with Mistress Chattan. Gradually more eyes were drawn to the scene the moment they set out along the street together. Whereas the town's curious women had been following developments between himself and young Lady Florilyn for two years or more, within minutes of his arrival on this day, startled speculation began circulating like a brushfire from house to house.

As Percy and Gwyneth walked out of the village, more eyes than either had any idea were following them from behind curtained windows. Everyone was asking the same thing: Who was the light-haired beauty on Mr. Percy's arm?

"Would you like to visit your old cottage?" said Percy as they went. "That is if it is still unoccupied."

Gwyneth thought a moment. "Perhaps not immediately," she replied. "I may want to do so alone. I hope you don't mind. I think to see it again will make my heart too full for words."

"I don't mind," rejoined Percy. "You will always have places within you that are yours alone."

"All I want to do today is sit and look at the sea," said Gwyneth with a smile. "From this side again."

They left the road, crossed the grassy expanse in the direction of the rising headland, and continued up the slope toward the promontory of Mochras Head. Percy had as yet said nothing about the great change that Gwyneth would find there.

⁓

If such was possible, at the sight of Steven walking into the sunroom unannounced, Florilyn drew herself up yet higher. Her face flushed red, and her heart filled with indignation. "Now I see who is the author of this subterfuge!" she cried. "Get out of here, Steven! Leave this room immediately!"

"Happily, Lady Florilyn," replied Steven. "Colville and I will leave together. Miss Lorimer, I believe, requested to have a word with you."

"I will have no words with her or anyone else! I told you to get out. Who is mistress of this house—me or you?"

"Neither, Lady Florilyn. Your mother is my mistress. I take my orders from her." Steven turned to Colville. "Would you please come with me, Colville?" he said. "We will leave the ladies to themselves."

"I take no orders from *you*, Stevie Muir," said Colville with a sneer. "I believe Lady Florilyn ordered you out. I suggest you obey her, or I will throw you back outside myself. If you force me to do so, I will not be gentle about it."

A peculiar smile crossed Steven's lips. It was clear he was not cowed. The expression enraged Colville, for he took it as mocking his threat. He stepped forward and laid a rude hand on Steven's arm.

Now Colville Burrenchobay was himself a powerful young man and stood some three inches above Steven. But the fact that he had all his life looked down on Stevie Muir as a weakling on this day proved his undoing. His overbearing confidence was not well founded.

Steven allowed himself to be shoved unceremoniously back toward the french doors, which stood still open. At the last instant, he spun suddenly and away from Colville's grasp. Before Colville knew what had happened, Steven placed two hands on Colville's shoulders and pushed him through to the outside with a force that nearly sent Colville to the ground. By the time he recovered himself, the doors were locked in front of him and the curtains pulled.

In impotent fury, he tried the handle then stood a moment, not relishing the idea of shouting and demanding entrance like a spurned schoolgirl. At length, imagining himself a squire who must defend the honor of a woman whom he had convinced himself he loved, he turned and sprinted for the front door of the house.

SIXTY-FIVE

The Compulsion of Love

I think at last I know why my father loved the sea," said Gwyneth as she and Percy sat on the overlook at Mochras Head, "but also why it made him sad. My mother is somewhere out there. I know he thinks of that every time he looks upon it. I think the sea will always make me sad when I gaze upon it, too, though perhaps in a quietly happy way. For now I know who she was."

As they had approached along the promontory, Percy explained about Lady Katherine's new home, which now loomed before them. Gwyneth was quiet for several minutes as they drew closer. Percy knew that her initial reaction was likely the same as his had been— disappointment that a house now stood on what had all her life been one of her "special places" of solitude.

It was a relatively small structure, for a manor house, especially by the standards of Westbrooke Manor or Burrenchobay Hall. Its design was simple, yet ornate, giving the impression of a miniature castle that had grown horizontally rather than in height, emerging out of the plateau of itself. In every respect Katherine had instructed the designers to make its every detail merge and blend in with its surroundings, so as to appear a natural part of the headland and coastline. This they had achieved admirably. It added to rather than detracted from the landscape surrounding it.

Its aspect was neither imposing nor high. She had not wanted to break the view of the sea from farther up the plateau. The gray stone structure, therefore, rose but one floor above the ground and was shaped roughly as a horseshoe opening to the sea. The courtyard in the center of the three wings had been left in its natural habitat of coastal grasses liberally scattered with stones and small boulders. The outer walls and roof of the house were by now nearly complete where it sat back about three hundred yards from the edge of the cliff.

They sat quietly talking for thirty or forty minutes. Finally Percy remembered the question he had been waiting so long to ask. "By the way," he said, "why did you not come to meet me here that day when we agreed to meet before I left Wales?"

"You were waiting for me?" said Gwyneth in surprise.

"Yes, I waited for hours. You never came."

"I was waiting for you at the beach by the harbor."

"On the beach! But I thought—" He paused as the light dawned on his memory. Slowly he nodded. "'At our special place, where land meets sea. . .'" he said reflectively. "I thought it was here. You thought I meant there. Were you really waiting for me all that time?"

"Finally I walked up from the harbor," she replied. "Then I heard the coach, and I saw you at the inn with Florilyn. She kissed you before you left, and I ran home in tears."

"Oh, Gwyneth. . .I *am* sorry!"

They both sat musing in silence.

"Who would have thought that it would be nearly four years before we would see one another again," said Percy, "or that, when we sat here again together looking out over the sea, we would be engaged." He paused a moment. "But when you left Llanfryniog, at least *you* didn't leave without saying good-bye like I did on that day."

"What do you mean?" asked Gwyneth. "I *didn't* say good-bye. You weren't even here."

"But still, you said good-bye to me in your own way." Percy pulled from his pocket the dried bouquet and note he had discovered at the cottage.

"You found it!" exclaimed Gwyneth with delight.

"I've been waiting until we were here again to show it to you."

"Oh Percy, do you really want to marry me?" asked Gwyneth simply.

"Gwyneth, how can you ask? I love you!"

"It seems that I have stepped into a dream too good to be true. But I love you, too, with all my heart."

At length Percy climbed to his feet. He offered his hand and pulled Gwyneth up beside him. "It is probably time that we see what destiny awaits us," he said.

They turned, and he led the way across the plateau, Gwyneth's hand in his, past Katherine's new house and toward the road and through the entry to the estate.

"Are you certain Lady Katherine will want us to stay at the manor?" asked Gwyneth.

"She will be delighted to see us both. Don't forget, I'm family. I have my own room." Percy paused and began laughing. "What am I saying? You are family, too, though no one knows it yet. We're *both* family!"

"What are you planning to tell them about me. . .about what I am doing here?"

Gwyneth's question reminded Percy of his uncle's earnest desire that his aunt be spared as much pain as possible. "They have to be told," he said seriously. "I haven't decided on a course of action yet. First of all, we must see how things stand when we arrive. I will have to speak with my aunt. The matter is delicate, yet I have no alternative but to tell her everything. But that can wait. For now I will simply say that I ran into you and encouraged you to come for a visit. That is entirely the truth. Then I will seek the best means to talk to her in private."

Finding herself suddenly alone in the sunroom, without an ally and with Rhawn Lorimer on one side of her and Steven Muir approaching from the french doors through which he had just deposited Colville Burrenchobay on the other, Florilyn did the only thing she could think to do under the circumstances. She made for the door on the opposite side of the room.

"Florilyn!" said Steven in a tone of command, calling her by her name.

She spun around. If wrath could burn, he would have been reduced to ashes on the spot. "How dare you address me in such a tone!"

"I have done what I could to serve you—"

"And I want no more of such service!"

"But you drive me to extremeties," he said, ignoring her interruption. "I am telling you now, as a friend and brother who loves you and cares more for you than you have any idea. . .you must not marry that man. At present he is a scoundrel, though I hope he may in time become something better. But as things stand, I will do all that is in my power to prevent you—"

"You. . .prevent *me*!" shrieked Florilyn in a paroxysm of rage. "What gives you the right to presume to know what is best for me?"

"The right of love, Florilyn. Even if it should cause you suffering, I *will* do my best for you, until you put it out of my power completely. I will do all that I am able to deliver you from the lies that man has told you. I will commit to whatever it takes to help the true self that was growing in you to waken again. I will give my life to strengthen yours. But one thing I will *not* do is stand by and watch you destroy your future."

Florilyn could hardly speak for the fury within her. Her lips quivered as she struggled to find her voice. The next words she heard, however, at last jolted her awake.

"Florilyn!" said Rhawn in a loud but measured voice.

Florilyn turned.

"Colville Burrenchobay is the father of my son," Rhawn added. "If you can marry him after the way you have seen him treat me for three years, while ignoring his own son, then perhaps you deserve each other. But he is a heartless man who will, I have no doubt, cast you adrift if such should suit his purpose just as he did me."

Florilyn stood staring like a statue, her face white as a sheet.

SIXTY-SIX

Surprise Reunion

*A*s Colville raced around the corner of the manor toward its front entrance, he scarcely noticed the young man and woman walking toward it from the entryway drive. He cast a brief glance toward them but did not slow his step.

Knowing well enough who it was, and liking neither the look on his face nor the fact that he burst through the door without slowing, Percy merely cast Gwyneth a brief look then bolted after Colville. Some mischief was afoot. He feared a dangerous situation was brewing. Gwyneth hurried after him.

From the moment Percy ran into the darkened entryway, it did not take long to descry where the trouble was coming from. High words and shouts echoed through the corridor. He listened a moment then darted toward them.

It was in hopes of forcing an acknowledgment from the father that Rhawn had insisted that Colville be present when they confront Florilyn. Fearing it could too easily turn ugly, Steven had reluctantly agreed, for he could do nothing without Rhawn. His concerns were about to be realized. Colville had been taken by surprise once. It would not happen again.

He had just run into the room and issued a warning threat to Steven to leave at once or pay the price when Percy shot in after him.

It took Percy but a second to size up the situation. The next instant he heard the shriek of his name.

"Percy!" cried Rhawn and flew to his arms as if he were a knight in shining armor come to set everything right.

Again, events conspired to throw off Colville's designs. But this time he tried to use it to his advantage. "There, Florilyn," he said with a smile of patronizing humor, "it is just as I told you. He is the father himself."

At the words, a sob escaped Rhawn's lips. Ignoring the charge and continuing to clasp her to him with one arm, Percy looked toward Steven for enlightenment.

"Hello, Percy. It is very good to see you," said Steven. "Rhawn and I have been having a private conversation with Florilyn. Colville seems intent upon intruding where he is not wanted."

"Then perhaps, Colville," said Percy, "you and I should leave them."

"I will not leave Florilyn alone with this madman," said Colville. "I was about to throw him out, Drummond, and take Florilyn away from this charade when you barged in. I don't know what you are doing here, but you might as well leave. This is between Muir and me. I will settle it in my own way."

Just then Gwyneth walked through the open door. She saw Percy with his arm around Rhawn Lorimer. Unlike many young women confronted with such a sight, her first thoughts were not jealous ones. She trusted Percy entirely. Though Rhawn had never spoken a civil word to her in her life, and in fact during her younger years had spoken many a cruel one, Gwyneth intuitively recognized pain on her face. She knew that Percy's embrace was that of a comforting brother. As the helpmeet she was already preparing to be, she moved toward Rhawn and slid her arm around her from the other side.

For several seconds no one recognized her. At last truth dawned.

"*Gwyneth!*" said Florilyn in surprise.

Gwyneth smiled sweetly. "Hello, Florilyn," she said.

In Florilyn's mind, however, the former friendship between them was but a distant memory. The poison of division had spread throughout her being. Recovering her initial surprise, her next thought was that

Gwyneth and Percy were somehow involved in this plot against Colville. "What are you doing here?" she said. Her tone was not friendly. "And what are *you* doing here, Percy? This is none of your concern."

"Steven?" said Percy, as he stepped into the middle of the room.

"Rhawn and I have been explaining to Florilyn," said Steven, "why she cannot marry Colville Burrenchobay."

"Marry him!" exclaimed Percy. "Is this true, Florilyn?"

"It is," Florilyn answered imperiously. "Colville and I are engaged."

"And you saw no reason to inform me?"

"I did not. You were no longer interested in me."

"That is not true."

"Percy!" now sobbed Rhawn, "he is the father of my son. Florilyn, he only wants to marry you for your money."

"That's a lie!" shouted Colville.

The volatile exchange momentarily silenced the room.

"He was always talking about how rich you would be one day," said Rhawn.

"I don't believe a word of it," said Florilyn.

"Yes, where is your proof?" said Colville, recovering himself with cool aplomb. "It's all lies. Come, Florilyn. They are all mad together. Let's get out of here."

"Gladly!"

They moved toward the door.

"A moment, Florilyn," said Percy, moving to block their way. "Would you indulge me with a brief word in private?"

"I will not! I am leaving with Colville."

"I would rather not insist, Florilyn. Please." Percy turned to Colville. "As you are a guest in this home, Colville, I believe I can safely speak on behalf of Lady Katherine in requesting you to take your leave."

"I will not take a step without Florilyn."

"Do you want me to summon the manservants to escort you forcibly from the premises?"

"What—two or three men twice my age?" laughed Colville.

"You are right," rejoined Percy. "They will hardly be necessary. Steven and I are well up to the task. Now, Florilyn," he said, taking his cousin's arm and leading her through the door and into the corridor, "come with me."

Unrepentant but powerless to argue, Florilyn squirmed to get free. Instead she found herself closeted a moment later with Percy in the adjacent sitting room. Steven, meanwhile, not relishing a further hostile encounter, reopened the curtains and slipped through the french doors and outside. Gwyneth led Rhawn after him. Colville found himself standing in an empty room.

Closing the door of the sitting room behind them, Percy turned to Florilyn. "You are much changed, Florilyn," he said. "I am sorry to say it does not become you. What happened?"

Florilyn looked away. She had not completely forgotten the feelings she had had for Percy and how much she had once desired to please him. Even in her present state, his words stung.

"You asked what Gwyneth and I are doing here," he went on. "What I am about to tell you, I implore you to breathe no word of until I make a full disclosure."

Florilyn's vanity flared up again. "You would place a muzzle on me?" she said.

"I think you will hold your tongue. The only person who will be hurt is your mother. I cannot believe, even now, that you would intentionally hurt her. So I have no choice but to hope you will comply with my request."

"What is it, then?" said Florilyn peevishly.

"Knowing something of what kind of man Colville Burrenchobay is, I cannot but imagine that his motives for wanting to marry you are mixed. What do you think he will say when he learns that you will inherit nothing from your father's estate and that you will no longer be known as the *Honorable* Florilyn Westbrooke?"

"What are you talking about? Courtenay inherits the title, not me."

"As sister of the viscount, you would still be deserving of the address of a viscount's daughter until he is married. That would obviously make a husband look good, especially one who might have political aspirations. What do you think he would say to know that you will not inherit one pound from your father's estate and to know that Courtenay will never be viscount?"

"That's absurd!" said Florilyn. "He is right—you are mad!"

"Listen to me, cousin," said Percy sternly. "Then make your choice—whether to send Colville away yourself or find him breaking your engagement when he learns that you have no claim to rights, privileges, title, or money and are not the prize in society's eyes he thought you. You may hate me for saying such a thing. All I ask is whether you know Colville Burrenchobay well enough to be absolutely *sure* of him."

The question jolted Florilyn. A glimmer of the "new Florilyn" flickered like a nearly extinguished candle coming back to life. It was a powerful and disturbing question. In her heart of hearts, she knew that she was *not* sure of Colville. One thing she did know, however, was that Percy Drummond would *never* lie. As she continued to listen, Florilyn's expression turned from anger to stunned disbelief. Slowly her pride began to wilt.

When Percy led her back into the sunroom a few minutes later, Colville had left the house through the front door. Through the window, Steven saw Percy and Florilyn come back into the room. He saw from Florilyn's countenance that her self-will had been defeated at last. The demon of division had been exorcised by the light of loving truth. The two disclosures concerning Rhawn and Gwyneth, coming one after the other, had finally penetrated the hard shell of Colville's deception, shattering the last vestige of pride she had allowed to reassert itself.

Percy led her to Steven. He took her gently and led her to a couch, then sat down beside her. Percy walked outside where he found Gwyneth and Rhawn talking quietly together. Rhawn was softly weeping in emotional exhaustion.

SIXTY-SEVEN

Disclosure

*C*ourtenay Westbrooke sat at the desk in his apartment on the third floor of Westbrooke Manor deep in thought. Before him was the most recent statement of his account in the Porthmadog Union Bank, which reflected the deposit of the check from Lord Litchfield's assistant of £1,000 he had received a week and a half earlier. The balance would be forthcoming within days.

Courtenay's brain was alive with the staggering possibilities presented by a cash balance of over £8,000. He had been perusing several flyers and brochures with the current offerings in the midlands horse market, thinking to himself that perhaps now he could afford to go after a major prize from one of the most distinguished stables. His was the mentality of one who assumed that money had been invented for one thing alone—to spend, and that as quickly as possible. He was still not fully appreciative of the fact that bank balances required regular supplementation to maintain themselves, nor that his forthcoming viscountcy came with a cash income that would be considered dubious by London's leading financiers. *Saving* for the proverbial rainy day was not an intrinsic element of his economic creed.

He had been hearing voices for some time. But as the feminine figured most prominently, his subconscious had ignored them. As things heated up two floors below him, however, the sounds intruded into his waking brain. He set down the flyer in his hand and listened. As by some primal instinct of the fighting male animal, men young and old, or it might be said, *boys* of all ages, are drawn even to the potential of conflict with a wide-eyed lust for violence. After a few more shouts, Courtenay rose to his feet and listened. Now it grew deathly quiet. He strained to hear more. A minute later he was out of his room and on his way for the stairs to investigate.

He flew down the stairs two at a time. The front door stood open. Outside Courtenay saw Colville with a look of angry consternation on his face. Perceiving no opportunity to get Florilyn alone, and having his own reasons for desiring to avoid Rhawn Lorimer in the company of so many allies, he was debating with himself whether he ought to simply get on his horse and beat a hasty retreat. "Colville," said Courtenay, running outside, "what's all the ruckus I hear?"

"That fool Stevie Muir hauled Rhawn Lorimer up here with her accusations. He's trying to discredit me in front of Florilyn."

"Why didn't you throw him out, or come find me and I would have?"

"The blackguard took me by surprise. They cornered Florilyn with their lies. Then that devil of a cousin of yours showed up and stuck his nose in."

"*Percy*. . .he's here?" exclaimed Courtenay. An expletive exploded from his mouth. "We'll see about this! Where are they?"

"I left Florilyn with him in the sunroom."

Courtenay turned and sprinted back inside and along the corridor. Colville followed, his eyes aflame. His fists were itching to redress the recent grievances against his pride, and these were odds he liked much better.

The two burst into the sunroom, ready to take out their anger on anyone who crossed them. They were, however, completely unprepared for the scene that met their eyes.

Percy had gone to find Katherine. After a brief and affectionate greeting, he had led his aunt and the boy back to join the others.

Katherine, Rhawn, Percy, and Gwyneth were speaking in low tones, with Rhawn's son in their midst. Gwyneth was telling Katherine where they had gone after leaving Llanfryniog and about Grannie and her father, though without divulging the reason for their sudden departure to Ireland.

On the couch across the room, Florilyn sat quietly weeping beside Steven Muir. One of her hands rested between his. A pulse of rage surged through Colville's frame.

At the sight of the two young men rushing into their midst, faces flushed and hands eager for a fight, Percy stepped away from the women and moved to intercept them.

Nothing could have been more to Courtenay's liking. An involuntary smirk passed over his lips.

Steven, too, rose and stepped protectively in front of Florilyn. Courtenay saw the movement and hesitated briefly. After the incident several days earlier, he was a little afraid of Steven. Not so, Colville Burrenchobay. Determined to be neither surprised nor foiled a second time, he charged like an angry bear.

"Defend yourself, Steven!" shouted Percy. "Don't stand on ceremony—he's dangerous!"

Florilyn and Rhawn screamed in a single voice. Percy shot a quick glance toward Gwyneth. She understood and hurried Rhawn, her son, and Katherine from the room.

Emboldened by Colville's aggression, Courtenay rushed Percy with a fierce series of blows. He had been waiting for this opportunity for a long time. He was not about to let it pass without giving full vent to his frustrated resentment against his goody-goody cousin.

Meanwhile, Colville landed several severe blows alongside Steven's head, one of which drew blood behind the ear. Steven was doing his best to evade or stop them, but with difficulty. Florilyn was yelling at them all to stop. Neither her brother nor Colville was inclined to back off from what they misperceived as a delicious advantage.

"Steven!" cried Percy again, not fearing Courtenay so much as he feared for Steven. "It's the whip the moneychangers need, not the gentle word. Defend yourself, man!"

Willing enough under the circumstances to bow to Percy's wisdom, ten seconds later Colville Burrenchobay was measuring the six-foot-two-inch length of his frame along the floor. Florilyn's shrieks stopped abruptly to see with what lightning speed Steven had rendered the threat to himself unconscious in front of her.

"Courtenay. . .Courtenay, please!" implored Percy. "I need to speak with you."

"Say it with your fists!' shouted Courtenay. "Take your own advice and defend yourself! Are you a coward?"

"I have no desire to fight you, Courtenay."

"It is too late for that!"

"Courtenay. . .*stop!*" It was now his sister's voice he heard.

"I will stop when this bounder has learned that we need no more of his interference."

"*Courtenay!*" cried Florilyn. "You've got to hear what Percy has to say."

For answer, several more wicked blows came battering toward Percy's head and body. But they did not continue much longer. Suddenly from behind, two huge arms clasped him round the chest. Finding himself caught in a straightjacket and held firmly against Steven Muir's massive chest, he writhed to free himself, but to no avail.

"You big lout!" he cried. "Unhand me, Muir! You will pay for this, I tell you! Release me, and I may not bring charges against you."

"Courtenay," said Florilyn, her voice softer now. "You *must* listen."

His audience at last a captive one, and by now his own righteous anger aroused, Percy walked close to Courtenay until he stood a foot in front of his face. "Courtenay," he said in a passionate and indignant voice, "you will be twenty-five in a matter of days. It is time you grew up and stopped behaving like a spoiled child who thinks he can do and have anything he wants. While I am loathe to call anyone a fool for fear of the fires of hell, you have acted the part of the fool of Proverbs. You are a foolish and self-centered young man. It is time to be a man. A *man*, Courtenay, not a boy. I have done the best I could to be a friend and faithful cousin to you. Before he died, I promised your father that I would do all that was in my power to help take care of your sister. With that vow came an equal commitment to you. I would have striven to do my best for you and Florilyn even without that promise. But you have foiled all my efforts to be your friend. You despised me since my first visit here. You have not loved or followed the truth. You have been selfish and conceited toward me and toward others. You have made no effort to follow the right. You have been rude toward the young woman I love. All her life you treated her pure heart and forgiving spirit with shameful disdain."

He paused, sensing Florilyn's unspoken question at his words. He turned toward her. "Yes, Florilyn," he said, nodding with a smile of acknowledgment, "I found Gwyneth in my own fir wood, as I think you knew I would. I have asked her to marry me."

"Oh, Percy," said Florilyn, rising and walking to him. "I am so happy for you."

He turned to meet her.

She embraced him as Courtenay, still powerless in Steven's grasp, looked on. Florilyn stepped back and now stood to face her brother. "Courtenay," she said, "Percy is our friend, not our enemy." Her voice was soft. The spell of lies at last was broken. "He has always been our friend. I don't know how I could have forgotten. Now you *need* to listen to him."

Slowly Steven relaxed his hold and stepped back.

"All right, then," spat Courtenay belligerently, "what is it?"

"You may prefer to sit down," said Percy.

"I will stand. I will submit to this childish show of power because you have me at a disadvantage," spat Courtenay. "But know this, *cousin*, in five days I will take great pleasure in throwing you out of this house—you and all your accomplices in whatever game you are playing."

"I do not think you will, Courtenay. I will not leave except by the word of the viscountess."

"In five days the manor will be mine. If you refuse my order, I will have you removed by force."

"Again, I think not, Courtenay. In five days the manor will *not* be yours."

"Don't talk bloody nonsense!"

"I speak the truth. You are not your father's rightful heir."

A stunned silence filled the room. Courtenay stared back speechless then broke into a laugh. "You are mad as a March hare! Who else would be his heir?"

Out of the corner of his eye, Percy saw Steven staring at him with an equally dumbfounded expression. "She whom your father commissioned me on his deathbed to find," he replied to Courtenay's question. "She who was his rightful heir by his first marriage, before he knew your mother."

"An outrageous claim!" cried Courtenay. "If my father had been married twice, I would know of it. Who is this mystery heir?" For the first time a hint of nervousness was evident in his tone.

"The very one whom you so long despised as too far beneath you even to deserve your contempt—she whom you know as Gwyneth Barrie."

Again a blank stare of incredulity met Percy's words. Steven's expression of disbelief drifted toward his own cousin. "She is but a peasant and guttersnipe!" he said. As he spoke, he laughed scornfully.

"Careful, Courtenay—she is the young woman who is to be my wife. I will let it pass this once. But do not insult her again, or I will give you cause to regret it. She is also your father's granddaughter."

The evident seriousness on his sister's face and the confidence with which Percy spoke at last succeeded in sobering Courtenay to the reality that there might be more to the claim than could so easily be laughed off. He believed not a word of it. But the mirth slowly died from his lips.

"I presume you have some sort of proof you intend to put forward in support of this preposterous notion," he said coolly.

As he spoke, on the floor Colville was returning to consciousness. His confused brain struggled to make sense of where he was. The only word that registered from out of the fog he now repeated in defense of the charge that had been brought against him.

"*Proof. . .*" he repeated in a slurred tongue, climbing groggily to his feet. "Proof. . .all lies. . .where's the proof?"

"I believe all the proof needed for the truth of Rhawn's words, Colville," said Florilyn, "may be seen clearly enough in the face of that little boy who just left with his mother. Steven," she said to Steven, "would you please escort Mr. Burrenchobay from the house. Our afternoon tea is over."

With one hand on his arm, Steven gently ushered Colville through the french doors. A pronounced stinging in the region of his right cheekbone was all the persuasion Colville needed to go quietly. Steven saw him safely to the front of the house, helped him mount his horse, and returned inside through the main front door. By the time he reached home, Colville's head was splitting, and he called for cold compresses.

Meanwhile, the three cousins were left alone in the sunroom.

"You spoke of proof," said Percy. "All the proof you may require shall be provided in due course."

"No doubt," rejoined Courtenay sullenly. "But my solicitor shall make inquiries."

"Florilyn," said Percy, "would you mind going to your mother? Tell her I need to speak with her in private. I will join her momentarily. You may return and tell me where to meet her."

Florilyn turned to go then hesitated. She gazed at Percy full in the face. "Percy. . .I am sorry," she said. "Can you ever forgive me for the dreadful things I said?"

Percy smiled. "You were forgiven without needing to ask."

She returned his smile, hugged him warmly, and left the room.

Percy and Courtenay exchanged a few more words in private.

SIXTY-EIGHT

Ladies of the Manor

The moment they were alone, Katherine gave Gwyneth a warm hug.

"Gwyneth, my dear!" she exclaimed. "How you have grown. You are beautiful!"

Gwyneth smiled with peaceful embarrassment.

"But what are you doing here? No one knew where you had disappeared to."

"I will leave that for Percy to explain, Lady Katherine," replied Gwyneth. "I apologize that we came unannounced."

"Think nothing of it. You are both more welcome than I can say."

As they were talking, Florilyn walked through the door. She glanced about. There were her mother, Gwyneth, and Rhawn. All three turned toward her as the door opened. Her eyes filled with tears at the sight. She walked to her mother. Katherine received her into her embrace, and Florilyn broke into great cleansing sobs. "Mother," she cried. "I am so sorry! I'm sorry I didn't trust you or come to you."

Katherine stroked her hair and held her as she had not done in years.

Florilyn wept until the storm gradually subsided. She sniffed and wiped at her eyes, then turned to Gwyneth. The two embraced. No words were needed.

Florilyn now approached Rhawn, whose tears were not yet altogether spent either. The two friends embraced, with mutual words of renewed affection. "Thank you, Rhawn," said Florilyn. "It took courage to do what you did and tell me the truth. I know you didn't want to. But you did it for me. I am sorry for all you have been through and for the terrible things I said. You are a true friend. I will never forget what you did for me today."

Just then Steven returned from outside after seeing Colville on his way and walked into the room. Florilyn turned and saw him, then came toward him with a peaceful, humble, embarrassed smile. He opened his arms, and she walked into them without hesitation.

"I'm sorry, Steven," she said softly. "I treated you terribly. I have no excuse. I forgot who you were—that you were my friend. . .and more than a friend."

"It is over now," he said tenderly. "It will be as if it never was."

Florilyn now turned again to Katherine. "Mother," she said, "Percy wants to see you alone. He asked me to tell him where you would like to meet him."

Katherine nodded. She and Florilyn spoke further for a few moments, and then she left the room.

⌒⌒⌒

Percy entered Katherine's private sitting room on the second floor a few minutes later.

His aunt was waiting for him.

"Hello, Aunt Katherine," he said with a smile. "At last I can give you a proper greeting!"

She rose and embraced him. "You seem to have come just in time."

"I had no idea about Florilyn's engagement."

"I told her she needed to write you. But she has been very different since your last visit."

"I noticed."

"I should have told you and your parents, but. . .I was embarrassed. I suppose I kept hoping Florilyn would come to her senses. How I prayed you would come!"

"I hope all that is over now. I am sorry I gave you no advance warning. Our trip was very sudden."

"You are always welcome, Percy—with or without warning. Though I will not be at the manor much longer, as you know. This may be your final visit."

"We shall see about that," replied Percy. "Though I must say this wasn't exactly the peaceful homecoming I envisioned," he added with a light laugh. "It appears Gwyneth and I walked into a hornets' nest!"

"It is as much my fault as anyone's," replied Katherine. "Steven asked my permission to confront Florilyn about her engagement to Colville. I had no idea it would turn so heated and violent."

"Colville has a terrible temper. But if it is any consolation, I think she will soon be breaking her engagement."

"Yes, she told me. She already seems her old self again. Colville had cast such a spell over her. I am very relieved. And Gwyneth—she is looking wonderful! Who could have imagined she would turn into such a beautiful young lady."

"Did either she or Florilyn tell you?"

"About what?"

"Gwyneth and I are engaged."

"Oh, Percy—that's wonderful! Although," she said pausing momentarily, "I had been holding out hope that one day I would be able to call you my son-in-law as well as my nephew."

"I am hoping that it won't be long before you will be able to call one your son-in-law who is every bit the man I am. . .if not more!" Percy paused and drew in a deep breath. "But time for all that later," he said. "Aunt Katherine," he added quietly, "I need to talk to you very seriously. I think we should sit down. What I have to say may be painful for you. This is not how I envisioned it. I did not want to tell you like this. But events today seem rather to have overtaken us. It is imperative you know the truth without delay."

"The truth about what, Percy?"

Percy went on to tell her the whole story.

She listened quietly, with occasional tears. "I think I knew it all along," she said when he had concluded. "A woman knows when she is not the only one living in a man's heart, even if the other is but a memory. When you wrote me after returning from Ireland, I knew you were trying to protect my feelings. You probably hoped I would think Roderick was involved in some business deal that he wanted you to look into. I appreciate what you tried to do. But when you were so evasive, I had the feeling even then that there must have been a child."

"I am sorry, Aunt Katherine. If there had been a gentler way, or any other way..."

"I know, Percy. You had to do what you felt was right. Under the circumstances, this may prove to be for everyone's good in the end."

"Even Courtenay's?"

"If it serves to humble him and make a true man of him, then of course. What is a title and property alongside character? I would rather see my children paupers, and me along with them, if that is what it takes to build the character of godliness into us all."

"Hopefully it will not require quite such extreme measures," said Percy. He drew in a deep breath then rose. "I asked the others to wait for us downstairs in the sitting room," he said. "I told them I would explain more after talking to you."

"Then let us keep them waiting no longer."

"There is one thing, Aunt Katherine.... I don't know how much you want me to say, or—"

"I would have no more secrets, Percy," said his aunt. "Tell them everything. Perhaps you should simply read the affidavit Roderick asked you to write out then tell about the letters and your going to Ireland and everything Mr. Barrie told you. After all these years, I would have light shed on it all. Please, you mustn't worry about my feelings. We must have the full truth."

Percy nodded seriously. "Perhaps Steven should take Rhawn home," he suggested. "Then the five of us can talk among ourselves."

Katherine thought a moment. "She has been through an emotional ordeal," she said. "She should not be alone right now. I think it would be good for her to remain here awhile, with her friends, perhaps for evening tea."

"And Steven?"

"Steven is as much a part of our family as anyone. He is Gwyneth's cousin. However. . .it may be that we should keep Roderick's disclosure among ourselves, at least for now. It will all come out soon enough, but. . .I shall talk to Steven. He will understand. He can keep Rhawn company while the five of us talk."

She rose, and they left the room and walked down one flight of stairs where the others were awaiting them in the east parlor. She walked straight to Gwyneth and folded her a second time into a loving embrace. "You dear, beautiful, mysterious young woman," she whispered into her ear, "Percy has told me everything. Welcome to the family!"

SIXTY-NINE

The Affidavit

*A*n hour later, after a break for tea and walk outside settling into old friendships, Katherine, Courtenay, Florilyn, Percy, and Gwyneth gathered upstairs in the sitting room of Katherine's apartment. Steven and Rhawn were outside in the stables where Steven was introducing Rhawn's son to the manor's horses.

"By now we all know why Percy and Gwyneth have returned," Katherine began. "There are pains to be borne, probably most severely by you, Courtenay, and myself. But the truth must come out. So I asked Percy to tell us everything." She turned toward Percy.

"Before Uncle Roderick died," Percy began, "he asked me to take down a statement he wanted to make. I know it may occur to you, Courtenay, to wonder why he made his confession to me rather than you or his solicitor or anyone else. I asked him that as well. His chief reason was simply that, should I prove unsuccessful in finding Gwyneth, whom he believed to be his granddaughter, then he saw no reason for any of this to come out at all. Telling me was his way of preserving confidentiality. I think he may have had some mistaken notion that my being a student of law gave the affidavit added veracity. It doesn't, of course. Nothing I took down from him carries the weight of a legal document. However, I think that may have influenced his thinking."

"If it is not a legal document," said Courtenay, "then what possible grounds do you have for thinking I intend to sit idly by and be deprived of my title and inheritance?"

"You asked for proof earlier," replied Percy. "Though it is not legally binding, I will give you what proof I am able for the moment in your father's own words. What additional proof there is will have to wait for another day, except to say that I have seen the parish records, both attesting to your father's first marriage and to the birth of Gwyneth's mother. Proving Gwyneth's maternity may be more difficult, but I am confident that proof will come in time."

"Go on, Percy," said Katherine. "Read Roderick's statement."

Percy nodded then unfolded the papers he had in his hand.

> *"To whom it may concern,"* Percy began aloud, *"especially to my dear wife Katherine, my family, and to Hamilton Murray, our faithful solicitor of many years:*
>
> *I make this affidavit on the 27th day of June in the year 1872 in the presence of my nephew, Percival Drummond, son of Edward and Mary Drummond of Glasgow. I am of sound mind, but failing body. . . .*
>
> *At sixteen years of age,"* Percy continued, *"as a spoiled son of what I thought was wealth, I left Wales on a youthful grand tour, as we called it in those days—to see the world and spend money and generally squander my youth on the altar of irresponsibility. It turned out that my father was not the wealthy man I took him for. Before my travels were over, I was nearly out of money. I found myself in Ireland chasing the fleeting dream of riches in the rivers of Wicklow, though what remained to be found was doubtful. There my heart was smitten with a young Irish lass of working, though not peasant stock. Her name was Avonmara O'Sullivan. . . ."*

Percy continued, not without many pauses and breaks, as Florilyn and Katherine listened with handkerchiefs in hand and eyes wet. At length he came to his uncle's final words.

"To you, Courtenay, if Percy is successful, you may hate me as well as him for what I have done and his part in it. I can only pray that it will make a man of you and that you will awaken to the claim of character sooner in your life than I did. You have the makings of goodness within you, my son. Heed their call and do not ignore them until it is too late."

Courtenay sat listening with a sullen scowl. As if it wasn't enough to be deprived of his inheritance in full view of this parcel of urchins, women, and cousins, he had to endure the further humiliation of being lectured at by his father from the grave!

"To you, my Flory, I have treasured our friendship of recent years. You have become a beautiful daughter to make a man proud—and I am assuredly proud of the young woman you have become. You will make your new husband a worthy and loving wife, and I am happy for you both."

Florilyn could contain herself no longer. She burst into sobs at her father's words. Percy waited.

"To you, my dear Katherine," he concluded at length, *"there are no words to tell you how sorry I am. You were the best wife a man could have—certainly far better than I deserved. Whatever happened before I met you, I only pray it will not cause you more pain than you can bear. But from the moment I met you, I loved you with all my heart. I love you now, and I will miss you until the day we meet again. Good-bye, my love."*

Percy glanced up, himself also blinking hard. Katherine was quietly weeping. Florilyn rose and went to her on the couch. Courtenay stood, his face stoic, and left the room. Percy and Gwyneth followed a moment later, leaving mother and daughter alone.

SEVENTY

Encounter in the Hills

*I*n that mysterious process by which *news* spreads of itself, word had circulated through the Westbrooke Manor staff that something was up, that some great change was at hand, and that Gwyneth was at the center of it. They had been told nothing as yet, but whispered speculation ran rampant.

Gwyneth noticed curious looks coming her way from Mrs. Drynwydd and Mrs. Llewellyn and others of her former fellow servants. Percy knew her well enough to know that Gwyneth felt that her place ought to be with them, *serving* the family rather than pretending to be part of it. During that evening's tea, during which Courtenay was conspicuously absent, Percy noticed her embarrassment as she glanced about occasionally, smiling awkwardly and almost apologetically as Mrs. Drynwydd poured tea into her cup.

He knew she felt out of place. Though Steven was her cousin, and had grown up no more an aristocrat than she, he had been part of the manor family and treated as such by Katherine for more than a year. Everything was suddenly new to her.

When Katherine showed Gwyneth to one of the available guest rooms on the second floor where she and Florilyn and Courtenay and Percy all had their rooms, she asked Katherine if it wouldn't be better for her to stay in the servants' quarters. For answer, Katherine merely gave her another hug. The seeming luxury of her new surroundings would take time for Gwyneth to become accustomed to.

At Steven's suggestion and after he had hitched the manor's large carriage to two horses, the four young people loaded into it and together accompanied Rhawn and her son home to Llanfryniog. It was well past nine o'clock and dark before Percy, Gwyneth, Steven, and Florilyn returned.

Of the four, notwithstanding her discomfort at being waited on by her former fellow servants, only Gwyneth was asleep by ten. The other three, in their rooms and alone with their thoughts and the gamut of emotions and reactions the day had produced, lay awake past midnight.

The day had not gone as Percy had anticipated. His chief concern had been for his aunt. However, she had absorbed the news of her husband's past with all the poise and equanimity he should have known to expect. Instead, his thoughts alternated between the two girls who had been at the center of the day's fray—Rhawn and Florilyn. He knew the next days would be hard for them, adjusting to the sudden rush of events that had come upon them like a flood. Rhawn, especially, would probably feel alone and easily despondent. They needed to get together again and allow time for the emotion of change to settle and dissipate amid conversation, laughter, and friendship.

He spoke to Steven early the next morning. Thus it was that shortly before noon, with a great lunch packed behind two of the horses, Steven, Rhawn, Florilyn, Percy, and Gwyneth set off for a long ride north and east into the hills of Snowdonia. The five were older now, quieter, full of many thoughts. New times were coming to them all. A good deal of laughter was interspersed with serious talk, but there were no races on this day. Profound changes had overtaken them in recent days. The future now spreading out before them contained many unknowns but also new opportunities. They were subdued yet also alive to those possibilities.

As they went, Percy gradually drew back and allowed the others to ride ahead. He watched them with a smile, reminded of the rides he had taken during his first summer here. Now Florilyn was riding at Steven's side, talking together as they hadn't for months. Gwyneth and Rhawn followed as if they were old friends. How different this was from the day when Rhawn had tried to use her wiles on him and they had encountered young Gwyneth watching from the treetops. *She* would now be the one giving orders, not Courtenay as he had that day... for this would be *her* land. It was a peaceful day. Many bonds had been renewed and strengthened, and new and deeper ones formed. These five, henceforth, would always be friends.

"Would you three mind continuing on without us?" said Percy as they made their way back toward the coast several hours later. "There is someplace I want to go with Gwyneth."

They parted ten minutes later, Steven riding between Rhawn and Florilyn down the descending slopes westward, while Percy and Gwyneth veered north and again into the hills.

"Where are we going?" asked Gwyneth.

"Can't you guess?" rejoined Percy.

"To my special lake?"

"I went there after you were gone," said Percy. "I had no idea whether I would ever see you again. I suppose I went to be close to you. I've wanted to be there again *with* you ever since."

"Did you see the horses?" asked Gwyneth.

"I've been there twice but saw the horses neither time. They have probably been waiting for you."

Gwyneth smiled, and they continued on.

They reached the overlook above the crystal green waters forty minutes later. They dismounted, tied the horses, and sat for a few minutes gazing down upon the peaceful scene.

"Is this really happening to me, Percy?" said Gwyneth softly. "Or am I dreaming back in our cottage down near the village...or in our home in Ireland?"

"If you are dreaming, how do you account for the fact that we are both having the same dream?"

"Maybe I am dreaming you into my dream, and whatever you say is part of my dream."

Percy laughed lightly. "I have the feeling you will realize that you are awake soon enough. If I know you, you will very soon find yourself thinking of the good your position will allow you to do."

"I hope so, Percy. If it is true. . .oh, I *do* want to do good. I want to do good for *people*."

"You will, Gwyneth. Maybe this is God's way of allowing you to spread your bouquets of goodness to many, and with more than flowers."

"When will. . . I cannot say it, Percy," began Gwyneth. "But when will, you know. . ."

"When will you inherit?"

"*If* I do."

"It will be as it has been for Courtenay—when you are twenty-five."

"That will not be for five years," said Gwyneth in a tone of relief. "I am glad of that. What will happen until then?"

"Aunt Katherine—and now we may both call her that. . .although, no. . .she is actually your. . .hmm, let me see. . .yes, she would be your step-grandmother. In any event, she will continue to be viscountess and trustee of the estate."

Gwyneth drew in a breath and let it out slowly. "That means I don't really have to do anything now," she said then thought a moment. "I would like to do something, though, for Rhawn," she said. "She is sad. I know it is from the consequences of what she used to be. But I still hurt for her."

"Being a friend is what she needs most of all. I think now Florilyn will be a friend to her again, too."

"What is Florilyn to *me* now, Percy? Is she my aunt, or my half aunt? It is very confusing."

Percy smiled. "I hadn't thought of it," he said. "But I think a half-aunt qualifies as an aunt."

"It would be hard to call her Aunt Florilyn."

Percy laughed. "Just promise that I am present when you spring an *Uncle* Courtenay on Courtenay!"

Gwyneth drew in a deep breath as she peered down toward the lake.

"I see no movement down there at all," she said. "I don't even see deer. They are always there. Something is wrong, Percy."

"Shall we walk down and see? Maybe the rabbits are there."

They rose. Again Gwyneth hesitated. A puzzled expression came over her face.

"What is it?" asked Percy.

"I hear something," replied Gwyneth softly.

Gradually intruded faintly into Percy's hearing what sounded like the far-off sounds of machinery, the dull thudding of wood, an occasional clank of metal. . .even, though he could not quite be sure, shouts of men's voices. "I hear it, too," he said. "What can it be? We are miles from any farm."

They hurried to their horses and rode toward the sounds. The terrain was steep, and the hills and peaks surrounding the lake were rocky and jagged. Gwyneth led the way for she knew these hills far better than Percy. In fifteen minutes, they crested the north-south ridge east of the lake. Below them at a distance of about half a mile, a crew of perhaps a dozen men, surrounded by at least twice that many horses, some pulling wagons, others hitched to strange-looking machines, were hard at work. Some of the men appeared to be removing large rocks from a wagon track or roadbed stretching out behind them, while others, ahead of the wagons and machinery, were cutting trees and removing brush and clearing out a way forward. Where the road came from, they had no idea. But they were obviously moving up the ridge in the direction of the lake.

"What are they doing, Percy?" asked Gwyneth.

"I have no idea. But I don't like the look of it."

"I thought all this land was Lord Snowdon's. . .or Lady Katherine's now."

"As did I. Perhaps they are on someone else's land. I don't know where the boundary is. I saw several surveyors out here once before. When I told Aunt Katherine about it, she wasn't completely sure where the boundary was."

"Should we tell Lady Katherine?"

"Without a doubt—and immediately. Gwyneth, you know these hills better than I. You lead the way back to the manor. . .and with as much speed as you think is safe!"

SEVENTY-ONE

The Lady and the Lord

*G*wyneth and Percy arrived at Westbrooke Manor an hour later, breathing hard and their two mounts lathered from the exertion.

By then Rhawn had returned to town. Steven and Florilyn, who were walking together back from the stables, saw them ride in.

Percy dismounted and ran for the house. "Tell them what we saw, Gwyneth," he said. "Maybe Steven knows something. I'll try to find Aunt Katherine!"

When Percy and Katherine emerged from the house two minutes later, Steven, Florilyn, and Gwyneth were standing beside the two sweating horses talking.

"Steven?" said Katherine as they approached.

"I know nothing about it," replied Steven, shaking his head.

"Do you know the place where Percy and Gwyneth saw the men? Do you know the lake?"

"I know it well."

"Is it near the boundary of the estate? Could it be someone else's land? Sir Armond's property borders ours to the northeast, I believe."

"There is no chance of that, Lady Katherine," said Steven. "The estate boundary lies two ridges east from that lake, not one. It is at least a half mile from where, if I have my bearings correct, Percy and Gwyneth describe seeing the men."

"How can you be sure?"

"After he hired me as a groom, your husband took me about to show me the extent of the estate. He was especially concerned that I knew where the boundaries were between his land and that of Mr. Burrenchobay. Whatever is going on. . .it is on *your* land, Lady Katherine."

Half an hour later, on fresh mounts, Katherine, Florilyn, Steven, Gwyneth, and Percy rode away from Westbrooke Manor northeast into the hills. As anxious as they were to make haste, they allowed Steven to set a pace that would not overly tax the horses. By the time they reached the final ridge and began the descent down the slope where the work was still in progress, the afternoon was well advanced.

Shadows from one of its two surrounding parallel ridges had nearly consumed the valley where the men were working, and their thoughts were turning to the dinner and beer that awaited them back at the inn in Bronaber. It happened that the mastermind of the project had ridden out at day's end to assess progress.

As they made their way down through the thickly wooded slope, Katherine nodded to Steven. The others slowed, and he rode on ahead. He made his way into the clearing and toward the scene. A few heads turned as he approached and reined in.

"Who's in charge here?" said Steven.

Other heads turned. A few comments filtered back through the ranks.

After a moment, a well-dressed man came forward from among them. He was obviously not one of the laborers. "I am Lord Coleraine Litchfield," he said. "And who might you be?"

"I am Steven Muir, factor of the Westbrooke Manor estate."

"Ah. . .Mr. Muir. Well, it is nice to meet my new neighbor."

"How do you mean, your neighbor?"

"I am the owner of this land."

Steven took in the statement calmly. "What are you doing here?" he asked.

"As you can see, my men are building a road."

"And this, you say, is your land?"

"It is."

"As of when?"

"Very recently."

"From whom did you purchase it?"

"From the Westbrooke estate."

"I see. That will come as a surprise to the trustee of the estate, who knows nothing about it." Still seated on his horse, Steven turned and signaled for Katherine to join him.

As she rode toward them, Lord Litchfield recognized the late viscount's widow. An indulgent smile came to his lips. "Lady Westbrooke," he said, "it seems we meet again."

"This man tells me that he is the owner of this land," said Steven.

Katherine had not liked Lord Litchfield from the first. It was with great difficulty that she now kept her anger in check. "That is a curious claim," she said, "in that I control the affairs of the estate and have heard nothing about it."

"The purchase was carried out through the new viscount," said Litchfield. "Your son, I believe."

"Courtenay sold you this land!"

"That is true."

"It is not his land. He has not inherited yet. None of this is his to sell."

"It will be in a matter of days."

"Do you mean to tell me that you are doing. . .whatever all this is. . . on my husband's land when it is not even yet legally yours?"

"Your son allowed me to commence my plans though the transaction will not be formally finalized for a few more days."

"But I do not give you permission. This is not his land."

"Three days. . .four days. . .what difference do a few hours make? He will be viscount, and this will be my land. Why should I not get under way?"

"Because at the moment you are trespassing, Lord Litchfield."

"Tut, tut, Lady Westbrooke. A mere technicality."

"Hardly a technicality, Lord Litchfield, when you consider the fact that although my son will indeed turn twenty-five in four days, he will not become viscount. . .not then, not ever. Whatever papers you may have signed are not legally binding."

"What are you talking about? He will become viscount in four days."

"I fear not, Lord Litchfield. Gwyneth dear," said Katherine, turning in her saddle and beckoning her forward.

Gwyneth urged her mount up to Katherine's side.

"Lord Litchfield," said Katherine, "may I introduce you to my husband's granddaughter and heir, the future viscountess and Lady Snowdon."

"Don't be absurd!" laughed Litchfield, sending his eyes in Gwyneth's direction. "She is a girl. . .and a young one at that."

"My son will not inherit, Lord Litchfield," said Katherine. "I will not trouble you with the legalities. However, I *will* trouble you to remove your men and equipment from our land. I will send Mr. Muir out tomorrow to make sure all activities have ceased and all equipment is gone."

At last Lord Litchfield found himself without words. But only briefly. "If what you say is true, Lady Westbrooke," he said. "Then there will be a lawsuit. I have paid your son a good deal of money."

"That is between you and him," rejoined Katherine. "He was not negotiating on behalf of the estate. Furthermore, I may be forced to bring a suit against you for trespassing and for the damage you have done to our land. Good day, Lord Litchfield. You will be hearing from my solicitor."

Speaking more boldly than she had ever spoken in her life, nearly trembling in righteous anger both toward Courtenay and Lord Litchfield for what they had tried to do behind her back, Katherine turned her mount around and galloped back to where Percy and Florilyn were waiting, followed by Steven and Gwyneth. She did not slow when she reached them but continued as fast as she was able up the ridge, into the trees, and back to the manor.

Somewhat calmed by the time she arrived home, Katherine was still infuriated at what Courtenay had tried to do. She went straight to her office and immediately drafted a letter to Hamilton Murray, informing him of what had taken place and requesting that he call at the manor as soon as possible. He must be made aware of Gwyneth's presence without delay.

Steven was on his way to Porthmadog with the letter shortly after breakfast the following morning.

SEVENTY-TWO

The Solicitor

*I*n Steven's absence, Katherine asked Percy to ride again into the
hills to make sure Litchfield's men and equipment were nowhere to be
seen. Gwyneth and Florilyn accompanied him. They set out after lunch.
They found the site vacant except for the scar through the land that
Litchfield had intended as the new road to the lake.

They returned through Llanfryniog. It was the first time Gwyneth
had been in the village again since the day of their arrival on the coach.

"I would like to see Grannie's cottage," said Gwyneth as they rode.
"Do you know if it is still vacant?"

"I don't know," replied Percy. "Do you, Florilyn?"

Florilyn shook her head.

"There is one way to find out," said Percy, turning and leading down
a narrow side street between the close-built stone houses. As they went,
he caught what seemed to be a brief glimpse of purple, which almost
the same instant disappeared down one of the narrow lanes leading
away from Grannie's cottage.

Gwyneth was quiet as they went. She had scampered among all
these streets and lanes as a child, as most of the villagers considered
her the peculiar stuttering "witch child" of Llanfryniog. The nostalgia
of the sights, sounds, and smells brought mingled pains and joys to her
heart. Riding down the town's main street, and now through its narrow

lanes, the eyes that followed the three young people all knew Florilyn and Percy. Not a soul recognized the light-haired girl between them nor would have guessed that she was the very one they had feared to speak to fifteen years before. Rumors about the sudden change in her fortunes would begin soon enough, as rumors always do. As yet no whisper had reached them that the urchin who had once left forgiveness bouquets on Llanfryniog's doors would soon wed their beloved young Scot and then, five years from now, would become the viscountess and mistress of the manor to whom they would pay their rents.

Percy and Gwyneth dismounted in front of Grannie's door. Percy tried the latch. The door opened on creaky hinges. He poked his head inside. "There's nobody here, Gwyneth," he said.

Slowly Gwyneth walked inside the poor cottage that had been a second home to her.

Sensing that it was time to let her ponder the past and future quietly and alone, Percy stepped back into the street. While Gwyneth renewed her memories, Percy helped Florilyn dismount. The two led their horses as they strolled up the lane.

"Remember the day we visited that creepy lady?" said Florilyn, pointing to the strange and weirdly appointed house at the end of the street.

"I do indeed. In fact, I thought I saw her a minute ago. It looked like she was scurrying away from Grannie's cottage."

Slowly they wandered toward the house. It was of wood, unusual in this place where stone predominated, painted in white and purple and of an architecture more reminiscent of Germany's Black Forest than north Wales. The roof was steep slanted, boasting atop it an occultish weathervane. Gargoyles and statues of fairies, trolls, goblins, and other strange figures sat round the small yard. The mere look of the place sent a shiver up Florilyn's spine.

A sign above the door, ornate with Celtic symbolism, read: MADAME FLEMING, PSYCHIC—FORTUNES AND FUTURES FORETOLD.

No one knew why the enigmatic "Madame Fleming" had come to this coastal village with her fortune-telling boutique or where she had come from. On the few occasions she chanced to be seen—in dresses and scarves of reds, pinks, and purples and with gaudy jewelry dangling from ears and neck and wrists—there was no mistaking her.

When they returned back along the street a few minutes later, Grannie's former neighbor was talking over a low fence with Gwyneth. None of them had any idea that they were being watched through one of Madame Fleming's curtained windows. Neither could they have divined what thoughts were racing through the devilish woman's cunning brain. Nor why, hearing rumors of a young, white-haired beauty newly arrived in the village, she had grown newly fearful of what clues to her own identity might have been left behind in Grannie's cottage.

". . .just left without a word," Grannie's neighbor was saying. "No one knew where she had gone."

"She is happy and well, Mrs. Hueil," said Gwyneth.

"She is alive! But how do you know, lassie?"

"I am Gwyneth, Mrs. Hueil."

The woman stared back at her speechless.

"The saints preserve us!" she said in disbelief. "*Gwyneth*. . .is it really you, lassie?"

Gwyneth smiled. "My father and Grannie are in Ireland, Mrs. Hueil. It is a long story. I came back with Percy for a visit."

Mrs. Hueil glanced toward Percy and Florilyn as they walked up the lane toward them.

"Mr. Drummond. . .you're back again, I see," she said then nodded with a timid smile toward Florilyn. She was dying to know whether any significance might be attached to Florilyn's being with Percy on this day, for the whole town knew of their broken engagement and her subsequent engagement to Colville Burrenchobay.

But the rumor mills would have no more grist to add to their grinding wheels on this day. When the three remounted their horses and rode the rest of the way through the village and out of town, they appeared no more nor less than what they were—three friends who had known each other a long time and had been seen together numerous times.

Steven returned in midafternoon to say that Hamilton Murray would call at the manor on the following day.

By eleven thirty the next morning, Katherine was seated with the solicitor in the manor's formal sitting room with Florilyn, Percy, Gwyneth, and Steven, whom she had asked to be present, also. She had just given Mr. Murray a brief account of the turn of events and introduced him to Gwyneth.

"Well, I must say these are unexpected developments indeed," said Murray as he and Gwyneth and Katherine resumed their seats. "However, I must confess that I knew something of it before I came. Your son has been busy, Lady Katherine. After you left me yesterday, Mr. Muir," he said, nodding toward Steven, "I received a telegram from one of London's noted barristers informing me that he was filing a suit on behalf of one Courtenay Westbrooke, son of the late Viscount Lord Snowdon, in substantiation of his claim as the rightful and legal heir to his father's title and property."

A few comments went round the room. No one was surprised at what Courtenay had done, though having managed it so quickly took them off guard.

"Obviously I need to research the legal background of the viscountcy and its unique stipulations of inheritance," said Murray. "I should also read the affidavit you told me about."

"I have it here," said Percy. He rose and handed Murray the folded papers.

Murray took them and read it in silence, nodding a few times as he did so. "Very interesting," he said when he had completed it. "Of course, it might have been advantageous had Roderick shared this with me. But I think we all understand his reasons for handling it as he did. A document such as this, in and of itself, would have little standing in a court of law. However, as supplemental evidence, especially if its facts can be confirmed elsewhere, by parish records of the marriage and births in question, there would be a strong case to be made to substantiate Miss Barrie as the viscount's heir—that is, of course, if her maternity and her mother's paternity can be likewise substantiated."

"Tell him what you found in Ireland, Percy," said Katherine.

Percy recounted the details of his two visits to Ireland, what he had seen in the parish record books, and his talk with Mrs. Maloney, Gwyneth's aunt, along with the details both of Morvern's birth and Gwyneth's.

Murray listened attentively, taking notes and occasionally asking questions. "Even with all this," he said when Percy was through, "I fear that in the hands of a capable, and perhaps unscrupulous, barrister, the case could be troublesome in court. Without the mother—I'm sorry, Miss Barrie," he added, turning to Gwyneth, "without *your* mother. . . or some substantiating record or testimony, we really have no absolute *proof* that you are Morvern Westbrooke's. . .a.k.a. Morvern O'Sullivan's daughter. And according to what you say, Mr. Drummond, about the nature of the birth and the superstitions voiced by the aunt's husband, it is probable that the birth was never entered in the parish register. At least you never saw it, isn't that correct?"

Percy nodded. "What do you mean by a substantiating testimony?" he asked.

"An eyewitness who could absolutely establish that Miss Barrie is in fact Lord Snowdon's granddaughter by his daughter Morvern, known as Morvern O'Sullivan—someone other than Miss Barrie's father or aunt."

"There was a midwife who attended the birth," said Percy. "They were all afraid of her, but she—" He stopped in midsentence as his eyes shot open.

Suddenly Mrs. Maloney's words came back into his brain with forceful clarity—"*She claimed to be able to see into the future. . .always wore purple. . .horrid earrings of snakes and ugly creatures. . .purple, purple, purple!*"

The next moment he was out of his chair and rushing toward the door. "This may mean nothing," he said, "but there is someone in town I must see immediately. Steven, would you mind helping me hitch up the small buggy?"

The two young men ran from the room, leaving the others staring after them in bewilderment.

SEVENTY-THREE

The Fleming

On this day Percy did not care who saw him or knew whom he had come into Llanfryniog to visit. He tied the horse to the iron post on the street. Moments later he was jingling the brass bell on Madame Fleming's front door.

Several seconds later the door opened. The face that appeared was older and more wrinkled even than Percy had expected. She did not seem surprised as she cast a brief glance behind him. "So you're alone this time, are you, Mr. Drummond," said Madame Fleming.

"That's right," said Percy abruptly. "I want to talk to you."

"Come in, come in. How can Madame Fleming be of service to you?" said the woman, leading Percy into her lair and closing the door behind him. Several candles burned inside, casting shadows upon the shelves and chairs and statues and tapestries and paintings with which the place was furnished. The bookshelf still stood against the far wall. The air was stifling with incense mingled with unpleasant odors of a more personal nature. The woman was dressed in several layers of thin, flowing purple material, her head wrapped in an orange scarf wound several times around a head mostly of gray that fell loosely over her shoulders. From her ears dangled two silver snakes. "You've had some reversals in love, I understand," she said as she waddled into the interior. "Come to see what your future holds, have you?"

"It's not my future I'm here to talk about," said Percy, "but yours. . . and your past." He stopped and stood in the middle of the crowded, dimly lit room.

The words jolted Madame Fleming, though she did not allow her reaction to show. She continued toward the small anteroom where she conducted her fortune-telling art until she realized Percy was not following her. She stopped and turned. "Come, young Drummond—come into my den where we may sit. I will look at your hand with the aid of my crystals and—"

"I have no intention of letting you look at my hand or any other part of me," said Percy. "I shall stay right here, and you shall answer my questions. I want to know where you came from before you arrived in Llanfryniog."

"Madame Fleming divulges nothing of her—"

"I want to know," interrupted Percy. "And you can stop the fake accent. You are no more Bulgarian than I am. Perhaps I should be more direct and simply ask if you came from Ireland. . .*Mrs. Faoiltiarna?*"

Even in the dim light, Percy saw the word hit her like a physical blow. Slowly she tottered on wobbly knees like a tree about to fall then staggered to a chair and sat down. "Where did you hear that name?" she said.

"It is my business where I heard it," replied Percy. "I see that you know it. You must know, too, that if those who know what you are and have cause against you. . .if they were to discover where you have been hiding all these years, it might not bode well for you."

Quickly Madame Fleming recovered herself. Her eyes flashed with anger. "It was all lies!" she spat. "What do my affairs have to do with you, young Drummond? Take care that you do not anger me, or evil may come to you when you least—"

"Don't threaten me with your mumbo jumbo," interrupted Percy. "You may be able to pull off your charade as a psychic with superstitious old men and women, but it will not work with me. Your threats mean nothing. I know that you practiced as a midwife in eastern Ireland before escaping with your life under threat of witchcraft. Unless you tell me what I want to know, I will expose you as a deceiver and fraud. I will contact the authorities in Arklow, informing them of your whereabouts. I think you know that the religious climate in Wales would not be friendly to the knowledge that witchcraft was being practiced in its midst."

A vile string of imprecations exploded from Madame Fleming's mouth.

"Guard your tongue!" shouted Percy. "Threaten or curse me again, and I will walk out of here and broadcast what I know. Now calm yourself. I have questions to ask, and I want answers. If you cooperate, I will promise to keep your secrets."

Thirty minutes later, Percy and Madame Fleming left the latter's house together. If either had qualms about being seen with the other, they did not show it. The proprietress of Madame Fleming, Ltd. was notably subdued from the interview recently concluded. But inside her dark soul, the fires of fury still burned hot.

They climbed into the buggy where it stood on the street. The springs groaned and tipped under the bulk of Llanfryniog's colorful seer. Percy sat down beside her, flipped the reins, and they bounded off. What those curious eyes who saw them might have thought would have been interesting to inquire.

It would have made an even more interesting inquiry to know what the erstwhile Mrs. Faoiltiarna, alias the Wolf Lady, alias Madame Fleming, thought to find herself gazing up at the stone walls of Westbrooke Manor as they rode toward it and, a few minutes later, being led toward its front door. What the manor residents and staff thought as word gradually spread concerning whom Percy had brought into their midst might have been yet more interesting to know.

Percy led her through the front doors. "Wait here," he said when they were inside. He disappeared up the main staircase, taking the steps two at a time.

The others were still gathered in the sitting room, having tea and waiting for him.

"Mr. Murray, I have with me," he began as all eyes turned toward him, "a woman who can, I believe, provide you the testimony you speak of. She is waiting downstairs."

"Who can that be?" asked Katherine.

"It is a long story, Aunt Katherine," replied Percy. "I heard about her when I was in Ireland. All the pieces did not fit together until we were talking a short while ago. Suddenly the light dawned, and I realized that the very woman who might hold the clues to prove Gwyneth's identity had left Ireland, changed her identity, and had been in Llanfryniog all along. She is not someone I would normally trust. However, Mr. Murray, that I know her former identity, I believe, gives us sufficient power over her that she will tell the truth. If you question her and take down her statement, along with Uncle Roderick's affidavit and the parish records. . .hopefully you will have enough documentation to meet Courtenay's challenge."

"Then let us see what the woman has to say," said Murray. "Lady Katherine, if you would provide me a room where I can interview the woman in private, I shall see what I can learn."

"I want to hear everything, too!" said Florilyn.

"I promised her confidentiality," said Percy. "She has a past she is anxious not be known. That I figured it out makes her hate me. But I promised not to tell her secrets if she would give Mr. Murray a full statement of the facts of Gwyneth's birth. We must let her speak with him alone."

"I will need a third party to witness to the attestation to insure its legality," said Murray. "You are of age, Mr. Drummond, and not directly related by blood to any of the principles involved. It would seem that you are the likely candidate."

Percy hesitated a moment. "Yes, I see what you mean," he said. "But I would prefer that Steven also be present, either as the primary witness or you can use both of us if you prefer. He has nothing to gain, and it could be argued that I do."

"A wise observation, Mr. Drummond," nodded Murray. "Two witnesses will be better than one."

Five minutes later, Percy showed Madame Fleming into a small office on the first floor that had several chairs and a writing table. He introduced her to Hamilton Murray then himself took a chair beside where Steven already sat across the room.

Madame Fleming sat down in one of the chairs while Murray took his place at the desk. With pen in hand, he wrote down a few preliminary remarks of time, date, place, and the names of Steven and Percy and himself as witnesses. Then he looked up at Madame Fleming. "Please tell me your name, for the record," he said.

The name she gave was neither of the names by which Percy knew her.

"Now tell me, please, in as much detail as possible, what you know of the parentage and birth of the young woman known as Gwyneth Barrie."

Madame Fleming cast a brief glance of wrath in Percy's direction, still incensed that another was capable of exerting power over her. "I was for many years a midwife in Arklow, on the eastern coast of Ireland," she began, almost as through clenched teeth. "A time came when I was called upon by a certain lady of the name Maighdlin O'Sullivan. Her granddaughter had been raised by her and had recently married and was with child. She employed me for the birthing."

"What was the granddaughter's name?" asked Murray.

"Morvern. . .Morvern O'Sullivan. That was the name Mrs. O'Sullivan gave me."

"Do you know the names of her parents?"

"No. They were either dead or gone, I don't know. She was raised by Mrs. O'Sullivan."

"And she was now married and expecting?"

"Yes."

"What was her husband's name?"

"Barrie. . .Codnor Barrie."

"So the expectant mother's married name was actually Morvern Barrie?"

"I suppose so."

"And then?"

"The time for the birthing came. I delivered the baby—a girl."

"Did they name the child immediately?"

"They did."

"What name did they give her?"

"Gwyneth."

"Was there anything unique or distinctive about the birth?"

"Nothing. The child was healthy, the mother was healthy. Only, the baby was born with pure white hair, not the red hair of the mother and, as I understand it, the grandmother as well. The mother's uncle—an irrational man of violent temper—threatened me on account of it. He said that I had brought a curse on the family and the white hair proved it. After that, because of him, my life was in danger. I left Ireland and came to Wales and changed my name."

Murray nodded and looked over his transcription of the conversation.

"Did you ever see any of them again?" he asked.

"The man Barrie and his daughter, of course," replied Madame Fleming. "It wasn't long after I arrived in Llanfryniog that he came here himself. I had had no idea that he was Welsh. One day I saw him in the village, and I knew in an instant who he was. I had my own reasons for not wanting him to recognize me. But I soon learned that he had come to Wales with the child. When I saw her for myself, even though it was from a distance when Mrs. Myfanawy was caring for her, I recognized her in an instant. There was no mistaking that hair. What the man and his girl were doing in Llanfryniog, I hadn't an idea. I later heard that the mother, the girl called Morvern, had died and that he was a widower alone with his baby. But there's no mistake that the child called Gwyneth Barrie was the same baby I delivered in Arklow."

Again Murray paused and looked over the transcript. "All right then," he said, rising from the desk. "I believe that is all I need for now. If I should need to question you further, Mr. Drummond, I believe, knows how to contact you."

Again Madame Fleming shot Percy a hateful glance then lifted her ponderous bulk from the chair.

"If you would just sign here," said Murray, handing her the pen.

She did so, with obvious displeasure.

"And you as well, Mr. Muir. . .and Mr. Drummond."

Steven walked across the room, still stunned by the amazing turn of events, and also signed the paper, as did Percy.

Finally Murray added his own signature. "With the parish records you located," he said to Percy, "along with the viscount's affidavit, and now this. . .I believe Miss Barrie's claim to be virtually unassailable. No court will overturn it."

Percy escorted Madame Fleming, whose curiosity was heightened by Murray's final words, out of the office and to the front door. They again climbed into the buggy, and he returned her to her home.

Not a word was spoken between them.

SEVENTY-FOUR

The Grandparents

*C*ourtenay's twenty-fifth birthday came and went without fanfare. He had not been seen since Percy's and Gwyneth's arrival.

It was a great relief, for the present at least, for Katherine to know that she would not be forced to depart for Glasgow in the immediate future. Several letters were dispatched to Percy's parents, informing them of developments.

Percy and Gwyneth planned to leave Llanfryniog for Scotland as soon as they were certain that Katherine and Florilyn would find no unexpected notices of eviction slid under their doors during the night. In thoroughly reviewing the legalities of the case, Hamilton Murray assured them that Courtenay could make no move against them. In the extremely unlikely event that he should prevail in court, if the matter went that far, it would be months, if not years, before any change would be enforced. Gradually Katherine began to breathe more easily.

Two days after Courtenay's birthday, Palmer Sutcliffe appeared at the manor requesting an interview with Katherine. He presented her with a legal demand for a return of £5,400 that had been paid to Courtenay, in two payments, the most recent £1,000 only two weeks previously, by Lord Litchfield as down payment for sale of one thousand acres of Westbrooke land. Katherine confessed herself completely unaware of the transaction. Be that as it may, rejoined Sutcliffe coolly, papers had been signed on

842

behalf of the estate and a large amount of money had changed hands. If that amount was not returned within a week, said Sutcliffe, interest at 4 percent would commence, to be added to the balance monthly, along with legal proceedings against the Westbrooke estate for fraud. Stunned by the charge, Katherine did her best to preserve her outward calm. She said that she was very sorry Lord Litchfield had not been more careful and had entered into a transaction with her son when he had no legal power to act on behalf of the estate. However, she hardly saw what she was able to do about it. She suggested he speak with the manor's solicitor. Another consultation between Katherine and Hamilton Murray followed almost immediately.

With their old friendship rekindled, drawn together on deeper spiritual levels by the blossoming maturity of their mutual womanhood, as well as by the fact that both had suffered at the hands of the same man, Florilyn and Rhawn saw one another nearly every day. The reciprocity of their friendship now sought more meaningful levels of communication and exchange than was possible when they were self-centered teens, for they now desired to become women of dignity and character. Gwyneth's presence at the manor, too, drew the best out of Florilyn. Their former friendship resumed, and Rhawn could not but be drawn into it. It was not long before the three young women were the best of friends. In spite of the fact that Gwyneth was several years younger than both, the two older girls sensed her calm, soft-spoken, and mystical union with God, made all the more profound as she now entered the fullness of her womanhood. It was only natural that Florilyn and Rhawn looked to Gwyneth as the unspoken spiritual head of their threefold cord of friendship. She had been attuning herself to the subtleties of the inner voice all her life. She had learned much that still lay years in the future for them. When they prayed together, however, Gwyneth remained curiously silent. Most of her prayers were prayers of listening. What she had to *say* to God, she said in her heart.

One day when Rhawn appeared at the manor to visit her friends, she wore a strange look on her face. "I have a favor to ask," she said.

Gwyneth and Florilyn waited.

"There is something I want to do. . .something I *need* to do. I am afraid of doing it alone. I have spoken with my parents, and they agree that it is time. I would like to ask the two of you to accompany me."

The three left the manor for town a short while later. They stopped at the Lorimer home where Mr. Lorimer had a buggy hitched and ready. He greeted Florilyn and Gwyneth and took charge of their horses while Rhawn went into the house for her son. A short while later the three girls and young boy, with Rhawn at the reins, set out northward.

By the time they reached their destination, Florilyn and Gwyneth knew what was in Rhawn's heart to do. At length Rhawn reined up in front of Burrenchobay Hall. With her friends at her side and her son's hand in hers, they walked to the front door. When it opened, she asked the butler to see Mr. and Mrs. Burrenchobay.

The wait of two minutes seemed like ten. When at last they heard footsteps approaching, Florilyn and Gwyneth stepped back. Florilyn had her own reasons for being apprehensive. She had not seen Colville's parents since breaking off the engagement. She had no idea what they might have been told.

What the butler had said, or whether they had suspected the truth before now, the expressions on the faces of the member of parliament and his wife were neither hostile nor unwelcoming. Lady Burrenchobay smiled, betraying slight nervousness. Her eyes flitted down to the boy at Rhawn's side. Instantly her eyes filled as the years fell away and she found herself looking at the very image of her son twenty-two years before.

"Hello, Sir Armond. . .Lady Burrenchobay," said Rhawn. "I know this is awkward, and I know you may hate me, and I won't blame you if you do, but you need to know. . .this has waited far too long. I would like to introduce you to your grandson, Amren. Amren, dear, this woman is your grandmother, and this man is your grandfather."

The boy smiled and nodded sheepishly, then held out his hand as he had obviously been told to do.

Swallowing hard and blinking a time or two, Sir Armond reached down and shook it. "A good firm handshake, my boy," he said in a husky voice. "That is a sign of character. Good for you."

Lady Burrenchobay, tears in her eyes, stooped down as her husband stood and stepped back. "Hello, Amren," she said, desperately trying to keep from breaking down altogether. "I am so happy to know you. Would you like to come in and see our house, and perhaps have some biscuits and milk?"

"Yes, ma'am," said Amren. "Thank you very much."

Lady Burrenchobay stood then turned to Rhawn and looked deep into her eyes. "Oh, my dear," she said, taking a step forward and embracing Rhawn affectionately. "I am so sorry for what you have been through. Thank you *so* much!" When she stepped back, she and Rhawn were both weeping.

Rhawn forced a smile then turned. "You both know Florilyn," she said.

"Yes. . .certainly, of course. Hello, Florilyn," said Sir Armond. Neither of Colville's parents knew the full details of what had transpired between Florilyn and their son. They only knew there had been some change. They did not yet know, however, that Florilyn had formally terminated the engagement.

"I would also like you to meet my friend, Gwyneth Barrie," said Rhawn. "You will be hearing more about her, I am certain, in the future. Gwyneth, please meet Sir Armond Burrenchobay and Lady Burrenchobay."

Gwyneth stepped forward, smiled, and shook hands with them both. "I am very pleased to meet you," she said simply. The man and woman returned her smile, disarmed by her penetrating expression and countenance.

Lady Burrenchobay turned again to Rhawn. "Come in, my dear," she said. "I think it is time you and I became better acquainted."

Rhawn looked back at her two friends. She smiled as if to say, *I will be okay now.*

"Shall we come back for you later?" said Florilyn.

"Don't worry about a thing," said Sir Armond. "I will take Rhawn and the little fellow back to Llanfryniog. Perhaps you will stay and have tea with us, Rhawn," he added to Rhawn. "Florilyn, if you would tell Styles that I will bring them home."

SEVENTY-FIVE

The Storm

*A*s the train pulled into the Glasgow station, Gwyneth stared out the window with wide-eyed anticipation.

"Do you remember that first day we met?" asked Percy beside her. "You said you wanted to see Glasgow one day. That's why you asked my name...so you would know who to look for when you came to Glasgow. Well, here we are...and you know my name!"

Gwyneth laughed. "I remember," she said. "I also said I wanted to visit London. Will you take me to London someday?"

"Your wish is my command!"

Having never before had occasion to meet Gwyneth when visiting Wales, Edward and Mary Drummond could not have been more delighted with their future daughter-in-law. After a few days in Glasgow, however, Gwyneth was anxious to see her father again. They had written him, but she wanted to tell him about everything that had happened in person.

She and Percy sailed from Glasgow to Dublin, where Codnor was waiting for them. Though the great change in her life was only a few weeks old, already there was an obvious change in Gwyneth's countenance. What a reunion they had with him and Grannie! Grannie seemed about to die of happiness at the double blessing that had come to Gwyneth. Percy also took her to meet Father O'Leary. With him accompanying them, they paid a visit to Gwyneth's aunt, Vanora Maloney, telling her about Percy's climb up to Percy's Table and revealing Gwyneth's engagement to Percy but not the full details of her altered social status.

With Gwyneth now heir to Westbrooke Manor and its title, her future was obviously in Snowdonia. Her father and Grannie, too, were anxious to return to Wales. What to do with the house on the lower slopes of Lugnaquilla remained uncertain, though Codnor would sell his flock to neighboring sheep farmers at whatever price they could afford. He and Grannie, they said, would try to be ready to sail for Wales by summer. With their former cottages still vacant, both planned to return to life as it had been before. Learning of their plans, however, Katherine would hear nothing of it. They would come live at the manor, she insisted, where Grannie would be well cared for by loving hands and where Gwyneth's father could help Steven with his duties and gradually replace aging Holin Radnor as the manor's groom. Steven could not have been more excited at the prospect of working with his uncle. He had missed shepherding. And Adela was greatly anticipating sitting in the library with her brother and reminiscing about their grandfather's library.

As for Katherine's new house on Mochras Head, due to be completed within a year, it was obvious that Courtenay would not be displacing her from the manor, at least anytime soon. After wondering briefly if she had been too hasty in constructing a new home, Katherine realized that Gwyneth and Percy, as Master and Mistress of Westbrooke Manor, would one day want to have a family of their own and occupy the manor's family quarters on the second floor. Therefore, she would herself take up residence in her new home whenever it suited Gwyneth for her to do so. Notwithstanding that she herself would be legal trustee of the estate until Gwyneth herself turned twenty-five, Katherine quickly began to defer to Gwyneth regarding future plans.

The glaring uncertainty about the future remained to be Courtenay. He returned from London after a month, clearly aware that the prospects of his legal contestation of Gwyneth's position were not favorable. He was rarely seen. What his future held was anyone's guess. Thus far, only Katherine knew of the financial dilemma facing him. Whether she would have bailed him out and cleared off his debt to Litchfield had she been able, she could not have said. But as her every available pound had been sunk into the construction of the new house, it would be two or three years before her resources would sufficiently accumulate to keep Courtenay from serious legal problems. If Litchfield pressed the matter to the extreme and brought charges of fraud against Courtenay, the specter of jail was not out of the question. But she did not see what she could do. She had no intention of asking for Edward's help.

In late May, a month after Percy's and Gwyneth's return from Ireland, a tremendous storm blew in off the North Atlantic, consuming Ireland in wind and hurricane tides. The battering spread through the Irish Sea to the west coast of Scotland and Wales, threatening to flood their low-lying coastal villages. The fishermen of Llanfryniog secured their boats in the harbor as best they could and prepared to ride out the siege, hoping they would not find their boats in splinters when it was over.

The worst of the storm hit between three and five o'clock in the morning. Whether anyone in north Wales was still asleep was doubtful. Most lay awake in their beds, listening to the dreadful tempest doing its best to blow the roofs from their houses. Thankfully those roofs were of heavy Welsh slates!

Percy finally rose about six thirty, thinking himself likely the first in the great mansion to venture from his room. Instead, he found Florilyn and Katherine already in the breakfast room with tea. Mrs. Drynwydd had just put out a pot of fresh coffee.

Steven joined them a few minutes later. "Is the roof still on?" he laughed.

"I thought my window would burst," said Florilyn. "I kept thinking the glass was about to shatter and the rain come splashing in all over my bed!"

"When it is light, Steven," said Katherine, "we will have to check all the upper floors and the garret for leaks."

"I will see to it, as well as the windows on the west and north of the building."

"Where's Gwyneth?" asked Percy, glancing about at the others. "I would expect her to be up at the crack of dawn. She loves tempestuous weather!"

"I think I heard her door close and footsteps in the hall," said Florilyn.

"When?"

"Earlier. . .an hour or more ago."

"Oh, no—then she's out in it!" laughed Percy.

"Do you think she's in any danger?" said Katherine.

"Not for a second," answered Percy. "She could no more be in danger from the weather than Steven could from a sheep. She loves whatever face nature puts on and fears none of them, except snow in the mountains. She does have a healthy regard for the perils of winter."

Percy went to the window and gazed out. The dawn was still dark and gray. Fierce winds whipped at the trees as if it would uproot them with a single blast. In spite of his words to Katherine, the sight sent a momentary shudder up his spine. This wind was stronger than he had ever seen. It could sweep Gwyneth off her feet in an instant. If she stood too near the cliff edge or too close to the sea at the harbor. . . He shuddered to think what might be the result.

After a cup of coffee and a few minutes more conversation, he excused himself, hurried back to his room, bundled himself in what protection from the elements he could, grabbed a second rain slicker, and then left the house by the back stairs and side door.

A great blast of wind nearly knocked him over as he came round the side wall of the house and into the seaward brunt of the storm. Recovering himself, he set off down the drive toward the plateau, bending hard into the face of the tumult. There were only two places where he expected to find Gwyneth. This time he would check *both*.

The rain had let up since the worst of its drenching onslaught between midnight and three. Percy trudged across the spongy, soaked turf toward Katherine's new house. As he passed the house, he could see clearly to the point of the promontory of Mochras Head. It was obvious that Gwyneth was not there or had been blown into the sea!

Percy turned toward town but then paused. He glanced back up at the newly constructed stone walls of Katherine's proposed home. A dozen or more openings where the windows would be installed seemed to look out upon the coastline as if from dead, hollow eye sockets. One day this house would be full of life, Percy thought. Those window-eyes would gaze out upon the countryside with light from within. As yet, however, the edifice was an empty shell awaiting the life of human touch, in the same way that the human animal had been an empty shell until implanted with the soul-life of God's divine touch.

Moved by some impulse, he turned and walked toward the house. He entered through one of several openings where doors, like the windows, would eventually be installed. He had been inside the house with Steven a time or two since his arrival back in Wales but had paid little attention to the details of its interior. Now he stood gazing about in the darkness of a stormy morning. All around him were the signs of construction—piles of boards, half-finished walls and ceilings, and bare floors. The wind whistled and sang through its many openings, up and down staircases, around corners, and through vacant rooms.

Slowly Percy made his way to the stone staircase at the center of the ground floor and up to the landing above the first floor. Something seemed to guide his steps. Ahead of him, the centerpiece of the entire house, envisioned in Katherine's mind's eye from the beginning, was what would be the large central sitting room, facing due west toward the promontory, its seaward wall comprised nearly in its entirety of three enormous windows, giving the entire room a spectacular vantage point of the promontory. The coastline stretched away north and south as far as the eye could see. The view straight ahead looked out westward toward Ireland, whose own coastline, Katherine hoped, on a clear day, might faintly be seen.

As Percy entered, across the great room, he saw a figure seated on the bare stone floor six or eight feet away from the opening of the largest central window.

The early riser knew whose footsteps were approaching behind her without turning.

Percy sat down beside her and took her hand in his.

"There could not be a house with a more beautiful view than this," said Gwyneth quietly.

"How long have you been here?" asked Percy.

"I don't know," replied Gwyneth. "The storm drew me. I think I have changed my mind about Lady Katherine's new house. It is the perfect place to have built it. How did you know where to find me?"

"I didn't. This time, if you weren't here, I was planning to check the harbor next!"

They sat for a few minutes in silence, gazing out at the wild, windy, gray sky and sea blended in turbulent motion. The sea appeared angry, but Gwyneth found it no less mesmerizing than on a day when its radiant blues and greens stretched westward to the land of her birth.

"As I was looking up at the house, with the empty windows," said Percy, "it reminded me of the empty eyes of the skull you saw in the cave."

"Don't remind me. It frightened me to death!"

"If ever a storm were going to wash the sand away from that old pirate again, this would be the time."

"Do you really think what I saw was the skull of the old pirate from Grannie's tale, the same man who gave her the coin?"

"I thought she said they found the man dead on the beach the next morning."

"Oh, that's right. Then who did the skull belong to?"

"Maybe there were two pirates. What if one of them made it to the cave, but the man Grannie saw didn't? We'll go look at low tide as soon as the storm passes!"

"Not me, Percy!"

"Then I will go myself."

"Well. . .maybe I will go with you."

SEVENTY-SIX

The Cave

*T*he idea of exploring the cave again did not leave Percy all day. By late afternoon the storm showed signs of easing. When night fell, the moon was making sporadic appearances between the clouds, and the wind had nearly ceased. By then Gwyneth's enthusiasm for the project had mounted as well.

When Percy appeared in the breakfast room the next morning, she was eagerly waiting for him. "The tide is rising, Percy," she said excitedly. "It will be high sometime before noon."

"What—you've already been out!"

"Of course," she laughed.

"Don't we need a low tide?" he asked.

"Yes, and low tide will be late in the afternoon when the sun is going down. It will be perfect—the sun will shine off the water straight into the cave!"

"This afternoon it is, then. We have a date with a pirate's skull!"

They were at the beach by three, walking leisurely hand in hand along the shoreline at the water's edge of the outgoing tide. It was obvious to Gwyneth's eyes that the storm had wreaked havoc with the coastline she knew so well. She scampered about looking at everything excitedly.

By four o'clock, the water had retreated most of the way out of the cave's mouth, and they crept inside.

"The cave floor is lower," said Gwyneth as they made their way into the darkness. "I can tell that the roof is higher above me. The outgoing tide must have removed at least six inches of sand."

"Can you remember where you saw the skull?"

"I don't know—about halfway back to the end, I think."

As their eyes accustomed to the darkness, Percy went to his knees and began to crawl about on all fours, his eyes probing and his hands feeling the sand. Back and forth he crawled, feeling about, digging with his fingers all around the area where Gwyneth thought the skull might have been.

"Wait. . .there, I felt something hard," he said at length. He brushed his hands about the spot again. "Yes, there it is—look," he said, removing bit of wet sand from the spot.

"Look, yes. . .I think it's a bit of bone!"

Percy continued to rub away the sand then scooped more away with his hand until the rounded top of a human cranium was clearly visible. "It's the pirate!"

"Oh Percy, let's leave him where he is. I don't think I can bear to see those horrid empty eyes again."

"We've got to solve the mystery. What was he doing here? I'll go get a spade from Chandos."

"Wait for me. I don't want to be left alone. . .with *him*!"

They ran out of the cave. In the distance, in the direction of the harbor, they saw two horses. As Percy ran toward them, he saw Steven and Florilyn.

"Where are you off to in such a hurry?" laughed Steven.

"I think we found the old pirate in the cave!" he replied. "I'm going to find a spade."

"Pirate!" exclaimed Steven, but already Percy was running toward the village.

A minute later Gwyneth came hurrying up. They dismounted and tied their horses at the harbor.

"What's this about a pirate, Gwyneth?" asked Florilyn.

"Haven't I ever told you about the pirate's skull I found?"

"No. . .ugh—that sounds horrid!"

"It was in the cave back there, after a terrific storm when the tide was low—just like today. You know the cave, Steven. All the children played in it. I never saw it after that. It was covered over with sand. Percy thinks we've found it again. He wants to dig it up."

"But why?"

"Because when Grannie was a girl, she saw a pirate who had washed up on the beach from a shipwreck. He gave her a gold coin."

"Gold!"

"The pirate said there was more. But by the next morning he was dead. Look—I've got the coin right here. Grannie gave it to me." She dug in her pocket and pulled out the coin.

Steven and Florilyn looked at it with wide eyes. "I want to see this pirate!" said Steven.

He ran on ahead. By the time Gwyneth and Florilyn followed him into the darkness of the cave, Steven was on his hands and knees where he saw evidence of Percy's clawing about the cave floor, digging in the hard-packed sand with his fingers.

When Percy returned five minutes later with a spade, Steven had uncovered the eye sockets that had struck such fear into thirteen-year-old Gwyneth Barrie. Immediately, Percy set in with the spade.

"Careful. . .careful," said Steven. "If the old fellow's head is still attached to the rest of him, you don't want to behead him."

"Steven. . .ugh!" exclaimed Florilyn.

Slowly as they dug down, the skull came more into view. Percy gently loosened the sand while Steven scooped it away with his hands. The two girls gradually moved back out of the cave into the sunlight. This was man's work. They had seen enough!

By now the day was reaching its end. Most of the village men were either on their way to Mistress Chattan's inn for a pint of ale or were walking home from their day's labors for evening tea.

The sun continued to settle toward the western horizon. As it did, it sent longer and longer shafts of light into the mouth of the cave where Percy and Steven continued with what seemed to Gwyneth and

Florilyn a gruesome task.

It did not take much more excavation before the excited young men were convinced that it was no mere skull Gwyneth had discovered seven years before but the entire skeleton of a man laying his full length toward the mouth of the cave, buried a foot beneath the surface. A few shards of clothing remained, preserved in the salty, sandy grave.

"Come look!" yelled Percy, his voice echoing to the outside through the cave mouth. "We've found the pirate. . .all of him!"

"I don't want to look!" Florilyn shouted back. "I would have nightmares for weeks."

But Gwyneth ventured slowly back inside. She stood for a moment looking down at the trench Percy and Steven had dug in the growing light. A bony human frame lay at the bottom of it, still more than half embedded in the hard sand.

"It looks like he was trying to crawl out of the cave," she said. "If he was trying to get away from the other man—the pirate who gave Grannie the coin—or if he was trying to find shelter in the cave, he should be facing the other direction."

"You're right," said Steven. "I hadn't thought of that. Why is he facing toward the cave mouth?"

"Maybe he came in here for shelter," suggested Percy, "but then was trapped by the incoming tide and tried to get out but then drowned."

By then the rays of the setting sun were sending their light from the level of the sea directly into the mouth of the cave, illuminating its wet walls of rock and sandy floor that sloped up toward the back of the cave. As Percy glanced about, it seemed as though the violent waters of the storm had also cleared away a good amount of the sand from the back of the cave wall. Slowly he wandered deeper inside where the rock ceiling above him sloped down to meet the cave floor. He dropped to his hands and knees to examine the farthest end of the cave.

"What have you found?" asked Steven, following him.

"I don't know, maybe nothing," replied Percy. "I remember being curious about this before. Now that the sunlight is shining on the back of the cave. . .it looks different. Some of the sand is gone. And look, there is a trickle of water coming out from somewhere."

"What's this," said Steven, stooping and probing with his hand. "It looks like. . ." He dug about harder. "There is a small hole that extends through the rock. . .or under it."

Percy scrambled back for the spade. Within seconds, he was again at Steven's side, digging away furiously at the base of what appeared as the back wall of the cave. After a minute he stopped, stretched out on his belly, and reached his hand through the opening he had made under the rock, feeling about with his fingers. In another moment, his hand poked through into an opening behind it. Immediately a rush of cool air met his face.

"There's a cavity behind the rock," he said. He stretched his arm as far as he could through the hole. "I'm moving my hand about. I think the cave goes farther back. It's been blocked up by sand!"

He pulled his arm out, grabbed the spade again, and now began digging harder than ever.

"I can feel back in there. There's definitely an opening! And I'm feeling something. . . . It feels like rope."

"Watch yourself," said Steven. "It might be alive!"

By now Gwyneth had come up behind them and was watching intently. Even Florilyn, hearing the conversation in the distance, crept a step or two into the cave mouth to listen.

Working together, Percy and Steven managed to excavate an opening a foot deep under the back wall of the cave. As it required digging out below the level of the cave floor, it would fill with sea water the moment the incoming tide reached it again. As soon as it did, their excavated tunnel would fill with sand.

"We've got to get a deeper opening," said Percy. "I need to squeeze in before the tide."

"You're not going to crawl back through there?" said Steven.

"I'm thinner than you. Somebody has to. We have to see what's there."

"And if the tide comes in, you'll be trapped inside! A hundred years from now someone will be digging up *your* skeleton."

"I have more faith in you than that," laughed Percy. "You won't let that happen to me."

"Then we need to dig a wider opening," said Steven. He took up the spade again.

Without looking too closely, Florilyn crept past the crypt where the silent skeleton lay. Both girls now watched the progress. They did not like the idea of Percy trying to crawl into what looked like an opening too small for a cat.

Fifteen minutes later, a tunnel through the cave floor under the sloping back wall appeared large enough for Percy to make an attempt.

"Percy, be careful!" said Florilyn.

"I don't know that I like this," said Gwyneth. "Once it turns, the tide rises quickly."

"Then you all keep an eye on it. The moment there is any danger, I promise I'll come right back out." Percy lay flat, the entire front of his body now wet, and began to wriggle and squeeze into the opening he and Steven had excavated. Inch by inch, he wormed his way into the darkness until his feet disappeared from sight.

"Percy!" wailed Florilyn.

As her voice echoed away, the cave fell silent.

The next sound they heard was Percy's voice. It sounded a mile away and echoed strangely off the stone walls of the cave.

"I'm inside a small chamber," he said. "It's nearly black. I can't see a thing. I'm feeling about. . .there's not room to stand. . .it's probably five feet by four feet. The larger cave must originally have included this little back part. There is definitely a rope and. . .now I'm feeling what I think are two or three cork floats. It must have washed in here when the cave was open. . .and. . .wait, there's something. . ."

The other three waited.

"There's some kind of box," Percy's voice echoed back again. "I can't see it, but. . .it's too heavy to lift. It's tangled up in the rope. Steven, hand your knife through. I'll try to cut away some of the rope."

Steven lay down and stretched his hand through the tunnel. A moment later, Percy's hand fumbled from the other side, grabbing for the knife. Again they waited.

"I've cut it away from this mess of rope," called Percy. "I can hardly move it...it feels like there's a lock...it must be made of metal, otherwise it would have rotted. Here, Steven, take your knife."

Again Steven reached through and retrieved his knife.

"I'll try to get the box into the opening. . . . I'll shove it your way... you're stronger than I am, Steven—if you can pull it through..." Grunting and pushing sounds followed as Percy struggled with whatever he had discovered.

Still on his stomach looking through the tunnel with what light the sun sent in, Steven saw the black end of a box some eight or nine inches square being pushed toward him from the inner portion of the cave.

"That's as far as I can move it," Percy called to him. "It's so heavy it wants to sink into the sand. I can't budge it another inch."

Steven stretched his hand as far as he could reach. It took several minutes and a great effort, but inch by inch he managed to pull the box through toward the open side of the cave. As the girls waited anxiously, behind them a wave sounded on the shoreline outside.

"Percy...the tide!" cried Florilyn. "Whatever is in there isn't worth you getting trapped!"

Gwyneth turned and ran out to the beach, glanced to her right and left, then out to sea, then hurried back inside. "The tide has turned, Percy," she said into the darkened tunnel of the cave floor. "Probably fifteen minutes ago."

"She's right, old man," said Steven. "I didn't want to mention it, but the bottom of this little tunnel we dug is getting soggy. It will fill up with water anytime. I've got the box. It's time you got out of there before this cave becomes known for *two* graves."

"Just give me another minute or two. I want to make sure there's nothing else in here."

"Like another pirate!"

"I don't know. But we may not have this chance again."

"Percy!" cried Florilyn again.

By the time the fading light of the sun began to reflect off Percy's white face as he wriggled back into the front of the cave, his hair was matted and wet, and his shirt and trousers soaked and caked with sand. Both girls let out great sighs of relief when he was through and back on his hands and knees.

Nearly the same moment the sun began to sink below the horizon. The briefly lit cave again grew dark.

"I'm getting out of here while I can still see," said Florilyn. "I don't want to trip and fall on that old pirate!"

Gwyneth followed her out. Percy and Steven together lugged the small chest behind them into the open air.

"This thing weighs a ton!" said Percy. "It must be made of solid lead."

"Are you going to open it?" said Florilyn excitedly.

"The box must be of brass or silver not to have rusted," began Steven, "but that lock is definitely rusted shut."

Percy turned and ran back inside the cave. He returned with the spade. Two whacks was all it took to demolish latch and lock together.

The four knelt down around it.

"Well, Gwyneth," said Percy. "If you are the future owner of all this, which I assume includes the land all the way down to the water's edge, I suppose technically this box belongs to you. You should do the honors."

"You discovered it, Percy," said Gwyneth. "I would rather you open it."

Percy reached out his hand, took hold of the broken latch, and pulled hard on the lid. The two rusted hinges on the other side shattered. The lid swung free and flew back.

Four gasps of disbelief sounded simultaneously at the sight that met their eyes in the golden light of the setting sun.

SEVENTY-SEVEN

Rebuke and Forgiveness

*I*t took some time for their stupefaction at what they had found, and their subsequent frenzied discussion of what it must be worth, to subside.

Steven at length sounded the practical note. "We need to get this back to the manor," he said. "We obviously can't carry it. I'll ride back and bring a buggy. Florilyn and I left our horses at the harbor."

"I'll go with you," said Florilyn, jumping to her feet.

"And we shall stand guard," added Percy.

"Do you really think all that gold is mine, Percy?" asked Gwyneth when they were again alone and dusk began to settle around them.

"It will be. I suppose it is Aunt Katherine's right now. Who else's would it be but yours?"

"You and Steven found it."

"All four of us found it. . .and on *your* land."

"What will be my land. Or *may* be. It's not mine yet. But this gold must belong to somebody."

"I doubt it. Look at these inscriptions," said Percy, removing one of the gold coins from the chest. I never paid much attention to the markings on Grannie's coin before. But these are all identical—and very old. Those pirates must have stumbled on some ancient site, maybe going back to King Alfred's time or earlier. I'm no expert, but I would guess these to be of Celtic origin from somewhere in Wales or Scotland or Ireland. Whatever the value of the gold, which is considerable, the historical value is probably greater."

"What should we do with it?"

"That will be up to you and Aunt Katherine."

After Steven and Percy had lugged the bog to the waiting buggy at the harbor, and once it was safely locked in the safe in the late viscount's office that evening, Katherine, Gwyneth, and Percy had a long discussion. They judged it best to say nothing to anyone for the present, even to Courtenay. They needed to consult with experts and seek legal advice without allowing rumors to begin circulating.

Meanwhile, Katherine told several of the leading men of the village about the skeleton that had been found. That would be fuel for rumor enough. She arranged for them to dig up the remains and bury them in the village cemetery beside the shipmate who had been found two generations before.

At first pass, Hamilton Murray agreed with Percy's assessment that the gold belonged to the Westbrooke estate where it had been found. He would look into the matter, he said. In the meantime, if they had need of any portion of it, he could arrange to sell some of the coins through confidential antiquarian sources.

A few weeks later, Percy and Gwyneth returned to Ireland to help Gwyneth's father with the return move to Wales. Codnor Barrie and Grannie arrived back in Llanfryniog in July. By now, all of North Wales knew that the former urchin and witch-child of Llanfryniog had all along been the viscount's secret granddaughter and was now the future viscountess and Lady Snowdon. This raised Codnor Barrie and Grannie almost to the level of royalty in the eyes of their former neighbors. Their arrival was greeted with great fanfare.

One person who was not rejoicing at the many changes coming to Westbrooke Manor was Courtenay Westbrooke. In his opinion, the place was becoming a home for peasants and vagabonds. The sooner he could get away from it the better. But he had bigger problems than Gwyneth and her family. His mother did not have the money to clear off his debt to Litchfield. She had as good as told him she wouldn't do so even if she did. Pride prevented him going cap in hand to his religious uncle, Percy's father, for a handout.

It killed him, but he knew there was only one way to hope to raise a portion of the cash needed to keep him out of jail. He would have to sell his racehorses. He had floated an offer to Lord Litchfield, offering his four thoroughbreds in exchange for the full sum. Though the reply had been sent in writing, he could feel Litchfield laughing in his face at the absurdity of the suggestion, concluding with a summary of the current amount due, including interest, and a renewed threat of legal action if the matter was not resolved in a timely fashion.

He might be able to get £2,500 for the four animals, £3,000 *if* he was lucky. That would hardly raise half the cash he needed. And where would he find buyers out in this wasteland of North Wales? He was in trouble, and he knew it. Litchfield's were no idle threats. He knew the man would have no qualms seeing him sent to prison. If he could just get his fastest horse into a race or two during the summer, perhaps the winnings would get him out of this pickle.

He walked into the new stables in an irritable temper, piqued to think that he might soon have to say good-bye to these magnificent horses and angry at the rest of the world for putting him in this position. He was especially angry at his father for his ridiculous deathbed pangs of conscience, at Percy for interfering when he could have simply let the thing drop, at his mother for all her religious claptrap, and most of all at the little fool Gwyneth Barrie for. . .just for being alive at all. Blast his father for his youthful indiscretion! Why couldn't he have just died and let his secret be buried with him.

As his eyes accustomed to the dim light, he saw someone standing in front of the stall of the jewel of his stable, a three-year-old reddish-brown filly from the South of France. He had had such high hopes for this animal.

As he walked closer, his pent-up frustration finally exploded. "Gwyneth, what are you doing here?" he cried angrily. "Get away from that horse!"

"She won't hurt me, Courtenay," said Gwyneth calmly.

"It's not you I'm worried about. Get back, I tell you. That is an expensive racehorse. You've meddled enough in my affairs. I won't have you disturbing my animals."

"I'm sorry, Courtenay," said Gwyneth as she stepped back.

"These horses of mine are extremely valuable. I don't want you near them, is that clear? What do you know about horses anyway? Because of you, I am being forced to sell them to pay a debt that I would not have if it weren't for you. You have caused me enough trouble without meddling with my thoroughbreds."

"I didn't mean to meddle."

"No, no. . .of course you didn't *mean* to," said Courtenay sarcastically. "You never mean anything but sweetness and light, do you? But I know your conniving little game. You wormed your way into the manor with my sister and mother years ago. Then somehow you deceived my father into thinking you were his heir. But it won't work, you little vixen. You are a crafty one, and you've got them all blinded to the truth, especially my imbecilic cousin. He is nothing but a fool. The two of you deserve one another. But I know your game, and it won't work. I will fight you in court. When I become viscount, don't come to me for any handouts. Enjoy it while you can, because the moment I am able, I will throw you and your father out in the street and never think twice about it, and that idiot Percy with you. Now get out of here, you stuttering little white-haired shrew, before you make me angry!"

Gwyneth's eyes stung from the bitter rebuke. She turned and ran from the barn.

From one of the library windows, Percy saw the familiar figure running down the drive then onto the plateau and down the incline toward her former home. She was running too fast, he thought. Gwyneth's was a spirit whose deep currents ran as calm placid waters, not as turbulent rapids. The sight of her flying across the grass seemed wrong.

He turned from the window, set down the book in his hand, and made for the stairway. He had a feeling he knew where he would find her. He did not hurry as he left the house but walked purposefully in the direction he had last seen her.

About twenty minutes later, he approached the still-vacant cottage. Behind it, where the pens and fences and coops and shelters for her animals had once been, he saw Gwyneth seated on the grass with her back to the house. Slowly he walked forward and sat down beside her. She was gently stroking the back of a small rabbit in her lap. She did not turn toward him.

"Bunny White Tail remembers you," he said.

She nodded.

"I see you coming here nearly every day. Are the animals beginning to return?"

Again Gwyneth nodded but kept her face down. No words were spoken for a minute or two.

"Gwyneth?" said Percy at length. "What is it?"

At last she turned toward him. Her eyes were red. Her face wore the most miserable, forlorn expression he had ever seen. She tried to speak but only succeeded in breaking out in fresh sobs.

"Gwyneth. . .what happened?" said Percy, stretching his arm around her.

"Oh, Percy. . .I don't know what to do!" she wailed, laying her head against his shoulder.

"About what?"

"About Courtenay. I don't want to have people think I am an important person. I don't want to inherit all this and have a title. I don't want it, Percy! Why shouldn't I let Courtenay have it?"

Percy waited before replying. Gradually Gwyneth's tears spent themselves. They sat several minutes in silence. In the distance, a doe with two fawns wandered out of a thicket of woods and seemed to think about coming closer. Several other rabbits scampered about the meadow in front of them.

"You know what I would say in answer to your question?" said Percy at length.

"I think so—that it is my duty. . .that I would probably treat the people more fairly than Courtenay would. . .that my grandfather—it is still hard to think of him as that. . .Lord Snowdon, that he would want me to accept my rightful inheritance."

"Why do you feel you should not?"

"I don't know. . .I just. . .it is hard to have people think bad things of me."

"Who thinks ill of you, Gwyneth?"

Again Gwyneth did not answer.

"What happened, Gwyneth? Something happened. What was it?"

"Do I have to tell you?"

"I won't make you, if that is what you mean. But I would like for you to tell me."

Gwyneth was quiet then drew in a long breath. "Courtenay was rude to me," she said. "He said cruel things. I don't know if it is worth it. It seems easier to simply let him have what he wants. People have been cruel to me all my life. But that doesn't make it easy. It still hurts. It hurts deep, Percy." Again Gwyneth began to gently weep.

"Gwyneth," said Percy at length, "it is obvious that Courtenay is selfish and immature, even in what just happened. He is not qualified to be viscount. He would probably double rents just to pay for his silly scheme of racing horses. If he is cruel to you, imagine what he would be like to his tenants. Do you want to be responsible for the cruelty he might inflict on others?"

Gwyneth sighed and slowly shook her head.

"If by some chance Courtenay matures and reforms and somehow is able to conquer his self-centeredness," Percy went on, "maybe when he is thirty-five or forty or fifty, if you feel he would make a compassionate landlord and viscount and you still do not like being in the position you are in. . .nothing would stop you from stepping aside at that point. People relinquish titles. You could do so then, and Courtenay would inherit. By then he might be of a character that you could trust to do good for the people."

"That is wise, Percy," said Gwyneth after a moment. "That is *very* wise. I had not thought of that. I don't have to make a decision right now that will be binding forever. I am still young, too. In my own way I may be just as immature as Courtenay. I need to grow inside, just like he does. After all, I will not even inherit for several years. Everything does not have to be decided immediately."

They sat and watched the rabbits and deer, though none made closer approach.

"Don't worry about Courtenay," said Percy at length. "I will have a talk with him and tell him to stay away from you. If he is rude to you again, he will have to answer to me for it."

"I would rather you did not talk to him, Percy."

"Why?"

"I don't want the two of you arguing over me. This is time for another forgiveness bouquet. Then you and I will think of what Courtenay said to me no more."

Percy sighed then nodded.

"I would rather march back to the house and take it out of his hide," he said, then paused and nodded. "But you are right."

It was silent a moment.

"So will you pick a handful of wildflowers on the way back?" he asked.

"I don't know," replied Gwyneth thoughtfully. "That would only make Courtenay laugh at my childishness. I think I must find something that will get the forgiveness deep inside him—some other kind of forgiveness bouquet than wildflowers."

Percy rose. Gwyneth set Bunny White Tail on the grass, and Percy helped her to her feet. They walked slowly back in the direction of the cottage.

"What does that mean?" said Percy, pointing to the words in Gaelic carved into the stones near the front door.

"Mor bhairne a Inbhear Dé" said Gwyneth. "That's what my father named the house."

"What does it mean?"

"It's my mother's name in Gaelic—Morvern from Arklow. He never wanted to forget her."

"Of course. Now I remember—I saw it at your house in Ireland! This was the clue I needed to find you. It was right in front of me all along!"

"If you had known what the Gaelic meant. . ."

SEVENTY-EIGHT

An Equine Bouquet

$\mathcal{P}$ercy and Gwyneth left the cottage, walked toward the coastline, up the edge of the promontory, then turned toward Katherine's new home and slowly made their way back in the direction of the manor. They had been so preoccupied that they had not noticed the single horse and buggy coming up the main road that had turned into the manor drive some time before. When they arrived back at the manor, they found the rest of the family, along with Hamilton Murray, waiting for them. Courtenay had been apprised of the fact that the family solicitor had come with news of the disposition of the estate. He declined to be present. A written notice of the same news in the form of a letter was, in fact, awaiting him in town at the post.

"I have come," Murray began when Katherine, Florilyn, Percy, Gwyneth, Steven, and Codnor were all seated, "with good news to report. Just yesterday I received word from the barrister in London who has been representing your son, Lady Katherine, informing me that all legal objections have been dropped. He had, he said, extensively researched both the Snowdon viscountcy as well as the evidence I had presented him concerning Miss Barrie's claim. He reached the conclusion that it was no longer in his interest to pursue the contest against her inheritance. He was therefore dropping the suit. He could not predict what would be his client's response, he said. He was likely perhaps to engage other counsel, though he assured me that no suit, after what his research had made clear, would succeed. After receiving his letter, therefore, I immediately filed the necessary documents concerning title, as well as your continuing trusteeship, Lady Katherine, until such time as Miss Barrie's formal assumption of her title."

Murray paused then walked to the couch where Gwyneth sat at Percy's side. He reached out his hand.

Slowly Gwyneth rose.

"May I be the first to congratulate you, Miss Barrie," said Murray, "or, I should say, now as the recognized heir apparent to your grandfather's viscountcy, Mistress of Snowdon."

The others rose and gathered around her, with many hugs and kisses and warm congratulations. Still ambivilant and uncertain, Gwyneth accepted their attentions with embarrassed gratitude.

As the young people were talking among themselves, Gwyneth's father sidled up to Katherine. "I think I have nearly begun to understand how all the pieces of this puzzle fit together," he said in a tone of wry humor. "You will of course continue to be *Lady* Westbrooke. . .but I wonder what people will call *me*. Do you suppose I will have to get used to wearing a top hat?"

Katherine laughed. "Who would make you, Codnor?" she said. "Surely not the future viscountess."

"I don't know—custom, convention, tradition. Maybe my Gwyneth will turn hoity-toity and uppity when she inherits."

"You don't really believe that. . . ."

"No," replied Codnor with a light chuckle.

"I cannot imagine a title having less power to go to anyone's head than Gwyneth's," added Katherine.

Already having had a long ride, and the afternoon drawing down upon them, Hamilton Murray willingly accepted Katherine's offer to spend the night at the manor. A brief conversation between Katherine and Gwyneth, largely bearing on the specifics of Courtenay's financial difficulties, resulted in a private meeting of some length between Murray and the two women after evening tea during which the disposition of a portion of the gold in the safe was discussed.

The result was, when he returned the next day to Porthmadog, that Hamilton Murray's briefcase carried one of the long-buried coins to have appraised. Gwyneth was desirous, with Katherine's blessing, of raising, she said, a sum of approximately £5,500.

Six weeks later, following the completion of the several aspects of her plan, Gwyneth set out alone one morning for a walk in the hills. Gathering this bouquet was something she needed to do alone, that the exercise might accomplish its full work within her. Forgiveness always comes with a price. It is a price whose payment deepens the wells of character within the human soul and draws both payer and payee closer to the heart of God. In the case of the latter, however, those results may not easily nor quickly be seen. As Gwyneth went, therefore, her prayers were full on behalf of Courtenay. It was not easy to find blooms at this time of year as autumn began, but she was determined to find them.

Later that afternoon, after watching for her opportunity, Gwyneth saw Courtenay approaching the stables. She hurried after him then paused at the door. "Courtenay," she called into the darkness.

A moment later his voice sounded from inside. "What do you want?" he said.

"May I see you for a moment?"

"No. Go away."

"Please, Courtenay. I know you do not want me going near your horses, but please. . .just for a moment."

Gwyneth heard a muttered oath, and then footsteps approached. Slowly Courtenay's scowling face came into view. "All right, here I am," he barked. "What do you want? I'm busy."

"I wanted to give you this," said Gwyneth. She handed him a small bouquet of wildflowers, tied with a short length of ribbon. She then turned and walked away.

Courtenay started to throw it to the ground, intending to grind the flowers in the dirt with his foot. At the last moment he noticed that among them was tied what appeared to be a tightly rolled slip of paper. Curious, he fumbled with it, letting the flowers drop to the ground as he did. He loosened it from the ribbon then unrolled the paper. He found that he was holding a three-inch by nine-inch parchment, along the top of which was imprinted the single word RECEIPT.

Below Courtenay read the words, *"Received of Gwyneth Barrie, on behalf of Courtenay Westbrooke, the sum of £5,379. All indebtedness, including interest, in repayment of earnest money deposit, paid in full."* It was signed, *"Lord Coleraine Litchfield."*

Thunderstruck, Courtenay stared at the paper in disbelief. He read over the words a second time then finally looked up.

Gwyneth was just disappearing into the house.

Quickly he stooped down, picked up the flowers she had spent three hours to find, and hurried after her. "Wait. . .Gwyneth, wait!" he called.

She turned and faced him.

"What is. . .I mean, is this. . .what does this mean—how did you. . ."

"I paid your bill," said Gwyneth simply.

"So. . .I don't understand. Do I now owe you the money?"

"No, Courtenay, you owe me nothing."

"But it was *my* debt."

"I know. But I took your debt on myself so that you would not have to pay it."

"Why would you do that?" he said, shaking his head in stunned disbelief.

"Because I care about you, Courtenay, and I want the best for you. After all, you are my half brother or my uncle or something—I still am a little confused about all that. I think you are my uncle. But most of all, you are a person God made and that makes you wonderful and special. I think I will even learn to love you in time. For now I wanted to do something for you to show you that I bear you no ill will despite that you are sometimes cruel to me. But I do not think you will be rude to me after this, because you will know that you are forgiven."

Speechless, Courtenay stared at her for another moment then turned, still holding both receipt and forgiveness bouquet, and walked slowly back in the direction of the stables.

SEVENTY-NINE

The Offer

*C*ourtenay excitedly read for the third time the letter that had come that morning. He could hardly believe the words on the page in front of him.

> *Dear Mr. Westbrooke,* he read.
>
> *A late scratch by one of the primary contenders in next month's Chester Open has left the field one entrant short. Because of the strong showing by your three-year-old Viscount's Pride in the Wales Handicap two months ago, the organizers would like to offer you this final slot in our field. Please reply as soon as possible. This year's entry fee is £225.*
>
>

I am,

Sincerely yours,

Garfield Smythe,

Chairman of the Organizing Committee,

The Chester Open

Courtenay set the letter down, his mind racing. This was the opportunity he had been waiting for! But he had spent his account completely dry engaging that imbecile of a barrister in London who now said there was nothing more he could do. Where could he lay his hands on £225?

For the rest of the day, Courtenay hung about more than was generally his custom. Early in the afternoon, Percy, Steven, and Codnor rode into the hills to check on the new flock of sheep they had taken to one of the high meadows a month earlier. He happened to know that Florilyn was in town visiting Rhawn Lorimer. He also knew that Gwyneth never remained cooped up inside on a nice day for long.

He busied himself in and about the stables, checking on his horses, dreaming and scheming what he dared hope might be a chance to compete in a major race. After about twenty minutes, he saw Gwyneth walking from the kitchen garden behind the house. Though shorter than any of the young people of the manor, the grace and dignity of her bearing made her appear taller than she actually was. Even wearing a worker's frock and with her hands soiled with dirt, one look was enough to command an observer's attention. Her entire countenance said that here was a young woman somehow set apart from her peers. As yet, however, because they were focused on himself, Courtenay's eyes were unseeing of all this. He came out from the shadow of the barn and, with pretended nonchalance, intercepted her.

"Hello, Courtenay," said Gwyneth sweetly.

"What are you doing today?" he asked.

"I was helping Mrs. Drynwydd pick the beans for tonight's dinner."

"If you are going to be viscountess one day, don't you think you should let the servants do that kind of work?"

"I will never want anyone waiting on me. Why should someone else do for me what I can do well enough for myself. Besides, I like to work."

An awkward silence followed.

"I say, uh. . .Gwyneth," began Courtenay, "you know my, uh—the racehorses that you, well. . .that you helped me keep?"

"Of course, Courtenay."

"I have a chance. . .that is, I've been invited to enter a big race next month."

"Oh, that's wonderful, Courtenay. Congratulations."

"Thank you," he said, smiling awkwardly. "It wouldn't have been possible if you hadn't. . .you know, done what you did."

Gwyneth smiled.

"Are you, uh. . .interested in horses?"

"I thought you knew that. I love all kinds of animals, especially horses."

"Do you think I should enter the race?"

"Oh yes—it sounds like just what you have wanted."

"Yes, well. . .actually, yes it is. I would be very excited about it if. . . well, you see, there is one little problem. I need £225 to enter the race."

"Don't you have that much?"

"I'm afraid not."

"And you are trying to find a way to ask if you could borrow it from me," said Gwyneth with the hint of a playful smile.

"I suppose that is about the size of it," replied Courtenay, with an uncharacteristically sheepish expression on his own face.

"What would you say if I just *gave* you the money instead of loaned it to you?"

"I would be very appreciative."

"It would be my investment in your horses."

"I suppose that is only fair, since I wouldn't even have them if it weren't for you. So how big a cut of the action would you want for your investment?"

"I'm not sure what you mean. What is a cut of the action?"

"What percentage of my winnings would be yours, and what percentage would be mine?"

"I don't want anything in return, Courtenay!" laughed Gwyneth. "Whatever you win would be yours."

"What about the entry fee—you know, the two-twenty-five?"

"If I give it to you, Courtenay, I would not expect it back. Don't you know what Jesus said—to do good and lend and give to others and expect nothing in return? I try to do what Jesus said, that is all. The money would be yours, Courtenay."

"Hmm. . .yes, well. . .there is that, I suppose, though I never thought of anything *He* said having to do with finances or racehorses."

"But," Gwyneth added, "there would be one condition."

"A condition—what kind of condition?"

"Would you be riding in the race yourself?"

Courtenay nodded.

"Then if I am going to invest in this race, I would want to give you riding lessons."

"What!" Courtenay began in a blustering tone. "Do you think that you are actually—" He stopped abruptly and managed to control himself. This was a gift horse into whose mouth he didn't want to look too closely! He drew in a deep breath, trying to find the wherewithal to swallow his gigantic pride—no mean feat for one like Courtenay— and put up with whatever absurdities were being hatched in Gwyneth's brain.

"Yes, Courtenay," said Gwyneth. "I know what you are thinking, that you are a superior horseman to me. But you are not all you could be. If you gave me two weeks with any of your horses, I would beat you in a race with you riding any of the others. I know how to talk to horses in a way you don't, Courtenay. You are not that good in the saddle. I can teach you to race much faster."

Momentarily Courtenay's calm gave way.

"How dare you propose to—" he began. Again he caught himself. This was galling, but if he wanted to race, he had no choice. "What exactly did you have in mind?" he said.

"Just to teach you how to talk to your horses, how to sit in the saddle, and how to ride faster. It will take me a few days to get you the £225. I will have to speak to my father and some other people. Would you like to start your riding lessons tomorrow?"

"Whatever you say," replied Courtenay with a supreme effort at self-control.

"Then we will take two horses to the wide sand south of the harbor tomorrow at low tide," said Gwyneth. "You should ride the horse you plan to race, and I will show you how fast it might be."

"I will be sure to bring my whip," said Courtenay with a touch of sarcasm.

"You will not need your whip, Courtenay. The only use it might have would be to show you, if you tried to use it, how much faster than you I can ride without it. But I would rather you did not bring it. I don't think you will ever need your whip again."

"We shall see about that."

For the next week, every day at low tide, Courtenay and Gwyneth met at the beach for Courtenay's riding lessons. By the third day, Courtenay ceased his objections. Whether he had begun to *see* into Gwyneth as a person was doubtful, but he was a sufficient horseman to recognize that she knew what she was about.

From the promontory above the beach, Percy, Florilyn, and Steven watched the proceedings every day with amusement. What they would not have given to be able to hear the conversation taking place on the sand below them.

"I have to hand it to Courtenay," said Percy. "He seems to be taking his medicine like a man."

"You probably know everything Gwyneth is saying to him," said Florilyn. "This is how she taught you to beat me."

" 'High, forward, and loose in the saddle,' " nodded Percy. " 'Be one with your horse. . .feel the rhythm. . .relax and let him run.' You're right—I can imagine exactly what she is saying!"

"Are we witnessing the beginning of Courtenay's transformation?" said Steven.

"I don't think I would go *that* far!" laughed Florilyn. "Although," she added in a thoughtful tone, "Gwyneth does have the power to get under the skin. If I can change, though it took me awhile, I suppose maybe Courtenay can, too. But I'm not holding my breath."

EIGHTY

The Race

*A*s the twelve entries in the Chester Derby entered the starting gate, few expected anything from the late entrant from the north coast of Wales, Viscount's Pride. At twenty-five to one, neither had the three-year-old garnered much activity with the punters and bookmakers, though a few late rumors that the filly's pedigree came from France and could surprise had aroused a mild flurry of interest. Most of the bets laid down, however, followed conventional wisdom and remained with the three favorites, the Empress, Red Heat, and Birdsong Meadow.

In the seats just above the rail about fifty yards from the finish line, however, sat a small cluster of visitors to the Cheshire city, some of whom, in the excitement of participation more than expectation of gain, held markers for the wagers they had placed on the long shot.

Katherine had invited any from the manor who desired to accompany them to watch the race. Mrs. Drynwydd and Mrs. Llewellyn, attired in their finest Sunday dresses, were beside themselves at the fun of such an adventure and behaving like two schoolgirls in the midst of the great crowd. This was the first horse race either had seen in their lives. They had speculated to the sum of ten shillings each and were now clutching their receipts as if the economy of the entire British Empire was at stake. Stuart Wyckham was more daring. He had invested a pound and now sat more nervous than excited, fearing the worst and regretting having been caught up in the prerace enthusiasm of the others. Florilyn had bet four pounds, Steven two. They had also invited Rhawn Lorimer to accompany them, and she had equaled Florilyn's bet. Adela Muir had declined to place a wager. Beside her, however, the mother whose son would carry the hopes of Snowdonia on his shoulders had invested five pounds. Only one of the company had sufficient personal prior experience with the techniques of Viscount's Pride's diminutive trainer to have reason for optimism. Percy was so convinced of Gwyneth's genius with animals that he had confidently placed a ten-pound note on the table in front of the skeptical bookie, who, he said, had no objection if the young Scotsman wanted to throw his money away, and he would be glad to take it. Gwyneth, most quietly confident of all, placed no bet. She had no desire to profit from the day's adventure. She was thinking more of the eternal consequences of her investment and what interest might be gained from it within Courtenay's heart.

Courtenay arranged to go ahead with the horse several days before. The contingent from the manor followed two days prior to the race, riding in two large carriages to Blaenau Ffestiniog, where they caught the train the rest of the way. A festive dinner at the hotel had capped off the adventure. Katherine and Adela treated the women to ice cream, and her housekeeper and cook thought they were in heaven. They invited Stuart Wyckham to accompany them. Glancing about at the four women, however, he declined and instead spent a boring evening in his room, wishing that Hollin Radnor had been up for the trip, or that Codnor Barrie did not possess such a keen sense of duty that compelled him to stay behind and keep watch over affairs at the manor.

Steven and Florilyn walked through the city with Percy, Gwyneth, and Rhawn. As they made their way back toward the hotel, Gwyneth and Florilyn were engaged in conversation with Steven and gradually moved ahead. Behind them Percy and Rhawn found themselves alone together.

"What is it like being without your little Amren for so long?" asked Percy.

"I miss him," replied Rhawn. "But it feels so good to be free of the duties of a mother for a few days. Sir Armond and Doris are like two little children in a candy store to have their grandson to themselves for three days. My parents are going to Burrenchobay Hall one evening as well. You don't know how much I appreciate your asking me along. I know I'm sort of the odd woman out—you and Gwyneth, Steven and Florilyn, you know—but I appreciate it."

"It was Gwyneth's idea."

Rhawn smiled. "Somehow, I am not surprised. She is an amazing girl," she said. "After how I treated her all those years when we were young, now she acts as if I am her best friend. You are a very lucky man."

"She cares for you, Rhawn. She *does* consider you a friend. I think she is proud of you, too, for not giving up, for growing, for becoming the person you are. I am proud of you, too."

"You have been so good to me, Percy. Whatever I may be growing into, I owe it to you."

"You have made your own choices, Rhawn. You've been strong and have grown through the adversity. Nobody's done that for you."

"But watching you helped me make good choices, Percy. I watched you making good choices. It had a profound impact on me. You were no saint either when you first came to Wales."

"Don't remind me!" laughed Percy.

"But you grew and changed. I know it seemed that I was just trying to get my hooks into you with all my flirting and conniving. . .but I was watching. It took awhile, but it began to get into me. I had never been around a boy who was unselfish and kind. Courtenay and Colville had no depth of character, yet all the girls for miles around swooned over them. Girls can be really stupid, Percy. They don't look for character. So they get into bad situations, just like I did. When I met you, I began to see that character mattered. Then I began to see that it mattered within my own heart most of all. Anyway, I am very grateful. You will always be special to me. I wish you and Gwyneth all the happiness in the world."

"Thank you, Rhawn," said Percy. "Is there. . . What is going on with Colville, now that you are seeing his parents regularly?"

"He was angry at first," answered Rhawn. "He always managed to be away when I went to visit. But we have exchanged some civil words since. I think he is getting used to the idea that Amren and I are in his life to stay."

"Has Amren been told that Colville is his father?"

"No, it's too soon for that."

"Do you think. . .I mean, is there any chance that you and Colville will marry one day?"

Rhawn smiled sadly. "I don't know, Percy. I suppose part of me does love him. Whether he loves me, or ever loved me—honestly, I don't know. He is the father of my son. Of course I wish we could be a family. His parents don't like things the way they are. But we all know that we have to give Colville time to adjust to it all. Whether he will decide he wants to become a man of character, much depends on that, too. I would not marry him unless I was convinced that I would be the only woman in his life. If by some chance he did ask me to marry him, he will have to show me that things have changed before I would accept him."

"Well, for all your sakes, I hope he is capable of that," said Percy. "It may be that your growth is having more of an effect on him than you realize."

It was after ten when the five young people returned to the hotel the night before the race.

"I hardly recognize Courtenay," said Katherine as she watched the horses lining up on the far side of the track. "I think he's lost nearly a stone in preparation for this race."

"He is still large for a jockey," said Steven from the other side of his mother. "But the loss of weight should help him be more competitive."

"Do you think he has a chance, Steven?" asked Florilyn beside him. "I just hope he isn't last. Can you imagine how impossible he would be to live with?"

Steven glanced past Florilyn and Rhawn to Gwyneth seated beside her. Her vision was fixed on Courtenay, her eyes glowing with a strange light.

"I'm not the one you should be asking," he replied after a moment.

Florilyn looked to her right.

Gwyneth sensed the movement and turned toward her. "Yes, he has a chance, Florilyn," she said calmly. "He will beat most of the others. I cannot say for certain that he will win. I can see that two of the others are very fast. But I *think* he may win."

Between them, Rhawn's thoughts were not on the race but on Colville Burrenchobay and the conversation she and Percy had had on the way back to the hotel the night before. *God,* she said silently, *I do pray that You would put within Colville's heart the desire to grow and to become a man of character.*

Her thoughts and prayers were interrupted by the starter's bugle. All eyes turned to the opposite side of the track. As if shot from a gun, the twelve horses exploded forward out of the gate. Instantly a great roar from the crowd went up. Along the back straight the twelve competitors quickly spread out almost in single file. The light, pinkish-gray Empress led the way into the first turn.

"Where's Courtenay!" shouted Katherine, glancing down toward Steven and Percy.

"I am afraid that's him bringing up the rear," said Steven. "But he has time to regroup."

Nothing more was said as they watched the field come round the curve and into the straight. Birdsong Meadow made a move out of the curve, passing the Empress on the outside and galloping out to half a length's lead. He was followed by the rest of the closely bunched field. Out of the curve, Courtenay swung wide and eased up on the rider in front of him.

As they came down the straight, slowly Gwyneth rose from her seat and leaned over the rail. She stared intently as they came on, as if trying to exert her will into Courtenay's brain and into the mighty frame of Viscount's Pride.

All around her the others were yelling frantically. "Courtenay. . .go, Courtenay!"

"Faster, Courtenay!"

"Courtenay, Courtenay!"

Stuart Wyckham was pounding his hat on his leg, yelling at the top of his lungs, "Move out around them, boy. No time to hold it back now!"

Mrs. Drynwydd and Mrs. Llewellyn had risen to their feet, all propriety abandoned, and were shouting in Welsh too thick for anyone around them to understand.

Only Gwyneth was silent as the field thundered past in front of them. Percy looked at her out of the corner of his eye. Her hands were together, as if clutching two imaginary reins, her elbows out, her upper body gently rocking, her lips moving with the silent words, *Be one. . .feel her rhythm.*

Percy smiled then turned his attention back to the race. "Go, Courtenay!" he cried. "Don't wait too long! Go!" He thought he detected Courtenay's head turn toward them for the briefest moment. Had he heard them calling his name? Or had he sensed Gwyneth's piercing stare?

As quickly as they flew down the straight, they were gone. Seconds later the field entered the far turn. Birdsong Meadow still led, followed by Red Heat and Empress neck and neck. Around the curve, none wanted to swing wide, and all held their positions. As the track again straightened, several swung out and flailed their whips as they flew down the backstretch. Courtenay alone among the twelve jockeys held no whip in his hand. He passed one more horse. Quickly the two behind him faded back. He swung out, drawing even with a cluster of four running side by side halfway down the far straight.

Gradually he inched ahead, pulled out half a length, then a length in front of the four, then swung back into the pole. Birdsong Meadow, Red Heat, and Empress led down the straight, no more than a half a length separating them, while two lengths back, a black stallion and a roan gelding tried desperately to hold the pace. In the gap between them and the cluster of four, rode Courtenay alone.

Into the final curve they came. The Empress appeared strong and gathering herself for another challenge. Red Heat began to fade. The roan drew even then passed him. Courtenay came alongside the stallion's rear and held position halfway through the curve. The black swung out to pass Red Heat, brushing Courtenay's left leg. He swung out but kept even. Red Heat faded behind them. The six who trailed fell back.

It was now a five-horse race.

They emerged into the final straight. A deafening roar from the crowd nearly drowned out the pounding hooves on the hard-packed dirt. The Empress came even with Birdsong Meadow. But the roan was gaining. Behind him the black stallion and Viscount's Pride were coming on strong less than a length back.

Suddenly Courtenay swung wide, too wide it seemed. An audible gasp sounded from the crowd. The sudden lurch appeared to have been caused by the stallion. But now Courtenay leaned far forward, elbows out, his entire frame moving in rhythm with the powerful beast beneath him. He appeared to be speaking into her ear. No one would ever know what was said.

As the two favorites and roan and stallion thundered toward the finish beside the pole, yards to their right, in the middle of the track and alone, Viscount's Pride came on at great speed.

Percy was on his feet and waving his hands wildly. "Courtenay....go, Courtenay!" he cried.

Steven and Florilyn and Katherine and Rhawn and Mrs. Drynwydd and Mrs. Llewellyn and Stuart Wyckham were yelling in a frenzy. "Courtenay, Courtenay! Go, Courtenay!"

Only Gwyneth stood calmly at the rail, saying nothing, a peaceful smile on her face as she watched the field thunder toward her.

As he passed them, Courtenay drew even with the Empress. He glanced briefly toward the stands. On his face was a great smile of exhilaration. Then he was gone, pounding toward the finish.

Courtenay flew across the line half a length ahead. Birdsong Meadow surged past the Empress by a nose at the line, followed by the black stallion in fourth.

The twenty-five-to-one long shot had triumphed in the Chester Derby!

Percy and Steven jumped out of their seats and ran through the tumultuous crowd for the winner's circle. They were followed by Florilyn and Rhawn. After all the excitement, Stuart Wyckham sat down in his seat thinking what he could do with his winnings, while beside him the housekeeper and cook were trying to compute what their winnings would be.

By the time they reached the winner's circle, Courtenay was being congratulated by the race organizers and presented with the first-place cup. Percy and Steven and Florilyn and Rhawn were swallowed in a great swarm. Courtenay saw them, finally dismounted, and made his way through the throng toward them.

"Magnificent race, Courtenay!" exclaimed Percy with a great smile, shaking his hand.

"Well done, man!" said Steven.

"Thanks," said Courtenay. "An amazing last two hundred yards. I don't know quite what happened myself."

Florilyn stepped forward and gave her brother a tight hug. There were tears in her eyes.

Rhawn hugged him, also. "I can't believe it, Courtenay," she said. "That was a fantastic ride."

"I don't know that I believe it myself!" laughed Courtenay.

Even as he was greeting the others, it was obvious that Courtenay's eyes were flitting about the sea of faces looking for someone else. But she stood a head shorter than everyone and was not easy to find in a crowd. At last he detected the head of white. He bumped and inched toward it.

A moment later, Gwyneth's face came into view.

Courtenay stopped and stood, his left hand holding the reins, staring down at her.

Gwyneth returned his gaze with an innocent and peaceful smile, as if she were not surprised in the least with the result. "Congratulations, Courtenay," she said. "That was masterful. I knew you could do it."

He smiled almost sheepishly then slowly began to shake his head in disbelief. "*You* did it, Gwyneth," he said. "Thank you. Thank you. . .for *everything*!"

EIGHTY-ONE

Mochras Head

*P*ercy remained in Wales throughout the fall, working every day with Steven and Codnor about the manor and grounds and at the new house. Never had he enjoyed hard, honest labor so much. Even Courtenay occasionally joined them.

As the year 1874 drew to a close, Edward and Mary Drummond made plans again to spend the Christmas holidays at Westbrooke Manor. There was not only much to celebrate, there were plans to be made and much to discuss. Percy was eager to talk over the future with his father and arrive at some resolution regarding his plans for his law studies.

The season would be highlighted by a family reunion with Edward and Katherine's parents, the earl and his wife, returning at last from China to retire from the mission field. Their future plans were not yet firm. Before leaving for China, they had sold their home and parted with most of their worldly possessions. Son and daughter were doing their utmost to persuade them to spend their remaining years with one or the other of them—at the vicarage in Glasgow or with Katherine in North Wales.

Edward and Mary, with the senior Mr. and Mrs. Drummond, arrived several days before Christmas. Katherine had seen her parents but once since their departure for China twelve years earlier. They were now in their late seventies. Though in good health, they were clearly slower of step and more stooped since she had seen them. The gray atop her head, however, signaled as great a change in their eyes as their increasing frailty did in hers. They had laid eyes on their three grandchildren but briefly since they were children, during a furlough from the mission some years before. Tears flowed freely throughout the day of their arrival. Three fine young adults now greeted them warmly, with handshakes and hugs, and, at least in the case of Percy and Florilyn, countenances of character to make them proud. Even Courtenay, who had avoided such gatherings in recent years, was present. He seemed genuinely glad to be part of the family again. The earl and his wife fell in love instantly with Percy's young fiancée. They perceived in her eyes the light of truth and immediately took her to their hearts as had Edward and Mary earlier in the year.

"So, Katherine," said the earl the next evening as the extended family gathered in the large sitting room, "this is where you think we should retire and live out our days? Edward has been doing his best to convince us that he and Mary should take us in."

"I am aware of that!" laughed Katherine, glancing at her brother with a smile. "But can Glasgow compare with the beautiful coast of Snowdonia? Surely you would be happier in the country."

"You would certainly have room for us. I had forgotten how huge the manor is."

"Actually, you would not be living in the manor, Father," said Katherine. "I have been building a new house out toward the promontory, about three-quarters of a mile from here. You probably saw it when you came up the hill."

"Why a new house?" asked Mrs. Drummond.

"After Roderick died, there was some question about the inheritance and my future," replied Katherine vaguely. "It seemed best that I have a place of my own and leave the manor for the new. . .uh, the new owner when that time came."

"This place is big enough for ten families," rejoined the earl.

"You may be right, Father. But young families need a home of their own. I did not want to be underfoot."

"Yes, well. . .I see what you mean. Right—can't have too many old people around when youngsters are scurrying about. Although I must say, on the mission field children multiply like rabbits. Their energy is exhilarating. I have to say, I hope to go to my grave with tiny little hands and feet nearby that occasionally cease their play long enough to climb into an old man's lap."

A pause came in the conversation. Katherine, Adela, and Florilyn rose to refill tea cups.

As they resumed their seats, Steven took the opportunity afforded by the lull to stand and look about the room. "If I might be permitted a few words," he said. All eyes turned toward him, wondering what the normally reticent young man had on his mind. He drew in a deep breath. He appeared uncharacteristically nervous. Had the company not been looking at him, some would have noticed a sudden reddening of Florilyn's cheeks as she buried her hands and eyes in her lap.

"For many years," Steven continued when he had composed himself, "I have admired from afar a certain one of our number, trying to find ways to serve her in whatever humble capacity I might despite the vast gulf that existed between our stations. I was but the son of a poor sheep-herding crofter and certainly never dreamed of a more personal or intimate approach. When the late viscount was kind enough to employ me at the manor, and when Lady Katherine added to that kindness by showing such trust as to make me her factor, my opportunities for service toward the one I speak of, though occasionally frustrated by herself, were increased by closer proximity. Yet I remained what I was— but a poor crofter in the guise of a factor. However, when suddenly a few months ago my dear cousin was revealed to be Lord Snowdon's granddaughter, hope sprang up in me that perhaps I myself might claim to be a *little* more than a mere peasant, even if not directly so. If I am not quite an aristocrat, perhaps I might claim sufficient standing to look a young lady of noble birth and character in the eye and tell her I love her. Therefore, after speaking to her mother, this I have done. Unbelievably, she reciprocated my sentiments. The result of all this is that I have the following announcement to make—that this afternoon I asked Miss Florilyn Westbrooke to be my wife, and she accepted me."

Even before the words were out of his mouth, Florilyn was on her feet and hurrying toward him. As they embraced, the room erupted in surprised exclamations. The two were quickly surrounded by their family and friends and smothered in hugs and backslaps and handshakes and kisses of congratulations.

Steven's announcement at last prompted Percy to talk seriously with his father and mother. Gwyneth had a similar conference with her father. The five then met together, Percy and Gwyneth seeking the combined counsel and wisdom of their three parents concerning their future and its timetable. No resolution was reached regarding Percy's plans to attend law school, though his father recommended, and Mary and Codnor agreed, that he should travel to Aberdeen within the coming months to reassess possibilities. Now that it seemed clear that his future was in Wales, he needed to decide where his heart was leading him about his studies and future profession.

Out of these discussions and the prayer that followed, one decision was reached. The wedding that would join their two families would be held in Wales in eighteen months, a year from the following June. At Percy's request, Vicar Edward Drummond would be presiding.

Two days after a festive and joyous Christmas, following a great Boxing Day "open house" at the manor to which the entire village had been invited, on a bright, sunny, cold afternoon, Gwyneth found Percy in the garden with his father and grandfather.

"Come join us, my dear!" said the earl, rising from the stone garden bench and greeting his grandson's future wife with an embracing hug of affection.

"I don't want to interrupt," said Gwyneth, "but Percy, would you walk to the promontory with me later?"

"Sure—it is a perfect day for a walk."

"Sit down, Gwyneth," said Edward. "We were just talking about you. Percy was telling my father about his adventure in Ireland trying to find you, when he didn't even know it was you he was trying to find!"

"I certainly never dreamed I would see Percy again," said Gwyneth. "No, that's not quite right," she added. "I *dreamed* of seeing Percy again every day. But I did not see how I ever would."

"I have to tell you," Percy's father went on, "I have tremendously enjoyed becoming acquainted with your father these last few days. He is a remarkable man."

"I could not agree more," smiled Gwyneth. "I don't know that I have ever seen him happier. For my sake he was willing to make a new life for us in Ireland. But he is, after all, a Welshman at heart. He is so happy to be back home, as is Grannie."

"But she is not actually your grandmother?"

"No, my great-great-aunt."

"And Steven. . ."

"Is my cousin. His mother Adela is my father's sister."

"Ah. . .I think I have it straight at last!" laughed Edward.

An hour later Percy and Gwyneth walked to the edge of the promontory, bundled in several layers of clothes, and sat down on the damp grass. The winter sun was slowly dying into the sea in front of them.

"This is one of my favorite places," said Gwyneth softly.

"One of *our* favorite places," rejoined Percy, "as long as you're not waiting for me at the harbor!"

"I have been coming here and sitting looking out over the sea since before I can remember," Gwyneth went on. "I always associated the mystery of the sea with my mother. Now I know what happened. I have been to Ireland. I have seen the land where I was born. Yet I love it here no less that the mystery has been solved."

"The sea is mysterious of itself," said Percy. "And we still don't know how that chest of gold came to be buried in the cave down there. That mystery may always baffle us."

"But we found it. Imagine, Percy—we actually found a buried treasure! It's a fairy tale!"

Percy turned toward Gwyneth. The setting sun had grown bright red at the wintry horizon. Whenever the sun shone just right, its rays turned Gwyneth's light hair into a luminescent crown of gold.

"More a fairy tale for me than you," said Percy as a smile played on his lips.

Gwyneth returned his gaze with a puzzled expression.

"I discovered the *real* treasure," he said, "though it took me sailing back and forth across the Celtic triangle to find it. What is a chest of old coins compared to the gold I found? I found *you!*"

Gwyneth smiled and laid her head on Percy's shoulder. He stretched his arm around her and drew her close.

"I love you, Gwyneth Barrie," said Percy.

"And I you, Percival Drummond. I may be your gold, but you are every girl's dream come true."

They sat watching the sun slowly set. The moment the final speck of its red disappeared, the sky immediately seemed to explode in color. But the brilliant sunset was short lived. It was winter and the atmosphere was too thin to sustain the colors for long. Within fifteen minutes, dark blues and purples of approaching night began to engulf them in a descending blanket of darkness.

"Just think if we could live our lives with this view all the time," said Percy, "overlooking the sea, watching every sunset."

"Perhaps we can," said Gwyneth.

"What do you mean?"

"Stand up, Percy, and turn around."

Percy rose to his feet then pulled Gwyneth up to his side. They turned their backs to the sea. There stood the outline of Katherine's new house against the night sky three hundred yards inland from the promontory.

"Are you thinking what I think you might be thinking?" said Percy slowly.

"I don't think Lady Katherine really wants to move to the new house," said Gwyneth.

"She is planning to. I've heard her say so."

"Only because she thinks she ought to," said Gwyneth. "She probably thinks we will want her to after I inherit. But we would get lost in the manor by ourselves. I would feel very awkward. It will always be Lady Katherine's home to me. The new house is not half so big. Why should *we* not live in the new house, where we can see the sea every day and let Katherine and Florilyn and Steven and Adela all remain at the manor."

"Gwyneth, that is a fantastic idea!"

"I will speak with Lady Katherine. We will do whatever she wants. As long as I am with you, Percy, I will be happy anywhere. But I cannot think of anything I would love more than to wake up every morning beside you and go to bed every night with the sound of the sea in our ears."

EIGHTY-TWO

Knotted Strands

*T*ears came to Katherine's eyes the next day when she realized what Gwyneth was suggesting.

"Oh, my dear girl!" she said, embracing Gwyneth with all the affection of true motherhood. "You would do that for me?"

"I would do whatever I could for you, Lady Katherine. Your happiness means more to me than anything."

"More than your own?"

"Of course."

Katherine shook her head in wonder. "I know you mean that with all your heart," she said, stepping away and smiling down at the girl who had become to her as an adopted daughter. "I would love to be able to remain at the manor. There would also be more room for my parents. I only decided to build the new house because I assumed I would have to find another place to live. Once we realized that Courtenay would not inherit, I must admit wondering if I had made a mistake. Still, the manor *will* be yours one day. Should it not be your home?"

"I would rather think of it as *yours*, Lady Katherine," replied Gwyneth. "The manor will be yours to live in and make use of as your own for as long as you wish it. If you would allow my family to live in your new house, I would be honored for you to remain at the manor."

"Then the new house shall be my wedding gift to you."

"To use, perhaps, but not to own," said Gwyneth. "The new house and land shall remain yours. In your name, I mean," said Gwyneth, "so that you will have them to pass on to Florilyn or Courtenay one day. You need to be mindful of your inheritance to them as well."

"Perhaps you are right. We do not need to decide all those particulars just now. But you have made me very happy, Gwyneth. Thank you!"

With the arrangement between the present and future viscountesses, work at the new house continued as rapidly as the winter weather would permit. Doors, windows, cabinetry, shelves, fixtures, fireplaces and other brick- and stonework, and paneling and trim, were all completed by early February. By that time Percy, Steven, Courtenay, and Codnor were in the process of painting those rooms whose walls had been plastered rather than paneled in wood. Carpet and drapes were ordered and in place by early April. By the end of the month, though sparse of furnishings, the new house was ready for Codnor, Gwyneth, and Grannie to take up residence within its new stone walls. What remained of their furniture in the two cottages in the village, as well as what had been shipped from Ireland, was carted to the new house. Katherine added many furnishings from the manor as well. For two weeks the entire company at the manor contributed to the move. Carts, buggies, and wagons moved back and forth between the two houses and the village bearing furniture, boxes, beds, crates, chairs, clothes, wardrobes, utensils, food, wall hangings, pictures, and tapestries. The men of the manor helped Codnor outfit the new stables with tack, tools, saddles, feed, and all things needful for the barn and workshop. Meanwhile, the women remained busy in Gwyneth's new kitchen and in making the bedrooms and other rooms of the house cozy and livable.

When at last the small Barrie family left the manor one evening after a great supper and prepared to spend their first night in their new home, it seemed as though some portion of the glory had departed. And indeed, life seemed dreary for a time in both houses. Even Gwyneth in the new house, notwithstanding her daily view of the sea, found it perhaps a little *too* quiet. But she saw Florilyn and Steven and Katherine and Adela daily. The path between the two houses was already well worn. Stuart Wyckham had planted a boxwood hedge and other shrubs alongside it. Gradually life returned to its old channels. Gwyneth ministered to Grannie and her father as she had in Ireland. Steven and Codnor continued to work on what interior details remained to be completed at the new house. Life between the two homes was soon flourishing as if they were one.

Percy spent much of the spring in Glasgow with his parents, taking up again his occasional legal work, and made a trip to Aberdeen to assess his options for resuming his law studies. Whenever he was in Wales, he took up residence in his former room at the manor.

Steven and Florilyn were married the following August. Percy stood beside Steven as best man, with Courtenay beside him. Gwyneth and Rhawn served as Florilyn's two maids of honor. Steven and Codnor, along with their work on the new house, and with the help of several able carpenters and joiners, had remodeled a portion of the wing of the manor that had been used in former times as servants' quarters. They had transformed it into an expansive apartment of seven rooms, occupying two floors, including a newly outfitted kitchen. It was ready by the day of the wedding. After a week's honeymoon by boat north through Scotland's western isles, the wedding couple took up residence in their new east-wing quarters.

Percy and Gwyneth were married a year later, in June of 1876. Percy would have chosen his father to be his best man had he not been officiating for the service. Those who stood before the proud vicar were the same six from the previous August. Edward's own son, however, was now the bridegroom. The ceremony was conducted on the flat plateau between the new house and the promontory of Mochras Head. The entire village was invited, and nearly every one of its number attended. Percy had always been a great favorite. And now, even if belatedly, those of the community embraced his new bride and their future viscountess as if they had always secretly known that she was something beyond the ordinary. A great feast and celebration was held afterward on the grounds of the new house. As the day was bright and warm, it lasted most of the day. The bride and groom did not depart in their honeymoon carriage—which would take them that night to Barmouth, thence to the Lincolnshire resort village of Cumberworth—until after six o'clock.

One of the surprise guests of the day was Colville Burrenchobay. He and Rhawn spent most of the afternoon together. He was even seen a time or two in the midst of the festivities engaged in what appeared to be cordial conversation with Styles Lorimer. Drawn together by their mutual grandson, the Lorimer and Burrenchobay families had been visiting with increasing frequency. How much the people of the community knew was doubtful. The truth was not long in coming out, however, when Colville began calling at the Lorimer home later that summer. A few buggy rides followed. After some time, these began to include young Amren. With unhurried wisdom, Rhawn allowed the two men in her life to become accustomed to each other slowly. By the time their engagement was announced the following year, Amren had begun calling Colville "Daddy." Colville and Rhawn were married and eventually had three more children. They took up residence in Burrenchobay Hall, which Colville inherited at the passing of his parents. As true as it is that most people do not change, anyone who *wants* to change is easily made capable of it by that desire. Influenced primarily by what he observed in Rhawn and Florilyn, a spark of that desire began to flicker to life within the heart of Colville Burrenchobay. He never stood for parliament, and though no one would have called him a saint, he turned out to be a surprisingly good father and was faithful to Rhawn for the rest of his life.

Grannie lived in the new house and was honored by the families and staff of both houses as matriarch of the extended clan of Westbrooke Manor and the new house. She lived to be ninety-seven and died in her own bed in the new house with Gwyneth and Adela at her side. Her passing was mourned by the entire village that had once scorned her.

Percy and Gwyneth spent three school terms in Aberdeen while Percy completed his law degree, returning with great joy to Wales every summer.

Gwyneth inherited the title of viscountess and all the property of the Westbrooke estate on her twenty-fifth birthday. The day-to-day affairs of the estate continued to function as they had. All the people of the village and manor addressed both she and Katherine either as "Viscountess" or "Lady Gwyneth" and "Lady Katherine."

Gwyneth's only order as the new first lady of Snowdonia was that someone from one of the two houses—she or Katherine or Percy or Steven or Florilyn or Courtenay or Codnor or Adela—should visit the village every day, whether for a pint of Mistress Chattan's ale or a visit to one of the shops or even simply a ride on horseback through the main street. She was determined that everyone should have easy and unrestricted access to the viscountess and her people and know that their concerns would always be listened to and their needs attended to.

Steven continued as factor for the entire estate and all the affairs concerning both houses. He attempted to make Codnor his co-factor and spoke to both Gwyneth and Katherine with the request to formalize the office and pay Gwyneth's father accordingly. But Codnor would have none of it. The humble man would happily serve as his nephew's assistant and his daughter's willing servant, he said, but would accept no title nor pay for his services.

Percy apprenticed for two years under Hamilton Murray, riding into Porthmadog weekly, then established his own law practice from an office in the new house on Mochras Head. More than half the local cases that came his way he performed *gratis*. The new viscountess was determined to *serve* her people, not profit from them. Percy's gradually expanding reputation throughout Snowdonia and North Wales, however, along with regular referrals from Hamilton Murray, kept his legal practice mostly in the black.

The earl and Mrs. Drummond moved to Westbrooke Manor and lived out their days with their daughter attending lovingly to their every need. They died within a year of each other, both aged eighty-eight.

Though an invitation was sent them, Vanora and Daibheid Maloney declined to attend Gwyneth's wedding. Now that Gwyneth knew the details of her own personal history and of the sufferings the O'Sullivan and Maloney side of her family had endured, she longed to know her Irish relatives and see the Welsh and Irish strains reconciled. She was conscious, however, that not all the suffering had been accidental. It was clear that Daibheid Maloney had inflicted his own share of grief upon others. Nor could she seek to win the man's favor on the basis of what she had become. True reconciliation must be based on a recognition of her father's character and a desire on the part of Maloney to make amends with the man he had scorned and rebuffed.

Gwyneth and her father, therefore, planned a trip to Ireland and a visit to the home of Vanora and Daibheid Maloney. Vanora was cordial but concerned about her husband's reaction. After humble apologies by Codnor for his contribution to the family rift, a gradual thaw began in the heart of Daibheid Maloney toward his former friend and coworker. Several more visits over three or four years culminated in Gwyneth at last revealing to Daibheid Maloney the full truth of her inheritance. Her aunt Vanora rejoiced, wept freely at last to have it out in the open, and embraced the daughter of her beloved sister. Gwyneth's desire was to help the family financially to the extent Daibheid Maloney's pride would allow. It was the least she could do for her mother's family. All she was able to accomplish, however, after consultation with her father, was to turn over the deed to the house and land on Lugnaquilla. As the purchase had originated as a gift from the late viscount, Daibheid Maloney accepted the gift more freely than would have been possible had he considered it charity from Gwyneth's hand. Friendship with several of Gwyneth's Irish cousins in future years, and their children with her children, followed.

Cousin Henry's treatise on love, which Edward and Percy had read in manuscript, was finally published in book form in 1880. It became one of the bestselling and most beloved books on the Christian life ever published, and in coming decades sold an astonishing twelve million copies.

Inspired by what he had read from his young cousin Henry, and under the continued influence of the pen of George MacDonald, Edward Drummond wrote a book simply called *The Commands of Jesus*, urging obedience as the central and only priority of Christianity.

D. L. Moody returned to Britain between 1882 and 1884. Kyvwlch

Gwarthegydd served as a volunteer for the evangelist's meetings in Wales. Henry Drummond was again involved in Moody's work.

Moody later recalled a memorable night during the tiring campaign.

> *"I was staying with a party of friends in a country house during my visit to England in 1884,"* he wrote. *"On Sunday evening as we sat around the fire, they asked me to read and expound some portion of Scripture. Being tired after the services of the day, I told them to ask Henry Drummond, who was one of the party. After some urging he drew a small Testament from his hip pocket, opened it at the thirteenth chapter of First Corinthians, and began to speak on the subject of Love.*
>
> *"It seemed to me that I had never heard anything so beautiful, and I determined not to rest until I brought Henry Drummond to America to deliver that address. Since then I have requested the principals of my schools to have it read before the students every year. The one great need in our Christian life is love, more love to God and to each other. Would that we could all move into that Love chapter, and live there."*

Gwyneth sold what remained of the chest of gold to the British Museum in London for an undisclosed sum. The research of the museum's historians had identified the gold as from a cache at the ancient Celtic site of Dolau Cothi that had disappeared shortly after its discovery in the previous century, thought to have been stolen by pirates and never heard of again.

The actual value of the gold was impossible to determine. Seeking the advice of Hamilton Murray, Katherine, Steven, her father, and her own husband-lawyer, Gwyneth received no more from the sale than sufficient to recoup most of the losses of previous generations and thus place the affairs of the estate on a permanently sound financial footing again. Beyond that, she did not feel it right to profit from the discovery in excess of need. Rather, she considered it her duty to allow the museum to determine whatever future the coins should have, whether to keep them or sell a portion of the find as artifacts to help support the museum and finance its future acquisitions.

When Madame Fleming, a.k.a the Wolf Lady, of dubious reputation in Arklow, Ireland, died of natural causes, Gwyneth ordered her house demolished and all its contents burned.

Courtenay continued to race his horses with somewhat regular success. He won several more events at various tracks in England, though never another at such long odds as at the Chester Derby. After great effort, he convinced Gwyneth to jockey for a few of these. Her success convinced Courtenay that he had indeed discovered the golden goose. She only laughed at his plea that she become his permanent jockey, saying that she had more important concerns on which to expend her energies. To please him, however, she agreed to ride in one race a year. Courtenay's racing activities at last made full use of his father's new stables at the manor. A reputation began to follow him as one of North Wales's leading owners and jockeys. He was often seen in close counsel with Gwyneth, the two walking side by side, Courtenay towering a foot above her, picking her brain about some aspect of horse training or race preparation and strategy. It was a sight none would have expected but which made Katherine's heart swell.

Courtenay met the daughter of a horse breeder from Barmouth at the annual Chester Derby of 1879. They were married two years later. After a year at the manor, an illness prevented his father-in-law being able to keep up with the work and oversight of his stables. Courtenay and his wife moved to the Barmouth estate, taking with them Courtenay's gradually growing stable of thoroughbreds. There Courtenay took over the daily operation of the farm and business. He and his wife visited Llanfryniog frequently, however, bringing their children to visit their cousins and grandmother, while Courtenay slipped away to hold counsel with Gwyneth and Steven, whose knowledge and wisdom about animals and racing he respected more and more with every passing year. He was never able to bring himself to draw close to Percy, and they never formed what would be called a warm relationship. As brothers-in-law, however, Courtenay and Steven became the best of friends.

By her choice, Adela Muir continued in the role of staff manager at the manor for the rest of her life. As Florilyn's mother-in-law and aunt of the viscountess, her status in the home was as a family member. But she had to work, she said. It was the natural order of things. She could never be happy living a life of leisure. She and Katherine read every new MacDonald book they could get their hands on. Indeed, the Scottish bard and seer from Huntly continued to produce best-selling books at such a rate that the MacDonald shelf in the manor library grew to encompass nearly three shelves full of many editions and several thumb-worn copies of each title.

Codnor Barrie never worked in the slate mine again. With his nephew Steven, he developed a breed of sheep especially suited to the climate of North Wales. Their flocks roamed the hills of Snowdonia, and their wool was highly prized throughout Britain.

Lord Coleraine Litchfield was censured by the House of Lords when it was discovered that he had entered into a contract to purchase a tract of land on the Lleyn Peninsula under false pretenses. The ensuing scandal made all the papers, sullying Litchfield's reputation with charges of embezzlement and fraud. Whether formal criminal charges would be brought remained in doubt. His secretarial assistant, Palmer Sutcliffe, fled the country and was last reported to be somewhere in France. Bagge, Litchfield, and Sutcliffe all went to their graves, in that order, never seeing the gold they had so lusted after, and the secret of what lay under the lake died with them.

No one ever knew about the gold under the emerald Snowdonian lake until years later. After a long and serious summer's draught, one of Percy's and Gwyneth's adventurous grandchildren was exploring in the hills and came across the long-hidden cave. Hurriedly he rode back excitedly to the new house to tell his grandmother, the viscountess, of his discovery.

Steven and Florilyn had four children—three boys and a girl. Only one of the boys took after Steven. He grew into a burly youngster who loved the out-of-doors. By the age of twelve, he was already being touted as a future sheepshearing champion.

An altogether unexpected visitor appeared one day at the new house on Mochras Head. The girl who answered the door was new to the area and did not recognize the plump figure standing before her in the finest dress and hat she owned.

"Begging your pardon, miss," said the woman, obviously nervous, "but would your mistress, the viscountess, I mean. . .is she at home, miss? If I could just have a word with her, you see."

The girl disappeared into the house. Gwyneth appeared a minute later dressed in a working frock, wiping her hands with a kitchen towel. Even on her usually placid countenance, the surprise was instantly visible.

"Hello, Mistress Chattan," she said. "It is nice to see you. Won't you come in?"

"No, Miss. . .I mean, begging your pardon—Lady Gwyneth, that is. I'll just stay here and say my piece."

"How can I be of service to you, Mistress Chattan?" asked Gwyneth.

From somewhere in the folds of her expansive dress, the innkeeper pulled a dry, faded cluster of what appeared to be dead wildflowers and grasses.

"Do you know this?" she asked, showing it to Gwyneth.

Gwyneth smiled. "Is it one of mine?" she said.

"You left it on my back door one day many years ago. I had been rude to you that day, you see. But like you always did, you returned me kindness for it. I'm sorry to say, I cursed you that day and threw this on the floor. But something made me pick it up the next day, and I can't say why, but I saved it all this time. I wanted you to know that I'm sorry for the times I was rude to you. You were a good girl, and you've become a fine lady, and I'm hoping you'll forgive me for whatever unkind words I spoke to you."

Gwyneth's eyes filled with tears. "Oh, Mistress Chattan, of course you are forgiven. You are a dear for saving one of my little forgiveness bouquets all this time!" She stepped forward and stretched her arms around the great bulk of the woman who was more than twice her size.

Mistress Chattan had not cried in years. Nor did she cry now. But she came dangerously close.

"Please. . . ," said Gwyneth as she stepped back, "won't you come in and have tea with me. I would enjoy it very much. I would like to show you the beautiful view of the sea from our sitting room."

With a nervous but appreciative smile, feeling greatly lightened from the release of her long-carried burden of conscience, Mistress Chattan nodded then followed Gwyneth inside.

Chandos Gwarthegydd married Mistress Chattan's niece from Dolgellau. The innkeeper's personal life had always been so shrouded in mystery that no one really knew where she had come from or whether she had living relatives at all. The identity of Chandos's bride was greeted with many questions. Little was learned, however, beyond the fact that she was the daughter of Mistress Chattan's brother. A beautifully incongruous relationship developed between the hulking young blacksmith and the aging aunt of his wife. The two young people took care of her during her final years with the most tender kindness imaginable. When the Keeper of the Ale died at the age of seventy-three, a handwritten will was found in her cash box, which Percy confirmed as legal and binding. It left the inn and all its contents to Chandos's wife. The building that housed the inn and pub was one of the few in the village that was privately owned and not the property of the viscount or viscountess of Snowdon.

Chandos continued blacksmithing with his father. An increasing amount of his time, however, was spent on his wife's new enterprise. They upgraded, restored, and added several rooms, turning it into a seacoast hotel of some repute. Many of those bound for the village on the north- or southbound coaches got out at the hotel and remained in Llanfryniog for several days. The pub of the newly renamed *Chattan Arms* continued to serve the best ale in Snowdonia.

Percy and Gwyneth had five children, three boys and two girls.

As Katherine's hair gradually turned a silvery white, her countenance took on more and more the radiance of that quiet, humble, peaceful, wise daughterhood that only lifelong attentiveness to the commands of Christ can produce in God's women. She continued to read and reread the works of the Scotsman, along with her brother's writings. With every passing year, she became more deeply convinced that the answers to life's quandaries were to be found in uncomplicated, practical obedience to the words of Jesus. All her grandchildren adored her and took every opportunity to scamper into her lap, where they felt at home, content, and at peace.

One morning in early summer, bright and warm, as Percy sat at the breakfast table with his tea, a girl of six and a boy of three walked into the room, rubbing their eyes and looking about.

"Daddy, where's mummy?" asked the girl.

"I don't know, sweetheart," replied Percy. "I haven't seen her this morning. Would you like something to eat?"

"Yes, please, Daddy."

After Percy had the two situated at the table, with glasses of milk and a plate of oatcakes in front of them, he left the house. A glance north and south along the promontory revealed nothing. He continued around the north wing of the house until his gaze opened toward the hills of Snowdonia eastward from the coastline.

On a green hillside in the distance he saw a simply dressed figure walking through the grass as it sloped up toward the inland ridge that overlooked Tremadog Bay. The light hair bathed in sunlight was unmistakable.

He smiled as he saw her stoop to the ground. He knew what she was doing. She was plucking wildflowers.

Gwyneth would always be Gwyneth, thought Percy with a full heart. Deep inside, she would never *really* be a viscountess, whatever people might call her. She would always be the mysterious daughter of the Snowdonian hills whose childlike nature spread life and goodness wherever she went.

Discussion Questions

From Across the Ancient Waters

1. In chapter 7, in discussing the village of Llanfyniog, it is said that its religion "tended to see God as an Almighty magician and shaman, rather than as the loving Creator-Father of humankind." What did you think of this description of a Christianity that mingled remnants of paganism with the Christian Gospel?

2. Nearly all of us have experienced family stresses not unlike what occurs between Percy and his parents. Share a similar experience from your life—either as a parent or as a teen. How was it handled, and what was the end result?

3. By chapter 25, nature begins to get more deeply into Percy's soul than he ever anticipated. God speaks to every human heart by unique means. Nature is one of those ways. What have been your experiences in detecting God's voice and presence in new ways, whether through nature or other manifestations of His Being?

4. Respond to Vicar Edward Drummond's sermon on prodigality and reconciliation in chapters 29–30. Do you like this kind of thought-provoking spiritual content in a novel? Were you challenged to make right any relationships in your life? Have you wondered, with Edward and Mary, about the role of the prodigal's parents in the parable, what they were doing and thinking while their son was away?

5. What arrows of prayer were you challenged to send to God for your own loved ones after reading chapter 33?

6. Read between the lines of chapter 68 and interpret what you think is going on in Percy's thoughts.

7. Has Percy made a sound decision (chapters 74–76)? He is facing an extremely difficult and delicate set of circumstances. When you were in similar situations, how did you arrive at clarity? Whom did you seek for counsel? If Percy had asked for your counsel in his predicament, what would have been your response?

8. What would you have said to Roderick Westbrooke in chapter 81 that Percy did not say?

The Treasure of the Celtic Triangle

1. Many readers of fiction agree with Thomas Jefferson that books of fiction and imagination are powerful to move us and "contribute to fix us in the principles and practice of virtue." Discuss Jefferson's comment in light of people who downplay the power of fiction. What are some of the fiction books that have been most influential in your life?

2. Did you like or dislike the literary device of using one fictional book within another—George MacDonald's *David Elginbrod* playing a pivotal role in this fictional story?

3. Often fiction is about watching characters grow. Some characters grow toward God, toward truth, toward goodness, and toward maturity. . .others grow away from them. When this series began, what did you expect of the various characters? Which ones surprised you?

4. How did you respond to Florilyn and Percy calling off their engagement? When the first book ended, did you think their decision to marry was a little too hasty? Did you see trouble on their horizon? Discuss how marriages might be strengthened if more couples had the humility and courage to honestly assess whether they were moving too quickly. How did you respond to Gwyneth's willingness to marry a man her father chose for her? Is her perspective—"I will learn to love him"—an adequate foundation for a good marriage?

5. Discuss Florilyn's changeability. Did you feel it was realistic that she altered so dramatically from the selfish girl she was before to seemingly becoming a young woman of strength and character. . .only to fall prey to Colville's deceptive charms? What do you consider was the chief cause of her "backsliding" in attitudes and outlook?

6. Who is the central character in *From Across the Ancient Waters* and *The Treasure of the Celtic Triangle*?

MICHAEL PHILLIPS (b. 1946) is one of the bestselling and most beloved Christian novelists of our generation, author of dozens of books of great diversity, both historical and contemporary.

Phillips began his distinguished writing career in 1977 with several nonfiction titles. Since that time, he has authored over twenty nonfiction books, most notably dealing with the nature and character of God and the fatherhood of God. His loyal readership through the years has come to depend on the signature tune running through all his writings—the personal call to what Phillips calls bold-thinking Christianity. After turning to the writing of novels in the mid-1980s, Phillips has penned some sixty fiction titles of wide-reaching scope and variety. The enormous breadth of his faithful audience is testimony that his writings are universal in their appeal.

He is also one of many in a rising generation of spiritual offspring of C. S. Lewis, George MacDonald, and the legacy of the Inklings. Phillips is widely known as George MacDonald's redactor, publisher, and biographer, whose vision and editorial expertise helped bring MacDonald back from obscurity when his realistic novels had been nearly forgotten. After discovering the writings of the Victorian Scotsman whose books were foundational in leading C. S. Lewis out of atheism into Christianity, Phillips made it his life's work to bring to public attention the literary and spiritual links between MacDonald and Lewis, and to promote the teachings of these giants of the past. If MacDonald is the "father of the Inklings," Phillips calls himself one of thousands of "sons of the Inklings." His multidimensional efforts helped ignite the MacDonald renaissance of recent years and have resulted in a new generation of readers having access to MacDonald's books again for themselves.

As one of those responsible for the widespread renewal of MacDonald's influence, Phillips is recognized as among the world's foremost purveyors of MacDonald's message, with particular insight into the Scotsman's heart and spiritual vision.

As his own volume of work reaches a stature of significance in its own right, Phillips is regarded as one of many successors to MacDonald's vision and spiritual legacy for a new generation.

For a complete listing of books by Michael Phillips,
see www.FatherOfTheInklings.com, or write to the author at:
P. O. Box 7003, Eureka, CA 95502.

19th-CENTURY SCOTLAND,
with Judith Pella
The Stonewycke Trilogy (1985–1986):
  The Heather Hills of Stonewycke
  Flight from Stonewycke
  The Lady of Stonewycke
The Stonewycke Legacy (1987–1988):
  A Stranger at Stonewycke
  Shadows over Stonewycke
  Treasure of Stonewycke
The Highland Collection (1987):
  Jamie MacLeod, Highland Lass
  Robbie Taggart, Highland Sailor

CALIFORNIA GOLD RUSH
The Journals of Corrie Belle Hollister (1990–1997):
  My Father's World, with Judith Pella
  Daughter of Grace, with Judith Pella
  On the Trail of the Truth
  A Place in the Sun
  Sea to Shining Sea
  Into the Long Dark Night
  Land of the Brave and the Free
  Grayfox
  A Home for the Heart
  The Braxtons of Miracle Springs
  A New Beginning

19th-CENTURY RUSSIA,
with Judith Pella
The Russians (1991–1992):
  The Crown and the Crucible
  A House Divided
  Travail and Triumph

WORLD WAR II & COLD WAR GERMANY
The Secret of the Rose (1993–1995):
The Eleventh Hour
A Rose Remembered
Escape to Freedom
Dawn of Liberty

WESTERN AMERICAN PRAIRIE
Mercy and Eagleflight (1996–1997):
Mercy and Eagleflight
A Dangerous Love

SPIRITUAL FANTASY (1998)
The Garden at the Edge of Beyond

CONTEMPORARY THRILLER
The Livingstone Chronicles (1997–2000):
Rift in Time
Hidden in Time

WORLD WAR I ENGLAND
The Secrets of Heathersleigh Hall (1998–2000):
Wild Grows the Heather in Devon
Wayward Winds
Heathersleigh Homecoming
A New Dawn over Devon

ANCIENT EPIC SCOTLAND
Caledonia (1999–2000):
Legend of the Celtic Stone
An Ancient Strife

CONTEMPORARY DRAMA
The Destiny Chronicles (2002):
Destiny Junction
King's Crossroads

AMERICAN CIVIL WAR
Shenandoah Sisters (2002–2004):
Angels Watching over Me
A Day to Pick Your Own Cotton
The Color of Your Skin Ain't the Color of Your Heart
Together Is All We Need
Carolina Cousins (2005–2007):
A Perilous Proposal
A Soldier's Lady
Never Too Late
Miss Katie's Rosewood
American Dreams (2005–2008):
Dream of Freedom
Dream of Life
Dream of Love

SCOTTISH DRAMA (2011)
Angel Harp
Heather Song

19th-CENTURY WALES
The Green Hills of Snowdonia (2012):
From Across the Ancient Waters
The Treasure of the Celtic Triangle